GAMEMASTER

THE BIODOME CHRONICLES BOOK 4

by

JESIKAH SUNDIN

ISBN: 978-0-9997721-8-8

Printed in the United States of America

Forest Tales Publishing
PO Box 84
Monroe, WA 98272
foresttalespublishing@gmail.com

This book is a work of fiction. Names, characters, places, and incidents are the product of the author's imagination or are used fictitiously. Any resemblance to actual events, locales, or persons, living or dead, is coincidental.

Cover design by MoorBooks Design
Interior Digital Illustration by Amalia Chitulescu
Interior design by Forest Tales Publishing
Map of New Eden Township by Andra Perju

DEDICATED TO

My father, Dennis Frantom

and

My children, Myles, Colin, and Violette

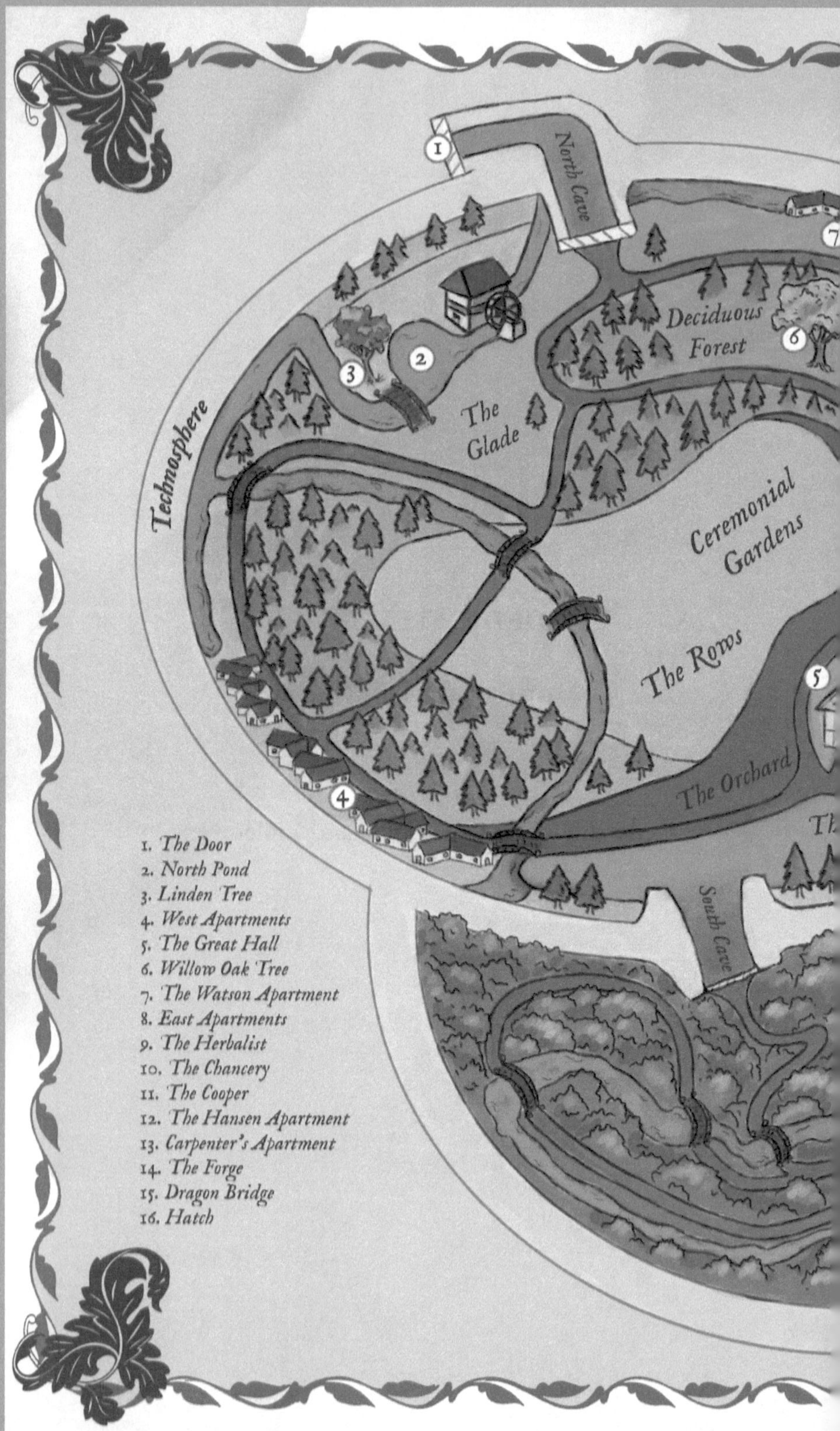

1. The Door
2. North Pond
3. Linden Tree
4. West Apartments
5. The Great Hall
6. Willow Oak Tree
7. The Watson Apartment
8. East Apartments
9. The Herbalist
10. The Chancery
11. The Cooper
12. The Hansen Apartment
13. Carpenter's Apartment
14. The Forge
15. Dragon Bridge
16. Hatch

New Eden Township

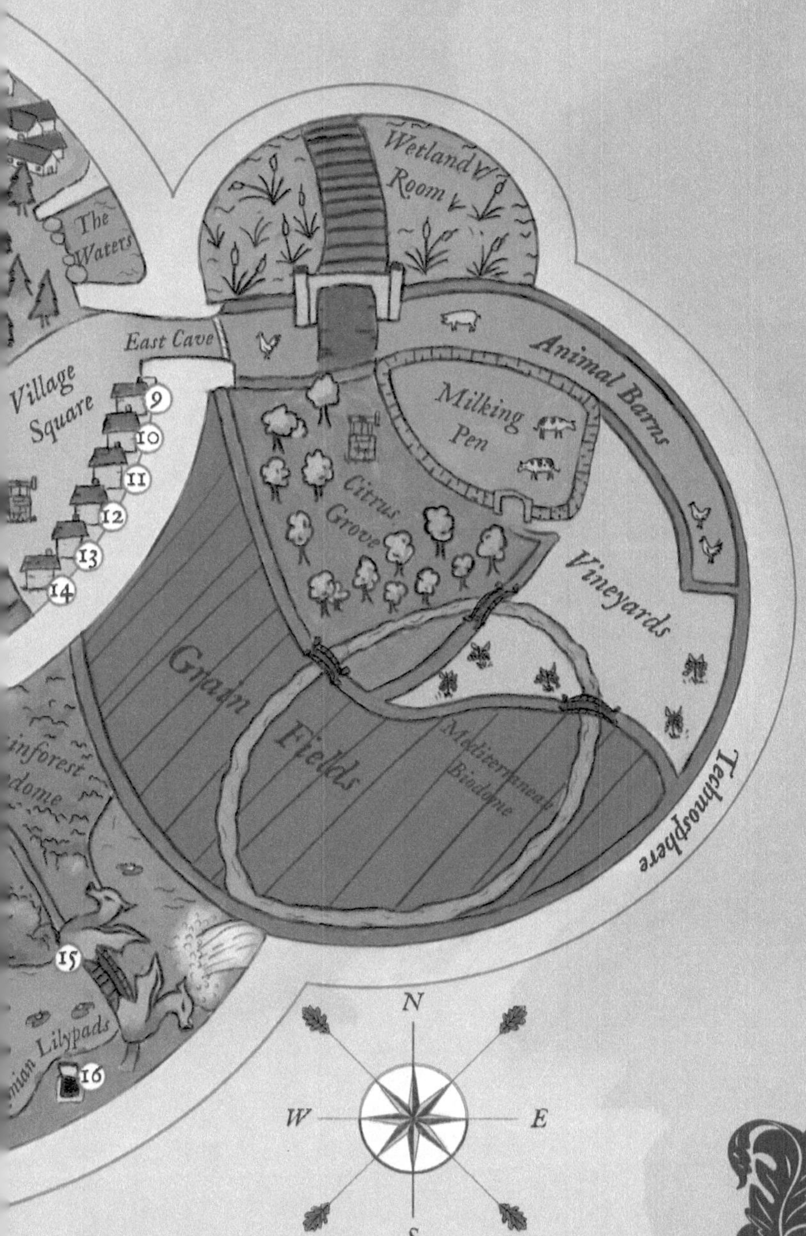

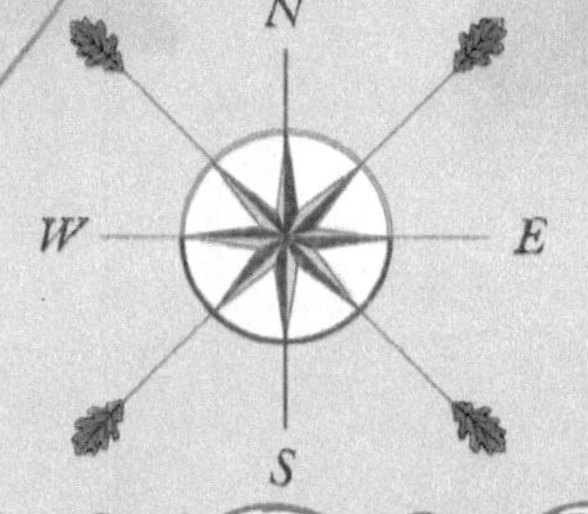

A means for full cryo-preservation and restoration remains a long way off still. However, recent medical progress is quickly advancing our ability to induce deep sleep states (i.e. torpor) with significantly reduced metabolic rates for humans over extended periods of time. NASA should leverage these advancements for spaceflight as they can potentially eliminate a number of very challenging technical hurdles, reduce the IMLEO for the system, and ultimately enable feasible and sustainable missions to Mars.

— John Bradford, SpaceWorks Enterprises Inc., 2013 *

No movement can afford to be caught in a time warp and exist in a state of suspended animation.

— Theodore Bikel, artist and activist, 2002 *

Chapter One

Dublin, Ireland

Sunday, March 24, 2058

3 years into Project Phase Two

The body had been dead for only one hour.

Fillion stared in horror, the bile churning in his gut. The deceased—a man in his forties with a wife and three children—lay on an exam table in the lab at New Eden Biospherics & Research. The eyeballs had bulged and cracked. Blood dribbled from the ears and mouth. Vessels in the face had popped, leaving a network of bluish lines across the unnaturally pale skin. The pale skin common to New Eden residents. Fillion pressed his fingers to his mouth, ready to throw up.

"This is the third death since yesterday," Michael said. He looked at Fillion from across the exam table.

Fillion whipped his gaze to the head scientist. "Third? Holy shit."

"Stasis works with the general population; adverse effects are extremely rare. Something in the genetic makeup of those inside New Eden clashes with the therapeutic-torpor procedure, though. It almost doesn't make sense. Especially the cooling period seizures." Michael lifted the sheet over the man, the movements sorrowful and respectful despite the clinical data he presented. "My theory is that the cellular structure in their DNA is far more different than their Earthen counterparts than previously believed. The limited space and depth, different diet, and atmosphere has conditioned their senses. Basically, they're highly sensitive."

Michael touched his Cranium, brows pinched, before glancing Fillion's way. "The biochemists and physicians recalibrated for a new core temperature and are ready to try again."

"No." Fillion backed away from the table. "No more blood on my hands. Who gave permission for these tests?"

"Your father." Michael swallowed and touched his Cranium, swiping at invisible commands. "He delivered orders to continue until the stasis tests pass viability."

Blood pounded in Fillion's ears. He tapped his fingers against his thigh in an angry rhythm. "I veto his order. Human experimentation is no longer allowed on N.E.T. premises. Is that understood?"

"I'm sorry, Mr. Nichols," Michael said in a near whisper. "You're not the owner yet."

"Were the test subjects from New Eden given a . . . choice?" Fillion choked on the last word.

"They are property of the lab." Michael pretended to study the holographic chart. "The next subject is ready, Mr. Nichols."

There was a long pause. Then Michael began speaking again. But the only sounds Fillion could hear were the flood of thoughts screaming in his head. Why were stasis tests even necessary? Nobody was going to Mars. This was an experiment, not a mission. Hanley had, once again, put him in a position of responsibility while granting him none of the power. Set up to fail, always. Maybe he was the one who was really in suspended animation. *Wake up!* he shouted over the screaming thoughts in his head. This wasn't the time to shut down. He needed to remain sharp.

The door slammed open, rattling the examination table; the dead man's hand fell over the edge.

Law enforcement moved swiftly in Fillion's direction. He took another step away from the table. Officer Brent McKee, whom Fillion knew well from his previous stint at New Eden, grabbed Fillion's hands and forced them behind his back with instructions to follow peacefully. Fillion tried to yank his arms free.

"Under what authority do you use physical force? Show me the warrant!"

"Mr. Nichols, your presence is required in the viewing gallery. We are authorized to use force if necessary."

Fillion's urge to fight fled with Officer McKee's warning. Force meant heavy sedation. No, he needed to keep his faculties intact.

Fillion began marching down the hallway to what felt like his own execution. The blood drained from his head in rapid fire, as if he were shot multiple times, his life spilled and splattered over the entire room. He couldn't watch. He couldn't see Hanley condone the killing of another innocent soul.

At the end of the hallway, he was shoved through a door and into a dimmed room filled with seats positioned theater style, facing a one-way mirror. Hanley stood when he entered, and a kind smile lit his face, a smile that never reached his eyes.

"Good of you to join us. They're bringing her in now. I'm confident stasis will work this time. NASA is eagerly awaiting our results."

Her?

A sob released deep in Fillion's chest and burst when they forced *her* into the room beyond the mirror. Long, golden hair had tangled into ratty clumps, and her emerald gaze leapt from object to object. Parts of her dress were torn and covered in filth. How long had they kept her confined? Restrained, she screamed and pleaded through tears to be let go, to be shown mercy. The men and women in white uniforms and masks moved like androids—precise, fluid, unfeeling.

"Willow!" Fillion threw his shoulder against the glass. His body stiffened with the impact. He rushed the glass again and again. "No! Let her go! Stop!"

She raised frightened eyes toward the glass, and he swore she saw him. Their eyes connected for one brief, terrifying second. In that moment, her body slowed, as if time in the room had slowed. Her arm escaped from a scientist's hold and she placed a trembling hand onto her heart. "I hate you," she growled through clenched teeth. A bright pain tightened his chest, like millions of glass shards piercing him all at once. The trembling hand lifted off her heart and gestured outward toward him, right before a nameless, faceless scientist inject- ed her in the arm with a long needle. She screamed and jumped toward the man, lifting her arm to strike in self-defense. But her legs buckled first, and she slid against the son of a bitch, sedated.

Hanley smirked. The triumphant grin widened when Willow was placed into the stasis chamber. The figures in lab coats tucked her simple, homespun skirt beneath her legs. A princess destined for eternal slumber in her glass cof- fin. Fillion wanted to kiss her, to wake the sleeping maiden. But he was trapped. A useless, pathetic prince. This dragon was just too powerful to slay on his own.

The scientists laid her out straight, strapping down her head, arms, and legs. They plugged her into a machine filled with coolant—and Fillion lost it. An animalistic sound roared from his body as he charged Hanley. But the offi- cers slammed their weight against him and shoved his face to the glass. He couldn't move. He couldn't look away. Hanley approached Fillion and leaned in close. The cold stare swallowed Fillion whole and he fought against the en- croaching darkness.

Drawing even closer, Hanley whispered, "She'll never be yours."

"You promised me," Fillion said, dragging in ragged breaths. "You told me if I married Akiko, you wouldn't harm her."

"But you're not really going to marry Akiko, are you?"

This couldn't be happening. Trusting Hanley was like holding a viper and trusting it to not strike. But, like the idiot he was, Fillion had caved and struck a bargain with the devil. What would have happened if he had just doxxed him like he had originally threatened? It was too late. Fillion squeezed shut his eyes. They would never open again. Somehow he knew, when Willow died, so would he. Synchronicity. Quantum entanglement. What happens to one is experi- enced by the other. Even death.

Hanley issued a command to proceed. The hum of a machine vibrated through the glass pressed against Fillion's face, making his teeth clatter. A loud thump echoed in the room. Then another. Air rushed from him as the chamber rattled from her seizures. Voices shouted. A raw, tortured scream sliced through the room and her agony split him wide open.

He knew the moment she died. The invisible thread that stitched their lives together snapped. Fire exploded inside of him as everything they were, everything they would never be, incinerated to fine ash. His chest heaved as he gasped for air, his heart pounding with violence. Convulsions wracked his entire body.

But the worst pain of all—he hadn't saved her. A scream scorched through his gut and left his mouth in a rush of fury.

Fillion jolted upright.

His limbs were no longer restrained, but his body was still convulsing and his lungs still gulped for air. Had he died?

The pitch black confused his already tumbling thoughts. His gaze darted around for any signs of life. Nothing.

Holding his breath, he touched his face to confirm he was solid, then recoiled. Cold sweat dripped down his clammy skin and coated his hair. Gross.

He had been dreaming. Another nightmare. Damn, that was the worst one yet.

Fillion stood on shaking legs and groped his way to the bathroom, stumbling down the narrow staircase from the attic bedroom. Queasiness roiled and rocked his gut as he grew dizzier by the second. God, he felt like a junkie coming down off a bad high. Too unsteady to walk, he crawled the rest of the way across the second-floor hallway in the dark and gripped the toilet seat just as he puked. Another layer of sweat broke out over his body as he spasmed again. Fillion wiped his mouth and curled up on the floor, circling his arms around his stomach.

His mind couldn't wrap around the idea that he was literally inheriting an entire quasi-Martian generation. He was a slave owner. The son of a killer. A line of killers. Legally, he was bound to his Legacy. There was no lawful refusal. No way to abdicate. His fate was sealed with the generations who believed he was the Son of Eden, the man of bedtime stories who would save them from the evils of the Outside world. Except, he was part of that evil. The sins of the father had visited the son.

A shudder wended its way down his body.

Only three more days.

Per his usual modus operandi, Hanley changed the game rules when it promised him the greatest gain. Or to create confusion as a way to slowly, methodically break someone's will. Usually both. The victim was unaware of the psychological murder taking place. Fillion, however, was conscious, and Hanley used that fact to his acute advantage.

About six months after Fillion turned nineteen, Hanley upped Fillion's Legacy trust maturity age to twenty-one to account for the lost time he had spent in juvenile detention. Hanley knew it would elevate Fillion's already toxic levels of anxiety over owning the company, thus making him more vulnerable to manipulation. Isolating him for six months from those he trusted by sending him on the World Tour, and then forcing him into the spotlight, only made a bad situation worse.

Breathe in. Breathe out.

But it hurt too much to breathe.

When the nausea settled, Fillion turned on the water for the shower. Emptiness buried him in a darkness blacker than the room. He didn't want the light on. Didn't want to see the weak man reflected back in the mirror. His normally racing mind had crashed, and he wasn't sure he wanted to force re-start. He stood in the hot stream and tried to collect himself. Stood there still when the water ran cold. Nothing. Absolutely nothing. He shut off the water but remained there, shivering while staring at the dark void.

He didn't know what to do. The bed was probably too gross from all the sweat. But he couldn't hide in the shower all night, either. Time to move forward and let the system crash do its job. Fillion rubbed a towel vigorously over his head and left the bathroom. It wasn't until he saw a pretty brunette in the hallway that he noticed the lights were on.

"Are you all right, Mr. Nichols?" Tracy asked.

Fillion froze. Naked. And had to process her question for a moment. Why in the hell was the service droid—the one that came with the house—on the second floor at this hour? What time was it? He lowered the towel, though it was a pointless move. Anyone who wanted to see something already had. The *An Garda Síochána* probably bugged his house before Fillion even arrived. Hell, they were probably running surveillance through Tracy. He didn't think to check after arriving four days ago, too tired from his travels during the World Tour—and too relieved to be free from Hanley's company.

"Mr. Nichols?"

"I'm fine," he ground out. "Reminder: You're not to enter the bedroom areas of the house without my permission. That's a privacy order."

"I heard screams and sounds of distress. Safety overrides privacy." She frowned to appear concerned. "Do I need to alert the guards?"

"I'm fine. I rolled over onto an external remote and turned the Imigicast on by accident."

"Well, that's a relief, Mr. Nichols." Tracy strode past him and continued down to the main level.

Fillion closed his eyes with a heavy sigh and bit the inside of his cheek. Sometimes stories just spilled out of him without effort. It was disgusting. "Shit. Dammit." He continued to swear, running up the stairs to the attic room, and then dressed with lightning speed. "Cranium, the time?" He squinted at the bright blue light as the Cranium flashed 1:47 in the morning. Snatching his jacket off a chair, he grabbed a pack of cigarettes and his wallet from the nightstand, then strode out of the house before Tracy could ask where he was going. Who the fuck cared? It was none of her damn business. Or the world's.

Where to now? The computer underground in Dublin? No. He didn't want to get sucked into that scene without Mack. Better to find a tourist night-club and blend in. Maybe. Right now, he couldn't think straight. He began walking with no destination in mind.

A car wheeled past, making his hood flap as he placed a cigarette in his mouth. Shielding the lighter with a jittery hand, he lit up and savored the first drag. Smoke escaped his mouth in a shuddering breath as he marched toward the unknown.

Head down and hood up, he focused only on his combat boots as they clomped across the damp concrete, treading along Philipsburgh Avenue. Neon signs and holographic advertisements flashed in his peripheral vision. Fingers of light clawed across the wet roads, clutching at the asphalt as the shimmering colors bled into the shadows. The night sky drizzled sporadic raindrops, and the tiny slips of water pricked his hand.

The garish retail storefronts gave way to more brick-and-mortar residential units, like his great-grandfather's terrace house. Homeless men and women huddled against the wrought iron gates surrounding a stone cathedral, begging him for money, food, anything to help them forget their pitiful existence. There was nothing he could do. He couldn't save them. He couldn't save himself. Helplessness overwhelmed him once more. But he forced his legs to keep marching onto Fairview Strand, away from the church and away from the homeless. Moving targets were less likely to get mugged.

Lost to his sinking thoughts, he barely registered the boarded-up storefront where his feet had taken him. The building was decorated in graffiti, and moss and ferns rooted in any crevice available, even the window panes. Trash coated the gated front yard, where people had tossed cans and wrappers like coins into a wishing well. The gate screeched as he pushed it open. He kicked through a few pieces of trash. An aluminum can clamored over the cement and rolled away, its tinny clatter harsh in the night's silence. Fillion strode up the front steps, then paused before the dark blue door.

On the other side were the remains of his great-grandpa Corlan's custom woodworking shop—now his. Antique machinery, molded sawdust, and rats were officially signed over to him three days earlier, per the specifications in his great-grandpa's will. Seven days before he turned twenty-one. Not a day sooner, and not a day later. Weird, but Fillion was too mentally fatigued to search for hidden meanings. The building was a giant heap of abandoned hope next to a pile of dilapidated dreams. And, yet, it was one of the most valuable possessions he owned. He reached for his keys but couldn't find them. Had he left them back at the house?

"Sir, face the camera and put your hands out."

Fillion thunked his head against the door. "Shit," he muttered, then turned around.

A holographic female *Garda* appeared a few feet from where he stood and locked a spotlight on him. It scanned his face in several motions. He held very still, barely breathing, until the scanner turned off with a loud, mechanical click. The officer blinked. "Identified as Fillion Malcolm Nichols. Male. Twenty years old. Non-chipped. What brings you to Fairview Strand at this hour, Mr. Nichols?"

He didn't answer right away. Instead, he fumbled with his pack of Marlboros, placing a new cigarette in his mouth. "I'm just passing through," he murmured. Where the hell was his lighter? He searched his pockets, pretending to act perfectly natural. The drone was gathering information on him—biometric responses, brain wave activity—looking for any markers that would indicate lies or overly nervous behavior. Probably checking to see if he was drunk, too. "Don't happen to have a lighter on you?" he asked.

"Smoking is bad for your health, Mr. Nichols. It is strongly advised that you seek help at an addiction clinic. The fair city of Dublin is happy to send a list of approved clinics to your message center."

"I appreciate the concern, but no thanks. Call me Fillion, please."

The female guard stood military style with hands folded behind her back, her green eyes barely registering a blink. "Did you plan on passing through the building, Mr. Nichols?"

He sighed, fingering the lighter in his pocket. Smart-ass drone. What could he tell her? He freaked out after a stress nightmare? Stormed out after an android caught him in the nude? The police station would laugh themselves into a stupor. And they were listening. And watching. Everything he said would go on public record. Hell, his wandering would probably be reported on the Net before business hours began. Everyone owned his life. Nothing was sacred. He just wanted to escape.

Wait.

An idea struck him, and he lifted his lighter out of his pocket and lit up.

Taking a long drag on his cigarette, he exhaled and said, "I'm waiting for a taxi, but I don't think my request went through. Wi-Fi dropped." He lifted a single shoulder in a small shrug. "I own this building. Family business. Check your probate records. Corlan Jayne was my great-grandfather."

"Verified," she said after a few seconds. "Where do you travel to at this hour?"

"Alchemy Nightclub and Venue."

"Please don't leave this location. I've ordered a taxi on your behalf. You should receive the receipt shortly in your message center."

"Thanks." Fillion winked with a one-sided smile. "I'm used to wandering around in other countries," he continued while puffing on his cigarette. "Never had the police order a taxi for me before. What gives?"

The holographic woman tilted her head like she was considering his question. "Mr. Nichols—"

"It's Fillion."

"Mr. Nichols, the guards are in pursuit of a dangerous man suspected of murder, last seen in this neighborhood. Have you seen him while *passing through*?" The drone shifted its hologram into an image of a man in his late twenties.

Fillion carefully studied the man's features. "No. Sorry."

The hologram faded back to the digital woman. "Thanks for your time."

"No prob," he replied under his breath. Thanks for his time? Did he actually have a choice?

The *Garda* drone departed. Fillion drew his eyebrows together and sank to the concrete steps. He casually looked over the dark neighborhood. A man suspected of murder? Did she know Fillion was the son of a killer? Lately, he couldn't tell if information like this was meant as a joke or was truly real. Six months with politicians, space agencies, and corporate magnates made him distrust everything, including himself.

Moves and countermoves.

He dragged on his cigarette while raking shaky fingers through his hair. Another *Garda* drone hovered over the sidewalk across the street, searchlights on. The rusted iron gate creaked in a gentle breeze and he startled, nearly dropping his cigarette. God, he felt so jumpy. Escape couldn't come fast enough.

The Cultural District was calling his name. Two nights ago, he had melted into the throbbing music, drowned himself in whiskey, and then walked along the River Liffey until he found a scenic spot to watch the sun rise. He had needed that release from all the pressure and expectations. Now it was Saturday night—well, Sunday morning—and the scene would be hot. A perfect way to forget his existence and discover another. But he was departing for Tokyo in a few hours with a scheduled in-flight video meeting with the NASA Mars team. On Monday, he had a *hanami* press junket with Akiko at *Shinjuku Gyoen* before heading back to Seattle—though she didn't know his immediate plans that day—and then off to California early Wednesday morning.

He groaned with the mental reminders and flicked his ashes. The *Garda* drone had linked his Cranium to a taxi order for Alchemy Nightclub and Venue. He was stuck. "Stuck."

But you're not really going to marry Akiko, are you?

The nightmare came back to him in flashes.

There were things Hanley refused to talk about due to Fillion's restraining order. At least, that was the excuse given. One subject concerned the rumors of a secret company. Another was Hanley's plans for the community of New Eden Township following project shutdown. Corporations were viewed the same as people in a court of law, and thus granted certain rights of privacy. Hanley didn't have to disclose these details. Financial information, yes. His future plans? No. Fillion was inheriting an unknown situation, and his employer was a monster—the son of one, too.

He leaned the back of his head against the woodshop door and studied the few stars that bled through the city's ambient light. Thoughts of the coming week plagued him. A disease with no cure. But, here in Dublin, sitting on his own piece of property, was surreal.

Shortly after turning thirteen, Fillion received a birthday card from his great-grandpa Corlan, who had died five months earlier—hand-delivered by an attorney his great-grandpa had secretly hired. Even more shocking, included inside was a living trust that bequeathed the house and woodworking shop to Fillion on March 20, 2058. Hanley was stunned, believing the family property in Ireland was rightfully Della's as the oldest surviving heir. Fillion's mom, however, was not as surprised, and she took Fillion and Lynden to Ireland during spring break to begin the probate process.

Had his great-grandpa known that Fillion would need a safe haven? A place where he had roots and memories to sustain his reality? Fillion had fallen into the attic room's bed four days ago, emotionally and mentally exhausted.

The bed where he had taken his first breath of life. Same with his sister.

The bedroom his mom, uncle, grandpa, and great-grandpa were born in as well.

For the first time, he had tasted freedom and the peace that accompanied this understanding. It was his home. *His.* Bound by the laws of inheritance, and protected by the Republic of Ireland. His mom could've filed a caveat to challenge the authenticity of the will, but she never did. And Hanley finally "insisted" Fillion enjoy his inheritance. He made sure that Fillion heard his opinions. What would Hanley do with the house and woodshop, anyway? Nothing. The point—like always—was for Fillion to feel guilt and shame.

A taxi pulled up, yanking Fillion from his thoughts. He rubbed out his cigarette on the road with his boot then slumped into the back seat. "Waverley Avenue."

"Are you shitting me?"

"Sorry, mate. Changed my mind. I'll leave a fat tip for your troubles."

"Damn Yanks," the driver muttered as he rolled out onto the road for the considerably shorter lift than was ordered. He looked at Fillion through the rearview mirror. "Flutered? Or just an ignorant American gobshite?"

Fillion met the driver's eyes. The man didn't know that the world's Eco-Prince sat in his taxi. Good. A smile teased the corner of Fillion's mouth. "Nah, just a sober eejit."

The older man laughed. "A lad like you should join in the *craic.*"

He ignored the driver and looked out the window, counting the house doors leading up to his. "Stop here. This is my place."

"Ya sure you don't want to head out to Temple Bar?"

"'Nothing good happens past 2 a.m.' Ever heard that expression?" The driver's answer was a thin smile. Fillion ignored him and paid the electronic bill with his Cranium, adding a sizable tip. "As promised."

"Thanks a million."

Inside the house, Fillion shuffled up the stairs.

Still in his clothes, he fell on top of the bed and blinked slowly as his body bounced on the springing mattress. He scooted up to the pillow and stared at the shadows on the ceiling.

"What's my legacy?" he whispered to the walls. His fingers inched over the comforter. Clawing toward something meaningful. Gritting his teeth, he rolled his eyes. Like it mattered. "I'm the first-born loser of a first-rate swindler," he answered for the brick and plaster. Angry laughter rumbled out of him. The dispirited sounds echoed in the empty room. He was mental. Talking to a freaking wall and praying to his ancestors like a Green Moron. Holed up in his very own hundred-forty-year-old house, and he was still muttering to himself like a homeless person. Classy.

He rolled over toward the shuttered window and cinched his eyes close. Reality was becoming soupier the closer he approached March 27: his birthday, and the first day he'd no longer be the master of only his life.

Three more days…

Cars and drones rushed by outside his window. It was like a sea of technology, and the waves of sound, set to the rhythm of traffic lights, eventually lulled him toward sleep—but not peace.

The nightmare returned. Except, this time, the dead body on the examination table was his.

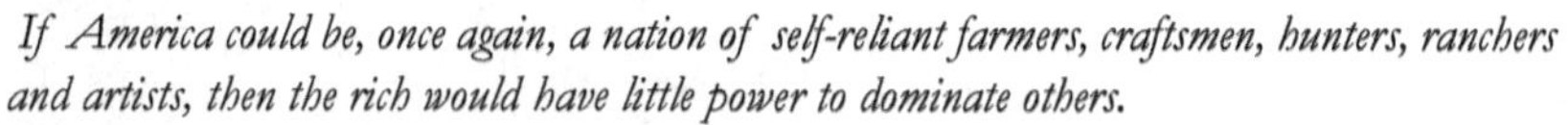

If America could be, once again, a nation of self-reliant farmers, craftsmen, hunters, ranchers and artists, then the rich would have little power to dominate others.

— Edward Abbey, author and essayist, 1989 *

The Anime Generation is failing to thrive. Not only do we struggle to find employment, the skills necessary to sustain our existence should capitalism fail has been programmed out of us, too. And, believe me, capitalism will fail if employment continues to trend for computers and robots over humans. Who will buy your products and services when governments and corporations—you—possess all the money in the world? Who will you control when people can't even drag themselves out of the gutter from hunger and disease?

— Fillion Nichols, World Tour speech in Dubai, November 22, 2057

Chapter Two

New Eden Township, Salton Sea, California

Sunday, March 24, 2058

A scientist in a white coat scurried by, weaving in and out of the families heading toward the village square. Leaf leaned his forearms along the upper deck's railing of his apartment and watched until the man disappeared around the bend. A long sigh heaved from Leaf's chest and his shoulders slumped.

He was ready to return inside and announce his departure when war cries emerged along the entire length of the village path. A passel of lads nimbly raced up various deciduous and evergreen trees. They each gripped the end of a long rope that was securely tied at the other end to a home's second story railing. The boys raced to each tie their end of rope around branches and trunks. Their mothers and sisters stood beside baskets of wash and gave encouraging cheers, while fathers and older brothers wagered good-naturedly on which boy would win. A gangling lad with brown, rumpled hair and a missing tooth lifted a fist in triumph to Leaf. He replied with a warm smile and a congratulatory nod. Soon, several ropes spanned the path, gently dipping toward the ground within arm's reach. The winning boy's mother had already lifted her arms to their rope, and pinned a wet cloak to the line to dry.

Memories of racing up trees with Skylar and Coal on laundry day, scraping knees and releasing their own war cries, lifted his heavy thoughts. He settled along the railing once more, deciding to enjoy the morning and allow his mind to clear and settle. Messages of import could wait. He was bound for The

Chancery this morn soon enough anyway.

Golden light sheathed the villagers who passed by along the trail in conversation. The trees creaked and groaned under the bio-breeze. A bird soared above the tree canopy. Its wings beat the air to remain aloft before swooping toward the tree line in an aerial dance. Leaf marveled at the bird's ability to take in the full scope of the bustle and restlessness below. Above its black, outstretched wings, the mosaic sky reflected a dull blue. Dull—an observation he could claim after peering into the vast, azure skies beyond The Door on more than one occasion.

"Alder?" Willow's voice sang out below, interrupting Leaf's musings. Light hair—belonging to his son—flashed in the bushes and then disappeared. "Where are you hiding?"

"Here!" Alder cried out with a giggle.

Willow whipped around toward a bush and placed hands on hips playfully. "You silly toad! You gave me quite a fright."

"Boo!" Alder said in response to the word "fright" and Willow smothered a laugh. His son was an endless source of amusement. And, at two-and-a-half years of age, he was a perpetual motion machine, too. As if reading Leaf's thoughts, Alder announced to his aunt, "Catch me!"

"Are you not tired of this game yet?"

Willow shook her head when Alder dashed from the bushes toward the village path. White-blond hair fell in curls and framed his round face, the unruly tresses bouncing as his small legs pumped quick-like toward the stairs. The steps slowed him down, however, and Willow caught up with mock exasperation.

"Alder Dylan Watson, you shall tire me out before the day has even begun." She tickled his side, and the boy giggled while squirming away. "Remember to be a good lad and remain quiet for your mother." Willow took Alder's hand and assisted him with each step. "Shall I fetch your wooden blocks?"

"Play with blocks!"

"Very well. Do mind your manners."

"Blocks please, Auntie Oak."

"There is a good lad."

The boy jumped up onto the deck from the last step with a squeal. "Remember," Willow began, crouching to eye level with Alder. She caressed his hand to match her gentle tone. "We need to use soft voices. Show me soft?" His son caressed her hand in return. Willow smiled and Alder grinned in reply, revealing a dimple. In a whisper, she said, "Now show me a soft voice."

"Roar!" Alder answered back, his dark eyes sparkling with mischief. Laughter sputtered from Willow's compressed lips. A giant grin stretched across Alder's cherubic features in delight, and Willow reached out and messed with his mop of hair. Alder ducked and ran around the stair rail and into the apartment. His small feet thumped across the wooden floor.

"You are doomed, Your Majesty," Willow said as she meandered next to Leaf.

He lifted the corner of his mouth in shared humor.

Willow pulled from her pocket a small bundle wrapped in cloth. "Ginger biscuits from Cook."

"My humble thanks." Leaf shifted on his feet and cleared his throat.

At times he felt embarrassed, knowing his actions led to Ember's condition. She carried their second child, with four weeks left until the estimated delivery date. It was a helpless feeling he could not shake, nor did he know how to respond thusly before the community. During Alder's birth, Leaf received a glimpse of his own father's anguish when Mother had died. Leaf knew if anything happened to Ember, he was partially to blame, and that was a loss he could not even begin to process.

Unlike her time with Alder, this pregnancy came with persistent sickness, general weakness, headaches, and now swelling. Brianna, her step-mother and the Township's midwife, reassured him that Ember would fare well, prescribing her rest and low doses of magnesium sulfate. Words meant to comfort, but they did not. For he and Ember both lost their mothers to childbirth. It was difficult to not dwell on his anxieties, especially as his wife's time drew near.

"Auntie Oak!" Alder peeked around the half-closed door. "Play with blocks!"

"Do we speak to our elders in demanding tones?" Leaf asked kindly, and Alder's eyes rounded when spotting him. "How does a gentleman speak to a lady?"

Alder straightened his little shoulders and raised his eyes to Willow. "Auntie Oak, please?" He ended with a bow of sorts and Leaf rewarded his son with a proud smile.

"How can I refuse such a *charming* gentleman?" Willow took Alder's hand and led him back into the apartment.

Leaf resumed his quiet thoughts as he peered out into the budding forest. New life unfurled and graced the once bare limbs with promises of renewal and hope. It was a time of rebirth, his favorite season of all. Sometimes the meditative ripples of nature's peace swelled inside of him. Sometimes, the angst of growing things that, everywhere, persevered to push through the darkness toward the light.

Outsiders did not share this connection to Gaia's rhythm. It was a perplexing enigma Leaf failed to comprehend. Though New Eden was cut off to test long-term survivability on Mars, there were times he felt more connected to the Earth outside its doors than the Outsiders who lived there.

A bird flitted from one branch to another, flapping away when Laurel's laughter cut through the village sounds. Corona hung on her arm as they traipsed along, lost to their excited chatter. At the intersection of paths, they slowed their steps and bowered their heads together—one with hair as light as day, the other dark as night—looking over their shoulders casually. Canyon waltzed up behind them in quick strides, carrying a bucket. Yesterday, the young man had pulverized roasted egg shells in a mortar and pestle to lime the various ponds this day.

"Good morning time, My Lord," Laurel called out. She lowered into a graceful curtsy as a soft pink hue bloomed upon her cheeks.

"Laurel. Corona," Canyon said with a dip of his head. "A fine morning to you both." The Son of Water breezed by and continued on his merry way toward the North Pond.

The girls giggled behind hands when Canyon was out of earshot, the pitch of their voices escalating as they climbed the stairs. Rounding the corner, Laurel stilled as she met Leaf's waiting gaze. Corona lowered her eyes respectfully.

"Does not Joannah need your assistance this *fine morning?*" Leaf asked.

"Yes, Your Majesty." Laurel smiled at him. Her long, golden hair danced in the breeze. Amber eyes blinked, then she feigned modesty, lowering her head as Corona had done earlier. "I simply left my apron behind and returned home to fetch it."

Leaf narrowed his eyes and studied Laurel. Every shop possessed extra aprons for this exact situation. A month away from twelve, his youngest sister was far too mature for her age. Or so he believed. Ember reminded him a week prior that she was not much older than Laurel when he began leaving flowers on her windowsill, a notion that only added to his worrisome thoughts.

"Corona chaperoned me through the woods as she is here for spinning lessons with Oaklee—pardon, with Her Highness." Laurel glanced at Corona with a friendly smile. "Is this not so?"

"Indeed," Corona volunteered.

The word "chaperone" caused Leaf's eyebrows to raise. "Well, do not keep Joannah waiting. We must honor our commitments."

"Yes, Your Majesty." Laurel lowered into a graceful curtsy. She kissed Corona on the cheek and said, "I shall see you at mid-day meal, *soeur de mon coeur.*" In a flutter, Laurel practically danced into the apartment with a long, melodramatic sigh. Corona hurried behind her with bashful footsteps.

Leaf scrubbed work-worn hands over his face, then ambled into the apartment. It was nearly time for his meeting. Alder played in the corner with his wooden blocks, building towers. Corona settled beside Willow for her morning lessons.

Down the hallway, he pushed in his bedchamber door—once belonging to his parents—and found Ember sitting on the edge of their cot. Dark circles lined her eyes and red-gold curls tumbled down her back and over her shoulders. A knitted shawl loosely wrapped her bare shoulders and arms. She had taken to wearing her thin, linen shift to bed for greater comfort. A smile greeted him as he shut the door. They gazed at one another for several heartbeats, before Leaf knelt at her feet.

"How do you fare, My Lady?" he asked softly, taking her hands. She placed his hands flush upon her rounded stomach and a kick answered in reply. They both smiled when their wee one kicked his hand once more. "She is a lively one," Leaf said.

"'She,' My Lord?" Ember's eyebrow arched with amusement. "You are rather sure."

"Oh yes. All the ladies in my home are feisty. I am wholly surrounded."

Ember lowered her lips to his and graced him with a chaste kiss. "When do you leave for The Chancery?"

"Now, actually." Leaf pulled the packet of ginger biscuits from his pocket. "Cook was kind enough to send these along with Willow for you."

"That is indeed most kind of her." Ember received the food and placed it upon their bedding. "Does Willow join you this morn?"

Leaf's eyebrows pinched together. Another kick pressed against his hand as he opened his mouth to respond. The feel of his child distracted him, and he caressed the spot where their unborn babe had touched him.

"Your thoughts are heavy this morn." Ember placed her hand on his cheek. "Allow me to carry away some of your concerns. I shall speak with her about the Ceremony."

He searched the dark brown depths of her eyes. They were the same shade as Alder's. The boy's eyes were starting to show the same intelligence that burned behind them, too. His wife possessed a gift for insight, a trait he found captivating. He need not answer her, for she already knew how he would reply. Moved by her love and support, even as she suffered, he cupped her face and pressed a light kiss of his own upon her lips.

"Thank you, My Lady, for gifting me with family," he whispered. "I am forever in your debt." Fears threatened to overcome him with his words. He quickly stood from his kneeling position and cleared his throat. "Shall Coal turn on his Cranium to meeting mode so you may listen in and participate?" Ember brushed away a tear, and his heart stuttered a beat. He thrust his fingers into his hair, blinking back sudden shyness.

"No, My Lord. I shall fare well. I wish for fresh air and plan to picnic in the meadow with Alder."

"May I join you during mid-day meal?"

"We would be honored by your company. I shall have Cook prepare an extra dish for our basket."

He took her hand and kissed her fingers, bowing deeply. Ember turned her head toward her shoulder as her eyelashes lowered. She was most beautiful, especially in the soft morning light, and he drew in a breath, lest he stop breathing altogether. "Until then, My Lady."

It did not take long for him to reach The Chancery near the East Cave in the village. The clank of Connor hammering on metal set a work rhythm as people moved about in various occupations. Clotheslines reached from home to tree along the entire length of the village path. Linens and modest articles of clothing billowed through the main square. Women with baskets and pins lowered into curtsies as he passed, while children ran through the endless curtains and makeshift hideaways, or shooed birds from perching upon the temporary lines.

The door to The Chancery was open, so Leaf let himself in with a soft "hello the house" to announce his presence. Chairs creaked as bodies rose to stand. Leaf dipped his head in acknowledgment to Jeff, Skylar, Coal, and Rain. Michael, however, remained in his chair. The Outsiders did not favor ceremony or custom, nor honor his position, even though he was minority owner of the lab that employed their services. Some of the scientists and officials were affable—such as Michael—but most were indifferent, and a few treated him as though he were unintelligent and coarse. It rankled Leaf's sensibilities, unaccustomed to rude treatment. Nor could his mind understand the cause for offense.

Movement in the corner beside the window drew Leaf's attention. A young woman with blood-red hair, curling upward at the chin, and thick, darkly rimmed hazel eyes, rose from her chair. A black mid-length skirt, edged in red and split in the front, draped over breeches that boasted multiple straps and metal brads. White lettering and designs were scrivened in elegant loops and shapes across her form-fitted, black tunic, and tight sleeves narrowed into silver rings that looped over the middle finger and thumb on each of her hands. Her attire and presentation were similar to how Coal now fashioned himself. Still, it was rather shocking on a lady. Nevertheless, he maintained a polite expression. The way she appraised him with mild blasé disinterest was reminiscent of another and, he knew, without introduction, that he stood before Fillion's sister.

"Welcome, My Lady," Leaf said with a bow. "It is a great honor to finally meet you."

She cracked a tiny smile. "Thanks. Yeah, nice to meet you, too."

"Hanley, at last, conceded permission for Lynden to enter New Eden," Coal said as a way of explanation. "He wishes for Lynden to represent the Nichols family in preparations for the Ascension Ceremony and Celebration."

"My wife shall be disappointed to have missed your visit."

"Lady Ember is not in New Eden?" Coal asked, his eyes widening.

"My apologies for the confusion. She is unwell this morning and rests at home." Leaf took his seat, and those standing eased into their chairs after him. To Lynden, he asked, "How fares your brother?"

"Just fine."

Something in her gaze suggested otherwise, but Leaf moved along, not wishing to press her further. "I, as well as many others, look forward to seeing Fillion once more. It has been far too long." She provided a faint smile and glanced away, shifting in her chair. The diffident body language was very much like her brother's and, for a moment, Leaf wondered how much Fillion had changed after the imprisonment and extended travels with Hanley. "Shall we proceed?" He nodded at Jeff, hoping to alleviate Lynden's discomfort.

They discussed, in detail, the press conference leading up to the Ceremony, which would take place in front of the large pomegranate tree in the courtyard Outside. After all the official documents were signed, Fillion and Hanley would mingle with the press and guests in attendance.

Michael relayed a message from Hanley that The Aether and The Elements were to stay in the background unless approached. And Hanley requested that those from New Eden refrain from hors d'oeuvres and beverages unless offered by the caterers. Leaf squinted his eyes as he listened to Hanley's assistant and lead scientist speak. Why were they not permitted to participate in the festivities as the invited guests they were?

When the room quieted, Lynden shared that Akiko Hirabayashi, Fillion's fiancée, would be in attendance and be Fillion's guest of honor at the Celebration inside New Eden Township the evening following the Ceremony. Hanley had appointed Lynden as Akiko's assistant and, as such, it was her duty to share with the others Akiko's requests. The word "duty" was said with disdain and Leaf stilled.

A flush colored Lynden's fair skin and she lowered her eyes. "Akiko requests that no one from New Eden speak to her directly. They may go through me instead, and I'll relay any replies she may have. Also, Akiko will bring her own cook to prepare her own food." The room silenced until nary a breath could be heard. Tears welled in Lynden's eyes and she looked up at the ceiling, crossing her arms over her chest as she whispered, "I'm so sorry."

"Forgive my ignorance," Leaf began. "Surely, as Fillion's intended, she understands that she not only insults her future husband but his family and all of his employees as well?"

Lynden's face relaxed into an expression devoid of any emotion. It happened so fast, he blinked in surprise. "That's the point."

"I am afraid I cannot be party to anything that not only dishonors Fillion but dishonors my home as well."

"You don't have a choice." Lynden spun in her seat toward the window, her body unmoving and stiff except for the black ring she twisted on her thumb.

"Of course I have a choice." Leaf stood, and those from New Eden followed suit. "I wish for a private moment with Coal and Lynden, if I may?"

"Certainly, Your Majesty," Skylar said with a bow. While lowered, he flashed Leaf a furtive glance and tapped his ear, then gestured with his head toward Michael. Before Leaf could reply, Skylar asked, "Shall we wait in the village?"

"Let us reconvene in a half-hour's time." Leaf dipped his head to Skylar, then faced Jeff, who nervously flitted his eyes away. "May I use The Chancery?"

"It is time for my mid-morning stroll," Jeff replied with practiced ease. "Take all the time you need." He leaned in toward Leaf and said, "Your presence is requested in the boardroom Wednesday morning." The lawyer handed Leaf a slip of paper, then strode from the office with Skylar and Rain close behind.

As quietly as possible, Leaf tucked the invitation into his pocket. An awkward silence descended upon the room. Offense thundered in Leaf's pulse. He studied Lynden as his thoughts attempted to compose polite conversation. Coal had moved next to her, leaning against the wall, his hand drawing comforting circles on her back. The gesture was both protective and tender, and Leaf understood the unspoken message. Michael poked at something in the air and Skylar's warning came rushing back.

"Did you record our session, sir?"

Michael forced a smile and tapped his Cranium. "Mr. Nichols asked to review the planning session since he was unable to attend."

"Is the recording saved or was it streamed to Hanley in real-time?"

"Real-time."

"And now?"

"My Cranium is turned off, Mr. Watson. In an act of amity, I'll place it in my pocket. You can trust me."

"Is that so?" Leaf said, allowing a thread of distemper into his voice. "Yet you recorded our session without first announcing your intentions."

"Coal," Michael said, "I believe I'll join Jeff on his stroll." The scientist paused before Leaf. "Hanley will ask what you had discussed in privacy. I'll let you and Coal decide that answer before we leave New Eden."

Leaf pinched his brows together and watched the man leave. Unable to gather himself quickly enough, he stared at the closed door long after it was shut. When his pulse resumed a manageable pace, he faced the Son of Fire. Time continued to stretch between them in thick silence.

Willing more patience, Leaf finally asked, "Please explain what you mean by my inability to have a choice."

"I am not allowed to share this with you, though you are The Aether and my King," Coal began quietly, "for I was required to sign contracts and nondisclosure statements with N.E.T." The tendons in his brother-in-law's neck flexed. "The penalty is permanent isolation from friends and family within the lab. I am so sorry for not speaking sooner, Your Majesty. I have been too terrified."

"Dear Lord in Heaven," Leaf said under his breath. "Please consider before sharing then, My Lord. For I am responsible to not only protect my family but the community as well. Therefore, I cannot guarantee that I can act as though I know nothing of what you may share."

Coal issued a curt nod and looked away. "To Earth," he began again, "I am a Martian who has fully assimilated. They accept me in part, as I mirror their culture and their ways. It is easy for me to forget what *I am*. However, whenever in the company of people from NASA, many at N.E.T., as well as those in other governmental agencies, I am reminded of what most of Earth does not yet know, but perhaps suspects."

"'What I am'? What are you?"

Coal locked eyes with Leaf. "Property."

"I beg your pardon?" The air rushed from his lungs. "Property of whom?"

"New Eden Biospherics & Research. According to human property laws, I am a product of science, born of genetic manipulation for experimental purposes and, therefore, the lab that created me must own my life for liability purposes." Coal clenched his jaw. "In the science communities and to the global governments, I am a slave—and so are you."

Leaf stared at Coal in horror for several heartbeats before he buried his face into his hands. Thoughts stabbed him one at a time as he tried to comprehend Coal's explanation. He thought of his wife and children, of Willow and Laurel, and rejected the reality that they were property, owned by another. If this were true, why did the project need to shut down? He was told, per law, experiments of this kind were permissible for a maximum of twenty-five years. A solid plan for the future had yet to be revealed. Hanley continually evaded this question.

"I need more details," Leaf said, his fingers trailing down his face. "I believe you, but I do not fully grasp what you share nor what this implies for New Eden."

Coal and Lynden both launched into definitions and descriptions, providing answers to each of Leaf's questions. The information grew more horrifying until the sense of foreboding completely entombed him. Why the second generation was not required to sign The Code suddenly made sense. But how had his father's money been woven into this scenario?

"Do I actually possess minority ownership of N.E.T.?" he asked when the conversation dimmed.

"I am not sure," Coal replied. "That is a question for Fillion."

Leaf grit his teeth and exhaled slowly. He shifted his eyes toward the window and found Lynden studying him. "Is it possible to request a private audience with your brother during his stay at N.E.T.? Or am I not allowed to make requests?"

"Make requests. Who cares what they say? But I'll let him know, no prob." She rose from her chair and sauntered toward him, and Leaf straightened his posture. "I'm sorry," she whispered, the pain surfacing on her features once more. "Akiko is not Fillion's idea—"

"I know, My Lady," Leaf said. "I was present when Hanley shared the news of an engagement contract with Fillion, and I witnessed your brother's refusal. I may be a simple man from a simple world, but I do understand laws and contracts." Leaf paused for a heartbeat and continued in a softer tone. "Fillion is a good man, and I am honored to call him family. I do not think little of him for his engagement, nor do I you for your appointed position to represent his fiancée's affairs during the Celebration."

He lowered into a slight bow. "Please relay to Miss Hirabayashi that we are honored by her visit and we shall do all in our power to ensure her comfort." Leaf clenched his jaw when rising. "However, she is entering *my* world. I will not insult the community with vain requests nor offend our Cook. As The Aether, given legal rights provided in The Code and in the Legacy drafted by Hanley Nichols, this is my decision. If Hanley wishes to reveal the falsehood of these rights, he shall have to inform me so himself and in writing, signed by witnesses."

A slow smile spread across Lynden's face. "I like you."

"Thank you."

"Akiko is going to cause an epic scene. Fillion might, too." Lynden lifted a hand and flipped her hair, shaking her head. "My brother is . . . intense. I think he might actually be losing his mind. But Akiko *is* crazy."

"I appreciate the warning," Leaf said simply. This was the emotion he noted in Lynden's gaze earlier. "We shall do our best to accommodate without dishonoring all involved."

"Good luck," she replied.

To Coal he said, "For now, I shall only share with Willow and Ember. The less who know until I can speak with Fillion, the better. If I choose to do otherwise, I shall inform you first of my intentions." He dipped his head in deference. "Thank you for sharing. I am deeply honored by your sacrifice."

"I have wished to tell you for so long. But I didn't know how. Then Michael started to share his discomforts over certain ideas––and treatments––and offered to support whatever line of communication I wished to open with you. To warn you." Coal dropped his voice. "Hanley has eyes and ears everywhere."

"You trust Michael?"

"I am undecided. Michael has been my advocate since Exchange Day, and my friend. There is much to recommend him."

"You do not worry he shall spy for Hanley?" Leaf crossed his arms over his chest and narrowed his eyes. "It all seems rather convenient."

"If Michael is being honest, he certainly understands the risks. I would remain guarded."

Leaf closed his eyes and attempted to regulate his emotions once more, needing to remain calm and level headed. "So," Leaf said with a disheartened sigh. "What I hear you saying is that we should play along with eyes wide open and our minds fully engaged, more so than before."

"Precisely," Coal replied. "I would even go so far as to say to not even trust Fillion. Hanley sets up many situations through him."

Leaf raised his eyebrows. "Should I distrust you as well?"

"I long to say that you can always trust me; however, I am a pawn being moved within the game just the same as anyone else involved." Coal's heated gaze billowed with fury. "Even though I am viewed no different than the robot who serves our drinks in meetings."

"I am beyond grieved and know not what to say," Leaf whispered. He considered his brother-in-law a heartbeat, then asked, "*Vous avez trouvé le bonheur à l'extérieur?*"

"I am a product of myself, Your Majesty. No man can steal my life, although they might try," Coal answered in English. He then peered Lynden's direction surreptitiously and added, "*Malgré les circonstances, j'ai la chance de connaître le bonheur.*"

Leaf smiled knowingly. "Such sources of happiness will drive a man to fight for his home, to protect the precious gift he has been given."

"To wage wars, if necessary."

"Indeed." Leaf extended his hand toward Coal, desiring to forge a partnership despite his brother-in-law's warnings. The Son of Fire gripped Leaf's hand with a grim smile and bowed his head.

The others returned shortly thereafter, and they resumed their meeting. Michael placed the Cranium back onto his ear with an announcement first that Hanley was listening in, but to act natural and to pretend otherwise. Leaf began with an apology to everyone and a quick explanation of his need to confirm the more private details of Fillion and Akiko's visitation to ensure their comfort, nearly choking on every word.

The walls of The Chancery seemed to crowd in and attack Leaf's waning self-control, and he wished for isolation. There was much to process, especially what purpose his family still served Hanley. Leaf had heard Hanley declare that he and his sisters no longer existed, and that to remove their presence and fingerprint on the world was an easy feat. In the same breath, Hanley was adamant that he did not wish for the world to know the Watson siblings were alive for he feared the ramifications. These threats proved empty and false in the end, and Leaf battled with occasional paranoia over the unexpected change in opinion. Far too unnerved to continue in present company, Leaf wrapped up the meeting and said his farewells to Coal and Lynden.

Outside The Chancery, he studied the length and direction of his shadow and determined the time. The honeysuckle scent of laundry soap wafted on the gentle breeze. Mothers and daughters took down and folded garments and bedding, then hung others in their place. Children giggled with games of hide-and-seek and chase, dashing in and out of the undulating linens.

How would he share that the second and third generations were *owned* by the very man they celebrated this week? The Son of Eden determined *every* aspect of their future.

The joyous atmosphere wrapped around Leaf, and his shoulders slumped with the burdens he carried once more. Turning toward the meadow, he left the village behind in search of his wife and son. It did not take long to find them. Ember stretched out on a woolen blanket and Alder picked the tall grass. Willow worked with her loom not too far away, beside the other weavers.

His wife's eyes moved his direction and Leaf lifted a finger to his mouth as he crept up behind Alder. Unaware, Alder continued to babble to himself, using a stiffer grass stem as a sword to unleash the violence of his imagination onto a hapless flower. Swift and sure, Leaf scooped up his son and blew raspberries upon his stomach. Alder squealed and giggled, squirming in his arms. Laughing, Leaf threw him up in the air and caught him, lowering his son to the ground.

"Father, run!" Alder commanded, lifting his grass blade. Unable to resist, Leaf trotted away, allowing Alder to chase him. Scrunching up his small face into a fierce expression, Alder pretended to stab Leaf in the leg and Leaf fell to the ground in response. His son jumped on him with a triumphant giggle. Leaf wrapped his arms around the boy's small body.

"Have you eaten your mid-day meal yet?" Leaf smoothed away a soft curl from his son's eye. "Every warrior must feast to celebrate his victory."

"No eat meal," Alder said, wiggling out of his arms. "Hungry, Father?"

"Yes, let us bask in your mother's beauty as we dine like heroes of old, shall we?" Per his usual way, Alder dashed away and leapt onto the blanket. Leaf sat up on his elbows and met Ember's amused gaze over the rustling grass and dancing wildflowers, the small smile confirming that she had heard every word he spoke to their son.

The sinking feeling settled in his stomach once more, but he pushed it aside for now. He would disappear for the remainder of the afternoon to organize his thoughts. This moment, however, belonged only to his family.

Epigenetics is the study of inherited changes in gene expression … changes that are inherited, but they are not inherent to our DNA. For instance, life experiences, which aren't directly coded in human DNA, can actually be passed on to children. Studies have shown that survivors of traumatic events may have effects in subsequent generations.

— Futurism.com, 2016 *

Like silt deposited on the cogs of a finely tuned machine after the seawater of a tsunami recedes, our experiences, and those of our forebears, are never gone, even if they have been forgotten. They become a part of us, a molecular residue holding fast to our genetic scaffolding.

— Discover magazine, 2013 *

Chapter Three

People watched Lynden's every move like she belonged to a freak show. Yeah, the circus came to town. Piss off. She stared straight ahead and pretended to not notice. She was invisible. Thin air. They didn't *really* see her. Not the real her, anyway.

Out in the village, she rubbed her arms as she glanced around as inconspicuously as possible. Coal wrapped up conversation with Skylar and Rain and laughed at something one of them said. The sound encouraged a small smile, but Lynden wiped it away as quickly as it formed. His laugh was infectious. But his smile was dangerous. And god she missed him. It had been a couple of weeks since their last visit together. He slid a glance her way, as if reading her thoughts. She looked the opposite direction. Easier to control her emotions this way.

Her bottom lip ring flicked in and out of her mouth as she nibbled on the silver hoop. Laundry was strung up all over town, fluttering in a light breeze. It looked like a costume closet had exploded on the set of an expansive period drama movie. There were kids everywhere. They laughed and played, and she watched their zig-zag movements from the corner of her eye.

An older girl fresh out of pigtails—somewhat tall and slender, with long, blond hair—froze and gaped at Coal, recovering her surprise quickly. He seemed to notice her at the same time.

"Good day, Laurel," he said.

This was Leaf's sister? Was Willow Oak nearby? Lynden's anxiety spiked and she reached for the ring on her thumb, twisting it around absently. *Breathe.* She took on a mildly aloof posture.

"My Lord, I did not know you visited this day."

Coal bowed before Laurel and she lowered her eyes and tucked her chin toward a shoulder. Was she flirting with him? Weird.

"I met with your brother to discuss the Ceremony and Celebration," he said.

"Of course." Laurel darted her eyes toward Lynden and smiled politely.

He tracked her movements and said, "I am honored to present Lynden Nichols, the Son of Eden's sister." He held Lynden's hand. "And this young lady," Coal said to her, "is Laurel Watson."

"My Lady." Laurel dropped into a curtsy. "A pleasure."

"Hey," Lynden replied. "Nice to meet you."

Laurel tilted her head in a pretty way and considered Lynden for a sec. Then she returned her focus back onto Coal and tapped the basket in her hand. "I wish I had time, for I long to talk more." Lynden eyed the basket, wondering what was hidden in there. She must have let her aloof expression slip, for Laurel glanced at her and angled the open top of the basket toward her for a better view. "Wood betony and vernal grass," she explained, then turned quickly back to Coal again. "Hay fever is especially irksome this year, it seems."

A kind smile curved her full mouth and Lynden felt a twinge of jealousy. What a joke. She was jealous of a girl half her age. No. That wasn't the source of her thoughts. Did her older sister share the same elfin looks? The jealousy mixed with insecurity, and Lynden stared past Laurel and took in the scenery. It was inevitable. She'd face Willow eventually. She might stop breathing. That'd be embarrassing. She better focus on breathing, just in case.

"Your sister and Her Highness are in the meadow over yonder," Laurel added. Lynden suppressed a groan.

"Thank you," Coal responded. "Please give Joannah my regards." A nanosecond later, Coal leaned toward Lynden and whispered, "Shall we?"

"What? Go frolicking in the meadow over yonder?" Lynden arched an eyebrow. "How cute."

A subtle smile lifted the corner of his mouth. "Actually, I am famished."

"No. Shocking!"

He leaned close again and whispered, "I am rather spent, Lyn. Nor do I wish to trespass upon my sister's poor health this day. Frolic in the meadow another time, perhaps?" The smile faded and a faraway look entered his eyes as he turned toward Michael. "Ready?"

No Ember? Or Willow? Now Lynden really was shocked. And relieved.

"Lead the way," the scientist answered.

Coal gripped her hand and moved through the pockets of people. She felt every pair of eyes. Heard every whisper. Apparently, holding Coal's hand was the equivalent to a ten-point magnitude earthquake. Would kissing him right here, right now—as if he were her last meal—be like Mount Vesuvius? She could almost envision the people choking on the ash of their prudish lifestyle. She was tougher than shit, though. The freak show was over. Time to take the circus to a new town.

Damn, she needed a distraction. Looking around, she realized her and

Coal's hands were swinging back and forth, like they were skipping. When did she start that? Well, why the hell not. With a conspiratorial smile Coal's direction, she tugged on his arm and skipped forward. A grin stretched over his face, and she soaked up the sight. He was seriously dangerous. Killed her every time.

Lynden issued a look of mock innocence. "You didn't say no frolicking to the woods."

"An oversight, you troublesome faerie," he said with a laugh. "I will be more precise with my words next time."

When they reached the forest, she slowed and spun to walk backwards. He gazed at her like she was a rare piece of art. Nobody looked at her like that. It was a level of appreciation that went beyond the physical and straight to the core of her as a person. The kind of appraisal that sent a hive of bumble bees into her body. She buzzed and felt the rush of wings, her insides dripping, gooey and sweet. And the soaring experience came complete with the sting of judgment for falling in love with such a man.

Lynden looked up at the pieced together sky, peeking out from behind tree limbs. That was her and Coal. Separated but one. Broken by inhumane laws, but together made whole.

She and Coal had the last laugh, too. One year ago, she became Mrs. Draken Smyth before Mack, who officiated their secret wedding. Not even Fillion knew. Nor would he ever. Mack even filed a marriage cert with the government, using their fake I.D.'s to make it official. The ceremony was simple and perfect, their vows exchanged up in the mountains beneath a lush canopy of stars. When they were alone, Coal shared New Eden's tradition of handfasting. This time, however, they made their promises in their real names. To him, she was Lynden Norah-Leigh Hansen. To cyberspace, she was Rainbow Leigh Smyth. To their families, they were the same as always. But, to her, she was good enough to be his. That's all that mattered. The end.

A man pulling a small hand cart passed them on the dirt road. He bowed his head with a quiet, "My Lord," to Coal. Lynden glanced over her shoulder and studied the dusted white sacks he hauled.

"Flour," Coal said, studying her face. "We will see The Mill in action on our way out, it appears."

All morning she felt stuck in a fairytale. Did they really just walk past a guy with a wooden wheel hand cart? With burlap sacks? Who wore one of those thin, fabric baby-bonnet type caps that tied under the chin? The man had his untied, though. The strings dangled down his neck and upper chest. God, people looked at her like *she* dressed funny.

"What the hell is he wearing on his head?"

Coal peered over his shoulder and back to her with amusement. "A coif. It is rather *en vogue* for men of industry in the Middle Ages."

She rolled her eyes. "Was that the miller?"

"No, *Mademoiselle*. I am happy to introduce you to the miller, though, if that is your desire."

Lynden shot him a side glance. "Your speech is thicker since we've been here."

"And this bothers you?"

"Nah. It's sexy."

"Anything for the lady," Coal said with a dimpled smile. Killed again. Damn. Look away.

The forest was pretty and serene. She half expected to find a dewy-eyed maiden singing to the wildlife, birds perched on her outstretched arms. Out of the corner of her eye, she watched Coal and tried to picture her husband in this world. What did he look like in a tunic? She'd never seen him in one. Did he wear one of those ridiculous coifs once upon a time? Had her brother? The last thought made her snicker. She couldn't help it. Coal peered her direction.

"This is crazy. I'm trying to picture you growing up here."

"Is it really so difficult?"

"You're so modern compared to them. Even when I first met you."

Coal rolled his bottom lip into his mouth for sec. He was uncomfortable. That was always his sign of nervousness. She stopped walking and flicked the platinum blond strands that fell over one of his dark brown eyes. With a shy smile, she curled her arms around his neck, nibbling on her lip ring. She was nervous, too.

"What are you thinking, Mr. Awesome?"

"This world should never end." He turned his head away from her. "I wish there was a way to help the Anime Gen through communities like this one. Perhaps they would not struggle so hard to eat or work. Earth needs a reboot."

Lynden's eyes widened a notch. Did Michael hear? She glanced at the scientist over Coal's shoulder. The guy stood a healthy distance back reading something on his Cranium. Working even as he took a walk through the woods. Geesh.

"You want to rewind progress?" she asked. "Like, for an entire generation?"

"I was speaking with Mack—"

"Oh god. First mistake."

He laughed and the rush of wings fluttered through her again. "True." Coal dipped down toward her, then straightened and glanced around, as if he had changed his mind about something. "Come along, *mon joli petit dragon.* The miller is a busy man this day." A smile tipped the side of his mouth up. It was a look that promised many things. The kind of things that would make her forget her own name.

"Your smoldering gaze sucks, Son of Fire."

"Every great man needs a flaw, I suppose."

Lynden groaned and pushed away from him. "Hey, Michael." The scientist looked over his screen, almost startled. "Come here."

He obeyed, scurrying up the rutted dirt path like a good little scientist-slash-personal-assistant. What a puppy. He was kind of adorable. Ten years older than her or so, he sported male pattern baldness like its poster child. He looked at her with large greenish-brownish-somethingish colored eyes and, she swore, his gaze quivered under her inspection. It was his discomfort around girls that made him all sorts of cute.

Lynden looped her arm with Michael and she could imagine his mouth getting dryer by the second. "Come on, Michael. You have a normal sized ego. *His* is too big to fit through The Door."

"It is all your fault, Lyn," Coal said in reply. "All day long I hear Mr. Awesome this and Mr. Awesome that."

"Ignore him," Lynden said, squeezing Michael's arm with hers. She forced Michael forward and cast Coal a flirtatious look on the down-low. "So, Michael," she began in a sing-song voice, returning acute attention onto him. "You live at the lab year-round?"

Michael flicked his eyes Coal's way and back to her. "Yes, I do. My work keeps me busy. I don't mind too much."

"I hear you'll become Fillion's personal assistant after the Ceremony?"

"That's correct," Michael said, bobbing his head.

Lynden patted his arm. "My condolences. My brother is . . . well, he's intense."

"I think we'll get along just fine." Michael offered a shaky smile.

"Do you have any siblings or are you an only?"

Michael lowered his head in a bashful way and Lynden smiled to herself. "I'm an only, Ms. Nichols. Are you and Mr. Nichols close?"

"Yep." Lynden forced a bored expression. "For two more days, Fillion and I are the same age. Our time of armistice is quickly coming to an end."

The scientist smiled, an honest-to-goodness smile. Aw, he was so stinking adorable. "Sounds like I should be extending my condolences to you, Ms. Nichols."

"Seriously. I'll take them." Lynden shook her head with an annoyed sigh. "Fillion's dictator mode is why I've demanded a month-long cease-fire each year since we were thirteen."

This time, Michael patted her arm in response. They were like an old couple. Coal had to be dying a little bit inside. Good. Served his male pride right. She and Michael continued to stroll, and she remained a good girl and used her upper crust social skills to keep conversation flowing with Michael— ignoring Coal entirely. Except when flirting with him over Michael's shoulder by flashing a disinterested look, as if irritated that he was still there.

The last of the apartments gave way to a towering stone wall, bordered by a layer of trees. The Mill appeared to her right. Behind her, Coal slowed to a stop when they stood at the forest's outskirts.

A few people bustled in and out of The Mill, and Lynden watched, intrigued. The creaking groan of hidden gears and the splash of moving water roared in her ears. A middle-aged man unloaded a sack of flour from his shoulder into a different wooden cart, next to a girl. With graceful movements, the girl threaded a needle through the top of a different sack.

Coal knotted his fingers with Lynden's and led her toward the enchanting scene. Michael stayed behind, muttering something about a report he needed to review.

A large pond pooled around the building like a watery skirt with lily pad polka dots. Ferns grew near the waterline and up against the abutment of a stone bridge. Across the bridge stood a large tree, newly budding.

"This is a breastshot waterwheel," Coal explained, dragging her toward the object of discussion. An enormous, rotating wooden wheel dropped partially below ground level compared to the rest of the building. "The North Pond is fed by a stream that circles the main biodome," he continued. "The Mill is situated along a weir, channeled out for a mill race. To make it operational, the sluice gate is opened." She looked to where he pointed. "The water spills out and into the wheel slats, then downstream through the tail race." She watched the water run through another gate in a stream toward the pond. "The stream continues from the pond underground, beneath the North Cave and surfaces on the west side of the cave entrance. It disappears beneath the apartments and surfaces through the gardens, then back beneath the apartments again."

Lynden faced him. "Did you repair any parts for this?"

"Let us peer in the window." Coal gestured toward the building.

In a few steps, they reached the storybook window and she traced the leaded panes. He pressed his nose to the glass and cupped his eyes to shield against the light. She did the same, and wow. Inside, metal, wood, and stone wheels and axles spun and rumbled. It was like looking at the innards of an oldschool watch. The man who had tossed a sack of flour into the cart now stood at a chute, catching freshly ground flour into another burlap sack. A different man used a lever-and-pulley system to hoist sacks of grain through a trap door in the ceiling. The wheat began its journey all the way up there?

"To answer your earlier question, yes." Lynden stood back and met Coal's eyes in their shared reflection in the window. "I have repaired small parts on the waterwheel as well as the interior machine."

"I will never look at a bag of flour the same again."

"It appears the miller is on the bin floor. Introductions shall have to wait until another time."

She attempted to sound like him. "Oh drat! Howsoever shall I fare with my disappointment?" She failed miserably.

He quietly laughed, though. The kind of laugh that communicated she was cute. Then, he grabbed her hand and pulled her into a jog.

"Hey! What are you doing?"

Coal smiled over his shoulder. "A surprise. Pretend you like them."

Their footsteps swished over the grass. They passed the girl stitching the sacks and the stone bridge. Upon reaching the giant tree, Coal rounded to the trunk's shadowed side, cradled her face, and promptly captured her lips with his. She stiffened in his arms at first with the unexpected affection. But she loosened up a few seconds later and curled her arms around his neck, tangling her fingers into his hair.

"Coal?" she whispered in between kisses. When he failed to respond, she whispered, "Mr. Awesome?"

"I have missed you, Lyn."

He trailed his mouth along her neck with seductive kisses, then tasted her lips once more. It had been two weeks since she had last seen Coal and, damn.

Finding her voice, she asked, "So, is this the surprise?"

Coal pulled away just enough for his breath to engage in foreplay with her mouth, and her heart performed flip-flops. "I ardently profess my love for you, Lynden Hansen," he whispered against her lips. "I am yours, body and soul, and seal my declarations beneath the sacred boughs of the linden tree."

She pushed him back a step and looked up, her eyes rounding a tad. "*The* linden tree?"

"Naturally."

Lynden issued a droll expression, then swiveled to face the trunk. "Where are your parents' initials?"

Coal grasped her hand and rounded to the trunk's other side and pointed at his father and birth mother's indentations. Next, his fingers trailed the rough bark until they skimmed over Connor and Brianna's initials.

"And here is my sister and Leaf's." He looked at her, his eyes hopeful. "May I etch our initials into the trunk, perhaps during the Celebration?"

Lynden played with her lip ring as her anxiety levels rose. "No. Sure. I don't know," she said, twisting the ring on her thumb. "I worry—"

"Yeah, I know." Coal circled his arms around her waist. "We do not break the law by carving our initials into this tree."

Michael cleared his throat. "Sorry to interrupt," he called out. "But, we need to get going."

"Drat," Coal swore. He lifted a corner of his mouth. "My babysitter tires easily of my adventures."

Lynden brushed her fingers across the numerous initials. "Perhaps you'll have to ardently profess your love for me tonight when we're alone."

"No, I can only do so once a day. You will have to wait until tomorrow."

"God, really?" Lynden groaned, punching him in the arm. "You're an ass."

"*Moi?*" Coal pivoted toward the trail. "I am wounded, *Mademoiselle.*"

"Yeah, this is me crying over your pain." Lynden stuck her tongue out at him and Coal laughed. "Pretend it's tomorrow."

"Alas, I cannot." Coal attempted a straight face. "Perhaps I can make amends to you this night through *other* forms of confession."

"The honor price is pretty steep. I don't know."

"I shall endeavor to work hard to regain your good opinion of me then."

Lynden rolled her eyes and casually flipped her hair. "This whole conversation is ridiculous." But secretly, she loved it. God, she was such a girl.

His response was a humored smile, meant more for himself. Then it was gone. Poof. Just like the panes of the biodome, she suddenly noticed. Sunlight heated her skin and burned her eyes as she lifted her gaze to take in the clear, blue skies. During their back-and-forth, they had crossed the bridge, entered the cave, and exited the biodomes. The freak show had officially left town.

He laced his fingers with hers and a sharp pain slashed through her chest again. To the world, he was her boy toy. Her gift from Daddy. She wanted to shut down the Net with statements of how he was the most honorable, kind, loving man she had ever known. When he touched her, he didn't just appreciate her body, he cherished *her*. His kisses erased every insecurity she kept close until her heart beat to the words beautiful, wanted, essential, loved . . . good enough.

Overwhelmed with his earlier gesture, Lynden tensed against the forming emotions and quietly said, "Thanks for the surprise."

He flashed a rueful smile and fingered the silver bracelet dangling from her wrist, a gift on their wedding day. Then, he lifted their joined hands and kissed her fingers.

They had finished their prayers and were on their way from the temple and passing under the great cherry tree known as the 'Kanzakura' or Holy Cherry, when they saw, standing near its stem, a youth of some twenty or twenty-one years. He was handsome, with a pale face and expressive eyes. In his hand he held a branch of cherry-blossom. He smiled pleasantly at Hanano, and she at him; then, bowing, he came forward and smilingly presented her with the blossom. Hanano blushed, and took the flowers. The youth bowed again and walked away; as did Hanano, who had a fluttering heart and felt very happy, for she thought that this youth must be the one sent by the God of Love in answer to her prayers.

— from "The Holy Cherry Tree of Musubi-no-Kami Temple" *

Chapter Four

Tokyo, Japan

Monday, March 25, 2058

A gentle breeze plucked a flurry of soft, pink petals from the forest of cherry trees at *Shinjuku Gyoen*. Ripped from their life source, the *sakura* petals traveled across the park like angry whispers. The manicured lawn bled pink where Fillion sat. Legs stretched out and crossed at the ankle, he draped an arm across the back of a wrought iron bench.

He exhaled a thin stream of smoke and glanced over his shoulder. The world whizzed and spun around him while his mind, for once, processed in slow motion. Eyes, everywhere he looked, seemed to study his every movement. He flicked the ashes and pretended not to notice. Or care.

Picnic blankets dotted beneath the pink trees for *hanami* celebrations. The forecast had been favorable this year, and the treasured trees bloomed early. A large group of young men and women, around his age, busied with setting up tables and paper lanterns not too far away. They would feast and drink *sake* late into the night. Fillion had attended a *yozakura* party once when sixteen. With *her.* A piece of ash fell on his fingers and he swore. Damn. He was mentally rambling again.

"*Tabako wa iya na kuse desu yo. Kekkongo toriaezu yameta hou ga ii deshou. Watashi ni haji wo kakasemasu.*"

Fillion bit the inside of his cheek. The light, modest quality of Akiko's voice reeked with class and charm and clawed at the remains of his unraveling state. The offending cigarette dangled loosely in his fingers, next to a pink petal that rested on his knee. He stared at the wisps of smoke, curling, reaching, then dissipating.

"*Kiiteimasu ka?*" A dainty hand, clad in rings and white-painted nails, brushed the petal off his pants in a single sweep.

He shifted toward Akiko and checked his response. Shoulder-length, rose-tinted hair—colored specifically for their *hanami* press junket—lifted in the breeze. The warm, mid-day light glowed off her smooth, ivory complexion. Earrings dangled and reached the thin straps of her designer dress, which left her small, elegant shoulders bare. Dark eyes spared him a quick glance, before her head returned to a dignified position.

To the world, his fiancée was the gold standard of beauty. To him, she was everything ugly in a human—fake, shallow, self-centered, and demanding. He loathed pretentious social-dictators. And when it came to governing their relationship, she was tyrannical. But only because she didn't own him, and that was apparently unacceptable. Like hell if he'd let her treat him as if he were the rug beneath her gild-slippered feet.

Akiko ignored his dark stare and, instead, smiled demurely for the media, which clamored a few feet away. Drones, androids, and humans snapped pictures, streamed live video, and shouted questions to him and Ms. Hirabayashi. She answered with intelligence while dipping her gaze and bunching her shoulders with grace. The media devoured her aura of bashful confidence as if half-starved.

The low hum of machines and their boisterous voices clashed with the Zen this park was meant to inspire. A peace he grappled at but couldn't cling to. Whatever. Fillion was a pro at acting natural in an unnatural situation and while in the company of someone he detested.

The dainty hand returned to his knee with a warning squeeze. She wanted to play coy? Fine. Give the people what they want. Leaning forward, Fillion pretended to nuzzle her cheek and she rested a hand on his chest in reply. Sentimental sounds from the onlookers cooed from every direction, and he almost gagged.

"The first thing I'll change in our marriage?" he whispered in her ear, using sultry tones. "Us. Name only. Separate bedrooms. No heirs." She released an angry gasp. He flashed his eyes to the media as a flirtatious grin spread on his face. "And," he began again, pressing a light kiss beneath her earlobe, "I'll smoke as many damn cigarettes as I want. Wherever I want."

She pulled away and locked eyes with him, her gaze promising a lengthy conversation later. Code for nuclear meltdown. Except there'd be no later. But she didn't know about his travel plans.

Fillion's mouth curved with satisfaction as her eyes narrowed. She recovered quickly, though. A shy smile touched her lips once more and he waited for the fake giggle. There it was.

It was spring. The cherry trees were in bloom. The fragility of life and death were immortalized through the ephemeral blossoms, and thus celebrated. But that was not why he and Akiko sat beneath the diaphanous rain of *sakura* petals. Their media stint was staged to capture the Japanese imagery of falling in love—an experience as beautiful and delicate as blossoms. It was said that as one story began, another ended, such as love, such as the cherry tree. Akiko played the blushing maiden to perfection. And . . . he was done. His smile widened with arrogance for a nanosecond before pushing off the bench.

Fillion didn't look back. Even when she called after him. He continued walking through the tangled mess of picnic-goers, refusing to acknowledge her or the drones chasing after him. Irritation boiled to the surface and past his self-control. He lifted a cigarette to his mouth, then slipped a hand into a pocket as if reaching for his lighter. Inside the pocket, his fingers found the personal EMP switch and pushed the trigger in the programmed rhythm. The drones and androids trailing behind crashed to the ground in a loud clang. Personal devices not on his person within a fifteen-foot radius were disabled, too. He wouldn't dwell on it, though. Collateral damage was an unfortunate given in any war.

It seemed like the entire park silenced into shock that moment. The crowds who sprawled beneath the profuse branches. The anthropomorphic robots. His fiancée. Control fondled his pride, arousing his ego. He'd cave this one time and allow the sweet rush. The personal signal boost offset the chunks of dignity the world took with each one of these ridiculous sessions. It was none of anyone's damn business who he fell in love with and what that looked like. Why did the world long to be fed lies?

In a matter of minutes, his name would circulate as a romantic hero among the *otaku* communities. At the same time that his and Akiko's names elicited sighs from the mouths of the delusional, his message center would flood with angry posts demanding repayment for vandalism. It wasn't the first time he'd taken out media drones; he wagered it wouldn't be his last time either. Everything in him wanted to turn around and flip off the journalistic parasites that were still operational. But he didn't.

He kept walking, shrouding falling petals in cigarette smoke. If his look didn't wilt the falling *sakura* petals, the caustic chemicals leaching from his mouth did. Good. He was satisfied with his modified metaphor. Love was a fairytale. Happily ever-afters would never be his reality. Especially with...

She'll never be yours.

Fillion slammed the door to that thought. Self-protection demanded that he feel nothing. Otherwise, the weight of the world would crush him within a blink of an eye.

He flipped the hood up from his assassin-style jacket and pulled until shadows covered his face. The botanical gardens of *Shinjuku Gyoen* couldn't disappear fast enough. It felt like eyes were still on him. Judging his every move. Recording his rage-filled exit. Only when he blended in with the stream of pedestrians choking the streets of Tokyo did the knots in his shoulders loosen a bit.

Bright lights flashed on screens attached to nearly every building. Drones whirred above the sea of heads. Every shop blared music. A tsunami of voices came from all directions and Fillion drowned in a riptide of sights and sounds. Digital limbs reached out toward him, but he ignored all attempts for attention. The holograms appeared in full-window advertisements or in human form along the sidewalk. Inside the shops, charisma clerks—mostly humans—consulted with consumers on the latest trends, which they wore, from short-skirted schoolgirl *kogyaru* outfits, to *yōfuku* westernized clothing to Tokyo street fashion.

All of it was a joke. Japan was more American than anything. Since the two countries melded their education systems, Japan's culture had become a mirage of what American corporations marketed to the world, and vice versa. Despite fashion trends, real Japanese school girls were a thing of the past. And cartoonish nowadays. Very few people went to traditional schools anymore. Westernized clothing was for mimicking the business class, not what cubicle monkeys actually wore. Most worked from home anyway. The underlying mockery of cultural hijacking seemed cruel to Fillion, except nobody cared. Japan wanted to be America, and America wanted to be Japan.

Fillion flicked the ashes of his cigarette and continued to push through the crowds.

Eerily lit, two-toned gazes darted his direction, but didn't linger long. Permanent cybernetic contact lenses were all the rage in Japan. People were flocking to the clinics to be fitted with the micro computer system that ran off of their brain waves, utilizing a transparent screen layer over their natural vision. It was reported to make Cranium technology obsolete within a couple of years.

"Are wa Fillion deshou?" a teenage girl asked her friend.

"Hontou da!"

A cluster of girls stared wide-eyed and tried to take pictures beside him as he walked, squealing and chattering with excitement. He was a good boy and refrained from rolling his eyes. He didn't give them a nanosecond of attention either and, instead, took longer strides.

Eventually, he reached Shinjuku Station and boarded the N'EX for Narita International Airport. He was supposed to have an "assistant" with him at all times and a chauffeur to whisk him away at will. Fillion enjoyed the anomaly, though. Very few things eased his mind like walking the city streets alone, regardless of country or continent. The trappings of wealth and self-importance nauseated him.

The express train departed and bodies swayed back and forth with the light motion. Fillion sat next to the window, watching the world pass by in a blur. Those around him stared vacantly at hidden privacy screens, fingers scrolling through the air in random patterns. In Japan, it was sometimes difficult to determine human from humanoid. Tech here was years ahead of other Westernized nations, despite the country's prolific Americanization. But he found an easy deduction. Robots didn't need to manipulate screens when connected to the Net. Fillion raised an eyebrow. In this car, at least a third of all the travelers were android. Incredible.

An old woman sat next to him, hunched over by an unnaturally extended life. When noting his quick, appraising look, she patted his hand and said in English, "You are far from home, Mr. Nichols. Do you leave our fine country so soon?"

"Still figuring out where I belong," he answered in Japanese.

He wasn't sure why he confessed that. Stupid. His small-talk skills would forever be the bane of his existence. Then, he wanted to laugh. Perhaps talking out loud like a homeless person all these years was to prepare him for this future. When Fillion reached Seattle, he planned on staying in a hotel until he figured out where to live stateside. He'd probably end up at Mack's until after the wedding.

"In June, our country will be proud to become your home, Mr. Nichols. It is a lucky month to marry."

The air stilled in his lungs. *"Arigatou gozaimasu,"* he said with a tight head bow. "You honor me." The words slipped out with sincerity despite the falsehood he felt in saying them. Had he spoken his thoughts aloud about staying with Mack? He couldn't remember.

The woman patted his hand one last time and then lowered her head. The elderly were not starstruck around him. Ever. It was refreshing. Creepy. But, preferred over the crazed *otaku* reactions from those younger.

An hour later, he passed through customs and boarded his private jet. Akiko had probably figured out his travel plans by now, and that he had left without her. Fillion's fingers trailed over the leather seats until he reached his favorite spot, near the back. A private jet was one of the few luxury items he afforded himself. He wasn't above commercial flights, but he wanted to be in control of his schedule. With his upcoming role as majority owner of New Eden Biospherics & Research and New Eden Township, that was a necessity.

Fillion still couldn't believe Hanley had changed his inheritance age and used his jail time as an excuse. He had been sentenced to twelve months of detention after being found guilty of two counts of employee sabotage in a trial that lasted the better part of a year. He only served five months, though, released for good behavior and to relieve overcrowding pressures. Detention was probably only a distraction, a plot point to hide the real story.

Bastard.

At least MIT had allowed him to take online courses while detained, despite their policy on granting credits toward a degree to incarcerated criminals. Perks of his celebrity status. And probably a large donation by Hanley. Still, those classes were the only things that kept him sane. And Mack. A smile teased Fillion's mouth as he thought of his best friend. God, he missed him.

The last time he had seen Mack was six months ago when Fillion graduated from MIT. In two-and-half-years, Fillion had earned a mathematics with computer science undergraduate degree, specializing in cryptography. And, because he had nothing but time on his hands, he had also obtained a double minor in music and in physics, focusing his physics electives on astrophysics and quantum mechanics. Yeah, he was a nerd. He didn't care.

The World Tour had kicked off the following day. For six months he had given elaborate, passion-filled speeches and charming interviews on employment reform to grant rights back to humans as preferred hires over their computer counterparts. He had attended state dinners, been wooed by space agencies, and pursued by governments.

The Elite applauded his convictions. But the gesture was hollow, meaningless. All they really wanted was his Byzantine blessing over their empires. Magically, everyone had forgotten his "troubled youth." Young as he was, he commanded astronomical amounts of money and wielded power over two worlds. Or so they thought. When the veneer of power and prestige was stripped away, he was still a puppet on a string.

While Hanley draped his cloak around his son and slipped his ring onto Fillion's finger, Fillion knew he was irrevocably cornered. If he doxxed Hanley, the Watsons would die. If he failed to marry Akiko, the Watsons would die. At times, during the Tour, he didn't give a damn anymore and just blew up, unable to tamp down the explosive emotions. Unable to cope under the pressure. Taking out media drones with an EMP switch—like today. Leaving mid-interview—also like today. Twisting words mid-speech to fit his own agenda instead of Hanley's. Regardless of what Hanley demanded, Fillion had a message: He would go down fighting.

Two more days…

God, he just wanted something—anything—to make sense. To feel like the ground beneath his feet was solid and real. No more games.

Games. An idea uploaded into his brain, and his entire body stilled. Even his breathing. For over three years, he'd wanted a private confrontation with a certain man. One who may have the details necessary to change the game and move Fillion into a position of real power. Today, the first day the restraining order was lifted, he could finally make it happen.

Opening up his calendar, he confirmed that his schedule was open the following morning. Perfect. He then sent a visitation request to Lewis Psychiatric Hospital and closed his screens to peer out the window. The Pacific Ocean stretched out as far as the eye could see. Fillion watched the jet's shadow skim across the glittering surface until his breathing resumed a normal pace.

Hours later, he landed at Sea-Tac Airport and took a cab downtown to the Fairmont Olympic Hotel. Being back in Seattle should elicit a twinge of nostalgia, he reasoned. This was "home" after all. But his muscles tightened even more. As the staff brought his luggage to his suite, Fillion sauntered into the bar. Stuck in a private room with people, who gawked at him, made his skin crawl.

The bartender leaned forward at his approach. "Double whiskey, neat," Fillion said as he eased onto a stool.

"ID?"

Fillion patted his pockets and swore under his breath. "Left my wallet with my belongings." And he forgot that he was no longer in Europe. The legal drinking age was ridiculously old in the States compared to the rest of the world.

"No worries, Mr. Nichols. I watched all your speeches. Especially liked the one in Dubai." The bartender lifted a corner of his mouth. Fillion didn't have a chance to reply. "On the house. Welcome back home, and happy early birthday."

Fillion cringed with his words but offered a single nod in a way of thanks.

Drink in hand, he took a sip and allowed the warmth to coat his insides. After leaving a large tip with a Cranium exchange, Fillion pivoted on his heel and moved toward the elevator. The metal doors glided open. He was halfway in when a woman shouted.

"Mr. Nichols!" The click of heels on the floor accelerated. "Mr. Fillion Nichols, please wait!" He sipped on his whiskey and swiveled toward the sound. A woman, perhaps in her upper thirties, wearing a hotel uniform and blond hair piled up high, halted her approach with an enormous smile. "Thank you for waiting. My name is Anna Kimberly. I am the director. On behalf of the Fairmont, we welcome you as our esteemed guest. I have assigned a service assistant to your suite. Please do not hesitate to let us know of any needs as they arise."

"Thanks." Fillion forced a fake smile and turned back toward the elevator.

"May we bring you a meal? I bet you're hungry after your long travels."

Actually, he was, now that she brought it up. He continued to stand in the doorway, preventing it from closing. "Sure. A cheeseburger and fries." Anna blinked, and the we're-here-to-serve-you smile remained plastered on her face. "Make sure it has bacon," he added. "Lots of it. Side of ranch, too."

"Yes, Mr. Nichols. Anything else?"

"Box seats for two to the symphony performance tomorrow night at Benaroya Hall." He lifted the cut crystal tumbler in his hand. "Another double whiskey, neat. That's all."

"Room service will bring your meal and drink within the hour. I'll have the front desk notify you once the tickets are secured. Do you prefer a call or message?"

"Message. And speaking of calls, I will *only* take front desk messages from my sister, Mackenzie Ferguson, and Draken Smyth. Refuse all other messages and inquiries."

"I understand, Mr. Nichols." They both looked to the glass entry doors where a small crowd had gathered. "Your privacy will be well guarded and respected."

"Thank you." He lifted his drink in salute and alerted the elevator to his floor by calling up the hotel screen on his Cranium. As the metal doors closed, he added, "After room service, I don't want to be disturbed."

The Service Assistant opened the doors to his suite, notified of his approach with the room key loaded into his Cranium. The android lowered her head as he entered and quietly shut the elegant wood door in his wake. Ignoring the robot, he approached the king-sized bed in a separate room and placed his whiskey on the nightstand.

His luggage rested near the bed, per his instruction. Fillion preferred to take care of his own clothing and personal belongings. The OCD in him wanted things arranged a certain way. Not to mention, it was refreshing to do something so simple, so ordinary.

Inside his carry-on suitcase, tucked between a week's worth of clothing, lay a wooden chess board. He thought about setting up a game to play against himself to burn off mental steam. No, he just needed to shut down. Gently, he tossed the board onto the bed and shuffled through his clothes.

Within minutes, he had two days' worth of clothing hung up and stowed away in a dresser. Pulling out a pair of flannel pajama bottoms, he undressed, throwing his jeans and shirt into the closet—the ones selected by Akiko for the press junket. Maybe he should burn them. The Service Assistant stepped toward the closet to care for his dirty laundry, but Fillion waved her off. When had she entered his room? Perv.

"In the future, only enter with permission," he said over his shoulder.

"Understood, Mr. Nichols."

The only non-clothing item remaining in his carry-on suitcase was a cherrywood box inlaid with abalone in the design of an oak tree. His fingers brushed along the high-gloss polish as the muscles in his chest tightened. He opened the lid and peered at the contents.

On top lay Willow's token, sealed in a clear plastic bag. The piece of rough spun linen was the most beautiful possession he owned, despite the burns, holes, and frayed edges. He slipped it out of the plastic and opened a fold and gazed at a brittle, browned willow oak leaf. Emotions tumbled through him. Memories of words and promises, the feel of her lips against his, the completeness he experienced when around her. He should have kept his distance. Deep down, he knew pursuing her would end in heartache—for both of them. Still, he couldn't let go. Didn't know how.

He placed the rag back into the plastic and reverently onto the bed. Fillion eyed the next item and gently peeled away the delicate tissue. Swaths of folded China silk in the shade of wood violets shimmered and rippled in the lighting. A wistful smile pulled on his lips and he straightened his back with a deep breath. Before replacing the tissue paper and sealing away Willow's token, he felt beneath the silk and verified that the stainless steel scissors and elaborate sewing kit were still in the box.

"What's your name?" Fillion asked, turning toward the Service Assistant.

Her eyes blinked and pink lips formed a smile. "Liz, at your service Mr. Nichols."

"Liz, this box is very important to me. No one is allowed to touch it."

"Yes, Mr. Nichols."

"Where is the safe?"

"On the other end of the closet."

Fillion strode over and studied the small safe, meant more for jewelry and wallets. "I need a larger one that will accommodate this box."

"I will return shortly with a larger safe." Liz paused and studied the cherrywood box to calculate the size, then left the room.

Fillion sank onto the bed and lowered his head. Travel fatigue was setting in. He sipped on his whiskey and peered around the room, absorbing the corporate opulence. A knock echoed through the suite and he sighed. A few moments later, the knock sounded again. He'd forgotten that Liz had left.

Wary, he opened the main door a crack and met the excited eyes of a young woman with a cart and tray. "Thanks," he said. "One sec. Don't leave."

He jogged back to his room and dug through his discarded pants until he found loose cash. He opened the door wider this time and the young woman wheeled the cart past the door, barely into his room. "That's good enough." Her eyes whipped to his shirtless state. "Here." Fillion took her hand and plunked the money into her palm as he pushed her out of the suite, closing the door.

"Wait!"

How he hated that word. Fillion braced himself and lifted a bored look her direction. He arched an eyebrow and leaned against the door's edge, crossing his arms over his chest. He knew what was coming. The starry-eyed look was a dead giveaway. Why he didn't shut the door right now, he had no clue.

"Would you sign my notepad?" She pointed to a Cranium screen.

"No." He looked at her name tag. "Jody, delete the photos, turn off your Cranium, and put it in your pocket. Or I'll fry it when you walk away."

She did as he commanded, looking a little flustered. But still, she remained. What the hell? Her eyes wandered over him and he pushed off the door to close it.

"You look different in real life." He shielded his body behind the door and thunked his forehead on the dark wood. She sighed. "Way better."

"Want my beauty secrets?" he asked, opening the door wider again. She missed the derisive tone entirely and smiled in that flattered school-girl way. "The reason I'm so goddamn gorgeous is because I'm part of a government experiment." Her eyebrows shot up. "You haven't heard?" She shook her head. "What kind of fangirl are you?" Light brown eyes widened and a blush heated her cheeks once more. "Fine. I'll tell you. There's a secret lunar colony where the government genetically engineers superior humans. I was born on the Moon."

"Really?"

"My birth certificate says Ireland because I need a Terran address. Being a citizen of both countries affords me more access to Earth. Why do you think my family is in the space colonization business? That's just my civilian job. I'm really a weapon. I stop people dead in their tracks, and that gives the government extra time to make their move."

"Oh my god."

Fillion lowered his tone and leaned closer. "I'm dangerous. I can do things most men can't." He bit his bottom lip and winked. Jody swallowed, looking him over again. "So, it's for your own protection that you stay away. We're being watched. Even now. OK?"

She looked over her shoulder. God, the human race was so stupid and gullible at times. Especially the *otaku*. They wanted to believe everything. It made him sick to behave this way. But he'd decided that if he couldn't beat them, he'd join them, and on his own terms.

"Don't tell anyone. Promise me?"

Her grin widened. "Promise."

"Good girl. Thanks for the food."

She started to speak again, but he shut the door in her face. His story would blaze across the Net by tomorrow. Guaranteed. Some days, like today, he really hated people.

Just as quickly as the rant formed, it dissolved into the black of his mind as the enticing smell of a hamburger hit his nose—and he moaned. Like, out loud. As if having a foodgasm. For a moment, Fillion peered around the suite for people's reaction to his slip. He was still alone. Good. On that happy note, he wheeled the cart into his room, hopped onto the bed, and put the tray on his lap. Eating a meal in solitude, closed off in a hotel room, had become the highlight of his adult life.

"I'm so lame," he muttered to himself.

Balancing the plate, he put the lid on the cart and stilled. On the bun's top was a piece of paper with Jody's message center number scrawled across it. Really? Yeah, not that kind of desperate. He flicked it off then grabbed a fry, dunked it in the ranch dressing, and popped it in his mouth. He swore his eyes rolled to the back of his head. So. Damn. Good. Next, he took a sizable bite into his cheeseburger. Juice dribbled down his fingers and mayo or ketch-up or something squeezed out the side with the pressure. A sound close to ecstasy emerged from somewhere deep in his throat and his head fell back as he chewed. He was so weird. And hungry. God, he could eat a dozen of these right now.

Liz returned a few minutes later, rolling a larger safe into his room and depositing it in his closet. "Will there be anything else, Mr. Nichols?"

"No. Guard the main door. I'm not taking any visitors and I don't want any disruptions. I'll message you any changes to those plans. Shut the bedroom door on your way out. Thanks."

She bowed her head and exited. Finally. Alone again. The tumbler of whiskey called his name and he replied. Amber liquid spilled down his throat and coated his muscles with instant warmth. The tension eased a notch. Another tumbler waited for him on the cart. This one he would sip more slowly. Nah. He just wanted to go to sleep and forget this day ever happened. Like most days.

A few seconds later, he placed the glass on the cart and turned off the lights. But he didn't lay down. He remained sitting on the edge of the bed. If he slept, the nightmares would return. If he stayed awake, his mind would rant the night away. While traveling, he often played chess late into the night with Hanley. Both quiet. Both studying the other.

Moves and countermoves.

He gripped his hair and closed his eyes, clenching his teeth when a chirp pinged in his head. His eyes flew open. Dammit. He had blocked Akiko's and Hanley's numbers for the day. Should have blocked more. He wasn't in the mood for business. Mack's name was announced and Fillion smiled with relief. He tapped his device and allowed the vid screen.

"A lunar colony?" Mack asked with a lopsided grin. "That's your best story yet."

"Damn. I think that's a new world record."

"You should mess with their bodies, not their minds," Mack deadpanned. "It's what they *really* want. Social cues, Fillion."

"I told her I could do things other men can't. For the rest of her life she'll wonder what that is. I did her a favor." Fillion ran a hand through his hair. "The mystery is far more fun."

Mack grinned. "Social. Cues."

"Like this one?" Fillion flipped off his friend.

"Good job."

"I aim to please."

"I hope *senpai* notices me." Mack batted his eyes.

A corner of Fillion's mouth curved up. "I like engineering my own conspiracy theories."

"Yeah. I've noticed. You've had a busy day, *bishounen*." Mack raised his eyebrows. "Walking out on Akiko. Taking out a robotic media army. Fleeing Japan. Revealing you're a weapon engineered by the government to stop people dead in their tracks with your beauty."

"Stalker much?"

"For a man who hates being in the spotlight, you sure know how to command it."

"Fuck you."

"Do I get to know what you can do that other men can't?" Mack bit down on his tongue suggestively.

"Maybe." Fillion pressed his lips together to keep from laughing. "What about dinner and a show first?"

"You mean like a real date?"

"Sure."

"Peachy. I'm in." Mack waggled his eyebrows. "You can romance me anytime, never-really-happened-husband."

Fillion shook his head, rolling his eyes. "Meet me in the Fairmont lobby at four-thirty tomorrow afternoon."

"See you then." Mack blew a kiss. "Glad you're back. Missed your smart ass."

"Yeah. We can hug it out tomorrow." Fillion drew his brows together and bit the inside of his cheek. In a softer voice, he said, "Need to catch some beauty sleep. The government is relying on me."

Mack studied him for a sec before morphing into mock-stoicism. "Carry on, soldier." He saluted Fillion as the screen went black.

Never-really-happened-husband. Fillion smirked. While in juvie, he and Mack married to gain visitation rights that were otherwise permitted to parents only. That gave them the two-hour, non-recorded window of time granted to newlyweds immediately following their wedding. A necessary move. After their "conjugal" visit, Mack signed power of attorney paperwork over Fillion's financial and mental health decisions to push back against a court-ordered mental health evaluation.

Hanley was pissed over the wedding and, later, over the power of attorney. He wanted to control Fillion through claims of mental instability. But Mack did what Mack does best: He negotiated. His friend found a solution that appeased Hanley's need to rebuild public image among shareholders while still ensuring Fillion's contract with Akiko's family remained intact. Three months later, he and Mack annulled their marriage and everyone walked away better than they were before, including Hanley and the Hirabayashi family.

"Partners for life," he whispered to the void. Fillion played with the black wedding band he still wore on his ring finger, though on his right hand. Mack still wore his, too. He could live a thousand lifetimes and still never find a better best friend than he had now. They were more like brothers, thick as blood. A long breath loosed from his chest, one he hadn't realized he'd been holding.

Yawning, Fillion picked up his discarded tumbler, desperate for any remaining drops. The first glimmer of a buzz was beginning to hit his head. Maybe he should order one more. No, he didn't want to interact with another Jody today.

Just as he was about to fall back onto the bed, a notification ping echoed in his head. Dammit. He forgot to remove his Cranium. Half-lidded, he attempted to read the message. But it was too blurry. Expanding the screen, he squinted against the bright light and burst into laughter.

> Mack: OMG. I so don't know what to wear. I'm going out
> with Fillion Nichols. What do you think? Outfit 1?

Fillion studied the first picture of Mack's utility kilt draped across his bed paired with a black shirt. A stuffed, cartoonish-looking bunny rabbit—probably Lynden's—was tossed on top of the clothing.

> Mack: Or outfit 2?

The next image revealed the exact same outfit. But the corner of the pic was taken up by half of Mack's face, biting his knuckles as if stifling a squeal. His friend had changed his hair to all-over white, the latest trend in the Anime Tech Movement; and, interestingly enough, it looked natural on him.

Fillion swiped the air.

> FNichols: Naked. It makes your dreamy, dark blue eyes
> pop.

> Mack: Rawr.

> FNichols: Sweet dreams of me.

> Mack: Best. Night. Ever.

This time, Fillion remembered to pull the Cranium off his head and placed it on the nightstand. The whiskey swished around in his head and the buzz seduced him with nothingness.

Just what he wanted.

Ay me! For aught that I could ever read,

Could ever hear by tale or history,

The course of true love never did run smooth.

— Lysander, in Shakespeare's *A Midsummer Night's Dream* *

Heartbreak is possibly the most unjust feeling. Unlike other unfortunate events—like a family member's death—we are the ones who get ourselves into it. If something goes awry, we're the culprits. …

But pain—like birth and death—is an inevitable part of life. Though I wouldn't want to experience that heartbreak again, I also wouldn't go back and change a thing.

— Sheena Sharma, dating consultant, 2015 *

Chapter Five

New Eden Township, Salton Sea, California

Tuesday, March 26, 2058

Apple blossoms sprinkled their tiny, blushed petals upon the woolen blanket Willow shared with Rain. It was morning and, this day, Willow had decided to lounge with a book in favor of the alternative. All others within the community flitted around in preparation for the coming Ceremony tomorrow and Celebration the day after. Her friend, Rain, embraced a similar idea of escape, much to Willow's delight. Each left to her own thoughts and adventures, Willow tried to get lost in the words. But she could not.

The Orchard was enchanting during the March and April months. The Old Biddies transformed by magic, their blushing branches proudly boasting a love affair with Spring. Inspired by a grove of faerie trees in profuse displays of peach, white, and pink, Willow selected *A Midsummer Night's Dream* by William Shakespeare to peruse until the mid-day meal. The scenery was far too beautiful for a book, though.

A deep sigh escaped her too-tight chest and she rolled to her back, resting the poetic words upon the ties of her kirtle bodice, and folded an arm behind her head. Knobby limbs dressed in delicate, elegant finery bobbed in the bio-breeze, releasing another shower of petals.

In truth, reading about lovers who gallivanted through the woods was more than her mind wished to ponder and imagine. Today marked the last day she was free of *him*. Tomorrow was a dreadful day, where her life married his in a matrimony of business and politics. And while she endured an entire community celebrating a man who no longer laid claim to the heart he was gifted, he would find solace and comfort in another.

Residents hid gossipy whispers behind hands when she passed by in the village square as the days sped toward this week's festivities. During meals in the Great Hall, some looked upon her with pity, others with silent reminders of how spirited, opinionated women were unwanted by men. Intelligence was prized and deeply respected; but in New Eden, a woman should be unassuming, despite her intellect. Her romance had become something of a moral story for younger maidens. She was a jilted woman—unheard of in their world—and rejected by the esteemed Son of Eden.

The community did not judge him the same way they blamed her—for he was an Outsider and the upcoming owner of New Eden Township, while she had known better. She had not controlled her behavior as a Noble lady should; as a Princess, no less. This is why, according to the wagging tongues, Fillion Nichols had pursued a more refined woman and why Coal Hansen preferred the Outside world rather than be reminded of the mistake of wanting to court her. The latest rumors reported that men now feared that any attentions from her might result in their sudden attraction to the Outside world.

Such rubbish.

How she longed to turn back time to when she had publicly gifted Fillion her father's Harvest token and allowed him to walk her home during the hour of rest. The community would have never known of her affection, nor her shame. Nor would Timothy have possessed fuel to question her reputation before all present in the Hall the day of the Great Fire—her sixteenth birthday.

She did not regret giving Fillion tokens of her affection nor indulging in fervent kisses, which had left her breathless and longing for more of him. From the very beginning, she knew he would break her heart. It was a pain she had feared despite her own weakness for him, a connection she could not sever nor control.

Still, she knew fighting for Fillion meant fighting for her home. They were entangled truths. Her pledges and promises were always in earnest. She loved him, could not stop if she tried, and seeing him once again would only stir these feelings even more. A relationship full of *nevers*, her thoughts whispered to her soul. Fillion was right. Pursuing her did end in pain, and she held her breath against the ache.

"If you continue to frown so, the tree might wither and die. I do so enjoy apples." Rain stretched out beside her on the blanket and pointed her gaze toward the gauzy clouds of blossoms.

Willow turned her study from her friend toward the apple tree as well. "Yes, it is a grave day indeed when such loveliness fails to cheer the soul."

"The trees appear as though they wear bridal veils, crowned in floral chaplets, do they not?"

"Indeed, and each blushing blossom a young bride."

Rain giggled. "A tree full of brides, 'tis a horrifying thought."

"Perhaps the branches quake with nerves rather than listlessly sway on the verge of swooning whenever the breeze whispers its sighs of sweet nothings."

"And the petals?"

Willow focused on a tiny, pink petal and whispered, "The decay of empty promises, delicate as hope and bruised with mourning. Soon, the bursting passion that once consumed the tree shall give way to leaves, and life will find new meaning, the blossoms all but forgotten."

Rain wove her fingers with Willow's. "Celebration day shall pass swiftly. I have made it my personal duty to ensure your goblet is always full and your feet dance rather than run."

"I do not wish to dance, though I have every intention to run." Willow forced a smile and shared a conspiratorial glance with Rain. "I shall not refuse a full goblet, however."

"Are you still cross with Coal?"

"Heavens, yes! 'Tis unforgivable that he should depart without introductions." Willow released an irritated breath. "Ember shares my offense, as she was in my company that morning. I am quite certain Coal shall receive a thorough chastisement upon the morrow."

Her friend smiled. "Coal Hansen in trouble?" Rain laughed to herself. "Oh, Willow. Lynden possesses an otherworldly beauty that defies proper description." The Daughter of Water rotated her gaze back to the tree and said wistfully, "Her hair is the color of ripe apples, skin kissed by faeries, and large, bright golden eyes. Her eyelids sparkled as if encrusted with dewy grass. And her mouth was painted the same sanguine hue as her hair. She was like an Outsider Faerie Queen."

Willow watched her friend, knowing the disappointment Rain suffered upon learning of Coal's attachment years prior. Though nothing compared to the anguish of waiting for Skylar Kane to realize his affections for her. It was quite obvious to all that the Son of Wind cared deeply for Rain and she him. And, yet, he pursued only friendship.

What would it be like to possess the same freedoms as men? To declare one's heart without taint or tarnish to one's reputation? Men were not seen as promiscuous or ungentlemanly for professing their admiration. Alas, Willow feared her hopelessly romantic friend would remain a maid—at least they would be together.

Rumors circulated of the disgraceful circumstances surrounding Rain's birth as well. Many believed she was the love child of Norah Daniels and Jeff Abrams. Even if true, Lady Rain was elegant, graceful, intelligent, and well-spoken. Any man would be richly blessed to have her for a wife. But the pettiness of such insignificant details surrounding her birth shaded her life with scandal.

In this, they shared a bond that other maidens of marriageable age did not understand. It was difficult enough that they were both head Nobles, an intimidating fact for most village men. Although, Willow did not desire to marry, even more so now that Fillion had found another woman with whom to share his life. The very sound of his name, spoken so casually in her private musings once more, upwelled the mud of her emotions and she grasped for safer thoughts.

Lightening her tone, Willow asked, "Was Lynden amiable?"

"She is a Nichols, no? Her demeanor was polite, but she carried the same aloof bearing as her brother." Rain released Willow's hand and rose to a sitting position. "She spoke only when spoken to and made brief eye contact on occasion to demonstrate that she was listening. Otherwise, she seemed overwhelmed by her surroundings."

"I imagine it is quite overwhelming." Willow gently tossed her book upon the blanket and rested up on her elbows. "It is the same reason I have yet to venture Outside of the biodomes. The very idea is frightening." This was not entirely true. She had far more frightening reasons for not venturing beyond the panes of her home. Reasons her friend need not be privy to, nor anyone beyond her home. Instead, she looked to her friend and bantered, "I applaud her bravery."

Rain laughed, the pleasant sound wrapping around Willow. "You are quite brave, Your Highness. I do believe you confuse bravery with stubbornness."

"Perhaps," Willow consented with a genuine smile. "I am rather mulish at times."

"Do you think he shall look far different? Similar to Coal in attire and grooming? I try to imagine him so and cannot."

Willow's stomach clenched and she fell back onto the blanket, draping an arm over her midsection. Never had she shared with Rain how she had first met Fillion, nor would she travel any farther along the roads of those memories. "My Lady, I do not wish to discuss him beyond required pleasantries."

"My apologies. However, I cannot recommend myself as your friend if I do not help you prepare for reintroductions upon the morrow."

"The element of surprise appeases me."

"It does not!" Rain shook her head. "For shame, Willow Oak Watson. I know you well enough to say with confidence that you are spinning tales."

"Mayhap I am," she said quietly, more so to herself. "My Lady, I shall not join the Ascension Ceremony in the courtyard Outside nor shall I grace *him* with my presence at the Celebration any longer than necessary. I shall make an appearance to ensure I do not embarrass my brother, and that is all. Nothing you or Ember may say shall change my mind."

Rain lifted a corner of her mouth. "For you are mulish?"

"Precisely." Willow turned her head away from Rain. "And it pains me too much. Have I not endured enough tragedy and scandal?"

"You are not even curious to see *her*?"

"No, not really." Willow rose to a stand and brushed petals from her dress. "I shall return shortly. I wish for a new book."

Rain repositioned onto her stomach and opened her book with a smile of understanding. Willow ducked beneath a low limb and then ambled along the worn footpath between the trees. Bees bombinated a cheerful tune as they paid social calls to each blossom. She tucked the book under one arm and extended the other to caress the soft petals with her fingertips as she passed. A gentle bio-breeze brushed along her skin and flurried strands of her hair as it stirred the sweet scent of an entire orchard in bloom. Petals twirled through the air, released upon the wind like the very sighs of tree maidens pining for the breeze to deliver another message from their lost love.

The last thought caused her breath to catch. Her entire being became leaden by thoughts of Fillion. Although he broke the heart he promised to guard and protect, she wished him the happiest of futures. She simply longed to live her life without reminders of him. It was not a difficult request. However, her friends and family did not seem to understand that their desire to help her face tomorrow and the day after only reopened the wounds. She was not disillusioned. Neither was she, now nineteen years of age, the innocent maiden who parted with her broken heart to a broken man. She knew it would be impossible to avoid the new owner, especially when her brother was The Aether and King of New Eden Township. There would be many opportunities to see each other. But alas, not tomorrow. Not during public affairs.

She pinched off two small twigs, weighted in apple blossoms, and wove them into the side strands she had twisted away from her face. A throat cleared a small distance away and she searched The Orchard until she spotted her brother striding toward where she lingered.

"Good morning time, Your Highness," Leaf said with a swift bow. His light green eyes darted around The Orchard. The unsettled demeanor was rather odd for Leaf, and she tightened her grip on the book. "I did not see you leave the apartment this morning," he said.

"My apologies. I rose with the birds this morn."

His face softened as his eyes rested upon the blossoms in her hair. "Do you fare well?"

"Have you traveled all this way simply to ask how I fare?"

"Is that so difficult to believe?" Concern touched his smile.

Willow drew her eyebrows together as suspicion leaked into her thoughts. "Are you worried that I shall embarrass you before all at the Celebration? For if you do, allow me to soothe your pride. I have no intention of attending the Celebration for long, nor will I sit at the head table."

"I have no such worries." Leaf crossed his arms over his chest and shifted his feet on the uneven ground. "My only thoughts were of you." She did not know how to reply and lowered her head. "Jeff informed me that Fillion's restraining order was lifted yesterday morning at midnight. He is now free to communicate to whomever he chooses at the lab and within our community prior to the Ceremony."

"Thank you for the news, Your Majesty." She watched a bee crawl over a blade of grass, too drunk on nectar to travel back to the hive just yet. "Does Coal plan to visit prior to tomorrow's festivities?"

"No, I do not believe so."

Leaf looked out toward The Rows. The filtered light further shadowed the dark circles forming under his eyes. For the past fortnight, fatigue had physically manifested on her brother's face. Drawing in a deep breath, he covered his face with his calloused hands, and Willow's heart faltered a beat. Whenever her brother appeared thusly, he guarded a secret, and she could feel the weight of the unknown press against her own fragile state. The impaired bee near his foot stumbled along toward the apple tree's trunk and crawled beneath a cast-off flower head.

"I need to speak privately with you, if I may?" Leaf's hands fell from his face. "A place where there is no danger of others walking in on our conversation. The rainforest is empty this day, and the Dragon Bridge is a secure location. I shall not take much of your time."

"The rainforest?" Willow issued a pleading look. "What of the observation deck?"

"The wind could carry our voices and those below could potentially overhear our conversation."

"I suppose." Willow twirled a strand of hair upon a finger and nibbled on her bottom lip. "I must return the book to the lending library first and notify Rain of our errand."

Her brother's shoulders relaxed a little. "Thank you, Your Highness. I shall await you in the South Cave."

Willow watched her brother depart, releasing the hair spun tight around her finger. It did not take long to accomplish her tasks. Rain sent her off with reassurances that she would await her return as well as guard the Greek tragedy Willow had deposited upon the woolen blanket.

A jaunt through the gardens toward the South Cave would actually be refreshing, she concluded. Pea bonnets bloomed in soft pinks over the triangulated birch posts, the leafy mounds lightly shading a colorful variety of lettuce and cabbage. Bean runners webbed through stalks of rustling sweet corn, merrily swaying above the sprawling squash vines. Large strawberry leaves, hiding cheery flowers, acted as green mulch beneath broccoli, cauliflower, and many other vegetables. Each garden area was designed in swirls and shapes. It was a sight most beautiful from the second story decks in the village, and the upper-most observation deck, too.

This morning, The Rows were filled with workers gathering greens and vegetables into baskets for evening meal and the upcoming feast. Those she passed tipped their heads and extended polite greetings. The gardeners typically treated her with respect, in honor of her brother and late father. She smiled kindly in reply and continued toward the back acre.

The November-sown field of winter wheat had grown tall and boasted a lush, verdant shade of emerald. Leaf was pleased that the newest conditioning field had passed into the early dough development stage already. Ripening would begin soon and the green would fade to shades of straw gold. The stalks murmured as she passed and Willow inhaled their subtle but sweet, earthy fragrance. She moseyed along the small dirt path and crossed the stone foot bridge. The creek babbled as it rushed beneath her feet and she listened to its excited chatter half-heartedly. On an opposite side of the narrow trail, a more recently planted field was dotted green with grassy tufts of tillering wheat. From this vantage, the South Cave yawned before her and she squared her shoulders in anticipation of what was to come.

Leaf leaned just inside the mouth of the cave with eyes closed and head resting against the stone wall. His well-toned arms crossed over his chest, tense with thoughts, she surmised. Upon hearing her approach, he lifted his head and bestowed a small nod of acknowledgment.

She slowed before him and whispered, "Your Majesty," with a small curtsy.

"We are alone now, *ma chère*. You may call me Leaf. You know how I feel about titles and formalities."

"Very well." Willow folded her hands at her waist. "Do you wish to speak here or shall we continue onward to the Dragon Bridge?"

"The bridge is preferable. The waterfall will drown out our exchange."

Heat enveloped her in a suffocating embrace as they entered the rainforest biodome. The jungle sang its raucous tune of life and she winced at the clashing sounds. Holding her hand, Leaf led her along the newly cut trail, remaining silent the entire way. Vines wound up trees and draped overhead. Orchids in whites, purples, and reds dotted limbs and trunks, their bearded faces beseeching Willow to pause and inhale their heady scent. The Dragon Bridge soon filled her sight and she sighed. It never failed to capture her imagination.

She caressed the arched railing as they glided across the bridge and over Step-Stone Pond. The Waterfall crashed in a misty roar and glimpses of rainbows shimmered through the silvered vapor.

Pulling her eyes away from the enchanting scene, she faced her brother and patiently waited for him to begin. He seemed to struggle with finding words, releasing the start of a word and stopping. Willow knit her eyebrows together just as her brother's shoulders slumped in defeat. He blinked a few times and finally began, in a tone so low that Willow had to come closer to discern his words.

"What I am about to share, I have not even discussed with Ember nor others within Nobility." Leaf searched her eyes and the steadfast veil slipped away. "I am overwhelmed. Nor can I grasp that the first generation would knowingly place their families in an oppressive position."

"You are frightening me." Willow attempted to calm her racing thoughts, but she could not.

"My apologies, but I fear you may be the only one I can trust, which is why I have sought your counsel. Especially as there is no other who knows Fillion as you do."

She nibbled the inside of her lip and blinked back the growing nerves. "I am listening."

"The day Coal visited, he and Lynden shared a most grievous revelation."

Her brother continued with details of his private discussion with the Son of Fire and Fillion's sister, as well as Michael's desire to support the community. Words died on her lips as Leaf's confession tumbled out in quavering tones. No longer could she hear the waterfall or the somewhat deafening noises competing in the jungle, only the sounds of Leaf's voice mixed with the pounding heartbeat thrumming in her ears. She canted forward, until her fore-arms rested on the bridge, and closed her eyes.

A memory echoed in her mind, so real, so tangible, it was if Fillion actually stood before her this moment. Dark hair played in the breeze and eyes as light as day reflected a keen intelligence. Anguish sharpened his features as he battled against the illusions of power that shackled him to a life and system he could not control. The rhythm of her pulse quickened with the sight of him, even if only in her mind's eye. Transported, she could almost feel the cool autumn breeze and hear the rustling sound of leaves colliding with earth in the private alcove along the village path.

"I just don't know how to do this," Fillion had said, his voice cracking with emotion as he spoke. *"Any relationship I pursue with you will end in pain, for both of us. I couldn't live with myself if Hanley harmed you because of me."*

"Hanley places my family in his Legacy and then punishes us for existing?" she had asked. *"I struggle to comprehend how he could be so heartless as to reduce my family to the equivalence of slaves. For who treats another with such cold indifference, as if they are property to do with at will?"*

"You exist because of Hanley, never forget that. The second gen is the product of human manipulation. You're a character to entertain scientific theories. Everything about your life is built on lies. I tried to tell you and Leaf this through Messenger Pigeon."

She had flared with indignation and spat, *"Well, I refuse to cower before Hanley. Your father shall not manipulate my family or home anymore."*

Willow opened her eyes and swiveled toward her brother, who stared at the waterfall, every muscle taut. Restless, she played with the ends of her tablet woven belt as she contemplated the fading memory. "Do you believe Fillion has known all along?"

"I am not sure," he said. "This is one of the reasons I wished to speak with you."

She lowered her eyes and watched her fidgeting fingers. "Well, the Dungeon Master spoke to us as though we were beneath him. Fillion, however, was forthcoming about his life and broke the law to save you, Leaf. He was willing to throw away his future to ensure our family had one. Still, many of his statements now seem questionable in light of this horrific information."

An ache throbbed in her chest and she pressed a hand flush against her heart as a tear dripped down her cheek. *"Honest men never need swear oaths of innocence. Their actions prove the integrity of their deeds."* Her mind wished to twist Fillion's warnings and comments. But her words—spoken to him the day Norah died— repeated over and over again in a tumbling swirl inside her head. Surely this was a sign.

She sought Leaf's eyes. "His actions do not reflect that of a man hiding an agenda, is this not so? Deeds defend a man's honor."

"Yes, an excellent point." Leaf plowed work-worn fingers through his hair and then down his face. "Shall we trust him, then? Coal gave caution that we were to trust no one, not even Fillion."

"I am not sure we have much choice in the matter."

Her brother looked away.

"What shall become of our generation? Of our home?" she asked. "Do we not have a say in our future?"

"I share your apprehensions, and not having answers is tearing me apart.

My family…" Leaf did not finish, allowing his words to trail off. Instead, he reached out and took her hand, no longer able to hide the emotions breaching his usually calm countenance. "Please, *ma chère*. Be at my side these next two days? I cannot face this alone. I shall bend on knee and beg of you if I must."

"Leaf —"

"I know the cost involved for you, Willow. But I need your strength and discernment, and so does New Eden." He paused and pleaded her silently for a moment, before whispering, "Please?"

Hot tears rolled down her face. She sucked in a heavy breath and fought against the sob gathering storm clouds within her. "Yes," she said in a trembling voice. "I shall join you——for the Ceremony, and the Celebration."

Leaf swooped in and pressed her against his chest, wrapping his arms around her back as he whispered, "Thank you."

She was unsure how long they clung to one another. But she did not mind, not wishing to return to The Orchard and pretend all was well. Once more, the shifting sands of their future kicked up against the winds of change. This time, however, control blew from their grasp, no longer offering a commodity of protection.

"Seeing him again, especially knowing what I do now, will break my heart into infinite pieces."

"I am indebted to you, Willow Oak." Leaf lifted her hand and kissed her fingers. "Whatever you ask of me, if it is within my power, I shall grant it."

Both winced with his words. What power did Leaf actually possess? Rather than point out the obvious, Willow nodded her head with gratitude and offered a faint smile.

The return back to the main biodome passed in blurred thoughts. A light morning glow softened her brother's features as he absorbed the main garden's pastoral scene and outlaying meadow. As a grown man of two-and-twenty, a devoted husband, an adoring father of one rambunctious son with another child due any day, a doting brother, and a dedicated king, Leaf still was not a man without his share of faults. But he was a man in love with his family and his kingdom, and it always showed.

Workers in the fields rose and bowed as she and Leaf strolled by. The Son of Earth smiled kindly, asking about their families and complimenting their diligent work. In the heart of the Ceremonial Garden, he touched her forearm and she paused, glancing over her shoulder at him. His expression mirrored the placid, unwavering strength he carried into life, but his eyes told a different story. He was afraid. So was she. Her lips tipped up in a gesture of reassurance and he drew in a shaky breath, before bowing and pivoting on his heel toward the gardeners in his care.

Willow peered out toward The Orchard where Rain had remained on her stomach, nose pressed to a book.

A single white petal danced through the air until its tenuous existence landed upon the living soil at Willow's feet. She knelt into the ashes of her loved ones and whispered, "In order to live, something must die, but death gives way to the resurrection of new life." The tip of the petal fluttered with her breaths.

Entranced by the sight, she scooped up a palm of tilth and buried the decay of empty promises, delicate as hope and bruised with mourning. "Ashes to ashes. Dust to dust."

Wiping the dirt from her hands, she left the remains of her loved ones and continued her journey back toward The Orchard. The regal Brides of Spring beckoned her, and she could not help but attend their blossomy reverie as their wintry maid-in-waiting.

Thousands of young Americans who were disenchanted with politics went off instead to set up their own experimental communities – the commune movement. And they turned to Arthur Tansley's idea of the ecosystem as a model for how to create a human system of order within the communes.

But they also fused it with cybernetic ideas drawn from computer theory, and out of this came a vision of strong, independent humans linked, just like in nature, in a network that was held together through feedback. The commune dwellers mimicked the ecosystem idea in their house meetings where they all had to say exactly what was on their minds at that moment – so information flowed freely round the system. And through that the communes were supposed to stabilise themselves.

But they didn't.

— Adam Curtis, documentary filmmaker *

Chapter Six

Portland, Oregon

Fillion sat across from Timothy and forced a dispassionate stare. But really, his insides were shaking. A strange chemical smell permeated the entire building, one Fillion couldn't place. The mental infirmary felt alive, too, writhing and groaning under the weight of delusional shadows—the shades of the afflicted inhabiting the facility.

In the waiting room, a persistent moaning soaked through the walls. The front desk attendant sifted through files and drummed her nails on the Formica surface. Each rhythmic click and tap was like a gunshot to Fillion's head. The other visiting family, waiting to be called back, also stared off into space, as if sitting in a vacuum. It made Fillion question if the sounds of neural-emotional agony were generated from his own mental instability.

He never found out.

Now, he sat in one of two highly secure visitation rooms and faced the man responsible for years of anguish and heartache inside the biodome. And damn. The older man had lost a significant amount of weight. The skin drooped on his face and neck. Light brown hair, sprinkled with gray, was trimmed short and fashionable, still as thick as before. The rest of him looked unkempt—a coffee stain on his white T-shirt, a small hole in the gray sweatpants—but his hair was groomed. Weird. Timothy crossed his legs and gripped the chair's arms. Casual but ready to pounce.

A mental health aid circled around where they sat, making one final sweep of the room. It was required protocol before she allowed privacy with a man who could lash out, turning a harmless object into a weapon. A small smile formed on Timothy's face. He blinked casually, tilting his head to the side like he was amused by something. Fillion had been flicking his bottom lip ring while lost to his thoughts and stopped, closing his mouth. The last time Timothy had seen him, he was dressed like a young man from the Middle Ages. He was a man of the world now.

"Everything is in order." The aid turned to Fillion. Professionalism dripped from her presence, contrary to the peevish way she looked at Timothy. "You have the emergency call switch?" He opened his hand and revealed the tiny device in his palm. The man across from him tensed a notch and Fillion studied the reactive body language from the corner of his eye. "OK," the aid said. "Call when you're done or if Mr. Kane threatens you in any way."

"Got it," Fillion said.

The door shut with a loud click. To not appear too eager, and to identify more body language cues from Timothy, Fillion made himself take in his surroundings. The visitation room was decorated tastefully in muted tones. Furniture was bolted down to the floor or to tables. Even the lamps were fastened down. With nonchalance, he rested his eyes back onto Timothy, who hadn't moved an inch. Probably never blinked, either.

Jerking the hair out of his eyes, Fillion said, "So."

"So." Timothy parroted, the smile growing a smidge. "To what do I owe the pleasure?"

"Pleasure isn't the word I'd use."

"Oh, come now," Timothy practically sang. "You derive a small form of pleasure from seeing me brought down so low."

Fillion smirked and leaned back in his chair. "Choices are a bitch sometimes."

"And yet, I regret nothing."

"And that sums up why you're here."

Timothy tilted his head again, the movements suggesting he saw right through Fillion. After a nanosecond, the older man muttered, "Indeed." The coldness in Timothy's eyes hardened and Fillion sobered as warning tingles alerted his animal instincts. How could a man smile and talk like the world was full of blues skies and sunshine and yet have eyes that reflected a disconnection to his own humanity? The hairs on Fillion's neck prickled. He hid the reaction by continuing the conversation.

"And how do you feel about your brother?"

Timothy lifted his eyebrows. "Who?"

"Hayden Kane."

"Ah, you know." Timothy smiled again, this time wide with satisfaction. "Well, *nephew*, now you understand why I wanted to keep the business in the family."

"And yet, *Hayden* thought differently. The Watsons are still heirs in the Legacy."

The former Wind Element laughed as if Fillion shared a humorous joke. "You are so naïve."

Fillion stood up and tossed the calling device into the air, catching it.

Timothy stopped laughing as he darted a glance to the door. In slow strides, Fillion walked toward the exit and nearly grinned when Timothy just about bolted from his chair. Before reaching the door, Fillion veered off to the left and stilled before a dumb painting of a family sharing a picnic on a beach.

Fillion wasn't naïve. And Timothy would be easy to crack. The man was always surrounded by adoring fans in the biodome and liked to be the center of attention. Always laughing. Always telling a story or sharing something interesting. He was probably lonely here. No friends. No wife who fell at his feet and did his bidding. No son to parade around as God's gift to biodome humankind. No enemy of the state to take down. Yet.

Fillion turned halfway toward Timothy and reached out toward the door. Timothy's eyes were riveted to Fillion's hand movements, but the charming smile remained on his otherwise tense features.

"Hanley wants to keep the whole business in the family?" Fillion asked. Timothy didn't answer. Instead, his eyes moved to Fillion's face and back to his hand. This was too easy. Fillion leaned his hand on the door for support and arched an eyebrow. "He sure has a strange way of going about that."

"Not really." Timothy finally met Fillion's inquisitive stare.

"No?"

"No."

"Then why are you here, *Uncle*? Shouldn't you be in New Eden preparing for project shutdown?"

Timothy broke into a smug grin. "You know why I am here."

"You mean the murder of Joel Watson?" Fillion pushed off the door and stepped toward Timothy. "The hacked death certs for the Watson children?" Another step closer. "The attempted faction to overthrow a throne?" Fillion leaned close into Timothy's personal space and half-whispered, "And conspired assault on Leaf with a threat to take his life?" They locked eyes and neither moved for several seconds. Fillion blinked and twisted toward an empty chair, easing in with blasé grace, as if he owned the entire world. "Those reasons?"

"I have been convicted of nothing. This conversation is ridiculous."

"The reason you haven't been convicted is because of me. Not for one second do I want you to forget that. Got it? I put you here." Timothy rolled his eyes and looked away. "Your future is mine. Don't believe me? Ask your brother. Oh wait. According to personnel, there's been no contact since he dropped you off here, right? Sad."

Timothy chuckled. "You sound so much like Hanley this moment."

"He groomed me."

"The next Gamemaster." Timothy chuckled again. "Must be a relief to finally have *real* power instead of being one of many puppets your father manipulates."

"We're both puppets, so whatever. Power is an illusion," Fillion murmured. He exhaled a heavy sigh. This place gave Fillion the creeps and so did Timothy. But he needed to keep his head straight and his ego amped up. God, he wanted to smoke. This game was getting old and he was getting nowhere. Leaning forward, Fillion rested his forearms on his knees. "Explain how Hanley plans to keep the business in the family but not place Skylar in the Legacy?"

"Whatever delusions you carry about owning my future, I still do not answer to you."

"Yeah, we'll see about that." Fillion's lips curled with arrogance as he shifted back in his chair, leaning on an angle and stretching out his legs. "This place is a goddamn resort compared to prison. Your choice."

Timothy sprung from his chair to tower over him in a show of intimidation. Fillion just smiled through the strands of hair draping over his face. One thing detention did teach him: No sudden movements. Stay calm. Don't fly off the handle. All hell broke loose when that happened. Reaching into his pocket, Fillion pulled out the call switch and rolled it between his fingers. Played with it. Brushed his thumb over the button. When deciphering codes, it wasn't always about what was obvious. It was also about the hidden—and Timothy got the silent message. The older man's eyes fixed on the device for several strained, awkward seconds and then he stretched, trying to play it cool.

Timothy eased back into his chair. "The Techsmith Guild uses a different communications backbone, separate from the Messenger Pigeon used by all others at N.E.T."

Fillion considered the confession. "Is it a different environment or a different server?"

"Yes."

"Makes sense." Fillion bit the inside of his cheek. He'd use a redundant system, too, optimizing covert activity through a separate server environment, set up similar to the existing server configuration. "This is strictly your and Hanley's communications?"

"The Techsmith Guild uses the production environment we set up. Hanley and I, however, continued to use the test environment as a means of communication. It was a server N.E.T. 'decommissioned' once the Guild server went live."

"I'll learn how the business plans to remain in the family?" Fillion asked. A smile stretched across Timothy's face and a shiver coursed up Fillion's spine in response. "And how Joel's money plays into all of this?"

"What makes you think his money has anything to do with this?"

"Don't play cute."

Fillion jerked the hair out of his eyes again. He hadn't even brushed it after his shower, leaving the hotel in disarray. Too hyped up about seeing Timothy and soupy after a restless night of sleep. Timothy looked eerily put together and Fillion probably looked part homeless right now. Annoying. Shit, he was mentally rambling.

Keeping up the aloof act, Fillion said, "His money has everything to do with it. You know it. I know it. No games."

Timothy made a tsk sound and shook his head. "Life is a game."

"Yeah, and you lost."

"Everyone loses in this game."

"That's some deep shit. You should start a line of 'we're all going to die, life's a game, loser' inspirational memes to entertain the people sheep of cyberspace." Fillion rose from the chair and tossed the call switch into the air, catching it with a sly look Timothy's direction. "No winners? What a glaring recommendation for you and *Hayden*."

Smugness smeared across the ever-friendly smile Timothy sported. "Any other questions, My Lord?"

"Nice. Actually, yeah. One more. The day Leaf stormed the Great Hall and blew his cover," Fillion said, tossing the device into the air once again, "you seemed shocked that the first gen were the only community members legally bound to The Code. Why is that?"

"Perhaps the same reason as all others."

Fillion sighed with exasperation. "And what reason is that?"

"The second generation are deemed adults in the community at age fifteen per The Code, given the same rights and the same consequences. Therefore, it stood to reason they were also bound to The Code as all other adults before them."

Fillion paused his movements and processed Timothy's logic a moment. "You believed this even though you knew the second gen were products of science? Property of the lab?"

"What difference does it make, really?" Timothy leaned forward in his chair and straightened his shoulders. "My shock concerned the consequences of having a second generation who suddenly believed they possessed more power than they actually do. The position of Aether should never have been revealed without legal action, as promised in The Code."

"I can't believe you willingly had children knowing what they'd become." Fillion grimaced with disgust. "God, you're sick."

Timothy lowered his eyes and looked away. "I was ensured certain amenities for my family."

"Do you still have them?"

The older man slowly moved his head and locked eyes with Fillion. "No."

A dispirited expression stole Timothy's features, matching the morose tone of his voice. Goosebumps erupted over Fillion's skin again. The weird feeling continued to unsettle Fillion and all other questions dissolved on his tongue. What wasn't Timothy sharing? It was clear the conversation was over, too. Fillion narrowed his eyes a notch and swiveled away toward the exit.

"I need to go."

"You'll come visit again?" Timothy masked the lonely tones with a friendly smile.

For a moment, Fillion felt a twinge of compassion. Then he remembered all the crimes Timothy committed, including murder, and shut the door on his emotions.

"If I do, it's only because I need more information." Fillion paused at the door and pushed the call switch. "As of tomorrow, I officially pay the bill for your cozy accommodations. Papers signed off and everything. Don't get too comfortable, though."

The door opened and the nurse peeked her head in, shooting a warning glance toward Timothy. "Everything OK?"

"Time for me to leave," Fillion said. He peered over his shoulder to the stricken expression on Timothy's face. With the droopy skin, he looked old and haggard. "Anything you want me to pass along to your family? I'll see them tomorrow."

Timothy lifted his eyes. "Tell them I fare well."

"Anything else?"

"No." He turned away.

Fillion bit the inside of his cheek again. Empathy warred with his logic and he didn't know what to do. "OK. I'll let you know how they're doing in our next visit." What the hell? That just slipped out and Fillion wanted to thunk his head on the door. Stupid.

His uncle looked up at him with hopeful eyes and nodded, glancing away again. Fillion tensed. Timothy didn't deserve his compassion or kindness. Was this a psychopathic game? He didn't know or want to find out.

The nurse shut the door. "This is for you, from Mr. Kane." She handed him an envelope. "I was instructed to give it to you after your visit."

"To pass along to his family?"

"No, records show that he gifted these belongings to a Mr. Fillion Nichols."

Spooked, he pocketed the envelope in his jacket with a single nod of thanks. The nurse gestured toward the waiting room in reply. Her face was bland, the light in her eyes sharp, but uncaring.

Were the mentally infirm withheld food as punishment? Timothy had lost a significant amount of weight, but he didn't look healthy. And he was really nervous about Fillion pushing the call switch. Originally, Fillion thought it had to do with his leaving. But perhaps not? How did they deal with threatening behavior? The waiting room was a straight shot down the long, sterile hallway and Fillion controlled the impulse to run out of the building. His skin was crawling, as if the ghosts of the mentally afflicted were passing through him, whispering to his mind to let go and embrace his future.

Down the hall, a thick metal door opened and a girl around his age was hauled out of the room by another militant aid. Like Timothy, she was wearing gray sweatpants and a white T-shirt. Light brown hair matted against her head, the strands chopped as if cut in a rage. It was her face that made the hair on his arms lift. Perfectly still, as if glass. Even her blue-green eyes. She stared at everything and nothing all at once. If he had passed her on the street, he'd conclude that she was android. Her movements contained the fluid shuffle of a robot, too.

As their paths crossed, Fillion lowered his eyes. The girl, however, whipped her head his direction, unnaturally fast, and gripped his upper arm.

"The walls are listening," she said in a static whisper. "They have ears." Fillion held his breath and lifted his eyes until they locked with hers. The void that existed moments ago was now brimming with a thousand lights as emotions danced across her face. "Don't trust him."

"Who?"

It seemed like time had slowed, but it all happened so fast. By the time the question left his mouth, a swarm of people had already entered the hallway, shouting orders. A male nurse pushed him against a wall and shielded his body. At least three workers came forward and used a low-res bio-electric sensor disruptor. The girl dropped to the ground, her body flopping from the shock as strained groans passed her clamped jaw. Then she just stilled. Like she had powered-down.

"Stop!" Fillion tried to move, but there were too many people blocking his way to the girl. "She didn't hurt me! Stop!"

The male aid turned toward him. "She's dangerous."

"Then why was she permitted to even leave that room, knowing I'd be walking down the hallway?"

"Misfire of information, our error."

Fillion gaped at the man. "So, it's your error, but she gets punished for it? You didn't even try to talk to her first." The man didn't answer, just stared back in that bland, stoic way of other health care professionals in this infirmary. God, was she set up so they could inflict pain on her? "I need to leave. Now."

"Yes, sir. Right this way."

A few minutes later, he checked out then walked outside and down the street to an alley where he rested the back of his head against a brick wall. The misty air coated him in a cold sheen of vapor. It bothered him and, strangely, he felt numb to it. Anxiety released as a slow pulse, eventually gaining speed until his whole body began to shake. He could be Timothy in a few years. He could be the girl. His sanity was already on the verge of cracking.

Clenching his eyes shut, Fillion grit his teeth against the waves of nausea and the images flashing in his mind from his dream. Don't trust who? Hanley often said that the walls were listening. What the hell? Willow was fine. Experimentation for stasis wasn't happening. Timothy was hiding information, but the Watsons weren't in imminent danger. He'd be the owner tomorrow and would ensure Willow's, Leaf's, and Laurel's safety. But, something about Timothy uncorked a bottle of repressed emotions, and numerous fears poured into him, gurgling with satisfaction. The girl didn't help.

He popped a cigarette and lit up, slumping against the brick wall once more. "Cranium, phone Dr. Della Jayne Nichols." The outgoing signal beeped. Once. Twice. Then nothing.

"Fillion?"

"Hey."

"I am in California. When do you plan to arrive?"

"Early tomorrow morning."

She paused. "What can I do for you?"

He flinched at the professional tone she used. "Is Hanley with you?"

"Yes."

"Got it." Fillion dragged on his cigarette with a trembling hand and darted his eyes around the alley and nearby street. "Can we talk privately for a sec?"

"Of course. One moment." The line silenced as he was placed on hold. A car horn honked at a bedraggled pedestrian crossing the street and Fillion dropped his cigarette. Swear words hissed from his mouth and he pushed off the wall. Bending over, he picked up the cigarette and wiped it off, just as his mom came on the line again. "I am now in a private room. Are you all right? You sound shaken up."

"The psych evals from when I was in detention," he began, and then puffed on the slightly dampened cigarette. Shit, he was so jumpy. "None of them said I was psychopathic, bipolar, schizophrenic?"

"No, Fillion. We have discussed this before. Several times, actually. Your racing thoughts and insomnia are mostly related to being exceptionally gifted, not bipolar. But, also, because you suffer from anxiety as well as post-traumatic stress disorder. The psychosis you've experienced is induced by your PTSD, not schizophrenic delusions." His mom's voice grew quiet and sympathetic. "What is troubling you this moment?"

Fillion exhaled a thin stream of smoke. "How ... how do you know the test results weren't tampered with?"

"You feel they were tampered with?"

"I don't know. Confused." He groaned and closed his eyes again. "Sometimes I swear I'm on the antisocial personality spectrum and the psychotic episodes and anxiety attacks are from resisting a genetic psychopathy. Is that even possible?" Multiple voices in his head murmured "son of a killer," each whisper and accusation a sharp stab. *Are you ready to discover what is real?* Opening his eyes, he watched a dog enter the alley and rummage through the piles of garbage lining the narrow street. "I'm repulsed by my behavior."

"The very fact that you are repulsed is a strong indicator that you do not have antisocial—"

"It's so easy to slip into a role to control and manipulate others and ... it's empowering, like I crave it, even though it also feels wrong. Stories come to me without trying. Reality is hard to distinguish sometimes. I'm probably schizophrenic. Shows up in young adulthood, right? Or maybe I'm a pathological liar? It doesn't matter how it's labeled. God, I'm so fake all the time. It's disgusting."

"Listen, Fillion," she said softly. "I promise you the reports were not tampered with. Everyone manipulates, even small children. Controlling others or situations is a common way to protect 'self' when we perceive danger or threats, real or imagined. And storytelling is in your blood." Her voice dropped to a whisper. "But you are *not* your father."

He quietly laughed. "And yet everyone says I am."

His mom hesitated. "Did someone just share this comparison or are you decompressing from your travels?"

"I'll tell you later. I'm out in the open. Shouldn't have called right now, but ... but ..." *The walls are listening. They have ears.*

"Are you by yourself?"

Don't trust him.

"I'm fine." Fillion squinted his eyes and gazed up at the dreary sky. Cars whizzed by not too far away. The dog—mangy and malnourished—nosed wrappers and bags and kept a nervous eye on Fillion. "I need to catch a train."

"All right. See you in the morning."

"Sure."

"Call back if you need to."

"Thanks. Appreciated."

Fillion threw the nub of his cigarette on the ground and rubbed it out. He reached into his pocket for another and pulled out the envelope instead. Whatever was inside, it was thin. Except a shape, like a ring, took up a corner space. He slipped the tip of his finger beneath an unsealed edge. Little by little, he tore open the paper, wincing with the ripping sounds, then peered inside.

"Shit," he swore between clenched teeth, followed by more swear words. Fillion gripped the hem of his shirt and grit his teeth. Was he being punked?

For a solid five minutes, he stared at the envelope, oscillating between curiosity and fury. What if the card revealed a clue to Hanley's next game move? He closed his eyes tight, grimacing against the heartache. He was tired of being jerked around. Tired of all the lies. While Hanley created an experiment to foster nurture through community bonds, Fillion was continually traumatized by the nature of his own psychopathic, emotionally abusive family. What kind of genetic memories would he pass along? Better they died with him.

The ghosts from the mental infirmary began whispering his name again—Mr. Nichols. *His father's name.* Begging him to return. Fillion gulped in a large breath to fight the forming tears. A cold sweat broke out on his forehead. The shaking in his hands grew stronger. Blinking back his escalating fear, he pulled out the playing card before he lost his nerve again.

"Twist of Fate," Fillion read aloud and then studied the card, featuring a court jester, who wore black and white against a red background. In the envelope's corner lay a simple gold wedding band. Was he to give Emily this ring? Perhaps for Skylar to use should he choose to marry? Or was Timothy commenting in some sick, metaphorical way about Fillion's upcoming marriage to Akiko? The envelope was empty. No note. No instructions.

He brushed his thumb over the jester and repeated the words under his breath. Thoughts glitched in and out of focus as more questions surfaced. What did the card mean? Whose fate? Fillion's or Timothy's or some other person? The fringes of his mind continued to grow hazy with each unanswered question. But it was a game. Not real. Didn't mean anything. Not really. Still, he pocketed the card and looked around the alley for watchful eyes. He was about to system crash.

Desperate to relieve the mental pressure, he opened his pack for another cigarette only to close the lid again. Not even in the mood to smoke. Hell had to be freezing over this moment. Disgusted with himself, he threw the half-used pack down the alley and began his walk back to the train station.

At the end of 1991 a giant experiment began in the Arizona desert. Its aim was to create from scratch a model for a whole self-organising world.

Biosphere 2 was a giant sealed world. Eight humans were locked in with a mass of flora and other fauna, and a balanced ecosystem was supposed to naturally emerge. …

The idea of nature that underpinned all these visions of self-organisation was a fantasy. A fantasy that was born at a time when those who ran the British empire were desperately trying to cling on to power as the dynamic forces of history whirled around them. So they turned to science to create a vision of a static world where everything is stable and your moral duty is to make sure that nothing ever changes.

The other problem with the self-organising system is that it cannot deal with power. Although it sees human beings all linked together in a system, its fundamental rule is that they must remain separate individuals. Alliances and coalitions would compromise the precious autonomy of the individual, and destabilise the system.

— Adam Curtis, documentary filmmaker *

Chapter Seven

Seattle, Washington

The train ride back to Seattle was a blur. Thoughts and scenarios continued to circulate one after the other. He wanted to hack into the so-called neglected server and read through the archived files. But not on public transit. Instead of returning to the hotel, Fillion took a cab to Mack's apartment. He wanted to pick up a few things before flying out to California.

Inside Mack's place, it was quiet. Outside the wall of windows, storm clouds gathered over the Salish Sea and rattled the glass. He watched for a few seconds, then forced his body forward.

Down the hallway he paused before his old room—the Black Hole No. 2—and gently pushed open the door. The coffin of his former bedroom welcomed him. Mack hadn't changed a thing. He walked in, entranced, blissfully swallowed whole. Nothing was left untouched by the black finger of death. Except one object. In the corner lay his bright blue guitar, and the side of his mouth quirked up.

Not wasting a single moment, he grabbed the guitar and plopped onto his bed, scooting up to the pillows. He rested his head onto the wood frame of his instrument and tuned it by ear. He plucked the first few strings and grinned with the rich tones. Closing his eyes, he let the music carry him away.

Song after song poured from him. He shifted from classical pieces to modern band covers. The angst that had been choking him for months surfaced with intensity and his muscles tensed with the overwhelming heartache. He strummed harder, gritting his teeth. His fingertips burned and he winced with the pain. Still he played.

Desperate for peace, he moved to a quieter number and leaned his ear against the body of his guitar as he plucked the notes, eyelids sliding shut once more. The song's tympanic beat moved to the rhythm of his pulse as he fingerpicked an old Catalan melody. Seven years ago, he had played this song as an ensemble piece with the Seattle Youth Orchestra at Benaroya Hall. One of the few moments he felt like himself, transported to a place where he knew, without question, that he belonged.

The pain in his fingers was growing intense and he clenched his jaw tighter with each pluck, eventually giving up. With a heavy sigh, he eased his fingers up on the neck and rested his other hand against the lower strings. Clapping cut through the silence. *The walls are listening. They have ears.* Fillion jerked his head up and peered around his room. Had he finally cracked?

"Shit," Fillion said under his breath when spotting Mack. He fell back against the pillows as his breathing tried to keep up with his pulse. "Your ninja skills cost me a life. Maybe two. What the hell?"

"Your guitar playing is like the Pied Piper, calling to me," Mack deadpanned. "This unseen power told me you were going to miss our appointment in the hotel lobby and to return home."

"Tracker?"

"Yup."

"How long?"

"Since you left the States."

Fillion raised his eyebrows. "Um, why?"

Mack sauntered over to his nightstand and pulled out the old-fashioned spiral notebook and wrote: *I don't trust H. Got your back, mate.*

Fillion nodded his head and looked away. "You could've told me with-out scaring the shit out of me."

"Nah," Mack grinned, lighting the page on fire. "It's way more fun to see potential energy become kinetic." His friend stomped out the flames then lowered onto the bed. "You look like shit."

"You're making my heart flutter. Stop it."

"Seriously. You looked like shit in the vid feed last night, too. But today, you look like you became one with your spirit animal—which, by the way, needs to change. 'Shit' is an animal by-product. Not an animal. Your poor *chakra*. How it suffers in the confusion." Mack studied him a few seconds, growing more serious when Fillion didn't humor him. "So, besides the obvious, what's up?"

"Nightmares." His friend nodded his head thoughtfully. Fillion drew in a shaky breath and turned toward the wall. Black entombed him and he swallowed. "I'm . . . I'm . . . crazy. Losing my mind. Probably lost it a long time ago."

Mack remained quiet. Adjusting his position on the bed, his friend continued to study him, then said, "Get what you came here for and let's go. Your carriage awaits."

He eased next to Mack on the edge of bed, setting his guitar against the wall. "Terrify, then kidnap me? What's next on the agenda?"

"A midnight stroll on the beach, followed by a hot make-out session." Mack slid him a straight look, but his lips twitched. "Then you'll propose, because I'm just that good and you miss being married to me. I'll feign surprise and will cry fake tears of joy, take a selfie of our happy moment to share with the world, make you suffer as I prolong the agony of my answer, but of course I'll say yes." Fillion rolled his eyes and Mack sighed, as if defeated. "Or, we can skip the symphony and head to The Crypt and welcome your twenty-first birthday like the badasses we are." His friend's face sobered even more and he silently pleaded, searching Fillion's eyes. "Break my heart gently."

Fillion lifted a shoulder in a slight shrug. "Can't use a fake ID. The last thing I need right now is legal trouble." He fell back onto the bed and stared at the ceiling. "I know. I'm lame and boring. On several levels."

"O ye of little faith." Mack shook his head with disgust and leaned back onto the bed next to him. "Bouncer owes me a favor. He'll look the other way. Promise." They turned their heads and locked eyes. "Ready to misbehave?"

"Drinks and dancing only. No girls."

"Yeah, yeah, vows of celibacy." Mack winked at him. "This is the root of why you look like shit, *desu*."

Fillion rose from the bed and trudged toward the closet. "I just came for the blue guitar and a fresh set of clothing."

"Hurry up then." Mack bit his pierced tongue suggestively. "The night is young and so are we. Time to activate our sexy *henshin* powers."

Almost an hour later—after changing clothes and finally doing something with his hair—they walked down the steps to The Crypt. Fillion dragged on a cigarette and leaned against the brick wall as Mack cozied up to the bouncer for a private conversation. A small group of young women walked by, flashing their IDs to the bouncer. They eyed Fillion with interest, but he looked around as if bored with the scene already. Hypnotic beats blared from the open doors. Multi-colored lights flashed and strobed. The bouncer's eyes shifted to Fillion then back to Mack. The older man handed Fillion's ID back to Mack with a brief nod. Mack gestured toward the entrance and Fillion pushed off the wall and snuffed out his cigarette.

The Crypt was packed. They angled around people and slid through pockets of zombified humanity, most hyped out on Brain, pure amphetamine. His friend threw flirtatious smiles and winks at every opportunity. But Fillion schooled his features and avoided eye contact.

The holographic deejay revved the crowd up and switched to a new song. On the dance floor, a sea of sweaty bodies undulated to the seductive beats, tweaking from amphetamines and ecstasy. Or the sheer thrill of feeling alive. Holographic confetti fell over their heads, stars bursting into mock-fireworks, mixed with real bubbles. Occasionally, a slow stream of fog would wrap around everyone's feet. This was life after death, a rave of black, empty souls. And damn. Joining the macabre celebration had never felt so good.

"A bottle of top-shelf whiskey for my friend here." Mack shouted to a woman behind the bar. The bartender leaned forward and spoke. "Yes, the whole damn bottle." Mack pushed a handful of gold coins toward the bartender, whose eyebrows shot up. "Make it two. Snappy." His friend turned to him. "Here you go, mate," Mack said, clicking their bottles together. "Cheers." They lifted their bottles up in salute and indulged in long drinks.

Fillion leaned back against the bar and studied the people nearby through lowered eyes. "Fly out with me in the morning?" he asked Mack. "I want to discuss a tech opportunity for the lab with you."

"No shop talk, *bishounen*." Mack shifted his eyes back to Fillion. "I prescribe to you a night of bad behavior. It's good for your *hikikomori* soul."

"My hero." Fillion issued a tight bow.

"Hellz yeah. Tonight, I'm your therapist." Mack scooted close and dropped his voice. "And since girls aren't on the menu for you, I'm your lover, too. So, drink up, lover. Time to hit the dance floor."

"Don't tell me what to do, bitch."

"You've come back to me!" Mack swung toward an innocent bystander walking past, grabbed her around the waist and spun her around, shouting, "He's back!" Plopping her back onto the ground, he high-fived a man nearby and shouted again. Then he sighed with satisfaction and leaned back against the bar. "Shit. I thought I'd lost you for good." Fillion enjoyed another long drink of whiskey, realizing he'd consumed a third of the bottle already. "So, what's the plan tonight, boss?" Mack asked, standing at attention.

Fillion stared at his drink. "Dance."

"God, when you give single-syllable commands like that I could *nosebleed*." He snagged the bottle of whiskey from Fillion's hand and gave it to the bartender with instructions to guard it with her life. Then, he pushed Fillion toward the dance floor. "Turn me on, lover."

They melted into the storm of raving zombies and Fillion let the vibrating thump take hold of his body. Whiskey had coated his senses and loosened his muscles and his mind, urging him to let go completely. To forget his responsibilities. The ache that writhed inside of him. Fears over his future and new fears from his visit to the mental hospital today. Easing his grip on reality, he embraced the moment. This moment. And he looked at his friend with a smile, a real one for once. Mack shouted that he needed to piss and would be right back. Touching moment over.

The music overwhelmed Fillion and he felt more tension release as he envisioned himself cut off from everyone around him. So lost in the moment, in fact, that he startled when a girl slinked up to his side. A coy smile curved her mouth, dark eyes laughing as she increased her erotic movements, pressing every inch of her against every inch of him. The lighting and her grinding motions made it impossible to focus well on her features. The alcohol firing in his system didn't help either. But he could tell she was pretty in a vintage pinup girl sort of way. Irresistibly feminine. His weakness. Nevertheless, everything about her screamed trouble. He angled away with a dismissive look. She ignored his refusal and slithered up and down the length of him from behind to the music's throbbing rhythm, her hands gripping his hips tight.

"Leave me alone," Fillion shouted over his shoulder. "Not interested."

She wrapped her arms around his chest from behind and said, "You want me. You've always wanted me. She even looks like me." Her hands began a slow, seductive descent. "Stop fighting it. Pretend I'm her so we can talk."

Fillion stilled. Her voice was familiar. Who was the "she" in question? Talk? About what? Weird. Casually, he turned around to see her face again. A huge mistake. The crowd jumped to the heavy beat and pushed him into her. She seized their collision and began kissing him along his jaw, his throat, and then down his neck before he could react, her hands slipping under his shirt and teasing the bare skin of his lower back. Fingers trailed his side until they dipped just below the waist of his pants. The touch tantalized him despite the twitchy movements. And, for a few seconds, he gave in to the arousal, eyes closed and mouth parted, breathing deep and long. It didn't matter if his body was interested, though. He wasn't and couldn't go there—wouldn't go there— especially in a public place. The word "no" formed on his tongue and his hand shot out to nudge her away when he felt a hard tap on his shoulder.

Mack raised his eyebrows at him, mouth set in a grim line. "I leave for five minutes and already you're cheating on me. Bastard." Fillion shoved away from the young woman, his heart racing. His friend looked to the girl. "He's my lover. Hands off."

A sultry laugh spilled out of her. "Come and find me when you're ready," she said to Fillion. Her smile was seductive, but her eyes were strangely ner- vous. Fearful even. "We'll talk the night away." With a final challenging look toward Mack, patting his cheek, she slid into the throng of dancers and disap- peared.

Leaning in close, Mack walked Fillion to the dance floor's perimeter floor. "As much as I tease you about your vows of celibacy, I get it. And you know that." Mack flicked his eyes around the room and Fillion did the same. People were watching him, probably taking pictures of him, too. Or he was just imagining it. He couldn't tell. His paranoia no longer had an off-switch.

Fillion ran a hand through his hair and sighed, trying not to flush. "It wasn't what it looked like. I swear."

"She's out to get you."

Ice crawled up Fillion's back with Mack's accusing tone. "Who?"

"Pinkie."

"What?!" Fillion's heart fell to his stomach and the room tilted. "Oh god." He stalked away a few steps. "I'm too lit and. . . Shit!"

Mack watched him closely, his face still serious. "We'll hit the floor again. But let's blend in at the bar for a while."

Fillion drew in a steady breath and made way to where his bottle of whis- key waited, hands trembling. Alcohol burned in his veins and slurred his thoughts and he blurted, "I'm walking chaos."

"I've noticed."

"It's nobody's damn business what I do." Rage swirled violently with the alcohol, and Fillion whirled to face Mack, gritting his teeth. "It's *my* life!"

"Yeah?"

"Yeah."

Mack handed him the bottle of whiskey with a wink. "We're men of power. Nobody owns us."

But his friend was wrong. The world owned Fillion and he, in turn, would own another world. What would Willow think of him if she somehow saw the images? What would government officials think? Business partners? His sister?

"Shit," he breathed under his breath again.

"Drink, lover. Then let's dance. Afterward, we'll crash your hotel room and engage in all sorts of unspeakable homosocial activities. Like spooning." Mack shrugged his eyebrows.

Normally, Fillion would force a quiet laugh for his friend's sake. But he couldn't.

Everyone loses in this game.

The card burned in his pocket, the jester silently mocking him. Fillion resisted the urge to crumple the paper in his hand.

"By the way," Mack began again, snapping Fillion out of his thoughts. "Happy birthday, mate."

The midnight bells tolled in The Crypt—the hour of the dead—and a cheer erupted. Fillion lifted his bottle of whiskey to his lips and welcomed the black.

This is the chapter of my story where I trade a lifetime of fear for a lifetime of freedom by learning how to fight. It's the part where I transform from victim to hero on every page that I write for the rest of my life.

—— Christy Ann Martine, Poet, "The Transformation," 21st century *

Chapter Eight

New Eden Township, Salton Sea, California
Wednesday, March 27, 2058

Lynden tried to get her brother's attention. But Fillion was like an ice sculpture, captured in a frozen position of quiet, controlled fury. Invisible emotions dripped off him and puddled at his feet. It was creepy. Leaning back in a large chair, a hand dangling over his mouth in concentration, and eyes riveted on an imaginary spot on the wall, Fillion listened as their dad droned on and on about Fillion's behavior since their World Tour ended. And, like the asshole Hanley was, he did it in front of a large audience, including Leaf—who was the lab's "special guest" pre-Ceremony—and a few other important individuals at N.E.T. She was pissed off at her brother. She had no clue who the girl was in the photo from The Crypt. Still, he didn't deserve this.

"…As the new majority owner, it's crucial your public image is spotless," their dad said, hands splayed on the long meeting table as he leaned forward. "Governments and corporations will not partner with a man who is destructive and an embarrassment. I didn't spend years building *you* up so *you* could destroy *your* Kingdom before *you* officially take possession. What you do behind closed doors is your business—"

"And mine," Akiko said, her voice as icy as Fillion's body language. "You embarrassed me and my family yet again. I refuse to be made a fool before the world."

"Indeed, Ms. Hirabayashi," Hanley said with an inveigling curve to his mouth. His eyes lingered on Akiko a beat too long before he bowed. What the…? Lynden's disgust continued when her dad said, "You honor my son and *me.* I will make this right for you."

A slow smile spread on Akiko's face and Lynden shivered. She hated that smile. In Japanese, Akiko replied that Hanley could begin by removing his slave King from the board room. And that there was only one rightful King, she continued, and "it" was an abomination for Hanley's son to share a title with "it."

Fillion swung her direction with lightning speed. "*Ore ga shitteiru ichiban kouketsu na hito da yo. Kare ya New Eden no juumin o hiningen no you ni atsukatte ikemasen. Wakatta?*"

Akiko pushed to a stand, took her glass of water, and threw the contents in Fillion's face. The entire room froze, like somehow the arctic chill had transferred from Fillion to the board room with his and Akiko's movements. Now, completely thawed, emotions visibly dripped from him and puddled at his feet as his stare grew hot. Fillion rose to a stand, sleek and confident, and peered at Akiko with such contempt, even Lynden felt intimidated. A tiny smirk curled his lips as he shook the water from his face, before raking fingers through his hair. Akiko gasped, wiping droplets off her cheek, and grimaced in outrage.

"I will make you into a man worthy of the world that worships you," she said to Fillion.

"Emasculate me some more," he snapped, leaning in close with a cocky smile. "It only makes your job that much harder." With a sharp turn he stamped toward the exit.

"This meeting isn't over yet." Hanley placed a hand on the door. "First, you must apologize to the executives who now support you as majority owner at N.E.T."

For several long, agonizing seconds, Fillion and their dad glared at one another. Then, her brother yanked open the door. Hanley grabbed his arm and Fillion jerked it away. "Don't touch me," her brother growled. "If you and the execs don't trust me to run this company, then let's cancel the Ceremony right now. Find yourself a new majority owner." Fillion cooled into arrogance and leaned against the door jamb with a smug smile. "That's my first move. Wanna play Gamemaster?"

"You refuse to apologize?"

"I refuse to cower before people who accuse me without facts and refrain from asking me my defense." Fillion wiped away the droplets chasing each other down his face. He turned his attention to Leaf. "I'll walk you back to The Door." Fillion locked eyes with Mack, then Coal, and gestured for them to come along, too.

Coal slid a hand beneath the table and placed it on her knee, and she wove her fingers with his for a few short seconds. Her husband's body was like a coiled snake ready to strike. She could almost feel the restless energy seeping through his fingers into hers, white hot and dangerous.

Akiko peered down her nose at Lynden with revulsion. Instead of pulling away under Akiko's obvious disapproval, Coal lifted Lynden's hand and publicly kissed her fingers. Disgusted, Akiko wrapped an arm around her stomach as if their PDA was more than Akiko's delicate constitution could handle. Poor thing could have the vapors for all Lynden cared.

With a sly, conspiratorial smile just for Lynden, Coal gently returned her hand to her lap. He was so wicked. She knew what he was thinking and god if she wasn't thinking the same thing. Their silently communicated fantasy was far better than any further move they could have made in reality to torment Akiko. It didn't last long, though.

Sinking dread filled her stomach with lead once again, and she studied her brother's face as he waited for Team Fillion to spring into action. Each of his features remained placid, save his eyes. They were blazing, an erupting volcano that oozed wrath. She quickly returned attention to Leaf when Fillion's fiery beams rested on her. Hell if she'd be the sacrifice to cool his temper. Throw in Akiko.

Leaf rose from the table and issued a bow to the room, meeting Lynden's eyes for a moment, then her mom's. He was freaking out, same as her. Twisting the ring on her thumb, she looked away. After the required New Eden formalities, the "slave King," as Akiko called him, marched toward the exit, head down, Mack and Coal at his side.

"When I return," Fillion continued, "there will be no more talk of my public image. In the future, I will be treated as innocent until proven guilty. And, if the execs in this room want to keep their jobs," he said, voice tight, "they'll apologize to *me*."

Their dad shook his head with a belittling chuckle. "Fillion, you don't understand—"

"You said what happens behind closed doors is my business. Right?" Her brother waited for their dad to respond. But Hanley remained still with a bored yet humored expression. "If I have to apologize to government officials and corporate partners for something I didn't do just to save face, that's one thing. I'll sacrifice my ego to protect my employees and New Eden. But that's not the situation right now, is it?" He didn't wait for an answer. Fillion shoved past their dad and left the board room. Leaf, Coal and Mack followed close behind.

Lynden almost gaped, stunned that Fillion actually had the last word. "Holy shit," she said under her breath. Her brother was angry for all the right reasons, too. Their dad had undermined him in front of friends, family, and employees. On *his* birthday. On *his* first day as owner.

A firm grip on her wrist startled Lynden and she flinched. Akiko grabbed her hand tighter and tugged.

"I need to fix my makeup," she said, blotting her face in search of water droplets. "Walk me to my suite."

"Yeah, OK." Lynden drew her hand back, absently rubbing her wrist. She rose and, on shaky legs, made way toward the door. Eyes tracked her movements in the thick silence. *Thin-air thoughts*, she chanted to herself. Nobody could really see her. She didn't exist.

Maybe she, the Eco-Princess, was the dog, not Michael. On a short leash, she was commanded to obey her master's will, or suffer the eternal shame of embarrassing her family before the world. As usual, Fillion could destroy things or throw tantrums. He was still heralded as "the hope of the future," even if sentenced to jail, or fined for vandalism, or emotionally volatile. But her? No second chances. No forgiveness. She was nothing in her dad's eyes. Just a tool to be used and discarded again and again.

"Ms. Hirabayashi," her mom said with a subtle look Lynden's way. "I was hoping for your company, actually. Perhaps you can share wedding details with me and Hanley over an early lunch?"

Her mom was rescuing her? Lynden played it cool and glanced around the room, as if the faux-medieval interior was interesting.

"I would be honored, Dr. Nichols," Akiko said with a less than thrilled smile in response.

"Wonderful." Her mom replied with a practiced smile of her own. "I will see you after you freshen up. Thank you, Lynden." A warm look softened her mom's face. "It is kind of you to assist Ms. Hirabayashi."

What the hell had gotten into her mom? "Of course," she said in reply. Lynden blanketed the shock, maintaining a relaxed stance and a bland face. To Akiko she said, "Your room isn't too far away."

"Is there a room with a better view?" Akiko asked Lynden, indignant. "I do not wish to reflect upon the biodomes. They are ugly and uninteresting." As they passed Hanley, Akiko's tone grew syrupy. "Mr. Nichols, thank you for your defense, as always."

Hanley glanced up from the heated discussion with the executives and offered Akiko a charming smile. Lynden could puke. She knew the look in her dad's eyes. She'd seen it plenty of times in men. Lust. Power. Control. All packaged behind a debonair look of trustworthiness. Hanley approached Akiko. "My son is fortunate to have an attentive woman to tame his *passion*."

"And yet he does not appreciate me."

"How could he not? You're perfect . . . for him."

Hanley flashed another inviting smile, and Akiko blushed. Like an honest-to-goodness, rosy-cheeked, moony-eyed blush. Yuck! Humiliation burned in her mom's eyes as she stared into a cup of tea. But, as usual, her mom schooled her composure and smiled politely at anyone who noticed in the room, as if Hanley hadn't openly flirted with their son's fiancée.

Before Lynden projectile-vomited all over the place, she gently took Akiko's hand and pulled her along. "Let's find you a new room."

Akiko retracted her hand and wiped it on her clothing. "Do not touch me."

Lynden rolled her eyes with a giant sigh and exited the boardroom. The door shut behind them with a bang and Lynden nearly jumped. Certain sounds still triggered her. For whatever reason, the sudden, loud grind of metal doors closing in the lab reminded her of when her assailant slammed the partially unhinged door in the back bedroom to block out the party. Many years had passed and, still, she startled.

Keeping her steps fluid, infused with attitude, Lynden moved forward. Akiko refused to walk by her side, trailing behind a few steps. God, Akiko thought she was the very essence of culture and beauty. Lynden wasn't this woman's servant. She wasn't her doormat either. All her life Lynden had bit her tongue and cowered in the face of public shame and rejection. Hell to the no. She refused to become subservient to her dad's ignominy another second of her life. Or just sit by while her dad marked Fillion's territory—and, this time, on a personal level that was deeply disturbing. She shuddered. How could her mom just sit there and look pretty? So freaking gross.

There was only one way to deal with alpha females: remind them who's top dog. And if Lynden was going to be treated like a dog, she'd damned well better lead the pack.

"Walk beside me." Lynden peered over her shoulder, flipping her hair while scanning Akiko from head to toe and back. Not finding anything interesting, she faced forward again. "I said, walk beside me."

"I do not walk beside those who indulge in debase, animal behavior with one of *them*."

Lynden spun on her heel and hurled Akiko up against a wall so fast, the bitch gasped for air from need rather than shock. "I'm Hanley's daughter, got that? You're beneath *me*. If Fillion is stupid enough to marry you, I'll still be above you in social standing. Why? Because *I'm Hanley's daughter*, his DNA, the Eco-Princess. You're only a blood-sucking leech. And don't even think about crawling in bed with my dad to try and gain power. You won't. He'll use you to get at Fillion like he does everyone else."

Akiko's face paled for a nanosecond before turning thunderously red. "How dare you insult me!"

"Ah, poor Ms. Hirabayashi," Lynden cooed in a mock-playful tone. "She can dish it but can't take it. Life must be so hard for you."

"At least I have friends and am regarded as desirable in society. You are the ugly duckling, a blemish to the Nichols name. This is why your father allows you to engage with his property." A slow, calculating smile crept up Akiko's face. "You are nothing. Why should he care if you mate like a rodent with a lab rat? It is a kindness he shows you after your tainted reputation."

The words stabbed deep and Lynden's stomach clenched as if punched. Her first instinct was to back up and look away and just absorb the injury. Instead, Lynden maintained eye contact and controlled her voice. "You don't deserve Fillion. He's a way better human than you'll ever be." Akiko's mouth parted, inflamed, but Lynden continued. "Yeah, I'm ugly and friendless. How original of you to point that out. At least I don't flirt with my fiancé's father to warm my cold heart and bed." With that, Lynden shoved away and sauntered down the hallway.

Akiko laughed. Not friendly. Not humorously. More like she delighted in Lynden's self-defense, as if Lynden's actions and words were adorably pathetic. Spooked, Lynden chanced a look over her shoulder, her heart in her throat. She wouldn't show fear, though. Dissolving all emotions, Lynden faced Akiko and crossed her arms over her chest as if bored.

"I always get what I want," Akiko said. She took slow, seductive steps toward Lynden and appraised her with a dismissive look. "I want Fillion. He is mine."

"OK, psycho, how's that working out for you?" Lynden kept her facial expressions still. "If you haven't figured out yet, my brother doesn't belong to anyone, especially *you*. In fact, he despises you, so good luck with that."

A satisfied smile touched Akiko's lips and Lynden resisted the urge to shiver—again. "I will do all that is necessary to get what I want. He will learn who he belongs to soon enough. Now—" Akiko snapped her fingers. "My room?"

"You're crazy." Lynden finally showed disgust. "Find your own damn room."

"You will take me to my room, now!"

Lynden lifted her eyebrow, actually finding Akiko's tantrum humorous. Really? Oh, she was so scared. Pivoting on her heel, Lynden tromped down the hallway, adding an extra swing to her hips to further goad Akiko. Either that or flip her off. But she had class. She just used it sparingly. Plus, Lynden knew the gesture wouldn't be as meaningful as swinging her ugly, friendless ass at Akiko.

It felt good to fight back. Coal would be so proud of her for not melting into the background. A few turns later, Lynden stood before Coal's room. Akiko was nowhere in sight, probably ran back to Hanley to tattle. She could imagine Akiko saying with a childish pout, "Lynden was mean to me! One of your children has embarrassed me and my family again. Wah!" Toughen up, Ms. Bat-Shit-Crazy. Lynden was never going to hear the end of how, yet again, she had proved a disappointment to her dad and, therefore, her brother.

Cringing at the thought, Lynden let herself into Coal's room and softly closed the door to all the pain. This was her sanctuary. Her happy place. She clutched her husband's pillow to her chest, closing her eyes as she breathed in his warmth, love, and safety. The world could say whatever it wanted about her, make her feel like she was nothing. In Coal's eyes, she was everything.

Fillion deserved to know that same feeling. She hoped he woke up from whatever nightmare in which he was living and did something about it, too.

When you deny employment to your fellow human, you deny them life. Not only do they lack a paycheck to meet basic needs, striking out on their own is nearly impossible. Laws in most countries prevent start-ups without piles of paperwork and licensing fees. You can't open a business without property, let alone one that's up to code. I checked and India is less stringent on building codes, but your country still demands exorbitant licensing fees and business taxes on a gradient scale based on caste. Where does this capital come from? If they can't afford groceries, they can't afford to invest in self-employment.

— Fillion Nichols, World Tour speech in India, February 17, 2058

Chapter Nine

Leaf held an apple blossom and studied the specimen. In three hours, he had yet to hear from Willow or another on Ember's state. His wife remained in bed with pains that were deemed irregular when he had left for the required meetings at the lab.

Nor could he discuss any more legal formalities in preparations for the Ceremony in five hours hence. Fillion's mind required more mental stimulation to remain levelheaded—a trait he had nearly forgotten about in the Son of Eden—which only wound up Leaf's anxious state even more. Tranquility was a commodity he would not know for some time, he had finally accepted. So, he would gather peace in small pockets, savoring each rushing moment.

Still, it was good to see his sworn brother again. Leaf had missed Fillion's analytical, anxious ways. Standing in his presence felt right, as if a long-lost part of himself had returned home. By the way Fillion slid relieved glances his way since shaking hands this morning, Leaf surmised Fillion felt similar.

He released the dainty flower and peered at his friend. They were finally alone after hours of meetings and formalities. Leaf wished to ask him about the validity of his ownership in the company. However, he was not sure if he should launch into this topic of conversation right away. He decided to tread gently.

He was rather curious about another topic anyway. Whatever Fillion was accused of had been clear to everyone else in the boardroom—the blurry photograph offered up as some kind of undeniable proof. Leaf had an inkling of what Hanley was implying. The photograph was clear enough. And yet...

Lifting his gaze, he asked, "The image shown in the boardroom—"

"I won't touch your sister." Fillion met his eyes briefly, then looked up at the dome ceiling. "Or any other woman in New Eden. Relax."

"What is your defense?"

"Like it makes a difference now. The execs have probably all turned in letters of resignations by this point. Bound to happen eventually." Fillion lifted a single shoulder in a faint shrug. "Hanley loyalists."

"Your explanations matter to me. I shall believe you."

Fillion sardonically chuckled and plucked a leaf from the tree. "I was at a bar—a, um, tavern. A girl came up to me, hoping to engage me in intimate activities. I said no. Mack sent her off. The end." Leaf studied the grass and his face warmed while Fillion continued. "The picture was taken while she tried to arouse my interest. I was drunk and feeling . . . lonely. So, for the stupidest ten seconds of my life, I caved to the temptation. But that's it. Nothing happened. The entire episode lasted a few short minutes."

"Such unseemly professions still exist in the world?" Leaf blinked back shyness with his question. Fillion held an unreadable expression for several beats, then issued a single, curt nod. Heartsick, Leaf continued. "The image was then sent to Hanley?"

"No." Fillion released another ill-humored chuckle. "It was posted on the Net for the entire world to enjoy, complete with outrageous commentaries and eye-witness accounts. Lucky me. Entertaining the masses once again. It's what I live for." He flicked the bruised leaf into the air, the lines around his eyes hardening. "Just another day in my wonderful life."

Leaf squinted as he regarded the man before him more closely. Fillion's countenance pulsed with a form of confidence that one of influence naturally radiates. His authority, however, lacked gentleness. It was all sharp edges and impatience, as if he braced for a fight at every turn, and no wonder.

"We both pledged things that I'm sure you now regret," Fillion began again when noting Leaf's inspection. "I release you. From everything. I won't hold you to oaths that partner you to me beyond business dealings."

Stepping toward Fillion, Leaf said, "I shall not withdraw my pledges or sentiments. If anything, I renew them with greater vigor than before."

Willow's words from yesterday—that deeds defend a man's honor— echoed fresh in his mind. Fillion could have denied any involvement with the image. Instead, he made a full confession. Leaf had not meant the question as a test of honor, but Fillion's honesty over a delicate topic had earned Leaf's respect.

Steady and sure, he gripped Fillion's forearm. "Many years have passed since last I saw you, but you are still my brother, my *family*, and I deem it a privilege to serve you all my days."

Fillion's head fell forward. "Leaf..."

"I know you would never wish to hurt Willow. She knows this truth as well, despite the heartache she nurses." Leaf dropped his voice. "I owe my life to you."

"I don't need repayment for anything. My family committed a crime against yours, remember? We're marching toward project shutdown, too."

"You have never owed reparations to my family."

"Dammit, Leaf!"

Fillion pulled away and raked trembling fingers through his hair. His eyes darted around The Orchard. "I learned the day I left..." The color drained from Fillion's face. "The day I left New Eden, I was informed that the second and third gens are—"

"Property of the lab."

Fillion winced, but he remained guarded. "Yes."

"I have heard only recently and have longed to discuss this topic with you in private."

"Did Hanley tell you?"

"No, another who prefers to remain anonymous. Apparently, there are grave consequences for lab employees who divulge details to me. I gather Hanley wishes for the element of surprise when I am scheduled to be made aware of my standing within society."

"I'll feign ignorance that you know. Shit." Fillion scuffed the grass. "For the record, I don't see anyone in New Eden as anything different than me. We're all human and born with the same rights. Things are going to get ugly, though. I'm part of the system. One of the bad guys."

"I disagree. You are far from—"

"I own you!" He clenched his teeth. "Do you get that? I'm in charge of your price tag and your future. And Hanley's not removed from this picture since he's still partial owner. I have no idea what in the hell he has planned, but it's big. The world will think I'm a part of his schemes, too, and I'm not sure if there's anything I can do about it." Fillion grabbed a handful of flowers and crushed them, his body shaking as he continued to grit his teeth. Slowly, his hand opened and the petals tumbled to the ground in bruised clumps. In a trembling whisper, Fillion asked, "How many know in New Eden?"

"So far, only Willow and I know. I will share with Ember soon." Leaf moved closer to Fillion. "Forgive me, but for a couple of days now I have longed to ask you this question: Do I possess real power as minority owner?"

"I'm not sure. I've only gained access to files and personnel at N.E.T. as of yesterday." Fillion shook his head again. "I'm screwed. You know that, right? It doesn't matter how much I value my life or yours. We're both going down with this huge, sinking boat and the captain has already abandoned ship." A low chuckle passed Fillion's lips. Leaf's skin prickled with goosebumps as the dispirited sound rolled over him. "Want to take back your re-swearing of fealty?"

"Of course not." Leaf leaned toward him. "I trust *you*, not systems, governments, or laws."

"The law and government aren't on your side, and they trump me."

"You hacked The Code of my government and changed our laws." Leaf lifted the corner of his mouth. "Perhaps there is a future for my generation with you as our King."

Fillion released a shaky breath. "Hope is for the weak-minded."

"I beg to differ. Hope is the very breath of life."

The Son of Eden lowered his eyes and scuffed at grass and stray blossoms once more. "It'll take time. Way more time than the two years we have left as a project."

"Then we should schedule another meeting solely to discuss this problem. Shall we request all head Nobles or just you and I initially?"

"Probably best if just you and me at first."

"Shall I arrange meetings through Michael? Or contact you personally through my Scroll?"

Fillion smiled. "I should get you a Cranium. You'd look badass."

"Alas," Leaf said with a laugh, "I shall not feel like one. Technology and I are not fast friends."

"You just need a better teacher. Yours is too distracting," Fillion said with a wink. "So happens I know a guy."

"Indeed." Leaf smiled in reply, then sobered, clearing his throat.

They were quiet for a moment, then Fillion stepped closer and dropped his voice. "I visited with Timothy yesterday." Leaf drew in a quiet breath. "There's a hidden—"

"Your Majesty!" Both he and Fillion jerked away and jumped toward the source. Laurel pushed away a rambling limb and ran toward them with panicked motions. "Your Majesty! You are needed, posthaste." His littlest sister placed a hand upon her stomach as she gasped for air, blanching upon noticing Fillion.

"Is Ember…?" He could not finish.

"Lady Brianna says you are to come quick."

Leaf nodded, woozy as the blood drained from his head. "Thank you, Laurel."

"I know my way to The Forge," Fillion said. "We'll see ourselves out."

"Thank you, Your Majesty." Leaf bowed.

"If I don't see you at the Ceremony, I'll know why. Enough from New Eden are coming. We signed all the docs already. Don't feel pressure from me, OK?"

Leaf grabbed his forearm once more and said solemnly, "You are a good man. Thank you."

"No worries. Congrats." Fillion smiled weakly. "It's a decent birth date."

"Fillion?" Laurel asked hesitantly, eyes rounding.

Fillion flicked a glance at Laurel with a polite smile before peering out over the fields. "Hey. Good to see you again, Laurel."

His youngest sister took in Fillion's full measure through the eyes of a budding young woman rather than a child, every enamored thought reflecting upon her face.

Narrowing his eyes at her, Leaf said, "*S'il te plait, prend sur toi et montre un peu de modestie. Dévisager quelqu'un n'est pas distingué ni apprécié par notre invité.*"

She ignored his correction, her focus firmly fastened upon the Son of Eden.

"You have changed much." Laurel blushed and lowered her head. "Your Majesty," she finished softly with an elegant curtsy.

Leaf cleared his throat and offered his arm to Laurel, who took it reluctantly. She attempted to steal a furtive glance Fillion's way once more, but Leaf maneuvered as if to step forward and Laurel swung her focus back to the uneven ground. To Fillion, he said, "I am honored to serve beside you, Son of Eden." Fillion replied with a tight nod, a muscle pulsing in his lower jaw. Turning away, Leaf said to Laurel, "Tell me of your day."

He was not sure he would make it home without assistance if his apprehensions were not silenced. Still lightheaded, he stepped forward, then took another step. Soon, he and Laurel found a rhythm, and her birdsong chatter filled his head with distractions—until they walked into their apartment.

Sounds of distress traveled from his bedchamber, and Leaf stood in the entryway, trying to compose himself. This was how he felt when Alder was born: helpless and listless with anxiety. His son played in the corner with his favored wooden blocks, looking toward the hallway with a slightly pinched face. Willow sat next to him, gripping the edge of her chair with whitened knuckles.

"I shall take Alder to the Great Hall for a treat," Laurel volunteered. A greenish pallor painted his littlest sister's skin.

"Yes, thank you."

"Alder, dear, would you like a biscuit?" Laurel asked in a cheerful tone. "Shall we visit Cook and sample her treats? Perhaps see if Auntie Rona and Uncle Blaze are available to join us?"

"Biscuits!" Alder jumped to his feet and grabbed Laurel's hand, pulling her toward the door. In a serious voice, Alder added, "Unca Baze eat all biscuits."

"Blaze is rather fond of treats, 'tis true," Laurel said. "I am sure he shall save you one."

"Unca Baze no share. Like Unca Coal."

Willow hid a smile when Alder's face scrunched into a stern expression. "You must not allow the Hansen men to steal your desserts," she said, then added, "Be a brave lad and stand your ground. Now run along with Auntie Laurel and mind your manners. Be sure to kiss Cook on her cheek."

Leaf waited until his son marched from their apartment, then faced his sister. "Willow, please stay with Ember. If I cannot remain, I would rather you be here with her."

"She is your wife. Your duty is to her before all else. Do not allow the anguish of decisions to plague you further this day."

"I cannot leave you to face the Ceremony alone. 'Tis my fault you are now attending. Do you think me so unfeeling?"

"Nonsense," Willow said, straightening her shoulders. "I shall have Rain and Skylar for company as well as Connor and Canyon. Coal shall be our guide, I imagine."

"No, Connor shall remain to lead in my and The Elements' absence should the need arise." Leaf sighed and scrubbed his hands over his face. "You are willing to act as Regent?"

"Oh, I had not thought of such. I must sign legal documents on your behalf?"

"Fillion and I already cared for those details with Jeff just now." His sister's face registered mild shock. Blinking shyly, she ironed out invisible wrinkles in her dress and touched her hair. Leaf softened his voice and continued. "Copies shall be ready to mock-sign for ceremonial purposes only."

Willow turned and peered out the latticed window. "I see."

"Media shall be present and may inquire about you and our colony, especially as they have not yet met you."

Her eyes rounded. "Technology ghosts?"

"Perhaps. Although Coal is charged with media interactions on behalf of New Eden Township and the lab, so you may not need reply at all."

"I see," she said again, her voice faint.

"Willow, I cannot lay this before you to face in my absence. I begged you to join me." He dropped his voice to a whisper. "Hanley is *not* to be trusted, and I worry immensely. The Outside world is hostile in many ways. I shall attend—"

"You shall do no such thing, Leaf Watson," Willow said, with arms akimbo. "Ember needs you and you shall be worthless out there when your heart and mind are entirely engaged with worries over your home and family. If anything were to happen to her in your absence, you would never forgive yourself." He lowered his eyes as she continued. "I shall not cower before Hanley's feet. Nor shall I . . . fear . . . the technology ghosts bent on haunting the Ceremony. Skylar and Coal shall assure my protection." She nibbled on her bottom lip and relaxed her posture. She began to fidget with the end of her belt. "I am only frightened of seeing Fillion. But I am no more made of glass than you. I shall not break."

"I do not deserve you, *ma chère*."

"Yes, this is entirely your fault: the Ceremony, the Celebration, the birth of your child, all this very day," she countered with a wry smile. Shooing him away, she continued. "Now go attend your wife and allow me to clean up this mess you have made in everyone's life."

Leaf smiled. "There are times I feel as though you say my company is preferred over that of a snake to placate me."

"Naturally."

He laughed. "You are a piece of work, Willow Oak."

She scoffed and pushed him toward his bedchamber. *"Tu seras père encore aujourd'hui et ce petit enfant aura la chance d'avoir ton amour pour la vie."*

Leaf's eyes filled with tears and he lowered his head. *"Et ce qui appartient à sa mère."*

"Yes, indeed." Willow's face softened. "All will be well. You shall see." Then her eyes widened. "Her? You fancy yourself a daughter?"

"I do."

He cast her a shy glance before knocking on his bedchamber door. Brianna opened the door, the hair around her forehead dampened from sweat. Joannah and Timna spoke in low tones with Ember as Leaf walked in. His wife gripped the sheets, her face grimacing as she labored through another pain.

The Herbalist wrung out a rag and wiped her face, whispering steady encouragements to breathe. There was absolutely nothing he could do. He felt embarrassed even, watching his wife suffer, knowing he was partially to blame. He lowered his head as he approached the bed.

Ember opened her eyes and locked onto him. A trembling smile touched her lips and he offered one in reply. "You came, My Lord."

"Of course," he whispered. "I am so very sorry, My Lady."

With a single look from Ember, Joannah and Timna moved to the room's other side with backs turned, hands busying with an occupation. Brianna joined the women and Leaf swallowed, glancing back to his wife. She extended a hand and he took it, kissing her fingers as he knelt onto the floor beside the bed.

Ember whispered low, "There is no reason to feel ashamed."

"There is naught else for me to do." He kissed her lightly across the lips. "I am humbled and deeply honored by your sacrifice, yet again."

"Your daughter comes this day. She is an impatient lass, it seems—" Ember drew in a deep breath and tensed, groaning with another pain. When it passed, she continued through heavy breaths. "It seems she could not wait until after the Ceremony."

"I was assured this was a fine day to be born."

"He fares well?"

"Yes, My Lady." Leaf paused a beat. "Willow shall attend in my stead." His wife tensed with another pain and she gripped his hand, moaning. Her hand loosened as she relaxed, breaths heavy once more; and Leaf experienced another dizzy spell, realizing he had stopped breathing. The air left his lungs all at once as he whispered, "I love you, Ember. I have been in love with you since first we met."

Ember searched his eyes and her bottom lip quivered. "Our children are blessed to have such a strong, honorable man for a father." Leaf closed his eyes, moved by her confession. She placed her fingers onto his lips. "We shall not say farewells." His shoulders began to shake and he looked away.

"Our babe comes early. How can I not be worried? 'Tis several weeks too soon."

"She shall fill our life with love and laughter. She simply cannot wait to do so."

He smiled, caressing Ember's cheek. "I hope she is as wise and compassionate as you."

"And not feisty?"

"I already know she is, My Lady," Leaf said, humored. "And I shall blame her spirited nature entirely on her Auntie Oaklee."

The smile faded on his wife's face as her eyes cinched shut with another contraction. Reverently, he brushed dampened strands of hair from Ember's face as she grit her teeth. If only he could take away her pain. If only he could prevent the sacrifice her body may demand so their child might live.

Either the well was very deep, or she fell very slowly, for she had plenty of time as she went down to look about her, and to wonder what was going to happen next.

— Alice's Adventures in Wonderland, 1865 *

Chapter Ten

The Door framed Earth as a barren, otherworldly realm. Did she chase a white rabbit toward an adventure? Willow often thought of Alice since she had lowered herself into the hatch three years ago. It was an orated story her father oft shared in the evenings to pass the time.

Sometimes she thought that Alice's adventures were real. How could they not be? For Willow had experienced many wondrous, terrifying, unexplainable things since her world converged with another. What she once believed was up was now down, and what was down appeared sideways. 'Twas an ever-changing paradigm. "Curiouser and curiouser," she whispered to herself. She startled when she realized she had spoken the thoughts aloud. Nevertheless, she plodded toward the luminous portal, clenching and unclenching her fists.

She dreaded the moment she would see *him*. But she would not embarrass her brother or New Eden. She would present herself as a proper Noblewoman. Or so she hoped. A weak, illogical part of her wished to please *him* as well, her new King. She despised herself for these unbidden notions, for Willow could no longer lay claim to his affections. Perhaps she never could and he was right, their relationship was merely an illusion. Nevertheless, her heart continually betrayed her good senses since the moment she agreed to attend the Ascension Ceremony and Celebration.

The Son of Fire waited nearby, dressed in dark finery she concluded was customary with Outsiders during celebratory events. Willow's heart leapt and galloped. She was certain her face had drained of all color as well. With his back to her, Coal slowly turned upon hearing their footsteps and delivered a soft smile meant only for her before greeting The Elements and Canyon, who stood directly behind her in the North Cave.

Willow stopped at the dividing line and released a slow breath. Heat bathed her exposed skin and she wrinkled her nose against the foreign smells. Light, pure and bright, blanketed the landscape in golden starshine as the sun's fingers caressed each object. Holding in a giggle, she cast her eyes to the heavenlies and extended her hand in introduction to the sun and her skin tingled beneath the auric magic. She drank in the sky, unable to get her fill of the rich, fathomless blue that stared back. The endlessness of everything was intimidating. Her whole life had been defined by beginnings and endings. The world beyond The Door seemed infinite.

Mingling voices and exotic music wrapped around her and, for a moment, she was not sure if she was lost in a dream or under an Outsider spell. If she left, would she return? This gnawing fear is what had kept her tucked safely within her castle of glass since the start of the Second Phase. Most in Nobility had visited the lab at least once since the The Door opened. Engineers who worked beneath Skylar cared for the many parts on the exterior walls as well. Still, she feared Hanley, despite her words to Leaf earlier. He may not harm her brother now that Leaf's identity was known to the world. But she had once shared a bond with his son, one Fillion feared would place her in danger.

"Your Highness," Coal said with a bow, interrupting her racing thoughts. The light reflected off his white blond hair, casting a soft aura around his head. For once, she could envision him as the angel he was commonly reported to be. All he needed were wings, and then perhaps he could fly her away to safety. He caught her staring. "You are lovely this evening."

"Thank you, My Lord." Willow dropped into a curtsy, and accepted Coal's extended arm.

He peered over her shoulder, a shadow falling over his face. "Is my sister well?"

"Aye. Ember is hale. There shall be much to celebrate this day, no?"

"Indeed," he whispered, nibbling on his bottom lip. He knew her attempt at optimism was weak. "No good tidings to share, then?"

"No, not yet."

They stepped through the Looking Glass and onto Earth. Willow closed her eyes as fiery tendrils of dry, brilliant air seared her skin. A multitude of sensations overwhelmed her all at once. But, then, within a measure of a blink, the intensity of heat dropped to a comfortable temperature and she opened her eyes. A strange black contraption moved over her head, keeping in time with her steps and she jumped back with alarm. The Nobles each held similar contraptions over their persons and she tilted her head, intrigued. Where had they come from?

"This is an umbrella. It is necessary until the sun sets, Your Highness. N.E.T. keeps them by The Door as a courtesy for visitors. My apologies, it is rather clunky in social situations, but the alternative is an unpleasant experience you do not wish to know. A shelter covers the stage area for the Ceremony, which will occur during sunset." Coal peered over his shoulder at the Nobles attending her, worry creasing his brows.

Nerves fluttered in her stomach with his strange behavior. Did he sense Ember's pain and anguish? Several times when they were children, he had known his sister was injured though she was not present. It was most strange, but perhaps a bond shared as twins. A diversion was necessary, before trepidation consumed her even more.

Finding her eyes a few heartbeats later, he offered, "You truly are most becoming this day, Oaklee."

"Flattery shall not erase my grievous offense with you," she admonished with a melodramatic lift of her head.

Coal slid a glance her way. "How ominously waggish."

"Please be warned, I am quite vexed."

"Frightening."

"Shall you hide Lynden from me this day as well, My Lord?"

The Son of Fire grinned with innocence. "Is this to be my only chastisement? My charms must be working despite your protests."

"Hardly. You think too highly of yourself."

"I have it on good authority that I possess only one flaw and thinking too highly of myself is not it."

She rolled her eyes with a humored groan. "This source of authority certainly does not know you as well as I, then."

Head down, Coal smiled, as if to himself, but an obvious uneasiness continued to surround him. Sights and smells inundated her, and she wished to further distract her own discomfort. Willow lifted fingers to block her nose, deciding instead to pluck a cherry blossom from the chaplet circling her head to breathe in and not the foul, unnatural stench saturating the air.

"The matriarchs and matrons placed so many flowers in my hair I fear I shall induce sternutation to those who breeze by or stand in my company," she said, with a casual glance at Rain. "A rather unkind reply to the hospitality given this fine evening."

Rain stifled a laugh behind her. "Perhaps the matriarchs simply wished for you to earn the Lord's blessing all evening time, Your Highness."

"Heaven knows I shall need each blessing to last this night."

"I find the transformation rather fetching," Rain added. "The Daughter of Earth should reflect a garden in Spring."

"Utterly ridiculous." She turned to Coal. "Do I resemble a bush in bloom?" He issued a distracted smile, almost nervous, sparing her a quick glance. "You know how I feel about being trussed up…"

Her voice trailed off as the gathering came into view. The sheer number of those in attendance had to be at least four or five times that of the residents within New Eden proper. Elegant women meandered through small groups in shimmering gowns boasting colors her eyes had never beheld, their immodest display of skin glowing in the golden light. Twinkling jewels draped along necks and dangled from ears. The men wore dark breeches and shirts beneath knee-length, form-fitted robes, similar to Coal.

"Dear Lord in Heaven," she whispered under her breath.

Willow peered at her simple linen garments comparatively and adjusted the copper leaf girdle hanging on her hips, a trousseau gift from Coal to Ember several years ago. The bone hook and copper leaf earrings, presented to her by Connor and Brianna upon her sixteenth birthday, fluttered against her neck in the breeze. She reached up to ensure her mother's carved dragon comb still fastened the crowned strands of corded braids to the back of her long tresses, which draped unbound to her waist in soft waves and manufactured curls. A matriarch had softly lined her eyes with charcoal, using a damp stick, and tattooed her hands with henna in swirls, dots, and Persian-inspired flowers.

"My words were in earnest," Coal whispered for her alone. He gently took her hand, the one fussing with her hair, and wound his fingers with hers. "Do not worry so over your appearance. The Outside world will find you enchanting, flowers and all. To them, you are a modern faerietale princess."

She offered a feeble smile. "I fear I shall faint."

"The air is thinner here than in New Eden." His face softened with concern. "I shall procure an essential oil for you to help with any undesirable smells. The acclimation takes time." Coal released her hand and touched his Cranium. She watched in fascination as his fingers flew through the air. "You will find alleviation soon, Oaklee." He tapped his Cranium and his free hand dropped back to his side. "I should have thought of these needs sooner."

A hush fell over the Outsiders. Even the music silenced, and Willow steadied herself. This was the moment she feared. Oh, how she longed for Leaf's easy way with people to fortify her trepidations!

The soft voices of those behind her quieted, the stillness slithering through the brambles of her tangled thoughts. Goblets and plates rested in motion, as if the Outsiders turned to stone as they openly appraised her appearance, only those whispering into ears dispelling the imagery. Willow lifted her chin and straightened her shoulders. Her knees began to buckle and her breath hitched in an attempt to strengthen her reserves; but any sound she made was drowned out by Coal's announcement.

"I am pleased to present the Daughter of Earth, Her Highness, Princess Willow Oak Watson of New Eden Township."

The whispers turned to excited chatter as the Outsiders took in her measure without apology. Lights blinked. Flashes hurt her eyes from several directions. Hands touched ears to activate devices. The title "Martian Princess" and "heiress" floated on the warm breeze to where she stood. She flinched, not knowing if they were compliments or insults.

Coal continued with introductions of those who accompanied her from their humble Township. Willow, however, secured her feet as her head grew dizzy. Panic took over and her eyes flitted from one Outsider to another. Faces melted together with the landscape. The images spun round and round in nauseating motions. Until she locked eyes with *him* and the world stilled.

But Iseult loved him, though she would have hated. She could not hate, for a tenderness more sharp than hatred tore her.

— *The Romance of Tristan and Iseult*, medieval folktale *

A tree grew inside my head.
A tree grew in.
Its roots are veins,
its branches nerves,
thoughts its tangled foliage
Your glance sets it on fire,
and its fruits of shade
are blood oranges
and pomegranates of flame.
> *Day breaks*
in the body's night.
There, within, inside my head,
the tree speaks.
> *Come closer—can you hear it?*

— Octavio Paz, poet, 1987 *

Chapter Eleven

er mouth parted. She could not move, save her fingers which twirled the cherry blossom stem frantically, back and forth. Attempting to appear natural, she lifted the delicate flower to her nose and inhaled the soft, sweet fragrance.

Black hair, with subtle casts of the indigo night, had grown long—nearly reaching mid-cheek—and partially draped across one eye. The strands were styled in a deliberately disheveled fashion, a look that released a flood of pleasurable sensations in her stomach. A single lead-toned ring pierced the corner of his bottom lip. And another, similar to a small sewing pin with tiny, pewter knobs on each end, pierced through an eyebrow partially hidden behind dark, angled strands. His right hand hooked into the pocket of his black breeches by his thumb, drawing attention to a black band around his ring finger. The word "Honor" appeared across the knuckles on his left hand, tattooed one calligraphic letter at a time. A different black ring graced the thumb on this hand; a joint dangled from his fingers. She nearly smiled with the familiar image.

His gray-blue eyes never wavered from hers. His face remained impassive and distant. Nevertheless, those eyes communicated a complication of emotions, similar to her own. Faint, swirling feelings drizzled through her like warm bio-rain drops, pleasant and uncomfortable simultaneously. It had been so long since the invisible thread that connected their lives had tugged on her heartstrings, and she nearly gasped with the force. Memories reeled through her mind's eye with the momentum. She had to look away before her knotted nerves unraveled into a pile of frayed sorrow.

But she could not look away for long. A woman with petal-pink hair and rich, dark eyes maneuvered to Fillion's side. Was this Akiko? She was breath-takingly beautiful, in face and in form. Willow pressed a hand to her stomach as the flutters of pleasure soured to the heavy, sinking sensations of abashment.

With a pointed expression, Akiko plucked the joint from Fillion's fingers and disposed of it with her ornamental shoes. Fillion blinked, long and slow, clenching his jaw. A dark storm gathered in his eyes, though his face remained bland. Akiko seemed nonplussed, however, and smiled with adoration, ensuring others took note of her great affections.

A scintillating necklace of diamonds draped down the woman's ivory skin, rising and falling with the swell of her breasts which practically spilled out of her pearl-toned, form-fitted gown. Still smiling at nearby guests, her dainty hand slid up Fillion's arm as she pressed herself against him with intimate familiarity. Willow studied the parched soil, mortified.

One observation surfaced above them all and lingered, however. An angry young man had left New Eden the day of the Great Fire. Now, without question, Willow stood before a grown man—in stature and in deportment. And never had her eyes beheld a more striking figure of casual power than Fillion Nichols.

Coal leaned toward her and whispered, "Your turn."

"I beg your pardon?" she whispered back, eyes wide. Her heart found its rhythm once more and beat erratically. "I must speak publicly?"

"Extend thanks, as you would in New Eden."

"Yes, My Lord. If you insist." Willow cleared her throat and folded her hands in front of her, drawing in a shaky breath. "On behalf of my family, The Elements, and all of New Eden Township," she intoned, placing a hand upon her heart, "thank you for your kind invitation as we celebrate the birth of a new era this day." Willow found Fillion's eyes and lowered to the ground in a grand curtsy. "And honor a man worthy of our admiration."

Applause rent the suffocating atmosphere and she remained bowed before him. Fillion appeared physically ill, unable to hide his struggle with her gesture. The grief weighing heavy in her stomach sank deeper, beckoning her heart to drown in the thousands of tears she had shed over his engagement. But, like the treacherous organ it was, it still beat strong with desire to please him.

A tall, fashionable man, perhaps of five-and-twenty, with light brown hair and sharp, magnetic hazel eyes, broke away from the gathering. He was handsome, yet vaguely familiar, his strides long and graceful until he stood before her with an outstretched hand. The Outsider custom to take the hand of a woman for any reason, especially simple greetings, irked her sensibilities. Still, she accepted his hand as she rose, wary to cause offense.

"Your Highness, it is an honor. I have waited many years to meet you. It seems you're unavailable or indisposed whenever I visit New Eden."

She blinked and forced her breathing to remain even. How is it that he appeared so young? Indeed, he appeared not much older than her own brother.

Hanley cocked his head. "Is Leaf with you?"

"No, Your Majesty." She attempted to withdraw her hand, but Hanley held fast.

"Mr. Nichols or sir, will do."

"Very well, sir."

He smiled at the onlookers. "Where is your brother?"

"An unexpected emergency keeps him in New Eden. He sends his heartfelt apologies to you and His Majesty, Fillion." Saying *his* name aloud in *his* presence increased the listless feelings moving through her. It was as if her body floated. Perhaps she had fallen down the rabbit hole after all.

"Emergency?"

"Of a personal nature, sir."

"Interesting." Hanley squeezed her hand a little tighter. "What could be so personal that he fails to do his duty and publicly stand beside his new business partner?"

Willow boldly met his eyes, although her body trembled. "His wife labors prematurely."

Hanley considered Coal for a moment. The Son of Fire remained expressionless, which only increased Willow's dismay.

He turned back to her. "Please send your brother and sister-in-law my congratulatory wishes." Leaning forward, Hanley slid a finger down her arm and whispered, "I see why my son *was* taken with you. But he's off-limits." Coal stiffened by her side and cleared his throat. Hanley ignored him and cupped her upper arm, pressing his fingers into her skin. "Don't try anything foolish, Willow Oak. You'll be held personally responsible for my son's public failure if you do."

"Sir, *The Word Today* is wrapping up with Dr. Nichols." Coal took a step closer to Willow, drawing to full height. "They are nearly ready for your pre-Ceremony interview."

"That so?"

Coal remained undeterred despite the patronizing humor dripping from Hanley's face. "Shall I inform them you are on your way?"

"Tell them five minutes." Hanley's eyes brazenly roamed over Willow's entire body with a satisfied grin. "Do we understand each other?" he asked her in velvet tones.

"Perfectly."

Shame burned her skin hot as he took a step back, releasing her hand and arm as he turned toward the gathering with affability and charm. She rubbed her fingers and held back tears once more.

"Please, enjoy yourself this evening, Your Highness," Hanley said, throwing more smiles at the decadent Outsiders. He gestured toward the shelter and Willow understood the message, lifting her chin a notch higher. "If you will excuse me," Hanley said. His fingers grazed along her upper arm and shoulder blade as he brushed by, and she shuddered. "Rain, Canyon, and . . . *Skylar*, welcome." Hanley eyed Skylar with a look akin to amusement before moving on.

"Please escort me to the garden over yonder," she said to Coal, clenching her teeth. "I refuse to be displayed for his pleasure."

Coal tensed further with her words, took a step and hesitated. "Oaklee—"

"The alternative is to flee back to New Eden and cause an even greater offense."

He whispered, "I am so sorry, Oaklee. His behavior is unpardonable."

"How does a woman defend her honor in this culture?"

"Our ideas of honor do not exist here," he said. The muscles in his neck knotted as he darted a look around the gathering. "One cannot treat another as human when they are not in touch with their own humanity." Hanley's voice floated from behind and Willow winced. Coal turned toward her and continued with a gentle nudge to walk. "The garden is shaded, a perfect location for you until the Ceremony. The media and guests will enjoy pictures of you in this setting."

"Are you frothing mad?" she spat. "That is all you can say after such a degrading moment?" She lowered her voice to a whispered growl. "And *him*, the man who—"

Coal stopped walking and cut her off, whispering barely above a breath. "My job is to ensure positive press for New Eden Township. This is not the night to tip back the scales of injustice with public defiance, especially against Hanley. That time shall come. Tonight, you must woo the world with your Martian charms. Not for Hanley's sake, but for Leaf's. For the community's."

"I am afraid I am not material for positive press, whatever that may mean. Nor do I possess *Martian* charms. Such nonsense." Willow angled her head away, though she watched her friend from the corner of her eye. "Really, Coal Hansen. I am disappointed."

A corner of his mouth lifted, but she noted that it faltered a heartbeat. "Normally, I would never argue with a lady. However, you shall look radiant in the garden, afire in the splendor of your fury. The world will be captivated with you." He looked over her shoulder toward Hanley, then back at her. "Come, Your Highness."

Willow gestured for Rain to join her, extending a hand. They linked arms and meandered through the throng of attendants, who were resplendent in their strange fashions and garish accessories. Many women wore dresses that matched their hair to perfection. Even men sported ostentatious hues in their hair. In contrast, she felt drab and childish, as if she were a girl attempting too hard to appear as though a woman.

She was grateful for the black contraption above her head, for it shielded her from others and from falling through the sky. Logically she knew the latter thought was not true. The inability to perceive depth and space begged to differ, however, even though the black contraption increased the illusion of falling deeper into the hole that had swallowed up her life.

Coal slowed in front of her as they ambled by Fillion. But, with a gentle touch from her, the Son of Fire continued as before. Her skin tingled where she knew *his* stare rested upon her. Nevertheless, she fixed her attention upon the back of Coal's head. Perhaps she should acknowledge the Son of Eden to maintain etiquette. Finding her bearings was of more importance, she decided. One more step, then another, the ground rushing beneath her feet, she filed through the gathering with head held high and with as much elegance and dignity as possible.

Upon reaching the modest garden, Coal gestured for her and Rain to sit upon a bench seat. He took their black contraptions and closed them, leaning them near where they sat. Willow fussed over the tucks and folds of her skirt and properly fanned the long length over her feet. Skylar and Canyon approached and settled on either side of the bench, as if guards. Feeling enclosed by both men comforted the otherwise overwhelming sense of space.

The Son of Fire studied the gardens and tapped the silver device strapped to his ear. "Yes, sir? Right away, sir." He tapped his Cranium again and rested his eyes on her. "My apologies, I will return shortly. Interview time." He looked to those in her company. "In the meantime, if a member of the press or party wishes to engage you in conversation, please do so. And remember," he added, dropping his voice, "Outsiders are not as socially considerate in the ways to which you are accustomed. Most mean no offense; they are ignorant of their rudeness."

Coal walked over to Skylar and leaned in. "Hanley jammed amplifier equipment and signals. Private conversations cannot be tapped if outside a seven-foot radius of the media's drones and Cranium tech." Skylar nodded with understanding and peered over Coal's shoulder, his focus sharp but wary. With a bow, the Son of Fire pivoted on his heel and strode into the crowd of people.

Willow fidgeted with her skirt a moment before watching the mingling crowds through lowered lashes. With a surreptitious glance at Skylar, she contemplated his resemblance to Hanley. It was truly uncanny. She had heard of such comparisons, but now she understood. Skylar shifted attention her direction with a frown. His gaze flicked back to the crowd when a small cluster of Outsiders broke into loud laughter, peering their direction. Rudeness, indeed. She needed another distraction.

The wild landscape just beyond where Skylar stood captured her attention. And, for a moment, she forgot all her worries and woes. A mosaic of colors—shifting in the waning sunlight and encroaching shadows—spilled in tranquil puddles across her agitated thoughts, cooling her mood instantly. Her imagination wished to jump and splash and play in the garden, caressing each leaf and smelling deep the scent of new life. The exotic flowers and vegetables continued to pique her curiosity until she left the bench to quietly shuffle along the narrow dirt path to explore this alien world. Her friends allowed her the solitude, knowing her well enough.

A bright pink flower brushed along the exposed skin of her hand and she fingered the soft petals in delight. A gentle breeze skipped across the flora, and the leaves sang a happy melody in reply. The sound of nature was a far contrast to the savage sounding beats and notes blaring from the stage area.

Near the imposing wrought iron fence, the most enchanting insect fluttered from flower to flower, and she gasped. Willow crept along for a closer look, giggling when the butterfly's white and brown wings gracefully danced through the air by her face. Or was it a moth? New Eden boasted many pollinators, but not butterflies or moths. They were deemed destructive to vegetation and linens unlike the other beneficial insects. Until this moment, she had only seen drawings of various specimens and could not contain the grin that stretched across her face. If she stood very still, she wondered if the insect would visit a flower woven into her braids. The butterfly-like insect wandered her way once more and she held her breath, tracking its movements with only her eyes.

"Wine?" someone asked from behind. She started with the sound, feeling foolish. Then, her heart fluttered as though a butterfly in flight upon recognizing Fillion. A man beside him, his looks as light as Fillion's were dark, regarded her with keen interest, as if memorizing her every detail. "Thought you could use a glass," Fillion said. "Maybe two." A ghost of a smile touched his lips.

"Very kind of you." She curtsied, her legs shaking. His voice was still reminiscent of a soft, mournful breeze, as when the soul of a winter wind sighs until the remnant leaves hum back the doleful tune. The very sound unfolded more tucked-away memories, and the confusion she labored against grew unbearable. Nevertheless, she rose and determined to remain cordial. "Felicitations this day, Your Majesty."

"Fillion."

"Fillion," she half-whispered. "Your intended is . . . she . . . I wish you every happiness."

The furtive smile dimmed as he handed her the goblet of wine. Their fingers touched and lingered half a heartbeat longer than necessary. Her breath danced, and she fought the flush wishing to color her cheeks. She was a woman grown and should be beyond first-blush responses. He, on the other hand, paled and softly chewed the inside of his lip.

"This is my friend, Mack," Fillion finally said, glancing at the man beside him. "He wanted to meet you before the Ceremony began."

The introduction was given with dispassion despite his obvious distress and Willow wrinkled her brows. With great effort, she pulled her gaze from Fillion and gave attention to Mack, refusing to cower under the man's continual inspection. Mack's eyes were a balmy shade of dark blue, reminiscent of the delphiniums Joannah grew in her herbal gardens. A rather striking color when contrasted with his shockingly white hair, arranged haphazardly around his head, as if he had just awoken from a restless slumber. His nose was pierced with a small silver hoop. A post, sporting a rounded, black knob, pierced his chin just below the center of his bottom lip. And, unlike Fillion's tall, narrow build, Mack was a tad shorter than his friend and more solidly built.

Mack extended a hand and she acquiesced to this custom once more. "Hey, nice to finally meet you," he said, shaking her hand. The act was barbaric; nevertheless, she smiled kindly.

"Yes, indeed. An honor." She retracted her hand from the man.

Mack seemed as though he desired to say more, but remained quiet, shifting on his feet. Willow enjoyed a dainty sip of wine and peered anywhere but at Fillion. An awkward silence ensued, and Mack looked between his friend and her, his face unreadable. Fillion's head remained downcast, but his eyes trailed over her, slowly, the pallor of his skin still a sickly shade. Did he simply come to stare at her? It was rude and ungentlemanly.

"I shall not keep you from your esteemed guests." Her throat was closing up the longer she remained in his presence. "Thank you once more for the wine, Your Majesty. If you will excuse me." She lifted her chin and moved to waltz past him.

"Wait."

The stone wall she had built around the grave site of her longings crumbled upon hearing the word "wait," and she could bridle her tongue no longer. Whipping her head back toward him, she asked, "Does it please you to place me on display as well? For the world to behold and admire *your property?*" Mack's eyebrows shot up, but Fillion remained indifferent, his eyes fastened to the dirt path. She took a step closer until they almost touched, a fist clenched at her side. "I will not allow your family to treat me as though I am nothing!"

"People are watching us," he said, taking a casual sip of wine.

Willow glimpsed the technology ghosts before her friends and blanched, touching her head as she grew dizzy. People gathered and watched her and Fillion's interactions as well. She imbibed a large sip of wine despite the queasy motions in her stomach.

"No, I don't find pleasure in any of this." Fillion watched the dark liquid swirl in his crystal goblet. He continued, as if pained, "I'd *never* put you on display."

"Although I am your—"

"Don't say it. Not here." He glanced over his shoulder, then at Mack. Leaning forward, he brushed long strands of unbound hair and braids from her shoulder and she tensed with the intimacy. "Willow," he breathed her name in her ear. The invisible thread tugged harder and her heart pounded in response. "How you and I feel isn't factored into this goddamn equation. We have duties and obligations. Please don't challenge me publicly tonight, no matter what it looks like."

His breath warmed her neck, and her eyelids, weighted with dreams of him, wished to slide shut and relish in the sensation of his nearness. He no longer smelled of cedar, earth, and wood smoke. Rather, he carried a scent she could not fathom how to describe, though she found it equally as alluring.

"Promise me."

"Why should I?"

Fillion whispered in her ear once more, his breath laced with wine. "Because, Hanley has something planned. He never shares the spotlight. He owns it. There's been talk of a secret company for years, and I think the unveiling will happen during the Ceremony while the world is watching. If not that, then something else. He's been trying to throw me off my game all day." His cheek grazed hers and he drew in a quiet breath, and her eyes finally closed. "I'm the best ally New Eden has," he continued, a slight shake to his voice. "I'm on your side, even if it looks like I'm not. Image." He paused. "Perception." He paused again. "Those two illusions are keys to power. *We* need public support. Remember that, no matter what. The future of New Eden depends on it."

"And allow my community and leaders to see me cower beneath Hanley's treatment and ideology? After all he has done to my family and home?"

Stepping aside, he murmured, "I'd never expect that from you."

"How do I know this is not a game you play with my heart?"

"Yes, I'm an asshole! Stop acting so surprised." Fillion clenched his jaw and ran a finger along the rim of his goblet, round and round. Time continued to build and still he traced the glass vessel's smoothed ledge, eventually choking out, "Promise me?"

"Your vulgarity does little to persuade me." Willow pressed her lips together. "Will I regret trusting you once more, *Master Fillion*?" He flinched. "Or shall I shore up the broken remnants you left behind?"

Shame clouded his eyes even though the rest of him remained hardened. In the past, he would have grinned with accusations of vulgarity, offering flirtatious witticisms with ease, desiring to spar words with her and best her temerity. The man before her, instead, seemed cautious, stoic, hollow even.

"Just so we're clear," he punctuated, "this isn't my attempt to seduce you back into a relationship. But, tonight, pretend like you give a damn. For New Eden Township. For your brother. Not me." He bit his bottom lip, vulnerability softening his features and the umbrage shading her emotions dissolved completely. With a nervous glance her way, he whispered, "Hate me tomorrow when everyone is sleeping off their hangovers. Hate me in front of New Eden. I don't care. Just not now. I need to remain focused."

Tears stung her eyes. She could not hate him. *The son of Della and the daughter of Joel*, her soul cried out in protest. How does one tell their heart to be silent when it beats true? Rubbing a variegated leaf, she quietly replied, "I shall not challenge you or Hanley publicly this night, with a caveat."

"Yes?"

"Your protection." Willow straightened her shoulders. "If I refuse to challenge Hanley, then I need to know you shall protect me if he or any other means me harm."

He searched her eyes a heartbeat. "Always."

"Then I give you my pledge, Your Majesty."

"Thank you." He issued a tight bow and reluctantly turned to leave.

"I could *never* hate you, Fillion." He lifted his shoulders and hung his head, and the broken pieces of her life stirred with his anguished movements. "You are a man worthy of admiration and honor."

"Yeah, you'll worship me like the saint I am when New Eden shuts down. Stop thinking with your heart," he snapped. "This isn't a fairytale. And I don't need your acceptance or affirmation to do my job."

His friend shot him a dark expression. "*Ittai doushitattenda yo?*"

"*Kanojo o touzake te iru. Kibou o sute tame.*"

Mack stared at his friend, long and hard. "No shit."

"*Hanley o shinjirarenai. Jibun jishin mo.*"

"*Shoujiki ni iu hou ga ii deshou. Otona dakara daijoubu.*"

Fillion shook his head as he dismissed his friend and turned to leave.

Scandalized by his final words with her, Willow spat, "Shall I quake with fear and anger before you, then? Simply because it lessens *your* grief? I think not." She maneuvered in front of Fillion. "I have defended my honor and heart against worse men than you."

"I side with her for the record," Mack said. "Team Willow."

Fillion angled toward his friend. "Shut up!"

She ignored Mack, and the way Fillion glared at his friend, and thrust her empty goblet into Fillion's hands while saying, "I do not fall to the whims of Outsider boyish fancies, Fillion Nichols. Nor do I bow before your egotistical notions of grandeur."

"Lessens *my* grief?" Fillion chuckled even though he appeared physically ill, his complexion ashen, eyes blazing but glassy. The deadened sound of his ill-humor caused the hair on her arms to rise. He leaned in close, their noses nearly touching, his breath mixing with hers, and ground out, "You have no fucking idea what you're talking about."

Willow reared back a small measure as if slapped. "You are quite right. I am merely a false princess locked away in a tower. I know nothing of grief. How kind of you to remind me."

Fillion stepped away to regain composure, as though he were stricken with nausea while wishing to remain a sturdy current of quiet anger. Holding back the cold, bitter winds gusting furiously inside of her, she braced against his dark atmosphere. This was the storm she had noted earlier, one that was making good work of tearing him apart piece by piece, along with anyone who stood in the way of his destruction. She wiped away an errant tear. Then another. She no longer recognized the man for whom eternity seemed a small price to pay in order to know his love and give hers in return. The man whom she had staked her reputation on so that he would revolutionize New Eden for noble reasons.

Did his behavior relate to Hanley's warning to her? Willow narrowed her eyes and studied the Son of Eden. He almost seemed repulsed by his own words and actions. Regardless, his desire for polite appearances and nothing more was made clear.

"Forgive me," she whispered. "I shall not trouble you a moment longer." Willow dipped into a curtsy then moved to walk away, sucking in a quick breath. The sorrowful expression on Mack's face deflated any hope of strength, though. He seemed just as astonished by his friend's behavior. Her legs wobbled, more so with each sharp ache that stabbed her chest.

"We're all pawns on a chess board," Fillion said as she passed. Dark eyebrows knit together as another shadow fell across his face. "I'm terrified to make the next move. Freaking out that . . . that—"

"You have said quite enough," Willow quietly interrupted. "Though my heart *grieves*, I truly hope you find every happiness you deserve." His eyes dulled, but he refrained from further comment. "Spin the tales, Son of Eden. Weave the stories together. Create your own reality."

He studied the empty goblets in his hands as she pushed past him. Technology ghosts seemed far safer company. Lifting her chin, she began a march toward where her friends awaited her return, only to be intercepted by Coal.

"Your Highness," he said. Willow whipped her head toward him and loosed a tense breath when spotting the otherworldly woman by his side. "The Ceremony will begin momentarily and your presence is requested upon the stage," he said.

Fillion brushed his thumb over a dark dribble on the goblet's rim. "You'll escort her?" he asked Coal.

"Yes, that is the plan. *Merde.* Your publicist is calling me." Coal touched his Cranium with a heavy sigh and an eye roll. He sobered quickly, however, appearing confused when Mack attempted to communicate a silent message. "Kerry?" Coal asked, turning away from Mack and facing Fillion. "Yes, my apologies. The Cranium is on his ear . . . He is in the garden." Her friend gave Fillion an apologetic look, who turned on his heel upon hearing Coal speak again, as if knowing what the Son of Fire would say. Mack followed close behind. "I will inform him that he is needed to greet the press with Ms. Hirabayashi. Yes, I will wait on the line for further instruction."

The woman by Coal's side pretended to stare at her brother, who strode toward the throngs of revelers, rather than meet Willow's gaze head-on. Outsider Faerie Queen, indeed. With head turned, Lynden's neck appeared long and graceful, giving way to a lithe form. Her skin shone alabaster in the dusky light, affectionately sprinkled with tiny, faint faerie kisses. Rain was right. Lynden's hair was an alluringly sanguine shade, the blood-red tresses falling gently to her chin in soft, ruffled waves. It was her eyes, however, that stole Willow's breath. They were soulful, wise beyond her years, and filled with equal parts fear and compassion, speaking of a tenderness that shied away from notice.

"You are more beautiful than I imagined," Willow said, blinking back shyness. "I have longed to meet you for many years."

Uncertainty—or was it disbelief?—cracked through Lynden's detached facade for half a heartbeat as she twisted a black ring around her thumb. A ring, Willow noted, that was similar to Fillion's. Lynden glanced at her brother's fading form, then back to Willow. "He's considered a genius. But I think he's only exceptionally gifted at being an idiot."

Laughter bubbled from Willow, despite the tension. "I prefer pigheaded."

"He mopes around too much." A tiny smile curved the corners of Lynden's mouth, similar to Fillion's expression of amusement. "Drama King."

"'Tis no wonder. Two worlds rest upon his shoulders, My Lady. I am inspired by his ability to remain standing beneath such weight. He is a man of commendable courage and perseverance."

"Yeah." Pride slipped into Lynden's features. But the expression disappeared as quickly as it formed. With a bored shrug, she said, "Still a pain in the ass."

"Your Highness?" Coal tapped his Cranium. "My apologies, but it is time. Fillion declined a last-minute interview so we are moving forward." He pulled from his pocket two brown bottles the length of his forefinger. "First, would you care to use diluted peppermint oil or lavender oil to lessen the unfamiliar pungency in the air?"

"Lavender, please." Coal handed her the bottle and she dabbed a drop beneath her nose. "Thank you, My Lord."

"Of course," he answered with a distracted smile. "Shall we?" Coal extended his arm to her.

Before taking Coal's arm, Willow gently squeezed Lynden's hand and said, "I hope we shall become friends, you and I."

Lynden blushed and removed her hand while turning to leave, her face an instant wall of stone. Coal pulled Lynden back and brushed a kiss across her lips before whispering in her ear. Willow lowered her eyes to provide privacy, embarrassed that she may have unwittingly caused offense. It was rather strange to see Coal affectionate in this way as well, though she had known of his relationship with Fillion's sister for years. Eventually, Coal stepped aside and Lynden graced her with a hint of a smile—the uncertainty riddling her gaze once more—and then she departed for the stage with a grace and stature allaying her obvious lack of surety.

"Thank you," Coal said. "Your offer of friendship was most kind."

"I am sincere and would relish her company, though I fear I have caused her distress."

"No, you have not, I assure you."

Without further explanation, he offered his arm once more. Willow placed her fingers upon his forearm, per the custom in New Eden, and allowed him to lead her toward the stage.

"You will sit with Hanley and Fillion," he began again. "Nobility of New Eden and high-ranking officials from the lab and NASA will be directly behind you."

As they passed the garden benches, her companions from New Eden joined her in a procession toward the stage. The Son of Fire continued speaking. "After Fillion pretends to sign the last document, the media will be allowed to ask questions. Be simple and quick, and hide any emotions you may feel."

"Hide my emotions? You ask too much of me," she teased with a trembling smile, one they both knew was false. He laughed politely, nonetheless.

When they reached the stage, Coal kissed her cheek with brotherly affection, taking her by surprise. "Oaklee," he began again, the nervous smile in place once more. "You make New Eden proud. I am honored to serve you."

"Please, My Lord. You shall embarrass us both."

"I was not even half as brave as you when facing Outsider media technology for the first time."

Willow swallowed and busied herself with inspecting the stage. She had never shared with another soul what had transpired at The Door the day of The Exchange. Shackled and bruised, Fillion had entered her world. This day, she felt similar while interacting with his.

"Yes," Willow began in reply. "Well, you see, I live with your sister who is second-in-command of the Techsmith Guild."

"True." Coal's eyes roamed over her face. "You look unwell."

"I shall fare well, worry not."

He nodded and turned attention toward the stage, assisting her up the stairs. "Simply give me a pleading look over your shoulder and I shall rescue you."

The surroundings overwhelmed her all at once. She could not reply, let alone move. A large, beautiful pomegranate tree shaded the back of the stage area, behind the tall chairs where NASA officials, The Elements, and Coal would sit. The fiery orange-red blossoms swayed in a warm breeze, the leaves glinting bronze in the evening light. It was as though the tree were on fire, and her breath caught.

A light touch on her forearm pulled her from the image to Fillion, who waited to escort her the remaining way across the stage. Over his shoulder, the sun set behind majestic steeples of land, the earthly spires aglow as if tipped with molten iron. Shades of red, pink, and orange blazed across the sky and pooled in his eyes as they held hers. Nature was alight in honor of his Kingship and the very sight ignited her soul. Despite the anguish and offense she carried, Willow took his offered hand, a bit breathless.

Slowly, they made way to the chairs positioned at center stage. Her body trembled with facing the unknown and her hand absently clamped tight around his. She had never seen so many people in all her life, let alone stood before such a crowd. Lights blinked and flashed from the attendees as a hush settled in anticipation. Technology ghosts wavered in front of the stage, their dead, transparent eyes staring right through her. The black hole in her mind yawned wider. She felt herself falling, the weightlessness all-consuming, the oblivion tempting.

Hanley cleared his throat and Fillion released her grip and reluctantly moved away, flashing a devilish grin for the crowd as they cheered and applauded under his attention. It was startling how fast he transformed. *Image*, her mind whispered. *Perception.* A heady warmth intoxicated her as she watched him prepare to fight for her home. But Hanley's cold stare, the one directed her way, chilled her heated blood into a shiver.

Death, like birth, has a momentum of its own. Her breathing was rapid and shallow like a woman in the transitional stage of labor. ...

With birth, we labor to bring a squalling baby into the room; what then, I ask with no small amount of exasperation, do we labor for in our dying?

— Eve Joseph, author, 2016 *

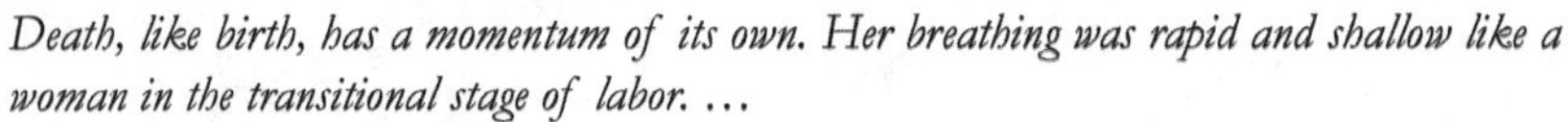

It does a man good to see his lady being brave while she has their baby . . . it inspires him.

— Ina May Gaskin, known from her work beginning in the 1970s as "the mother of authentic midwifery" *

Chapter Twelve

Leaf watched as Brianna patted her step-daughter's cheek, which was pale and sheened with sweat. "Ember, stay with us, darling," Brianna said. "You need to push."

Leaf's chest constricted when a soft whimper escaped his wife's compressed lips, her jaw clamped in agony. Dark rings bruised the delicate skin beneath her eyes. Hair that was normally springing with red-gold curls lay lifeless in strings of sweat-dampened strands.

Timna gripped Ember's wrist and stared at a wall. "Her blood pressure is still dangerously high," the Naturopath finally said. "Another dose of magnesium sulfate, please." Joannah stirred a spoonful of Epsom salts and honey into water to dissolve, adding a pinch of freshly grated ginger to aid the nausea. "Ember," Timna cooed, as she held the cup to the woman's lips. "This shall hopefully help ease the ache in your head."

But his wife pushed the drink away with another whimper. Earlier, she had retched and then suffered dry heaves, an unfortunate side effect of the mineral, despite the small doses administered. She had suffered from nausea and vomiting most of this pregnancy, but this was different.

He cradled Ember's face and caressed her cheek with his thumb. A particularly painful contraction had just ended and she now lay limp in relief. Hours had passed in a similar pattern, and her heartiness had waned to lethargy.

"My Lady?" Leaf whispered. Dark brown eyes squinted open in hazy focus. "Ember Lenore Watson—fight, my love." She dipped her head slightly in response. Tears burned behind his eyes, but he held back, determined to remain steady for her sake. He scooped up her head and held the tumbler to her chapped lips, tipping it up. "Small sips." She complied, drinking most of the contents before crying out from another pain that clutched her body.

"Push!" Brianna shouted. Ember tried but her muscles were weakened from exhaustion and, perhaps, another side effect from the mineral. His mother-in-law tapped his shoulder. "Leaf, she needs assistance."

"What shall I do?"

"Sit behind her and support her body. Timna and Joannah will cup her heels so she can bear down more easily."

"I am burning," Ember mumbled, her words slurred and listless. "I feel as though the sun has set in my body."

"Remove her shift," Brianna ordered. She looked to Leaf. "It is the magnesium." She had given the same explanation the last time Ember voiced her discomfort. Leaf had questioned using the mineral. But Brianna worried that Ember may have preeclampsia, given the headaches and swelling. Ember's mother had died of a stroke in delivery. There was a good reason, he knew, that Brianna treated the symptoms suffered by that woman's daughter—whom she now considered her own—with utmost seriousness.

Joannah and Timna gently removed his wife's shift and dribbled water from a drenched rag over her face and bare skin. He slipped in behind Ember, positioning himself against the wall, and the women leaned her weakened body onto him.

All curves and softness—even now, Leaf's eyes roamed over her breasts and rounded stomach. Seeing his wife full with child was a form of beauty unparalleled. Yet, if she lived, he would ensure her body was never figured in this way again. He could not endure the anguish of watching his wife suffer so. He could not watch death try to take her, and their unborn child.

"Hold her arms so she can push away from you with the next contraction," Brianna ordered. Ember moaned into a frail scream as her body spasmed, and the sound tore at him. "Fight Leaf's hold, Ember. Dig in your heels. Push against Timna and Joannah's hands and tilt your hips upward." His wife fought the resistance they provided, muscles shaking, and she screamed out again through teeth clamped tight. "I see a head!" Brianna looked up and smiled at Leaf.

Ember's body collapsed as the contraction receded, her cheek pressed flush to his chest. Tears and sweat dripped down her face as she stared transfixed across the room. "Beautiful..." she whispered, eerily breathless. "I am not sure I can endure—"

"No!" Brianna shouted, and Leaf's heart stopped with the sharp sound. "Ember, focus! Your child is almost here. One more push, my darling. As long as you draw breath and your heart beats, fight. Fight for your unborn child. Fight for the life you deserve together!"

Leaf stifled the urge to gather Ember to himself and beg her forgiveness. The shame was overwhelming. Instead, he grazed his nose along the hairline near her ear, and whispered, "You are my family. My life. And I refuse to let go of you. Do not leave me, my love. Please. Alder needs you. Our babe should know her mother's arms and her love." Ember's body seized with another contraction. Leaf held her tight and shouted, "Push, my love! Push against us."

The cry that shuddered through his wife's body vibrated through his, then faded into the faint, sluggish cry of a newborn. Tears wet his cheeks as his fear turned into laughter. Leaf pressed a long kiss to Ember's head. His heart was bursting into a million pieces of relief and joy. A feeble smile lit her pale face and he brushed away a tear sliding along her cheek, and then another.

"You have a daughter," Brianna said, vigorously rubbing the child with prepared linens. The cry grew lusty and Brianna placed the girl onto Ember's stomach, satisfied as the child's wails reached a crescendo. "Speak to her," Brianna encouraged. "She longs for your voice."

"Our little joy," Ember slurred. Their daughter quieted and searched for her mother. His wife drew in a deep breath and brushed a trembling finger along their daughter's cheek. "Your mother and father love you, sweetling."

Leaf kissed Ember on the neck, then upon her shoulder. "You have humbled me this day," he whispered. "How courageous you are, My Lady." He rested his head against his wife's and happily soaked in the sight of their small babe. "She is beautiful," he breathed, overcome. A tremulous cry quavered upon their daughter's lips and he smiled, a blissful warmth saturating his entire being with the sound. It was the same sweeping intensity of rapture as when falling in love, every thought and sensation deep and all-consuming.

The smile slipped from Ember's face and she cinched her eyelids shut. Her body shook as muscles contracted, and a sound of anguish left his wife's mouth. Brianna gradually looked up from the end of the bed when Ember unexpectedly clenched against another hard labor pain. It was the sort of movement that communicated fear without a single word.

"Ember, please listen to me," she soothed. "Do not rest, darling. Hold your precious daughter and will yourself to find additional strength."

The air rushed from Leaf. "Twins," he breathed.

Ember cradled their daughter to her with one arm as she pushed against Leaf's arm, digging in her heels and lifting her hips as Brianna had instructed. "I cannot," she cried out. "Too weak..."

"The head is crowning... Now the shoulders," Brianna said with an encouraging smile. "You are doing so well my strong, brave girl. One last push and—"

His mother-in-law never finished her sentence. A second babe quivered a first cry, and Brianna rubbed the tiny body with brisk motions. "Another daughter," she declared, beaming. Tears fell down her flushed, work-worn face. Leaf laughed again, unable to hold back his elation. Two daughters! "Her cry is weak." Brianna turned to Timna and Joannah. "Lower Ember so I can deliver the placenta. Then let us place this precious lass in Leaf's tunic." She looked to Leaf. "She needs skin-to-skin bonding and the comfort of a steady heartbeat. Your girl will draw strength from you."

Ember's breaths came quick and shallow. Timna lifted their first daughter and temporarily placed her into Leaf's arms as they maneuvered Ember to a new position. Tiny fingers curled around Leaf's finger, and pride swelled until he feared he could no longer contain the surging emotions.

"I love you, my wee lass," he whispered in her ear.

Far too soon, his daughter was taken and placed to her mother's breast. Brianna pressed down onto Ember's stomach, massaging and compressing. His eyes shifted from watching Brianna concentrate on post-delivery tasks to Joannah, who approached him with his second daughter.

"Forgive my familiarity, Your Majesty," Joannah began. "If you hold up your tunic, I shall place her upon your chest." Leaf nodded his understanding. "She is lovely," Joannah murmured as he wrapped his arms around his second daughter.

"Yes, she is." He caressed her downy head, playing with the damp curls. "Joannah?" The Herbalist met his eyes. "Would you kindly announce the happy news to Laurel, Corona, and Blaze first, and then to the vigil? I am sure they heard the cries and are eager with anticipation."

"With honor, Your Majesty," Joannah said, dropping into a curtsy before quietly leaving the bedchamber.

Candlelight flickered on the walls and blanketed his family in golden light. Leaf sat next to his wife, and nuzzled the top of their younger daughter's head with soft kisses. "You are strong and resourceful, my precious daughter," he whispered, followed by more words of love. Ember weakly gripped his hand, and he turned his head to her as she smiled, her eyes sliding shut. Their older daughter suckled, latching on with eagerness, and he quietly chuckled. A woman with an appetite. "You are the feisty one, I believe," he said, and Ember's smile widened with his words.

Timna and Brianna worked in silence and, soon, Ember fell asleep, her breaths even and peaceful. She still needed to bathe in tinctured mineral water to prevent infection, as would their daughters. Hopefully the women would first grace his wife with a measure of rest.

Brianna removed his oldest daughter from Ember's breast and tied a ribbon around her ankle. "You are a pretty package, tied in a bow," she sang softly to her granddaughter. "Now we shall know you are the oldest twin. Not that you would let us forget."

His daughter squalled in protest, yearning to return to her mother's embrace. Timna gently slid the youngest from his tunic, and Brianna rested the oldest upon his chest in replacement. Leaf studied her, admiring each tiny, pink finger and toe, her small ears, and dainty nose, trying to determine if the sisters were identical. The low-lit room made it difficult to discern differences, however.

A grin pulled at the corner of his mouth as her sister quivered with a quiet, shaky cry in the sudden cold. Where the oldest proudly proclaimed her opinions, the youngest mewled, soft-spoken even at birth, even in the evening's chill. The warmth of her mother soothed her quickly, though, and she began to instinctively root around.

"She desires to nurse," Brianna whispered with a delighted smile. The lines of worry on her forehead relaxed. "Strong and resourceful, indeed." His youngest needed a little encouragement, unlike her sister, but she eventually began to suckle. Surprisingly, Ember slept through it all. "She shall recover," his mother-in-law said, noting the concern upon his face. "A healthy one, she is. Never one for infections, even when chills and fevers visit homes."

Leaf nodded and swallowed. "I am forever indebted to you, My Lady."

Warmth softened her features as she inspected Ember and caressed the granddaughter in her step-daughter's arms. "You are a romantic, Leaf Watson."

He pressed a kiss upon his oldest daughter's head to hide the flush.

"And a good man." She rose to a stand and stretched her lower back. "I shall return within the hour to bathe your girls. But I shall sit outside your chamber door should you need anything. Rest, Your Majesty. I wager it shall be the last chance you have for some time."

The door shut, leaving him alone with his wife and daughters. Alder would have his hands full one day. Leaf knew from experience. He could not help but smile with his thoughts, nuzzling his oldest daughter's soft head with his cheek. A thin blanket covered his wife and younger daughter. The candle-light turned Ember's strawberry strands amber. His thumb caressed Ember's fingers, still secure in his, and he pushed aside the lingering fear.

In seven days, he and Ember would announce their daughters' names to the community in a New Life Ceremony, held in the Ceremonial Garden within The Rows. Until then, their names would remain secret. He played with the ribbon around his daughter's ankle.

Leaf closed his eyes and meditated on his beautiful girls, his son, and his wife, forgetting entirely about the Ascension Ceremony and Celebration, that the Biospherics lab owned his family, or that his sister braved this evening without his protection. He was falling in love, and his heart concerned itself with little else.

More than 2,000 people gathered outside Biosphere 2 yesterday morning to greet the project's eight crew members as they emerged, gaunt and pale but smiling, after two years in the giant terrarium.

Trumpets sounded a fanfare and the crowd rose to its feet and applauded as the four men and four women stepped through the airlock doors and walked down a red carpet at about 8:25 a.m.

— *The Arizona Daily Star*, September 27, 1993 *

Chapter Thirteen

hanley launched into his opening lines. Ease and charm dripped from each word in a predictable rhythm. Not that anyone else noticed. To Fillion, the words were alive. A terrifying animal that seduced the senses while injecting its venom.

Seconds ticked away—the tempo torture, its persistent march baneful—as he stood before the public gallows. The gathering of thousands nodded with awe-infused sincerity whenever Hanley suspended a word or thought in their minds for a beat. Two beats. Twittered chuckles erupted at the appropriate humored pauses. Fillion's rising panic transformed each laugh into mocking jeers. He was a joke. The punch line.

Spine straight, he sat with hands clasped in his lap, as PR had drilled into him. His princely bearing did little to ease his jitters or embed confidence. Willow's shallow, quick breaths increased his own. She was freaking out, a raging storm contained by brittle self-control. So was he. There were no reassurances.

"… My son has always been my weakness."

Hanley smiled at Fillion.

"Since he was a small boy, I knew he would become a great man. A powerful man. One who surpassed even my deeds. A man other men would want to be. I suppose all fathers feel this way about their sons. And like other fathers, my pride knows no bounds. From infancy, I have dedicated my life to him, pouring all that I am, all that I have into my son, my heir …"

Fillion studied a misshaped nail hammered flush into the stage floor. Still serving its original purpose, but only after being beaten into submission after resistance. His hands twitched to cover his ears and scream. *The first phase is charm*, he chanted in his mind on repeat. Nothing was real. Every word was twisted and false.

"… Most are content to live their lives and pretend away their troubles. They fabricate a gray that doesn't exist on the black-and-white chess board of life. You either live or die, one serving the other in a looping cycle."

Everyone is a pawn on a chess board, awaiting your move, Son of Eden.

Fillion winced. Was Hanley suggesting that Fillion determined who lived and died?

"People want to forget that they are players in the game of life with actions that impact others. Impact the greater game. They possess *real* power to make a change, to make a difference. Instead, they choose the illusionary, gray path of apathy. The rules once guiding a passion-driven life, once filling them with fervor, slip through their fingers like dust, as does their world and their place in it …"

Willow's breaths grew more rapid. She gripped her fingers until the tips purpled. God, he had never hated himself so completely as he did right this very moment. Did she see her dad die every time Hanley spoke fake words of exaltation? Her dad reduced to dirt beneath everyone's feet so Fillion's life could rise up as the one worthy of worship? He couldn't bring himself to look at her. Terrified he might see his defeated reflection in her eyes. He'd do *anything* for her. But, in the end, it still wouldn't be enough. Nothing would ever reverse the crimes his family had committed against hers.

He blinked hard, tight, attempting to gather his bleeding thoughts. Turning back toward the crowd, he bit down on the inside of his cheek until a metallic taste coated his mouth. The hands folded in his lap were shaking.

"… What is worth fighting for? What burns inside of you? What are you willing to sacrifice to defend reality? Knowing the answers to these questions is what sets world-changers apart from the others." The kiln firing Hanley's insatiable greed burned red-hot as he declared, "Fillion Malcolm Nichols *is* a world-changer."

The audience cheered with approval.

"He is not afraid to fight, even at the cost of his freedom."

The words were like a heavy punch to the gut, sharp and painful. Did Hanley set him up with the undercover cop to validate this future moment? Intentionally provoke him at the lab until he snapped and pushed back, so his actions went on public record? Allow him to sit in juvenile detention in order defend claims that he'd be willing to give up freedoms as a soldier of truth? Every master storyteller knows to show and not tell. With little explanation, the world knew Hanley's words were true. For years, they had watched his son fall, only to rise and fight again.

"… He's not afraid to blend in with the everyday man and rally behind him. To get his hands dirty and work alongside the downtrodden …"

From the front row, Mack's eyes shifted from Hanley to Fillion and anger darkened his friend's features.

"… Not afraid to burn with passion for his convictions. Burn for New

Eden Township." Hanley deliberately paused again. "How many of you have seen my son's tattoo? The one on his right arm?"

Murmurs rippled through the gathering.

"Yes. It's the symbol for New Eden Enterprises, and it's on fire."

Willow stiffened.

Hanley slammed a fist into the podium, his usual calm, unwavering voice rising with excitement. Willow jumped with a sharp gasp.

"On fire for the future! On fire for the past! On fire for change! And on fire for New Eden Township! His Legacy!"

A swelling roar of support thundered through the crowd. Akiko grabbed Lynden's arm, her dark eyes shuttering with orgasmic delight as she fed off his popularity. His sister shrugged her off with a piercing glare and moved more toward their mom.

"My son is a world-changer, a king among men."

Hanley bowed to him and Fillion felt the bile rise. The crowd whispered with the reverence Hanley's move was meant to inspire. When Hanley straightened, he stared down at the podium, overcome. Fillion went numb. Each second was torture. Just as the tension became unbearably awkward, Hanley lifted his head and locked eyes with his audience and quietly continued.

"Please welcome General Stephen Claussen, owner of Stellar Dock Corp., and previous director of Mars Operations for the National Aeronautics and Space Administration following the first Journey to Mars mission." Hanley turned and clapped his welcome along with the sobered gathering.

Air rushed back into Fillion's lungs with the close of Hanley's speech. Dubious still, he trained his eyes on the Stellar Dock Corp.'s owner as he approached the podium. A man of extensive military background, an astronaut on the first Mars mission twenty years ago, Claussen proved an imposing figure with wide shoulders, a firm jaw, crew-cut silvered hair, and his dark blue uniform pressed tight against him.

Fillion stood, as instructed by PR, smiling meaningless acknowledgments to the other NASA officials seated behind him. Willow rose by his side, taking his lead. God, he hated these media games. Pretend everything was perfect. Smile for the crowd. Love every minute of being in the spotlight. Whore away the little self-respect and dignity left. He wanted to gouge his eyes out!

Movement snapped Fillion out of his rant. Brows deeply creased, Claussen tried to navigate the podium's mechanics. Each swipe was precise, every move sharp. A soldier even when loading a speech. Fillion quirked his eyebrow, watching the older man fight the war on communications technology. This was going to be a long night. The crackling rumble of low conversation moved in waves punctuated by a drunkard's laugh.

Annoyed but remaining the very image of aloof politeness, Fillion shifted on his feet and shot a discreet plea to his publicist, Kerry. She understood the message and, having assistants busy with other tasks, rushed onto the stage, mumbling loud enough for people to hear about slight technical difficulties. Her red-painted fingernails flew through the air and loaded the man's speech direct from his Cranium. Finally. Her cherry-red lips broke into a celebratory grin as she quickly shuffled out of the public's view and back to the stage's shadows.

"Please, sit," the general said, not even looking Fillion's way.

Dismissed? Asshole. Fillion bit back a snarky reply.

Nah. Low enough so only the general and Hanley could hear, he said, "I was wondering if I needed your permission to sit at my own ceremony. Now I know. Thanks." He sat. The man stared at him, long and calculating. Fillion was intimidated. It worked. Still, he graciously added, "Whenever you're ready." Yeah, if Fillion had to endure another marketing pitch about his greatness, he might system crash.

The general moved his inspection to the gathering, silently waiting for people to pick up on his cue. They did. The audience became deathly still. Where Hanley excited the masses, Claussen chilled them in place. The polite smile did little to soften the hard lines of the man's face. His eyes, however, held a lively glimmer of emotion. Was it excitement? Anxiety? Confidence? Whatever. It made no difference. Hanley had forged a partnership with this man and others within NASA way before Fillion had come of trust majority.

"Thank you," the general began, ready to launch into the speech wavering above the podium. "Today records a moment in history humankind will remember for generations to come. Human ingenuity and determination has unlocked the secrets to interplanetary travel and, now . . . viable long-term homesteading."

Fillion gripped the arm of his chair.

"Since before the first Apollo missions," Claussen continued, "the United States government had envisioned a future of exploration and space commerce. Those very visions, sacrifices, triumphs, and failures led to unimaginable feats. But let's back up even more and appreciate an even wider perspective first." The man brushed another serious gaze over the gathering. "Only one hundred and seventy-nine years have passed since the invention of the electric light bulb. Eighty-two years after this simple but revolutionary piece of every-day technology, a human orbited Earth for the first time. Eight years later, a man walked on the surface of the Moon. It would be sixty years before another man walked upon a non-Terran or non-lunar surface, placing the first human footprint onto the Red Planet. I should say woman, actually." The crowd laughed as Claussen turned with a grin toward a woman in a navy blue NASA uniform, her dark hair, streaked with purples, pulled tight in a ponytail. "And here we are today, in the post-industrial era. Not only can humankind boast a population that comprises android members, but also the sheer victory of scientifically colonizing Luna and Mars."

The crowd's building roar of pride battered against Fillion's waning sanity.

"Today, NASA forges an unforgettable partnership with New Eden Biospherics & Research as its government-sponsored socio-psychological experiment marches toward project shutdown. But it's not the end. No, this new era has only just begun. Human experimentation has *never* produced a generation quite like the Second Generation of New Eden Township."

The general scrutinized Willow like he was ready to make a purchase. She lifted her chin and angled her head in defiance. The general flicked a satisfied look Hanley's way. The black clouds gathering inside of her visibly thundered in response. Eyes blazing, lips flushed with anger, cheeks pinked with humiliation, and chest rising and falling in a furious rhythm, everything about her radiated temerity in the face of fear and indignity.

This very look had always weakened Fillion into a solid mass of dumbstruck stupidity. She was beautifully terrifying, and he felt himself slipping off the edge of reason. Sliding toward emotions that would destroy him. Destroy everything. Destroy her. Instead of fighting the attraction, he let the world pale as his entire being begged to be swept up and carried off in her nebula of rage. To become wholly consumed by her strength and courage.

He locked eyes with her. An electrifying rush of power surged through his body, emboldening, awakening, blazing. This was his life. His reality. Nobody owned him or dictated his future. The jester poked at him through his pocket. The hell with Fate. With genetics.

"Fierce and ancient," Claussen murmured. Fillion pulled his focus away from Willow's intensity to the general's as the man spoke again. "A future Martian Queen, perhaps. The traits necessary for a hostile planet. Scientists live in HABs and only for short durations, psychologically unable to cope with the extreme environment and isolation. But her. . . Stand up."

Willow didn't even hesitate. She rose from her chair and threw back her shoulders, spine straight, hands clenching folds of her skirt, her eyes target-locked onto the general's.

A smile twitched the corners of Claussen's mouth. "A perfect specimen, am I right?" The gathering clapped and cheered. Tears glistened Willow's eyes, but she remained still. "She has been conditioned to endure these hardships and bends the known limits of the human psyche," he continued. "Her DNA is not imprinted with Earth like ours. Rather, it clings to a Martian world she has never truly known yet has always lived."

The glimmer returned to his eyes as he made a show of inspecting Willow. Again. As if she were up for auction. Spoke of her like she wasn't before him ready to unleash her tempestuous atmosphere, one capable of leveling this entire compound. Not seeing her as fully human, but as a product to advance humankind's superiority. As the key to the future, securing dominance by making the United States the first nation to colonize Mars, thus staking claim in a new capitalist frontier.

Hell no.

Blood rushed in Fillion's ears and he shot to his feet and snatched Willow's hand from the safety of her skirt. "The air out here is thinner than in New Eden. Let me help you sit. Take it slow." She blinked back the tears and eased into her seat, head downcast. "Better?"

"Yes, thank you."

He looked to Kerry. "A glass of wine for Ms. Watson. I'll take one, too." The publicist nodded and scurried off. He lowered into his seat, ready to destroy something. "Go on," he said to Claussen, not looking his way. "Sorry for the interruption," he added, to soften the moment.

He felt the general's eyes on him. One second. Two seconds. Then, the official scrolled to the next part of his speech and carried on. But Fillion stopped listening. The general's voice was even, measured, moving with very little fluctuation. Fillion thought of the way Claussen commanded technology and the patience in waiting for several thousand people to pick up on social cues.

Kerry glided back onto the stage and deposited a glass of wine first into Willow's hands and then into his. Fillion met her eyes and silently mouthed his thanks. She smiled and attempted to exit the stage as if invisible. He stared into his glass, making the dark liquid swirl. Taking a sip, he closed his eyes against the ache, forcing himself to pay attention to Claussen's monotone delivery.

"… Dr. Della Jayne Nichols, author and scientist behind the Theory of Reconstructing Universal Society and Trusteeship, has significantly advanced knowledge in transgenerational epigenetic inheritance unlike any other studies and experiments to date. Our fine nation, the world—no, two worlds—owes much to this remarkable woman."

Claussen gestured toward Fillion's mom, and Willow gasped. Like she was seeing her for the first time. Weird. Had she never met his mom in all her visits to New Eden? He didn't have to look at Willow to know what she was thinking. His mom was beautiful, unnaturally so. And, she looked young enough to pass as Fillion's slightly older sister thanks to biotech and gene therapy. Stylish black hair shone with faint violet hues in the spotlight, which his mom brushed from her shoulder as she displayed a stunning smile for the crowd. Her gray eyes, however, dimmed despite the attention she normally craved. The remorse was nice, but a little too late.

Like him, she was unable to escape the chains that shackled her to the pain of what their family had done. But unlike him, it was all her fault. She held the power necessary to end this nightmare and didn't.

Why in the hell didn't she run N.E.T.? Synapses were firing at rapid speed; so much so, he almost didn't hear Claussen say his name.

"Fillion Nichols, CEO and president of New Eden Biospherics & Research," the general said, angling toward him. Fillion drew in an angry breath as the imposing man continued speaking. "I watched as you used your World Tour as a platform to broadcast your impassioned convictions for reform and change, and all to aid your flailing generation. Listened as you discussed the future with governments, scientists, and civilians. You are a man of vision, a world-changer as your father declared. I am eager to stride into this new era of interplanetary homesteading with you. Perhaps, together, we can make a difference, to turn ideas into realities. On behalf of NASA, the U.S. government, and science, congratulations on your newest appointment, and happy birthday."

"Thank you," Fillion somehow managed in reply.

The gathering cheered, some even whistled. He placed his glass of wine on the stage floor and marched over to the podium. He clasped Claussen's hand in a firm shake while smiling wide for the cameras. *Image. Perception.* The magician's trick. Lights flashed and blinded him. Murmurs mixed with applause.

Handshake complete, the general started to pull away. But Fillion wasn't done. This was his night. His future. Fillion gripped Claussen's hand tight and pierced him with a hard stare. The panicking voice of his publicist rang in his head with urgent instructions to sit down. This whole night was orchestrated. Fillion was supposed to sit and look pretty, not give speeches. The hell with that. He met the apoplectic stare of his publicist and winked. Then he launched his reply.

"A great man recently shared with me that hope is the very breath of life," Fillion began, and loud enough to be picked up on the microphone. He faced Claussen and raised an eyebrow. "Together, may we turn ideas into realities that matter in the end. The kind worthy of the hope men like us breathe into the masses of humanity who hang on our every word. They're desperate for a meaningful life. The difference we make should honor them." He let go of Claussen's hand and pointed to the cameras, then the nobility visiting from New Eden. "The people who *freely* enable our power so we might, in turn, better *their* future." He paused as a wicked smile slowly formed. Checkmate. "Do you agree?"

"I couldn't have said it better nor as eloquently," Claussen replied, far too quickly. A man of rules and order. Good. He'd break every single one just to watch him squirm and regain composure. "You are a true pioneer, Mr. Nichols."

"We'll see." Fillion narrowed his eyes and stepped aside.

Before Fillion could sit down, Hanley had joined him and Claussen, carrying a black leather portfolio. It was just a prop. Like everything. Copies of the signed legal docs were inside, the originals tucked away safe with each respective lawyer. The audience didn't know that, though. Fillion found Willow's eyes and subtly gestured with his head for her to come and join their group. She quietly settled beside him, ignoring both Hanley and Stephen, her head held high, jaw set, a wildfire in her gaze.

Pulling a pen from his pocket, Hanley first pretended to sign each page. When complete, he passed the pen to Fillion. His hand flourished over the first signature. He shuffled the page and mock-signed the one after. The next page, however, wasn't signed. His brows furrowed, and he lifted the paper off the podium an inch. Had they missed a document earlier? He tried to skim over the wording, but Hanley leaned his arm in the way, until the paper rested onto the podium again.

"Right here," Hanley said, pointing to the signature line.

Fillion's pen hovered over the line. His lawyer had been meticulous. No way would he miss a document.

"Fillion," Hanley said, chuckling. "Everyone is waiting."

Hand shaking, he slipped the document into the signed pile—unsigned—and moved to the last doc. A copied one. Refusing to look at Hanley. But he could tell that the man was pissed by the way he flashed a smile for the audience.

He put the pen in Willow's hand and leaned toward her ear, whispering, "Trace over Leaf's signature. Don't sign a blank line. No matter what anyone says." She nodded then proceeded to follow his directions to the last page.

The final document required Claussen's fake signature. Once that was garnered, the audience erupted into applause. Hanley extended a hand first to Fillion, then to their guests.

"Willow Oak Watson and General Stephen Claussen," Hanley said. Fillion pivoted on his heel to escort Willow back to her chair, but Hanley grabbed his arm. Dammit. "The birth of a new era." Hanley appeared reflective. "Hope that breathes life and empowers a future." His grip tightened until Fillion felt Hanley's nails digging in despite the layers of clothing.

Gamemaster didn't like his move? Tough shit.

Fillion casually shrugged away from Hanley's touch and fixed his rumpled sleeve. Fury demanded that he beat the triumphant smirk off of Hanley's face. Instead, Fillion straightened his suit jacket and lifted a fake smile to the crowd.

This week I had the pleasure of touring the medieval village historical sites, Wharram Percy, Little Oxendon, and Clipston. The homes were simple and their lives were labor-intensive. Brought back many memories as I touched cob walls and walked through old garden plots. I was not prepared for how much hard work went into surviving. New Eden Township taught me many things, not only about the interdependency necessary for sustainable living, but about how ignorant I was about my origins and my intrinsic value as a human being. We have this cultural stigma that delayed gratification will be too emotionally traumatic to bear. But I suggest the opposite. Perhaps instant gratification has traumatized our growth until we—the human race—have lost touch with our ability to survive, emotionally, physically, and mentally.

— Fillion Nichols, World Tour speech in London, December 16, 2057

Chapter Fourteen

Fillion attempted to appear bored, patient even, as he and the rest of the world waited for Hanley to continue. An earthquake was rumbling inside of him, though.

"Are you ready to hear more inspiring words from the newest owner?" Hanley asked the gathering and grinned with the answering cheers. "Well then, without further ado, I give you the man of the hour, my son, Fillion Nichols." Hanley slid out from behind the podium and walked back to his chair, leaving Fillion alone.

What the—?

The whites of Kerry's eyes rounded and then a flurry of activity erupted by the side of the stage. "Quick, load up the . . . the. . ." She snapped her fingers while thinking. "The state dinner speech from London. Enough time has passed." She looked at Fillion and spoke in their private channel. "Improvise. Switch up words and details as much as possible." He answered with a faint nod as he continued to placate the crowd.

"Welcome," Fillion began.

He skimmed over the loaded speech and held his breath. This felt fake. *He* felt fake. Rattled, he tapped the side of his thigh to a silent tune. Smile. Look pretty. Pretend to sign the already signed contract. *Not give a formal address.* Why wasn't that one document signed? What were the contractual contents? His lawyer was in the crowd; he'd meet with him at first opportunity.

Slowly exhaling, Fillion closed the speech screen hovering in front of him but kept his Cranium open. Kerry asked what he was doing, but he ignored her. He didn't know what he was doing. All he knew is that he had walked into a trap and he needed to claw his way back out. It probably didn't matter what he said. Frustrated, he opened his mouth and spoke the first thoughts that materialized.

"It's strange to receive honor and praise for a job I haven't spent one full day in yet." His voice held a slight tremble, but he soldiered on. "Tonight, we celebrate my birthright. A future determined for me. But isn't that how the future feels? So much in our lives is beyond our control. It's almost easy to forget how many things *we can* control." He peered at Willow. "We are given opportunities to spin the stories of our lives."

Willow attempted a weak smile of encouragement, but she was still somewhere between pissed off and freaking out.

Images of the spinning wheel he had built for her flashed in his mind's eye. He had felt so lame and corny. It was a stupid romantic gesture from a seventeen-year-old boy. Now, as a twenty-one-year-old man, the memory of each splinter, every aching muscle, the way his fingers shook as he gripped the knife and carved their initials into a newly crafted leg made from linden wood, empowered Fillion.

Love has little to do with romance and everything to do with honor.

Feeling more confident, he swept a gaze over the crowd and continued, his voice stronger.

"The Aether of New Eden Township, Leaf Watson, once asked me if I had ever grown clothes from seed." A few people chuckled at the archaic absurdity of Leaf's question. "Yet, that is how it truly begins. We are to spin the stories of our lives and weave them together until a reality solidifies, one that properly clothes our future and reflects the truest part of our self. This,"—he gestured to his clothing—"is an illusion. Our lives do not appear ready-made, already manufactured, reflecting our individual fashion taste and socio-economic preference. There is a process. A beginning. We must labor to reach an end result that matters."

Fillion paused and his publicist gave him a thumbs-up.

"For most of my life, that's how I viewed my future—ready-made, already manufactured. A product I inherited. Not a beginning to a process that would transform my life. Not *real* people. I resented my Legacy and fought my future." He looked at Hanley. "For years, I had waged the wrong war."

Their gazes sparked as steel clashed with steel. Hanley appeared in his element and Fillion's silent declaration almost faltered.

Right as Fillion was about to thrust and parry another round, an emergency notification paraded across the bottom of his screen. A small smile curved Hanley's mouth and goosebumps chilled Fillion's skin. But he forced his expression to remain steady. He tapped the notification, then tucked a strand of hair behind his ear to make the movement appear natural. As the message loaded, he refocused on the audience and continued. "The people of New Eden Township—"

The words incinerated to ash on his tongue.

Mr. Fillion Nichols,

We regret to inform you that Timothy Kane was found dead in his room this morning. The first response team and postmortem biometric readout confirmed cardiac arrest. At your earliest convenience, please collect his ashes for New Eden Township, per his prearranged funeral instructions.

With Our Sympathy,
Dr. Dana Nelson

Fillion's heart pounded to life in his ears right before plummeting to his gut. People shifted on their feet and whispered to one another as they waited for him to continue. Fillion registered this somehow. But he didn't see the crowd anymore. The world was quickly fading to black. He fought to remain present. He needed an anchor. Gradually, as if he moved through mud, he peered over his shoulder and met Skylar's eyes. A crease appeared between his cousin's eyebrows in response.

Fear shivered through Fillion and he faced the crowd once more, determined to continue on. The alternative wasn't an option. Not in front of the world. Not this night. A sickening pain wended its way up from his gut and tightened his chest.

The walls are listening. They have ears. Don't trust him.

Fillion gripped the podium, his feet positioned shoulder length apart, a slight bend to his knees. The world was still dimming. Talk. He needed to keep talking.

"The people of New Eden Township are my future," he began again. Fear shifted to fury and quickly blazed into a raging fire inside his veins. "My birthright isn't property. It's a responsibility to generations of people who have given years of their life to New Eden Biospherics & Research. In return, my company will honor their sacrifices by *fighting* for the very best future possible for each individual post-project shutdown." He paused while people murmured reactions. After a few seconds, he bowed his head. "Thank you."

Hanley clapped for Fillion and moved his direction, the anger and disapproval evident with each step despite his smiles for the crowd. Fillion refused to let the Gamemaster win. Period.

To emphasize this point, Fillion added, "This concludes our opening events. Please enjoy the food and drinks, and stay as long as you like. Thank you for generously supporting the future of New Eden Biospherics & Research." Applause thundered around the stage and Fillion marched over to where Willow sat, pushing past Hanley, and offered his hand. "Your Highness?"

"The media is allotted time for questions," Hanley hissed from behind.

Fillion twisted and snapped over his shoulder, "Plot twist. Deal with it." He took Willow's hand and led her off the stage to Coal. "Take her back to New Eden. All of them."

Kerry raced over, a panicked look in her eyes. "What are you doing, Mr. Nichols?"

"Her brother needs her this evening," Fillion answered coolly. "Her sister-in-law is in labor."

"And...?"

"And what?" He blinked back the anger.

"What about the press?"

"Do you really need me to reply to that question?"

His publicist lowered her eyes. "No, Mr. Nichols."

"Good. I'll think of something." Fillion shot his gaze over Kerry's shoulder to Hanley, who left the NASA team and now strode across the stage to where Fillion, the Nobles, and his publicist huddled in the shadows behind a large speaker. "First," he said to Coal, "get Willow back inside New Eden. Stat."

"You allowed her to be publicly shamed," Coal seethed. "Now you ask her to endure further humiliation by being dismissed? Have you no conscience?" He lowered his voice to a near whisper. "You never deserved her."

Fillion swallowed back the nausea. He didn't have time to fight with Coal's hero complex or explain his actions. Instead, he grabbed Coal's arm. "Stay with your sister, if you want. When you return, don't eat or drink anything here tonight. If you need something, let me, Lyn, or Mack know, and *only* one of us."

Questions burned in Coal's gaze, as well as a multitude of promises; but he spun toward Willow and offered his arm.

"I am scandalized," Willow choked out.

Hanley began walking down the stairs.

She took a step closer to Fillion and he bit the inside of his cheek. Images flashed in his mind of ratty hair and torn clothing, of Willow pleading for the scientists to have mercy. Then a scream, raw and tortured, pierced his thoughts. Not now. His mind couldn't slip away right now. But he could feel his emotional finger trembling violently on his mind's trigger.

"Listen well, Fillion Nichols," she whispered for his ears alone, "I shall never become a *specimen* for their pleasure—"

"Willow," Fillion rushed out, "you need to leave. *Now.*"

Coal didn't hesitate another nanosecond, pulling her away before Fillion finished delivering his last word. She yanked her arm away but complied. The Nobles circled around Willow and then folded into the milling clusters of attendees congregating near the stage.

Hanley followed his gaze. "Your promise to 'the people of New Eden Township' is pointless."

"Damn. That's cliché, even for you." Fillion cocked his eyebrow with manufactured arrogance to counterbalance the queasy motions in his gut. "Come on, you can do way better. Try harder. Impress me for once."

"There you are!" Akiko half-wailed as she angled through the crowd. Her fingers angrily tapped the exposed skin of her crossed arms.

Hanley lifted a satisfied smile and moved back a few steps to give the illusion of privacy. The music was deafening, but Fillion swore he heard Hanley whistle a happy tune of triumph. A sound that reminded him of another and a fresh surge of fear hit him.

Timothy was dead.

He couldn't breathe.

How in the hell would he tell Skylar?

Don't trust him.

Akiko rose on tip-toes and kissed Fillion on the lips just as a demon horde of journalists rounded the corner. He jerked away and wiped his mouth.

"Don't."

"Of course you need water," she purred through smiles for the cameras. Turning eyes onto Kerry, she snapped her fingers and commanded, "Get him water! He just delivered a speech. How is it you were hired to do this job? Where is your team?" She shook her head and fussed with Fillion's suit jacket. "I will find you a new publicist who will remember that you are a king among men."

"Kerry," Fillion said, turning toward her, "I'm fine. Thank you for your and your team's excellent care and sharp attention to details this evening. It's a success so far."

Akiko stiffened. "You—"

"You are not in charge of my staff and will treat my employees with respect."

The journalists silenced. Several heads peeked out from behind their equipment for the measure of a single heartbeat. Then a gunfire of rapid clicks and hushed orders to keep filming dispelled the shock.

Cornered, Akiko narrowed her eyes to slits right before demurring into a submissive posture, hands clasped in her lap, eyes lowered, her back straight as she bent in *saikeirei* to express her public remorse and esteem. When she rose, Fillion pressed his arms to his side and bowed only his head in acceptance. Relief softened her smile, which she ensured every camera captured, even though his bow confirmed that she was his inferior.

He needed to keep talking. To keep moving.

Fillion forced himself to address Hanley to sustain normalcy, attempting to sound as polished as possible for the eavesdroppers. "An emergency called Ms. Watson and her entourage back to New Eden. My apologies for the disruption. Give me ten minutes and we'll gather the NASA officials for Q-and-A."

"On stage?" Hanley asked, clearly mocking him, a glass of wine now in his hand.

"Do you have a better idea?"

"Whatever you decide." Hanley lifted his glass of wine in salute. "You're calling the shots tonight."

"Nice." Rolling his eyes, Fillion turned to Kerry and lowered his voice. "Ten minutes. On the stage, with or without an audience. Q-and-A only. Broadcast our apologies about Ms. Watson's departure."

"Yes, Mr. Nichols. Anything else?"

He took in a deep breath and slid a quick glance to Akiko. "Yeah, actually. Before Q-and-A, release a counter statement to the questionable image of me on the Net. Confirm that the girl who danced with me last night was Ms. Hirabayashi. The girl looks similar enough for the statement to be believable."

Akiko pressed her lips together. "I would never—"

"Birthday surprise. Fun times." Fillion winked. "Or do you want to be publicly shamed when the media asks me questions about last night?"

His fiancée didn't reply for once, but her answer was written all over her face.

"Kerry, you know what to do."

A slow smile teased Kerry's cherry-red lips. "You have ten minutes, Mr. Nichols." She breezed by Fillion and marched into the parasites, redirecting their attention onto her.

"Well done," Hanley murmured. He sipped his wine and meandered the opposite direction.

Was that actual praise? Fillion paused with confusion. And, if he were honest, a touch of pride. Hanley approved of *him*? Publicly? In front of Akiko? The world stopped spinning for a few sands of time until reality came crashing back. No. This was the necessary future Hanley had prepared him for. He was praising himself.

Bastard.

Then another thought hit him. Was everything set up as a test? To see how the new Gamemaster would react under pressure? Was Timothy Kane dead or alive? Paranoia flared to life and Fillion swore under his breath. He hated this. Fillion faced the biodomes, digging his nails into his palm as his fist clenched tighter.

Akiko cozied up against him, pressing her body into his. "You are still thinking of that rodent." Her cultured tones morphed into shrill screeches in his head. "I see the longing in your eyes."

"Don't speak of—"

"You are *mine*."

The declaration ricocheted through his emptiness.

Aware of every camera, of every pair of eyes owning every second of his existence, he cupped Akiko's face and lowered close to her lips. Satisfaction and excitement warmed her gaze and she lifted her face to him. Only then did he whisper, "You're the rat."

Fillion untangled himself and strode toward the bar. Disgust coated his body where she had touched him. God, he needed another glass of wine. No, the whole bottle. People parted for him. Whispered in ears as he passed. Flashed secretive smiles and invitations his way.

He ignored it all and imagined himself standing before Willow and her hurricane-force winds that gusted at the injustice. The fury whipping around him until nothing remained.

He needed her. Needed her courage and strength.

It shamed him. Regardless of how he treated her, she always pushed him to be a greater version of himself. Not for her sake, but for *his*. Even tonight. Even when he was a complete asshole out of fear of what Hanley might do.

Once again, it was like she could see through all the games to the real him. It bent his mind.

Was he a man of commendable strength? A man worthy of honor?

Fillion looked up at the moon, waxing crescent. Aldebaran, the brightest star in the constellation of Taurus, appeared in the darkening night. The world moved around him in dizzying speeds, smudges of color in a drab landscape. A blur of sounds. His mind, however, slowed with wonder as he considered his actions at the event, flitting thoughts dawning into deeper understanding.

He had spun the tales. Wove the stories together. Publicly created and declared a reality all his own.

The independence would cost him.

Hanley wouldn't let Fillion's demonstration go without punishment. And, just like that, the moment of wonder gave way to a shudder as fear caressed his spine.

Timothy was dead.

Dead.

Son of killer.

His chest tightened. Every breath burned. His mind began slipping away. No. Not tonight. Not right now. He pushed against the panic attack. The media awaited his return. Willow was now safe within New Eden. Coal accompanied her home.

Though his hand trembled, he reached out for a much-needed glass of wine and knocked it over. The glass shattered on the ground. Nearby conversations stopped. People stared. The bartender smiled and told Fillion not to worry about it. Faces spiraled in and out of focus.

But all Fillion could see was dark red liquid, oozing over the parched soil and splattering the bar's front panel. Swearing under his breath, he spun on his heel and shoved his way through the crowd, back toward the stage.

For the first time since child labor laws were enacted in the early twentieth century, school attendance has dropped. The rising rate of childhood illiteracy is a digrace. Children can't attend Cyberschools when they can't afford the technology and Internet connections necessary to do so. The most highly educated generation who has ever walked the planet is now raising the most uneducated generation since the Industrial Revolution. That irony is on you, the people who can change this future and create a new reality for millions of people across the globe.

— Fillion Nichols, World Tour speech in Washington D.C., January 8, 2058

Chapter Fifteen

Thursday, March 28, 2058

Leaf awoke with his body bent in an uncomfortable sitting position, a small head nuzzled into his ribcage, and his hand intertwined with Ember's. Alder had climbed into his and Ember's bed in the night and now lay pressed into Leaf's side, sweaty and rosy-cheeked. Soft, golden curls fell over his forehead in angelic form, his lips pink and flushed from sleep.

On Alder's other side lay Ember. She remained asleep, despite their son's foot which bumped into her exposed leg as his heel wiggled back and forth. Alder had kicked off the covers in his restlessness. Even in sleep their son was a perpetual motion machine.

Dressed in a thin shift, unlaced in the front, Ember held their youngest daughter to her breast. Golden-red curls fell over her pillow and spilled across her bare shoulder, her long eyelashes framing her upper cheek. His wife's skin held a waxen pallor despite the shared warmth of their bed. Her breath came in deep and slow, their daughter's head rising and falling with the motions. Perhaps she had lost too much blood. He would consult Lady Brianna shortly and ask for Cook to prepare a meal rich in iron.

His oldest daughter—curled upon his chest—released a soft grunt and moved her arm until her fingers gripped the neckline of his tunic. Leaf smiled and kissed her head, before securing his arms around her tiny body and easing to the edge of the bed, slowly releasing Ember's fingers from his own.

Alder wasted no time in his absence and scooted up to Leaf's pillow to fold into the warmth he had left behind. His son's eyelids fluttered closed as his forefinger and thumb caressed the pillowcase's soft linen in self-soothing motions. Leaf pulled the blankets up to properly cover his wife and daughter and up to Alder's bare shoulders. Where were his nightclothes? His son had a penchant for shedding them soon after they were placed on him. Amused, Leaf rubbed his small back in slow circles until Alder's breathing grew steady and rhythmic.

Leaf stretched his neck and shoulders before stepping out into the hallway toward the living room. Though he wished to remain in bed, his mind dashed about with worries and his body ached. He was also hungry. Before retiring to Laurel's room, Lady Brianna had left bread, jam, and cider out for an easy morning meal.

He made every effort to remain quiet as he trundled through his home, but he practically stumbled into the living room, exhaustion like anchors on his feet. His daughter released another soft grunt with his movements. Vocal, even in her sleep. He nearly chuckled in the silence but halted his steps instead.

By the latticed window, unaware of his entrance, stood Willow. Her long woolen nightgown brushed across the wooden floor and her hair, left unbound, tumbled to her waist in soft waves, recently brushed. She peered out into the dawning forest while spinning a strand of gold upon a finger. Gray light filtered through the window and stretched across the walls as the sun rose, still well below the dome's horizon line.

Why was she not at the Hansen residence?

After their early return from the Ceremony, Coal had visited for a spell to check on his sister and new nieces, and with news of how he had left Willow in the care of his father. The Son of Fire had departed before Leaf could speak with him privately about the Ceremony. The lack of any notable details bothered Leaf late into the night, for he knew Coal intentionally avoided the subject. The curving slump of Willow's shoulders as well as her unexpected presence only confirmed his trepidations.

The floorboards creaked when he took another step and Willow peered over her shoulder. Guilt tightened the muscles in Leaf's chest. What had she endured at the Ceremony? With trembling fingers, she quickly brushed at the silent tears coursing down her cheeks and lifted a weary smile.

"Good morning—" Willow inhaled a sharp breath when noting the small head peeking out from his tunic. A genuine grin brightened her features and she rushed over on tip-toes. "Oh, she is lovely!"

"The eldest and stronger of the sisters."

"Hello, darling. I am ever so pleased to meet you." Willow traced his daughter's cheek with a single finger, then lifted tear-stained eyes to his. "Are the sisters identical?"

"We are not yet certain."

Willow nibbled on her bottom lip, though she smiled. A tear gathered on her eyelash before falling. "I am so very happy for you, Leaf. Mother and Father would have delighted in your beautiful children."

"Indeed," Leaf whispered. "I believe they do."

Another tear ran down her cheek with his proclamation.

Straightening her shoulders, Willow tucked strands of hair behind her ear. "Did Coal pass through last night?"

"Yes, he visited with Ember and met our wee lasses."

"I am glad. He was rather agitated. I believe he sensed Ember's anguish and feared her loss without a proper goodbye or last words."

Leaf nodded his head while stifling a yawn. He did not have the stamina to share how Ember had passed a large number of heavy blood clots since delivery. Lady Brianna and Timna assisted Ember several times during the night when she awoke to find a decent pool of blood upon the soft leather absorption mat, soaking though the stuffed hay, moss, and various medicinal herbs. His wife grew weaker and weaker still. His mother-in-law insisted that Ember would fare well, but Leaf was not yet convinced. Helplessness continued to plague his every breath.

"Did you not stay with the Hansens?" he asked. "Coal shared that he had left you in his father's care."

"I could not sleep and decided upon my own bed early this morn." She spoke these words while caressing his daughter's cheek once more. "I informed Laurel before departing, never you worry."

"The hour is young yet. Have you slept at all?"

A small crease appeared between her brows. The skin around her eyes swelled red and her lips had chapped with evidence of her grief. By the window lay Willow's hair brush and several handkerchiefs.

"Do not look at me so," she whispered, finally meeting his eyes. "I am no more made of glass than you."

"Willow—"

"Please, Leaf. Last night exists no longer. I have watched the moon set and the sun rise with a new day."

His pulse thrummed audibly in his ears.

"'You are a mighty oak, strong and resourceful,'" Willow continued in a distant voice, echoing Father's words of encouragement to her. Words Leaf had spoken to his youngest. "Until this morn," she said, "I had not realized the depth of my strength."

Her words twisted around him like the hair upon her finger. Grieved, he held his daughter closer and rested his cheek upon her head. A gentleman would never ask a lady to divulge her sorrows. But anger flared as he looked on, helplessly, as her heart ached. He was weary of feeling helpless.

There were several cruel ways to break a man. Hanley was not beyond harming Willow to torment Fillion and weaken Leaf's grip on power within New Eden. Though he gathered that her anguish lay solely with Fillion and not his father. A small comfort, but one he clung to as he struggled with how to reply.

Finally, he found his voice. "*Ma chère*, Coal assured me that you fared well."

"For I do. Worry not, dear brother," she whispered back, throwing him a warm smile. "May I hold her?"

He nodded and she strode across the living room to fetch her shawl, granting him modesty as he lifted his tunic. His daughter released a quavering cry in the morning chill and Willow, with back turned, giggled at the robust sound. "She is ready," he said with a lopsided grin. His daughter's arms and legs flailed in the open air, her face reddened by her mighty opinions.

Willow scooped his daughter into her arms and wrapped her in the finely knitted cashmere shawl. "*Mon coeur*," she whispered followed by a gentle shush. "Your father needs to rest his arms, little love." His sister danced light steps to the window, where she rocked his babe in her arms to a French lullaby. She placed her forefinger into his daughter's mouth who latched on, suckling with eagerness. The loud protest quieted to tremulous mewls until sleep claimed his wee one once more.

Leaf opened the jam crock on the cupboard and slathered the raspberry preserves onto a crust of bread. Every movement felt slow and forced and awkward. The knife even slipped from his grip while spreading the jam and clattered upon the floor. Willow halted her lullaby for half a heartbeat, adding a bounce to her sway when singing once more. He snatched a cleaning rag from the shelf below and wiped the utensil, then placed the knife back upon the trencher full of day-old bread. He blinked back the sleep and removed the waxed linen from the pitcher and poured a tumbler of cider. His hand shook, his muscles achy and stiff. And all this from simply supporting his wife as she delivered not one but two precious lives into their family. How Ember could sleep through the enormity of pain her body still suffered, he knew not.

A sigh, long and slow, left his tightened chest.

He did not have the fortitude for tonight's Celebration. He could barely manage the simple procedure of breaking his fast, let alone hosting a grand feast. Nor could he endure the tedious hours of waiting to see how Willow fared, once again, in his absence.

The bread and jam turned to sawdust on his tongue. He swallowed anyway. The cider washed away the remaining crumbs but, still, the foul taste remained. Something was not quite right. He watched his sister care for his daughter, a smile warming her face though her eyes glittered with a strange mixture of fury and grief.

Leaf sipped his cider, then approached the window. "You returned early from the Ceremony, I understand."

"She resembles you, Leaf. Do you see her mouth? Like yours and Father's. Laurel's, too."

His shoulders fell. "I would think the Outside world would have enchanted you."

"I saw the most beautiful creature." Willow lifted her eyes. "I do believe it was a moth, for it appeared at sunset." Her eyes widened. "Oh, the sunset! The sky wove together a tapestry of burnished golds and pinks and orange. I was positively breathless with wonder."

"Were many people present?"

"Thousands. I grew dizzy with the swelling numbers."

"The guests were kind to you, I hope?"

She smiled softly at his daughter. "Does her sister share similar features?"

His jaw tightened. "Willow Oak Watson—"

"The moon has set and the sun is rising." Angry tears pooled in her bloodshot eyes. "Let us speak of pleasant things."

"Tonight is the Celebration. Am I to remain ignorant of offenses committed against you?"

"Fillion Nichols is a conceited, vulgar knave. Are you now pleased?" A tear slid off her cheek and onto the shawl as her body trembled, every muscle clenched. "Do not look at me so, Leaf Watson. I am a woman grown and allowed to grieve without confession!"

"Do you still love him?" The words were out before he could stop his question.

Her head whipped toward his, the storm that wailed inside of her gathering strength. "Are you mad? Why should I love a man who tramples upon my heart without remorse or apology?"

The truth, however, shone bright in her eyes despite her vehement words. And this, Leaf ventured, was the true source of her fury. His sister's eyes could never lie. Soulful, very much like Mother's, brimming with the same feral spirit and well of convictions. He could still remember Mother's voice, earthy and whimsical, calling Willow her faerie child and Leaf her little man.

A wobbly, faint cry emerged down the hallway, pulling him from his memories. He had left his chamber door open should Ember or Alder have need of him. His eldest lass released a cry of her own, as if in reply to her little sister. Both he and Willow smiled with the same realization.

"They shall conspire against me one day," Leaf said with a chuckle. "Able to communicate through a bond I shall never understand."

"Indeed." Willow rubbed her nose with his daughter's, grinning. "Invisible threads, knitting one heart to the other." The smile slipped from her face and she drew in a shaky breath, before whispering, "A beautiful, unshakable bond."

Gently, he placed his fingers on Willow's forearm and she frowned. Holding back another sigh, he disguised his attempts at comfort by asking, "Can we trust him?" Willow rested her temple upon the window sill and watched the newly budding trees move in a gentle bio-breeze. "Please, *ma chère*. I need your wisdom and insight."

"Though I find fault with Fillion's untoward behavior last eve, dishonesty is not among my grievances. He is a man of honor where *you* are concerned." The crease appeared between her brows once more. "He declared before all that he shall fight for the residents of New Eden Township."

A faint cry quivered in the air once again and Leaf angled toward the hallway. "I should attend Ember." He reached for his oldest daughter when she bellowed in reply. "Perhaps they miss each other's company. Until last night, they have not known separation."

"Beautiful," his sister whispered. A tear rolled down her cheek and she blotted it away with the back of her hand. "Do you need assistance?"

"Lady Brianna shall assist me."

"If you need—"

"It would give me tremendous comfort if you found sleep, even if for but a small measure of time. This night shall be taxing for us both."

She lowered her head and clasped her hands at her waist. "Yes, of course." Willow issued a shallow curtsy, gathered her belongings, and disappeared down the hallway toward her bedchamber, refusing to meet his eyes.

Leaf entered his own bedchamber with Lady Brianna close behind. Alder still lay curled upon his pillow, sleeping through the newborn cries. Lucky lad, Leaf thought to himself with a small smile. His daughters quieted when sensing each other's presence and tiny bumps appeared on Leaf's arms. Invisible threads, indeed.

"My Lord," Ember greeted in a weak voice. "I am not well."

Leaf leaned down and kissed his wife's forehead. Her skin was cold and clammy, her lips pale. He exchanged a concerned look with his mother-in-law, then said to his wife, "I am here, my love. How shall I care for you?"

"I need Mother…"

Lady Brianna stepped forward and took her step-daughter's hand, before lifting the blankets to find another large pool of blood.

There is so much beauty in letting go of pain, watching scars turn into butterflies before they fly away.

— Christy Ann Martine, Poet, "Metamorphosis," 21st century *

A pocket of loneliness transformed into a rainbow of butterflies and fluttered away despite their punctured wings. A layer of oppression melted off of her with their escape and a tiny spark of hope flickered in her darkness.

— Lynden Nichols

Chapter Sixteen

Lynden sat on the edge of the bed and slipped her feet to the floor. The chill air caressed her bare skin and she shivered. Her husband continued to sleep, though it was mid-morning. Maybe she could sneak away and enjoy a long, hot shower—alone. Coal liked to hog all the hot water.

She rolled her shoulders and stretched her back. Her muscles were fatigued from stress and anxiety. The past few days had been so intense. Tonight, feasting in New Eden, would be no different. Actually, she knew it would be worse. The residents were celebrating her brother's Ascension. Her entire family would be on display. It was bad enough that she was seen as Coal's unwed lover, a woman of ill repute for their community. Shame burned her face, and she flicked her bottom lip ring in and out of her mouth. What would happen if they ever learned the truth?

Bury the emotions.

They were not allowed to hurt her and know it.

She was tougher than shit.

Lynden pushed off the bed just as Coal snaked an arm around her waist and pulled her back. "A few more minutes," he murmured into the pillow.

"Go ahead." Lynden peered over her shoulder. Coal smiled, though his eyes remained closed, his face partially pressed into a pillow. His light blond hair spilled around his face in a mess. God, he was so sexy. Heat curled upward from her core in a delicious rush. She should wrap the sheets around them. Tease and seduce him with playful promises. Kiss him until he moaned her name in surrender. Instead, she blurted, "Really? Holding me hostage?"

"Come back to bed, my love."

He tugged her toward him and she caved, but not without an irritated sigh. The warmth of his body was divine and she sank into his embrace. He secured her against his body, his arm and leg draped over her own, his face buried into her neck as his fingers began playing with her hair. It was like she was his teddy bear, and she bit back a forming smile.

"What do you find so amusing?" His hot breath tickled her neck. He repositioned himself even closer to her.

"Nothing," she whispered, but he was already asleep. Figured. She didn't know anyone who fell asleep as fast as Coal. Sometimes she swore he was out before his head even hit the pillow. Wide-awake and now trapped, Lynden had no choice but to let her thoughts wander.

After the Ascension Ceremony's opening events ended, Coal had disappeared for a couple hours. His twin sister had delivered healthy twin girls and the biodome community celebrated their births late into the night. All the while, a crowd numbering over three thousand celebrated her brother's birthday until the early morning hours.

When Coal had returned, she learned that the people of New Eden didn't name their children for seven days. The mother and infant mortality rates were too high during the first week after birth, he explained. Lynden didn't know how to feel about that. No resident was denied medical services or obstetric care. But they clung to ideologies that worshiped the cycle of life and death. Even at the cost of women and children. The women of New Eden were often shamed into marriage to pop out babies so their colony could multiply. Creepier still, The Code mentioned a naming ceremony, like it was her dad's plan all along for the residents to sacrifice their own for the experiment. She shuddered and sought comfort from Coal's embrace, pulling the blankets higher.

Despite Coal's morbid explanation, he had seemed ecstatic. At twenty, he now had one nephew and two nieces. And she was their secret aunt. It was weird. But not as creepy as the idea of already being a mother of three children.

Nevertheless, she touched her stomach. The skylight above their bed streamed beams of light into their small room. She watched as the trace wisp of a cirrus cloud moved across the blue sky. Coal's hand, the one tangled in her hair, released her strands and slowly traveled down her body to the hand she rested on her stomach, weaving his fingers with hers. Like he knew what she was thinking. He wasn't asleep? Lynden held her breath as tears pricked her eyes.

"I love you," he whispered to the beating pulse in her neck.

She whispered back, "I'm sorry."

"Do not take blame for the actions of another."

She stared at the sky through the thick glass and blinked, long and slow. She had little experience with babies. Her only encounters were with the small handful of women receiving pre-job interview makeovers at her clinic, who couldn't afford childcare. Lynden didn't want to punish these women for something they couldn't help—economically and socially. Most were transitioning homeless anyway. Or recovering prostitutes. So she welcomed them all, regardless of their life situation.

Three weeks ago, a mother had brought her newborn, the only baby Lynden had ever held in her entire life. He was so tiny, and she freaked out, especially when he began crying. His mother was in the middle of color processing and couldn't comfort him. Lynden was clueless on what to do. Especially since the mother breastfed, unable to afford formula.

Coal—who had visited for lunch that day between meetings—had scooped the baby from Lynden's arms and walked him around, patting his back while softly singing lullabies in French. Lynden had felt like a complete idiot. A man had better maternal instincts than her.

That was the moment she knew that her husband wanted children of his own. He wouldn't look at her, his anger at the injustice of their situation rolling off of him in huge waves, despite the gentle songs he sang. Coal cradled the baby to his chest as if he were his own son, a sight that left her feeling strangely empty and incomplete. And turned on as hell.

What was it like to be pregnant? To feel a baby growing inside your body? To produce life? Women complained about how children ruined their bodies and their lives. Screaming at them in public for having emotions and opinions, like they were dogs to be trained instead of fellow human beings. Her own parents treated her like the accident she knew she was. Fillion was the golden child. She was never meant to be.

Lynden watched the sky again, pushing back the rising emotions.

Unlike her progressive, corporate-run society, her husband's world celebrated children and considered each one a gift. A gift that she could never give him because the lab would own their child's life.

Swallowing back her remorse, she said, "I know you want children."

"Dozens of them."

She could feel his smile against the skin of her neck. The asshole was messing with her. He wanted to be playful? Fine. Worked for her, too.

"Dozens? So now I'm your broodmare?"

"You would make a wonderful mother." Coal leaned up on his elbow and studied her face with a sleepy gaze. "Adventurous, playful, empathetic, and fiercely protective."

"We'll never know. God, it pisses me off."

"We do not need children to know. It is in your nature." He kissed her lips softly. "Shall I introduce you to wee Alder this morning? I believe you will find him as charming as me."

"I feel sorry for your sister already."

Dimples appeared. "Why? She adores me."

Lynden groaned and pushed his chest, but he tightened his hold.

Coal's smile widened as he murmured, "You adore me, too, *Mademoiselle*."

Rolling onto her side to face him, Lynden combed her fingers into his hair and pretended to scratch behind his ears. "Who's a good boy?" she asked in a syrupy voice. "You are. Oh yes, you are."

He pulled the sheets over their heads and grabbed her hands from his hair. She squealed, followed by a laugh, when he rolled her onto her back, grinning. His rascally kind. *Oh shit.*

In achingly slow movements, he lowered her hands above her head as his mouth found hers, his kiss seductive for only a second. Then his kiss was searing and hungry. He didn't want to waste time. Neither did she. The heat of his body touched hers and she melted into the bed in swirling pools of pleasure. Stardust painted the night sky of her heart with each kiss, each touch. His lips left her mouth to explore her neck, then her breasts. She arched into him as a sigh left her body. He released her hands and she dug her fingertips into his skin as she trailed her hands across his shoulders and down his chest, memorizing the feel of his muscles as he moved beneath her touch.

Three loud knocks shook their door, loud enough to wake the dead. "Open up!" a familiar voice demanded.

Coal locked eyes with Lynden, the sheet still pulled over their heads. "Let us pretend we did not hear her…"

He lowered to kiss Lynden once more but she pressed her fingers to his lips, stopping his descent. "Ms. Bat-Shit-Crazy will knock all day long, just to prove her alpha bitch status."

She removed her fingers from his lips. A corner of her husband's mouth quirked up. "To be continued, then," he whispered but dipped down to kiss her anyway—slowly this time—his movements and touch sensual and erotic. Her hands finished their journey down his chest to his abdomen, pulling his hips toward hers. She shivered, losing herself to him once more.

Akiko knocked on the door again, repeating her demand. Lynden groaned and let her hands fall to the bed in defeat. Coal eased away and walked into the bathroom with one last sinful look Lynden's way. Dammit. He'd steal all the hot water.

"Your smoldering gaze still sucks, Mr. Awesome!"

Through the bathroom door, he said, "Drat. I suppose I…"

Another set of knocks drowned out his words. Annoyed, Lynden ripped the sheets from the bed and wrapped herself in the white cotton. Drawing in a deep breath, she exhaled slowly through clenched teeth, mentally preparing herself to face the she-demon on the other side of the door.

Thin-air thoughts.

Toughen up.

She visualized herself as a cat—a mighty huntress, sleek, sexy, sinew and strength combined with grace and cunning—and strode toward the door, yanking it open.

"What?"

Disgust tightened the corners of Akiko's mouth. Yeah, Lynden's ugly, friendless ass was naked.

"Where is Fillion?"

"How the hell should I know?"

"He is not in here?"

Akiko tried to look over Lynden's shoulder and so Lynden swung the door wider and dramatically gestured toward the room. Her and Coal's formal attire was strewn all over the floor. But, really, she wanted to grimace with disgust. Come on. Her brother in her room while she was naked? Yuck!

Straightening her shoulders, Akiko said, "Message Fillion and ask him where he is."

Lynden laughed with disbelief. "Yeah, I never played those juvenile games, and I don't plan on starting." The shower turned on and Lynden pressed her lips together. "Did you ask Kerry or Michael?"

"No, you are my assistant. Why would I do your job?"

Rolling her eyes, Lynden shut the door and touched the holographic lock. It clicked closed. She waited for Akiko to throw a tantrum and pound on the door, watching the light beneath the door for movement. Nothing happened, as if they were having a staring contest through the solid metal. A few seconds later, the shadow beneath the door disappeared.

That was it? Shaking her head, Lynden tossed the sheet back onto the bed and moved toward the bathroom. A stone in her gut churned, however. It wasn't like Akiko to be submissive—especially with her. Unsettled, Lynden slid open the shower curtain and stepped in to join Coal. Like hell she'd face Akiko and take a cold shower on the same morning.

Are hackers a threat? The degree of threat presented by any conduct, whether legal or illegal, depends on the actions and intent of the individual and the harm they cause.

— Mike Mitnick, hacker, 2000 *

Chapter Seventeen

A drip of sweat traveled down Fillion's forehead and ran the length of his cheek. Damn it was hot. He and Mack had snuck inside the Mediterranean biodome's technosphere, while the lab slept off their hangovers, and were now holed up in the stifling engine room. Fillion figured the technosphere with the farthest access point on the property was the safest place to hack into Messenger Pigeon. But, damn, it was hot.

Fillion sat on the concrete floor, his back to the curved wall. His gaze drifted from the screen to his surroundings. Pipes, coated in condensation, zig-zagged above their heads. Turbines and motors thrummed from far down the bending hallway. A waterproof computer system arched with the concrete wall's curvature, occupying a six-by-eight-foot space. Various knobs, switches, and holographic controls filled a backboard.

Fillion wiped away more gathering sweat before it could run into his already bloodshot, burning eyes. Mack lounged in a chair next to the controls, stripped down to his boxer briefs. His friend had the right idea. Fillion unbuttoned his shirt and tossed it aside.

The port sniffer he had loaded onto his Cranium blinked with activity.

"Another hit," Fillion said.

He circled the data with his finger to highlight the IP address and then dragged it to a layered screen to dump into his contacts. He swiped the sidebar and brought up a fresh layer and plugged in the newest IP address into the server settings for Messenger Pigeon. He then signed in as the administrator to view the archived messages. He studied various hex values first, then moved on to the content. The archives obfuscated any user names but, thankfully, the

MAC addresses were still visible.

Mack swiveled in the chair, his eyes half-shut. "Recognize any of the devices?"

"Nope. Reading communication content."

"More pleas to the Dark Lord's henchmen for time off and pay raises?"

Fillion squinted his eyes as he skimmed through the archives. "Engineering chatter."

"The kind that makes a man horny? Or the kind that puts him to sleep?"

"You? The latter."

Mack laughed. "I think you're flirting with me."

Fillion suppressed the urge to groan. "Another dead end." He dragged the IP address from his contacts to another folder to save for future use.

"Do you think Timothy was distracting you?"

"Maybe." Fillion scrolled down the streaming data, looking for another hit. "Not that I can confront him again."

"I'll interrogate him."

"He's dead, remember?"

Mack leaned forward, eyes wide. "What? When? Didn't you see him, like, two days ago?"

The hair on the back of Fillion's neck prickled. He looked over the screens to his friend. "I . . . I didn't tell you?"

"Uh, no." A shadow darkened Mack's expression as he scooted the chair closer. "The so-called neglected server, yes. Timothy's death, no."

Fillion closed his eyes and leaned his head on the back wall. "Shit. Sorry, mate. My mind . . . I swore . . . Dammit."

His friend was quiet a beat. "So what happened?"

"Cardiac arrest. Found dead in his room yesterday."

"Creepy." Mack shuddered. "When did you find out?"

"In the middle of my improvised speech last night."

His friend didn't reply, his face said it all. Shock. Anger. Disgust.

"And no, I haven't said anything to Skylar yet." Fillion focused on the screens again. "I'm . . . I'm not even sure if it's real."

Mack nodded his head, his movements slow and thoughtful. "Damn. I thought you sent Willow packing to be a dominating ass."

Fillion lifted a single shoulder in a weary shrug and returned to his mission. He didn't want to talk about her. He didn't really want to talk about Timothy's death, either. Both thoughts were too terrifying, especially if Timothy really was dead. Still, despite all efforts, his mental faculties had deteriorated far too much, and the haunting questions finally formed into another nightmare.

Had Timothy died because Fillion had visited him? Because Timothy shared confidential information? And how had Hanley known? It couldn't be coincidence. The message was delivered at a critical moment. If that bastard was willing to kill his own brother—

His chest tightened. He gasped for breath. Dizziness tingled throughout his entire body. Thoughts slammed into him one after another.

Not one full day as owner and already someone had died.

Because Fillion had asserted authority.

God, it was all his fault.

Would someone be punished for his act of rebellion last night?

Fillion's throat was swelling shut.

Like he was choking on Timothy's ashes.

Timothy had died because of him.

Because he pushed against Hanley.

A warning to back off.

Bright, warbled light shone overhead. A shadowed silhouette of Hanley leaned over Fillion and blocked part of the lighting. The world spun as his mind dimmed.

You will make an excellent Gamemaster one day. But do not ever forget that this game is over only *when I say so.*

"Stop!"

Had he shouted that aloud? He couldn't tell. Reality was soupy.

Fillion ripped the Cranium off his head. He grimaced while clutching his hair, rocking back and forth. He pulled his knees up to his chest and tucked his head down. His breath grew more ragged, his body shaking, as his head swarmed with accusations. Old fears. New nightmares. Visions of Willow convulsing with seizures in a glass coffin. Her raw scream clawing at him until grief took over and shredded what remained of his pulse.

"Save me," she called out to him. Dry, brittle leaves coated her throat as she spoke. Fillion jerked his head up and stared in horror at the corpse before him. Eyes shrunk into her skull, milky and unseeing. Hair, once golden blond, hanging in dingy strings. Entire clumps missing, revealing bald patches on her head. "Fillion..." She lifted a hand of rotting flesh, alive with maggots, bones exposed. Her blue lips parted and she begged him once more. "Save me..."

Fillion pushed his body back to the wall. He gagged, pressing a fist to his mouth.

"I need you..."

He squeezed his eyes shut and focused on his breathing.

"Son of Eden, protect me."

The vision had changed. Her voice was now honey-sweet and earthy, containing a musical lilt that entranced his pulse. He ignored the siren's call, his eyes remaining closed. But damn it was hard. He wanted to soak in the sight of her ethereal image. To feel her body against his. To drink in her breath as her hair fell across his face. But it was a trap. Not real. She wasn't real.

Maybe she'd never been real. Maybe New Eden was all in his head, too. Was he real? Was this a programmed simulation and he was simply in suspended animation? Part of a different experiment? He tried to dig through deeply buried memories for any clues. But it was black. Everything was black.

"Wake up!" he screamed to his mind. "Wake up, goddammit!"

"Fillion, focus on me."

"Go away!"

"Fillion!"

The sharp sound snapped at Fillion's focus.

"That's it," the voice encouraged. "Look at me."

Fillion blinked rapidly as his mind floated into a hazy, distant mirage of reality. Or what he considered reality. Hands cradled his head as a face drew near.

"Look at me, mate." Mack smiled at him, concern softening his gaze. "Hey."

"Hey."

His friend was about to reply when footsteps marched around the narrow, curved corridor and abruptly stopped.

"Oh, god. Sorry." Red crept up an engineer's neck and face as he gaped at Fillion and Mack. "I, uh—"

"Want to join us?" Mack asked the man. A flirtatious smile curved his friend's mouth while he raked the engineer over with a wolfish gaze.

Fillion blinked again. What the hell was Mack talking about? Join their hack? Then he saw it. Mack straddling Fillion's hips, wearing only his boxers and cupping Fillion's face. Fillion shirtless, covered in sweat and breathing heavy. The engineer stared at Fillion, flushing even more.

"We're not his type," Fillion said to Mack with a shrug. To the engineer he said, "Open your mouth to *anyone* and you'll be without a job. For all eternity."

"Got it."

"Tell your division that this sector is closed off until further notice, my mandate."

"Yes, Mr. Nichols." The engineer peered at him one last time then hurried the other direction.

Mack started laughing and Fillion rolled his eyes, giving his friend a shove. But Mack anchored his balance and wiggled his eyebrows.

"You're so his type, lover." Mack tried to keep a straight face. "He considered my offer."

"I didn't think you'd share me with another man."

Mack's lips twitched. "The engineering chatter got to me, *desu*."

Fillion released a weak laugh despite the ache in his chest. He couldn't help it. Though his laugh sounded more like a wheeze. Mack rolled off of him and leaned up against the wall.

"Holy shit, you scared me," his friend said after few seconds. "I thought I was going to have to hold you down and call in for reinforcements. Then I-so-want-you-engineer showed up."

"It's my fault," Fillion choked out. "Timothy died because of me. How am I—"

"His choices, mate. Not yours. He made a bad deal."

They locked eyes. Fillion's breath still came in quick. "Who cares? The message is still the same."

"Exactly what that *kisama* wants you to think. It doesn't matter what you do or don't do."

Fillion dropped his gaze to the willow oak tattooed on his forearm. The one his sister had surprised him with a year ago. The long, narrow leaves poked at his conscience until he whispered, "It matters to me."

"Then what's the plan, boss?"

He cringed at the word "boss" and gripped his discarded Cranium. "Find answers."

"Saddle up."

Fillion slipped the Cranium back onto his ear. He tapped at the command prompt screen and restarted the port sniffer to hunt for communications within the main Messenger Pigeon server. His movements were automatic, which was good. His breath was still somewhat ragged, and his thoughts moved as if swimming through a raging river of mud. The distraction was necessary, he knew. But he would rather curl up on the concrete and power down.

Mack crossed his arms over his chest and watched the activity, silent. A few more hits, still nothing. Biting the inside of his cheek, Fillion left the main Messenger Pigeon network and connected to the Techsmith Guild and began sniffing around again.

"Hit," Fillion said.

He swapped out his current Intranet IP address with this newest find and logged in as the administrator once again. The server's archive files opened up, ticking with activity. Fillion brought up his keyword searches to quickly explore the content. Then, both he and Mack stilled as they monitored communications over the past forty-eight hours in search of specific Legacy details and the MAC addresses belonging to Hanley's and Timothy's devices.

"Maybe I should adjust my keyword searches," Fillion mumbled.

"Meh. We've got everything in there except the toe of a crocodile and the blood of a virgin. Although *that* shouldn't be too hard to come by here. Shit, we didn't check the phases of the moon, either. That's probably it. Time to dance naked in the forest, *bishounen*." Mack deflated against the wall next to him, then popped back up in a rush. "There," Mack said as he pointed to hex values.

Fillion studied a notepad screen and compared the numbers and letters. "That's Skylar's device. Off by one digit."

"I see it now. Timothy's would end with an eight."

"This isn't the neglected server."

"How so?"

"Pathetic." Fillion bit his bottom lip. "You're getting dull, mate."

Mack's face fell with humor. "Smart-ass."

"I was up all night. Delivering speeches, kissing babies, and shit." Fillion lifted his eyebrow and slid his friend a side glance. "What's your excuse?"

"Yeah, well you were formed from the night. It's your playground."

A flicker of a smile teased Fillion's lips. "Quit your jealous gritching. Makes you sound even more pathetic."

Mack flipped him off with both hands and Fillion fully grinned.

He began the process all over again with another recognized port value on the Techsmith Guild network. He opened up the archive files and his stomach lurched. He wasn't even sure if he was breathing. Nothing. Absolutely nothing. The archive had been wiped clean. Not even basic set-up activity communications. His panic revved up once again.

"Purged," Mack said, followed by an explosion of swear words. "He knew."

"How am I going to do this?" Fillion held his Cranium straight and angled Mack's direction. "I'm leading blind."

"I don't know, mate."

The shaky sound in Mack's voice amplified Fillion's flaring paranoia. He felt his chest tighten again. His hands were trembling so bad, he couldn't close out the screen.

"Hey, stay with me. Don't fade." Mack pivoted to fully face Fillion. "We'll figure this out. I promise."

"I'll . . . I'll never forgive myself if . . . if Hanley hurts her or her family."

"Fillion, listen to me. You. Can't. Save. Her."

"You think I don't know that already?" he snapped. "Jesus…"

"You're not hearing me," Mack snapped back. "You can't save someone who doesn't need saving."

Fillion groaned and thunked his head on the cement wall. "Shit, Mack. Make sense. Get to the point." Sweat dribbled down his cheek and he clenched his teeth. God, he needed a cigarette. But smoking wasn't permitted in the technosphere. The stress and withdrawals and all-night social pressure were killing him. Mack still hadn't responded, either, amping up Fillion's irritation level even more. "Do you have a point?" he demanded, rolling his eyes. "Or am I supposed to decode your cryptic inspirational speech as part my journey to enlightenment?"

Mack hesitated for a nanosecond. "He never planned on letting you become majority owner beyond paper titles." Fillion groaned again—tired of hearing the obvious—and Mack's lips formed a thin line, his brows hanging low over his eyes. "Stop being a dick and hear me out."

The muscles in Fillion's stomach tightened. He dragged in a shaky breath and studied his hands, nodding his head for Mack to continue.

"He's controlling you through Willow and Leaf. As long as your focus remains on saving the Watsons, he's free to do whatever the hell he wants. Killing them would make you unusable. For anything. But the threat? Look at you. You're like a quivering, gelatinous mass who believes every lie. Every fucking lie that you're powerless even though you quote the anecdote. To everyone." Mack leaned in close. "Regardless of your mighty displays, he knows you'll bend. You always do. The pattern is *pathetically* predictable." Fillion shot his friend a glare. "So don't bend. Be a solid force. Do whatever the fuck you want and damn the consequences."

"He had his brother killed and purged the neglected server because I talked to Timothy! What if—"

"Cut the strings, Fillion. Cut every fucking tie and walk away."

"You know I can't and you know why."

Mack's expression clouded with fury. "Image," he taunted. "Perception."

Fillion flinched and turned away. Those two words. They would haunt him all his days. An angry tear escaped and he swiped it away quickly, not wanting his friend to see. Sometimes he thought it would be easier if he just wasn't alive anymore. The pain of each empty heartbeat was too great. The cost was too much. But he wouldn't do that Lynden. Or to the residents of New Eden, who believed he would save them from the evils of the Outside world. It was laughable, all of it. But their dependency anchored him to whatever nightmarish version of reality he was interacting with at any given moment.

Movement snagged his attention. His gaze darted over to the hallway leading toward the engines. A familiar-looking holographic woman flickered in and out of focus. A copper drone hovered above her head. Copper? Fillion squinted his eyes. Drones were almost always stainless steel. She smiled at him and his heart stopped beating for a second.

"How do you do, Fillion Nichols?"

Did Mack see her? The way Fillion's mind was glitching—moving with the murky, disoriented waves that crashed against his paranoia—he knew that he was hallucinating again. Or was his mind slipping back into the correct reality? He wasn't so sure about anything, anymore.

She tilted her head. "Are you ready to discover what is real?"

His breath caught. Tremors started up again. His breathing grew rapid. Did Hanley know where he was? Of course he did. Hanley knew every move Fillion made. Even in the underground. There was no escape.

"Let's get back to work," Mack said, his voice still sharp.

The hologram winked out. Even the drone disappeared. Clarity buzzed inside Fillion's head once more. He whipped his head toward his friend, a drip of sweat falling into his eyes with the movement.

Mack closed his eyes and rolled his neck. "There's one more hit to investigate before we can leave this hell-hole. Damn, it's like an inferno in here."

Fillion loosed a tight breath. His friend hadn't seen the hologram. Or heard her utter the same words she spoke to Fillion on Exchange Day.

Focus.

A yawn left Fillion's compressed lips. Exhaustion always triggered his PTSD and psychotic episodes. He wanted to crawl into bed and forget the world. But he'd only have a few hours, if that. *Time* magazine was coming out mid-afternoon for an interview and photo shoot, complete with a fashion design team. An interview Fillion couldn't refuse, even if he was puking his brains out. Shit. He was mentally rambling.

Focus.

He turned the screen back on and stared at the data without seeing it. Another yawn surfaced and he stifled its escape as he attempted to concentrate. He'd never seen Mack this fired up before. Or quote Hanley's words as weapons in an argument. Those two words churned in Fillion's gut and scraped across the raw edges of his mind. He couldn't do this. Couldn't concentrate with Mack pissed off at him. Fillion turned the screen back off and locked eyes with his best friend, his partner.

"You're my bitch," he said with an apologetic half-smile. "Not the other way around."

Mack started laughing. "That's the spirit."

Fillion wanted to keep smiling for his friend. But humor slipped away as his eyes burned with emotion. Apologies weren't his forte, but Mack deserved one. "I'm sorry."

His friend pressed his forehead to Fillion's and gripped his face. One of the most intimate, vulnerable gestures Mack had ever done with him. No playing. No pretend flirting. Instead, the same intensity reflected back at him.

"I can't stand by and watch him destroy you," Mack said. "And you're letting him, Fillion. *Fight.*"

"I'm afraid."

"I know, mate. I know." His friend tried to smile but he couldn't either. "*Fight.*"

Fillion swallowed back the ever-rising panic. "I'm trying."

"To win, to destroy. Not for feel-good boundary lines that will blow away the next time Hanley decides he's done humoring your attempts at control."

"To win."

Mack grinned now. "To destroy."

"To make a reality all my own."

"Hellz yeah." Mack patted his cheek and moved away.

Fillion used his discarded shirt to wipe the sweat from his face. "Professional negotiator. Motivational speaker. Director of operations at TalBOT Industries. Did I forget anything?"

"I am many things. It's true. But you forgot warrior-between-the-sheets and Robot Overlord." Mack waggled his eyebrows. "And your husband."

"Legally that never happened."

"I was there, zucchini. So were you."

Humor rumbled out of Fillion with the queerplatonic term for partner, and his shoulders relaxed a notch. He looked at his friend again and lifted an eyebrow. "What about vice president of New Eden Biospherics & Research?"

"Yeah?"

"Yeah."

"I'm not sure you can afford me."

Fillion grinned. "I'll sweeten the deal." He lowered his voice to a stage whisper. "You can rename the lab's five meeting rooms to anything you want. *Anything.* It'll be your first official order of business."

"You know I can't resist naming meeting rooms." Mack bit his lower lip as his eyes rolled to the back of his head in a look of ecstasy. "Turns me on. Every. Damn. Time."

"Well?" Fillion lifted his shoulder in a faint shrug. "Do I have myself a new VP?"

"The meeting room names remain, even if I leave."

"Or if I fire you."

"What?" Mack placed a hand to his heart. "Fire me? I don't care if you're a dominating asshole. Never say the 'D-word' in my presence. *Never.*"

"Divorce?"

Mack lifted his fingers to form a cross and hissed.

"OK. Fine. The meeting room names remain even if you leave and I'll never say the 'D-word' in your presence."

"Deal." Mack extended his hand.

Fillion shook his friend's hand. "Out with it. What are the names?"

"I present to you the Kübler-Ross stages of grief." Mack held a straight expression. But his lips twitched. "The first room is Denial."

Fillion burst into laughter. "I get dibs on scheduling meetings in Anger and Depression."

Mack bit down on his tongue suggestively. "Bargaining is sexy."

"But never Acceptance," they said at the same time, resulting in more laughter.

"Acceptance will be the saddest room," Mack threw out. "Always empty. Forever alone."

Fillion's stomach hurt, they were laughing so hard. Like they were children who found knock-knock jokes that didn't make sense the funniest shit on the planet. But, after what seemed like an eternity, he eventually regained control over himself, refusing to look at Mack. Because if he did, he'd lose it again. God, he was so freaking tired.

Still, feeling lighter, he turned his Cranium back on and pulled up a blank email screen.

"Uh, what are you doing, *bishounen*?"

Fillion smirked. "Sending a note to Michael to make the changes official with instructions to order new door plaques."

"My work here is done."

"What the hell. You can't leave. Not yet. You've barely clocked four minutes." He sobered as he stared at his email signature: "CEO and President." "I . . . I need you. I can't do this alone. Of course, the board will have to approve your appointment, but I'll ensure it happens."

A soft smile played across Mack's lips. "Let's finish this hack before we pass out, *boss*."

"We found the neglected server," Fillion mumbled. "The last hit is pointless."

"A *real* hacker wouldn't walk away without investigating *every* lead."

"Maybe I'm not real."

"Fake Fillion, snap! Snap!"

With his middle finger and a bored expression, Fillion brought up the command prompt screen and repeated the steps as before. Passing out sounded like a better option. But he'd appease Mack. It was the least he could do. His friend smiled at Fillion's not-so-subtle reply to his demands. Archive files opened up in a new layer and Fillion expanded the screen.

"What's this?" Mack asked, leaning in closer.

Fillion squinted to focus better. "More engineering chatter, it looks like."

"I don't think so. Hey, give me your Cranium."

Mack took the device out of Fillion's hand and placed it on his ear. Pinching the corners of the latest archives layer, he pulled out and expanded the screen even more.

"Look at the MAC addresses." He pointed to the notepad.

Fillion compared the first six hex values Mack had indicated to the notepad screen and target-locked onto the MAC address assigned to the manufac-tured tech produced by New Eden Biospherics & Research. Weird. Computer systems and engines inside the technosphere communicated. But not like this.

"There's Hanley's device." Mack pointed to the screen. "He's messaging back and forth with these N.E.T. devices."

"Androids?" Fillion lifted an eyebrow. "I've only seen Rosa bots on the property, though."

Mack remained silent as he read through the content. Fillion leaned over Mack's shoulder and skimmed over the random instructions and replies.

"This is on the Techsmith Guild network, right?" Mack asked.

"Yeah."

The content exchange was mostly mundane housekeeping check-ins, like system updates, software patch repairs, meaningless back-and-forth. But not like computer system autoreplies. The messages definitely had a human touch. More fluid. Each comment or check-in unique, even if they were about the same topic. He was ready to give up when his gaze snagged on a sentence.

Pointing at the screen, he asked, "Did you see this? He's giving this device commands to solicit sex with a hacker in the Seattle underground to steal his or her Cranium." Fillion didn't recognize the hacker's handle, but there were so many.

Mack went very still. A few seconds later he began swearing under his breath. Holding on to the Cranium to keep the screen straight, he turned his head to face Fillion. "Where's the inception paperwork for these devices?"

"N.E.T. has a searchable centralized database."

"Good."

Over Mack's shoulder, Fillion highlighted the MAC address for the de-vice in question and plunked it into a hidden search bar on a separate screen. A new screen appeared with results, all under a folder titled "M." Mack tapped the parent folder and a password screen popped up. Fillion reached over and entered his administrator password. A second later an "access denied" dialog box appeared.

"Do you know Hanley's?" Mack asked.

Fillion was too tired to be pissed off over access denial. In truth, it wasn't surprising. He reached over Mack's shoulder again and swiped in Hanley's password, one he had decrypted earlier that morning. The screen refreshed to a hidden database with lab access granted only to Hanley.

"MELISSA Project," Fillion whispered to himself.

Once again, Mack went very still. This time, however, the unnatural, catatonic stare Mack held while reading through the hidden file made the hairs on the back of Fillion's neck prickle for the second time since beginning this hack.

"Oh god." Mack's finger stopped scrolling and his mouth fell open. "Re-becca Nakamura."

"Who?"

Mack ignored him and began muttering other names. "Andra Black, Car-olyn Knight, Bran Davis, Jeff Abrams—" The unnatural stillness returned and the whites of Mack's eyes widened.

Fillion pulled the Cranium off of Mack's ear. "Jeff Abrams?"

"Do you know Andra Black?"

"Wait. You freaked out with the first name. Rebecca Nakamura?"

"Tell me about your visit with Timothy again," Mack replied, ignoring him once more. "Don't leave out any details."

"Re-hash from what point?"

"From the beginning."

"Seriously?"

"All. Details."

Fillion slid a nervous glance to his friend.

"There's something you're not telling me, pretty boy," Mack clarified. "Bit dump."

"I'm not sure it's real."

"Tell me anyway. We'll sort it out."

"I . . . I sometimes think I see and hear things that never happen."

"Different than the Willow trips?"

"Yeah."

"OK." Mack nodded his head, the movements sluggish. "Same sights and sounds or different every time?"

"Different."

"And what makes you think it isn't real?"

"Black spots in my memory."

Mack's face darkened. "How long?"

"Four, five months."

"Triggers?"

"Unpredictable." Fillion placed his Cranium on the ground. Data streamed upward on two screens and he blinked. "There was a girl—"

"Like the story already."

Fillion let his head fall back to the wall as he closed his eyes. Another drip of sweat traveled down his face. "She didn't seem human." He continued to tell his friend about the strange girl with choppy brown hair, the warning she spoke, and how she powered-down after the aides used a disruptor. "I don't want to hack into their system or hire the underground and get caught, and I can't ask about her due to privacy laws."

"Unless you file a claim. Injured when she attacked you or something." Mack shrugged. "Then you'd know for sure."

"Or be admitted for psychosis after the world stops laughing their asses off."

His friend's brows hung low over his eyes. "I believe you."

"Peachy."

"No, I mean it. While you were in juvie, Gremlin sent your marriage proposal answer back to me through an Untraceable."

Fillion turned toward Mack. "Like a cybernetic cloak of invisibility?"

"Yeah. Freaky shit. Not even bio stats. I asked my dad about it and he said a human cybernetic experiment existed a couple decades back called the ME-

LISSA Project: Modulated Engineered Living Information Socio-cybernetic Systems Android." Mack wiped his arm across his forehead. "The project was shut down by the government after massive issues, including death."

"Transhumans," Fillion said under his breath. "Holy shit."

"Black market ops."

"Computer underground?"

"From these files, it appears so."

Fillion strapped his Cranium back to his ear and turned it off. "Her warning—"

"Hanley's words, I know."

Goosebumps shivered across Fillion's skin, despite the thick heat. "What does this have to do with Andra Black?"

"Her current address is listed as the same mental infirmary that Timothy was checked into."

Nausea swirled in Fillion's gut. "And Jeff Abrams?"

"The inception doc said he was part of the original MELISSA Project."

Jeff's strange body twitches suddenly made sense. Was his nervous system damaged? And why was Hanley involved in this black ops? Fillion pulled his knees up to his chest and started to lower his head when he remembered another name.

"Who is Rebecca Nakamura?" Fillion asked. "You reacted like you know her. Do you?"

"Yeah. So do you." Mack shifted on the concrete and nervously met his gaze. Fillion knitted his brows in response. With another uncertain look, Mack finally confessed: "It's Pinkie."

At first, Fillion wasn't sure he heard him correctly. Then a thousand thoughts hit him all at once, followed by a wave of rage and disgust.

"Don't freak out on me," Mack said, raising his hands in surrender.

"What the—"

"Let me explain," Mack interjected, eyes wide.

"How long have you known?"

Mack drew in a tight breath and exhaled slowly. "The week after Lynden was hospitalized. I bribed someone in the underground with a large sum of cash—"

Fillion grabbed his discarded shirt and stood up.

"Stop, mate," Mack said. "Don't leave like this."

"I'm mentally breaking down. Just back off. Give me space to cool." Fillion shoved past Mack and marched toward the exit, buttoning his shirt as he moved. God, he was so pissed off. In a surge of fury, he kicked open the door and slammed it shut. He stabbed fingers through his rumpled strands, tucking longer pieces behind his ears.

For three years Mack had known Pinkie's identity. Three. Freaking. Years. What the hell? He didn't want to think of the implications for intentionally withholding information Fillion had sought since before Lynden's assault. It made Fillion wonder what else Mack was hiding from him. And that was a thought Fillion couldn't entertain right now. Not with all the other new information he had just learned.

Hanley was involved in another human trafficking operation. What did this have to do with New Eden? The Techsmith Guild? Could it even be linked to Joel Watson's death?

Did Hanley kill Timothy to protect his involvement with the MELISSA Project? Or to warn Fillion to back off? Probably both. Hanley always played multiple plot points at once.

Rant after rant formed, hot and heavy. Fillion's mind was sinking into an ocean of black water, his pulse drowning in one betrayal after another. He just needed to be alone. Needed to sleep. No more mental stimulation or paranoia. Time to power down and defrag.

The morning sun glinted off the biodome panes and burned his eyes. He passed custodians hired to clean up the property after the previous night's events. Passed Guardian Angels and scientists. People greeted him, but he ignored everyone. Didn't make eye contact or acknowledge their existence.

Fillion placed his thumb onto the biometric stat reader at the lab's main entrance until he heard a click. He swung open the door and strode into the temperate forest.

"Where have you been?" a woman demanded. One who looked exactly like Pinkie.

He came to a halt, sucking in a sharp breath. In the middle of the dirt path stood Akiko, arms crossed over her chest. Was he hallucinating again? He swallowed and blinked back the confusion. His pulse thumped loudly in his ears.

"Well?" Akiko asked. "I have looked for you all morning."

"Business," Fillion answered.

"Outside of the lab?" She ambled toward him, slow and seductive. "Did you crawl into your rodent's bed last night?"

Fillion rolled his eyes and moved to step around her, but she put out her arm. "Don't," he seethed. "I don't owe you an explanation for anything. We're a business arrangement, nothing more."

She laughed at him. The cruel sound echoed in the forest and wormed through Fillion's doubt. This was real. He wasn't imagining this conversation. He must have looked bewildered because her humor faded into a haughty smile, ripe with jealousy.

"Fillion," she cooed, straightening his wrinkled shirt. "Do not be childish. A powerful man always needs a more powerful woman by his side."

She smiled once more and then moved to kiss his cheek, but he stepped back. They locked eyes for a nanosecond before he spun on his heel and continued his escape. Revulsion rippled through him. He wasn't her project or trophy. He wasn't anyone's pawn. Yet, as the thought angrily shouted away in his mind, he knew it wasn't true. He was everyone's pawn. Even Mack's, apparently.

A few minutes later, he slammed the door to his room and bit back a forming scream. Exhaustion sighed through him instead. He didn't know how he was going to function tonight. He opened his nightstand and pulled out a bottle of pills prescribed for anxiety. If he took one, he would be dead to the world for the rest of the day. No, he'd better wait until tomorrow. Fillion put the pills back and lit a cigarette instead. His fingers shook as he enjoyed a long drag, exhaling long and slow.

On his bed lay an outfit the design team had selected for the photo shoot: a slate gray tunic with dark sliver trim, solid black jeans, two studded leather belts, and black combat boots. A note rested on top with instructions to report to the outside courtyard at 3:30 p.m. for an upcoming "The Future Meets the Past" digital spread in *Time*.

Placing the cigarette in his mouth, he crouched beneath his bed and pulled out the cherrywood box. His fingers caressed the abalone oak tree before opening the lid. The harvest token Willow had gifted him lay on top. Smoke curled from his lips as he stared at his future, and his past.

"Damn the consequences," he muttered to himself, rubbing out his cigarette in an ashtray. "To win. To destroy."

He pushed the box back beneath his bed, threw the clothes onto a nearby chair, and set the external alarm on his Cranium. Then he fell onto his bed, no longer afraid of his nightmares. Reality had become far more terrifying.

Adams: Do you see your role as the experiment's Gamemaster different than your father's previous role?

Fillion: We're different people, so it's only natural we'd lead and strategize differently, too. And, unlike Hanley, I've lived in the game world. I'm intimately acquainted with The Code. He theorizes, but I've put vision into action. The biggest takeaway is understanding that the residents of New Eden Township stopped pretending a long time ago. This is their world, their life, and we must respect it and their collective voice as a community. I hope, as the new Gamemaster, to help our world see them as fellow human beings instead of characters testing a scientific hypothesis.

— Fillion Nichols, on _Atoms to Adams Daily Show_, March 27, 2058

Chapter Eighteen

Willow paced behind the head table while curling a long strand of hair onto her finger. The scents of roasted goat and herb-seasoned vegetables wafted from the kitchen. Wood crackled and sparked in the hearth across the Hall, accompanying her padded footfalls and the occasional creak of the wooden chairs where Rain and Skylar sat. Candelabras overhead and single candles upon each table flickered in twinkling patterns, decorated liberally with vines from the rainforest, wildflowers from the meadow, and with garlands and bows made from linen and hemp scraps.

The room glowed with the magic Willow imagined existed in faerie halls. Yet the beauty and wonderment did little to distract her from the memories of the Ceremony. Her stomach muscles remained clenched into vicious knots. She pressed a hand to her midsection for relief, though none came. Walking the length of the head table and back was far from ladylike deportment, but moving employed her myriad apprehensions more constructively. Otherwise, she feared she might go mad.

Movement outside the latticed window caught her eye. The tension in her gut twisted painfully. With a quiet gasp, she leaned onto the sill, her nose nearly pressed to the cold glass. Evening light shaded the biodome in dusky grays and lavender, but she could still make out the approaching party with Connor in the lead.

"They arrive," she said, turning to Rain and Skylar.

Willow smoothed the skirt of her dress and fidgeted with the cherry blossom chaplet circling her head. She then dashed to the front of the head table, hands clasped at her waist, shoulders back, her chin lifted ever so slightly. The Daughter of Water prepared herself as well, while casting sly glances Willow's way. Skylar, on the other hand, simply rose from his chair, his stare fixed upon the stone floor. He appeared as distraught as Willow felt and, hopefully, concealed. She had little choice in this evening's festivities.

A headache bloomed at her temples. The delicate skin around her eyes remained somewhat swollen despite the comfrey cream she had applied for relief. She probably still appeared ghastly, despite the warmth from the hearth. Willow pinched her cheeks a few times and then checked to see if anyone had noticed her momentary slip in vanity.

The kitchen staff had assured Willow that the Great Hall would remain empty until evening meal. The hour of rest had begun a quarter of an hour prior and guaranteed a modicum of privacy, which she appreciated. Despite her inexperience as a hostess, she was charged with greeting the Nichols family and NASA officials on her brother's behalf before the Celebration began.

Ember remained weak following birth. Though Brianna declared that the community's Fire Element and Queen would recover in due time, Leaf was not so convinced. The youngest twin needed attentions as well, especially that of her father's warmth and steady heartbeat. Besides Ember, Leaf was the only one their wee daughter responded well to with notable improvements.

Willow agreed without protest to attend their guests prior to Leaf's arrival. Nor did she share with Leaf the way Hanley and the owner of Stellar Dock Corp. had publicly shamed her before the world. Her brother carried enough burdens and need not worry so over her. These details she would share once life resembled normal, which she was beginning to fear was a fanciful notion.

The large doors opened, yanking her from her reverie, and Willow bit back a startled response. She shoved aside her aching and placed a hand upon her heart as she gracefully lowered into a grand curtsy, the skirt of her dress rippling across the floor.

"Welcome to New Eden," she said when the party halted before her. "May health and happiness be yours during your stay."

"Thank you," Fillion quietly replied.

His entourage murmured and whispered, the hushed judgment pricking her already fragile confidence. After rising on unsteady feet, Willow turned her head toward her shoulder in modesty. She maintained a regal bearing, unable to yet look upon him, though she felt his eyes upon her.

"Lady Rain, please request libations for our guests."

"Yes, Your Highness." Rain dipped into a curtsy and then moved toward the kitchens.

Willow gestured toward the head table. "Let us sit and enjoy each other's company before evening feast commences." No one moved, as if they did not understand her meaning. "It shall become more difficult to talk as a group once the musicians start up and the community breaks bread."

Connor strode past her with a head bow and an encouraging smile. The whisper-soft sounds of shoes stepping across the stone floor followed in his wake. She felt terribly foolish and out of fashion. How did women host parties with foreign guests on Earth? People slipped past her in quiet conversations, commenting on the Great Hall and decorations. She mustered confidence to look up, terrified to meet Hanley's or the general's eyes. Instead, she met *his* eyes, and her pulse quickened in response.

Fillion stood directly in front of her in a linen tunic similar to those of New Eden. Sleeves draped to his forearm, edged in tablet woven trim, echoing the hem of his tunic. A black undershirt hugged his arms to his wrists. The garment was cinched around his waist by two leather belts, one of which hung at an angle down his hip. His breeches boasted a fathomless shade of black made from a thick, coarse material and appeared painted onto his legs, they were so tight, unlike the loose linen variety worn within the biodome. His solid black combat boots, an Outsider garb term she had learned from Coal, laced partway up his calf. Fatigue and tension colored his complexion and he appeared as battered as she felt. Still, he cut a dashing figure, a blend of her world and his, and Willow's head grew faint. Until she noticed her father's harvest token folded over his lower belt and her feverish musings gave way to indignation.

"Your Majesty," Willow acknowledged curtly, dipping her head.

Warmth suffused her neck and face, more so when she chided herself for being so transparent. Fillion pressed his arms to his side and bowed deeply to her, his back straight. Willow's entire being arrested with astonishment at his grand gesture. Akiko released a sharp sound that echoed off the stones, her face pinching with disgust and horror. A cutting silence descended upon their group in response. Coal's eyes rounded, as did Lynden's. Had Willow caused offense? She blushed even more, angry with her ignorance on how to properly host Outsiders. After several heartbeats, Fillion rose and locked eyes with her.

The invisible thread stitching their lives together tugged at her heart until the pressure in her chest stole her very breath. And she almost stepped toward him, simply to breathe again, as if he held the power to grant her life. He appeared to have a similar conflict, a look akin to longing bleeding through his impassive expression. Why did he wear her father's harvest token? Did he mean to publicly mock the heart she had gifted him before the community?

"Your Highness," he finally said in reply.

Willow's heart fluttered violently in her chest and she spun toward the head table, vexed. What sort of woman pined for another woman's man? For a man who publicly declared that she was no longer wanted? Who had spat imprecations at her barely a day prior?

The doors to the kitchen swung open—saving Willow from her spiraling thoughts—and several maids marched through with pitchers of wine and cider. Willow found her seat, smiling her thanks to Rain.

"Ms. Watson?" A man from NASA leaned forward on the table. "Will your brother join us tonight?"

"Yes, sir. He shall arrive shortly."

"His wife gave birth to twins?" a woman asked.

Willow stared at her fidgeting hands and quietly answered, "Twin daughters, madam."

"Are they premature?"

"Yes, madam."

"I take it the mother and babies are healthy and experienced only minor complications, then?"

Unmarried women did not speak openly of births, especially before men, and she felt the worrisome eyes of the kitchen maids upon her. Willow shot Coal a pleading look, unsure of how else to communicate her discomfort.

"Madam," Coal interjected casually. "If it were otherwise, we would not be here, for the community would be in mourning."

Everyone nodded, as if the obvious were a great revelation. Willow drew in a fortifying breath and forced herself to make eye contact. Were all Outsiders this bold and inconsiderate? Wishing to know the intimate details of a perfect stranger and her moment of near-death as she gave birth? She ground her teeth as she thought over Coal's instructions, that one could not extend honor if they lacked connection to their own humanity.

A momentary silence fell over their table as the kitchen maids consulted guests as to which libation they preferred. Hanley waited for Willow to notice him as she inspected the table. And, when she did, he leered at her openly, his eyes roaming over her curves and exposed skin with a look akin to appreciation. She attempted to hide her shudder by looking the other way, her gaze landing on another man in a NASA uniform.

"What are their names?" the man asked her. Did he believe she had silently required him to speak simply by looking upon him? The blood rushed to her cheeks once more, especially when realizing all eyes now pointed her direction while awaiting her answer.

"The community of New Eden will learn in a New Life Ceremony, six days from today, sir," Coal answered for her once more, much to Willow's relief. "For now, they are known as the Watson lasses."

"Fascinating," the man replied. "We look forward to joining your colony, Mr. Hansen, and studying your rudimentary civilization."

Rudimentary? Willow gripped her fingers to hold back her rising temper.

Fillion stilled in his chair, his skin paling to a sickening shade. His friend, Mack, flashed Willow an apologetic frown before returning his focus onto Coal.

"Excellent notion," Coal replied with a charming smile. "We have much to teach you about survival and class, sir. Modern technology and progressive beliefs are both poor replacements for true human values of decency, after all."

Hanley chuckled, though Willow knew that he was not amused. "Equality and human decency are values that transcend cultures," he said. "New Eden Township doesn't lay claim to them."

"Indeed," Coal replied, bowing his head in deference. "Nor did I mean to imply otherwise. Though one could argue that a civilization strengthened by core values of human equality and decency can hardly be considered rudimentary. Even savages held slaves, did they not?"

"The Son of Fire," Hanley said, clapping his hands. "His words always burn with passion." Others at the table clapped with Hanley, and Coal clenched his jaw.

"And burn with truth," Fillion added quietly, a dangerous form of quiet that chilled the table into an uncomfortable silence. The Son of Eden ran a finger along the rim of his empty tumbler.

Coal's gaze flicked to Fillion and then to Hanley, before focusing on a splintered divot marring the table surface before his seat.

Willow scrambled for a new topic of discussion. However, she did not possess her brother's way with people, his ease in conversation. Light, meaningless subjects, which placated the awkward silence and served no greater purpose, irritated her person. She would rather contemplate subjects of the soul or commune with nature to satisfy her need for relationship.

"Fillion?" a woman asked.

Willow nearly gaped when realizing the voice belonged to Della. Her son had inherited her soft-spoken quality as well as her otherworldly beauty. The entire table seemed riveted by her every movement. Willow struggled to envision her practical, no-nonsense father with such an elegant woman, failing further to comprehend the basis for their attachment.

Della tilted her head. "Perhaps you can share a few of your experiences from your stay in New Eden? I am sure the future colonists are eager to hear what is in store for them." When she finished, her gray-blue eyes, so much like her son's, slid Willow's direction as she lifted a kind smile. Did she suspect Willow's discomfort and inexperience?

Fillion cleared his throat and leaned back in his chair. "I worked with Coal's father in The Forge as a carpenter—"

"That's right. You were a blacksmith," the NASA woman said to Coal, interrupting Fillion, and not bothering to hide her admiration for the Son of Fire.

"I still am, madam." Coal picked at the splintered divot, ignoring her inspection of him. "I assist my father to complete orders in a smithy located within the lab when I am not working as a liaison for New Eden Enterprises and its affiliates."

"Perhaps you could give us a demonstration sometime this week."

"If Mr. Nichols works it into the lab's schedule, I will oblige."

Della smiled after Coal's reply, redirecting focus back onto her, and away from the unexpected tangent in conversation. Willow felt a twinge of jealousy at how effortlessly the woman commanded attention. Fillion's mother opened her mouth to speak, but paused when Killie, the head kitchen maid, repeated the choice of wine or cider to Akiko. Fillion's fiancée appeared to not hear Killie; instead, she stared straight ahead, her mouth set in a firm line. Willow blinked back the shock and embarrassment. Rain shared the look. Killie looked to Willow for instruction, her face glowing red.

"My Lady," Willow began, "would you care for wine or cider this evening? I shall pour for you, if you prefer."

Akiko's eyes hardened with distaste, but she ignored Willow as well.

"Akiko," Fillion said. "Answer her."

"I do not speak with *them*." She turned a hateful stare to Willow. "Especially her."

Willow should have looked away, but she refused to appear subservient to this woman. Furious winds gusted at the injustice of Akiko's treatment and insinuations, winds that had screamed inside of her since yesterday. Narrowing her eyes, Willow lifted her chin a notch and peered down her nose at her.

"Killie, it appears her Ladyship does not desire refreshment. Please alert the kitchen staff that she will not be served. If she wishes for food or wine, she shall serve herself."

Every pair of eyes at the table widened with Willow's instruction, even Hanley's.

The silence stretched for several loud heartbeats before Fillion addressed Akiko. His voice remained controlled as he spoke in a different language, but it was clear that he was issuing commands. From the corner of her eye, Willow could see Hanley smile with amusement. The others focused on the table and delicately cleared their throats.

When Fillion finished, Akiko's mouth fell open as she glowered in outrage. Then, collecting herself, a smile formed, beautiful in its cruelty. She laughed at Fillion before returning focus onto Willow. "I am not beneath you, *rodent*."

"You wish to address me now, do you?" Willow straightened her shoulders. "I simply conveyed your wishes, taking pains to accommodate your sensibilities."

Akiko pinched Lynden's arm. "Do not fail me again. You were to speak for me."

"Akiko!" Fillion shouted. His voice boomed off the stones.

Lynden flinched, before she shrank back, averting her eyes. Several kitchen maids squeaked and jumped back as well.

Fillion peered at his sister and softened his tone. "I'm so sorry, Lyn. Are you OK?" Lynden nodded. He then glared at Akiko. "We'll talk later."

Coal postured as if ready to throttle Akiko but remained silent, his gaze darting between Fillion and Hanley as he took Lynden's hand. How was this woman allowed to treat Hanley's daughter with such abhorrent disrespect?

Willow rose from her seat, unable to bridle her tongue a moment longer. "You shall refrain from harming my guests, My Lady. Do so again, and I shall have you escorted out of New Eden."

"How dare—"

"You had expressed yourself quite clearly that it was *beneath you* to be served by my people; therefore I made it known that you would rather serve yourself." Willow clenched her fists at her side. "Unless you wish to speak to Killie—now that you are speaking to me—and make other arrangements?"

"This is a perfect example of environmental conditioning," Hanley whispered loudly, leaning toward the general. "New Eden breeds the exact race needed for survival. She acts on instinct to protect the weakest in the pride."

Connor pushed out of his chair and leaned forward across the table until the muscles in his arms flexed with definition. "You will not speak of Her Highness or any other in such distasteful terms."

"Scientific observations, old friend. I meant no harm. Or have you forgotten the experiment status of your colony? NASA reps aren't here on holiday." Hanley gestured for Connor to resume his seat. "Let's not quarrel."

Connor did not move.

Tears swelled in Willow's eyes and she looked away lest the table witness her shame. Her heart ached for Lynden as well. Willow's father would never had aligned with insults nor allowed another to physically abuse his daughters. In the periphery, she could see Akiko form a satisfied smile. Willow grit her teeth while resisting the urge to claw the haughtiness right off that woman's perfectly beautiful face.

"Ms. Hirabayashi," Hanley began again, his eyes sliding from Connor to Akiko, "I concur with Ms. Watson's statement. Speak civilly or return to the lab, your choice. This night isn't about *your* needs."

Akiko's delicate features first registered red-faced shock before she blanched. Tears sprung to her eyes as she held Hanley's gaze. When Hanley looked away, Akiko's lips trembled and she promptly studied her lap. "Wine," she said loud enough for all to hear.

"Please sit, Your Highness," Hanley said to Willow.

"I shall do as I please."

He dipped his head ever so slightly in consent, as if he were King instead of her brother and Fillion. Their gazes locked as she continued to challenge him from across the table. His eyes were gleaming, seemingly pleased with her defiance.

Akiko delicately hiccupped and broke the tension. Her body trembled while suppressing the urge to weep. How strange that one so self-assured could be brought down so easily. As if her entire value and worth dangled precariously by Hanley's public approval. Willow paused. Queasy sensations stirred her stomach and she bit back a wave of revulsion. Her father's words—that people cry out to be loved since their first breath—echoed in the angry chambers of her heart. She would not add to this woman's many sorrows, though she wished to remove her from present company.

Willow gently coaxed the wine pitcher from Killie's hands. "My Lady," she said kindly to Akiko. "Allow me to fill your goblet in amity." She poured the wine first for Akiko and then for herself. "May good cheer be ours this evening." She lifted her goblet and imbibed a dainty sip before returning to her seat. "Killie, I shall share the choicest food from my plate with her Ladyship."

The table gaped at her once more. Except Fillion, who stared at his empty goblet, a scowl knitted between his dark brows. But not for long. The large entry doors opened and Leaf strode in, diverting everyone's attention. Willow stood as custom dictated, along with Skylar, Rain, Coal, and Connor. The Outsiders slowly followed suit, save Akiko, who remained in a posture of humiliation. However, beneath long lashes, jealousy pooled in Akiko's dark brown eyes as she stared, unflinching, at Willow.

<u>Adams</u>: *What do the people of New Eden think of our world?*

<u>Fillion</u>: *That's a tough question to answer since I haven't spoken to anyone from New Eden in over three years. Today is not only Ascension Day, but acquaintance day, too. However, before The Door opened, second gen residents couldn't fathom expansive space or global connectivity. Large-scale concepts are difficult to comprehend when all they've known is a four-square-mile radius their whole lives. If that's changed, I'll find out soon.*

— Fillion Nichols, on *Atoms to Adams Daily Show*, March 27, 2058

Chapter Nineteen

The drone of fidgety conversation and nervous banter hummed across the Great Hall. The fluid yet monotonous sounds melted into the voices at the head table. Leaf struggled to pay heed as Hanley regaled any who could hear of New Eden Enterprise's recent success in outfitting the dust bowl interior of the United States with new irrigation using desalinated ocean water, similar to how DesertSEA had reforested the great deserts of the world. The topic would normally interest Leaf. Instead, he stifled a yawn just as the musicians began plucking yet another gentle melody from the stage.

"Father?" A small hand rested on Leaf's forearm.

Hanley halted his speech mid-sentence. The head table quieted, all eyes on Alder. His son shrank back from the curious stares and buried his face into the folds of Leaf's tunic.

"Yes, lad?" he asked, bending in his seat to shield his son.

Alder murmured, "Sit with you, Father?"

"Of course."

Leaf scooped up his son, who promptly tucked his small cheek to Leaf's chest as he curled into his lap. Aware of the attention he and his son had garnered, Leaf pretended to take in the swelling scene of fabricated merriment until his gaze landed on Laurel, who stood beside his seat.

"Thank you for your kind attentions." He offered a warm smile to his youngest sister. "I shall care for Alder now."

Laurel dipped into a curtsy and slid into an empty chair next to Willow.

"He favors your family," Della said to Connor when the conversation failed to resume as before.

"Yes, a handsome lad," Connor replied in kind, though his words remained stiff. Then, wistfully, he added, "He reminds me much of Coal, actually."

Leaf resisted the urge to grip his son's small body tighter. Anger dangerously flared at the periphery of his self-control. Connor furtively cast him a knowing look before following Della's gaze. She studied Coal's and Lynden's empty chairs with a worrisome expression. Had Coal shared with his father? Della shifted her attention to her lap.

Shortly after the feast, the Son of Fire and Fillion's sister had departed for a walk, slowly retreating toward the inky night just beyond the Great Hall doors. Villagers had parted for them, most wearing frowns of disapproval or turning away as Lynden passed by. Leaf felt only sorrow for Fillion's sister, for he knew Coal would wed her if the law allowed. Ignorant though they may be, the community's response to her presence shamed Leaf. A few years earlier, he would have shared their disdain for her and Coal's immoral choices, upholding rules and traditions as he was raised to do. Now he questioned everything.

"Politics, business, and formalities," Hanley murmured, appearing reflective as he watched the community, same as Leaf. "Time to address New Eden. The handover speech won't take long."

"Should not Lord Coal and your daughter be present, sir?" Leaf asked.

"It's growing late. I have an early flight in the morning."

As much as Leaf would normally wish to argue, returning home to Ember had never sounded so fine. He missed his wife and daughters and worried much over them. To stifle another yawn, Leaf kissed Alder's head before untangling his son to leave in Laurel's care once more.

But Alder wrapped his arms around his neck in protest. "No, Father," he said softly.

"I shall be on stage. Will this bother you, son?"

In answer, Alder buried his head into Leaf's neck and began sucking on his thumb. Since this morning, Alder had remained close to Leaf's side and regressed slightly in behavior. Far too much excitement and life changes in a single day. He kissed his son's head again then stood, securing Alder's small body in his arms.

Fillion lifted a wine pitcher and refilled Willow's goblet. "Join us on stage?" the Son of Eden asked her, surveying the Great Hall as he did so.

Willow focused on the wine settling in her goblet, blinking back emotion Leaf could not read. "If you so desire," she eventually answered, each word clipped.

"Drink up and drink fast, then."

Their eyes touched for but a moment. She grabbed her goblet of wine and tipped it back as daintily as possible, then rose on steady feet.

Akiko rose as well, but Fillion turned to her and said, "No."

"You will leave me alone? With *them*?" she whispered back. Her lips pressed into a thin line.

"You're not standing beside me on stage."

"What will people—"

"Later." Fillion drawled out the word, almost as a growl. "After this is over, we'll talk. Right now? Sit in the chair and wait or return to the lab." An arrogant smile hardened Fillion's already grim visage.

"Michael," Akiko snapped. "Escort me to the lab."

The lead scientist stepped forward but halted when Fillion lifted a hand for him to stop.

"Seth," Fillion directed at the Guardian Angel who had accompanied the party. "Please walk Ms. Hirabayashi to her room."

"Yes, Mr. Nichols," Seth replied, encouraging Akiko to follow him.

"Oh, and Seth?" Fillion threw over his shoulder. "If you see Coal and Lynden, send them back to the Great Hall, please." Fillion flashed Hanley a look Leaf could only describe as dangerous, then marched toward the stage.

In his wake, the flame of conversation snuffed out like candles in the wind. The music followed suit. The wispy smoke of anticipation rose from each resident as they watched New Eden's guests replace the musicians upon the stage.

"Sky," Leaf whispered, pulling the Son of Wind close when they reached the stairs to the stage. "I ask a favor."

"Anything, Your Majesty."

Leaf pretended to adjust Alder in his arms and whispered, "Record the speech."

Skylar's eyes shone with understanding, though his face remained unchanging.

Leaf tipped his head and continued up the stairs and onto the stage.

When the Nobles and NASA representatives settled, Hanley stepped forward and turned on his Cranium. The residents simply shifted in their seats and waited, no longer afraid of Outsider technology as before. Leaf peered over his shoulder at Skylar, who replied with a single head nod.

An image wavered before the assembly: mountains cutting into an azure sky. Bright-colored wildflowers, in alien shades, skirted the looking glass-like waters of a lake. Clouds appeared to float upon the surface like mythological boats. Mouths parted in wonder and a low susurrus of appreciation rippled through the once motionless bodies. Beside him, even Willow gasped, her eyes bespeaking enchantment. Hanley lifted his finger and moved the image to another. Fields and rolling hills reflected endless shades of green. A vibrant rainbow arced across a gray sky before disappearing completely into a blanket of downy clouds smudged in light and shadows.

"Rainforest?" Alder breathed into Leaf's neck.

"No, this biome is not in New Eden," Leaf whispered back. Alder resumed sucking on his thumb while rubbing the neck trim of Leaf's tunic in a self-soothing rhythm. "Beautiful though, is it not?" His son did not answer.

"The land of your ancestors—Earth. The planet beyond The Door," Hanley spoke to the bewitched masses. "Every prism of color, each line and curve of life that tantalizes our senses, the water particles that comprise every breath and nourish each heartbeat, is the work of a closed-loop system." Hanley took a step toward the edge of the stage with a friendly smile. "All governed by a cradle-to-cradle cycle enabling our very existence."

Hanley's face glowed with strange colors from the screen.

"'In order to live, something must die,'" Hanley chanted.

The picture on the screen flashed to one of the most horrific images Leaf had ever beheld. Gasps and quiet cries of alarm sprung from the gathering. Bedraggled men and women in layers of threadbare clothing, covered in dirt and grime, faces gaunt, sat with backs to a wall in a village surrounded by rivers of rubbish. Heads hung in a posture of defeat or rested upon a black road. Children hid under a thick paper material, small fingers, far too bony, gripping the edges to hide from the rain.

"This, too, is the land of your ancestors—Earth. The planet beyond The Door. A world ravaged by unemployment and hunger."

Hanley swiped the air and the image changed to a village Leaf failed to comprehend. Rectangular buildings shot into the sky, clustered together and in such quantity that nature could not coexist with the dwellings and shops. How did one live without forests and grass fields? Or farms? People crowded every space, it seemed. Strange technology flew through the air and rolled upon the roads. Multi-colored lights beamed from walls, devices, the roads, and even from the sparse trees dotted throughout the village. The busyness offended Leaf and he squinted his eyes to simply feel more focused. Then he noticed how many walls were green, as though plants grew skyward in desperation, rather than blanket the soil as nature intended.

"A world ravaged by overcrowding and urban sprawl."

The Great Hall doors creaked open, normally not a noticeable sound. The silence was horrifyingly thick, however. Coal and Lynden eased into the Hall as Hanley began speaking again, and a smile crept up his face.

"A world under siege by social depravity, offering any temptation the mind could conjure."

The village scene faded into a shirtless man intimately kissing an immodestly attired woman, while hemmed in by a large crowd in a low-lit room. Warmth crept up Leaf's face as his sleep-deprived mind blanked with confusion. Perhaps he was not seeing clearly. Or his hazy mind conjured up images from plays of light and shadows. He squinted his eyes to focus better. In the assembly, parents turned their children around and glowered at Hanley. A few younger women turned away as well. Angry whispers circulated quickly, their bodies now a bubbling stew pot of activity. The image changed again to the same couple, and this time their faces were clear.

"Dear Lord," Willow gasped, clapping a hand over her mouth. Mortified, his sister turned around, as did Rain and most other women in attendance.

"Hanley," Connor seethed from behind. "You go too far!"

But the former Fire Element's voice was smothered by the outcry of disapproval as villagers demanded an explanation from their community's Golden Boy.

The Son of Fire slowly shifted his attention to the stage, murder in his eyes as he locked onto Hanley and shouted, "Shall we turn around so you may remove the knives and watch us bleed out?" Without waiting for a reply, he shoved his way out of the Great Hall, slamming the large door in his and Lynden's wake. Connor flew down the stage stairs, pushed through the crowd, and followed after Coal.

When the Great Hall doors slammed shut once again, Fillion charged the stage front. But not quickly enough. Leaf's heart plummeted to his stomach when the next image revealed the Son of Fire plugged into a strange contraption. The community quieted once more, stricken by the nightmarish machine holding Coal. Another image appeared of him fighting a man in an exotic landscape, blood streaming from his nose and mouth.

"But fear not. There is a solution." Hanley brought up an image of bio-dome clusters in a desolate, rust-colored landscape set against a yellow-brown sky. "Civilization needs a reboot. New Eden Township is our model and our answer." His lips tipped up in the barest smile as he chanted the remainder of New Eden's motto, "…but death makes way for the resurrection of new life."

The crowd began murmuring once again, pointing to the image in dismay and confusion.

"What is this?" Fillion quietly demanded beside Hanley.

"New Eden, Mars-side. Beautiful, isn't it? And yes, it's real."

Blood rushed from Fillion's face until a greenish pallor remained.

A faint glimmer of understanding dawned in Leaf's mind and the haze of sleepiness cleared as anger boiled to a rage in his veins.

"Enough!" he called out. "These images are grossly inappropriate."

With a smirk, Hanley turned off his Cranium and faced Leaf. "There is a point. I assure you."

"We shall discuss any further points privately before another is made."

"Are *you* giving *me* orders, Son of Earth?" Hanley stepped toward Leaf.

"Back off," Fillion interjected, moving in front of Leaf. "This is not the speech we discussed."

"Interesting." Hanley's gaze sharpened. "But when you change speeches mid-delivery, it's acceptable?"

"Lynden is your daughter!"

"She's an adult and earns her own reputation. You can't keep blaming me for everything, Fillion."

"Are you for real?!"

"What makes you think any of this is real?" Hanley casually gestured to the building and to the people. Fillion stilled, his eyes wild and haunted, his breaths shallow. "It's a simulation, a coded program," Hanley continued. "Everyone is a character in N.E.T."

"Where . . . where did you get those images of Coal and Lynden?" Fillion blinked several times in a row, hard and tight.

"Has your mind been slipping lately?" Hanley raised his eyebrows. "Seeing hallucinations? Black spots in your memory?"

For a moment, Leaf believed Hanley might truly be concerned. The worrisome expression he held was convincing enough. But it was a lie. No offer of help or consolation was given for the visible pain Fillion suffered under Hanley's inspection. Rather, the man appeared pleased beneath the overtures.

Leaf gripped Alder, afraid to move. He flashed his sister a warning look to remain silent. He could almost feel her hurricane-force winds gaining strength with every breath she took. He wished to defend Fillion, to say anything to break the intensity, but the feel of his son's rhythmic breath on his neck anchored Leaf's fury.

Hanley and Fillion remained locked onto each other, almost unaware of their surroundings. Until an invisible force snapped Fillion to attention. As if a previously buoyant thought suddenly gained weight and pulled him under. His ashen countenance burned red, his spine straight, shoulders flung back, eyes now level with his tormentor.

Each word slow and punctuated, Fillion repeated his question. "Where. Did you. Get those images?"

"Did you or didn't you bargain for the residents to remain in a biodome?"

Fillion hesitated a heartbeat. "Answer. Me."

"Look at them." Hanley pointed to the villagers. "I did you a favor."

"You're disgusting!"

"To think, until now a whole generation lived without seeing mountains or a rainbow arc across the expansive sky." Hanley leaned close. "Son of Eden," he whispered dark and low, "how will you save them from the evils of the Outside world?"

"Leave," Fillion commanded. "Take the reps with you."

Hanley chuckled. "I'm not afraid of you."

"You should be."

"Never pick on men more powerful than you. Haven't you learned this lesson yet?"

Fillion lifted a corner of his mouth in an arrogant taunt. But Leaf noticed how his smile quivered. "I'm majority owner. Did you make a bad move, Gamemaster?"

"You misunderstand me, as always, Fillion—"

"Leave!"

The gathering hushed as Fillion's normally quiet voice thundered off the stones and rafters.

Hanley stared at his son, the cruelty in his eyes hardening despite the smile on his lips. Then his gaze shifted behind Leaf and Fillion. "Skylar, my condolences on the recent death of your father. The medical records on the type of cardiac arrest indicate his death was quick."

The air in Leaf's lungs stopped moving. Timothy had died? He turned to find Skylar gritting back astonished tears, feet fastened to the stage shoulder length apart, back straight, hands curled tight at his sides. Gasps circulated around the room.

Hanley inclined his head as if confused. "Fillion hasn't informed you yet? My apologies. How rude of me. He's known since yesterday and so I figured . . . well, then..." Hanley's eyes appeared to be laughing when he returned attention to Fillion. "I'll *leave* him to it, then, since he's majority owner."

He dipped his head at Fillion. When passing Willow, Hanley slowed, his eyes trailing over her in a salacious gesture, a satisfied curve to his lips. Leaf made to move, but Fillion gripped his arm and shook his head with warning. To Leaf's horror, Willow met Hanley's eyes, unabashedly, delivering a heated promise of her own, chin lifted, eyes blazing. His sister dared to fight back, publicly? Leaf was not sure he was breathing anymore. The man's smile widened at her spirited response. Then, the minority owner whistled a cheerful tune as he marched off the stage. Leaf could throttle Fillion this moment. Why had he held him back from defending Willow's honor?

Dr. Nichols shot Skylar an apologetic frown from the front of the stage—her eyes sharp and angry despite the defeated slump of her shoulders—before hesitantly following Hanley and the NASA representatives out of the Great Hall. The giant doors groaned shut, much too loud amid the gathering's disquietude.

In the front row, Lady Emily's body slackened. Her knees gave way and her body crumpled headlong toward the stone floor. Two men caught her before her head could smack the ground. Voices shouted all at once and chaos quickly rippled through the villagers in response. Outrage. Grief. Terror. Skylar darted off the stage to his mother and sisters. Rain joined him, holding Gale-Anne as Skylar comforted Windlyn and delivered instructions for his mother's care.

Fillion released Leaf's arm, swearing without care of the women and children present. But Leaf pushed his personal offense to the side in order to process the more immediate issue.

"So it is true?" Leaf asked, heart pounding. "Timothy has died?"

"According to the mental infirmary. His ashes are ready for pick-up. Not even twelve hours after time of death."

"I see."

"No." Fillion's gaze skittered to Leaf's and then over the agitated crowd. "No, you don't. Ceremonies of Death in the Outside don't follow the same timeline as New Eden. Autopsies are required. Hanley—"

"Perhaps this conversation should be saved for later." Willow folded her arms across her chest. "The community needs direction before they disperse and allow the sun to set upon their anger and confusion."

Fillion lifted his shoulders and chewed the inside of his bottom lip.

Willow was correct. Leaf blew out a slow breath as he focused on the residents once more. A headache burned behind his eyes, strained and heavy with exhaustion. He could barely hold a conversation at the dinner table. He could not fathom how to comfort and direct the whole of New Eden this moment. Alder shifted in Leaf's arms and murmured incoherently in his sleep, his little fingers rubbing the hem of Leaf's tunic once more.

Willow tucked a wild curl behind Alder's ear, a worried smile pulling at her lips. Would this be Alder's future one day? Would Leaf's son and daughters stand upon this very stage and manage the villagers in their care? Or would they struggle in a New World, one filled with unspeakable beauties and unspeakable horrors as shown this evening?

Fillion studied Willow, a crease between his dark brows. A muscle in his jaw worked furiously as his teeth clenched. He appeared as though risen from the dead, ashen tones warming his clammy skin, dark circles under his eyes pronounced and sharp.

"This was his plan," Fillion muttered, closing his eyes in a wave on grief. He hissed a curse and turned his back to the villagers. "Hanley actually wanted to appear the bad guy"—he looked at Leaf down his shoulder—"and for me to become the pitied hero."

"It makes little sense," Leaf replied. "What benefit is there to gain in such a plan?"

"Then do nothing."

Leaf whipped his head toward his sister. "Do *nothing*? I am confused. Did you not just tell us to give New Eden direction?"

She remained focused on Fillion. "A man once told me that power was an illusion."

"Willow—"

Fillion ignored Leaf and asked Willow, "What do you suggest?"

"I shall lead New Eden while you both attend other matters of import."

"She shall *not* perform our jobs when we are present and perfectly capable," Leaf asserted to Fillion. "Hanley was given quarters to speak because *we* allowed him."

"I'm done playing into his plan," Fillion said.

"And so New Eden should suffer for your pride?"

"My pride?" Fillion lowered his voice. "I'm not the one offended by Willow's initiative."

Leaf's mouth fell open. "I beg your pardon? Her independence is not the cause of my offense."

"Then what are we debating about?" Fillion rolled his eyes and shook his head. "You've always been threatened by her—"

"This . . . this outrage and grief is our responsibility."

"Says the man who wanted to disrupt the game three years ago."

"Are you two quite done?" Willow placed hands on hips. "Men of power are the most illogical creatures. They fight over inane, meaningless subjects, yet discuss the endless possibilities of diplomacies when they should, instead, fight. Shall we focus, then?"

"You're not a meaningless subject."

Willow blinked back the surprise with Fillion's quiet words, then squared her shoulders, her eyes blazing anew. "Leaf, attend Coal."

"And leave the community? I appreciate your input—"

"Do not condescend to me, *Your Majesty*. Coal is your brother. He needs your reassurance more than the community at present. As your First Representative, I shall fare well in your absence and so shall the villagers, never you worry."

"A Nichols should apologize on behalf of the lab and reassure all that we are not relocating to Mars, under any circumstances," Leaf insisted. "How else will the residents learn to trust new leadership?"

Willow shook her head. "I daresay the community managed well enough with only Noble houses for leadership prior to the Second Phase. Nor do we know Hanley's reasons for setting up Fillion as he did." She touched Leaf's forearm and softened her voice. "You are exhausted, brother. Go before you fall asleep on your feet. The villagers shall understand."

In a graceful move, she pivoted toward Fillion, brows raised in challenge. Her eyes darted to the Harvest token draped over his belt, then back to his waiting gaze.

"I'll go with Skylar," he volunteered.

Willow spun on her heel and marched toward center stage. Leaf groaned in exasperation. His sister could be so infuriating at times. Why he allowed her to usurp his authority yet again, he knew not. He was about to chase after her when Alder lifted his head and rubbed his eyes through a yawn.

"Mother?" he murmured. Alder's gaze settled on Fillion before ducking back into the crook of Leaf's neck. "Want Mother."

"Yes, lad. I shall bring you home." Leaf sighed and reluctantly trudged down the steps. The Son of Eden squeezed by him toward Mack and Skylar. "Fillion," Leaf said, and grit his teeth. The Outsider paused, lifting an eyebrow. "I shall not put my sister in harm's way. Hanley—"

"New Eden!" his sister shouted above the roar of voices. "Quiet your hearts!"

Villagers in the front row turned to neighbors to pass back his sister's request over the undulating maelstrom of limbs and voices. Fillion angled to get a glance at the gathering, then swiveled attention back to Leaf.

"Do not trifle with her faithfulness or her honor," Leaf whispered in warning. "This very morning, I found her weeping over *you*."

Fillion's ashen features sickened further. Heartbeats passed in thick, crackling heat as their fury and fears remained locked in a whirling stream of silent debates and confessions. The Great Hall eventually hushed in anticipation of Willow's words. In that moment, Fillion lowered his eyes and turned away, cutting his way through the crowd until he reached Skylar, who leaned in when Fillion began whispering in his ear. Fillion then placed a gold ring in the Son of Wind's palm. Skylar stared at the ring a few heartbeats before nodding and gesturing toward the exit. Timna, Joannah, and a man holding Lady Emily moved toward the double doors, with Mack, Skylar, and his sisters close behind.

Leaf's stomach tightened. He could not imagine learning of his own father's death in such an insulting way. Despite grievances against Timothy, the community bowed their heads, many lifting hoods in mourning to honor the Kanes.

When the gathering focused on Willow once more, Leaf slipped out of the doors unnoticed. Gravel crunched beneath his feet. Orange light flickered from a slew of lanterns lining the path.

The walk home did little to ease his distress. If anything, each weary step gave leave for his fury to lay siege to his thoughts. Anger flashed in electrifying strikes. His heart thundered. This night, Hanley declared war on New Eden. And Leaf's family. The villagers stirred beneath the fear and outrage. But Leaf understood what was not said. Hanley was not truly offering the community a choice. As property of New Eden Biospherics & Research, the decision had already been made. His only consolation was that Fillion appeared sickened with disbelief.

Alder stirred as Leaf climbed the stairs leading to their home. The front door opened when Leaf ascended the final step and Connor stepped out, surprise written on his face when their eyes met.

"I was on my way to lend you my support, Your Majesty," Connor whispered across the night-shaded deck. "Hanley still at the Great Hall?"

"No, he and his guests left. Fillion demanded their exit."

"Good, though I fear it is too little too late."

"Indeed, My Lord."

Silence, sharp and heavy, stretched between them. The sound of leaves tousled by the night wind rushed in his ears. Leaf drew in a much-needed breath and laid his burdens before Connor's feet, reporting Fillion and Hanley's fight, Hanley's words to Skylar, the shock befalling Lady Emily, and Fillion's encouragement of Willow's temerity with Hanley. "My sister is now caring for the community."

"She shall do you proud." Connor's large hand rested on Leaf's shoulder. His distraught gaze then rested on Alder. "Here, let me take the lad."

A sleeping Alder easily rolled from Leaf's arm into Connor's warm embrace. Leaf settled the lantern onto the deck and then shook the weight from his arms, pushing out a slow, measured breath. "How is Coal?" he finally asked.

"Breathing fire," Connor whispered. "Presently he is with Ember. She has a way of soothing him."

Leaf nodded then buried his face into his hands and squeezed his eyes shut. Pain swelled at his temples and behind his eyes. What could he say to his brother-in-law? To Lynden? His head pounded with every beat of his heart. A dispirited sigh escaped Leaf's lips as his fingers dragged down his face before his arms fell back to his sides.

"I shall ready the lad for bed and then assist Willow in the Great Hall," Connor spoke softly. "My wife has left to attend another."

Connor's voice sounded as hollow as Leaf felt. The past few days had certainly carved a giant hole in his fortitude. A newborn's muffled cry swayed on the night breeze. His chest panged at the sound. Without another word, Leaf opened his apartment door and stepped into his candle-lit home.

Lynden's head snapped up from the corner. She quickly wiped at her eyes and masked any trace of emotion. Connor smiled at her kindly before walking past toward Alder's room. When they were alone, Leaf spoke.

"My Lady, I am grieved for how you have suffered this evening." He knelt by her chair and lowered his head. "Please name your honor price. I am entirely at your service."

"It's fine." She twisted a black ring around her thumb.

"No, My Lady, it is far from fine. I am ashamed for how you were disgraced before New Eden."

"Let it go. I'm used to it. But Coal..." Lynden peered up at the ceiling and blinked back the forming tears. "He didn't deserve his community's disgust because of me. I knew . . . told him once . . . never mind." She whipped her gaze to the window and nibbled on her lip piercing.

Leaf's heart sank. Gently, he took her hand and pressed the back to his forehead in honor. "You are family, My Lady. I shall make this right for you and Coal."

Her mouth parted with his words. A tear slipped past her defenses and rolled down her flushed cheek. Leaf cleared his throat and blinked back his shyness, releasing her hand as he rose.

"Care to join me? I wish to speak with Coal."

Lynden shook her head and resumed a meditative watch out the window.

Reluctantly, he turned away and stepped toward his bedchamber. In the hallway he could hear the low rumble of Coal's voice. Leaf knocked on his chamber door, quietly pushing the iron ring in until the door gave way and creaked open. "Am I intruding?"

"No, Your Majesty," Ember answered. "Please enter."

She beckoned him in with her free hand. Their youngest daughter rested upon her shoulder, swaddled tight in spare blankets. Coal sat beside her, holding the eldest in his arms, rocking her slowly. The Son of Fire refused to meet his eyes, clenching his jaw. The muscles in Coal's neck flexed and bulged, his arms knotted in fury despite the gentleness with which he held his wee niece.

"My Lord," Leaf began. "I ask your forgiveness. The handover speech discussed yesterday was entirely different from what Hanley presented."

"I do not fault you."

"Nevertheless, your honor with an unmarried woman was called into question before all. I am the one who allowed Hanley to speak before the community."

Coal's eyes flicked to his. "She is married, Your Majesty."

"I believe I misheard you." Leaf looked to Ember for explanation. But she busied herself with their youngest daughter. Astonished, he straightened his shoulders. "You have engaged in relations with a *married woman*?"

"She is my wife," Coal whispered. Leaf's eyes widened and his mouth slackened. "We wed in secret."

"Does your father know?"

"Besides Mack, you and Ember are the only others who know. The consequences are grave."

Leaf continued to stare in disbelief. "How grave?"

"Arrest and legal troubles for Lynden."

"Fillion does not know, then?"

"No. It would only cause him trouble."

"Dear Lord," Leaf sighed. "This is a right mess." He paced to the other end of the room and sagged against the wall. "I know not what to say."

"Do not judge me, Son of Earth."

"Coal Hansen," Leaf seethed. "You have always been impetuous and a bit foolhardy, but I fear you have never understood trouble as you may find yourself in one day because of your actions. And at what cost? Lynden shall suffer as shall your family, including Fillion, who is innocent."

"Nobody owns me." Fire flashed in Coal's dark eyes. "Not the lab, not New Eden, nor the petty laws of greedy men. Every revolution has a price. Both Lynden and I understood the cost. She is worth it. *I* am worth it. If Fillion is truly a man of honor and commendable strength, as Willow declared before all last night, then he will do what is right before *his* family."

Leaf's eldest daughter released a stuttered cry. Coal bowed his head and rocked her, his features softening as she fell back into a peaceful sleep. Then, with lips trembling, eyes glistening red, the Son of Fire lifted his head and whispered, "If you had known that you were property and of the cost associated with having children, would you have desired a family?" He paused. "And knowing now, do you regret the lives of your son and daughters? Or marrying my sister *in secret* on Exchange Day?"

Leaf held Coal's gaze, a terrible pain wending its way from his gut, tightening his throat. Coal had shared their cruel reality with Ember. He could not look upon his wife in shame.

"This," Coal whispered again, "is how I feel. Except Lynden could never carry my child, for the lab would take our babe for another to raise within New Eden. She would lose all maternal rights. Where is the justice?" Coal grit his teeth. "Where is the honor? Explain this to me, Your Majesty."

Leaf swallowed. "Do you believe tonight's exhibition is Hanley's punishment for your silent stand?"

"Of course." Coal focused on his niece. "Very little slips by his notice."

"Yet he does not prosecute you..." Leaf's eyes rounded as the blood rushed from his head. "Fillion," he whispered under his breath.

"Where is the Son of Eden?" Ember asked, raising an eyebrow at Leaf's change in behavior.

"Attending Skylar and his family." Leaf regarded his wife warily. "Timothy passed away yesterday. Cardiac arrest."

"*Merde*," Coal muttered.

The youngest daughter released a soft, quivering cry. "There, there, sweetling." Ember offered her finger for their daughter's pacification.

The room fell silent. There was nothing left to say. Leaf looked away from his wife and onto a wall sconce to focus his tumbling thoughts. A molten drip of fat slipped down a tallow candle. Leaf trailed the descent until the drip cooled and hardened. His stomach tightened at the sight. He could not say why, exactly. But he knew this: Coal's words burned, their truth a mighty fire that roared and consumed. The discomfort impossible to ignore.

"My Lord," Leaf began, pushing off the wall and stumbling toward his brother-in-law. "I am most sorry for my earlier judgment. Do you forgive me?" He held out his hand, which Coal shook without hesitation. Relieved, Leaf continued. "I stand with you and am prepared to fight."

"No matter the cost?"

Leaf eased onto the edge of his bed and caressed his daughter's cheek. "No matter the cost."

In recent months, the founder of Tesla, SpaceX, and OpenAI has repeatedly hinted at these ambitions, and then, earlier this week, The Wall Street Journal reported that Musk has now launched a company called Neuralink that aims to implant tiny electrodes in the brain "that may one day upload and download thoughts."…

Researchers could also develop genetic techniques to modify neurons so that machines can "read and write" to them from outside our bodies. Or they could develop nano-robots that we ingest into our bodies for the same purpose.

*— Wired, 2017 **

Chapter Twenty

Portland, Oregon
Monday, April 1, 2058

The mental infirmary's astringent smell burned Fillion's nose. Taking shallow breaths, he settled his attention on the wall over Mack's shoulder. Tiny, grinning faces appeared in the spackle, their smiles gruesome and cruel. The ceiling tiles were no different. Or the shadows cast from a large, waxy looking plant, looming in a corner of the waiting room. His mind was prone to matrixing, especially in a place where the shadows of the afflicted writhed with life.

Fillion pulled up a message screen and swiped a request for his mom to chat later. He had questions. A crumbling mountain of questions burying him alive. He was about to close up his screen when an auto-reply came through. Out of the office. Brows furrowed, he swiped a new message to her personal center then slashed the air to exit his holographic interface.

Mack jerked his head toward the door that separated the waiting room from the mental infirmary, a spooked look in his eyes. An undecipherable sound—more like a moan than a word—seeped through the walls again. A nanosecond later, Fillion's friend schooled his features to a bored expression as he repositioned himself in his chair.

Fillion understood. This place was creepy. The ghosts of the disturbed had beckoned him since they walked in. Calling to him. Whispering his name.

"Mr. Nichols?"

Fillion almost jumped out of his skin. He kept his cool, though his hands gripped the hem of his shirt. A woman in a white coat, with emerald-green hair, tapped an invisible screen while standing in the doorway that was, not even a second ago, closed.

"I'm Dr. Nelson. Right this way."

Fillion jerked a strand of hair out of his eyes and grabbed his messenger bag. He approached Dr. Nelson while conjuring up the Dungeon Master role, hoping he reflected nonchalant confidence. It made him sick to be so fake. But exuding a bored yet arrogant swagger was the only way he knew how to fill the cracks in his mind. Mental flaws that this place happily exposed and treated.

Mack walked close behind him, like he might embrace Fillion in fright or use him as a human shield. Fillion pushed back a nervous snicker. He'd never seen his friend so jittery before. And they'd seen a lot of freaky shit in the underground and while walking the city streets. So much for expecting Mack to visit when Fillion was finally committed.

Keeping his head down, Fillion followed the woman down a bleak hallway. The same hallway where he'd met the strange girl just a few days earlier. His eyes darted left then right, even though the hallway remained empty. Still, he heard her voice in his head. With clarity. Like it traveled through his Cranium.

Don't trust him.

What the hell? He kept his face devoid of any discernible emotion in case security cameras were watching him. In fact, he knew they were. Was Hanley playing a joke on him right now? Were people sitting in a room somewhere, laughing their asses off at his expense? Did Timothy join them?

Fillion wasn't convinced that the former Wind Element was actually dead. Did this Twist of Fate card point at this clue? Timothy came from a line of con artists and willingly participated in a psychological game. Whatever. Fillion's relatives wouldn't break him. Not today, at least. Still, the thought of Timothy roaming free put Fillion's animal instincts hyperalert. This was a perfect set-up for Hanley to gaslight. He could almost hear his dad's calm voice explaining that any Timothy sightings were all in Fillion's head.

Was he safe? Was his sister?

Dr. Nelson slowed before a door and gestured for Fillion and Mack to enter. The room was as sterile as the hallway with the type of organization exhibited by someone with OCD: monochromatic furniture and framed photos in straight lines, intersecting at right angles, equally spaced. Fillion enjoyed the tint and shade spectrum and the clean lines, feeling a sense of semblance and order. It was probably a test and he just failed. Miserably. He looked around for the one line that was slightly askew. The kind that over-thinkers like him would fixate on and mentally ramble about until they couldn't take it anymore and snapped. After a quick appraisal, his pattern-seeking gaze didn't discern any unwanted angles. And, probably because he was a special kind of mental, not finding a flaw when he was expecting one bothered him even more.

However, across the room from the desk, a brittle plant hung from the ceiling. Its rust-brown, spear-like leaves clawed the air in tangled chaos. The dead vegetal matter was so random and obnoxious, that it was easy to forgive its disorderly state, for it was equally as unnatural as the geometric, colorless environment that housed it. Mack noticed the same plant compared to the rest of the space, and his eyes widened a notch before relaxing to his usual unimpressed expression as his gaze cut back to the desk. Fillion followed his stare.

A dark bronze urn, the same color as the dead plant, took up the corner of the woman's desk and the hair rose on the back of Fillion's neck. How did he know this was Timothy? He hadn't identified the corpse. In Fillion's estimation, as his property or with Timothy under contract with the lab, his uncle's body should have been returned to N.E.T. Was the speed at which the body was handled normal procedure in a mental facility like this one? He didn't know and didn't trust any explanation he'd be given during his visit.

The walls are listening. They have ears.

The voice spoke in his head again and, this time, Fillion flinched. Neither Mack nor Dr. Nelson noticed. But did the cameras? He needed a distraction. Stat. Fiddling with his Cranium, like he was re-securing it to his ear, Fillion turned on his device. A privacy screen wavered in his vision. He needed to load a spectrum analyzer to see if any signals matched the unique frequency that could manipulate the bone conductor in his Cranium. But he didn't want to attract attention. Fillion glanced at his friend.

"Please, take a seat," Dr. Nelson said, pulling him from his thoughts. "I won't take much of your time. I know you're a busy man, especially this week. A few forms need in-person signatures, and you're listed as the responsible party for Mr. Kane's arrangements."

Fillion eased into a chair, angling away from Mack. While Dr. Nelson shuffled paperwork, Fillion launched the spectrum analyzer app. Data began streaming upward. Keeping his voice neutral, he asked, "How long had Timothy been dead before he was discovered?"

"The biometric readout confirmed the body had been deceased for around seven hours."

Don't trust him.

Good. She spoke to him again. Like she knew what he was doing. Maybe she did. His app began analyzing the signal.

"What caused the cardiac arrest?" he asked.

She stared at him for several seconds, then cocked her head to the side. "Are you implying that Mr. Kane died of unnatural causes?"

"No implications. Just questions." Fillion leaned back in his chair and crossed a leg over his knee. His screen highlighted a source, the name and account details encrypted. Access to messaging, however, remained open. Interesting. Pretending to pick off a piece of lint from his sleeve, he asked, "Your residents have biometric sensor implants for health monitoring? Or do you use external sensors for checkups and postmortem diagnosis?"

"Mr. Nichols, here is the first form that requires your signature." She slid a document over her desk and offered a pen. "Take your time reading the fine print."

Fillion took the single sheet of paper and handed it to Mack. "While he reads it over, I'd like you to prepare another document releasing all of Timothy's medical and mental health records over to me."

"Mr. Nichols—"

"It's Fillion, and either do so now or after my lawyer speaks with you. Your choice."

"I didn't realize you were an investigator, Mr. Nichols." A tiny flicker of a smile began to form, cold and taunting.

He replied with a similar smile. "I'm many things, Dr. Nelson, most of which you don't want to deal with. Trust me." His smile disappeared. "Now, the medical and mental health release forms?"

"Of course." She heaved a big sigh, like his request was a terrible burden. Tapping the air again, her faced hardened to an unreadable expression.

Fillion brought up a message screen. Mack remained engrossed in the form and didn't notice.

<u>FNichols</u>: Don't trust who?

<u>Unknown</u>: The Gamemaster. You blocked him. Wrong move.

<u>Fillion</u> held his breath.

<u>Unknown</u>: He knows you're here. /comm

"There." Dr. Nelson gave a final tap. "The forms should be delivered soon. Anything else?"

Fillion faced Mack and lifted his eyebrow, trying to act cool. But, god, his heart was in his throat. His friend handed Fillion the form. "It checks out. Appears standard."

"Is this your lawyer?" Dr. Nelson asked.

Mack openly laughed. Fillion tapped off his Cranium and smirked to play along. "Sure." Taking a pen, he skimmed over the document and then signed at the flagged line, mumbling, "He's many things, too."

"More things than you," Mack deadpanned.

Fillion slid a sly, humored look his way, then faced Dr. Nelson. "He teaches women's studies when he's not working for me."

"It's a very important job," Mack added with an official looking nod. "So many women fail to understand their potential. I help them unlock this secret so that they, too, can climax in life."

Fillion bit the inside of his cheek and pretended to peruse the document one last time.

"But," Mack drawled out slowly, "Mr. Nichols retains me as a professional negotiator and to consult on business operations. Isn't this right, Mr. Nichols?"

"Right."

Smart-ass.

"Many things…" Mack winked at Fillion with exaggeration.

Dr. Nelson eyed Mack with cool curiosity. "I don't think I caught your name."

Mack sniffed and leaned back in his chair, stretching out his legs. He draped an arm across the back of Fillion's chair. "What's the next form requiring Mr. Nichols' signature?"

She stiffened while shuffling the papers on her desk to hide the flush warming her face. Fillion hid a smile. Mack played her at her own game.

The next twenty minutes, they continued in this cycle. Mack first read the document while Dr. Nelson verbally explained the form to Fillion. A woman from the front desk eventually slipped in to pass off the medical and mental health record release forms.

Once all the documents were signed, Dr. Nelson asked, "Any questions before I see you out?"

Fillion hesitated for a sec. Hanley knew he was here. What if his next request resulted in another death? He blew out a slow breath. Not his fault. None of this was his fault. He blinked black the rising panic. But it was pointless. From the corner of his eye, he looked at Mack, who gave a faint nod in response.

To win. To destroy.

"Yes, actually." Fillion leaned forward in his chair. "Please set up a visit today with Ms. Andra Black."

"Who?"

"Property of New Eden Biospherics & Research. She was committed here four years ago."

"Mr. Nichols—"

"No games." Fillion dropped his voice to a threatening whisper. "I have all the documentation. I know she exists, and I know what she is, and I know who created her."

"Your documentation is incorrect, I'm afraid." Dr. Nelson looked at him and then Mack, before returning to her screen. "There are no patients here by that name."

"Prove it."

Dr. Nelson chuckled and rose from her chair. "Thanks for coming by, and don't forget the urn. All documents are now signed. Please give your mother my regards." She turned and reached for the door.

"How much is he paying you?"

"Excuse me?" She whipped his direction. "Don't insult me—"

"I'll double it."

She released the door handle.

Fillion lifted a smug grin. He walked over to where she stood, each step smooth and seductive. Slowly, he lifted his eyes to hers, as if taking in her measure. "Let's get something straight. *I own* New Eden Biospherics & Research. Everything. Including classified operations." He leaned forward until he was a breath away from her body, trapping her by the door. "I'll double what he offered you," he whispered in her ear. "Just this once. For your silence. But after that?" He hovered a couple seconds and let the question hang between them. Listening to her quick breaths as they pulsed against his skin. Then, he pushed away to meet her eyes. "You'll follow the law or I'll expose you."

"Won't that expose you, too?" She inclined her head in challenge, though she was clearly flustered. "Money is traceable."

Fillion dipped his gaze to her mouth and bit his bottom lip, then grinned. "I already know what jail is like. But he doesn't and neither do *you*. And, unlike you, I could probably buy my innocence. So could he." Her mouth fell open with the first sign of true understanding since he'd walked in this room. Spinning on his heel, he gracefully walked back toward Mack. Over his shoulder, he said, "No games. Don't fuck with me and I won't fuck with you."

"Fine." She smoothed out her white lab coat, her cheeks tinged pink. "I'll arrange for visitation. Wait here."

A few minutes later, four armed aides escorted their small party down the same hallway to a metal door. Dr. Nelson used a biometric scanner for entry and ushered them into the maximum-security ward. Another hallway opened up, reminiscent of dorm cells from juvenile detention. Dark, splattered stains spotted the concrete here and there. Sterile, cement block walls framed the narrow passageway. A light overhead flickered, and Fillion narrowed his eyes. The ceiling lamps used carbon nanotube bulbs, unlike the LED variety found in the rest of the facility. Was the wiring shorting out?

"We had a power surge the other day," Dr. Nelson said, following his gaze. "Custodians have yet to fix this wing. The lighting in maximum security is on battery backup still."

"Transformer blowout?" From his vantage, Fillion could see another faint flicker at the opposite end of the long hallway. The older woman simply smiled, grim and haunting. Without another word, she marched forward with a gesture to follow.

Moans could be heard behind cement walls. Bruised fingers pressed into slotted windows from behind cell doors. An occasional pair of eyes tracked their movements, too. Mack jumped into Fillion when a metal door thunderously rattled as they strode by. A body slammed into it again with a roaring scream, shouting, "I hear you!" over and over again. Dr. Nelson continued walking, unfazed.

"This is her dorm." Dr. Nelson stepped back as the two aides lifted EMP guns. One of them also carried a syringe, and the other a low-res sonic disruptor.

The slotted window to peer into her cell was black. She didn't have light? With bionic eyes, she probably didn't need it anyway.

The head psychiatrist pushed an intercom button and spoke. "Andra, this is Dr. Nelson. Lay on the bed, face toward the ceiling. We are entering and armed. Please be advised that we have EMP guns and will not hesitate to kill you."

"Not necessary," Mack said when she released the button. "I have a Rec-Mode switch and will force hibernation if necessary."

Dr. Nelson lifted a corner of her mouth. "Malfunctioning human cybernetic systems produce aggressive and unpredictable behavior. She's smarter and stronger than all of us combined."

"I don't argue with computer chips," Mack tossed back.

"You can't control transhumans."

"*You* can't. *I* can. Step aside. I'll go in first." He looked at the aides. "Alone."

"I'm sorry, I can't assume the liability."

"I didn't ask your permission." Mack pushed the intercom button. "Andra, this is Mack Ferguson, director of operations and robotics specialist from TalBOT Industries and unofficial VP of New Eden Biospherics & Research. I'm about to enter. I won't harm you, promise. But Dr. Nelson and her minions will if you attack. May I enter? Tap the wall once for no and twice for yes."

"Mr. Ferguson, you're not in charge and—"

"Shhh…"

Everyone quieted. Fillion moved out of the way for Mack, who leaned his ear to the wall. Two knocks rapped loud and clear in the hallway. "Open the door," he said to Dr. Nelson.

"I can hear you!" A loud bang rattled from down the hallway. And another. The guttural screech of the man's cries faded into walls. "I can hear you!"

"As I've said," Dr. Nelson practically sang out, "I will *not* assume liability."

Mack stared at the cell containing the delusional man and blinked when another round of hysterics started up again. To the others, he probably appeared bored, perhaps even inconvenienced by the demented. But Fillion could see Mack pumping calm into his system with each quiet intake of breath, as if the spores of self-control were airborne. Hell, maybe they were. Fillion forced himself to breathe, too. He was about to lose his shit.

Everyone loses in this game.

The card in his pocket seemed to whisper these words. Taunting him to keep making more pathetic moves. Laughing at his attempts to appear confident. Fate had a twisted sense of humor. But he was tired of being the butt of every joke.

"Now," Fillion practically barked, growing impatient.

Nonplussed, Dr. Nelson turned on her Cranium. "I would like video consent from both of you that New Eden Biospherics & Research and TalBOT Industries will hold Lewis Psychiatric Hospital harmless."

"New Eden Biospherics & Research will not find fault with Lewis Psychiatric Hospital in the event of injury or loss of life while interacting on Friday, March 29, 2058 with Andra Black, resident…?"

"564118953."

"Resident 564118953," Fillion finished and looked to Mack.

"What he said. Add TalBOT Industries to his statement."

Satisfied, she stepped forward. Entry required three steps: retina verification, thumbprint reading, and a key loaded into Dr. Nelson's Cranium. A sharp hiss filled the hallway as the pneumatics depressurized, releasing the lock.

Mack grabbed the handle and disappeared into the room without a backwards glance. The nanotube filaments flickered and winked out as the door shut behind him, plunging the hallway in darkness. No sound traveled out of the sealed room. But the hysterics continued a few cells down. Fillion did his best to ignore the man. And his warning.

A few minutes passed. Fillion's heart galloped in his chest. An aide muffled a cough. Dr. Nelson exhaled loud and dramatic. She moved to cross her arms over her chest when a dim light burst through the slit. Her arms fell back to her side. Mack's face appeared in the window. He locked onto Fillion and beckoned him to come inside.

Dr. Nelson peeked into the room and then pushed the intercom button. "Andra, lay down on the bed again, face up. Mr. Nichols is entering."

A few seconds later, he stepped into a slice of light. The flashlight setting on Mack's Cranium revealed grooved etchings on the walls and ceiling. Most were shallow depressions of nightmarish beasts and otherworldly settings. Impressed, Fillion tapped on his flashlight controls and then trailed his fingers over the concrete blocks. The ceiling appeared to be a perfect replica of the winter night sky in the Northern hemisphere. The Hunter, Orion, stretched from one corner of the small room to the other. Rigel, Betelgeuse, Belatrix, Saiph, Alnitak, Alnilam, and Mintaka—each star in Orion's constellation was accounted for and carved into the stone with precise alignment.

Fillion blew the dust off his fingers and focused on the bed. Short, shaggy brown hair glinted in the low light, belonging to a figure in a supine position. Fillion's shoulders slumped, his jaw releasing its clench. He wasn't crazy. Their incident in the hallway had really happened.

His gaze traveled down the length of her thin body, noting the braless curve of her breasts beneath the standard issue white T-shirt and a full tattooed sleeve on one arm of a sword ablaze in swirling tendrils of fire. Her hands were dirty with ragged, chipped fingernails and blood scabbed tips, and a large purple bruise sprawled across her right foot.

"Why are you he-here?" Her voice glitched on the last word.

"You know why," Fillion answered quietly. "Your foot, fingers—are they in pain?"

"I am pain." Andra's head swiveled his direction, her movements unnaturally slow and smooth. Lights swam inside her blue-green eyes.

Mack crouched on the floor beside Andra. "Like I said earlier, we won't hurt you. Promise."

"You can't hurt me."

His friend's smile fell. Moving a tad closer, still in a crouched position, he whispered, "What have they done to you?"

Andra's gaze snapped to Mack's fingers as he crept toward where she lay. He lifted both hands to show that he was unarmed, his body perfectly still.

"Let me help you." He lowered one hand to the floor for balance. "Do your cybernetics have inner sanctum controls?"

"I'm a puppet on a string."

"Have you tried to download one yourself?"

"Pinocchio safeguards are encrypted into my cybernetics."

Fillion wanted to vomit.

"Want one?" Mack crept forward again.

"In exchange for what, Mackenzie Patton Campbell Ferguson the

Third?"

"Nothing. But we have questions and you have answers."

"I already de-delivered my message."

"The offer still stands," Mack spoke softly. She didn't reply. "I can also repair your vocal glitch. Sounds recent. Pronunciation hasn't degenerated yet. Simple software patch." Mack moved another breath closer. "Any nerve pain?"

"Why do you care?"

"Because I'm a nice guy." Mack winked. He looked at Fillion. "But him? A complete pain in the ass."

Her gaze swung back to Fillion. "The walls kn-know you're here, Fillion Malcolm Nichols."

"Let's outfit you with inner sanctum controls. Make it harder for the walls to listen in." Fillion studied the cell blocks again. "Where's the spy glass in this room?"

Andra pointed to a corner opposite from her bed. "I already looped the feed." Static softened her voice, similar to when she spoke to him earlier this week. He realized this was her whisper, loud enough to fully hear nearby, but too scratchy for those in the background to make out.

"Anything else we should know before Mack begins?" he asked.

"The Gamemaster knows what you're doing."

Fillion's throat tightened. "Good."

"Come closer."

"No."

A slow, animatronic smile formed on her face. "Afraid of me?"

"Terrified."

"He won't kill me."

"What?" Every nerve winced to attention.

"You're afraid he'll kill me if we talk. No. Not me." She paused for a nano-second. Her body flushed, as if ashamed. "You're afraid The Gamemaster will issue kill orders again." Shame dissolved and fear stuttered across her face. The reaction seemed mechanical, too pronounced. She sat up within a blink and slammed against the wall, making herself as small as possible. A whimper es-caped her lips. But her eyes, they remained riveted onto Fillion, back-lit with blue, her pupils dilating. Then, with a voice that was eerily devoid of any emo-tion or fluctuation, she asked, "Did I read your m-mind correctly, Son of Eden?"

Blood rushed from his head. How the hell did she translate conscious thought from his bioelectricity? Digital telepathy had been around for decades. Proper tech stimulating the visual cortex could send and receive messages through the Net. She obviously had a brain-computer interfacing implant; she had already communicated to his Cranium. But telepathy from conscious thought? Impossible.

Nevertheless, Fillion pulled the Cranium off his head and placed it on the floor by his feet. The flashlight sprayed across her bed, illuminating an image of a scaled beast with blood dripping from its claws. Blood, he realized, that was her own. He lifted his shoulders a notch and looped his thumb into his pocket, angling his face away.

"With inner sanctum controls," she spoke to Mack, her modulated voice resuming as before, "I can block *all* incoming messages?"

"That's the idea," he answered cautiously. "You can be selective, too."

"Auto recordings?"

"Ah." Mack placed a hand on the edge of her bed and whispered, "That's an audio-visual problem. But similar fix. I have a software cocktail your cybernetics will slurp up."

"You have interesting asymmetrical features. But your left eye is a quarter shade darker than your right eye."

Mack smiled. "Most say my lips are my best facial feature."

"May I feel your face?"

"Plan on snapping my neck?"

"And Fillion's."

His smile widened. "Then go ahead, *bijin*."

Fillion shot his friend a wide-eyed warning.

"Beautiful woman? . . . Your compliment is-is verified." A shy smile flitted across her lips, the most synced, human reaction Fillion had noted yet. Mack's face remained bland, but he saw his friend's lip twitch. Her eyes rounded and glowed bright. "Really?"

"Girl Scout's honor." Mack's gaze slipped to Fillion as he theatrically whispered, "I'm having impure thoughts."

Fillion cracked a shaky smile in reply just as a flash of light shot toward Mack from the bed. His friend's quiet chuckle turned into a sharp intake of breath. A grunt punctured the silence as a body hit the floor. Fillion startled back a step, blinking away the black spots in his vision. How had she blinded them?

"Mack?!" Fillion called out, taking another step back. His gaze jumped around the room frantically until his vision cleared.

Mack lay flat on his back beside the bolted down bed. Andra straddled his hips, pinning down his arms, bearing her teeth in a predatory snarl. Fillion backpedaled to the far corner. Maybe he should have charged for the door. Called in the aides to tranquilize her. Something. Instead, he slipped a hand into his pocket and scraped around for his personal EMP switch. He didn't want to kill her. But he would and without a second thought.

"I-I don't want to do this," she confessed to Mack. Expressions flitted across her face with every racing beat of Fillion's heart. Sad. Happy. Angry. Eyes lighting up. Going dim. Showing teeth in a wide grin, before snapping at his friend. She dragged in a heavy breath and pleaded in a sliding pitch, "Make it s-stop. Make him sto—"

Before she could finish the last word, the light winked out behind her eyes. Her body collapsed onto Mack's in a graceful fall. "Goodnight, *robotto hime*," Mack whispered. They remained still for what seemed like an eternity, sucking in air, trying to convince their hearts to calm. Eventually, Mack craned his neck to peer at Fillion and uncurled his fingers. The RecMode switch. "Distracted her with one hand while slowly moving forward."

Fillion shook his head in relief. "Scared the shit out of me. What the hell happened to her?"

"Malfunctioning."

"I got that."

"Something fried part of her cybernetics, methinks. Maybe related to the power surge issue."

"You think she caused it?"

"Dunno."

Fillion crouched next to Mack. "Here, let me help." He scooped her up—shocked by her heavier-than-should-be weight—and placed her on the bed. "Still planning to install an inner sanctum?"

"Hell yeah. And bio-hack." Mack wiggled his eyebrows. "Firewall installation was just a cover, *desu*."

"We need a warrant first."

"Knew you'd freak out." Mack sat on the edge of the bed and turned Andra's head and ran a fingertip over her cervical vertebrae. "She's your property. New Eden tech. Registered MAC address to prove it." He picked at something with the tip of his nail until a flesh-like flap opened. "You're just inspecting your investment. Upgrading software. Fixing outdated parts. Blah, blah, blah. Hey, bring over my bag."

Fillion placed Mack's messenger bag onto the bed. She looked so human while hibernating. Gently, Fillion lifted her hand up and inspected each blood-crusted fingertip. Had she engraved the walls with her own nails? Of course she had, he realized with growing horror. They wouldn't trust her with a chisel and hammer. Grieved, he lay her hand back across her chest and then reached out with two fingers and closed her eyes.

"Bio-hacking," he muttered under his breath. Turning to Mack he asked, "Making a mirror file?"

"Yup. We'll digest the info later." His friend dug around the bag until he pulled out cables, connecting his device to Andra's hidden port. "Mirror, mirror on the wall," Mack chanted, "who's the sexiest of them all?" His Cranium dinged with the sudden connection and Mack slid a flirtatious look to Fillion. "It's me."

"Yeah, your robot seduction skills are impressive."

"They can't resist me."

Fillion allowed a genuine smile to form. "If only you had skills with fully human girls. Pathetic."

"Pathetic like you?"

"I have skills. I just choose self-control."

"Keep telling yourself that, pretty boy. Your vows of celibacy are eating you alive from the inside out."

Fillion lifted his shoulder in a near indiscernible shrug, smile still in place.

"Speaking of girls," Mack murmured, his fingers brushing and tapping the air. "I heard a rumor about you and Akiko."

"Mack," Fillion began, and paused with the rising panic. Images of Willow in the stasis chamber, the sound of her raw scream, strobed his mind.

"What would you do if a girl you thought was dead suddenly came back from the grave?"

His friend smiled with the familiar question. "Is she cute or creepy looking?"

"Beautiful," he whispered. "Strong and fearless, too."

Mack grabbed his Cranium and turned his head to face Fillion, the whites of his eyes large in the artificial light. "I'd finally grow a pair of balls and break contract with the witch. Damn the consequences. End my vows of celibacy and make zombie girl never want to die again except for when I touch her."

"Yeah. All that." Fillion walked away to gather himself. Closing his eyes, he took in a deep breath and exhaled slowly through clenched teeth. "I blocked all comm with Hanley and Akiko, too."

"You grew a large pair."

He didn't reply. There was nothing left to say on the subject. Mack knew him well.

Minutes continued to stretch. Fillion walked around the room and studied each picture on the wall. The beasts fascinated him. He peered up at Orion. Did she feel hunted? Or was she the hunter? And who or what were the beasts in her life? He had ideas, but he didn't know her past. What drives a person to sell their living body to science on the black market? Was she *that* desperate for money?

"Almost done," Mack said. "There." He looked up at Fillion. "Inner sanctum installed. Fixed her vocal glitch. And I snapped the strings connecting her to Hanley. She can be a real girl now."

"Hero of the people."

"Damn straight."

"Let's go. I need a cigarette."

Mack threw his cables in his bag and strode toward the door. "Ready?"

Fillion glanced at Andra, his eyebrows pushing together. "Should I relocate her to the lab?"

"Let's review her files first."

He nodded and opened the door, slipping into the hallway, Mack close behind him. Dr. Nelson rose from a folding chair that wasn't there before. The aides shifted on their feet, darting glances to the cell door as it closed.

"Recovery mode will last for another thirty minutes or so, then she'll reboot," Mack said. "We've completed our annual inspection and installed software patches. She shouldn't malfunction anymore. Expect sporadic check-ups in the future."

"With more warning. I need at least a week's notice."

Mack grinned. "Nah. You did fine today." He turned toward the exit. "Mr. Nichols, be sure to send Dr. Nelson a gold star sticker for over-performing despite her underwhelming lack of confidence."

"Quite the jester, aren't you Mr. Ferguson?"

Fillion's heart stopped. But, somehow, he kept moving forward. Mack's banter warbled in Fillion's muffled thoughts. He touched the card in his pocket and considered his friend in his peripheral. Was Mack part of the clue? Twice now Mack had hid information from him. First Pinkie's identity and then his intentions to bio-hack Andra.

Pinkie.

What were her parting words to Fillion at The Crypt? Something about talking the night away?

He shot a sharp glance to his friend. Mack raised his eyebrows in question but remained silent. Fillion shook his head and focused on taking steps. On breathing. On getting Timothy's ashes and leaving this mental house of mirrors. Tiny faces grinned at him from the textured walls. A door rumbled as they passed by.

"I can hear you!"

Nanoparticles and nanotechnology is a sort of term reserved for very small particles. ... Millions of them fit within a grain of sand. And our idea was to functionalize these nanoparticles, to make them do what we want. ... Essentially the idea is simple. You just swallow a pill with nanoparticles, and they're decorated with antibodies or molecules that detect other molecules. They course through your body. And because the core of these particles are magnetic, you can call them somewhere ... and you can ask them what they saw. The analogy in medicine is: Imagine you want to explore Parisian culture, and you do it by flying a helicopter over Paris once a year. That's what doctors do now. And what we're hoping to do is, these little particles go out and mingle with the people, we call them back to one place and, we ask them, hey, what did you see? Did you find cancer? Did you see something that looks like a fragile plaque for a heart attack? Did you see too much sodium? What did you see?

— Andrew Conrad, head of Life Sciences for Google X, 2014 *

Chapter Twenty-One

New Eden Township, Salton Sea, California

Wednesday, April 3, 2058

Fillion jolted awake. He wasn't sure exactly when he had fallen asleep at the desk. Or what triggered his return to consciousness. But the light through the window mocked his disorientation. The last he remembered, everything was dark. The holographic screen provided the only source of illumination as he reviewed old files and research notes, trying to catch up on business and familiarize himself with operations. He covered a yawn and peered around his office at N.E.T.

Paperwork spread across the large, ebony wood desk, a gift from his sister for his birthday. A few documents and file folders lay on the floor by his feet. His Cranium had fallen off in his sleep and hovered above a partially opened drawer. A pen was tucked behind his ear, where his Cranium had once been. The twilight of his mind registered all of these objects but failed to make sense of them. Whatever.

He was reaching for his pack of cigarettes when the window rattled. Fillion's eyes darted to the scene outside. The large olive tree bent in a gust that skipped through the permaculture forest garden. Nothing more. His mind, like usual, was playing tricks on him. Blinking back the sleepiness, he started to look away when a figure materialized outside the window. Fillion froze in his chair, eyes wide, disbelieving. The man's sandy brown hair ruffled in the wind. His smirk widened in satisfaction. The standard-issue white T-shirt from the mental infirmary pressed against his body with another gust.

At the opposite end of the room, a knock sounded followed by a groaning creak. Fillion whipped toward his office door as it opened. Michael popped his head in, cheerful as usual.

"Mr. Nichols, have a minute?"

Fillion snapped his gaze back to the window. Timothy was gone. What the… He cut off his mental expletives mid-sentence. He'd clearly imagined the whole interaction. Spooked nonetheless, he gestured to a chair and ran a trembling hand through his disheveled hair. The documents on the floor caught his eye. He bent over to retrieve them, shuffling them into the mess taking over his desk, hoping the fidgeting hid his shaking.

"Sleep here all night?" Michael asked him.

"Unintentionally."

"It happens."

"What do you need?" Fillion fell back in his chair and raised an eyebrow.

"We've been monitoring Ember Watson's health this past week and—"

"Wait." Fillion leaned forward on his desk, crossing his arms over the piles of paperwork. "Monitoring?"

"Yes."

"Postpartum visits from scientists at the lab?"

"No." Michael cleared his throat and tapped the air. "Sending you the health report. Sorry. Thought it had already been sent to you."

Fillion tapped his ear then remembered the pen. Rolling his eyes, he tossed the pen onto his desk and retrieved his Cranium. A few seconds later he peered at a spreadsheet. A column of real-time stats fluctuated every so often. He filtered to isolate data from March twenty-seventh to the present. Her red blood cell count had dipped considerably post-delivery, dipping even further within two days of the twins' births. Then, strangely, the numbers began to climb again, and at a rate that didn't seem natural. At least, to Fillion's limited medical knowledge it didn't seem accurate.

"Is the bio-stat algorithm corrupted?" he asked Michael, leveling a gaze over his screen.

"No, no the numbers are all correct."

"How do you know? Did you draw blood to compare hemoglobin lab results?"

Michael smiled. "Not necessary. The lab perfected the nanotech years before. It's self-correcting."

Fillion stilled. Nanotech? "What the hell are you talking about?"

"Are you OK?" Michael shifted forward in his chair. "You seem a bit green."

"What nanotech?"

"OK. Well, the biotech was developed fifteen years ago in the lab for civilian space travel and interplanetary homesteading. The nanobots bind with sublingual DNA-based vaccinations and are released in the bloodstream and then multiply within the subject's bone marrow as needed."

"To replace medics?"

"Yes, exactly!" Michael beamed. "Sharp like your old man."

Fillion ignored Michael's comment. He flicked his lighter, then puffed on his cigarette. His heart was ready to pound out of his chest. Despite his grogginess, his mind began analyzing the info in rapid fire. "So," he said, smoke curling from his lips, "this nanotech begins the transhuman process?"

"You don't miss much do you, Mr. Nichols? N.E.T. has created a revolutionary portless cybernetic system."

"The cybernetics," he began, his throat tightening, "do they adhere to the brain at all? Digital telepathy capabilities?"

Michael brushed his finger across the air in front of his face. "Sending you another doc. My apologies again. I guess we're still transitioning to new ownership. So, the short answer: Various nanobots within the binding are assigned to assist specific organs and biochemistry. Though the self-correcting aspect allows them to change assignments as needed. One assignment is an ultra-fine mesh designed to form over various parts of the brain, similar to the idea of neural lace."

"Does the cerebral mesh have built-in firewalls?"

"Yes, with Pinocchio safeguards so individuals can't hack to mod or destroy themselves." Michael smiled. "We wouldn't want humans wandering around with superhero capabilities, right? Or commit suicide and make it look like our product is malfunctioning."

"Holy shit." Fillion flicked his cigarette's ashes and then closed his eyes as his stomach rolled with nausea. "New Eden is inoculated?"

"Yes, two months after your arrest. The Techsmith Guild folks were inoculated as children. We . . . tested the final product on them . . . uploading small amounts of engineering and tech knowledge to their brains while they slept."

Fillion's eyes bugged out. He couldn't help it. Perhaps this would explain Ember's strange intuitive abilities. Did they upload info to her about the residents or future plot designs? Did she really love Leaf? Or was she conditioned by thought control to prefer him above all other males in New Eden? He was about to reply when Michael continued.

"The mother-child mortality rate has decreased notably. Not as many hemorrhaging incidents that result in death. Postpartum infections heal without medicine in most cases, too. Also, a high percentage of newborns make it past the seven-day black period."

"Was the first gen inoculated?"

"No, only the second and third gens have biotech."

"MAC addresses assigned per registered DNA?"

"Actually, instead of MAC addresses, we certified and patented a human DNA device marker with the government."

"Unlike the transhumans from the MELISSA Project."

Michael hesitated. "Yes. They were—"

"Wiped out."

"What?" Michael leaned back in his chair, his Adam's apple bobbing. "They were destroyed? I thought—"

"Their DNA was wiped out. Unregistered. To become untraceable."

"Oh that..." Michael exhaled slowly in relief. "Yes. It was necessary. The experiments were classified."

"By the government?"

"Military, actually. Needed to protect our human experiments from bio-hackers and activists. But, most importantly, from other governments turning our cybernetics against us and creating insurgents."

Fillion rubbed his temples, eyes cinched shut. Puzzle pieces were snapping into place and the image was more horrifying than he had previously imagined. Hanley had created the ultimate control group to test his cybernetic product on as well as to make advancements in transgenerational epigenetics. And the perfect seed colony for New Eden Mars-side.

Did Connor fully understand this?

Probably not. He was spoon-fed ideas that aligned with his own personal beliefs and convictions, just like everyone else inside New Eden. Connor genuinely loved his children. Fillion swallowed against the pang in his chest and refocused his mental energy.

What did this have to Joel Watson's money? Hanley was the richest man on Earth, and not just on paper. Or so Fillion thought. Hanley was a master illusionist, though. Did the funds have to do with project shutdown? To launch his new business?

Fillion placed the cigarette in his mouth and asked, between drags, "I need a comprehensive financial report since project inception."

"That'll take a while. I'll send your request to accounting right now."

"Thanks. Oh, and is Dr. Nichols aware of the inoculations?"

"I, uh . . . I assume so. She's never participated in any company meetings on the project though."

Fillion stared at the ceiling and exhaled smoke, a million thoughts uploading to his brain at once.

"Anything else, Mr. Nichols?"

"No."

Michael rose from the chair. "Well, if you need anything, you know where to find me."

"Appreciate it." Fillion rose and walked to his office door and opened it for Michael.

"By the way, congratulations. The news reached the lab a half-hour ago. It's all over the Net."

Fillion shut the door and stepped toward Michael, lowering his voice. "News?"

The small, wiry man paled. "Your partnership with New Eden Space Ventures." Michael placed a supportive hand on Fillion's arm. "I'll call medical. You really do look sick."

"Just give me a moment."

Fillion forced himself to take a breath. Then another. He stumbled toward his desk and slumped into his chair. He'd check the news, but not with Michael watching. His self-control was wobbling dangerously on his mental triggers. He could feel the panic leaching into his bloodstream.

This was the secret company rumored for years. How the hell did he partner with Hanley? It wasn't in any of the transfer of power and inheritance paperwork signed with each respective lawyer. And Fillion's lawyer didn't know anything about an unsigned doc. His attorney had verified everything with John and had received a copy of the paperwork already signed—nothing missing, nothing added. Fillion's mind really was slipping, and it was getting worse.

"Can I do anything for you, Mr. Nichols?"

"The ashes from Lewis Psychiatric Hospital—"

"Oh!" Michael strode back to the seat opposite Fillion and tapped his Cranium. "Forensics sent a report early this morning. Sending it to you now." He looked up over his screen. "The DNA sample checked out. Timothy Kane."

Fillion slumped further in relief. "Thanks."

"No prob." Michael stood and began walking to the door, then paused. "Still going to the New Life Ceremony today?"

"Oh shit!" Fillion rubbed out his cigarette and shot to his feet. "When is it?"

"Two hours."

"I owe you," he tossed over his shoulder as he darted out of his office.

In a few short minutes, Fillion entered his quarters and turned on the shower. He sent a quick note to Mack requesting a private on-site meeting, followed by a similar message to his mom, then undressed. The hot water splashed on his face, down his shoulders and body. A part of him wanted to scrub until his skin bled, to try and remove the filth of what Hanley had done to hundreds of people against their will.

Did Joel learn of this plan somehow? Was Claire set up as Aether to punish Timothy? Or as a way for Hanley to control him? Dangling the office of Aether out there as reward? Like, secure Joel Watson's funds and remove him from game play, and then Skylar will be Aether? Knowing Hanley, he probably convinced Timothy that ownership was always meant to remain in the family—granting the Kanes certain amenities to secure Timothy's trust—but that, in the meantime, placing the Watsons in the Legacy was a necessary game move. One that would benefit the Nichols and Kane families in the end.

Why was that sum of money so damn important?

Or was it just a distraction? A meaningless plot point to motivate Timothy and nothing more? To make Fillion and Leaf feel like they had some semblance of control and leverage for negotiations?

Maybe Hanley's plan all along was to slowly kill off his inner circle of friends. As simple as that. No other reasons or clues or game moves.

Fillion choked back the rising bile and turned off the water. Rosa had taken most of his clothes to launder, so he grabbed a black dress shirt and rolled up the sleeves to his elbows. Then, he pulled on a loose jacket. Mainly to hide his forearm tattoo from Willow.

A notification pinged as Fillion tied his boot laces. Mack responded that he was already on his way down to California. Good. Probably saw the news this morning and hopped on a train. Fillion had wanted to dive into the mirror file and investigate Hanley's activity, but he had to focus on other work-related issues first. Maybe Mack had made headway. Or maybe they should just hire the underground to digest and organize the information. Shit, he was mentally rambling.

Focus.

But, he couldn't.

Fillion was so pissed, he was going numb under the endless layers of fury and disgust. And he didn't trust his own mind. Or anyone at the lab. He wanted Mack to go through all the docs in his office one by one to see if his friend could find the partnership agreement. It wouldn't be beyond Hanley to buy off Fillion's lawyer. Or sneak paperwork into Fillion's office to mess with his sanity and credibility.

Strapping on his Cranium, he checked his message center for any replies from his mom. Only an auto-reply. Out of the office. Again. No response from her personal center, either. Fillion drew in a sharp breath, then launched a browser to peruse the news headlines. Images flashed up of Fillion shaking Hanley's hand at the Ascension Ceremony, with Willow in the background, shoulders back, her expression fierce. He tapped the top article and began reading.

> *The Nichols empire expands again. This time, it's stretching toward the real Mars.*
>
> *Global tycoon Hanley Nichols has taken over Stellar Dock Corp., the interstellar private venture started by famed Mars explorer Gen. Stephen Claussen, a close business associate. The company is now called New Eden Space Ventures.*
>
> *The name does more than pay homage to Nichols' previous effort, New Eden Biospherics & Research, known for its Mars colony simulation in the California desert. With a Nichols at each helm, the two companies will work closely together to turn simulation into reality.*
>
> *"New Eden Space Ventures marks the birth of a new era," Nichols said in a statement released today. "Interplanetary travel and homesteading has been our hope for many years, a hope that breathes new life and empowers a future for all. Here's our chance. I'm proud that my son, Fillion Nichols, agrees and has paved the way for his generation to know and experience a new life, a better life."*
>
> *Fillion Nichols, 21, became the new CEO and president of the biodome experiment last month.*
>
> *Sources speculate that the second generation of New Eden Township will become the first civilian colonists on Mars. Once established, Hanley Nichols hinted at opening up residency to the general public, using New Eden Township Earth-side as a training ground.*

Fillion grabbed his Cranium and threw it across the room with a guttural scream. The silver device bounced off the door and rolled across the floor. He pressed his cheek to the wall by his bed and grit, "Can you hear me, *Hayden*? I'm going to finish you. I'm the Gamemaster. Understand? Not you. *Me.*"

He grabbed his wallet and a pack of cigarettes, then shoved off the bed and retrieved the Cranium from the floor. Fillion slammed his door and marched toward the lab's exit. As he passed rooms, people stood and clapped, congratulating him on the partnership with New Eden Space Ventures. Fillion scanned the faces as he passed, each smile a stab to his heart.

Michael caught up to him. "This has really boosted morale."

Fillion didn't reply. Couldn't reply.

"We feared the end of our jobs with project shutdown," Michael added. "Now we know that you will not only fight for the residents of New Eden, but those employed at the lab as well."

Fillion nodded and continued toward the exit. A sick part of him understood. People were willing to do just about anything for jobs. They didn't see the residents of New Eden as fellow humans, but their ticket to a better future. A better life. God, he hated it when Hanley was right. In any way. Regardless of how minimal. Michael continued to follow him.

"I'm on my way to the New Life Ceremony," Fillion said. "Do you need something?"

"I just received word that media and protesters with a human rights activist group are at the gate." Michael turned when Fillion halted his steps. "I'm escorting you to The Door with security. I messaged them to meet us at the entrance."

"Protesters? Already?" Fillion's head fell back as he groaned. "Enough security to hide me?"

"Yes, that's the plan."

"Thanks, Michael."

"I'm on your side." The scientist stared openly at Fillion. "New Eden is too."

"Dangerous words."

A shaky smiled touched the corners of Michael's mouth. "I know."

Fillion narrowed his eyes and studied Michael a few seconds before moving forward. Inside the forest entry, six security guards with EMP guns stood at the ready and formed around Fillion.

The forest's dim, cool light gave way to a blast of heat as their group marched out of the lab and into the desert. Shouts grew from the wrought iron gate. Fillion kept his face straight, his focus on the biodomes. But, from the corner of his eye, he glimpsed protest signs, angry fists, grimacing faces. Far more activists than he expected. Insults were hurled his direction. People screamed slogans.

"Free the people, slave owners!"

"Humanity is not an experiment!"

"You signed a death sentence!"

The voices quieted for a moment and a man shouted, "Son of a killer!"

Fillion's steps fumbled. Michael grabbed his elbow and kept him moving.

"Do the residents of New Eden know their days on Earth are numbered?" a holographic journalist shouted above the voices.

The question sparked new fervor and people clamored at the gate with greater intensity than before.

"Like father, like son!"

"Monster!"

"Humanity is not an experiment!"

"Son of a killer!"

"Free the people, slave owners!"

The Door came into focus ahead. Fillion focused on his feet, and not the voices at the gate that mixed with the accusatory voices in his own head. Grief churned in his gut. Fury burned in his veins. His boots kicked up dust with every step. A gentle breeze swept the particles away. Fillion blinked, long and slow. He needed to remain grounded.

Sunlight hit the grooves in The Door and the symbol of New Eden Enterprises appeared on fire. Several years ago, he believed this was a sign from Fate that he would find redemption. He had been dragged to The Door in chains, bruised, beaten, and ready to set fire to the entire world. The card in his pocket laughed at his memories. He was so stupid. So naïve. New Eden Township was his life, and his death. Redemption was a fool's hope.

Michael opened The Door and stepped aside for Fillion. "Message me before you return to the lab. Security will remain positioned here."

"Seal The Door behind me," Fillion said, flicking a glance over Michael's shoulder to the protesters. "In case someone breaches the gates and gets past security."

Michael agreed, and Fillion walked inside the North Cave without another word or backwards glance. The Door screeched shut and Fillion was swallowed whole by the unlit black of cave walls. A few seconds later the hermetic seal pressurized into place.

He sagged against a wall as the sob he'd been holding in fought for release. Chest tight, his breaths came in quick and shallow. His body shook as hot, angry tears finally fell. He whipped toward the cave wall and threw a punch, then another. The skin tore from his knuckles and he hissed in pain. Yet the ache didn't come close to cutting through the internal pain. His fist connected with stone again. A flash brightened behind his eyes with the contact. There. Finally. A pain he could control.

Fillion leaned his forehead against the rock. The coolness soothed his flushed skin. His fingers clawed at the stone as another sob released. Grief moaned from his emptiness, a desperate, hollow sound. His body heaved for breath. He gulped again. Rage hit him in a fresh wave, and he push away from the wall and paced a short distance, clutching his hair.

Wake up! his mind shouted. *Wake up!*

He needed to shove back the emotions. Redirect the despair, the anger. Save this energy for a real fight. Forcing his mind to a blank state was impossible. Words and images continued to showcase all angles, highlighting his festering wounds, moving in and out of focus. Nevertheless, he wiped his face, hardened his features, and strode toward the faint glow of New Eden.

Perhaps to love is to learn
to walk through this world.
To learn to be silent
like the oak and the linden of the fable.
To learn to see.
Your glance scatters seeds.
It planted a tree.
                    I talk
because you shake its leaves.

— Octavio Paz, poet, 1987 *

Chapter Twenty-Two

The villagers bustled about in preparations for the New Life Ceremony, to take place before midday meal. Discord and fear lifted momentarily to celebrate the new lives who would officially join their community.

Alder tinkered in The Forge with Connor, allowing Willow the personal time she desperately sought to ready before the Ceremony. Her brother and sister-in-law presently knelt in The Rows with their newborn daughters, to pray and reconnect with loved ones. When Willow had walked by a few moments earlier, Ember's strawberry blond curls had glinted with hints of copper in the late morning light. An overall healthy glow presented a stark contrast to her pallor the previous week. The recovery was miraculous, indeed. Leaf finally seemed happy, too, his smiles more ready and full, despite the current of tension rippling through New Eden since the Ascension Celebration.

Willow lifted her face to a pocket of reflective sunlight as the bio-wind filtered through the wisps of hair that escaped her braided crown. The forest murmured and whispered, the leaves aflutter in anticipation of the new names they would hear for the first time, and then carry into the coming days and years. Her hand caressed the sticky bark of an evergreen, her fingertips an extension of her understanding as she meandered toward her apartment once more.

Sweat cooled the back of her neck with the breeze. She wrinkled her nose at the smell wafting from her person. She had left work early to change and freshen up, saving a pitcher of water especially for this purpose.

Today marked the beginning of shearing season in the Mediterranean dome. She wrangled goats, alpacas, and a rambunctious Alder, unsure of which presented the heartier struggle. Dark alpaca fibers now mixed with brown, white, and black goat hair on her work dress. Willow puffed in annoyance at the flyaway strands falling into her eyes. Shearing season was always such a hassle. She found stray fibers for weeks, even after the apartment, linens, and garments were scrubbed clean. There was no help for it.

Another pool of sunshine drenched her in muted golden light by the stairs leading to her apartment. Willow paused and lifted her face once again, eyes closed. Her heart sang with happiness, for soon she would know the names of her nieces.

The lyrics to a merry tune formed on her tongue. She sang aloud as she pushed in the iron ring and entered her home, only to choke back the melody. A black shadow—the shape of a man—moved in the corner near the window. Willow jumped back, a hand flying to her chest.

"Dear Lord in Heaven!"

"Is Leaf with you?" Fillion blinked nervously and searched over her shoulder before meeting her frightened gaze once more.

She collected herself and postured as a Noblewoman, back straight, hands folded at her waist. "He is in the Ceremonial Garden with Lady Ember."

His eyes seemed to darken, swirling gray-blues and silvers in a tempest of violent emotions. The intensity only brought more attention to his unexpected presence. He was far too beautiful for a man, even more so when his strong emotions thundered in a visible display rather than hide behind fabricated arrogance and confidence. The draw nearly overwhelmed her. Still, she somehow maintained eye contact in the strained silence, though her insides quivered with standing before him—alone.

"Did I miss the naming—"

"No, Your Majesty. 'Tis at the end of antemeridian duties, right before midday meal."

Willow had to look away and fussed with her dress, aware of every animal hair, of the way she reeked of barns and sweat. But when she glanced up, her vanity dissipated. Fillion's eyes glossed red as he stared out the latticed window, every muscle taught. He was striking. A fierce storm contained within a man. Her gaze caressed the lines of his profile, unsure of how to respond to his strained silence. His shoulders bunched higher than usual and a fist covered his mouth in an anxious gesture of self-control. Red gashes upon his knuckles seized her attention and she gasped.

"Forgive me, but are you well?"

A crease appeared between his eyebrows. "The fake docs we signed at the Ascension Ceremony," he said, voice trembling, "was there one with my and Leaf's signatures missing?"

"Yes, indeed. You cautioned me to not sign it."

His shoulders relaxed a notch only to begin shaking as he drew in a ragged breath. He lowered his head into his hands and turned away. She quietly stepped toward him, her pulse thrumming wildly in her ears.

"I'm sorry." He dropped his hands. She halted her movements, biting back a startled response. He slashed furiously at the tears. "I'm so sorry."

"Fillion—"

"I didn't do it. I didn't sign the doc. I didn't…" The words faded as he covered his mouth again with his injured hand, turning his head toward the window, and away from her. "I'm . . . I'm seriously freaking out."

"Come, sit." She touched his forearm and then gestured to a chair. "Allow me to see to your hand."

"Don't. No kindness. It just makes it harder." He stepped back. "I can't do this. Tell Leaf I'm sorry."

"Pardon?" Willow crossed her arms over her chest and inclined her head in question. "You speak in riddles."

Fillion dismissed her with a single look of repugnance and then strode toward the door. Willow groaned with exasperation and grabbed his uninjured hand before he could reach the door, pulling him back toward her.

"Oh no, Your Majesty. You shall not run from me."

"I. Can't. Do. This!"

"Do you plan to explain yourself? Or am I merely an object to punish for your pain whenever situations now present opportunities?"

"Don't flatter yourself."

Willow narrowed her eyes and regarded the empty man before her, weary of the emotional games. Since reconnecting, he behaved toward her as if he were plucking petals from daisies——he loved her, he loved her not.

The violent emotions in his gaze sharpened further in silent fury and her heart clenched in response. He was naught but a wounded animal, striking out in blind fear and grief. Perhaps he needed a fight, a way for him to process his internal torment and anger. She understood, for she was much the same. The winds of justice gusting furiously inside of her had needed release for quite some time now. Ready to unleash her own storm, she straightened her spine and lifted her chin.

"How will your betrothed feel about you holding hands with a *rodent?*" Willow asked.

"I don't care what she thinks. It's all over anyway. Everything. It's all damned." He stared at their entwined fingers. "Anything I touch is damned."

"Fillion, we need to talk."

He chuckled bitterly and rolled his eyes. "Does it matter what I say? I'm already the bad guy."

"I suppose arrogant, self-centered men do not feel the need to answer to anyone"—

He interrupted and shouted, "Let's cut the shit and get to the point!"

—"and they use women for their own pleasure without care for her heart or reputation!" she finished. "You are—"

"Trash. A pig," Fillion tossed out derisively. "Vulgar. Selfish. Did I miss anything?"

Her eyes flared. "You mock my pain?"

"God, I'm so sick of this. You think you're the only one who suffers? I'm losing my fucking mind!"

"Do not use profanity in my presence."

"Any other requests, *Your Highness?*"

"Release my hand at once."

He hesitantly met her eyes. "I'll let go if you promise to let go of me."

"My heart cannot bear another promise made to you, especially this one." She sagged for a moment then yelled, "Do not even ask it of me!" Her angry breaths mixed with his, her face inches away. Tears streamed down her cheeks and across her lips. Willow turned her head toward her shoulder and whispered, "For I am made of glass after all." She dragged in a shuddering breath and cried out, "I have only loved you, Fillion. My heart remained faithful though I knew you would break it."

"Your love," Fillion choked out, "is all I've ever wanted and never deserved."

"Yet you jilted me! And for *her!*"

"I didn't have a choice!" he shouted back. The blood drained from her head and her legs nearly gave way. He softened his voice and continued. "Hanley contracted my engagement when I was in New Eden. Then he used it to blackmail me by threatening your and Leaf's lives."

"I beg your pardon?"

"Afterward I learned"—he closed his eyes tight and swallowed, weaving his injured fingers with her other hand—"I learned that we could never be together and . . . and..." He did not finish his thought as a blush crept up his neck and face. Her throat was closing up, her pulse wild with panic. Finally, he opened his eyes and blurted, "Willow Oak Watson, I know this sounds like dumb, melodramatic romantic sentiments, especially after how I've treated you recently, but I'd . . . I'd—"

"Fillion, no you shall not—"

"In a heartbeat. I wouldn't think twice."

Willow stared at their hands in horror, his blood now smearing into her skin. "Your Majesty, you cannot proclaim this sacred vow to me." She removed her hands from his and took several steps back. "You are to marry another. She alone deserves these sentiments."

"I don't love her."

The world fell silent for several long heartbeats.

"Is that all I am to you? Flesh for your pleasure?"

"God, no." Fillion hesitantly stepped toward her again. "I'm . . . I'm in awe of your strength and courage. Your intelligence arouses me until I can't think straight. You empower me to be real, to fight for what matters, to care about myself and others." He threw out his arms. "I'm crazy. For you. *Literally.* And I don't know what to do about it. I'm damned if I fight for you and I'm damned if I don't!"

They stood so close, she could feel the warmth of his body even though they did not dare touch. Energy, hot and crackling, arced between his breath and hers. He dropped his gaze to her lips and watched as her chest rose and fell with mutual longing.

"You challenge me," he continued. "It's cliché and stupid and I feel ridiculous saying it, but you make me want to become the man you believe me to be."

"The man *you are*," she softly corrected, locking eyes with him once again. His arms fell back to his side.

"Forgive me?" he choked out. "Please. For everything. I don't know how to do this. I've never known how to do this. I'm freaking out…"

Her eyes filled with fresh grief. "I forgive you, Your Majesty."

"Fillion."

"Fillion," she whispered back.

"I'd do *anything* for you, Willow. Nothing will change this. No laws. No experiment. No relationship full of *nevers*."

"And your betrothed?"

"I broke off our engagement. I'll absorb the consequences." He flicked his gaze to hers, then darted focus back to the floor. "She's not you. No one will ever be . . . *you*."

Warmth heated her skin and her pulse throbbed once again. Yet, somehow, she kept her mind focused and asked, "And your agreement with Hanley?"

"Doesn't matter what I do or don't do." Fillion's lips curled in disgust. "He'd find another way to use your life as a bargaining chip."

"I shall not gift him the satisfaction of watching me cower at his feet!" she spat.

He did not comment. Instead, fear guttered behind his gaze, feral, bewildered, as if he were ready to crawl out of his skin. The indignation drained from her in response until a chill pricked at the back of her neck.

The red gashes on his knuckles drew her attention once more. She reached out and hesitantly took his hand in hers. The contact sent a jolt of excitement through her and myriad sensations trickled out to each limb, clear down to her toes. He tensed, and she darted a side-glance his direction and found his gaze riveted to her face. His countenance darkened with the same confusion as the day he arrived in New Eden years ago, as if he could not discern if she were real—a rather perplexing reaction.

"Do not leave," she whispered. With light steps, she dashed to her room and retrieved comfrey cream from her toilette basket. She then sank into a chair beside him. "Your hand, please."

Willow dabbed two fingers into the medicinal cream and soothed the compound over his injuries. His fingers were long and beautiful, calloused just upon the tips, and well groomed. Musician's hands, she realized. She could not help but imagine the full shape of his mouth and the fervor of his gaze as her fingers slid across his. If her touch affected him, she did not know. His face remained a blur of emotions as before when she finally chanced a look.

"How did your hand earn such affliction?"

"I fought a wall." A faint smile played at the corners of his mouth. He shrugged in that certain way of his, subtle yet communicating so much. "I lost."

"Dare I ask how the wall offended you so?"

"I had to fight something." He twisted to peer out the window and murmured, "To know I was still alive, and able control to my pain."

She stopped her ministrations. "You are frightening me, Your Majesty. Were you attacked?"

Gradually, he faced her once more and studied her for a few erratic heartbeats before whispering, "Hanley emotionally murdered me today."

"Oh…" She could not finish she was so grieved by his confession.

A distraction was needed while she gathered her wits. Oaklee studied his hand. The lightly slathered cream over his injuries glistened in the filtered light and she pursed her lips. The wounds needed to be wrapped. But she had given her pieces of linen and hemp to the community scrap bin yesterday morn. Then she remembered her hair. Nimbly, she unwound the braided strands of her crown to retrieve the ribbon woven into her plaits. Hair tumbled down her shoulders and back. Gray eyes trailed after each motion with keen intelligence, as if she were a cipher he needed to solve; and she did her best to ignore him lest she succumb to the pleasurable turbulence in her stomach. Willow shuffled across the room and retrieved a pair of shears from her sewing basket and nervously met his gaze upon return.

"Your hand once more," she quietly requested.

He lifted his hand, and she wrapped it with the ribbon. She tied it off, snipped the excess amount, then placed the shears in her lap.

They sat in awkward silence, bashful, listening to the trees shush the biodome in a gentle song. Nature's comforting gesture soothed her, and she momentarily closed her eyes. Memories of autumn days swelled in her heart, of his kiss beneath a yew tree, and his kiss in her parent's chamber, both drenched, covered in ash, as she wore Ember's wedding gown.

"Everything," he whispered and hesitated. "Everything about you is so beautiful."

"Your Majesty," she protested meekly, too embarrassed to meet his waiting gaze. She fussed with the unbrushed hair hanging in waves down her back, far too aware of the animal fibers coating her dress and the way she must smell. To redirect focus, she asked, "How has Hanley harmed you this morn?"

Fillion ducked his head until long strands of black hair covered most of his face. "This morning Hanley unveiled New Eden Space Ventures. The media declared that the lab and I had partnered with him."

"Did you partner with him?"

He laughed, bitter and hollow. "You know the answer to that question." Cutting a glance her way, he said, "Probably a hack-back for when Mack zombified N.E.T.'s servers and I hacked into the biodome's emergency system."

A hack-back? Her fingers spun the shears in her lap, spinning them over and over while she attempted to make sense of his explanation. "If you did not sign an agreement, how is a partnership legally possible?"

"I don't know. I have no clue what is going on. Hanley keeps throwing attacks my way. And then Akiko—" Fillion groaned. "Shit! That's why he wanted me to marry into the Hirabayashi family." His head fell back with another groan followed by more vulgarity. "Akiko's dad owns a leading medical Smart tech company. He probably supplies the biotech to the lab. Shit. Shit. *Shit.* I should have known this. Verified these facts sooner. But I fell for every goddamn trap Hanley created for me—"

"I am confused," Willow interrupted. She gripped the shears so tight, her knuckles grew white. "What is New Eden Space Ventures and the terms of your partnership?"

"Hanley bought Stellar Dock Corp. from General Claussen within hours of being able to claim majority ownership status again. I need to research lab relationship details prior to my Ascension. But this answers how Hanley built New Eden Township Mars-side. Now Hanley owns an actual Martian biodome city, has a viable interstellar human transport systems, and I"—he grimaced, teeth clenched, eyes bloodshot—"I own a generation of super humans genetically modified to become Martians."

The shears clattered to the floor as Willow clapped her hands over her mouth.

"No one is going to Mars," he practically hissed. "Hanley and affiliates won't lay a goddamn finger on anyone without consent. And they don't have it from me. Not really."

The fear gave way to indignation and she spat, "Or the people of New Eden Township."

"Especially that."

Fillion resumed his study out the window. The fingers of his uninjured hand furiously tapped a rhythm on his thigh. Emotions whorled around him in a wild tempest. He attempted a poise more confident than when first she saw him, back straighter and head held higher. Fear, however, continued to paint his countenance with unearthly tones.

"This story gets worse," he eventually said, almost a hush. "But I . . . I don't have the words to explain right now. It's complicated."

She dipped her head into a bow. "Although I know my influence is little compared to Leaf's, I shall lend you my ear whenever you wish to talk, Your Majesty."

"Always, Willow. I always want to talk with you. You're the reality I'm fighting for."

Breath fluttered from her chest as a blush warmed her cheeks. He could not hide his embarrassment either. In fact, he appeared shocked by his own words.

Their chairs creaked in the stillness as they shifted away from each other in polite awareness. Willow bent to pick up the shears from the floor, her mind galloping with his news. How could the story possibly be worse? Before she could contemplate any number of possible horrors, Fillion began speaking again.

"I feel like my whole life has been played out in slow motion." He examined the ribbon tied around his hand. "A single day feels like years. But things are going to start moving fast as we sprint toward the finish line. And fight. God, we need to put up one hell of a fight. I can't let New Eden Space Ventures take over the human experiment." He nibbled on his bottom lip before murmuring, "After today, I don't know when I'll see you again."

"Simply return to me, My King."

"Thanks for the first aid." He quirked a bashful smile. "And the argument."

She did not know what first aid meant, but gathered it related to dressing his wounds. "'Twas nothing, Your Majesty."

"Fillion."

She whispered, "Fillion."

"The Ceremony will start soon."

"Yes. I should ready myself."

"Yeah, sure. See you around, Maiden." He came to his feet and offered another shy smile, faint and shaky, as though he were more nervous than shy.

Willow stood and lowered into a curtsy. As she rose, Fillion bowed his head and kissed her, a bandaged hand touching her cheek as his lips and breath warmed hers. Before she registered what had transpired, he whispered, "You really are beautiful," lightly pressing his mouth to hers one last time in farewell. He then strode out of her apartment, his shoulders raised, the door quietly closing behind him.

For several heartbeats, she stood where he had left her before running to the latticed window. His tall form descended the steps in a nimble gait. And, when he was at last out of sight, she closed the shutters.

He had kissed her. Darkness swathed the room in shadows, hiding her sudden febrile state, as she raised blood-stained fingertips to her lips.

To forget how to dig the earth and tend the soil is to forget ourselves.

— Mahatma Gandhi, 20th century*

This outward spring and garden are a reflection of the inward garden.

— Rumi, 13th century *

Chapter Twenty-Three

A gentle breeze played with his youngest daughter's reddish-blond strands and flurried leaves and blossoms in the heart-shaped Ceremonial Garden. Leaf gazed at her in wonderment. She was beautiful, from her pinked cheeks and long, fair eyelashes, to her lips which hinted at a smile while she slept.

Alder buried his face into Leaf's leg, sucking his thumb while watching Brother Markus and the gathering with one eye. Beside them, Ember cradled the eldest sister who, even now, demanded to be heard above the blessings and prayers. A smile tugged the corners of Leaf's mouth.

"Today, we welcome new life into our community," Brother Markus intoned. "May Heavenly Father walk beside thee all the days of your life wee ones. May you know your value and share your love with us as we love you in return. We honor you Daughters, future wives and mothers of New Eden, and God's handmaidens. The labor of your hands and the gift of life you bring shall sustain our community."

Brother Markus dipped his fingers in liturgical oil and anointed the babe in Leaf's arms. Alder raised big eyes and clutched Leaf's leg tighter when the monk lifted his gnarled finger toward the eldest's forehead and drew a heart upon her forehead with the same liturgical oil. She squalled in protest. A tiny, clenched fist emerged from her swaddling blankets as she wailed. Villagers chuckled.

"Your Majesty," Brother Markus continued with amusement, "please introduce us to your newest family members."

"With pleasure, Brother." Leaf held his daughter up for all to see. "I present to you the youngest twin. She is known as Fia for 'flame' and Lenore for 'light.'"

"Welcome, Fia Lenore Watson," the community greeted in reply.

Laurel and Willow both blotted away tears as the girl's name left their lips. Coal grinned, and he tipped his head to Leaf for honoring the Fire Element house. Fillion, however, stood as though a dark statue, each feature as still as stone, save his eyes which flitted around from face to face as if he were making calculations, or fighting against waves of anxiety. Nevertheless, Leaf's gaze skipped past the Son of Eden and continued to acknowledge as many hearty welcomes as possible.

When the community quieted, Brother Markus sprinkled holy water upon his daughter's head. "'The Lord bless you and keep you,'" he chanted from the Holy Scriptures. "'The Lord make His face shine upon you, and be gracious to you; The Lord lift up His countenance upon you, and give you peace.'" Lifting two fingers, the monk brushed the air in *signum crucis* as he said, "*In nomine Patris, et Filii, et Spiritus Sancti.* Amen."

"Amen," the villagers repeated.

Leaf angled toward Ember who rocked the still-crying babe in her arms. "I present to you the oldest twin," he said, unable to hold back a chuckle. "She is known as Terra for 'Earth' and Oak after her feisty Aunt." Laughter rippled through the gathering. Even Fillion cracked a tiny smile, the first clear emotion Leaf had witnessed since his arrival in The Rows.

"A lass after my own heart," Willow declared proudly.

Leaf softened his gaze. "And one who beautifully possesses your indomitable spirit."

"I am deeply honored." She lowered into a curtsy, a hand draped across her heart. "*Merci beaucoup, mon cher frère et soeur.*"

"Welcome, Terra Oak Watson," the community practically sang out, followed by more laughter when Terra released a lusty, quivering wail in reply.

Brother Markus intoned the same benediction over Terra as he had Fia, then sprinkled holy water upon her fair-haired head. Terra stopped her protests and blinked her eyes when the water droplets touched her flushed skin.

"Water soothes you, does it, sweetling?" Ember cooed, kissing their daughter's cheek. His wife then rubbed Terra's bottom lip with their daughter's own tiny fingers until Terra latched onto her pointer and middle fingers eagerly in pacification.

Heads bowed reverently when the Daughter of Water entered the circle with her sister, Lady Mist, and began singing the traditional song of mourning to the elements and to family past and present. The same song also performed at the third Ceremony of Death. Sinking to the living soil, they each gathered a pinch and lightly rubbed the tilth where the oil and water of Terra's and Fia's baptisms and anointings had fallen. Lore told of how the memories of loved ones became absorbed through the ashes, their spirits connecting through the bond provided in the holy water.

Terra's infant blue eyes fluttered closed with Rain's and Mist's ethereal voices. Her small body shuddered a hiccup every so often as she merrily suckled upon her fingers. Her other hand, now released from her swaddling blankets, curled around the hem of Ember's bodice. Would she rub pillows and linens to self-soothe as Alder? Leaf studied his wee Fia, her face relaxed and skin unblemished from tears. Unlike her older sister and brother, Fia radiated peace, both when awake and when lost to pleasant dreams. In many ways, both his twin daughters reminded him of his sister.

For years he had viewed Willow's emotional displays as unladylike deportment and, ultimately, as a sign of weakness. Yet, as he considered his sister, he finally recognized—fully—the unshakable strength behind her tears. She did not bend to tradition for tradition's sake, nor the strictures of society simply because they exist—unlike him. Nor did he believe she was led by emotion and emotion alone. Passion and justice guided by compassion infused every word spoken, each deed of her hand, and the very breath of her silence when she listened to what was not said and studied what was not shown. She was not without fault or annoyances. At times her righteous indignation caught fire and set everything within sight ablaze, testing every fiber of patience he possessed. Still, how often had she proved him wrong over the past few years? And how long had she awaited *him* to understand *her* while he accused her of trying to control his every thought, word, and deed? Shame heated his skin and he ducked his head from onlookers.

"Father?" Alder tugged on Leaf's breeches.

"Yes, lad?"

"Faeries take her." Alder pointed to Terra with pinched brows and a disapproving frown. "No soft voice."

Leaf squatted down to be eye level with his son, holding in a smile. "She is ours, forever. A gift we shall cherish."

"No like her."

"Believe me, lad, you shall one day. She will lend you her strength and her voice when you find yours lacking."

Alder glared at Terra, unconvinced.

The ritual song ended and Leaf straightened, rubbing Alder's back as he stood.

"Would the family of Terra and Fia please come forward?" Brother Markus asked.

Members of the Watson and Hansen households circled around Leaf, Ember, and their children. Connor placed his hand upon Leaf's shoulder with a sideways smile for his granddaughter.

"Family, lift a hand in support," Brother Markus said, bowing his head in honor. Rain and Mist placed small scoops of living soil in each outstretched hand. "Family," the monk began again, "you connect each Daughter to her ancestors and you will also shape her future. Your heritage will continue in their children, and their children's children. What shall be their legacy?"

"Love, family, and community," they all replied in unison.

From the sidelines, Leaf glimpsed Fillion shift on his feet as his mouth parted with their ritual words, before tucking his chin to this chest. He knew what the Son of Eden was thinking, and he knew he was unable to reconcile those very thoughts within himself.

Returning focus to the family circle, Leaf watched as Connor curled his fingers closed and turned his palm toward the soil. The family followed suit. On a quiet count of three they each opened their fingers and watched as dark, rich soil fell back to the earth.

"Ashes to ashes, dust to dust," Brother Markus intoned. "In order to live, something must die, but death gives way to the resurrection of new life." He bowed first at Terra and then at Fia. "Welcome, Daughters of Earth and Fire."

"Welcome, Daughters of Earth and Fire," the community chanted, each picking up a scoop of soil and allowing the tilth to slip through their fingers and back to the gardens.

Their family returned to stand amid the gathering. When Leaf and Ember were once more alone at the center of the Ceremonial Garden, the monk continued. "Your Majesty, please call forth whom you wish to appoint as Godparents."

Leaf locked eyes with his friend and sworn brother. "Skylar Greysen Kane, would you do our family the honor of becoming Terra and Fia's Godparent?"

Skylar's grief-stricken features softened and he bowed deeply. "The honor is all mine, Your Majesty." His friend entered the Ceremonial Garden and knelt before Leaf.

"Anyone else?" Brother Markus asked.

"Yes, one more." Leaf turned to the Son of Eden, whose eyes widened in response. "Fillion Malcolm Nichols, would you do our family the honor of becoming Terra and Fia's Godparent?"

"I—" Fillion stopped, the refusal clear in his eyes. He darted a look to Willow then back to Leaf, before issuing a single, curt nod and joining Skylar in the soil.

Brother Markus slipped in front of Leaf and Ember. Liturgical oil dripped from his trembling pointer finger as he drew a heart first upon Skylar's forehead and then Fillion's. The Son of Eden swallowed as he blanched. Beneath long, dark strands, his gaze shifted toward Willow as he knelt in the soil. Leaf cast a furtive glance at his sister, who returned Fillion's intense stare with one of her own. He studied Fillion once more, noting the ribbon tied around his fingers. Had they met, in private? Surely his sister would not be so insensible. How had he injured his hand? He narrowed his eyes as the monk recited a blessing over both kneeling men.

"Place the wee ones in their arms," Brother Markus instructed.

Skylar easily cradled Fia and offered her a smile. Ember lowered before Fillion and offered Terra, but he made no move to receive her, his body stiff, eyes wide, his mouth slack in a look of terror.

Fillion lowered his head until hair fell over his face. "I've never held a baby before," he whispered to Ember.

"Hold your arms as Skylar," she whispered back. "I shall place her within your embrace." Fillion mimicked the movement and Ember gently laid Terra in his arms. "Simply support her head as you are doing now." Warmth immediately colored Fillion's neck and face and as he hid behind his hair once more. "Son of Eden," Ember whispered, leaning in close, "one day your own children and grandchildren shall esteem you as a man worthy of great honor. They shall speak of you for generations." She rose and, when beside Leaf, quietly added, "I have a hunch, and I am rarely wrong."

Leaf was grateful his eldest daughter had finally found peace, for he was not sure Fillion would survive if she were crying. The flush had given way to an unnaturally pale countenance, his chest rising and falling in quick succession, with shoulders knotted as if he might jump into action with any unexpected disturbance. Yet, the look in his eyes—regret mixed with wonder—shone clearly as he studied Terra's face.

Alder tugged on Leaf's breeches once more, redirecting his thoughts. "Up, father?"

"Sorry, lad," Leaf whispered. "I shall have to take your sister back shortly. Can I hold you during midday meal?" His son nodded, though his eyes tracked the elderly man in woolen robes.

"My Lord," Brother Markus said to Skylar. "Do you adopt Terra and Fia Watson as your own, to protect and serve, to defend and honor, all the days of your life?"

"I do," Skylar declared. The monk placed a hand upon Skylar's bowed head and spoke a benediction to seal the Son of Wind's pledge.

"Son of Eden," Brother Markus said, while stepping toward Fillion. "Do you adopt Terra and Fia Watson as your own, to protect and serve, to defend and honor, all the days of your life?"

Fillion lifted steady eyes to the monk. "Yes," he breathed. "Alder, too." He turned to face Leaf and declared, "I'll fight for your family and New Eden until my last breath."

Pride beat in Leaf's chest. Humbled, he bowed deeply at the waist to honor Fillion's sacrifices. When he rose, he sucked in a breath when noting how all of New Eden had lowered to one knee before the man cloaked in weaves of mourning, cradling new life in fluttering swathes of white.

"Hail, Son of Eden," a man shouted from the crowd.

The gardens immediately hushed with charged silence.

Moved by the image, Leaf shouted, "Hail, Son of Eden!"

The community roared back the proclamation, and Leaf swore the biodome panes shook with each exultation.

Adams: You've hinted at lessons the world could learn from New Eden Township in speeches during your World Tour. What is one example us Earthlings could learn from our Martian comrades?

Fillion: Honor.

[silence]

Adams: Can you expand on that?

Fillion: The fact that you're asking me to define a common word in our vocabulary says it all: It can't be understood except through experience. Try it out in your interpersonal relationships and then let me know what you think "honor" means.

— Fillion Nichols, on _Atoms to Adams Daily Show_, March 27, 2058

Chapter Twenty-Four

The crowd had finally ended their cheers and now quietly murmured. God, the shame was overwhelming. What would New Eden think of him once they learned the truth of their situation? Of his betrayal? Even if he was framed. Better to grow numb. He couldn't afford to shut down right now. After the New Life Ceremony was complete, he had to return to the lab and declare war on Hanley. And the media. Shit, he still needed to deliver the ashes to Skylar, too, now that the forensics DNA test came back with a positive ID.

Fillion chanced a look at the villagers from behind long strands. He expected to see hundreds of eyes pointed his direction. But they focused on each other or watched the Watsons. Ember held Terra close and swayed. The motion was mesmerizing to his out-of-sync brain. And a reminder of how his arms had trembled noticeably during the return hand-off.

Focus.

He pivoted toward the monk for direction when Mack materialized, angling through the crowd until he stopped behind Coal, his eyes wild with panic. What the . . . How did he arrive so soon? Michael granted him entrance without Fillion's permission? Then he remembered. He had given Mack full security clearance. Fillion squinted his eyes. Was his friend—right here, right now—even real?

The world tipped on its side. Fillion wobbled, though he was planted firmly on his knees in the soil before the monk.

He was still reeling from holding something so completely innocent and codependent. Forget Ember's words of his own children. Images of Terra tormented his already elevated anxiety. Her tiny body falling from his arms. Blood soaking into the soil as her head split open. Limbs bent at unnatural angles. A cry silenced far too soon. And all because of him.

New Eden was wrong. He wasn't worthy to be hailed. He was the son of a killer. Death pulsed in his veins and claimed his blood. The very blood that now partnered with him to destroy what remained of his heart and soul. And destroy the legacy created by the first generation for the second and third gens. A legacy he'd never know for himself.

Dizziness swam circles around Fillion's head once more. He flicked a wary gaze to where'd he last seen Mack, spooked when his friend still stood behind Coal. Maybe he wasn't losing his mind, after all.

To test this theory, Fillion lifted an eyebrow in question.

His friend mouthed the word "emergency."

Willow noted Fillion's stare and peered over her shoulder until her gaze connected with Mack's. His friend leaned down and whispered in her ear. Her mouth fell open, and she gaped at Coal as the blood drained from her head. Neither Coal nor Leaf noticed Mack's or Willow's reactions, however. Forget his earlier sentiments. Fillion's mind was still playing tricks on him. Hell, he even thought he'd seen Timothy that morning.

"You may rise," the monk said to both Fillion and Skylar.

Fillion brushed the dirt from his black pants. Though Brother Markus hadn't dismissed him, Fillion pressed his arms tight to his side, back straight, eyes to the ground, and bowed at a sharp angle, first to Leaf and then to Ember. He then spun on his heel and strode toward Mack. His friend had now gained Coal's attention, as well as Connor's and Brianna's. Once at Willow's side, Fillion turned his back to Mack to appear natural, but not without first dipping his head in a near-indiscernible nod.

"Let us close in prayer," Brother Markus spoke over the restless gathering. Heads bowed in respect, hands clasped at waists. The monk began chanting more ceremonial words and his voice sliced through the static silence.

"We need to go," Mack whispered into Fillion's ear from behind. "Now."

Fillion nodded his head, his heart in his throat. What the hell had Mack so worked up? And, despite his doubts, Fillion knew that his friend was truly here. He wasn't crazy—at this particular moment.

He turned to leave, but Willow grabbed his uninjured hand.

"Protect him, as if he were me," she whispered.

"Who?" But he knew. And with that his mind went immediately to Lynden. Was she in trouble? Had something happened to her? Was Coal to blame?

Willow dropped her voice even lower. "Protect Coal, please."

"I don't even know what happened yet. What if I can't?"

Her hand touched her heart and then she pressed her palm to his chest, exactly over his broken-heart tattoo.

His brain skidded to a complete stop. Their eyes locked as he tried to make sense of her hurried declaration. She gifted her heart to him? Again? Words failed to form. And he stared, as usual, like a complete idiot. The world continued to dissolve around him. He wanted to lose himself to her confession. Wrap each feeling of acceptance around himself until he disappeared into the unfathomable beauty she offered him. But, just as the prayer ended and heads lifted, Mack grabbed his shirt and pulled him away.

Villagers turned their backs to Coal as he cut through the crowd. Mothers covered the eyes of their younger daughters. Men spit on the ground beside where Coal walked, calling him an adulterer and hissing words about dishonor. But when Fillion passed through, heads bowed and women lowered into curtsies. The rage Fillion had pushed aside came barreling back.

Hanley had ensured that Lynden would never be welcome in New Eden. He had discredited Coal's influence within his community.

"*Kono yaro!*" he cursed under his breath.

They stomped through The Orchard. Branches switched Coal's back and petals exploded into the air with each thwack. Fillion caught a tree limb as it swung back his direction. He steadied the limb then ducked beneath. Coal continued to move through the trees like a machine. A pissed-off mass of rippling muscle and temper. Fillion rolled his eyes and continued to block the flying tree limbs.

The forest's dappled shadows soon swallowed their marching forms. Fillion looked for workers moving through the brambled trails. Once he was sure they were alone, he would stop Mack and demand an explanation. But he didn't have to. Coal grabbed Mack's arm and swung him around.

"Is she safe?" he asked Mack.

"She's in jail."

"What?!" Fillion snapped.

"Arrested early this morning."

"Someone better start explaining things. *Now,*" Fillion seethed.

Coal's face reddened as every muscle in his body knotted. "I will destroy him."

"Her," Mack said quietly. "Akiko's work."

The ground beneath Fillion's feet tilted again.

"You better tell him," his friend leveled at Coal.

Coal hesitated. "Are you in trouble with the law as well?"

"Don't worry about me. You, however…" Mack gestured to Fillion. "He's going to kill you if you don't start confession time."

Coal straightened his shoulders and peered down his nose at Fillion. They tolerated each other. Had for the past year and only for Lynden's sake. He wasn't charmed by Coal's noble arrogance or hot-headed bluster, unlike Mack and Lynden. Growing impatient with Coal's pissing contest, Fillion exhaled loudly. Coal blinked and a drop of fear bled into his gaze. Good. Maybe the giant of a man would shrink his ego a few more notches and finally bit dump.

Or not.

"Why is my sister in jail?" Fillion quietly shot at Coal, his voice like a silencer on a gun.

"Lynden . . . is my wife," Coal confessed. "We married a year ago under our false identifications."

A muscle in Fillion's jaw worked back and forth. His rage was about to blow. "Who married you—" He stopped, and whipped his head toward Mack. Fillion stumbled back a couple of steps. "You illegally married *my* sister behind *my* back?"

Mack nodded his head. "I'd do it all over again, too."

"What the—"

"This isn't about you, mate."

"The hell it isn't!" Fillion marched up to Mack and shoved his shoulder. "Who do you think will be forced to clean up the legal shit that has splattered all over this place because of what you did? And, god, Hanley already took a public dump on me this morning."

"Forced?" Mack shook his head. "Listen to you. Tell me you wouldn't marry Willow if an opportunity presented itself."

Fillion grit his teeth. "I don't believe in marriage."

Mack rolled his eyes and stepped aside. "Get your head out of your ass. That's the shit you're seeing."

"Nice. I expect others to manipulate me, but not you."

Mack's face fell. "I'm not manipulating you."

"Right. You're not at fault. You and *him*"—Fillion pointed at Coal—"didn't shove me between a rock and hard place with the law. It's all in my head, which is apparently up my ass." Fillion pushed away from Mack. "You made a bad deal, mate."

"I don't make bad deals."

Fillion spit on the ground and then strode down the dirt path toward the North Cave.

"Police are waiting at the lab to arrest Coal!" Mack shouted at his retreating form. "Akiko is expected to arrive soon, too!"

"What do you want from me?!" Fillion shouted back. "I didn't write the law! I didn't create Frankenstein's monster!"

"I am *not* a monster." Coal's fingers curled into fists. "I am a man, born free."

Fillion's shoulders slumped forward and he softened his voice. "I know. I don't blame you. I blame him," he finished, looking at Mack. "He knew there was nothing I could do about the consequences."

"Defeatist much?" Mack shot back. They glared at each other. His friend eventually sobered and intoned: "To win. To destroy."

"You didn't tell me," Fillion said, his voice hushed. "First Pinkie. Then bio-hacking Andra. Now *this*. What else are keeping from me, Mack?"

"It's not like that…"

"You were the *only* person I trusted."

"You still can. I'm on your side. You know that."

"No," Fillion choked out. "I don't know."

Mack's face turned a sickly shade of white. "Then he wins."

"We're all losers in this game."

"I disagree," Coal interjected. "He shall not win. As long as I draw breath, I shall fight for New Eden until he loses, whatever the cost."

Fillion sighed through his nose, long and slow. "How does your hero complex plan to fight arrest?" he derided. "Can't battle this one with your hammer, Thor."

"How adorable," Coal retorted. He smiled at Mack. "I do believe he attempted humor." To Fillion, he asked, "Would you like to be introduced to my *hammer?*"

"I'll pass."

Despite all attempts to remain mad at Mack, one look was all it took for both of them to burst into laughter. Dammit. His friend always had that effect on him—the light to Fillion's dark.

"Maybe Farm Boy can do things other men can't too," Mack deadpanned. Fillion lost it again.

Coal, however, watched them both with a look of patient perseverance. When he'd apparently had enough, he murmured, "Naturally."

A slow grin spread on Mack's face as his eyes swept over Coal from head to toe and back up again.

"I know that look," Coal said, crossing his muscled arms over his chest. "Whatever scheme hatched inside that feathered brain of yours, the answer is no."

"So touchy," Mack tossed out with a tsk. "Well, Mr. I'm-a-free-man-with-a-bigger-hammer-than-yours, I have a business proposition for you."

"No!" Both Coal and Fillion shouted simultaneously.

Mack raised his hands in mock-surrender. "Even Fillion will approve, if he'll trust me one more time." His friend slid him an apologetic side glance, but his smile dripped with pointed barbs. "To prove my fealty since I've grossly failed to do so over the past eighteen years."

"Mack—"

"Shhh . . . I'm monologuing. You said stupid things while you were angry. I get it. Lovers spat. We can kiss and make up later. But not now. We'll make Farm Boy blush." Mack closed his eyes as he stretched his neck and shook out his hands while jumping on the tips of his toes. Then his eyes snapped open and his body stilled. He adjusted his utilikilt, cleared his throat dramatically, and *finally* continued. "Now, as I was saying. I have a business proposition for you, Farm Boy, one that will require work relocation. But I don't think you'll mind, given the alternative and the easier access to Rainbow. Of course, I'll pay for all moving expenses."

"I could not live—"

"You're an illegal alien who is actively running from the law. Only hell can save you, *bakayarō*. Well, besides your obvious manliness, mythological Norse looks, and your *hammer*."

"Wipe your *nosebleed*," Fillion murmured. "Pathetic."

"Look at him!"

"He's crushing on you," Fillion tossed out to Coal, bored. "Mack has a thing for hammers."

"I do," Mack added with a serious head nod. "They like to bang things, *desu*."

"He also likes big, morally superior blond men."

"Actually, I prefer skinny asses, arrogant smirks, and artificial black hair," Mack said with a wink at Fillion. "But big blond men who Hulk Smash are nice, too." He bit down on his tongue suggestively at Coal, then slapped a hand across his own thigh. "OK, bitches. The scary witch arrives soon and wolves circle our den."

"So, what's the catch?" Fillion asked. "You said 'business' proposition."

"He works for us." Mack's grin returned. "Intel."

"Think you can handle that?" Fillion asked Coal. The corner of his mouth tipped up, smug and taunting.

The Son of Fire just glowered at him.

"We'll take his smoldering gaze as a 'yes,'" Mack said. Coal cracked a tiny smile when Mack blew him a kiss. "I think he likes me," Mack mock-whispered to Fillion. "Dreams really do come true."

"Focus, mate."

Mack opened his mouth to reply, but Coal cut in. "Should I agree to hide in the underground, how shall I evade the police? And then what? I cannot live there forever."

Fillion studied Coal, his mind whirling with escalating apprehensions. He had to admit, Mack's plan was viable. But, first, he needed to confirm the sickening fear eating away at his insides.

"Mack," Fillion said. "Do you have quick access to check a pulse and fingerprints?"

"Um, yeah. Why?"

"We need to secure Coal first before he can work intel."

Mack slowly turned to face Coal, eyebrows pushed together.

"Police could track him right now," Fillion said.

"Chipped?"

"Cerebral mesh. Biotech nanobots, possibly from HiraMed. Portless cybernetics homegrown in the lab and administered through sublingual DNA-based inoculations. MELISSA Project was phase one and two. New Eden the final rollout."

"Holy shit," Mack breathed, eyes wide. "N.E.T. is mass-producing transhumans?"

"For interplanetary colonization."

"Speak plainly," Coal demanded. "How am I to be 'secured'? What do you even mean?"

"You're part robot," Fillion said.

Coal blinked slowly, as if he were about to unleash the wrath of Valhalla on them both. "I grow weary of all these jokes."

"He's not joking, mate," Mack said.

"How is this possible?"

Concern darkened Mack's gaze. "I'll explain later." He tapped his Cranium and poked at the air. His eyes darted back and forth as information streamed upward on his screen. "Does your mom know?" he asked, flicking a glance at Fillion.

"Not sure. Just learned this morning. Been trying to reach her for several days. No response."

Mack grew intense as he locked onto Fillion over his screen. "Still seeing things? Dark spots in your memory?"

"Yeah." Fillion looked away, too embarrassed to face Coal.

"We'll talk later, too."

"Good. Similar thoughts."

Coal snapped a twig off a nearby tree and rolled the stem back and forth between his fingers. "How did Akiko learn of my marriage to Lynden?"

"A blood contract from Satan to maintain peace in hell," Mack murmured without looking up. "Truth: Disloyal hackers approached me with an offer to keep it hush if I paid a pretty sum. My guess? She paid it, but not to keep it hush."

Fillion bit the inside of his cheek. He should have had her watched. Akiko blew up when he broke contract with her family following the Ascension Celebration. But not for long. Her tantrum turned to syrup within minutes. She even parted the next morning on peaceful terms. He didn't think more on it, too relieved to be free and too distracted by Timothy's death. And just tired. Fatigued to the marrow of his bones.

"Cheeky buggers," Mack muttered under his breath, carving a circle in the air with his finger. "Ah, gotcha!" He looked to Coal. "Found the command center to your cybernetics. Encryption was impressive. I'll give them that. Cutting the strings . . . and . . . there. You're a real boy now."

Coal rolled in his bottom lip, the fear painted on each of his hardened features.

"Loading up inner sanctum software and then you'll be set to run and hide. Feel anything? Dizzy? Nauseous?"

"No."

"Interesting."

The nausea in Fillion's stomach intensified, however. Coal may not feel anything, but Fillion's emotional system was about ready to crash. Mack's brows hung low over his eyes as he watched his screen, but Fillion knew Mack was covertly watching him, too. A cold sweat broke out on Fillion's forehead. Pain bloomed behind his eyes.

"Hey, we got this," Mack whispered to him. "To win. To destroy."

Fillion swallowed. "To create a reality all my own."

"It's going to happen."

"Yeah," Fillion whispered back, though not convinced. "When is Lynden's bail hearing?"

"Tomorrow, mid-day."

"I'll fly out early morning." Fillion scuffed at the dirt path with his boot. "God, this is a mess."

Mack grunted in agreement while poking at his screen. "Think we can sneak Coal out by disguising him as a protester at the gate?"

"Possibly." Fillion glanced at Coal, then back to Mack. "You saw the headlines?"

"Yup. That *kisama* has made his last move."

Coal flicked the twig into the air. "Who are the protesters?"

Fillion tucked his thumbs into his belt loop and lifted his shoulders and angled his head away. But, quietly, he began explaining everything he learned that morning to Coal, including Ember's miraculous recovery and Pinkie's and Jeff's connections to the MELISSA Project. The Son of Fire didn't move. He didn't even appear to be breathing. He remained still during the entire explanation, his gaze intensifying with each word. Even when Fillion finished. Leaves rustled in a breeze and Fillion swore it sounded like the crack and cackle of flames. The air became dense, too, as if Coal sucked the oxygen from the atmosphere to feed the inferno of his fury.

"Done," Mack said, breaking the tension. "You're secure."

"I am a dragon among men," Coal grit between clenched teeth, ending with an angry chuckle. "He shall burn alive until he screams for mercy, but he shall find none from me."

Fillion's eyebrows shot up in surprise.

"Good," Mack answered when Fillion remained quiet. "Contain that fire to survive in the underground. You'll need it." He looked at Fillion. "To think, Ms. Willow-o'-the-wisp is possibly more machine than you."

"Yeah."

The muscles in his stomach spasmed again. Fillion peered up through the evergreen branches to the geodesic sky. His mind was racing faster than his pulse. Mack's comment didn't help, either. Especially as Fillion was starting to suspect that he was inoculated, too. A man of magic . . . he clenched his teeth until he thought they'd crack.

Since the beginning, he had considered Willow nature and he the machine. This time his world tipped completely upside down. He tried touching one thought and then another, but they slipped from his mental grasp and fell into the endless black of his mind.

He sauntered off the trail into the woods. He could feel Coal's and Mack's stares, but he continued on without explanation. Moss draped over roughened tree bark. His fingers grazed the feathery, chartreuse tips. Brittle leaves crunched beneath his footsteps. With this boot tip, he nudged away the forest layer to the rich, black soil beneath.

This world was both real and fake, natural and machine, life and death. Bio-wind tousled his hair across his eyes. The hem of his black coat flapped to the rhythm of the invisible. Tree branches swayed and groaned with an ocean wave of fluttering green leaves.

Beyond these panes, millions of people hungered for jobs, for food, for purpose. Their bodies poisoned from machine waste and processed living, despite the organic labels slapped onto everything. Why should a healthy, functioning ecosystem and community belong to Mars? Earth needed this more than a barren wasteland of a planet. More than corporations, governments, or scientific journals. Humanity was desperate for hope, one that breathed life and empowered new beginnings.

Willow's words of forgiveness and love whispered from the black to his spiraling mind. The noise in his head came to an abrupt stop. All the voices, all the expectations, every demand needing his attention—gone. In the deafening void, his fingers played with the edge of the ribbon she had tied around his throbbing fingers.

This was the reality he wanted.

The one he was fighting for, like he had confessed to Willow.

The jester in his pocket laughed. Fillion's fingers curled around the playing card in his pocket until the paper crumpled into a ball. He was the Gamemaster. He moved the pieces on the board. Fate be damned.

The forest awakened to life. All the sounds came rushing back in. His mind amped up to full acceleration again. His anxiety fed in a frenzied delight, gnawing away at one thought and then another. But, now, he had a target lock on an idea.

A reality.

Fillion slowly turned around and faced Mack and Coal. "What if . . . what if the experiment status of New Eden was changed to a communal asylum? The CSRP status remains. Perhaps I can bargain with the government to lift Frankenstein laws on the residents in exchange for 'x' number of youth offenders per year."

"I'm not sure the feds will budge with registered transhumans at their employ," Mack said. "Robotics ethics and laws are slippery devils."

"Earth needs a reboot," Coal added, eyes locked onto Fillion. "I will do whatever necessary to preserve New Eden and help the Outside world."

A reboot. He couldn't have said it better. Fillion offered a Coal a faint smile of appreciation then said to Mack, "We need a back door. It may be the only way for me to legally dissolve this fake partnership and free New Eden." Fillion sauntered back their way, then passed them as he continued down the path. "Figure it out," he tossed over his shoulder to Mack.

"Sure thing, boss."

Fillion paused on the dirt trail and peered back at his life partner. "Coming?"

"What of me?" Coal flipped back.

"Hide behind The Mill. Mack or I will come for you tonight."

Coal bowed. "Thank you. I shall say my proper goodbyes to family first." The Son of Fire tipped his head one last time, then jogged back toward The Rows.

"That sparkle in your eye?" Mack said to Fillion. "It's hella sexy. Turns me on."

"Everything turns you on."

"True." Mack laughed. "But that spark of life? I haven't seen it since you were twelve, before the world fell apart. I'd like to think it's me, but—"

"It's definitely you," Fillion cut in with a half-smile.

Mack returned the look.

Fillion didn't have to say anything else. Apology accepted, and he was forgiven, too.

A few minutes later, the security team opened The Door at Fillion's request. Police walked up as they exited, along with Michael. Sweat dripped down the scientist's face as he rushed up to Fillion.

"More protesters have arrived."

Fillion looked over Michael's shoulder to the gate, ignoring the officers.

"NASA called for you," he continued, obviously buying time. "Same with JAXA, CNSA, the ESA, and Hanley. Actually, he's called three times for you."

"Lynden…?" Fillion croaked in reply, despite all efforts to remain in control.

"The media is exploding."

"Mr. Nichols," an officer interjected. "We have a warrant for the arrest of Coal Hansen, wanted for fraud. Is he with you?"

Fillion didn't hesitate. "No, he's not." He relaxed into a bored postured.

"We'll need to search New Eden," the officer continued. "Move aside."

"Sorry, warrant or not, you're not permitted to enter." Fillion stepped toward the lab and gestured for the police follow. "Let's discuss further in my office."

"This is a court-ordered arrest, Mr. Nichols."

"Well, that's disappointing. I preferred police-gone-rogue." Fillion turned around and rolled his eyes. "Here's the issue: To enter New Eden requires government security clearance at the federal level. This is a government-sanctioned human experiment. Over two hundred people in this dome have never seen law enforcement. To roll in with guns raised and threats about harboring a fugitive would create irreparable psychological trauma." Fillion lifted his shoulder in a faint shrug. "I'm sure your department would be thrilled with the lawsuits that would pour in from all over the world. But I'm even more convinced they'll squeal and drop like fangirls over the legal hell I'll unleash."

"You resist complying, Mr. Nichols?"

Fillion swiveled to face Michael. "Ping the chief of police. Tell him to meet me in person within the hour. At the lab."

The officers chuckled at, what he knew, to be pretentious absurdity. The spoiled rich kid thought he could throw around his weight. Idiots. Fillion lifted his eyebrow at the group, smirk in place, then waltzed past them toward the lab. Tuning out the rising shouts from the gate, he brought up a screen and messaged the security team to continue blocking The Door and to use sonic disruption if necessary. The police didn't follow after him. He knew they were doing their job. But so was he.

The crowd roared when he came into sight, flinging verbal knives his way.

"Humanity is not an experiment!"

No shit. Fillion wanted to shout those words back to the simpletons on the other side of the gate. Green Morons. All of them. Utopic idealism wasn't magic. Goodness and order weren't restored by shouting words of hate and shame. The villagers weren't any different. A new fury writhed to life inside of Fillion with the memory of how the community turned on Coal. They didn't even give him a chance to explain the situation. Not one opportunity to defend himself. God, he hated mob mentality and moral superiority.

"Free the people, slave owners!"

A rock hit a security guard in the head. Fillion ducked. Mack hissed swear words under his breath, then pushed Fillion to keep moving. But he couldn't, even when more rocks sliced through the air at them.

"Monster!"

Something snapped inside of him. A giant explosion of fight-or-flight, and the former won. Fillion pushed through the security guards and marched toward the gate. The protesters threw more rocks, screaming, gyrating with hate, lathered up with their own self-importance in the name of human freedom. But, really, they just loved the sounds of their own voices. They knew nothing.

Nothing.

"Like father like son!"

"Son of a killer!"

A rock hit his leg. Another hit his shoulder. He threw his hands up and protected his face when more rocks sailed through the air. Still, he marched forward. The security team scrambled to reassemble around him, but Fillion just stepped around their efforts.

Media droids and human journalists shoved their way to the gate's front or activated their drones to rise above the masses. Questions were hurtled at him, sharper than the rocks. He felt the sting, each cut and scrape, but kept marching.

He reached the gate.

The angry world hushed. Arms lowered. Faces relaxed. Hundreds of eyes stared at Fillion in anticipation, and he stared back. He was a story. An enigma. A name to hate and a name to love. Bits of code strung together on the Net. Not a real person. Yet, here he was before them, flesh and blood. Seconds turned into a minute and still he said nothing, and neither did they. He remained grounded, back and shoulders straight, head lifted high.

Image.

They thought he was a coward? They thought he was soulless? Let them get a look at the monster they got off on. Orgasming at the expense of his happiness. Violating his life over and over again. It was easy to throw rocks and accusations from a distance. But he silently challenged their reality face-to-face. World leaders didn't do this. CEOs and Corporate Kings didn't do this.

Perception.

A journalist seized the silence and threw out a question about Lynden's latest scandal. Fillion shifted his focus onto him, blinked slowly, then turned around. That journalist, and all the others like him, could kiss his ass. The world didn't get a front-row seat to his suffering, or his sister's.

He wasn't a character on the Net.

Life wasn't a game.

He wasn't a vessel for anyone's entertainment. Or political platform.

Free the people, slave owners. It took everything within Fillion to not scream this back at the top of his lungs to all the people who judged him from the other side of the gate. But he was tired of hate, of feeling powerless. Tired of feeling tired. Most of all, he was battle weary of being nothing more than another piece of trash for the masses to throw into their mythological fires of Gehenna.

Hell was real, and he'd been living it inside his mind for far too long.

Mack winked as Fillion strode back into his company. The security team moved back into formation and became a human shield again. The lab entrance was just around the bend. The spell now broken, protesters resumed circle-jerking their angry, utopic rants. The illusion of his presence at the gate a mere mirage in the desert. Power was like that, he realized. The illusion remained in constant flux and adaptation.

As fickle as the wind.

They entered the lab and the security team dispersed when he continued on toward his office. Employees in open lab rooms stood as he walked by. A Rosa bot halted her steps, her head tracking his movements until he rounded the corner. Weird. But he rolled with it. At his office, he opened the door and walked in ahead of Mack and Michael, only to bite back a groan. Akiko leaned over his desk, sifting through paperwork. Her assistants—more like servants—watched from the other end of the room.

"Fillion," Akiko cooed. Her dark eyes trailed over him with each seductive step his direction. "We need to finish discussing details for the wedding."

"Your imaginary wedding?" he asked. "Fortunately, I'm busy." She tried to caress his face and he backed up a step. "Don't touch me."

"We have less than two months. Guest lists and menu options are due this week." Akiko smiled, sweet and indulgent. "Your father and mine have been talking and—"

"Get. Out."

"You always were so childish." She waltzed past him and pointed at his chair. "You should sit so we can finish our discussion like adults."

Mack's eyes widened a notch and slid his direction.

"Michael," Fillion said, turning to his assistant. "Please call security. Ms. Hirabayashi needs to be escorted from the building and safely past the gates. Have her access to N.E.T. revoked."

"Yes, Mr. Nichols." Michael brought up a screen.

Akiko laughed and shook her head as she lowered into a guest chair. "Sending me away does not change our contract or our wedding plans."

Fillion curled his fingers around her chair's wooden arms and leaned down toward her face. "You hurt my sister."

"You smell like that *rodent* you fancy," she spat in disgust.

"Don't ever hurt me or my sister again."

Fillion pushed off the chair and walked to the door, opening it for her. But she remained seated, arms crossed, her eyes blazing.

"You threaten me, Fillion Nichols?"

He chose not to reply. Instead, he continued to hold the door expectantly.

"We are still under contract!" she snapped, digging her nails into the chair. "You do not dismiss me!"

"I'm not a product and you do *not* own me!" Fillion shouted back and slammed the door. "Or my sister!"

"Once again, you behave like a child," she sneered prettily. "Your tantrum is embarrassing."

If he didn't leave now, he might strangle her elegant neck. A cigarette was calling his name back in his room too. He swung the door back open but didn't get far. Three security guards arrived before he could escape.

"Fillion, dear," Akiko practically sang as she rose from the chair and strode toward him. "How about filet mignon made from the choicest *Kobe*? Or salmon in white wine sauce perhaps?"

"You choose." His lips curled in a taunting grin. "I won't be there."

"I always get what I want, and I want *you*."

"There's a first for everything." Fillion mock-bowed. "I'm honored to be the asshole who ruined your winning streak."

"I will forget this insult and lift charges against your sister if—"

"Thanks for admitting to extortion before witnesses. Makes my job easier."

Akiko's mouth fell open. "You may be beautiful, Fillion, but your heart is ugly."

"Goodbye, Akiko. You'll be hearing from my lawyer." He opened the door wider and directed his focus to the floor. The muscle in his jaw began working back and forth again. "This is your social cue to leave," he quietly derided. "You're dismissed."

"Your father—"

"Doesn't own me, either."

"So naïve." Akiko smiled, the hatred scarring each beautiful feature on her face. "Your father raised you to be a king among men, not a wimpy boy who throws fits full of delusions. I will fix his mistakes. *You* will hear from *my* lawyer. The lab owes my father. You will pay, one way or the other." Then she marched out of the room, her assistants scurrying behind her with heads down.

Fillion shut the door, then trudged to his desk and crumpled into his office chair.

Michael finally blinked and a touch of color returned to his face.

Mack, however, chuckled and fell into a chair before offering Fillion a cigarette. "Light up, *bishounen*. The big pair of balls you grew needs a smoke break."

Fillion placed the much-needed cigarette between his lips and flicked his lighter. His eyelids closed shut while he dragged once, then twice. God, that never got old. He didn't realize how much his body was shaking until he went to flick the ashes. Mack pretended to the study the room, instead of him. But Fillion knew better. His friend always had an eye on him.

"The scary witch is gone," Mack drawled. "Next task: the wolves. We have a brawny damsel in distress to save."

"Brawny damsel?" Michael asked, confused.

"I was referring to Coal." Mack puffed on his cigarette. "He has pretty long eyelashes and sexy dimples, am I right?"

"Well, uh, I..." Michael blushed bright red and suddenly appeared interested in his screen.

Fillion lifted his eyebrow. "Oh hell. You too?"

"Quit your jealous gritching," Mack tossed out. Fillion flipped him off, which made Mack grin. "Have you looked at him, pretty boy? Like actually *looked at him*? Coal is every man's fantasy. Right, Michael?"

"No," Michael shook his head vigorously. "Not like that. Never like that. I'm a whole decade older. And, he's with your sister."

When Michael resumed interest in his screen, Mack mouthed to Fillion, "So like that."

Fillion smirked. He knew Mack drooled over Coal and had for a long time. But, for some reason, thinking of Michael crushing on Coal was kind of cute. And explained a lot. Actually, it explained everything. A thread of relief touched the tightness in his chest. Maybe Michael was trustworthy after all.

"Mr. Nichols." Michael glanced over his screen, all business once again. "The chief of police is here. Security is escorting him here."

"Time to fight the wolves," Mack murmured, making smoke circles as he exhaled. "Ready, boss?"

"Thanks, Michael." Fillion stood and straightened out his shirt. Then he took one last puff on his cigarette before rubbing it out, when a thought hit him. Slowly, he lifted his head and met Mack's waiting gaze. "Why aren't you in trouble with the law?"

Mack leaned back in the chair and sniffed, placing his combat boots on the edge of Fillion's desk. His head fell back as he exhaled a thin stream of smoke, saying, "The FBI owes me a favor."

"A *favor*?"

"OK, you're right. They owe me two favors."

"The hell?" Fillion quietly laughed.

"It was more like 'oh my god,' but we'll leave that story for another time." Mack flicked the ashes, then leveled his gaze onto Fillion. "To win."

"To destroy."

"Cut the ties. Call the shots."

"Moves and countermoves."

This time, Fillion uttered the words with confidence. He refused to go backwards and become a slave once again. Nobody owned him.

Wake up! He called out to his emerging mind, the one crawling out of suspended animation on hands and knees. *Wake up!*

He wasn't a character on the Net.

He wasn't a vessel for anyone's entertainment.

The elements that comprised his life mattered.

Wake up!

His fingers played with the edges of the crumpled-up player's card in his pocket until it rolled into his palm. A knock on the door sounded. As Fillion strode over to greet the chief of police, he tossed Fate's final play into the trash.

Your mind is a walled garden. Even death cannot touch the flowers blooming there.

— Dr. Robert Ford, in *Westworld*, 2016 *

Stability's the beginning of the end. We only walk by continually beginning to fall forward.

— Milgrim, in *Zero History*, by William Gibson, 2010 *

Chapter Twenty-Five

Wednesday, April 4, 2058

Fillion pushed around files of information across his screen. He was determined to read every word in the MELISSA Project's folders by morning. Not necessarily to comprehend fully, but to highlight specifics for further investigation later. Plus, his mind was too wound up to rest. It was either this, other work details needing his attention, or mentally ranting the night away.

"I need help," he mumbled to himself. God, still talking to himself. Would it ever end? Fillion stared at the wall by his bed, disgusted. "Hey, Hanley, you pervert," he muttered to the wall. "Stop listening to me."

His gaze leaped around his darkened room. Waiting for some kind of reply.

Nothing appeared. No rebuttal signal. He didn't feel any different. Whatever. That asshole's days were numbered. Fillion was gathering every scrap of evidence he could find. The mind game was about to spin. Fillion was now the Gamemaster—he moved the pawns on the chessboard—and Hanley was going to find himself in forced retirement. Bonus if orange became his new dress code, too.

Puzzle pieces were *finally* coming together. Bio-hacking and body augmentations had been around for decades. Hell, he'd considered a few enhancements himself. Now it didn't matter. Seemed Hanley had made that choice for him, like usual. That is, if Fillion and Mack's suspicions proved true. At least he wasn't chipped. So demeaning. He wasn't the government's pet. Or a corporation's.

In Europe and some parts of Asia, citizens were required to get chipped. Identity mining and digital cloning were rampant. It was getting harder for security to remain ahead of implanted consumer tech.

But biotech developed by New Eden Biospherics & Research was a game changer in the science community, not only for transgenerational epigenetics but also for the transhumanism movement. The dark irony wasn't lost on Fillion.

Isolation, confinement, and extreme environment syndrome? No. Villagers preferred their close quarters. Most couldn't perceive visual depth beyond the limitations of the biodome. Not enough far distances for the retina to focus on. When faced with the expanses beyond The Door, villagers routinely cowered or threw up their hands as protective measures. The lab had labeled their reaction "the sky is falling syndrome."

Imprinted by Earth? Not really. Not like all other globally connected humans. Role-players had done their job well. The second and third gens could only comprehend the closed-loop cycle of their Martian biosphere. The reality of Earth, of the greater ecosystem's enormity, was incomprehensible.

Self-correcting medical biotech to heal and avert major medical crises? Yes. The mother-infant mortality rate had dropped to record low levels—lower rates than even the most progressive industrial nation. Very few adversely reacted to foreign viral and bacterial infections too. A guarantee that a Martian colony could multiply and be fruitful. But, so far, no plans to release this tech to the public sector to aid mothers and infants who still died on Earth from poor or limited health care. Bastard.

Cybernetic programming capability to alter human genetics to withstand changes in gravity, atmosphere, and other space-related trials? Possibly. In fact, Fillion found evidence that tests would begin on randomly selected individuals in New Eden. He tagged those studies for Michael.

All human experimentation would end. Effective immediately.

Even so, he had to admit that the community would flourish in a biodome city Mars-side. The rest of the world realized this, too. Since his father's press release, Fillion's message center had overflowed with business propositions from several mega-corporations wanting to use New Eden for privatized space opportunities. The hell with them. The next people to use New Eden would be the homeless, the jobless, the juvenile delinquents—the ones who needed every opportunity to fight the system that had failed them.

Fillion bit back a yawn as he loaded another file to audit. So far, the information and discoveries that should have elicited shock instead flat-lined. After discovering Jeff was from the original MELISSA Project, it wasn't a stretch to learn that other members of The Elements were too. All but Connor. He was the control.

How was he going to tell Leaf? The Son of Earth was going to flip. And when Leaf was pissed, the ground quaked and the sky turned red. A man made for peace, but he was a formidable weapon in war. Even Willow knew to check her responses when her brother switched from life-giver to destruction mode. The side of Fillion's mouth pulled up. He couldn't wait to sic Leaf on the world.

A muscle in Fillion's neck ached from laying at a weird angle on his pillow. He blinked long and hard. His eyes burned from strain, from auditing, and from too much emotion in a single day. Hell, what time was it? Mack should be taking off soon to meet up with Coal.

Following a late dinner, Fillion had studied schematics for the biodome until he found two viable points of entry away from the public eye. One was a hidden gate at the property's back end, now covered by oleander bushes. The other was through the technosphere into the rainforest biodome. According to the digital 3D rendering, the hidden pressurized door opened to a small alcove behind the waterfall. Fillion had always wondered how Guardian Angels worked on hydrotech without prying eyes. Villagers believed Step Stone Pond earned its name from the large Amazonian-type lily pads dotting the water. Turns out that actual stepping stones lay six inches below the water's surface and led directly to the hidden alcove.

Nevertheless, Fillion informed Coal via vid that he'd have to swim across the murky pond. Mack's lips twitched the entire time Fillion was explaining the plan to Coal. The Son of Fire didn't need to know about any stepping stones. Maybe the damn man might cool off a notch or two.

Mack would meet Coal in the technosphere with dry clothes and a wig—women's clothing. How Mack found women's clothing large enough for Coal, Fillion had no clue. But his friend was motivated, and for multiple reasons. They'd leave N.E.T through the back gate and try to blend in with the protesters camping around the corner. If anyone stopped them, Mack would pretend to make out with Coal. Regardless, they'd stagger down Eden's Gate Road like lust-driven drunkards to the chauffeur Mack had arranged.

Lynden was going to kill Mack if Coal didn't first. Fillion couldn't help the grin that formed in the darkness. His friend was finally living out his Coal fantasy. And he could almost hear his sister threaten Mack's manhood when learning of his friend's latest scheme.

The humor quickly disappeared as his thoughts focused on Lyn. A pang sliced through his chest. She had to be afraid right now. There was no way to contact her. But he was flying out at first light, scheduled to arrive in Seattle two hours before her bail hearing. If all went according to his plan, he would have time to pick up his lawyer and demand a private moment with Lyn.

Akiko was going to pay for this stunt. Attack him? Fine. But his sister was off-limits. So was screwing with the residents of New Eden.

The overhead vent turned on with a loud whoosh. Fillion's gaze darted away from the holographic screen to each dark corner in his room. The lab was cloaked in silence, making him extra jumpy. Hell, everything made him jumpy these days. Reality blurred and smudged to shades of truth way too much, tinted with enough lies that Fillion's mind target-locked to hunt out inconsistent patterns in his ever-shifting perception. Necessary to stay on top of Hanley's moves. But damn. It made him question everything. All. The. Time.

Focus.

He resumed auditing the research findings. And read the same sentence three times in a row before giving up. Maybe he should shower. Or go for a walk.

Or not.

He minimized the "M" files and brought up a message screen with a note to Michael giving detailed instructions for a personal delivery to the Watson home the next day. The package would contain a message for Leaf—asking him to schedule a vid conference with Fillion and his lawyer—and a gift for Willow. Fillion released a slow breath with the latter bit. Continuing to pursue her might end in more pain. But, god, she was worth every second of torture he'd know. And what was he thinking, kissing her? There was no thought. Not when around her. All intelligence just poofed into the stratosphere of his social anxiety until his stupid, awkward self could only stare, helpless. Always.

It was annoying.

Before he turned into a corny, sentimental cretin, he brought up the recent financials for the handover. "Buyout," he murmured under his breath as he swiped each letter into a search bar. When signing docs, he hadn't paid that close attention to Hanley's majority ownership buyout, paid by shareholders and New Eden Biospherics & Research. At their levels of affluence, money was money. But he had a suspicion. One that'd have to wait on its answer a bit longer. The numbers moved in and out of focus as Fillion's eyes teared with another yawn.

A chill brushed along his bare torso from the vent. The cooler air was welcome, though. Kept him awake, and he needed to stay awake. After today, he was afraid of what nightmares would visit him. He'd crash at Mack's after the hearing and his meeting with Leaf. Somewhere safe. Somewhere he knew Hanley couldn't touch him.

The information on his screen formed a river of blue, streaming one direction. His eyes tracked. And that's about it. He stared at the numbers without actually seeing them.

Maybe he needed a cigarette.

Stifling another yawn, Fillion sat up and stretched his neck and shoulders. He twisted to readjust his pillows when a soft rap echoed in his room.

His pulse jumped to this throat. Probably only Mack. Just as a precaution, Fillion slid his screen over to the security camera he had installed. There, in the hallway's darkness, his friend's white hair glowed.

"In a sec," he hollered toward the door, relieved.

Fillion grabbed a cigarette, then cupped his mouth to light up as he crept across the floor. Orange flickered in the black and his pulse calmed with the habitual trigger. Opening up his door a crack, he taunted, "Finally get to man-handle Coal and you're getting cold feet?"

"He broke my nose once." Mack slid past Fillion into the room. "He'd do it again."

"Maybe he needs a safe word."

Even in the darkness, Fillion could see the outline of Mack's middle finger.

"I'm gentle."

Fillion grunted in humor as he shut the door. "Not interested."

"You're adorable when shy, *bishounen*."

Mack slapped Fillion's ass and then swaggered across the room in the holographic screen's low light. He paused by the nightstand and groped for a pack of cigarettes in the dark, celebrating when making contact.

"Need a light?" Fillion asked.

With a stick dangling between his lips, Mack murmured, "Come hither, pretty boy." Fillion grinned and leaned in toward his friend until the end of his cigarette touched Mack's. In between drags, his friend asked, "How's your head?"

"Hurting."

"Yeah. Figured." Mack exhaled slowly and opened a screen on his Cranium as he eased onto the edge of the bed. Bright blue light bathed his friend in an ethereal glow, his hair like illuminated icicles. They squinted at each other as their eyes adjusted, blinking. "Ready?"

"I don't think I have another existential crisis left in me."

"Gubbish," Mack muttered under his breath. "After I'm done, you should feel more in control though."

"You . . . you think my anxiety and PTSD—"

"Is anxiety and PTSD." The cigarette bobbed in Mack's mouth as he spoke. "Were you required to get additional vaccinations before The Tour?"

"Yeah, through the Department of Health. Part of my travel papers."

"Shots, sublingual, both…?"

"Both."

"The black spots in your memory, they've only appeared the past four, six months?"

"Along with persistent nausea."

Mack studied him over his screen. "Like an overdrive of anxiety?"

"Increase in emotional dysregulation to the point where I question my reality. Every. Freaking. Moment." Fillion lifted his shoulder in a slight shrug. "Maybe I should. Hell, we could be AI, and our machine consciousness breakdown is part of a different experiment on behalf of humanity's quest for knowledge and progressive advancement. The backstory could just be to test empathy capabilities." He slid a sly look to Mack. "*Desu*."

"I knew you had another existential crisis left in you." Mack waggled his eyebrows and bit his tongue. "OK, I'm diving deep. Breathe in slowly and relax…"

Fillion puffed on his cigarette and then another in silence while his friend concentrated. The ever-present twinge of nausea was growing. Eventually he leaned forward, his head in his hands, his elbows digging into his knees. Smoke curled upward from the ash tray. Tiny wraiths escaping with the frayed shreds of calm he had worked so hard to keep. Familiar panic touched his pulse. And his ever-racing mind. Especially when his gut clenched with heavy, queasy motions.

How had Hanley influenced or controlled Fillion's thoughts?

His body?

He focused his attentions on the shadowed ceiling above Mack's head. Anything to deflect from dissecting those two questions. Small divots dotted the ceiling tiles. His eyes began making quick work of patterns. Constellations appeared—Orion, Pegasus, Virgo, and ones he conjured from imaginary lines and dots. Smoke hazed past his vision, like clouds passing through the night sky. Another roll of nausea hit Fillion as Mack's fingers danced through the air. Fillion's focus shot back to his friend.

"What'd you do?"

Mack's eyebrows hung low over his eyes. "Your system is different than Coal's and Andra's."

Bile rose in a violent wave and he gagged.

"H-how?" Fillion somehow managed to ask.

Mack removed the cigarette from his mouth. "It's more complex. More covert. Not as much medical coding, but what's there is concerning. Trying to find central command." His gaze darted Fillion's way for a nanosec. "Feel anything different?"

"Worse."

"Well, shit. So much for being gentle." Mack frowned, a strange look for his happy-go-lucky friend. "Sorry, mate. Need a bucket?"

"I hope not."

"Want me to kill all operations?"

Fillion bit the inside of his cheek. He didn't know. Well, yeah he did. All his life he suffered from anxiety. An illness with no cure except through never-ending therapy and prescription medications. Hope sparked with a sudden thought.

"No." Fillion found Mack's eyes over the screen. "Kill any control linked to Hanley. I want inner sanctum. Switch off Pinocchio safeguards. And . . . and program me."

"Uh, how?"

"Target bots to latch onto neurotransmitters, coded to balance out gamma-Aminobutyric acid, serotonin, dopamine, and epinephrine responses."

"I'm not a bio-chemist, mate."

"Maybe program a pulse into the nanobot electrons. Self-administered bio-electric therapy."

Mack's expression didn't change.

"Forget it," Fillion said. "Just cut strings for now."

His friend's frown deepened. "Hanley has an attack program. Any attempt to mutate or hack will punish you."

"How?"

"Not sure."

"I don't care."

"Fillion—"

"You're the one who told me to cut every tie and walk away."

They stared at each other. Mack looked away first, his body deflating.

"Hanley won't kill me."

"Yeah, but he'll make you suffer until you wish you were dead."

"Too late for that."

Mack heaved a loud sigh and began swearing in Japanese.

"You're not the one hurting me, Mack."

"I know. I know." Mack closed his eyes and cracked his neck in several sharp movements. "Get a bucket."

Fillion strode into the bathroom, returned with a wastebasket and sat down again. "Ready."

But he wasn't. Oh god, the pain. His body seized then released what felt like the entirety of his twenty-one years of life in one violent spasm. He dragged in large breaths, groaning when his body convulsed again. And again. And again. Mack tried to give reassurances but Fillion couldn't hear a goddamn thing over his retching and the blood rushing in his ears. And, shit, was he grateful for that song of life galloping in his veins. It was the only way he knew he hadn't died yet.

"I'm rearranging your code. Deleting strings. Stitching new operations. Central command is buried deep. Diving further. Hang on."

It's a simulation, a coded program. Everyone is a character in N.E.T.

Fillion shoved Hanley's taunt back to the shadows where it belonged. The message clawed at him nonetheless. His life was programmable, like a drone. His literal fear now reality. A sob buried deep fought for release. He didn't have the energy to grieve anymore. Whatever was left of him was dedicated to war.

"A Gamemaster ponders the hidden," Fillion whispered to himself.

"Say again?" Mack asked.

His friend's voice grew distant and reverberated, as if Fillion had fallen into a tunnel. And he was falling—down, down, down into the coffin of his mind.

His body trembled with warning and then he vomited again. Cold sweat coated his skin, his breathing ragged. Fillion wiped his mouth and stared out into black and the black stared back. Not menacing, but expectant. A gentle current moved through him and coiled around his mind, encouraging him to keep falling.

So he did.

Highways of information surged through his head in ribbons of neon light. The softly buzzing current coiled tighter around his waning sense of reality until awareness constricted out of focus.

Still he was falling.

Falling.

Falling.

He cried out when crashing hard onto a decayed mass of pixelated leaves in a glitching digitized forest. His words were carried away by a cold, biting wind, one he had never experienced before—a hurtling gust of weeping anger and gnashing sorrow. Dark clouds seeped through the geodesic panes in his mind's eye and gathered in a thunderous song of destruction and triumph. Warm rain showered in drips of blood, soaking into the soil and coating his skin.

Fillion gaped, mesmerized. Allowed nature's nebula of rage to heal his own. Dark strands of hair whipped across his face. His jacket flapped and snapped with each word that blew from this place of grief to storm the static atmosphere around him.

"Fillion, look at me."

He jumped back and sucked in a sharp breath. Where did her voice come from? His entire system froze. Error messages flashed in his periphery. The forest of trees stilled in a gentle breeze, glitching in and out of focus. He touched his face. A cold sweat beaded on his forehead, not blood rain. Fillion's heart thrummed hard against his ribs. What the hell was happening? Fear slithered into his veins and ice crystallized up his spine. He twisted to peer the other direction when *she* appeared, wreathed in visions of golden light. Like an angel.

"My King, you shall find a solution to shatter the illusions he has cast."

You really are the perfect solution.

The trembling finger at the trigger of his emotional stability finally pulled. A shot to his entire system. His life splattered and sprayed out in all directions as Hanley's familiar words hit his brain. The forest blurred. A sharp pain bloomed behind his eyes.

Willow continued, unaware of his struggle. "Spin the tales, My King. Weave them together. Make a reality all your own."

They trust you, Son of Eden . . . A man of magic, one who will save them from the evils of the Outside world.

The nameless, faceless scientists placed Willow's body into the stasis chamber. A roar scorched his throat as he charged the glass. The world fuzzed and spun. A loud screech wailed in his head and he grabbed his ears, his teeth grinding until the sound stopped. Giant trees towered over him and rustled in the bio-breeze. They marched toward him, like protesters. He staggered back a step and blinked rapidly. His chest heaved. Breathe. He needed to breathe.

"Fillion?" Willow shrieked. She clapped her hands over her mouth, eyes wide with growing terror.

She was alive.

Wait. She was alive?

Where was he?

She'll never be yours.

Bile violently churned in his stomach. He didn't want to puke anymore. But he was so sickened by Hanley. And that he . . . that he would experiment on his own son. The sob in Fillion's throat loosened and he finally gulped in a large breath. And then another. He bent over and clutched his head as the world tilted again.

Voices streamed in and out of focus.

Different stories speaking at once.

Different realities.

A convergence of multiple dimensions.

Fillion cinched his eyes closed as another spasm hit. The glass that was pressed to his face began to shake. A body thumped with seizures. Voices shouted.

"You will make an excellent Gamemaster one day," Hanley whispered in his ear. "But do not ever forget that this game is over *only* when I say so."

Fire exploded in his vision and burned through his body. The ground rushed up to meet him. And then he was falling.

Falling.

Falling.

"Fillion!"

A hand touched his face, cool and gentle.

"Fillion, look at me!"

Pain brightened in a searing flash, then everything went dark.

Fillion's eyes snapped open to pitch-black emptiness. Was he in a coffin? No. He could see his hands, legs, and his clothing with sharp clarity. In fact, it appeared as if his skin wavered with a faint bluish glow. Why didn't the black absorb the light? His fingers clawed the dark where he lay. No floor that he could discern. What the hell?

"Hello?" Fillion called out.

Strange. His voice held a tinny quality not present before. No echo either.

Maybe he blacked out. Why didn't he feel panic? Or dread? He should feel many things. Yet his emotions and his normally racing thoughts seemed unnaturally flat. Not that he didn't acknowledge emotions or his cognitive functions. They were still intact. But he had a sense of control over himself. It was like an astral projection—his spirit, separated from his body, on an empty plane of consciousness.

He rolled onto his knees. The nonexistent floor proved present despite the physics that shouted otherwise. Was he suspended by light vibrations? Or zero gravity? Slowly, he came to a stand and turned to fully investigate this inter-dimensional space—and stopped.

"Look at me now, dammit!"

A searing light sliced through the darkness. Fillion threw up his hands to block the intensity. It was if someone lifted the lid to this digital coffin. He opened his mouth to scream, but the light swallowed him whole and his body evaporated.

The world came into focus in a single blink. Literally. One moment, he was fighting the elements and convergent realities. The next, he was in his lab quarters, curled up on the floor and clutching a sour-smelling wastebasket with a light shining directly into his eyes. He was shaking so bad his teeth were clacking together.

"Hey." Mack crouched on the floor beside him. He turned off his Cranium's flashlight. "Your eyes are finally focusing."

"Wh-what happened?"

"I think you rebooted to reset the repairs I made."

"Holy sh-shit."

"The code is rigged. I can't fix you tonight. Not fully. But you're safe now. Dammit, you're safe." Tears streamed down Mack's face. "I've never been so scared in my life."

Fillion reached out a trembling hand and tried to wipe away the tears on his best friend's face. And failed. Miserably. Instead, he ended up tapping

Mack's cheek several times before giving up with an embarrassed smile and eye roll.

His friend grinned, and then started laughing. "Love you, too, mate."

"D-did you s-save evidence for c-court?"

"Yup. A mirror file is intact."

"Good. What kind of a-attack?"

Mack laid out flat on the floor with a long, quavering sigh. "Didn't make sense. Medical coding. My guess? Probably flooding you with cortisol production to trigger your PTSD and anxiety."

They grew silent, both lost to their fears and internal rants. Eventually, Mack rolled onto his side and stared. Like he was calculating data and trying to make sense of his demi-robotic friend who quivered beside him on the floor. Fillion wasn't bothered by his cybernetics or Mack's inspection, just beyond pissed at being violated and assaulted. Perhaps someone in the underground could help Mack reprogram his coding to treat anxiety and depression. Help his mind calm, like in the black hole he experienced while rebooting. No more meds or self-doubt. Control over his triggers. Shit, he was about to cry.

Instead, Fillion arched his eyebrow and stared at Mack. "Bit dump," he encouraged.

"Father forgive me, for I have sinned."

"Absolved. F-for life."

"I am now your official fake boy."

"Shocking."

"No, I was your fake boy before. Now I'm your *fake boy, desu.*"

"I already f-fainted for you. If you want a repeat p-performance, you'll have to try harder."

Mack winked. "I'm a gentle lover."

"Keep telling y-yourself that."

"Smart-ass." His friend studied him in that strange way again. Almost hesitant. "The reason you're safe is because I set up a man-in-the-middle. I want to observe how and when Hanley attacks you."

"And attack back?"

"Hellz yeah."

Fillion grabbed Mack's shirt and murmured, "You're the best fake boy. Ever."

"Are we going to spoon?"

"Something like that."

Mack hesitated a beat. "Seriously?"

"No." His friend flipped him off. Again. Fillion grinned at the sound of Mack's laughter. God, he loved that sound. "Help me up, mate." Fillion came to a stand on shaking legs with Mack's assistance. When grounded, he grabbed Mack's shirt again and pulled him into an embrace. His friend nearly crushed him and the humor quickly faded into quiet sobs. He'd never seen his friend cry like this. Not once. Tear up? Sure. But Mack was full-on weeping. Fillion closed his eyes and whispered, "Love you."

"If something happened—"

"You saved my nanobot ass, Robot Overlord."

"Life debt accepted, *koibito*," Mack said, pulling away and wiping at his face with a lopsided smile.

Fillion returned the smile. "Partners for life."

"Shit, I need another cigarette."

He tossed his pack Mack's way. "Go rescue that hulking damsel in distress of yours. I'll be fine."

"I'd protest, but your voice is back." Mack lit up and tossed the pack back. "Repairs are working."

"See you in a few hours. Promise."

"Walk into that courtroom like you own the judicial system."

"Damn straight."

"Turn me on."

Fillion shoved his friend toward the door. "Go. Coal is probably waiting for you. Wet."

"A wet man," Mack playfully murmured, his eyes rolling to the back of his head in a mock-look of ecstasy. "Smexy." Then he slid Fillion a straight look. "Farm Boy is dying a thousand deaths tonight. You can take the boy out of New Eden—"

"Yeah, yeah…"

"So, of course, I'm taking pictures of Farm Boy in drag for Rainbow."

Fillion burst into laughter. "Please wait to show her until I'm there."

"Naturally," Mack said in a voice like Coal's. Fillion lost it again. God, it felt good to laugh. "Hey, at drop-off, you want me to ask the hackers to start media rumors about Akiko's revenge? Garner social justice sympathizers as initial pushback?"

"Start a smear campaign against Hanley, too. Forging docs. Fake partnership. Along those lines only. No doxxing. Not yet. Soon, though."

"Best. Day. Ever."

"See you on the other side, mate."

His friend pulled him into one last embrace, then slipped into the hallway like the chain-smoking ninja he was. Fillion stared at the closed door, absently turning the black wedding band on his finger. Now that his friend had left, Fillion allowed anger to replace the waning nausea swirling in his gut. Mack needed to remain focused to get Coal safely out of New Eden. He'd share the ugly details with him later.

It made sense. All of it. He didn't have to check the financials to know the end of this dark tale. Or what Joel's money had to do with everything. The man was set up in a long con. Timothy, too. Marriage to Akiko wasn't to secure custom biotech from HiraMed, either. Fillion needed the cash flow beyond whatever Hanley had planned post-project shutdown to secure jobs at the lab and to pay out first gen for their twenty-five years of service per their contractual agreements. And definitely for the lawsuits that would crop up after the first gen learned the truth about their children and grandchildren.

Did you or didn't you bargain for the residents to remain in a biodome?

The human experiment's end at New Eden also meant the end of government and corporate contracts. Shareholders would sell out for the latest venture.

Set up to fail. Always. New Eden Biospherics & Lab would sink into the sands of the Salton Sea, and Hanley would publicly blame Fillion for mismanagement. The world would believe him, too. They always did. After all, he was just the first-born loser of a first-rate swindler.

His legacy.

Slowly, Fillion turned toward the wall by his bed. "Game over."

Adams: Willow Oak Watson is a surprise stand-in today as we've never met her in the three years since New Eden opened its doors. Did you spend much time with her during your stay? And, if so, what would you like the world to know about our Martian princess?

Fillion: Yes, I spent time with Ms. Watson—the whole Watson family, actually. Willow Oak Watson is . . . she's strength personified. I deeply respect her intelligence and authenticity. I've traveled to all seven continents and met people from nearly every corner of the world, and I've never known any woman like her.

Adams: [laughs] You better not let Ms. Hirabayashi hear you!

Fillion: Maybe you shouldn't have invited her to this interview, then. Akiko is a big girl and can handle it. But publicly suggesting she's jealous and shallow? That's the real offense. Whatever angle you want to spin for ratings. Right, Akiko?

Akiko: [laughs] He is just teasing you, Jennifer. You know how Fillion feels about the media.

Fillion: How do I feel about the media, Akiko? And false charm? Tell her.

— Fillion Nichols, on *Atoms to Adams Daily Show,* March 27, 2058

Chapter Twenty-Six

Wednesday, April 5, 2058

Loosen your hold a tad," Willow encouraged. Corona's fingers relaxed until the fibers drafted with more ease. Mohair yarn spun smooth and tight, much better compared to the lumpy threads that had been winding onto the bobbin. "Lovely! Remember to keep a consistent treadle rhythm. Changes in speed may affect yarn uniformity as well."

Rona's face pinched in concentration as she watched her feet, then her fingers, then her feet again. "How is my treadle rhythm now, Your Highness?" she asked.

"Much improved. Before long you shall be able to spin in your sleep!"

Ember's sister beamed under the praise. Satisfied, Willow moved away to a nearby chair, picked up her lap loom, and resumed tablet weaving a hemp belt. The familiar creaking lull of the spinning wheel sang in the background as her fingers busied with their task. One she could practically do with eyes closed, which allowed her to continue to appraise Rona's spinning without intruding in her space. Unlike other Hansens, Corona possessed a more timid spirit, always gentle and soft-spoken.

In the corner, Alder played with his blocks and a few twigs he had collected on the way home from the Great Hall. His imagination babbled on as the twigs jumped over the tower blocks. He would need a new activity soon. His energy was endless, it seemed.

Down the hall, Ember emerged from her chamber, a babe on each arm. She was still dressed in a shift. Fatigue colored half-moons below her eyes, but her gaze glimmered with contentment. "Good morrow, Rona," she said. "You are here early this morn."

"Yes," her sister replied, somewhat distracted. Her face pinched up more as she concentrated on her task and continued. "Mother needs me to assist on rounds later this afternoon."

"Perhaps you can assist me, too, for but a moment? That is, if Willow can spare you?"

Corona peered at Willow for permission. "Of course," she granted. "Care for family first, then the community."

The spinning wheel slowed to a stop. Corona gingerly placed a piece of linen over the drafting basket, then approached Ember with outstretched hands. Fia nestled into her Auntie's embrace with a hiccupped sigh.

"I shall lay Terra on my cot. Fia is still a wee bit restless. Would you watch the twins while I speak with Willow?"

When Ember turned back toward the hallway, Alder leapt to his feet and dashed over to where she stood and pulled on her shift. "Mother! Up?"

"Yes, lad. I shall return shortly and you can sit upon my lap."

His lower lip trembled and he ducked his head.

"Alder," Willow said, crouching beside him. "Shall you sit with me while we wait for Mother?" He took her offered hand, though reluctantly. With one last glance at Ember, Alder turned and followed Willow to her seat. He climbed up and tucked his head onto her chest and began sucking on his thumb. She smoothed the curls from his forehead and murmured, "I have a job for you."

"I work. Like Father and Papa."

"Yes, you are a hard worker. Shall I show you the task?"

The distraction worked. He perked up and leaned over the chair's edge as Willow rummaged through her sewing basket until she found a skein of unusable yarn. Brown eyes twinkled with curiosity as she placed the lumpy salvage into his hands.

"I need knots. Many knots."

"I work knots," Alder said with a serious head nod. "For Auntie Oak."

She kissed his forehead. "Papa showed you how to knot rope?"

"Yes," he answered simply. "In Forge."

"Knotting yarn is similar. Do you wish for me to show you? Or do you wish to try on your own first?"

Two cherubic dimples appeared with his grin. "I try first."

"Excellent. If you knot yarn well, I shall show you how to finger knit next." His brown eyes widened with glee, widening further when Ember stepped into the living room.

"Mother!" Alder scrambled off of Willow's lap, clutching the yarn, and ran into Ember's embrace. "I knot for Auntie Oak!"

"Wonderful, sweetling." Ember lowered into a seat and then scooped up Alder. "My, I do believe you have grown."

"I big," Alder said, puffing out his little chest. "Unca Blaze say so."

"Well, Uncle Blaze would know. He is a tall lad too."

Alder turned the ball of yarn around in his hands and nuzzled in close to Ember with a look of peace. Willow picked up her lap loom and resumed weaving while mother and son cuddled and murmured back and forth with each other.

A few heartbeats later, Ember caught her eye and Willow paused. "Fillion sent a video message for you."

"Indeed?"

"Shall I play it for you here? Or do you wish for privacy in your chamber?"

Willow curled a strand of hair around her finger and nibbled her bottom lip.

"There is no one present who would admonish your unchaperoned message," Ember teased.

"The silliness of it all," Willow huffed. She reached for Ember's offered Cranium and turned the metallic object over in her hand. "So small and yet so very intimidating."

"Yes, at first. 'Tis true. The message will load in a matter of two taps."

Ember continued with a series of simple instructions, including how to reply. A few heartbeats later, Willow sat upon her bed and turned on the Cranium strapped to her ear, remembering to keep her eyes straight. Tap number one. An image of Fillion, behind a dark wooden desk and slouching in a large black chair, filled her vision. He was far too dashing a figure.

The "play" button was easy to locate in the lower corner. Tap number two and Fillion came to life. Willow held her breath, with awe and trepidation. The magic of Outsider technology remained far too surreal to accept. Sheaves of paper littered his desk. A picture of a fantastical city awash in twinkling lights and rain puddles decorated the wall behind where he sat. The details were too small to fully appreciate. Perhaps one day she could see the picture upon his wall and study his alien world.

Fillion blinked softly, a shy gesture and yet entirely characteristic of his aloof bearing. It was then she noticed his eyes. Her pent-up breath left in a gust right before she clapped a hand over her mouth. His eyes—they were clear and bright, and he stared at the camera as though she were the very light of day after a long, dark night. A tempest still brewed behind the swirling silvers and blues. But he was not consumed by raging storms as before. Nor did he appear sickly. A healthy glow radiated from his countenance. What had transpired in a single day? She could weep for joy!

Slowly, he lifted a sheet of paper with words scrawled in a curious print.

Coal is safe and hidden.

Now she did weep, utterly relieved.

Fillion flicked a contraption in his hand and a tiny flame appeared. Fire licked the paper's edges which he tossed into a metal bucket he had lifted into view. Black smoke wafted past his face, right before he spoke.

"I know you don't fall to the whims of Outsider boyish fancies. But if you're listening to this, I win. Resistance is futile." A dark eyebrow arched as a taunting smile played across his lips. "You can't resist me. Even if I'm a technology ghost." The arrogant knave had the audacity to wink at her! Perhaps she should not have prayed for his irksome witticisms to return. "Go to the woods skirting the stairs," he continued. "Beneath a giant fern is a gift. You'll know it when you see it." He blinked slowly, the way he so often communicated with her. "See you around, Maiden."

The message ended and Willow stared, bewildered. A gift? For *her*? The day before, Fillion appeared as though he walked the edge of his sanity. Now, he dared to flirt with her as a technology ghost? Would he ever make sense? A smile formed the more she contemplated his obvious rebirth in character and temperament. This was the man she remembered. The man whom she was willing to stake her reputation on, to give her love and to receive his in return, and to work with to revolutionize New Eden.

Gently, she removed the Cranium from her head and placed it on her end table. Leaf was currently visiting the lab. He had left their apartment in a thunderous march, nearly slamming the door behind him. Alder awoke with the raucous sounds, as did the twins. Had Fillion sent him a separate message regarding New Eden Space Ventures? Willow had not shared with her brother, knowing that Fillion would in due time.

Somewhat dazed, Willow shuffled down the hallway and into the living room. She was not easily given to romantic notions. The promise of a hidden gift from Fillion out in the woods shattered any attempts at ladylike deportment, however.

Ember said nothing as she left the apartment. Her knowing smile spoke words aplenty. Willow refused to blush at the implications. Dare she accept a gift from a man not her betrothed? A man who had jilted her previously, even if justified? A lady—a princess and heir in a Legacy—would not behave so. This very thought set fire in her veins. New Eden did not own her reputation. They did not decide her matrimonial worth nor her value as a woman. She alone owned her reputation and, if she chose to gift it to a man who did not play by their social rules, so be it.

Fresh air bathed her flushed skin, laden with the smells of tilth and evergreens. The forest called to her, extending its finger and beckoning her closer. With each defiant step down the stairs, the binding strings of oppression snapped away until she fairly floated to the base of the biodome. No one would control her—not her brother, not society, and certainly not Hanley Nichols.

Ferns clustered around the base of several trees. Willow walked the tree-lined edge until her gaze caught on a scintillating light. Dew dampened her dress as she knelt in the wild grass and decaying leaves. Nestled beneath emerald fronds lay a carved box inlaid with an iridescent material in the shape of an oak tree. Her breath caught. The wood shone, as though perpetually glossed with water though dry, and reflected rich, reddish-brown tones.

Nervously, she peered over her shoulder and then pulled the box close, surprised by its heaviness. She trailed her finger over the oak tree design, marveling at the colors within the white material. She wished to inspect the contents, but not with watching eyes. Lifting the box, she casually returned to her apartment.

Rona now joined Ember in the living room. As she entered, their eyes fixed on the box.

"I shall retire to my chamber for a short spell," she told Corona. "I have mending in the corner you can stitch until I return to resume spinning lessons."

Rona dipped into a shallow curtsy as Willow continued into the hallway.

On her bed, Willow opened the lid of the box and wondered at the silence—not a creak or groan or click came from its sleek metal hinge. Inside, a folded piece of paper rested atop white, crinkly paper. She plucked the note from the box and smothered a smile at the sight of Fillion's strange penmanship.

Willow-
May it shimmer like water for you.
F. M. N.

Intrigued, she peeled back the delicate, flimsy paper and gasped. Ripples of light and shadows shimmered over the violet shades of fabric, reminiscent of the North Pond when reflecting the vibrant lavenders and grays of dusk. The China silk was cool to the touch and far softer than she imagined. And heavy. Goodness, the weight was astonishing. A giggle escaped her lips, followed by a delighted squeal. She gathered the fabric from the box, giggling once more when realizing Fillion had gifted her yardage for one full dress, with enough remaining for underclothes. Did the silk truly travel all the way from China? How wondrous a thought!

Gently, she placed the folds of silk upon her bed. From the corner of her eye, something in the box glinted in the sunlight. She peeked inside the box once more. Shears! The shiniest, most beautiful pair of shears her eyes had ever beheld. She lifted them and smiled upon seeing her reflection. Willow touched strands of flyaway hair and nibbled on her bottom lip as she inspected a narrow rectangle of her face. He thought her beautiful, and she could not help but blush at the memory of his words. She lowered the shears and turned them over in her hands, grinning when she found her name etched into the top blade.

Positively giddy, she looked inside the box to discover more delights. Spools of thread in a rainbow of colors, including the silk's exact shade—twenty spools in all! Her pulse fluttered wildly with excitement. Now she could embroider touches of color without the accompanying guilt that came with sneaking away scraps from the kitchen compost. She lined the spools on her bed beside the shears and then pulled out two packets of metal needles. Her eyes widened at the fine points and slim eyes. "Incredible," she murmured. She had only ever seen needles made of bone.

She peeked inside the box to ensure she had not missed any of his thoughtful gifts and stilled. At the bottom, etched into the wood, were the initials "F+W" in a similar fashion to the initials he had carved into the leg of her spinning wheel.

"Thank you, Fillion." She traced each letter. "Yes, it shimmered like water for me."

Willow placed each object back into the box and then lay upon her bed, lazily trailing her finger over the oak tree's edges and lines, forgetting to reply with a video message of her own. She was unsure how long she lay upon her cot, lost to reverie and grief, but she knew the moment Leaf had returned. Anger and bitterness chilled the air almost immediately with frenzied whispers of war. Footsteps echoed down the hallway and halted at her door. She sat up and fussed with her hair and then straightened her shoulders as she awaited his knock and request to enter.

When he finally strode into her chamber, his eyes were blazing, his jaw set until hard lines diminished any trace of the steadfast calm so familiar to his features.

He knew.

Every tree, every growing thing as it
Grows says this truth: You harvest what

You sow. With life as short as a half-
Taken breath, don't plant anything but

Love.

— Rumi, 13th century *

Chapter Twenty-Seven

Monday, April 8, 2058

Leaf fidgeted in his seat with a sidelong glance to Skylar. The Son of Wind, however, busied himself aligning the stone knight and monstrous beast figurines on the edge of Jeff's desk until they formed opposing lines.

The door creaked opened, and Jeff's walking stick struck the wooden plank floors. Leaf and Skylar rose and bowed as the town barrister walked into his Chancery.

"My Lords, your presence is unexpected." Jeff considered first Leaf and then Skylar, scuffing unevenly toward his walnut desk. "Did I forget a meeting?"

"No, not at all," Leaf answered. "Is this a poor time for discussion?"

"My schedule is open. How may I assist you, Your Majesty?" Jeff eased into his chair with a slight grimace. With trembling hands, he set his walking stick against the wall.

"We need testimony and confession," Leaf began. "I shall explain more in moments. Before we start, may Lord Skylar record our conversation?"

Jeff smiled kindly. "Well, that depends on who is the confessor and the topic of conversation."

"Ah, yes." Leaf leaned forward in his chair. "We need your confession, actually. On the MELISSA Project, if you would so oblige."

The twitch in Jeff's eyes stilled as his face registered a heartbeat of shock. "We are men of intelligence, I won't pretend otherwise." Jeff licked his lips nervously and tried to smile, but the emotion fell short. "Forgive me, I am at a loss for words this moment."

"Understandable," Leaf offered with a tight smile of his own. "I felt very much the same a few days prior."

Jeff wiped his forehead with a handkerchief. "How did you stumble upon archaic news like that of the MELISSA Project?"

"Not until we have permission to record our conversation."

Jeff smiled in earnest now. "The student has become the master."

Leaf dipped his head in honor to acknowledge the compliment.

"Proceed," Jeff finally acquiesced, albeit softly, refusing to meet Leaf's eyes.

"Thank you." Leaf watched as Skylar set up recording and then continued. "Jeff Abrams, three days past I learned of the MELISSA Project and New Eden Biospherics & Research's involvement in its experiments, past and present."

"Present?" Jeff blinked back a look of surprise.

Leaf ignored him. "I wish to ask you questions. For the record, do I have permission to record our interview?"

"Yes." Lines creased Jeff's forehead, his gaze unsettled. "I grant permission to be questioned and for our conversation to be recorded."

"Excellent. My humble thanks, My Lord."

"Of course." Jeff lifted a shaky smile.

"When did you become involved in the MELISSA Project?"

"In 2035, months before Moving Day. The original idea was that I would not need external technology in order to submit required legal documentation to the state and to New Eden Biospherics & Research. A few weeks before Moving Day, it became clear that the experimental surgery had failed. My body rejected the cybernetic system implant—"

"Do you still have one?" Skylar interjected.

Jeff's dark brows pushed together once more. "Yes, I do. Though it's not operational. The surgery to remove the implant would have caused immediate brain damage and possible death. Instead, I chose to live with irreparable nerve damage and the understanding that it would grow worse over time. Eventually, when the scar tissue stops blood flow to the brain, I will have a stroke. If cancer from the mutated cells doesn't deal the death blow first."

Leaf dropped his gaze and focused on his hands, his knuckles white. His stomach, however, knotted tighter than his interlocked fingers. "Did New Eden Biospherics & Research perform the surgery?"

"I am under contractual silence."

"I see." Leaf shifted in his chair. "Was becoming transhuman a condition for joining New Eden Township as the town barrister?"

Jeff's gaze darted away. "I cannot speak for others, only myself, if that's your angle."

Others? Now it was Leaf's turn to blink back shock. Did Jeff hint at information he was not at liberty to share? Sliding a furtive look to Skylar, Leaf said, "You are our only town barrister."

"Fair enough." Jeff twisted in his chair and rubbed his knee, his mouth compressed in a tight line. "Yes, to enter as a lawyer in a technology-free world, a cybernetic implant was required. Though I chose this path with full understanding of the risks. When the surgery failed, I was compelled to enter for the experiment's duration or take up residence in a mental infirmary. And here we are."

The courtly smile remained in place, though bitterness sharpened the edges. Leaf shifted to speak to Skylar when Jeff's hip hit the desk as he came to an abrupt stand. The stone knights and beasts clattered as they tipped over. "Thank you for your visit, gentlemen."

"My Lord, it is I who thank you—"

"I am next." Jeff's smile faltered.

The skin on Leaf's arms prickled.

"Just as well," Jeff began again in a sing-song voice. "I have no desire to return to the Outside world anyway."

The implications of Jeff's words wormed and writhed inside Leaf with a million realized fears.

"I have accepted my future, Son of Earth." Jeff maneuvered around the desk. His attention flitted to objects around the room, to anything save Leaf and Skylar. "May we speak off the record?"

Skylar's questioning gaze connected to Leaf's. The Son of Wind removed the Cranium from his ear and placed it inside a bag dangling from his waist.

Satisfied, Jeff sat on the edge of his desk and began righting the fallen soldiers and monsters. "Do you seek legal counsel?" he asked without looking up.

"Was my father transhuman?"

"Son of Earth—"

"You speak of strokes and cancers, but what of cardiac arrest?" Leaf grit his teeth as fury dislodged his self-control another notch. Jeff's twitching fingers tried to right a fallen soldier but could not find the proper balance. "I deserve confirmation and answers, for I know not what to believe anymore. More than deserve," Leaf asserted. "I am a victim of these choices and demand justice, not only for myself, but for others in the second and third generations."

"Justice is a word." Jeff finally looked at Leaf. "It's definition subject to the law."

"You were given a choice!" Leaf shouted as he shot to his feet. "You chose with full knowledge and understanding! My generation and the one that follows me has been grossly violated!"

Jeff's face paled. "What are you insinuating, Your Majesty?"

"You truly do not know?" Skylar asked, placing a warning hand on Leaf's chest until Leaf provided a less confrontational distance. "The inoculations our community received three years ago under state mandate—"

"No…" Jeff shook his head vigorously, his skin growing even more sickly. "Please tell me Hanley did not do what I believe you are suggesting."

"A portless cybernetic system, transferred through sublingual DNA-based vaccinations," Skylar answered, "with nanotechnology that is fully controllable by New Eden Biospherics & Research."

"N.E.T. controls the second and third generations?"

"The Techsmith Guild was the first New Eden rollout and the control group."

"Forgive me," Jeff whispered. His posture curved inward as he blotted his forehead once more with a handkerchief. He remained silent a long while, righting the last fallen soldier. "Do you have evidence of being controlled?" he finally asked.

"No." Leaf crossed his arms over his chest. "And even so, we do not possess legal rights as *human property* of the lab."

"As what?!" But Leaf did not expand further. Jeff eased to a stand and hobbled back to his seat, where he collapsed with a strangled groan. "Oh God," he whispered to the ceiling. "What have we done?" The barrister's eyes closed, lips drawn thin and pale, brows puckered, as though lost to prayer. Perhaps he was. Leaf had released a slurry of prayers these past few days as well. But he was past supplication and ready for war. Slowly, with movements ripe with weariness, Jeff leveled his gaze back to Leaf. "Is Connor aware?"

"Yes, My Lord. He knows of our human property status, not that I know of the MELISSA Project."

"And Fillion?"

"Fillion appears to also be inoculated with the same technology and suffering from outside control."

"Indeed?" Jeff's eyebrows lifted. "Does he have credible evidence?"

"Yes, My Lord."

"And of the second and third generations being bound by human property laws."

Leaf nodded. "Fillion also has a witness in a mental infirmary."

"Excellent," Jeff sighed. "Excellent."

"Is Connor transhuman?" Skylar asked.

Jeff pulled in a deep breath. "No." He darted an apologetic look to Leaf. "He was the only head Noble who was fully human."

Anger seared across Leaf's vision, as though the world bled bright red. "Why are you not dead yet?" he practically growled.

"And who would replace me?" Jeff drummed his fingers on the desk. "Hanley still needs my legal services within New Eden, it appears. Probably until project shutdown." He tipped one knight over, and then another. Two soldiers remained standing, swords drawn at the three beasts who circled them. "We didn't know," he whispered. "I'm so sorry. If we had known…"

"Perhaps *the fallen* did," Skylar countered.

"How so?"

Skylar murmured, "Many things were once heard on the wind."

Jeff considered Skylar's suggestion and then knocked over a beast. "There is merit in what you say, especially in light of Timothy's faction."

"Timothy died of cardiac arrest hours following Fillion's visit to him the day prior to Ascension," Leaf added. "According to Mack, any trace of activity was newly purged from Techsmith Guild servers, too."

"Correlation is not the same as causation, though," Jeff said. "Credible evidence is paramount when dealing with monsters and men."

"Indeed," Skylar agreed. "But my father was no longer needed, unlike you, My Lord. If anything, any attempt at retaliation could reveal Hanley's potential unlawful dealings. Thus far, it appears he has operated within the laws and bylaws of the state of California and the United States."

"I see." Jeff slid the position of a monster closer to a knight. "And who provided you this legal information?"

"Fillion's lawyer, who informed us yestreen in the privacy of my home before Sunday Feast." Leaf waited for Jeff to meet his eyes and, when he did, he said, "Moves and countermoves."

"Indeed." Jeff dipped his head with approval and Leaf released a breath he did not realize he had been holding. "How shall I help you counterstrike, Your Majesty?"

"As property of the lab, what are my legal options?"

"You are legal heir in Hanley's Legacy and granted all rights and powers accordingly, as outlined in The Code as well as other supporting documents." Jeff smiled kindly. "Inheritance trumps human property laws."

"I am not owned?" Leaf choked out.

"If you are truly human property, then you are bound to the lab who owns you. But you are not like the others, no. You have mobility freedoms and legal rights both in court and as a business owner that other human property would never know."

Shame pricked at Leaf's pounding heart as he chanced a look at Skylar before addressing Jeff once more. "And my family?"

"Children are heirs to the same Legacy and are, therefore, protected."

Crumpling into a chair, he hid his face behind dirt-smudged hands as a sob broke loose. His children were safe. His sisters, too. Ember, however, remained unprotected. Another sob pulsed through him. He wiped furiously at his eyes and looked up, embarrassed by his uncharacteristic outburst. Jeff played with a carved soldier. Skylar, however, stared at his lap, head bowed, shoulders rounded in defeat.

"I am so sorry, Sky," Leaf offered to his friend.

"Do not place this upon yourself, Leaf," Skylar whispered back, without releasing his focus from his lap. "We do not have adequate details yet to presume answers. But you are not to blame, nor do I begrudge you your relief."

"I do not deserve you, brother."

"No, it is I who does not deserve you."

"Then it is settled," Leaf said with a sideways smile. "We are horrible excuses for men and must find pity in one another."

"Political sons, to the very end." Skylar gifted Leaf a small smile in return.

Leaf gripped Skylar's forearm and declared, "You shall know freedom, Skylar Kane. I will not allow the lab, Hanley Nichols, or any other to further harm New Eden Township. Our fathers will not have died in vain."

Skylar tried to pull away, a slip of emotions tumbling across his face. But Leaf held fast, his grip growing tighter.

"Your father is also a victim," Leaf said quietly.

"He tried to kill you and burn down New Eden," Skylar gritted between clenched teeth. "He threatened Lady Ember."

"Yes, 'tis true what you speak." Leaf offered no other explanation or comfort. The Son of Wind inhaled a shuddering breath and then bowed over their joined hands. Skylar may find disgust in Leaf's claims, but Leaf knew his friend understood that what Leaf declared was also true. "I do not defend his actions."

"I know, Your Majesty."

"As you said," Leaf continued quietly, "we do not have enough information to form conclusions. However, we have enough to understand that Timothy was motivated for his family's protection."

"Or power."

"Yes, for truth, My Lord. But with power came freedoms and legal rights for his children and his children's children and so forth. Who else would know Hanley better than his own brother?"

"Brother?" Jeff asked, shock stilling his twitching eyes a second time. "Timothy and Hanley are brothers?"

"Half-brothers," Leaf offered.

"Interesting." Jeff leaned back in his chair. "Interesting," he repeated under his breath. "How long have you known their relational tie?"

"Since the Great Fire. And Hanley's real name is Hayden Kane."

Jeff sighed, long and slow. "I am overwhelmed. I have known both men since we were in our teens, and never once was there any suggestion of kinship or alternate identities."

"There could not be, for Hanley's mother was in hiding from his father with the aid of the government."

"And she happened to move to the same area as Timothy Kane's family?" Jeff asked, bewildered. "Seems irrational, given her need to hide."

Leaf answered with a shrug. "Fillion and Mack have a mountain of details if you are so inclined."

"I'll contact Fillion and request a consult."

"Thank you, My Lord."

"You still have not answered my earlier question," Jeff parried. "Do you seek legal counsel?"

"The risk is great."

"I am well aware of the risk, Your Majesty."

Leaf studied his mentor, his friend, and a man he considered a father-figure. He smiled. "We have much to discuss."

An hour or so later, Leaf parted ways with Jeff and then Skylar, and headed directly toward The Forge. The tangy stench of vinegar permeated the smoky air. Connor busied with polishing work tools, unaware of Leaf's presence. This gave him opportunity to study his father-in-law for a few brief moments, noting the tension in his jaw, the carbon-stained fingers, wrinkles around his eyes and mouth, and long blond hair pulling free from a leather tie.

"My Lord," he said, walking into the light. "Is this a bad time for you?"

Connor looked up, surprised. "No, of course not. I am always at your service."

Quietly, Leaf closed the shop doors and blinked with the sudden darkness. Orange firelight flickered across Connor's face as he gestured to the bench opposite him at the work table. Without another word, the former Fire Element pulled a shovel from a bucket of vinegar solution and rubbed knitted steel wool over the rust.

"What troubles you, son?" Connor asked without looking up.

Leaf eased onto the bench and just as casually asked, "Are you under contractual silence over the MELISSA Project?"

Dark eyes darted to his. The scrape of steel wool on a rusted shovel resumed once more, and more vigorously, before he replied. "Yes, though I am inclined to disregard binding words since you hint at knowing what you should not."

"Why should I not?"

"Your father—"

"Lied to me. I was not adequately prepared for the enormity of responsibility I would be burdened to carry." Leaf clenched his jaw. "His unnatural condition, as well as Jeff's, Norah's, and Timothy's should have been disclosed to me as Aether."

"You assume that Claire was also unnatural and aware of Joel's condition."

"Was she fully human?"

Connor laid the shovel across the bench and leaned forward, softly answering, "Yes, son. Nor did she know of Joel."

"How can you be sure?"

"Joel came back from Africa without her and immediately signed up to join New Eden as a head Noble. Claire was an afterthought to Hanley, as we now know. Your father was a devout rule-follower and loyal to his agreements. I would find it uncharacteristic if he disclosed details of the MELISSA Project to anyone, including his wife."

Leaf considered Connor's words and released a long, slow breath. "But you are not transhuman."

"No, I am not." Connor picked up the knitted steel wool and began scrubbing once more. Leaf winced with the grating sounds, trying to contain his building fury, especially when the man continued. "I was deemed the back-up should their cybernetic systems cause early death."

"Dr. Nichols knew this."

"I presume so," Connor said. "She never attended meetings nor did we speak of the Project when together."

"Perhaps another reason as to why she gave you the Death card."

Connor's broad shoulders sagged as firelight carved grief across his knotted features with Leaf's accusing tones. He chanced a look across the table. "Hanley could not harm me from the Outside the same way he could the other Elements."

"Are you suggesting..." Leaf started and stopped, coming to a stand. "Forgive me, My Lord. I fear I am too angry to continue our conversation and remain civilized."

"Leaf Watson," Connor said gently. "You should be angry."

"Why did you not tell me?" he immediately shouted back at Connor. "When my father died, let alone when we learned of my generation's enslavement, you should have told me! I shall never comprehend how you decided the wiser choice was my ignorance, Connor Hansen!" Leaf grabbed the shovel off the table and threw it across the shop. It hit the back wall with a loud clang. A shelf unhinged and baskets with metal tools fell with a thunderous clatter. Leaf did not flinch, nor care, as he continued. "Do you stand with New Eden or with Hanley Nichols? Choose now, for I will no longer associate with those who enable his success, and neither will my family."

The older man eased from his seat and walked around the table, unable to look upon Leaf. His shoulders slumped inward, his steps dragging. When close, Connor placed a hand on Leaf's shoulder. "You are right. I should have told you, and I have failed in my duty to protect your family." He lifted his head, every muscle taut, pools of fire flickering in his gaze. "I shall carry that guilt to my grave. I think of every decision I have made involving Hanley and possess nothing but remorse for each and every one." Connor withdrew his hand and twisted away. "My wife, my beloved Cami, joined New Eden and died, because of my connection to Hanley. The community no longer welcomes my son, because of Hanley. I oversaw the Techsmith Guild, unaware that they had infected my daughter with their latest prototype. My friends…" Connor's body began to shake, his voice choking. "My lifelong friends are dead, because of Hanley. Be angry, Leaf Watson. Be angry and declare war, for I did not. Do not cower behind honor and traditions and believe they will make you a better man."

Before Leaf could reply, Connor fell to his knees and grabbed Leaf's hands and pressed them to his forehead. "I stand with New Eden, and you, My King, my son. Please…" Grief halted his plea.

"Why did you not tell me?" Leaf asked once more.

"Out of respect for your father. I did not wish to alter your perception of him with information I knew you would not understand." Connor looked up, tears streaking through soot and grime. "How could I have guessed what Hanley would do? Has done. I believed the inoculation story for what he presented it to be, as did all others. Jeff had confirmed the state was making a legal request."

Leaf lowered to the ground before Connor and grabbed him from behind the head until their foreheads touched. "I forgive you," he grit, each word hard. "No more secrets. It matters not to me what I may or may not understand, for someone surely will and can advise me. If you withhold information again and I discover this? I shall deem it an act of treason and disown you."

Connor pulled Leaf into a crushing embrace. "You are wise."

"Fear makes enemies of us all, as Ember would say."

"My daughter is also wise."

"Indeed," Leaf whispered, pulling away. "Wiser than us both, I daresay."

Connor stared at the forge's glowing embers, seemingly lost to his thoughts.

A muscle in Leaf's jaw pulsed as he continued to clench his teeth. "Fillion is on his way to the underground and shall negotiate for a campaign. Ember has agreed to edit the videos Skylar will make of New Eden, before sending them off to Coal who will then broadcast from the underground, provided we have support. I have employed other Techsmith Guild members as well."

"You have contact with Coal?" Connor turned from the fire, emotion still brimming in his gaze. "Does he fare well?"

"No, not yet. I have only spoken with Mack, who informed me that Coal now resides in his city's computer underground." Leaf still failed to comprehend exactly what constituted an underground community, or why it was necessary. The images Hanley shared of the Outside world still haunted Leaf's mind. "I met with Fillion's lawyer in private yesterday evening as well, though not over our campaign recordings."

"Well, then, what shall your videos contain?"

Leaf allowed a small smile of triumph to appear as he rose, giving Connor a hand. When they stood, he answered, "Eco-Crafting Eden—Resurrected."

The former Fire Element's gaze snapped to Leaf's, and Leaf's smile widened a notch.

"I understand you were once a King," Leaf said.

"Yes," Connor replied. "Though my position was not real. I led a normal life during the week and played King on the weekends."

"Fillion sent video clips to both Ember and Skylar, including in- and out-of-character interviews. I have seen the former Elements pretend my world into existence, as if our future lives were as imagined as the game you played."

Connor flinched. "How shall I serve you?"

"Your new duty within the Techsmith Guild is to oversee this project."

"As a director?"

"Precisely. Spring Harvest and Beltane fast approach. New Eden Township shall bring in the May with a bold statement for the Outside world."

Connor bowed. "Your Majesty."

Leaf pushed open the door and had every intention of departing without further exchange. But he could not. The despair and fury were as foreign to his nature as the Outside world. Twisting away from the afternoon light, he marched back toward his father-in-law and threw his arms around the older man. Connor crushed Leaf to himself. This moment, he was not King. He was simply a man, broken and demanding justice. A memory surfaced with the feel of Connor's fatherly comfort, and Leaf's heart broke anew.

Tears had crawled down Leaf's heated face then, as they threatened to do now. His father had found him behind a tree near the South Cave, then fifteen and angry and humiliated after a group of village boys shamed him before all their peers. Unlike them, Leaf had begun additional studies under Jeff and worked one less day each week as a result. Even Skylar was excused from additional studies in lieu of more apprenticeship hours to meet the demands of their community's growing population.

"Son," his father had begun, crouching beside him. "I heard—"

"I am no longer needed," Leaf charged. "For I do not work for the portion I am given. They said I should leave and spare the community the burden."

"You are needed. Do not ever feel unworthy or insignificant," his father offered gently.

"Easy declarations." He had glared through the tears. "Your name is not Leaf and your father is not the Earth Element. Nor is your father requiring you to continue an education deemed unnecessary by the community. I am not like the others, and how they revel in reminding me so!"

A black shadow had slithered over his father's expression with the venom in Leaf's tone. Leaf had hoped his father would leave, feeling just as ashamed. Instead, his father gathered him into a tight embrace and whispered, "A leaf's sole purpose is to nourish the tree, from the newly budding green on each branch to the decaying yellow that litters the roots. The tree is a community, an ecosystem, and you are a necessary and noble ingredient to sustain its very existence."

He left Leaf beneath the tree to contemplate his words.

Many times since then, Leaf had felt he was still beneath the swaying branches, desperate to understand why he had to care for his sisters instead of the many willing matrons, work harder than other apprentices in the fields, and learn the laws and systems of a world upon which he had never set eyes.

A world that had become a blight upon his community.

Drawing in a deep breath, he pulled away from Connor and offered a bow, then stepped out into the fading afternoon light. It was now the hour of rest. The village square lay vacant as he marched across the barren ground toward the leaf-littered forest trail.

"A leaf's sole purpose is to nourish the tree," he whispered to himself, staring up at the fluttering green dotting each branch. He pulled his cloak tighter around his shoulders and pushed along the trail until he reached a sprawling oak tree. There, he slid down the giant trunk and found solace behind several large clusters of ferns.

For if you suffer your people to be ill-educated, and their manners to be corrupted from their infancy, and then punish them for those crimes to which their first education disposed them, what else is to be concluded from this, but that you first make thieves and then punish them.

— Thomas More, *Utopia*, 16th century *

Chapter Twenty-Eight

Seattle, Washington

Friday, April 12, 2058

Lynden fiddled for the keys in her pocket. Unlike most buildings, her modest shack of an office still used analog tech.

The rain seemed to drop in fully formed puddles. Trash melted into the street and floated down storm drains while thunderous plops of gutter water splattered onto the sidewalk outside her non-profit agency. She scrunched up her face in disgust. Then felt bad. Several homeless people were soaked through, huddled together under an overhang at the abandoned storefront next door.

God, what a shitty day. Really, a whole series of shitty days strung together.

The key slid into the last lock. "Finally," she muttered. She shoved the door open. A bell tinkled overhead. Another archaic throwback.

Drips of water pooled onto the chipped and cracked concrete flooring where she stood. Quickly, she removed her coat and tossed it into the wet towel bin. Her teeth clattered in the sudden chill. What temp was it? She waltzed over to the thermostat and groaned, cranking up the heat. Stupid thing. Probably was broken again. Old buildings equaled permits for repairs. Permits took lifetimes to process. So many freaking repairs needed. She dumped her lunch bag and keys on her desk and meandered to the back room, turning on lights as she went.

In the stock room, she pushed aside fresh towels and salon-grade capes. There. An old tarp. Something she used when painting the walls a few months back. Braving the weather, she dashed back outside to the shivering people next door and offered the tarp. A woman snatched it from her with a snarl. Lynden was used to drugged-out and animal-like responses from the homeless—especially the cold and hungry ones. After seeing New Eden, she understood what Coal had meant by a reboot. The two cultures might as well be galaxies apart rather than sharing the same planet.

The bell tinkled overhead as she walked back in, and she bolted the door behind her. Honestly, she was surprised more people didn't break into abandoned buildings out of desperation. She guessed there were scarier things to fear than hunger and weather. Like police drones. Lynden shuddered. They were brutal, and nobody gave a shit about how they terrorized the streets. Ever. Most homeless were chipped, too, making them easy targets. Disciplinary action could be made offsite. No human-to-human contact necessary.

The police. After being part of the underground and operating a social service clinic, a single night in jail wasn't as terrifying as she thought it would be. Most in the correctional facility tripped over backwards to ensure her protection. The Eco-Princess behind bars. Nichols child number two in a tumble with the law. Even without their show of protecting Daddy's little girl, she knew how to handle herself. Family was something else entirely.

Fillion was like an icy firestorm. He strode into the courtroom for her bail hearing—confident, aloof, and mad as hell—practically razing everyone and everything around him to ground zero. Especially when noting Hanley's presence. And John by his side.

Hostility and false charm curved Fillion's and Hanley's tight-lipped smiles as they stared at each other. The courtroom paused with the ripple of tension exploding between the two. Lynden had never truly known chilled silence until that moment. Then her brother and his lawyer took over, upstaging every effort Hanley made to be part of Operation Rescue Lynden.

Never—not once in her pathetic life—had her dad *not* commanded the spotlight.

Why the hell was he at her bail hearing anyway? Probably to control media coverage and boost his image as the doting father. But that didn't happen, and she didn't want to speak to him. Conversations with Hanley tilted toward condescension—he the victim and Lynden the stupid, worthless eternal thorn in his bleeding side.

In the end, Lynden was, yet again, an object exploited in a public move for power. Business as usual.

Back straight, cool smiles for the courtroom and journalists, and eyes glinting like a blade's sharp edge, Fillion sailed past Hanley when court was adjourned. The media missed nothing. Images and accounts of Fillion's bravado plastered the Net on how he saved his dumb sister from another family scandal. Headlines *still* hinted at bad blood within the Nichols Empire six days later, complete with growing speculations and leaked sources.

Tech Heiress Akiko Hirabayashi exacts her revenge on Fillion Nichols with false charges.

Civil war declared within Nichols family over human experiment laws.

Partnership between Nichols and Nichols faked, sources say.

Son battles father in the race to colonize Mars with civilians.

Lynden Nichols stars in another publicity stunt for family operations.

Following Fillion's epic exit, she was released to the care of his lawyer and Mack. A lawsuit was filed two days later. Strangely, all records of her marriage had disappeared, and her and Coal's fake IDs with it. Seems she and Coal were set up by hacktivists as an April Fools' Day joke to raise awareness of inhumane human property laws—April 1st, her and Coal's one-year wedding anniversary.

Mack just winked at her.

That damn man and his damn scheming. She was so pissed. Every revolution had its price. Lynden didn't want to go to prison. But she also didn't want to hide her marriage to Coal from the world. The world that now knew Coal's status—the one record that wasn't disputed or erased, which is why he remained in hiding. Fillion would be required, by law, to take action against Coal. Nothing about their situation was a joke. His freedom was worth her sacrifice and it was her right, as Coal's *real* spouse, to fight for him. Fillion had chewed her out like a petulant child for flippantly disregarding his protection when she threw it back in his face.

"Lyn, prison is *not* the underground. Not even close," he practically growled at her. "At your age, you'd skip juvie and go right into adult intake."

"I forgot that you're the perennial martyr and hero of the people and I'm just the annoying damsel in distress," Lynden had snapped back. "You and Hanley are media attention whores. Poor you, all day every day."

Fillion's face had crumbled. "If you can't see the difference between me and Hanley—" he choked out in a devastated whisper. "Never mind . . . I'm done trying to prove myself to you."

He had walked out of Mack's apartment and she hadn't seen him since.

God, she was such a bitch sometimes. The guilt was overwhelming. Living in his shadow demanded drastic measures, and she felt trapped. A feeling she knew Fillion understood. Unlike him, Lynden had built a life and a workable future with her forbidden romance for over three years. And, while Fillion felt justified talking down to her, he'd go to jail all over again for the Watsons if it meant bucking the system. The hypocritical double-standard was infuriating.

Male pride. Yuck! Especially his Dictator Mode.

Whatever. There was no way to win. None. The system was far too corrupt, and her brother had basically declared war before witnesses. She'd let the hacktivists take over. Their collective power was immeasurably bigger than her influence, anyway.

Tonight, after work, she'd invite Fillion over and make his favorite dinner. Atone for her careless words. He had probably cooled off by now. He'd never walk away from her. Not really. In the meantime, she needed to pick up her life and keep moving forward.

Lynden slumped into her chair and docked her Cranium to catch up on messages. It had been well over a week since she'd been in her clinic. Her heart and soul. Beautiful people ruled the world all around her and monopolized the media. But here? She gave second chances. It was an ugly business run by an ugly girl who transformed transitioning homeless and a few recovering whores and drug addicts into respectable citizens with respectable jobs.

Mack had lined up contacts in various industries, and Fillion promised kickbacks to the same contacts for hiring human employees, larger kick-backs and investments for hiring from Lynden's agency. It worked. With Fillion's kickbacks and the government's tax credits for hiring those with incarceration records, a steady stream of employment requests had come in since Life Link opened. Hopefully her latest scandal didn't result in canceled contracts or industry blacklisting.

Otherwise, with nothing constructive to do, she'd fester and spiral into an abyss of grief. She'd see Coal again. She knew that. Still, the comm silence right now was unbearable. Distractions were essential.

Messages flooded her work center. Lynden closed her eyes a beat, willing her heart to calm, and then launched into replies. Yes, Life Link would continue. Yes, she still had a screened list of humans seeking employment. No, she wasn't indenturing residents from New Eden on behalf of her brother. Gross. Human trafficking operations belonged to Hanley. Wrong Mr. Nichols. Disgusted, she made a list of monsters who asked that question and flagged their businesses to be removed from Fillion's kickback incentive.

An hour sped by. Followed by another hour. Today was purely for admin duties. Workforce assimilation would resume on Monday: screenings, interviews, makeovers, temporary housing for new hires. She had a whole team set up to collect donations from local businesses to furnish the temp houses, as well as stock shelves with food and closets with clothes. Employment contracts were guaranteed for six months, unless new hires failed in the most basic of duties. So far, so good. Only a few rotten apples in the bunch. Most would cut off their right arm for honest work with honest pay and temp housing. A few in her program were approaching the four-month mark, and their employers had already sent out renewal contracts.

More messages poured in. First, a break. Coffee was calling her name. And a cigarette. But she'd settle for coffee. Blindly, she reached for a blur of rainbows while reading a new message, flicking and nibbling her lip ring in concentration. Her fingers made contact. The new unicorn mug, a gift from her brother to replace the one she broke last year, slid into her vision. Aaaand, it was empty. *Kawaii*-style ceramic eyes reflected her disappointment. The unicorn always looked guilty. It was creepy.

"Soul-sucking coffee thief," she muttered to the mug.

Lynden stood up and stretched. Empty mug in hand, she wandered toward the small kitchen to refuel when she heard a knock. Or was it the wind? Sheets of rain dumped outside as trees bent to the wind's wailing. A solid piece of trash must have hit her door. She resumed her quest when the sound came again. The hairs on the back of her neck prickled. No, that was definitely a knock. The lights overhead flickered with the next gust and Lynden swore under breath.

Mug back on her desk and pepper spray in hand, she crept out of her office toward the entry. Bars lined the windows and several deadbolts armed the front door. The sign on the door, written but also illustrated for the illiterate, clearly communicated "closed." Logic told her it was probably a journalist. Animal instincts told her otherwise. Who the hell would venture out in this squall?

The hooded figured knocked again, this time more desperate. Rain streaks distorted the face from view.

"We're closed!" Lynden shouted over the howling weather. Lights flickered again.

"Lyn, I need to speak with you!" a woman shouted back. The woman glanced over her shoulder and then stared at the door, shivering.

"And who the hell are you?"

"Lyn, please."

Only a handful of people called her "Lyn." Most in this neighborhood knew her as Rainbow or used her full name. The voice was hard to distinguish over the rain, though.

Heart thrumming in her throat, Lynden unbolted the door and opened it a crack to see past the rain-streaked window. The woman wore combat boots, similar to ones Lynden had. Ripped black pants, with bondage chains connecting the legs, bunched into the boots as if the pants were too long for her. Pants, Lynden noted, that looked eerily close to an old pair she had stuffed into the back of her closet. The jacket—oh god. Forget the jacket. Her eyes. Gray eyes peeked out from deep inside a large hood and blinked.

"Mom?"

"May I come in, please?" her mom asked, rubbing hands over her jacketed arms.

Lynden opened the door wider and gestured for Della to enter, quickly turning locks in her wake. They stared at each other for what seemed like an eternity before Lynden blurted, "Why are you in my clothes?"

"Is your clinic secure?"

"Of course. Mack regularly does bug sweeps." Lynden flipped her hair and shifted weight on her feet. Water puddled onto the concrete floor. Again. "Your coat," she said simply, hand out.

Hesitant, Della slinked out of one of Lynden's kimono-style jackets. The sleeves engulfed her mom's smaller frame and the bottom hem reached her knees. Lynden knew she was tall, but damn. Her mom was swimming in her old garments. Della glanced over her shoulder again when Lynden tossed the sopping wet jacket into the towel bin with her own. It was strange, seeing her mom here. At her own place of work. One she created without a shred of help or acknowledgment from her parents. Until this moment, her mom had never visited Life Link.

And until this moment, she'd never seen her mom in anything other than a dress.

It was freaky weird.

Animal instincts kicked up again. *Breathe*, she reminded herself. Posturing into cat-like grace, Lynden sauntered toward the back kitchen and poured Della a cup of coffee before refilling the unicorn mug she had abandoned on her desk. Stupid guilty eyes.

"I was like you when I was younger," her mom said when Lynden returned. A smile? Like they were meeting at a country club to discuss the latest fashion?

She eased into her chair, eyebrow arched. "You've never once been like me."

"Forgive me." Della dropped her gaze and studied the mug in her hands. "I meant your passion for social services."

"Right."

"Thank you for the coffee."

"Have you cracked? Why the hell are you in my clothes? And here? During typhoon weather alerts?"

Her mom's gaze darting around the office. Coffee splashed over the mug's rim and onto her hands, but she didn't flinch. Lynden's eyebrow arched higher.

"I need your help."

"Well, for starters, military green is *not* your color." Lynden rolled her eyes. "Did you break into Mack's apartment? Why are you in my clothes?"

"Atoning for my sins." Her voice was weak. She genuinely looked afraid. And so small. So very small.

This wasn't her mom. Couldn't be her mom. Dr. Della Jayne Nichols was poised class itself. A seductress and mind manipulator. Drips of coffee fell off her mom's hand and onto the black pants. The woman didn't clean up the spill or try to hide the stain.

Atoning.

The word lodged itself into Lynden's racing mind. "OK," she drawled out carefully. "If my clothes help you atone, whatever."

"I need a makeover."

A shiver crawled down her spine. "My clinic is closed today."

"Lynden, *please*."

A gust shook the window panes. Her mom dropped the coffee cup and jumped to her feet, gaze snapping to the street. Ceramic shattered on the concrete floor. Dark liquid splattered over the storm-gray walls. Then everything went dark. The hum of electricity evaporated with the lights. Shadowed bars stretched across the room and over her mom's face. For several seconds, the only sound that could be heard were the raindrops pounding on the glass and her mom's rapid breathing.

Their gaze touched a few secs later and Lynden softly asked, "Are you in trouble?"

"So you will help me?"

Lynden started with how her mom flipped the question around. The mind manipulator wasn't entirely gone. Still, she found herself nodding, albeit reluctantly. She opened her mouth to speak again but stopped when the power flickered back on. Good. No electricity equaled limited makeover options.

"Let me call Coral and see if she's available."

"Nobody can reveal that I was here."

Her eyebrow lifted again. "Coral is trustworthy."

"Thank you." Her mom reached out and took Lynden's hands in hers. "I also have a request for the underground."

The hell? This seriously couldn't be her mom. But, if Della was going to use her, Lynden would use her back. Anything to see Coal. Relaxing into feigned indifference, she asked, "What kind of contact?"

"Hackers."

"And you're not asking Fillion or Mack because...?"

"It would not be safe for them to know."

Anger ripped through Lynden and her mouth fell slack, then clenched. "Fillion might be a dominating asshole, but I'll never betray him."

The unicorn stared at her with guilty eyes. Traitor. Fine, yes. She'd already betrayed her brother with her spiteful words.

Atoning.

"I will not betray him." Her mom offered a shaky smile, reeling Lynden back to the present. "Promise. My atonement is for him." She paused a beat and squeezed Lynden's hands. "And for you."

She withdrew her hands and took a step back.

"Tell me what's going on first."

Dr. Nichols resumed her seat and flicked a nervous glance to Lynden.

Then her mom began to share, and Lynden swore her heart stopped beating.

This changed everything.

The Celtic word Saille [Willow tree] itself became the word sally, meaning a sudden out-burst of action, expression or emotion …

Being known as the first to arrive and the last to leave, seasonally-speaking, the hazy yellow appearance is, along with the arrival of the Robin, the first indication that Spring has arrived. The golden brilliance of the Willow in the autumn remains long after her fellows have shed all their finery …

Saille has further connection to the Death Goddesses for the Celts … Funerary flints, shaped as Willow leaves, have been found in graves from the Old Stone Age, demonstrating clearly that Willow has been a part of our lives for a very, very long time. This Tree has been associated with death, grief and cemeteries, the leaves themselves symbolizing unrequited love or the loss of a lover.

— The Order of Bards, Ovates & Druids *

Chapter Twenty-Nine

New Eden Township, Salton Sea, California
Tuesday, April 15, 2058

everal hours past sunrise, the meadow still glistened from the prior night's bio-rain. Nevertheless, Willow and other weavers busied themselves behind looms, the hems of their dresses damp and soiled. Apprentices skirted burlap drop cloths around each loom, only to realign them multiple times as young children ran past or tugged on the coarse fabric while playing.

Spring Harvest came as it did each year, per tradition, following the close of Alder Month. Leaf rose before sunrise to join the opening revelry in The Rows. The fifteenth of April moon, the first day of Willow Month in the Celtic calendar, was also the first day of Spring in New Eden. Musicians with wooden flutes played merry tunes to accompany the birds, and women prepared simple circlets made from young willow branches and linen ribbons. The head farmers, led by their Son of Earth, drank a hearty goblet of honey mead to honor the flowers and bees. Leaf, with the assistance of Alder, then left a goblet of honey mead in the heart of the Ceremonial Garden for the faeries to find, and Spring Harvest officially began.

Willow's poor nephew believed his job was to commence Harvest. All morning he insisted, "Close Alder," demanding that he end the first Spring ceremony, misunderstanding the references around him. Willow stifled back an amused laugh with the memory. He would learn, as did she. It came with being named after Sacred Trees that also were Celtic lunar months.

Spring Harvest was a small affair with little ceremony other than welcoming the first day of Willow Month with song and mead. It was a day cloaked in joy and sorrow—joy that life shall spring anew, and sorrow for those in eternal winter. Willow glanced toward The Rows, a somber line to her lips. Families dotted the gardens and buried a willow leaf in the living soil in remembrance of each lost loved one. Before attending their purpose, she and Laurel had each buried a soft golden leaf, one for Mother and another for Father.

Her brother's laughter cut through her sullen thoughts. Head tilted back, his deep rumble filled the meadow with his mirth. A strange sound after his bruised, brooding mood these past few days. So much so, even the weavers and apprentices around her stopped their work and took note of Leaf's untroubled behavior, darting surprised looks her way. Other gardeners joined in the laughter and lifted another round of wooden mugs filled with mead in salute. Clapping a man on the back, Leaf turned and strode toward the wheat fields. It was then Willow recognized the false cheerfulness. Happiness slid from his features and stiffness crept into his easy gait. He picked up a scythe and joined the reapers, the humor moments earlier a mockery of the pain her family carried.

The women who gathered the newly felled wheat began a new song for the reapers. Willow closed her eyes and allowed their melody to comfort the ache in her heart for her brother, for her community. The villagers still did not know of the second and third generations' transformation, nor that they were owned by the lab. The women sang a merry ditty of a lover's spat, and several laughed at the witty lyrics as they sang.

A day of joy and sorrow.

"Happy first of Willow Month," a familiar voice declared. Willow's eyelids popped open as Rain rested a circlet upon her pinned braids. "A willow crown for my favorite Willow in New Eden."

"Spring is content to taunt me each year," she replied with a half-smile.

"For truth." Rain's fingers twisted together—knotting, unknotting—while she shifted on her feet. "Come, share a walk with me."

"Perhaps at mid-day meal, My Lady."

Oh, how she wished to escape the mess of weaving on this miserably wet day. Alas, flax was among the harvest crops, and the spinners and weavers had yet to process all the newly sheared goat and alpaca fleece. Rain pressed her lips together in a near scowl.

"Mistress Katie, I have business to discuss with the Earth Element's First Representative," Rain announced, much to Willow's horror. "I shall not keep her long."

"Go, Your Highness," Mistress Katie encouraged, looking up from the apprentices she instructed. "We shall fare well in your absence."

Willow studied the loom shuttle in her hand. Whatever had inspired Rain to behave so? Rather than express her annoyance before all present, Willow resigned to her lot. "A short walk, My Lady."

Arm in arm, Rain led Willow along The Orchard trail, around The Rows, toward the wheat fields. They walked in silence, dipping their heads to acknowledge greetings and honors given. Willow peered over her shoulder as they passed the last of the wheat fields. Rain ignored her, keeping to her own thoughts. It was rather strange behavior for her lively friend to remain this quiet for so long, or to leave the bustling company of villagers, let alone inserting her authority over Willow's work schedule.

The West Apartments—homes that remained vacant for the second wave of colonists—stood tall and shadowed against the stone biodome wall. The emptiness unsettled Willow and she halted her steps.

"This is hardly a short walk," Willow tossed out with a disgruntled sigh.

Rain turned and grabbed both of Willow's hands, her eyes darting over Willow's shoulders, brows deeply furrowed. "From my father's shop, I saw Hanley enter The Forge with representatives from NASA."

"Here? Today?" Willow drew in a tight breath and pursed her lips. "I thought Fillion had secured New Eden from his visits?"

"As did I." Rain leaned in closer and dropped her voice. "I spoke with Jeff before fetching you and apparently a protective order is in motion, but not finalized. The court hearing is tomorrow. Unless a judge rules otherwise, he is permitted upon the property as minority owner."

"Despicable man!" Willow stomped a few paces away from Rain. "Fillion is not at the lab?"

"Jeff shares he is in Seattle and not responding to communication attempts."

Anger billowed through Willow's veins. Rain was wise to force her to walk away from the community, for she would surely gain unwanted attention and set the tongues wagging with her temper. Even so, other Nobles needed to know. The wheat fields bent and rustled in a gentle breeze. Her eyes skipped over the tousled grain until she found her brother. "We must alert His Majesty."

"Skylar shall inform him." Rain tugged on Willow's hand, yanking her back. "Let us gather your sisters and hide in the Mediterranean Dome until that arse leaves."

"Rain Daniels!"

"Well, he is. I shall not apologize for my unladylike language." Rain crossed arms over her chest and tapped her fingers. "Do not be so pretentious, or shall we discuss *your behavior* since Fillion returned?"

Willow rolled her eyes. "Yes, he is indeed an arse."

"Which one, Your Highness?" Rain laughed, her hand fluttering in the air. "Mr. Nichols or Mr. Nichols?"

"Dear Lord in Heaven, you are incorrigible." She snatched Rain's hand in the air and tugged, a playfully pointed look on her face as she did so. "Yet, I would not have you any other way."

"Nor I your appreciation for all things scandalous, though you pretend otherwise."

"You wound me." She slid Rain a mischievous side glance, and Rain grinned in triumph.

Despite their shared humor, they warily ambled arm in arm toward the fields, both scouting for the unwelcome party. Children dashed about and mothers scolded. Eligible young men strutted by the younger women, shoving each other to gain their unassuming attentions. The familiar heightened her unease, knowing that Hanley mingled among her people. Where, she knew not. This was her day, the first of Willow Month, and he was a blemish upon their dawning Spring.

Did he know that Fillion was unreachable at present?

Were the NASA representatives still moving into the West Apartments next month?

Willow gnawed her bottom lip as more questions swirled about in her head as though tumbling leaves across the meadow.

The fields gave way to The Rows and still no sight of the horrid man. Pink, dew-glistened petals fluttered past in The Orchard and dotted the wild grass. She lifted her free hand to the breeze and caught a tattered petal in her palm.

"The decay of empty promises, delicate as hope and bruised with mourning," Willow murmured to herself.

Rain squeezed her hand in reply.

Blossomed tree maidens whispered to turn back, to run away. Her heart thrummed wildly in her chest with each rustled warning. Instead, Willow rested her head on Rain's shoulder as they meandered over the rutted trail. "Thank you, my dear friend, for everything."

Her friend opened her mouth to reply then pushed Willow behind a cherry tree. Through the tangle of branches, Connor's unmistakable deep voice could be heard, followed by Hanley's. Unlike Fillion's soft yet biting tone, Hanley's voice was like a song—smooth, melodious, and alluring. When he spoke, people listened in rapt attention while holding ridiculous expressions of awe and amusement. He was handsome, too, and quite aware of his own charms and seductive mannerisms. At the Ascension Celebration, Willow was continually disgusted by how village women blushed, especially so when he smiled their way—smiling flirtatiously while his wife hung on his arm sending wanton smiles of her own to the men. Were people's hearts such toys to be trifled with?

"How old do you think Hanley truly is?" Willow whispered to her friend.

Rain scrunched up her nose and shuddered. "Do you wish to curdle my breakfast?" she whispered back. "I surely hope not, for I so enjoyed Cook's cinnamon-berry pastries this morn—"

Her friend's reply ended in a gasp.

Though they whispered and huddled behind a tree, and though The Orchard and gardens writhed with activity and voices, Hanley turned his head directly their way. His eyes locked with Willow's and she clutched Rain's hand tight in hers as gooseflesh prickled down her arms and neck. How had he known where she was so precisely? His gaze had not stuttered in search but glided her way like a choreographed move in a graceful dance. A satisfied smile played across his lips as he tipped his head in casual greeting. Fire billowed through her veins once more and she lifted her chin and glowered back. His smile grew wider for a mere heartbeat before nonchalantly returning attentions to Connor and the NASA representatives. But before striding toward The Rows, he flashed her one more knowing, furtive smile.

"Impossible," Rain breathed, eyes round.

"Nothing is impossible for monsters," Willow gritted. "Or so monsters would have us believe. Well, he shall not satiate his ego with my fears." She removed her hand from Rain's and marched toward the village square, arms straight, fists clenched. "Nor yours," she snapped over her shoulder. "Back straight, My Lady, head held high, and let us find my sisters."

She would not tell Rain that her legs were quaking, or that her head was swimming in dark pools of terror. Had Hanley come to punish her for interfering with Fillion's public image? How had the world reacted to Fillion ending his betrothal to Akiko? Only Leaf and Ember knew of this threat, or so she thought. Perhaps her brother had shared with Rain and Skylar as an extra measure of precaution. Of course he had, she corrected, for they were Elements and Hanley threatened more than just her family. The community also would suffer—had already suffered.

Willow glanced back at her friend with sharper understanding and smiled grimly. Rain caught up and they hurried their steps down the forest path toward Ember. Several minutes later they burst into the apartment and dashed toward the main bedchamber, softly knocking on the solid wood door.

Ember creaked open the door and whispered, "Hanley has come to New Eden?"

Willow's mouth fell open a beat before replying, "How is it you know?"

"His Cranium communicates to mine whenever he visits the lab." Ember opened her door wider. Upon her bed, Alder lay curled up on his father's pillow asleep. The twins lay beside him, also in angelic slumber. "Let us speak in the living room."

Once in the main quarters, Rain said, "Fillion is not among his party, nor is he answering communication attempts from Jeff or Skylar."

"I do not trust that Hanley's motives are tied only to NASA today," Willow seethed.

"Nor I," Ember and Rain said in unison.

"New residents on the day of new beginnings seems like a move he would make," Ember said. "Though, his visits are always scheduled and announced."

"Precisely," Rain quickly replied.

"My Lady," Willow said to Rain. "Please stay with Ember. I shall fetch Laurel."

"Do not fear for me and the children" Ember placed a hand on Willow's forearm but spoke to Rain. "Please accompany Oaklee and ensure her and Laurel's safety."

"Yes, Your Highness." Rain lowered into a shallow curtsy.

Back in the forest, Willow broke into a run toward the village square. Mayhap she was overreacting, or behaving with the paranoia Hanley wished for her to experience, and his visit was as innocuous as it appeared. Fluttering leaves of emotions and thoughts continued to tumble through her mind. She simply knew too much now to react otherwise. No, ignoring the man and the potential threat his presence posed was not an option.

Her steps slowed to a stop and she gulped in much needed air.

From the village square she studied The Rows and wheat fields. On the edge near the West Apartments, she could make out the rigid silhouette of Leaf, Skylar, Hanley, and the NASA representatives in huddled conversation. Rain trotted up next to her, heaving for breath as well. A drip of sweat slipped down Willow's cheek as she took in the undulating motion of her community at work. Rain grabbed her hand and they started to turn toward the apothecary, but Willow dithered.

Ethan, a young man near her age, strode toward the pump well. A yoke straddled his shoulders with water buckets dangling on each end. She was not sure why she remained and rudely watched him with her feet firmly planted on the compacted earth. Perhaps it was the strange, contorted look upon his face. As if he were in pain but confused by the feeling. She took a step toward him, momentarily forgetting her sister. Then halted. Her nails dug into Rain's arm as her friend clutched Willow's sleeve. It happened all so fast.

One moment Ethan was walking and, within a blink of her eye, he lay crumpled in a heap by the well in an unnatural position. A trickle of blood dripped from his eyes, nose, and mouth.

Heart-shattering screams echoed in an eerie chorus, rising from the apartments, The Rows, and even muted wails from inside the Mediterranean dome.

A sickly shade painted Rain's skin as she stared wide-eyed at Ethan, her trembling fingers pressed to her lips. Screams and sobs continued to fill the biodome from every direction. Willow's voice joined the dirge, releasing Laurel's name to the grief-filled wind. Untangling herself from Rain, she bolted straight for the apothecary. Craftsmen and villagers poured out from the apartments and shops, terror stricken, and did not pay her heed. Sliding in the dirt, she stopped before the shop and reached for the iron ring when the door swung open.

"Laurel!" Willow cried out. She yanked her sister into a fierce hug murmuring, "Oh darling, oh darling," over and over again.

"Whatever has happened?" Laurel eventually asked. "I heard many screams. 'Twas frightening while all alone in a dark shop."

Willow pulled away, tears wetting her cheeks. "Ethan Combley gruesomely died right before my eyes."

"How had he—"

Laurel's amber gaze darted around the village square before she clapped a hand over her mouth and pointed in horror. Dread swirled in Willow's gut as she turned. Zachery Davis sobbed while carrying the limp body of his nine-year-old son through the gaping crowd. Similar to Ethan, small drips of blood oozed from the lad's eyes, nose, and mouth.

Stifling a cry, Laurel buried her face into Willow's shoulder, quaking. "Where is Leaf?"

"The wheat fields."

Laurel pushed away, panic written across her dainty features. "Alder! The twins!"

"They are safe with Ember back in the apartment."

"How do you know they are safe?"

"I…" Willow sucked in a sharp breath. Were they still safe?

"Corona! Blaze!" Laurel practically shrieked. "I must find them!"

"No, you may not leave my side." Willow cupped her sister's face until their foreheads touched, and whispered, "We shall not separate, for it is not safe."

"But—"

"Laurel, if they are dead, there is naught we can do to save them."

Willow hated herself for being so blunt. Her sister accepted the unfeeling logic, burying her head into Willow's shoulder once more, and began weeping. More cries and screams pierced the air and the tiny hairs on Willow's neck stood on end. Villagers parted for another family to pass through. Fourteen-year-old Becky Feldon hung limp in her eldest brother's arms. A drop of blood from her mouth splattered onto the dirt, her eyes vacant and unseeing, her head bobbing with each jostled step.

"What is happening?" Laurel asked, her face now pressed into Willow's neck. "Is there a plague?"

"A plague?" Willow repeated in a tiny voice.

"Yes, in a medicinal book Joannah uses, there is mention of a horrific plague that sweeps through villages, taking the young and old first."

"Dear Lord, I surely hope not." Talk of plagues billowed the rage still boiling in Willow's veins. Was this to be her punishment? To watch her community die off for falling in love with a monster's son? "Come," Willow whispered in Laurel's hair. "I shall escort you to our apartment."

"Will you not stay?"

"No, darling. Leaf shall need my assistance." And she wished to confront Hanley Nichols with promises of her own.

"I could help, too."

"Yes, indeed." Willow kissed her head. "Our sister shall need your company."

Laurel stepped away and tugged on Willow's hand as she entered the dark apothecary shop. "First, we need an herb sachet."

"Whatever for?"

"The medicinal book recommends packets of herbs for well-being and protection."

"What pestilence do you speak of?" Willow ran her fingers across clay jars on a shelf to distract her galloping nerves.

"I shall find the reference."

Laurel pulled out a book and frantically flipped through the pages. Herbal scents wafted through the small shop and Willow inhaled deeply. Surely her sister's imagination was leaping into the blackest abyss it could find. Fear was muddling her senses, too. If indeed a plague, how had her community become infected? Were they not inoculated against Outsider diseases?

"Here it is!" Laurel waved her over and began reading. "An account by Friar John Clyn of Leinster, Ireland, in August of 1348. 'That disease entirely stripped vills, cities, castles and towns of inhabitants of men, so that scarcely anyone would be able to live in them. The plague was so contagious that thous touching the dead or even the sick were immediately infected and died, and the one confessing and the confessor were together led to the grave. Many died from carbuncles and from ulcers and pustules that could be seen on shins and under the armpits; some died, as if in a frenzy, from pain of the head, others from spitting blood…" Her sister's word died off. "The lad and village girl, they had blood dripping from their face as if suffering from pain of the head."

Images of Ethan collapsing by the well sprinted through Willow's mind anew. Should they return to Ember and the children? Did they carry contagion? She re-read the passage in Joannah's book. "What herbs are recommended?"

"Meadowsweet, wild marjoram, sage, clove, campanula root, angelica, rosemary, horehound, camphor, lavender, and wormwood." Laurel looked up. "These were brewed into a Four Thieves Vinegar, but we shall carry them as an herbal ward in our bodices."

Willow swiveled on her heel and marched to the clay jars as Laurel rummaged through herbal bouquets drying from the rafters.

"Our wormwood stores are empty," Laurel spoke slowly, as if in concentration. "Cedar possesses similar properties…"

Gently, Willow placed the clay jars on the counter and watched as her sister fastidiously created sachets, her brows pinched. Since a wee lass, Laurel provided nurturing strength in the midst of troubles, be it problems big or small. Willow adored these qualities in her sister. However, the more Willow contemplated the unfolding events, the more horrified she became. The account in Joannah's tome seemed plausible, but Willow could not rationalize the suddenness of it all. Had more died in a similar fashion? Were they from the second generation as well? Had Hanley planned his unannounced visit thusly to coincide with this "plague"?

Rain jogged into the apothecary, a hand on her chest and tears on the edge of falling. "Oh Willow…" Her friend swallowed and looked between her and Laurel. "Several have perished—at least six reported deaths."

Laurel ducked her head and busied with herbs to hide her forming tears.

"Are they all under the age of twenty-two?" Willow asked.

Rain simply nodded as the correlation dawned in her eyes. "Do you think—"

"Yes," Willow cut in quickly, flashing a look of warning to Rain.

"Do you think what?" Laurel asked, unaware of their silent exchange.

"Oh, that…" Rain cleared her throat and wiped away a tear. "My brothers and sister are safe," she informed, and Willow nearly sighed with relief over the news and the change in topic. "The Hansen and Kane families are accounted for as well."

Laurel smiled through her tears. "Thank you, My Lady. I despaired, not knowing."

"Connor asked that I check on Ember and the children and report back to the Great Hall," Rain added. "Leaf has called a town meeting for those who are not attending the families in bereavement."

"There," Laurel said, lifting up several sachets. "Place this in your bodice." She handed one to Rain and another to Willow. "They shall help protect against the plague," Laurel added when Rain stared, confused.

"The plague?" Rain asked, looking to Willow for clarification. A sickly shade returned to her friend's skin and Rain reached out for the counter when her legs wobbled. "Have Timna or Joannah confirmed this?"

"No, not yet." Laurel nibbled on her fingernails as she peered through the open doorway. "Shall we leave now to avoid possible contagion?"

"Wise plan, darling." Willow looped her arm through Rain's, cutting another look of warning to Rain. "Joannah and New Eden are lucky to have your herbal skills."

Laurel beamed up at Willow under the praise in the way children often do. Approaching womanhood had already changed so much about her sister. But Willow hoped Laurel's incurable optimism and nurturing strength did not dissolve with childhood.

"I love you, Frog," Willow whispered into her sister's hair as she pulled her close and kissed her head. "You are my joy."

"Must you call me *that*?" Laurel playfully protested. "How will a man ever find me fetching if I am called 'Frog'?"

Rain softly laughed, a strange sound amidst the somber trees and sorrow-laden breeze.

"Do not marry," Willow countered. "Let us grow old together and enjoy our matronly freedoms and scandalize all the men with our mighty opinions."

"Do not marry and scandalize all the men?" Laurel gaped at her sister. "Have you lost your wits?"

"Every last one."

"Sometimes I feel as though I know you not at all. Lady Rain, please speak sense into my sister's lofty head."

"Your sister is a romantic beneath the overtures."

"I have never been a romantic, Rain Daniels, and you know it." Willow huffed an angry breath. "Ladies, we are not objects to receive or be given away, nor does the community own our reputations. We do. Games to fetch a man are grossly unappealing." Laurel wrinkled her brow and ducked her head, as though embarrassed. Willow squeezed her sister's hand affectionately and softened her voice. "A man should fall in love with *you*, darling, not his ideals of who you ought to be."

"Is this how Fillion treats you?" Laurel asked.

"His soul is beautiful, but he is afraid and often confused on how to have a meaningful relationship. I fear his heart may be broken beyond repair." Willow studied the geodesic sky to hide her forming blush. "A vexing man in many ways, but also the only man who has ever appreciated and defended my temerity. There are times I believe he intentionally riles me up simply to argue."

"He is a fool to tempt Fate so." Rain shot her a small, playful smile, a haunting look on her ghostly face. "A dashing fool, yes, but you shall destroy him one day."

"I believe"—Willow touched the warmth creeping up her cheeks—"I believe he wishes to be destroyed."

That final word lingered uncomfortably in Willow's thoughts.

Their love was destructive.

Her breath caught on a sob. Six innocents had died this day.

She groped for Laurel's and Rain's hands and then dashed along the forest trail in mournful silence. Sounds of weeping seeped through the walls of homes they passed by. The lack of Laurel's typical birdsong chatter pulled on Willow's heart until it hurt to breathe. The quiet was painful in a way she had never experienced before. Was she to blame for New Eden's grief? For the deaths of so many who died far too young?

Willow wanted to bury herself in the living soil as an offering for her generation in eternal winter. Spring was an illusion.

Global unemployment rates have increased to seventy-one percent this year. Unacceptable. In the past fifteen years, since the robotics laws changed to consider humanoid androids as citizens in most countries, human beings have taken a back seat in progression. Computerized employees are a virus to our sustainability as a people, our black plague. Hope is being buried in mass graves worldwide, and you've turned a blind eye to our suffering.

— Fillion Nichols, World Tour speech in Japan, December 3, 2057

Chapter Thirty

Seattle, Washington

The large rusted doors squealed opened. Fillion stepped into the Den of Iniquity beside Mack and Lynden. Lustful and drug-hazed eyes turned their direction. Music blared orgasmic beats, and wall-to-wall screens flashed various porn fetishes.

Fillion pulled his hood farther over his face. Hoping to blur his identity, he wore more facial piercings than usual and dark make-up around his eyes. Long, black strands fell over half of his face. Lynden did her best to obscure recognition, too. Mack, however, never hid. Didn't need to. The world knew TalBOT Industries offloaded e-waste to various computer underground communities around the globe, and hired out their hackers and engineers, too. But Fillion? Since his arrest at seventeen, he had no reason to be here other than to cause trouble.

And he was about to do just that.

Hands reached out and touched his body in invitation. Fillion's skin shuddered with each caress, but he kept his face schooled. He hated leeches and tweakers. Actually, he hated the system that birthed them. It was a dysfunctional cycle with no end.

Several people—male, female, non-binary—launched themselves into Mack's arms. He kissed them back with grins and winks, slapping their asses before moving on. Lynden pressed herself closer to Fillion, and he put a protective arm around her shoulders. This room triggered them both. Mack put on a flamboyant show to redirect the spotlight away from the siblings. But his friend also craved every nanosec of attention.

There was a time Fillion had lost himself to sex. To the gratifying rush and thrill. Escaped through endorphins that temporarily medicated his traumatized heart. The desire to feel connected and wanted was strong, and he sought that earnestly with any gender during that time in his life. But they didn't really want him. Not the real him, at least. He was an object to be used and discarded. Mack didn't have the same burning desire to belong, like Fillion. His friend was literally a lover to humanity, no strings attached. But, to Fillion, giving away a piece of himself was intentional.

Very few pleasures existed in life, though. He didn't care that people hooked up. Despite his need for meaning, it was hard to remain celibate at times, especially when loneliness and stress screamed for comfort. Fear kept him in check. Life changed at sixteen when the media declared him the sexiest and wealthiest man alive. When people looked at him now, that's all they saw—an opportunity to upgrade their pathetic existence.

But this? The Den of Iniquity was a violation against humanity to keep whores in employment. Not everyone here was a prostitute or hired out. Still, to own another for pleasure was vile.

And now he was a human trafficker as well.

A twinge of nausea rolled in Fillion's gut.

Today he would fight the system, for them. What was the point of having power and influence if it only served self? He didn't choose to be born wealthy. He didn't choose to inherit The Legacy. He didn't earn his job. He could have easily been *them*. Guilt mutated into a cancer that multiplied and ate away at his conscience until there was only one solution. Fight. Hanley had weight, but so did he. And if Hanley was going to immortalize his son through nano-bioengineering and transhumanism, then Fillion wanted to be remembered for living a life worthy of the people whose only choice was to depend on him. Even if they would use him and discard him as the cycle demanded from the emotionally bankrupt.

Bodies continued to reach out to his. He stared ahead, aloof, disinterested, forcing his mind to call up other images than the ones offered. Absently, he slipped his free hand into his pocket and wrapped a dainty silver chain around his finger. A silver chain belonging to his mom's linden leaf necklace. A necklace he discovered a couple days ago on top of his pillow at Mack's apartment. No note. No message from his mom. And he still couldn't reach her. Neither could Mack, who tried hacking into her Cranium. Nothing. Lynden, overhearing their conversation, didn't offer up any new info either.

Spooky.

What the hell was up with his mom?

Fillion dropped his arm from his sister's shoulder when they angled into the next room. From here, it was like navigating a cement and pipe labyrinth, complete with beasts. People walked past, some barely recognizable as human after so many augmentations, some with invisible black-light tattoos and glowing eyes. Water trickled from ceiling seams, down molding walls, into rust-colored puddles on the floor. Lights flickered or remained eternally dimmed. Unmarked metal doors dotted the hallways here and there. Most doors led nowhere.

The hacking circle camped near the computer underground's back end, near the game arena. Wanderers couldn't find either areas. Only those in the know. It kept operations safer that way.

His sister bumped into him, knocking him out of his head.

"You OK?" Fillion asked Lynden.

She stopped biting on her nail and leveled a look at him. "Peachy."

"You're shivering."

"It's freaking cold down here."

Fillion stepped over a puddle then cut a glance back her way. "You'd tell me if it was something else, right?"

"Trembling with excitement at seeing Farm Boy, methinks," Mack threw over his shoulder.

"Oh please. We've gone longer than this between visits."

Mack swiveled on his heel to walk backwards. "Or have you already seen him?"

"Since my arrest?"

"That's the context, *Niji Doragon Ōjo.*"

Rainbow dragon princess? Fillion arched a humored brow at his friend. But Mack didn't notice. His crazy friend was too busy pinning Lynden with a humored look of his own.

"Since you're so smart and stuff, you tell me." His sister's face turned to stone, every muscle hardening, her eyes cold. The warning didn't work. Mack pulled on a strand of Lyn's hair. "Get off!" She batted his hand away and side-kicked his legs. Laughing, Mack jumped out of reach and then grinned. Tongue out and eyes wide, he wagged his tongue piercing at her, before spinning to walk forward again, an exaggerated dance to his step. "Asshole," Lyn muttered under her breath. "Don't try anything cute," she shot at Fillion.

"I'm already cuter than Mack" he replied quickly. His friend scratched his bare ass beneath his kilt.

"Oh my god," Lyn groaned. "Gross, Mackenzie!"

Thunderous roars rumbled through the walls bordering the gaming arena. They continued past and entered an unlit hallway. At the passageway's end stood a single, nondescript door, marked only by a dim overhead black light. Mack lifted his hand to knock and stilled when the door creaked open. A shape dressed in inky shades, skin unnaturally pale, with black, pupil-less eyes glided into the doorway and paused, dark eyebrows raised in surprise.

"Shit," Mack sighed.

Fangs appeared in a salacious grin. "Mr. Ferguson and Miss Lee, a delight, as always. I was just visiting with Mr. Smyth." Obsidian eyes moved Fillion's direction in lewd inspection. Mel licked their fangs in a hungry gesture. "Mr. Jayne, in the flesh. How many years has it been, now?"

"Mel," Fillion said. "We're visiting Amanda."

"Interesting." Mel tilted their head.

"She's expecting us," Mack drawled, as if bored. "Alas, we can't pass through your shadowy soul." He stepped back and gestured for Mel to move. "After you."

"Such manners." Mel caressed Mack's cheek with a single long finger. "Such lies."

"This doesn't concern project management."

"Mr. Jayne's business is PM's concern. Underlings need protection from street-level wars and poisoned money."

Mack sniffed and adjusted his utility kilt. "What do you want?"

"You know what I want." Black eyes roamed over Fillion. Their fanged grin widened when Fillion morphed into a posture of disinterest.

A reddish drip fell from the ceiling and plopped into a rust-hued puddle by Fillion's foot.

"I'm not for sale."

"Everyone has a price, Mr. Jayne."

"Let's go—" Fillion spun on his heel to walk away and jerked to a stop when bony fingers gripped his arm. "Don't touch me."

"Your price, Mr. Jayne, is involving PM."

He shrugged Mel's claws off of him. "And?"

"And a private moment with me."

"For?"

"The nature of privacy, Mr. Jayne, is that it does not involve others."

Fillion rolled his eyes. "If you want my poisoned money, you'll play by my rules."

"I run this game, Mr. Jayne."

"My money. My rules."

The demon tilted their head, fangs bared, and quietly hissed, "My underground. My hackers."

The plink of another drop echoed in the tense silence that followed.

More rust-colored drips shook free from their cement coffin when the walls rumbled from the neighboring game arena. Nobody moved. Not even when a droplet landed on Fillion's forehead and ran down his cheek. Lyn's eyes winced at the sight.

"Tears of blood," Mel taunted. "A savior's curse."

The crowd's roar tapered off and, with it, the shower of tinted rainwater.

"Shall we?" Mel pointed down the dark hallway. "I will not take much of your time, Mr. Jayne."

Fillion flicked Mack a glance beneath lowered lashes and wiped away the drop to hide his actions. The answer was subtle, a tiny dip of his head, Mack's eyes cutting to Lynden.

"You won't touch me," Fillion said to Mel. "Promise?"

"I am not a barbarian, Mr. Jayne."

"I don't care what you are," he snapped. "I won't go anywhere alone with you until I get a promise that you—and your *underlings*—won't touch me, physically or electronically."

"You have my word." Mel glided past Fillion and faded into the shadows. "Come, Mr. Jayne."

Mack and Lynden stepped into the hacker's circle and shut the door behind them. They couldn't show fear. Or any emotion other than arrogant confidence. The underground sniffed out weakness and feasted on it. But Lyn's worried gaze met his for a nanosec as she closed the door. He offered her a tight smile before disappearing down the dark hallway.

It didn't take long to catch up with the underground's demon. Their black robes billowed as they moved, as if floating on an imaginary breeze. The main hallway had flooded with people while Fillion's party had congregated at the hacker circle's door. Game sessions must have ended until the next round that night. Fillion tugged on his hood and lowered his head. Large men circled around Mel until the crowds thinned to only a trickle. Where had they come from? Just as quickly as the guards appeared, they disappeared into the walls. Fillion stared at the cement and plaster, curious. Fingers shaking, he reached out and touched solid matter. Was he still seeing things?

"The walls are listening, Mr. Jayne," Mel said over their shoulder. "They have ears."

Ice shards prickled down Fillion's spine. "Who told you that?"

"I believe you mean, whom have I told that to?"

Fillion's heart jumped to his throat. Had Hanley negotiated with Mel for MELISSA Project operations? Of course he had. Mel ran the Seattle computer underground. The demon had probably known Hanley for decades. Another layer of betrayal coated Fillion's resolve. He would uncover and dismantle every one of Hanley's plot points in this game. And he'd drag Mel down with him if necessary. The computer underground's undeads weren't immortal. They were characters playing a part, just like everything else in this damned world.

Mel inserted an old-fashioned skeleton key into a door lock. A faint, bluish glow poured from the keyhole and then a click. A pitch-black room yawned before Fillion. What else was hiding in the walls? He blinked back the rising panic and stepped forward. Show no fear. No weakness. The door shut behind him in a whining groan. Forgetting himself, he spun toward the closed-off hallway in a terrified flash and right into Mel.

"For the record, Mr. Jayne, I did not touch you."

The undead's breath pulsed onto Fillion's cheek. He slowly stepped back, thumbs tucked into his pants pockets, his shoulders lifting a notch higher. Focus. He needed to keep up the illusion of power.

Lights awakened overhead to a dusky level. Mel's fangs brushed their lower lip in a suggestive smile. Instinctively, Fillion took another step back, noting the canopied bed in the far corner, a small desk to his immediate right, and a dressing screen to the left, next to two overstuffed chairs. Biting the inside of his cheek, he hesitantly met Mel's black stare with as much arrogance as he could conjure.

"You are a beautiful creature," the demon said. "If you offered yourself to me, I would grant you anything you desired."

"No—"

"Relax. That is not why I brought you here, Mr. Jayne."

"Get to the point then."

Mel gestured to the large chairs and took a seat only after Fillion obeyed. "You are a frightened rabbit. I have not laid a snare for you, my pet."

Fillion remained tight-lipped. Unmoving. Unblinking.

My pet?

"The walls are secure inside my private chambers."

"Good for you."

"Mr. Ferguson is your hired samurai. The underground is crawling with government spies, more so than ever these days, as you both know. Why do you risk exposing yourself, and possibly Mr. Smyth, instead of operations per usual?"

Fillion shifted in his seat. "I didn't know you cared so much, Mel."

A breathy laugh. "If an Eco-Prince visits my doorstep in the flesh, perhaps it is because a Corporate King still sits on a capitalist throne made of glass ceilings."

"You didn't care before." Fillion grit his teeth. "Did this Corporate King pay you to look the other way *then?*"

Black eyes glimmered. "Do you plan to shatter his throne now?"

"Answer my question."

"It is not an interesting question."

You ask the wrong question. A Gamemaster doesn't ask the obvious. He ponders the hidden.

Anger bubbled to a raging boil from deep inside Fillion. He gripped the hem of his jacket and clenched his teeth until he thought they'd crack as question after question uploaded into his brain.

How many MELISSA Project test subjects hid in the Seattle underground? Abroad?

Why was Andra in a mental infirmary instead of in Jett's care inside the underground's safe house?

What part had Mel played in the black ops science experiments?

Was Hanley still paying Mel to placate Fillion?

Is this how Hanley knew exactly what his children were doing all those years ago?

"What's your legacy?"

The hell? Fillion bit back a groan. Out of all the questions he could ask, that's the one his stupid brain settled on? God, he was an idiot.

"This question entertains me."

Seriously? It took every effort for Fillion to keep his fury in check, especially when Mel goaded him further with a slow, calculating smile.

"I make deals with devils," they answered. "What sort of devil are you, Mr. Jayne?"

He didn't hesitate. "The son of a killer."

"What deal are you proposing to Amanda, son of a killer?"

"New life for the dead."

"You cannot reanimate what is already dead."

"True, but death gives way to the resurrection of *new life.*" He paused a beat. "New Eden still doesn't understand the subtext."

Mel leaned back in their chair. "Ah, you clever creature. So you know of them."

"I am one of them."

The demon blinked. Fillion was unsure if he had ever seen Mel blink before.

He continued. "I'm pulling MELISSA Project operations out of the underground. Don't stop me. I'll destroy you."

Fangs bared over pale lips in a predatory snarl.

"Shatter the glass throne it is, then. I will back Amanda's contract decisions." Mel rose from the chair in a graceful move. "You owe me a personal favor, Mr. Jayne."

A cruel smile curled Fillion's lips in reply. "I owe you nothing."

"My underground—"

"My money. The same poisoned money keeping the underground alive. Or do you want me to pull all donations and employment opportunities?"

Mel tilted their head. "And, like that, a new Corporate King is born." They walked toward the door. "You entertain me, Mr. Nichols."

Fillion inspected the empty hallway when he left Mel's private chamber. How did the guards move through the walls? Or did he imagine it? Lighting up a cigarette, he breathed deeply and exhaled onto the yellowed plaster. The smoke curled against solid matter and then dissipated into the air. With brows creased, arms stretched out, and the cigarette now dangling from his mouth, his trembling fingers ran along both walls as he strode down various hallways toward the hacker's circle, discovering nothing. Shit. Maybe his mind wasn't as secure since Mack's man-in-the-middle redirect as they thought. Or Mel's comments about the walls having ears were a tip-off that Hanley was aware of Fillion's location. Probably both.

"You live," Amanda tossed over her shoulder as she let Fillion in. "Did you have to sell your soul to them?"

"Mel sold their soul to me."

Amanda halted her steps. "Are you shitting me?"

"I'm special." Fillion lifted a corner of his mouth. "Good to see you, by the way."

"Yeah, it's been ages."

Hackers behind desks and on couches followed him with their eyes as he walked past. Several others busied with net-running through cyberspace in virtual reality chairs. In the far corner, Lyn perched on Coal's lap, nose-to-nose in conversation. Mack was draped across a mountain of floor cushions; he patted a seat beside him when he spotted Fillion.

Fillion walked by a friend from juvenile detention. "Hey Blue, nice to see you outside the system."

"No kidding." The hacker brushed royal blue strands out of his face. "This is Myles," he nodded toward a hacker seated beside him. "He'll be working on your case."

"Thanks," Fillion said to the wiry young man with shaggy brown hair. "Don't let Blue steal all the cred," he ended with lopsided smile and then continued to Mack.

Sprawling next to his friend on the floor, Fillion lowered his hood and shook his hair out of his eyes. "Did you tell Amanda?" he asked Mack.

"Nah. Just flirting with the vixen while waiting on you."

"I'm trying not to gag." Amanda's face grimaced as she looked at the couple in the corner. "Mack isn't helping."

Fillion glanced at his sister and Coal. "Finally, someone who isn't crushing on him."

"Hey, Farm Boy," Mack called out, wiggling his eyebrows. "Reunion over. Chatty time."

Lynden slinked off of Coal's lap and sauntered over to their group, Coal close behind her. As the lovers settled, Fillion slouched back against his pillows and caught Amanda up on the latest research news out of New Eden, his plans to dox Hanley, the forged partnership, Eco-Crafting Eden II, and his own rigged cybernetic system. But Fillion couldn't look away from his brother-in-law. Dark circles bruised Coal's eyes, his mouth turned slightly down. His hair was oily and messy, despite being tied back. A smudge of underground grime swiped across the right side of his forehead. A part of Fillion was relieved he was safe. Another part of him delighted in seeing the Son of Fire brought down a few pegs.

"Mole life suits you," he eventually greeted him with a taunting side-smile. "The homeless aura brings out your stunning complexion." Fillion winked.

"Does not everything?" Coal responded, crossing bare arms over his chest. His words became vapor and faded into the dank shadows while red dragon scales slithered around his upper arm and disappeared into his sleeveless shirt. "Shall we discuss business now?" he asked. "Or do you wish for more verbal foreplay?"

Vapor exhaled from his nose in a big puff and quickly dissipated. Yet, despite the obvious chill, Coal remained exposed.

"Bit dump," Fillion casually threw out, pretending to busy himself with something interesting on his sleeve.

"I found Bran Davis, Carolyn Knight, and a few others. They are willing to testify provided you grant certain protections and amenities."

"What's their price?"

"To live in New Eden with new identities."

Fillion sighed, long and slow, and looked up. "And if New Eden shuts down?"

"It will not." This time Coal smirked. "Unlike you, I do not nurse greedily upon Hanley's venom."

A few choice words exploded in Fillion's head, screaming for release. Instead he lifted his eyebrow in bored dismissal. Ignoring Coal was a better insult to the man's noble arrogance.

"Mack"—Fillion angled his head toward his friend—"teach Amanda how to cut their strings and build inner sanctum walls. I'll safely relocate them to New Eden *after* we get their recorded testimonies." He paused a beat, then said to the group, "And *if* the project is shut down, I'll treat them the same as I would any other resident." Fillion raked fingers through his hair and drawled at Coal, "Work for you, *My Lord?*"

Coal grinned, full of charm yet wolfish. The urge to roll his eyes hit Fillion hard, but he remained a good boy. He liked Coal. A lot. But the Son of Fire insisted on a perpetual pissing contest. This was now Fillion's game. He moved the pawns and he didn't give a shit how Coal felt about that fact.

"I'll take that as a yes," he muttered when Coal didn't reply. "One last thing?"

"Yes, *Your Majesty?*"

Fillion locked eyes with his brother-in-law and softly said, "Thank you."

The tendons in Coal's neck relaxed. "Of course." He dipped his head in a bow.

"Anyone giving you trouble?"

Coal sucked in his bottom lip for a nanosec. "Not terribly."

"Good. Let me know if someone crosses that line."

"My size alone is intimidating enough for most."

Mack bit his bottom lip in a suggestive look, and Coal pushed his shoulder playfully.

"Don't get comfortable," Fillion continued. "Ever. Always watch your back."

"Does *His Majesty* actually care about me?"

Now he rolled his eyes. "I care about my sister."

"And Oaklee." Coal flashed a look of innocence. "How you must suffer knowing your life is only valuable in saving mine."

"I suffer more knowing hulking damsels-in-distress, like you, still need saving."

Coal erupted in laughter. "Perhaps Mack should outfit me in a skirt then."

"Hell no," Lynden interjected. "You'd distract him too much with your legs."

"And easy access to your hammer," Mack added with a wink.

Amanda grimaced again. "We need Mack to focus."

Mack deadpanned, "I focus, o ye of little faith."

The Son of Fire placed muscled arms behind his head in a stretch and Fillion couldn't help the stab of jealousy. And Coal knew it. Watching for a reaction from the corner of his eye. A thin smile of satisfaction appeared, teasing, mocking, challenging.

"Anything else to report?" Fillion asked, ignoring the hot-headed bastard. Again.

"Not really."

"OK. Get the testimonies. Then work with Leaf in interviewing residents. I want the Eco-Crafting Eden II campaign viral in two weeks. Three weeks if we must lag. We'll dox Hanley and any dirt we dig up on Akiko a week after the campaign hits the Net."

Coal mumbled his understanding.

"How are the hounds doing?" Fillion asked Amanda. "I need leads. Reports. Cracks. All of it."

"Working on it," Amanda answered. "Mack just delivered Andra's mirror files the other day. Assigned Nadine and Violette."

"Perfect," Mack said. "She-devils with mad skills." He turned to Fillion. "Had to wait, too, for TalBOT industries to schedule an appointment with Gremlin, like today. Sorry, mate."

"No worries. I get it."

"Nadine and Violette are two of my best hounds," Amanda continued. "They'll begin tonight and work around the clock to digest Andra's files and decrypt her central cybernetics in comparison to Coal's."

"And mine." Fillion looked to Mack. "Send her a copy of my file."

"Sure thing, boss."

"I need info. Stat," Fillion said to Amanda. "So does my lawyer. And before the campaign, so we can decide if Andra is safe to relocate to the lab or better off institutionalized."

Amanda nodded. "Consider it done."

Coal leaned forward. "I forgot to mention, there still remains no news of Pinkie. She has been missing in the underground for nearly three weeks."

"She's here," Fillion said. "Nowhere else for her to go."

"I shall continue to investigate."

A heavy silence descended on the group. Fillion shifted on his pillows and quietly asked Coal, "Do you need anything?"

"If others can survive in such conditions, then so can I."

"You'd let me know, though, right?"

"Focus on weaning off of Hanley's teats, not my discomforts."

Mack burst into loud laughter. Fillion flipped off both Coal and Mack, adding a steady stream of swear words in Japanese, which only made Coal's satisfied smile widen.

"Damn peacocks," Lynden said, flipping her hair. "Are you done playing?" she asked Coal, scratching behind his ear. "Who's a good alpha dog? You are. Oh yes, you are!"

"Focus," Amanda practically barked. "I've got things to do."

Fillion pulled his gaze from Coal and Lynden's flirtatious wrestling and back onto Amanda. "One more favor?"

"Depends."

"I'm looking for Della Jayne Nichols." Lynden whipped her head his direction, her face suddenly void of any emotion. Fillion focused on Amanda again. "Can you help me locate her?"

"You didn't hear?"

Fillion's throat tightened. "Hear what?"

Amanda inspected her nails, almost as if she were afraid to look at them. "News broke about an hour ago."

"Our Craniums are off," Mack explained. "GPS grid phantoms, *desu*."

"We won't disclose your visit. You have my word." Amanda stood up and sauntered away.

They turned on their Craniums and stared at their loading screens, waiting. Fillion swiped his finger across his dashboard and brought up a Xandria page and stifled a gasp.

"Holy shit," Mack whispered.

Fillion's entire system numbed as he read headline after headline. His mom's plane was discovered in the Atlantic Ocean, near Ireland. The pilot's body washed ashore onto one of the remote islands. Her body had yet to be found.

"She knew," Fillion murmured. His fingers wrapped around the linden leaf necklace in his pocket. "She fucking knew."

"What do you mean she knew?" Mack paled to a ghostly shade he'd never seen on his friend before. "Suicide?"

"Or murder."

Mack leaned toward him and whispered, "You think Hanley would murder her?"

"To keep her quiet about something, yes."

His friend's eyes watered. "I'm so sorry, mate."

He couldn't break down right now. Not in the underground. Control was already a fragile thing. His heart, though, was shattering into a billion sharp pieces, each one cutting deep with every breath he took. Anger stung hot behind his eyes. A tremor started in his hands and spread until his entire body clenched with the effort to remain still. Better to employ his mind than become absorbed by the torrent of emotions shredding away violently in his chest.

Think. He needed redirect attention. The hackers were watching. And listening.

Fillion found his sister's gaze. "Come to Ireland with me?"

"Now?"

"After court tomorrow. We'll talk with the authorities together."

Lyn watched her fingers twist the black band on her thumb. "Yeah. Sure," she softly answered.

"Oh god," Mack rushed out while gaping at his screen. "Fillion, check your dashboard."

A slurry of emergency messages blinked red. Fillion swore he stopped breathing. Mack removed his Cranium and buried his head into his hands. What the hell was going on? Did they find his mom? Had Hanley died, too?

The first message was from Michael, who quickly let Fillion know that Hanley was at the lab. When was this? Two hours ago. Fillion's pulse was in a full gallop now. Images of Willow in a torn dress and ratty hair flitting across his mind's eye. Her screams echoing in his head. His mom sinking to the bottom of the Atlantic.

With a shaking finger, he tapped the next message from Jeff, who also relayed Hanley's unannounced visit. And a similar message from Skylar. Another message from Jeff popped up, but he couldn't understand the barrister. His voice was wobbling too much. His body twitching more than usual. Fillion closed out this message and opened another, from Ember. The violence in his chest became a raging tornado, ripping through his nerves. He motioned for Coal to move closer, who sucked in a sharp breath at his sister's disheveled state. Fillion turned on the external audio.

"Fillion please come to New Eden posthaste. There is not a delicate way to share this news. Forgive me—" An emotional damn broke and Ember began weeping, blotting her eyes with her sleeve. She tried to speak again but couldn't. After a few measured breaths, she began again. "Ten individuals from the second generation dropped dead before mid-day meal. Leaf is attempting to keep the community from rioting. Hanley is still here and has joined Leaf in the Great Hall. Please, Your Majesty, please hurry."

The video message winked out as a baby mewled in the background.

A roar ripped through the room as Coal launched to his feet and paced, muscles bulging. He pulled his hair free from the tie and threw the band across the room with another scream. Hackers removed Craniums and virtual reality goggles, coming to a stand, mouths falling open at the show of strength prowling through the room.

"Draken…" Mack spoke softly, taking a tentative step toward Coal. "Don't do anything stupid, like Hulk—"

Mack's words were cut off by another roar right before Coal swung his fist at the wall. Pieces of rotting plaster exploded through the room. Dust poofed into the air. Coal pulled his hand out of the wall and threw another punch.

Lynden cowered and covered her head, eyes squeezed tight, each time Coal screamed and unleashed his fury. He only stopped when Amanda pulled a gun and the safety unlocked in a loud click—an intentional feature.

"Enough!" Amanda shouted.

Blood dripped down Coal's hands. His chest heaved, his breath hissing through gritted teeth. The gun was pointed directly at his head, but he didn't flinch. Maybe he didn't understand what it was? Or that a single shot was all it would take to kill him? The underground didn't issue empty threats. Most here didn't even give warnings. One less body to care for meant more resources for everyone else.

"I'm approaching your left," Fillion said. Amanda lowered her arm but didn't engage the safety. "Hey," Fillion whispered to Coal as he neared.

"Spare me your lofty speeches of protection," Coal growled.

"Amanda," Fillion said to the hacking lead behind him, though his eyes remained fixed onto the Son of Fire. "Change of plans. Mobilize the hackers. I want every dark, disgusting secret about Hanley viral by this afternoon. I'll double what I offered, too, and grant bonuses for the dirtiest information. I want to stir up conspiracies and speculations in the wake of . . . of Della's death."

"Code Black!" Amanda shouted to her hackers. "We have a target."

Feet shuffled and chairs scraped across the cement flooring. Fillion didn't dare look away from Coal to watch the bustling activity behind him. "One last thing."

"What?" Amanda snapped.

"Scratch Eco-Crafting Eden II. I'm setting up live feed of New Eden. I want the world to witness the Ceremonies of Death. Use New Eden Enterprises' servers. Hell, use the lab's, too, if you want."

"I need two zombies!" Amanda shouted to the team.

"Hacktivist disclosure," he continued to Amanda. "I'm under military silence over New Eden right now. Not a single link back to me or Mack."

"Got it."

The Son of Fire pushed his brows together and sized up Fillion in a quick sweep.

"Want to breathe fire?" Fillion asked his brother-in-law quietly. "Fine. Me, too. But don't burn yourself and incinerate our plans in the process."

"You know noth—"

"I'm not done." Fillion took a step closer and harshly whispered, "You almost got yourself killed. Amanda would've shot you and dumped your body without a care. You're in the underground, *Dragon*." Coal rolled his bottom lip into his mouth a sec and then released it.

Fillion shoved away and marched back to his sister and Mack. "Hey, Amanda?"

"What is it now?"

"Let Draken push the big red button. He gets to burn Hanley alive." To Coal: "An honor price."

Amanda considered Coal a moment, dubious. "You'll behave?"

Coal bowed. "Yes, madam. I shall control my temper. My sincerest apologies."

"I don't give warnings." Amanda returned to her screen, back turned.

One look at his sister and Fillion almost lost it. Tears threatened to form, but he pushed them back. Grieving wasn't a luxury he had at the moment. At least, not here. It wasn't safe. Control was currency in the underground and he was maneuvering for dominance.

"We can't leave Coal here," Lynden whispered to him. "He won't survive."

"I can't risk getting caught by the government, Lyn," Fillion whispered back. "Be realistic."

"Please…"

He dragged in a shaky breath. "Coal stays."

"Fillion—"

"You know I'm right." He searched her eyes, begging her to forgive him. To forgive Coal, who would give up his life for New Eden without a second thought. "We leave for N.E.T. in ten."

He didn't want to miss the look on Hanley's face when the shitstorm hit.

Hacking is exploiting security controls either in a technical, physical or a human-based element.

— Mike Mitnick, hacker, 2011 *

Feelings are real. They often become one's reality. But they are not always based on truth.

—Leaf Watson

Chapter Thirty-One

New Eden Township, Salton Sea, California

The Great Hall silenced in an unnatural fog of confusion following Hanley's shocking reveal—a cybernetic brain sickness. A digital plague, he explained further, only affecting those inoculated with technology from HiraMed, owned and operated by Akiko Hirabayashi's family.

Now all of New Eden knew of the second generation's transformation at the hands of the lab's deception—a wrong they could not properly fight nor cure.

The air thickened around Leaf, and his breaths grew shallow. "Justice is just a word," he whispered to himself, "defined by the law."

Hanley cut a sly glance his way, eyes bright.

Before Leaf could address the community, Hanley continued. "I understand your confusion. The world has changed since New Eden sealed her doors over twenty years ago. Technology and medical advancements especially. But why would I bring in technology that would harm you or your children? Your lives are valuable to me." He walked to the edge of the stage, a hand on his heart. "The week after Moving Day, the United States Congress passed liability laws for labs who employ human volunteers for science. Research start dates under six months old were grandfathered into the new law. As a result, all generations born inside New Eden Township are now wards of the lab." Hanley smiled warmly and dipped his head. "I think of your children as my own."

Pressing his lips together, he continued to stare at the crowd. "I've done all in my power to ensure your community's happiness and sustainability. Your sacrifices over the years are many, and it was time for change, for a better future and a better hope, the very breath of life."

Hanley smiled at Leaf with the last statement, as if Leaf were in agreement, and Leaf's heart sank. Those were his words to Fillion.

"Numerous young lives have been saved since their inoculations," Hanley began again. "Even Timna and Joannah report far fewer illnesses and deaths since December 2054. So much so, it is shocking when death now visits."

Susurrations vibrated through the room, hurried and high-pitched.

"How do we protect our children from digital plagues?" a mother in the crowd shouted to the stage, followed by murmurs of agreement.

"What is a ward of the lab, exactly?"

"Blood is on your hands!"

"Our children do not belong to you!"

"What shall become of us all?"

Leaf's lips trembled. His spine straightened, though he lowered his lashes and studied the stage floor to hide his growing shame. He was a failure, a ridiculous excuse for a King. How many chances had he been given to protect his community? Their ignorance did not produce bliss. It became a death sentence. New Eden should have known of their enslavement and transformation by now, and they should have received the news from him.

Not the enemy.

They still believed Joel Watson died of natural causes and that Timothy Kane worked alone to move his son into a position of greater power. Nor did they understand the full extent of the Techsmith Guild's purpose. How many other deaths had Timothy falsified in order to award insurance money and inheritances to the lab?

"All good questions," Hanley shouted back, though kindly, and repeated his words again until the crowd quieted. "I'll be sure to relay each one to Fillion. Currently, my son is dealing with legal fallout after ending his betrothal to Akiko Hirabayashi. Otherwise he would be present to hear your grieving hearts and do his duty to care for your community."

Mouths fell open in shock. The Son of Eden had jilted a woman once already. But twice? 'Twas beyond dishonorable to the community, especially as his ungentlemanly behavior may have resulted in the deaths of New Eden's children. Hanley did not accuse Akiko of revenge, but the insinuation was there all the same, as well as Fillion's implied guilt.

Leaf could see the feeling of betrayal in their eyes. The Son of Eden, the man of bedtime stories, had not protected them from the evils of the Outside world. Nor had the lab or any Outsider present.

He knew this, for he felt the same emotion move violently through him. It was a powerful realization that nearly swept him away with its overwhelming clarity.

They were a people betrayed. Every single one of them.

Ribbons of light poured in from the latticed windows and touched the natural linens and blood-drained faces. Villagers glowed in spectral shades, mouths agape and eyes wide. It was a look that would haunt Leaf all the days of his life. Then, within a blink, within a single beat of his thundering heart, the community began weeping for justice—shrill, battle-born, the cries of souls terrified and broken. The stones cried back their echoing wails until the Great Hall shook with their collective grief.

Leaf was lifting his hands in a plea and beginning to shout for attention when villagers rushed at various Outsiders. A scientist was shoved to the ground and kicked in the head and gut. A NASA representative was pulled from the stage and held as residents—men and women both—delivered blows to the man's face. A different scientist ran out of the building ahead of a mob of villagers who shouted blistering threats at his back.

A tiny piece of Leaf savored the hostility. New Eden was powerless. They were reduced to violence as a means of expression. But this was not the world his mother and father had died to create. Nor the nature that was nurtured from infancy in each resident born inside the biodomes. In this moment, New Eden felt more alien to him than the whole of Earth beyond the panes. With these thoughts came a different sense of clarity, as if a strange fog dissipated in his mind.

How could he even possibly entertain any semblance of approval over his community's response? Had his own bitterness poisoned his heart? Or was he mad with grief as well?

His gaze darted over the crowd in search of his sister. Had she and Rain slipped in during Hanley's speech? He did not think so, and not knowing added to his increasing terror. And yet he desperately wished to know how Ember and the children fared. Had any died in the attack?

For once, Hanley appeared afraid. He stumbled back a few steps before recovering his typical unruffled demeanor. The NASA representatives huddled in a cluster on the far corner of the stage. Connor, Skylar, and Canyon formed a shield around the visiting men and women, but Leaf was not so sure their attempted defense would succeed. In fact, he feared that protecting the per-ceived enemy might pull the Nobles unwittingly into the community's fear-driven rampage.

Did the community still trust the Noble families?

"Trust is paramount inside our forming world," his father had often stressed. "If we cannot depend on our community, then we have lost the heart and soul behind rebuilding what has been lost to the Outside world."

Women shrieked and children cried. The energy rippling off the crowd devoured the charged emotions with vigor, growing stronger and more malig-nant. Another scientist was dragged by his feet into a group who descended upon him in a frenzy. The body of a beaten NASA representative was thrown through an open window, followed by cheers. A sound that chilled Leaf's blood.

He struggled to breathe, every muscle catatonic. The Great Hall dimmed in and out of focus as his mind drowned in rushing streams of terror. He had never felt so utterly helpless—a ridiculous excuse for a King. How did one stop a violent riot? New Eden did not possess a police force. They were a peaceful colony until recent years.

Until Hanley was granted access to their closed-off lives.

Until Timothy killed Leaf's father and stoked a faction.

Betrayal burned anew and Leaf's frozen state thawed into action. He would not hide behind hands to process. *He would no longer hide.* The Aether was meant to hold an invisible crown of power. But he was flesh and blood, not an idea and not an experiment.

"You have created monsters of good men!" he shouted at Hanley. "Stop them before more lives are lost to your lies!"

"Good men are just monsters in disguise."

Leaf drew in another shallow, shuddering breath. "Where is your humanity?"

"This is humanity," Hanley answered so calmly that the hair on Leaf's neck prickled. "Human beings are the evils of the Outside world. This is why I have transcended your generation into something better, something greater. I have gifted you immortality."

"You are not my God nor am I your creation," Leaf spat. "I am flesh and blood, born of a man and woman, and so are *they*!" He pointed to the protesting masses.

"And now you are a miracle of life, reborn twice." Hanley smiled at Leaf as if he were a simpleton. "The sacrifices of New Eden will benefit entire worlds."

"I never volunteered for your experiment," Leaf choked out. "Neither had the children who died today."

Hanley cocked his head. "I have always wondered how New Eden would react in times of violence and social war. Interesting how it is the fear of technology, of immortal life, that has revealed the inner monster. Death has a way of keeping humans connected to each other. But life? That is what we ultimately fear."

"It is *fear* that makes enemies of us all, not life."

Guilt stabbed his chest. Families suffered losses today he could not even begin to fathom as a parent and hoped he never would. Kin now dead by a plague controlled by Outside forces. Were lives so expendable in the Outside world? Had entire populations lost connection to their origins? To their humanity? Even if they had, he would not allow New Eden to regress to an Outsider's soulless view of one another any more than they already had. His father's vision and warning were right.

"Skylar!"

"Yes, Your Majesty," Skylar quickly answered.

"Notify the authorities posthaste."

Skylar nodded and touched his Cranium, pulling up a screen.

"The police will arrest villagers and remove them from N.E.T. property," Hanley said to Leaf, a slight shake to his head. "You will expose the colony to court-ordered investigations and trials. Several villagers will probably be charged with assault and imprisoned. New Eden may be forced to shut down sooner than scheduled too."

The Son of Wind frowned and looked to Leaf for direction. But he did not know what to do. Could he trust Hanley's warning? Though the monster breathed lies, he traded in truths. Leaf's shoulders slumped forward.

"Connor, a word if you please."

"There is a solution." Hanley continued to smile, an affable expression. The Great Hall quaked with anger and Hanley had the audacity to smile. "You will become a hero, a king New Eden will never forget," the man added.

Connor stepped away from the NASA representatives to Leaf's side. "Son?"

"Is what Hanley speaks true?"

"Yes, I am afraid so," Connor whispered back, a muscle flicking in his jaw. "The police will use tear gas and sonic disruption for crowd control, which will disable the innocent and aggressors equally. Residents will be arrested and tried for assault, even without intervention right now. The victims will undoubtedly press charges."

Leaf studied the community once more, his pulse throbbing in his ears. Tear gas? Was it a poison that killed or temporarily disabled? And what was sonic disruption? Would either weapon cause permanent damage?

A baby squalled near the stage. At the hearth, children tearfully clutched each other while mothers and grandmothers circled around them. The main exit and the back door through the kitchen remained barred by men holding chairs and candlesticks to blockade Outsiders. A female scientist, hiding under a table, was hauled out by her hair and tossed into the crowd. Her screams for help were cut off by the battle cries of men who no longer hesitated to raise a fist against the fairer sex.

Leaf wanted to retch.

Perhaps project shutdown was the answer. Men who justified violence for their grief deserved imprisonment, especially violence against women. Still, he could not shake the paranoia that any decision he made ultimately led to Hanley's desired outcome. Or that Leaf would be cast the villain for whatever transpired from this point forward, for he had grossly failed his community. Hanley capitalized on his inexperience and mistakes and exposed Leaf for the man he was—an inept leader and a coward.

Nevertheless, his duty as King, as The Aether, was to protect his community. His reputation mattered not. For once there were no more Outsiders to punish, would they turn on each other? The Techsmith Guild? Or the Noble families? He could not allow this response to escalate any further.

"Grab men you trust," Leaf directed at Connor. "Arm them with shovels and pitchforks, and attempt to control the crowd."

"And harm our own?" Connor asked in disbelief.

Leaf squinted his eyes, blinking rapidly. Could he actually order forced physical submission? What was the right decision in this situation? He knew not. A shallow, ragged breath escaped his tightened chest. Knots twisted his gut in queasy motions. No, he decided. He may have acted as a coward in sheltering New Eden, but he was a good man who believed in the goodness of others.

"Find men and women who are willing to douse unruly villagers with well water," he spoke to Connor once more. "Perhaps we can shock them to attention first."

"As I said, I have a solution," Hanley casually tossed out. "Violence won't be necessary to subdue violence. I could make it end."

"You set me up," Leaf half-sobbed. "Does it matter which course of action I take?"

"Choices always matter." Hanley stepped closer. "For instance, Fillion chose to be unavailable today, and your family was not chosen as a sacrifice. Both choices significantly impact today's tragedy."

Connor practically growled and yelled, "You chose to tarnish my son's reputation before his community!"

"He chose to dishonor his own upbringing. That's on him, not me."

"And what of your choice to not disclose my generation's potential human property status to those who signed The Code on Moving Day?" Spittle flew from Leaf's mouth. "Or to disclose the nature of the state-mandated inoculations to the same residents whose children you vaccinated with HiraMed technology three years prior? How does this impact your solution?"

"The mother-infant mortality rate has decreased to world-record lows. For the ten children who died today, dozens more have lived and their mothers with them." Hanley shrugged. "You disagree with this choice? I understand your own wife was saved by this technology." To Connor: "Your daughter."

Leaf looked away. The nausea in his stomach roiled with every wheezy breath. Dizziness buzzed bright in his head and limbs as panic increased another terrifying notch. "Connor, please ready men and women to bucket water from the well."

"Yes, Your Majesty." Connor flashed Hanley a searing glare and then strode across the stage, down the stairs, and into the angry crowd.

"How have the residents actually suffered by my experiment?" Hanley asked in a low voice. "Think, Leaf. You have heard the stories of Fillion's world. Seen the images. I gave the second and third gens life."

Once again, Leaf floundered. Hanley brought up points he could not adequately refute.

"You have a choice," Hanley continued. "Just like your parents gifted you a new life, a different life, you can do the same for your children and their children."

"If I do not make this choice?" Leaf asked, his eyes stinging. "What shall become of my children's generation?"

Hanley ducked his head to force Leaf to look at him, and whispered, "Earth is already overpopulated, with virtually no jobs. Government contracts end with project shutdown. N.E.T. doesn't have other means of cash flow now that Fillion broke contract with the Hirabayashi family."

Blood rushed from Leaf's head. "You would sacrifice an entire people?"

"In order to live, something must die," Hanley whispered, as if they shared a secret. "Your generation is an integral part of a closed loop system. My solution, the one I'm offering you, involves resurrection and rebirth."

Leaf stared, paralyzed by indecision. He was almost afraid to blink. "How is that even possible?"

"Mars." Hanley paused a beat and straightened. "An entire biodome city on Mars needs citizens. I have the means to transport every resident of New Eden to a new home free of Outsider interference. Just think of it, Leaf. You would have complete control to rule in peace.”

Leaf scrubbed his face with trembling fingers. “What of Fillion? What role does he play in this future scenario?”

“That is *his* choice.”

The word “choice” echoed in Leaf’s head until he thought he would burst.

“Your family would be safe from other cybernetic plagues and attacks, and from project shutdown.”

A tear slipped past the edge of Leaf’s control and fell.

“Other villagers as well.”

Hanley smiled as he tapped his Cranium, a soft look that radiated an empathy and kindness that did not reach his eyes. A single piece of paper appeared before Leaf’s vision. “Just sign here, and I will stop the riot.”

The stylus grew heavy in Leaf’s fingers. Thoughts spun faster and faster. How could he even possibly make a decision like this without first consulting The Elements? Or his community? And yet, if he failed to do so, would New Eden Township destroy herself today? Would he doom his generation and his children’s to death?

Long and thin, the stylus rolled between his fingers effortlessly. More effortlessly than the muddy details Leaf tried to consider.

“I am curious”—he cleared his tightened throat—“why not forge my signature as you did with Fillion’s?”

“Is that what you believe happened?” Hanley laughed. “Fillion suffers from disassociation. His grip on reality is slipping.”

“Neither his lawyer nor Jeff could locate a signed partnership agreement between the lab and New Eden Space Ventures.” Leaf forced himself to meet Hanley’s humored gaze. “Willow recalls an unsigned form at the Ascension Ceremony, to which neither she nor Fillion added signatures.”

A woman’s scream shrieked above the gathering’s outrage and Leaf flinched. From the corner of his eye, he could see that the large doors were now opened. Connor had somehow disarmed the mob of men standing guard at the Great Hall’s exit. Villagers squeezed out of the doors and into the open to escape the fights still waging and breaking out.

“Maybe the error lies with both lawyers and not me.” Hanley leaned in close. “Fillion has black spots in his memory. They’re growing worse. Have you ever heard of the term ‘disassociation’?”

“I am familiar with the word,” Leaf clipped in reply.

“Fillion moves between detachment from reality and loss of reality. Disassociation and psychosis. He’s not stable. I’m trying to help him feel in control and give him purpose, but he’s convinced I’m the enemy.” Hanley sighed, deep and heartfelt. “When have I personally harmed you or the residents? Others have, but not me. This colony is a lifelong investment of mine.” Leaf drew breath to reply, but Hanley quickly interjected, “Do you regret living in New Eden? Would you rather struggle to survive out there?” He pointed to the fractured sky. "What do *you* want, Leaf Watson? Let me help you."

"Do not answer him," Willow snapped beside Hanley. When had his sister entered? Neither he nor Hanley had noticed her arrival. "He is a snake."

"Ember—"

"They are all safe." Willow lifted her chin a notch and glowered at Hanley. "Fillion is on his way to New Eden. The Techsmith Guild's communication director asked that I relay a message to you on her behalf."

"Every second we spend in discussion," Hanley said to Leaf, "is another opportunity for New Eden's violence to—"

Willow cut him off. "An Executive Order signed by His Majesty revokes permissions for Hanley Nichols and Leaf Watson to cross the line at The Door. You are no longer authorized to stand on my soil, sir."

"Are all women in New Eden this fierce?" Hanley slid her an amused smile as he circled around her. From behind, he whispered close to ear while looking at Leaf, "Or has Fillion groomed you to be afraid of me?"

"I do not fear you."

Hanley chuckled with the shake in her voice. "No wonder Fillion can't resist you. All bark and misguided passion." He paused before her once more and quietly taunted her. "Just like him."

A gust of fury surfaced across Willow's entire body—fingers curled into fists, eyes blazing, her posture taller—right before she slapped Hanley across the face with the hurricane's release. His head snapped to the side with the force. Shock colored his face as he stretched his jaw and rubbed his cheek. Leaf sucked in a sharp gasp along with the NASA representatives and Nobles.

Sneering, she taunted back, "I assure you that I do more than bark." Hanley's gaze sharpened into steel blades. With mocking delight, she asked, "Do you still find my passion's aim misguided?"

Hanley swiveled on his heel and snapped his finger. A man from NASA rushed to his side. "Let's go. The doors are now unblocked."

"Fillion was right," she shouted at Hanley's back. "You are a monster!"

"Fillion is delusional!" Hanley replied back, touching the temple of his head. "His mind is broken."

"His mind is brilliant."

"Indeed. He's a master manipulator, and you've been fooled."

Willow's expression curled with fire and ash at his implications.

"You really believe he loves you?" Hanley chuckled again. "That out of all the women in the world, he chose *you*?"

"He speaks true of his affections."

"You're a hallucination that haunts him. A fantasy. Half the time he doesn't know if you're real." A piteous smile curved Hanley's mouth. "I am not the bad guy, Your Highness. I only want to help you and New Eden."

"You lie."

Hanley sighed, long and slow. "I didn't want to show you this. But I'm afraid you leave me little choice."

He turned on his Cranium and his fingers brushed the air. Willow's handprint smarted red on his cheek. Eventually, an image shimmered in the air of a man with dark hair in the middle of a crowd and her smile dimmed. The picture was blurry, as Leaf remembered, but it was clear the man's eyes were closed and his head tipped back in a look of enjoyment. An immodestly attired woman was kissing his neck while her body scandalously clung to his.

"This could be anyone," Willow said, arms akimbo, her neck heating in a mortified blush.

Hanley pointed to the man's hands. The word "honor" was spelled out one letter at a time across the man's fingers.

"This is a trick," she forced out on a choke.

Hanley swiped the image from the air and turned off his Cranium. "Leaf will confirm it's true. He was in the boardroom the day Fillion was reprimanded for his destructive behavior."

Fists clenched at her sides, she shouted, "You are a—"

"Willow, let him go." Leaf gently touched her arm. She bit her lower lip to hold back the angry tears and angled her face toward her shoulder. "We need to assist Connor in subduing the community."

"Did you tell your brother?" Hanley stepped close to Willow. His gaze swept over her with brazen satisfaction. "That you are to blame?"

"Blame for what?" Leaf demanded.

"I warned you," Hanley whispered. His eyes rested on Willow's lips, the corners of his mouth creeping up. "Perhaps your passion is misguided after all."

A sudden roll of gasps and cries pierced through the echoing rage, and Leaf turned toward the source. Buckets of water splashed onto the rioting villagers in wave after wave. The assembly line Connor set up moved swiftly to circle every fight, not giving the protesters a chance to work back up. The Great Hall quieted enough that Leaf took action, forgetting about Hanley and his guests.

"Get to your knees!" he boomed. "Unless you are holding a bucket or protecting children, fall to your knees or I shall be forced to use stronger methods."

Connor halted the dousing and repeated Leaf's instructions.

One by one, residents lowered and knelt in blood-tinged water.

Relieved, Leaf glanced back to Hanley, but the man was no longer there.

"The snake slithered away, it seems," Willow quietly said, a tremble to her voice. "Rain and I shall attend the women and children. Leave the clean-up to us as well."

He nodded. "Skylar, Canyon, assist me in quarantining the rioters." To Willow: "Those who participated in fights shall clean the Great Hall before evening meal, and I shall supervise."

"Very well, Your Majesty." Head held high and back straight, his sister marched from the stage, lifting the hem of her skirt as she made way to the hearth.

Skylar gripped his forearm and whispered, "I recorded everything."

"Thank you, Sky." Leaf grabbed his friend in a quick embrace and then jumped from the stage and into the kneeling crowd.

Too afraid to meet the eyes of community.
Too afraid not to.

Romeo: O, speak again, bright angel! For thou art
As glorious to this night, being o'er my head,
As is a wingèd messenger of heaven
Unto the white, upturnèd, wondering eyes
Of mortals that fall back to gaze on him
When he bestrides the lazy-puffing clouds
And sails upon the bosom of the air.

Juliet: O Romeo, Romeo! Wherefore art thou Romeo?
Deny thy father and refuse thy name.
Or, if thou wilt not, be but sworn my love,
And I'll no longer be a Capulet.

— from Shakespeare's _Romeo and Juliet_ *

Chapter Thirty-Two

Breath came quick. Dust kicked up into a golden cloud as he ran. The setting sun glared off the biodome panes and pierced his eyes. He didn't hear the protesters camped at the gate. Or the mechanical hiss of The Door sealing behind him. Sweat dripped into Fillion's bloodshot eyes.

He was too late.

Fear ripped through his chest in agonizing waves. The tangle of dark emotions he had labored to hold in for hours now balanced on a razor's edge. Already he could feel the cut, the slice deepening under the mounting pressure. The sanity Mack demi-restored bleeding out.

The riot in New Eden ended almost as quickly as it started, according to witnesses from the lab. Leaf issued a mandatory lockdown except during evening meal, which had been rescheduled for two hours past its usual time. An injured scientist shared how the Great Hall emptied in a matter of minutes as villagers returned to their homes under the threat that Leaf would ex-communicate anyone who disobeyed. The only residents allowed to leave their homes were the Noble families, the kitchen staff, and those responsible for cleaning the Great Hall.

Six scientists and four NASA representatives had sustained significant injuries.

Fillion spoke to two different FBI agents over the incident in the domes. The official statement from the government: the riots never happened. To reveal the riot would risk revealing the bio-engineering which could lead to private sector knowledge of the top-secret MELISSA Project, or insinuate psychological instability. Fillion had no choice but to follow orders at this point. Decades-old military and NASA contracts were involved. Contracts he was still wading through. Government-forced project shutdown wasn't an option he could flirt with either.

The Ceremonies of Death could no longer be broadcast as originally planned. Mack zipped messages to Amanda to stand by for further directions. Fillion needed another angle, some other way to garner public support without appearing gimmicky or desperate. An organic campaign needed to rise from the ashes from this shitstorm to win New Eden's freedom in court and to change the experiment status, and stat. Ideas churned and grated. Nothing viable had emerged, but an image for the world would rise up eventually. Probably once he had a chance to speak with Leaf face-to-face.

Hanley had vacated the premises an hour before Fillion arrived. The exact hour his true identity leaked onto the Net—son of the notorious serial killer and con artist Anderson Kane—and older half-brother of Timothy Kane. Minutes before Fillion dashed out of the lab, Hanley appeared on several news channels in tears over his wife's presumed death.

Rage exploded into wings of fury and, without realizing it, Fillion started running. Past Mack and Lynden. Out of the lab, past one angry mob and straight toward the den of another.

Free the people, slave owners!

A guard hermetically sealed The Door behind Fillion. For safety reasons, biodome access was temporarily revoked for everyone save Fillion and Mack. Fillion's executive order to restrict Hanley and Leaf from crossing worlds was illegal, as they were business partners. Still, both partners were required to adhere to Fillion's authorization change until a court deemed Fillion's policy unlawful. Hopefully the court tomorrow would side with Fillion's request for a restraining order against Hanley.

If his head had been screwed on right, he would have thought of the extra protective measure to revoke clearance sooner. Hell, he still wasn't sure if he was seeing things or not. Reality continued to fuzz in and out of focus.

A sob loosened in his chest and he fought its release. The muscles in his legs burned. His jaw clenched tight. Fillion sucked in a large gulp of air and pushed himself to run faster.

Soon, the darkening forest swallowed his fevered body in a cool breath.

Fire licked at his lungs and his legs shook. Desperate for air, Fillion slowed and bent over his knees. Rocks, leaves, and wild grass swayed in nauseating motions as the world spun. He gripped his hair and squeezed his eyes shut until the feeling passed. He needed to find Leaf. Or Jeff. Shit, the dome's silence was eerie. A chill touched his flushed skin and he shivered. Mentally he kicked himself to keep moving. Where to go first? Squinting, he scanned his surroundings and calculated distance to the Watson apartment and The Chancery.

The apartment was closer.

He trotted off the trail and into the underbrush next to the willow oak tree. Through the thicket of moss-draped branches and ferns, The Waters sparkled silver with the last touches of dusk. The Watson apartment was to the left. He switched back the other direction while grinding his teeth, the buzzing in his head growing louder. The same precursory buzz that appeared before his mind glitched. Weird. He had been fine for almost two weeks now.

Had his cybernetic's security been compromised?

Was Hanley trying to attack his system as punishment?

Was he bio-engineered to shut off when blood pressure and adrenaline reached certain levels?

Or was he reaching his PTSD trigger point?

Waves of thoughts continued to crash against the jagged cliffs of his mind. Emotions erupted and splattered, as delicate and fleeting as spindrift.

His vision shifted. Forest dissolved into ocean. Black hair coiled and undulated in death's soft current, blood-red lips parted in a silent scream, gray eyes vacant, her hands, arms, and legs gracefully positioned as if attached to marionette strings while floating, weightless, to the seafloor.

Had his mom suffered? Did she die before her plane collided with water? Or had she drowned, eyes opened wide with terror? No one held her hand as she slipped away from this world. No last rites or final goodbyes. And, yet, she knew her death was coming. Fillion touched the linden leaf necklace in his pocket and fought the emerging sob once more.

The watery grave drained away and the woods returned in a hazy glitch. He almost screamed his mom's name and dove into his mind after her. But it wasn't real. Still, just to make sure, he touched his clothes and skin. Perfectly dry.

Another cut, another slice. More of his sanity bleeding out.

God, he just wanted to curl up in the ferns and let his body melt into the forest floor until the tree roots cradled his skeletal remains.

Focus. He needed to focus.

Fillion drew in a deep breath, held it, then released it slowly, moving his head side to side to stretch the knotted muscles. Then stopped.

A flash of white in the canopy caught his eye. His already faltering breath stuttered more with hope. Long yellow leaves fluttered in a siren's song, pulling his vision up until he stared, utterly captivated. Strands of gold danced in the wind, and evening light framed her tear-blotched face. The folds of her linen skirt dipped into the sky and rippled wildly, a white flag to his warring state.

His heart surrendered, completely.

Still out of breath, he gripped a lower branch and started climbing—panting like a lovesick fool. "I'm so lame," he muttered to himself. He should find Leaf and Jeff. Doxxing Hanley and dragging Akiko through the mud placed an even larger target on the people of New Eden. Another attack was imminent. Hell, it could be happening this very moment, and here he was, climbing a damn tree.

But Fillion needed strength. He needed courage.

He needed Willow.

The ground grew distant. His boot slipped and he gripped a tree branch, muttering under his breath. This was such a dumb idea. His body was crashing under the acute stress. The robotics side of him could shut down at any moment. Invisible threads yanked him upward, though. It was the strangest sensation. Synchronicity. Quantum entanglement. What affected one, affected the other.

Even death.

A twig snapped beneath his foot and fell to the forest floor in a soft thud. The whites of Willow's eyes practically glowed as she gaped. "Fillion…" His whispered name echoed every tear she had ever shed, right before she twisted away.

Confused by her dismissal, he halted all motion and studied the fractured sky and fluttering trees, waiting. The branch swayed beneath his boot. A soft breeze skipped by. No glitching focus or fading images. Could he trust his mind right now? Just a few minutes ago he battled the edge of his breaking point. A virtual ocean and his mom's drowning body taunted his grief. Willow often appeared in his darkest moments. With her back turned and arms hugged tight around her legs, he hesitated to trust his faculties.

Did she blame him for the deaths today? For his mom's death? Did she even know about Della yet? Another mental laceration, this one deep and searing, and his hold on the branch loosened.

The old him would climb back down the tree and use arrogance and anger to hide his heartache. The new him, the one that refused to be treated like the shit people scraped off their shoes, reached for the nearest solid limb, fingers now curled tight, and resumed climbing.

Fillion scaled the fabled oak tree until he anchored himself on a branch just below the one she perched on. Eye-level, he searched her slitted green graze, darkened by the encroaching night. Fingers of reflective light caressed her cheek and tear-glistened lashes. The neckline of her bodice had fallen forward and he watched, jealous, as another finger of light caressed the curve of her breasts.

Softly he blinked and met her gaze once more. "You'll have to push me out of this tree to reject me."

"Tempting," she threw back, harshly.

"Hate me. Fine. I told you one day it would happen. But I deserve an explanation."

Willow grimaced and spat out, "How many times shall you betray my trust?"

"Still not an explanation."

"Hanley showed me an image of you—"

"*Hanley*? Seriously?!" Fillion huffed a disgusted laugh.

She lifted her chin. "Was it a trick?"

"No, it's real." He lifted a hand in surrender when she drew in a sharp, angry breath. He continued before she exploded. "That picture was a set-up. He's used it several times now to demean my character, first against my employees, board members, my sister, Leaf, and now you. Did I enjoy the moment?

Yeah. For a few stupid seconds. That's it. Nothing happened. *Nothing.* I told her no. Mack told her no. But dammit, Willow, there was a brief moment when I wanted to escape my loneliness and anxiety. Selfish, I know. And Hanley knew this. He knew how lonely and stressed out I was and set up the picture. But I never meant to hurt *you*, or anyone." Fillion offered his hand and whispered, "I'm so, so sorry."

"She was touching you intimately." Willow dropped her gaze to a golden leaf in her fingers, ignoring his hand. "Even if for a few seconds, the moment still happened."

"This was before my Ascension Ceremony, when I was still engaged to Akiko. I . . . I was suffering from cybernetic attacks and . . . and. . ." The words failed to form as angry tears took their place. Silently he cursed his nervous stammering and grasped for mental focus. "I'm the son of a killer."

Her eyes flicked to his, eyebrows pinched together.

Fillion swallowed. "The world can't make up its mind if I should be destroyed or worshiped. Strangers have violated my life since before I ever heard your name. This won't be the last image of me to surface with claims. Or the last person to try and create a scandal for political or monetary gains—"

"Why do you look upon me as though I am an apparition or a figment of your imagination?"

Shit. He hadn't see this one coming. The abrupt change in topic sent his mind spinning, too. Shame crept up his neck and face as he caved inward even more. "Did Leaf share . . . about me?"

"My dear brother has a poor habit of not sharing many things with me."

"Your question," he started, voice cracking. "I'm crazy. See things that aren't there. Have since I was twelve."

The whites of her eyes glistened. "Then it is true? I am nothing more than a fantasy to you?"

He drew in a shuddering breath, then confessed from the beginning. Being beaten up at twelve following her death, earning a broken arm and ribs. The names he was called. Hanley. So much about Hanley. His PTSD and anxiety disorder. His vow of celibacy and why. Living in juvenile detention. Marrying Mack to secure power over his own money and mental health decisions, followed by their annulment. Going to MIT. The six-month World Tour. His great-grandpa's house and woodshop in Ireland. And, finally, the attacks on his cybernetic system.

He didn't leave a detail out. She deserved to know everything about him. Because then, and only then, would he know if the daughter of Joel and the son of Della were real. Or if love was nothing more than a fairytale programmed by his mind as another way to cope with the abuse. Maybe even programmed by Hanley to break his spirit.

"You're usually a corpse when I hallucinate about you. Like you've just dug yourself out of a grave, begging me to save you." Fillion glanced up shyly. "Before I met you, I'd try. I'd try so hard to save you. I needed to prove that I wasn't a child-killing psychopath like Hanley. The delusions helped me feel less powerless, less guilty." He lifted a shoulder in a slight shrug. "After I met you"—he cleared his throat and looked out into the darkening forest—"after I met you, I hallucinated about us being together."

"Oh, Fillion…"

"Creepy, I know." Fillion couldn't meet her eyes as his face flushed hot. "I get it. I'm disturbing. *This* is disturbing. If you're weirded out by me, which I'd be surprised if you weren't, or don't want to see me again or, I don't know. Whatever." He bit the inside of his cheek, desperate to find a piece of himself still intact. Something that still felt whole and unviolated. Pissed, he tore a leaf from a twig and flicked it into the breeze.

"This is the *real* me," he croaked, watching the leaf disappear into dusk's shadows. "I'm not noble like Leaf. Or a social justice warrior like Coal. I'm . . . I'm scared and angry and fight my broken mind every second of every day. And, if I'm not fighting my mind, I'm fighting the world's perception of me."

He clenched his jaw. "All I can do is offer what little is left of me to New Eden. To you, if you'll still . . . still have me. But it won't be enough. Hell, I can't even save myself. I'm trying, though. I'm trying so hard to be what *I need*. I take strides forward, and Hanley knocks me back."

"A despicable, evil man! How could a father be so vile to his own son?!" Willow grit between clenched teeth. "I am not a toy he created for his pleasure and neither are *you*!"

His gaze fluttered to hers. "I don't know how to slay this dragon, but I won't stop trying."

"Allow me to pick up my sword and fight alongside you, My King—"

"My mom is dead," he interjected. "Her plane crashed into the ocean this morning. They can't find her body." Grief finally loosened from his chest and he heaved for breath. Even in the limited light, he could see the blood drain from Willow's face. "I never told her I loved her. Not once. But I did."

Willow laced her fingers with his and squeezed. Tears streaked down her ghostly features in strange, reflective lines. He ducked his head until hair covered part of his face, trying to control the riptide of emotions crashing his system. The forest began to dissolve into ocean once more and his body lightened and bobbed, as if floating. Fillion jerked his head up and clutched a limb until the bark bit at his skin.

"She knew she was going to die," he blurted out, desperate to remain present. "I don't know how or why. But I can't process this. Or what happened today in New Eden."

"The deaths today are unimaginably horrific and cruel," Willow said, barely breathing. "Children bled from their eyes, mouths, and ears."

Bile coated Fillion's knotting throat.

"Hanley spoke of their deaths as a necessary sacrifice for mothers and babes to survive childbearing in higher numbers." A hurricane of violent emotions swirled around her as she cried out, beating her heart with a clenched fist. "He warned me that I would be to blame if your public image fell. But children—merciful God, he murdered children in our name…" She looked at him, eyes swollen and bruised, lips cracked with grief. A haunting, mewling wail left her rigid body, and she sputtered through tears, "Hanley is the devil incarnate.

But he shall never own my soul nor the soul of New Eden."

"If Hanley actually harmed you to control or punish me—" He cut himself off and turned away. A blush crept up his neck once more. "I have reoccurring nightmares that he does. I've watched you die so many times."

Willow's mouth fell open with his admission then clamped shut. "Fillion Nichols, do not feed his illusions," she hurled in a gust of fury, and the twisting, painful churning in his gut intensified. "If you watch me die, it shall be in old age after a lifetime of fighting each other."

"You don't know that."

She shifted on the branch's edge. "Hanley gains from your fear. Perhaps it is time you gained from his."

"What?" Fillion's head snapped up.

"Perhaps it is—"

"No, I heard you." He stared at her, his mind calculating new angles and possibilities. An idea simmered on the surface, one he tried to grasp at. But it was still out of reach. "I released his real identity to the media today. Puts a giant target on my back, yours too. Retaliation in New Eden will happen again to punish me and he'll use my 'failure' to resurrect his public image. But, right now, he's deflecting by trying to gain sympathy over Mom's death."

"I speak of other fears."

Fillion picked at the moss and bark on a branch to give his racing mind an occupation. "Can't parse your meaning. What other fears?"

"He has convinced you that the true battle is for your mind and re-directs your energy to defend your coherency and intelligence." She peered at the golden leaf in her hand. "But it is your heart he wishes to own, for you were made to love and to love passionately." Willow's eyes flashed to his and she whispered, "Your name, Fillion Nichols, is forever carved into the boughs of my heart. Hanley knows this and despises how he cannot control our affections."

"My name..." Fillion grimaced and scratched his nails over the bark. "Even after knowing everything my family has done to yours? To others?"

"Especially after knowing everything. You are so very easy to love." She cupped his cheek with her hand once more. Fillion flinched, shame burning his skin. "My King," she began again gently, "you possess the most beautiful soul of any man I have ever known. But, dear Lord in Heaven, how you vex me so. Sacrifices I am willing to endure, fear not."

Her words were meant to be humorous. Heavy emotions lined her face, however. Holding her arm out straight, she released the golden leaf and watched it flutter into the shadows. "Please forgive me, Fillion," she said, hiccupping back more tears. But it was no use. They fell anyway. "I am utterly ashamed of myself. I should have never doubted you."

"Deflecting blame is Hanley's life-support." He wiped a tear from her cheek with his thumb. "Oaklee—"

"Oaklee?"

A bashful smile touched the corners of his mouth. The forest hushed as his bleeding heart crept to the edge of reason. The same calming silence he experienced in the woods during the New Life Ceremony. Anxiety disappeared. His racing mind quieted to one central thought: his story belonged with hers. Their lives were meant to weave together. She was right. Hanley may control Fillion's mind, but he didn't control his heart. Everything he was, everything he wanted to be, leaped off the edge in an exhilarating rush and plummeted toward his destruction. Consequences be damned.

"Yes, *Oaklee*, daughter of Joel . . . I want a relationship full of *forevers* with you."

Her eyes burned with understanding right before she leaped off the edge after him. They would crash together.

"Son of Della, I fear I have fallen to the whim of your Outsider fancies and shall never recover."

Joy surged through his shattered heart. It didn't invalidate the anger or the betrayal. Didn't soothe the disgust souring his gut. Instead, scintillating beams of control shot from each transparent piece of his life and illuminated Hanley's illusions until he could truly see them for the flimsy, sickening, power-grabbing shams they were. Hanley was the first-born loser of a first-rate swindler—the legacy he embodied. Fillion's legacy, however, would be comprised of entirely different elements.

Bark dug into his palm as he gripped a limb to lean in closer. Her breath trembled with his when he stopped short of her lips. "I love you, Willow Oak Watson. I will *never* stop loving you."

She whispered back, "I shall *never* cease loving you."

"*Never* stop flirting with your wit."

"*Never* tire of how you look at me as though a stunned goat."

"A stunned goat?!" Fillion arched an eyebrow.

Willow harrumphed with mock-annoyance, placing a hand on her hip. "Yes, a stunned goat. I half-expect you to fall over with arms and legs out stiff."

"That's because you make me stupid."

"Oh dear, how dreadful."

A hint of smile played across his lips. "Terrifying."

"Well, then," she sang out. "Since I make you stupid, I shall *never* feel anything but awe at the brilliant workings of your arrogant mind."

"Then I'll *never* tire of pissing you off."

Willow pulled back. "I beg your pardon?"

"It *never* fails to humor me and you *never* fail to disappoint."

"Then I shall endeavor to never satisfy your pigheadedness."

A corner of his mouth quirked up. "Pity."

She tilted her head closer to his. "Indeed, for I was about to grant you permission to kiss me."

Fillion's eyebrows shot up.

Mortification heated her skin. But she refused to look away or adjust her posture. God, he loved it when she bucked New Eden's non-progressive system.

"Talking dirty." He inched back a few notches and winked. "Scandalous."

The setting sun leaped from the sky and melted into her eyes. "I never realized your sensibilities were easily offended by a woman's confession."

"I like a brazen woman who speaks her mind. Especially about kissing me."

"Fillion Nichols!"

"Willow Oak Watson!" He lifted an eyebrow again.

"You vex me so."

"Liar," he said, sticking out his tongue. "You keep saying that, but I don't believe you."

"Pity," she threw back at him, lifting her eyebrow to mock his.

His smile widened. "You're a brat."

"You like it."

"No." He leaned in closer and whispered, "I love it." Biting his lower lip in a goading grin, he said, "Put me out of my misery."

"Begging now, are we? And what of your egotistical notions of grandeur?"

"Worthless notions."

She narrowed her eyes into an impish scowl. "Do not push me."

"Or what, *Your Highness?*"

"Or I shall push you out of my tree."

Fillion fully grinned now, he couldn't help himself. "No you won't. You can do way better than that. Try again." Leaning in closer, he flirtatiously whispered, "Kiss me and then what?"

Willow groaned, attempting to playfully shove him away but he didn't budge. Rolling her eyes, she snapped, "Pigheaded cad—"

His lips captured her fury and made it his own before she could finish. Wind tore through the forest that same moment, and he wanted to laugh. Their hearts were free-falling faster, harder, no end in sight. Her hair whipped around them and tickled his face. He could die this moment. God, her touch, just the feel of her. Every dark emotion he carried vanished as he ached for more, more, more.

Another gust moved through the trees. Branches groaned and swayed, moving to the rhythm of their kiss—wild, melodious, and erotic.

Leaving her lips, his mouth roamed her neck until he nibbled on her earlobe. "You're so beautiful," he whispered in her ear. "So beautiful it's painful." Fluttered breaths pulsed on his cheek in reply. He smiled, trailing light kisses down her neck to her collarbone. Creamy skin and soft curves lured him farther down. And he wanted to. He desperately wanted to know her breasts, to explore every dip and rise of her body. Instead, he dragged his lips back to hers in a bruising kiss.

Gently biting her lower lip, he tugged while slipping his hand beneath her skirt and around her calf, slowly, seductively, wrapping her leg around his waist until their hips crashed. Fillion's body went supernova. She arched toward him in a breathless sigh that formed his name. Fire curled through his veins at the sound. He was burning, turning to ash as her fingers roved over his chest, behind his neck, and disheveled his hair. Gripping fistfuls of his strands, she gracefully fell back against the tree trunk. Pain tingled in his scalp as she dragged him toward her with the momentum. A moan escaped Fillion with her dominance, and she smiled. *She smiled.* Damn.

That look—the headiness in her eyes, the tilt of her swollen lips, the way her breasts rose and fell with each quivering breath, skin flushed, a waterfall of golden hair rippling down her arms—it was hella sexy. The very definition of *sekushī.* He blinked, unable to think. Unable to speak. Was he even breathing? For years, he feared being the asshole who ruined her. But this unexpected alpha sensuality? Holy shit. She was ruining him, and he stared, paralyzed, like a freaking idiot.

"Stunned goat," she whispered.

"Huh?"

A satisfied grin curved the corners of her mouth. What the hell was she talking about? Intelligence slowly trickled back into his dumbstruck brain. And then it hit him.

Kiss him *and then* prove he turned into a stunned goat.

Fillion lost it. God, she was such a brat. Laughter rolled out of him, more so when she perched on the tree like a smug cat that had caught its prey. They smiled at each other for what seemed like an eternity. And Fillion knew what he wanted to do.

The necklace, previously tucked safe in his pocket, dangled between his fingers and glinted in the soft light. Shyly, he placed the gift in her hand, saying, "*Korekara zutto, ore no jinsei wa anata no mono desu. Zutto eien ni sasagemasu.*" Mouth parted, she gaped at the silver linden leaf, recognizing the symbol of New Eden's fabled tale of love and loss. "I now see that you have always owned my life and always will," he whispered, translating his words. "I give it to you."

Tears sparkled on her lashes in the ambient light. "You honor me, Fillion."

"Joel started the linden tree story in New Eden after gifting this necklace to my mom on Moving Day." He softly kissed her lips. "I offer you a different promise. Nothing will separate us again. Not different worlds. Not inhumane laws. Nothing. We control our fate."

Willow clasped the silver chain around her neck and then caressed the heart-shaped linden leaf, overcome. In some strange way, giving her a piece of his loss felt right. It didn't bring Joel back. But now she had a piece of her dad's heart. A piece, Fillion realized, that he and Willow together completed.

The story Leaf had shared years ago about the tree maiden's tear blazed through Fillion's mind. Tragedy had separated him from Willow long enough. They weren't their parents, even if their genetic memories coded their DNA. The sins of the father shouldn't fall on the children. It was time to write a new legend for the famed linden tree in New Eden. Another tale about how a tree maiden's tears created love and freedom, not betrayal and enslavement.

Fillion reached out and touched the linden leaf charm in Willow's fingers and murmured, "Love and truth."

"The silk," she sighed, appearing not to have heard him. "So soft and beautiful. Thank you, My King. The folds luxuriously shimmered like water for me."

"Good."

"I am moved by your lovely gesture, and that you remembered."

"When I was in China, I had the silk custom-colored for you. The cherrywood box was custom-made for you, too, from Japan."

"Truly? How wondrous." She kissed the linden leaf charm, then kissed him. "I fear I have nothing of consequence to offer you in return."

"Nothing?" He traced his finger along her cheek. "You've given me your heart, not once, not even twice. Many times. You grieved for me when I didn't know how." His thumb trailed across her bottom lip. "Anything you want, just tell me," he whispered. "Anything."

For a few, intense nanoseconds, he and Willow searched each other's eyes, memorizing every fragile emotion. Dusky light curved across her face in dappled shadows. The world decayed all around them. Death painted everything black. A closed loop system demanded sacrifices for life to continue and flourish. But, this moment, they just were and always had been a boy and a girl.

Drink up and drink fast, his mind murmured. He had a job to do.

Momentary happiness slipped back behind his paranoia as he contemplated the forest floor far below. It was so dark he could only make out the ferns, which were tiny dots. Dizziness swam circles in his head at the sight. He had climbed a tree instead of warning Leaf of how he had doxxed Hanley. Panic sparked his blood and the mounting pressure in his head returned in a single, sharp breath.

"I need to warn Leaf," he said, his gaze darting around the forest.

"Yes, of course."

"Come with me?"

"Leaf is in the Great Hall," Willow offered, softly.

With a final glance, she swung her leg over a branch and began to descend. She moved like water down the tree, fluid and graceful. Him? Fillion's legs shook as he awkwardly groped for branches and limbs. Anything. The soles of his boots gripped bark and moss in welcomed traction. A small comfort. Eventually, he jumped from the lowest branch to the leaf-littered ground, raking fingers through his mussed hair in relief.

They strode through the forest, quick and silent. Leaves and wild grass fluttered in another gust laced with the scents of cooking spices and roasted vegetables. Birds roosted in branches along the trail, fluffing their feathers in the wind. Life continued on as always. But he was caught between free-falling and feeling buried alive.

Was Willow battling guilt, like him? A logical, fed-up part of him shrugged off the shame for indulging in momentary happiness. Their worlds were crumbling to ruins. Declaring their love had become a defiant act of control instead of something normal people did. Hell, being "normal" wasn't a luxury he knew. Ever. Yet, despite believing that he had nothing to be ashamed of, a festering, grieving side of him roiled and sickened. The corpses of second generation villagers, ages ranging from eight to nineteen, were being prepared for a mass cremation ceremony. They died as a game move to punish Fillion into submission, and more could die in revenge for Fillion's bold move today. His reply? Sitting in a tree with Willow, flirting and kissing.

He was seriously mental. Or maybe grief and regret pushed him to ensure Willow knew him—the *real* him—and his love for her. It was too late to make things right with his mom. But Willow was still alive, and so was he.

What would Hanley try next?

Didn't matter. As much as Fillion wanted to puke at that thought, he couldn't let that *kisama* win. Fillion hadn't killed anyone. Neither had Willow. They were innocent, he kept reminding himself. When Hanley couldn't control Fillion, he controlled how others viewed him. Emotional torment. Mental torture. Always. All the while, Hanley would hide the bloodstains on his hands. Hell no. Fillion refused to let him get off on any form of pleasure over this situation.

The Great Hall shifted into view as they rounded a corner in The Orchard. Candles lined each window and, inside, he could see wheeled candelabras glowing overhead. Tension knotted in his stomach at what he'd find, of what Leaf would share. If he were honest, he was also afraid Leaf would finally disown their friendship.

Lanterns flickered along the walkway leading to the large double doors. The image was haunting, his and Willow's movements funereal. Inhaling deeply, he schooled his features and lifted his shoulders, then paused. The world around him digitized for one fleeting nanosecond. Tilting his head, he blinked. Cobblestone and lanterns returned, clear as before.

"Fillion…" Willow staggered, as if drunk.

He didn't have time to ask her what was wrong. Mid-step, her body became boneless. Head lolled to the side, knees buckled, fingers limp in his. Then she was falling backward on the gradual slope, like a rag doll tossed aside. He caught her around the waist seconds before her head smacked the ground.

An emergency message beeped on his Cranium. "What the…?" First, he needed to deal with the emergency in his arms.

Gently, he lay her on the gravel where she fell and tapped her cheek, saying her name over and over again. Not a single response. Not even a muscle twitch. "No, no, no, no…!" he practically sobbed. Fillion's panic exploded, and he shook her shoulders. Nothing. Green eyes stared straight ahead, unfocused. Grabbing her wrist, he felt for a pulse. There. Something. Her heartbeat was steady. Blonde strands flew over her stilled face with the breeze. Reflective light dusted her in macabre shades, pale skin washed in bluish, dark shadows, as if a corpse. He tucked her flyaway hair behind an ear and tried to think of what to do. Was she in stasis? Recovery mode?

Images of her tattered, soiled dress in a glass coffin replayed on a loop in his mind. And he suddenly knew, that nightmare was an implant. A foreshadowing to send him into terror and disable his mental faculties for when the actual moment arrived.

"I'll destroy him," he whispered into her hair.

Stretched out beside her, he leaned on his elbow and bent toward her mouth until his lips touched hers in a soft, mournful kiss. He choked back a sob as he pulled away. Of course, she wouldn't stir. This wasn't a fairytale. He wasn't really a prince, and he she wasn't really a princess. This wasn't a spell.

God, he was an idiot.

Touching his Cranium, he started to call Mack and remembered the message. Before he could tap his dashboard, the emergency text popped up on his screen.

HNichols: Ashes, ashes, they all fall down. Game over.

No tree, it is said, can grow to heaven unless its roots reach down to hell.

— Carl Jung, Swiss psychiatrist, 1950 *

My heart is broken and I grieve, for I have known love. Your heart is broken and you grieve, for you have not.

— Willow Oak Watson

Chapter Thirty-Three

The Great Hall doors burst open and villagers dashed out. Horror twisted their lantern-lit faces. Small pebbles kicked up as they barreled past. Fillion crouched over Willow to shield her from the stampede and rocks. The mob didn't spare him a look. Or, if they had, they didn't care.

Screams from the village square and the East apartments ripped through the night air. Fillion's head shot up and his gaze darted over the inky darkness. The villagers from the Great Hall slowed momentarily with the wails and then faded into The Orchard and temperate forest. An eerie silence followed. The only sound his labored breaths.

Hanley's message still flashed in his vision. A war beat, loud and fierce, drummed in Fillion's chest. It was as if all the sick, bruised, torn pieces of his heart fused together in a single cosmic explosion of self-respect. Mack was right. For years Fillion would rage only to throw down boundary lines that Hanley could manipulate.

Hints of lavender brushed against Fillion's nose as he buried his face into Willow's neck and mourned. A warm, comforting light glowed bright in his glitching mind. Fathomless blue skies stretched into an endless, cloudless horizon. Tall grass and wildflowers in a kaleidoscope of colors danced to the rhythm of a Celtic drum beating in the distance. A cool, heady breeze brushed along his bare skin, and he sighed. Beneath him lay Willow, her green eyes smiling as her fingertip traced along the curve of his jaw, inviting him closer. Happiness rippled to each point in his body as his lips grew drunk on hers. Each touch and kiss was lazy, almost playful, broken by smiles and an occasional laugh. They were free, not a single care in the world, and his heart clenched. This is the reality he wanted. The reality he would have and deserved.

Darkness returned in a flash. He dragged in a trembling breath, not ready to let go of his dream. Or her.

She was alive.

This nightmare wasn't his fault. He wasn't deserving of Hanley's abuse, and neither were the hundreds of innocent lives in New Eden. Image. Perception. The two illusionary keys to power were just that: illusions. The only power Hanley had over him was what Fillion granted. And Hanley no longer had permission to victim-blame and gaslight Fillion into submission. Emotional abuse was the true plague on his mind, cybernetics and genetics be damned. The violations ravaged and diseased and destroyed parts of him he may never see whole and healed. Parts he may grieve over for the rest of his life. But there were still so many beautiful parts of himself that he wanted to salvage, to protect and heal, starting now.

"Wrong," Fillion said for his Cranium to transcribe back to Hanley while sitting back up. "I'm the Gamemaster. This is now *my* game and we play by *my* rules. All previous claims you held are forfeit."

Message sent. He could've typed it out himself. But he wanted to say each word out loud and release his declaration to the atmosphere he breathed in, the very air that sustained all of life in New Eden. To feed each storm particle with righteous anger as it shredded through his core processor, ripping away Hanley's grip and washing away the stains of shame.

Reverently, Fillion scooped Willow into his arms and marched toward the Great Hall, lightning in his vision and thunder in his steps. Wind buffeted through the stone columns and archways right as he reached the doors. A nearby lantern blew over and skidded across the gravel, the candle snuffed out. Willow's dress whipped and snapped against his legs and his hair flurried around his head in the charged air. Black strands blew into his eyes, momentarily blocking his vision, but he kept marching until he passed the threshold and entered the Great Hall.

Inside, the tables and benches had been stacked against the far wall. Stones glistened with puddles of soapy water near buckets, with rags strewn all over the room. Among the buckets, scattered bodies lay in unnatural positions on the floor. Connor directed first-generation villagers as they checked pulses, heads, and limbs. Blood pooled around the head of a young man in his late teens. A few villagers wept over bodies.

Fillion dared another step inside, his insides shaking. Disgust slithered down his spine and settled in his belly. This . . . this was far more terrifying than he had previously imagined. He thought only the Watsons were under attack. All the unresponsive bodies, they were second and inoculated third gens. Even a toddler lay helpless beside his young mother.

"Are they alive?" Fillion asked no one in particular. Heads whipped his direction and Connor's shoulders sagged in relief, until he noticed Willow's body in Fillion's arms.

"Yes, Your Majesty," Connor replied, on the verge of tears. "So far, all are alive, even the injured."

"Where is Leaf?"

Connor turned and pointed toward the stage. Leaf's body lay in a supine position, legs together and arms tucked at his sides. The Son of Earth appeared stretched out for cremation and Fillion shuddered. Forcing his feet to move, Fillion lumbered toward Leaf and, with care, placed Willow beside him. Emerald eyes in a softer shade than Willow's stared at the rafters above, unfocused.

"Alder and the twins?" Fillion asked, touching Willow's cheek one last time before standing. "Is anyone with them?"

"*Merde!*" Connor spat. "My wife is with Corona and Blaze at home under lockdown." The tendons in his neck bulged as a tear slid down his cheek. "My children, my grandchildren…"

Fillion lowered his voice. "You're not to blame."

"'Tis already too late. Damage is done."

"You didn't earn this punishment. Nobody here did." Fillion studied the bodies on the floor. "Hanley is a virus that has been corrupting our lives for years. But a virus needs a host to thrive, an oversight on my part until now. Everyone in New Eden is under my protection."

Their eyes locked.

"We need groups to go door to door and gather information, stat. Otherwise the Great Hall will crowd with panic," Fillion said. "Each group needs volunteers who can stay with second-gen parents. They'll watch the parents and care for the non-vaccinated children. Joannah and Timna can go with the groups to treat injuries."

"Allow me to help, Your Majesty," a man said, coming forward. He stopped before Fillion, a curious expression on his face as he studied Fillion's. "My name is Gareth, and I shall organize groups as you say."

Fillion grabbed his hand and shook it. "I know who you are. I've seen you play a gittern a few times during Sunday Feasts, right?"

"Aye, that is me." Gareth bowed his head.

"Thanks, Gareth. I'm going to stay headquartered in the Great Hall if you need anything. Remind families to stay in their homes for safety. We'll bring food to them."

The man strode off toward a group of first-generation villagers by the kitchen doors. Fillion watched for a bit, studying body language and counting head nods. Then he swung attention back to Connor.

"The food in the kitchens?" Fillion began again. "Appoint another team of people to ration out food, also door to door. No evening meal tonight."

The former Fire Element scanned the room until his gaze landed on a woman with copper hair. "Kyra," he quietly called out, gesturing for her to join him and Fillion. She jogged over, skin flushed and eyes guarded. She considered Fillion a wary moment longer before dropping into a shallow curtsy.

"My Lord?" she addressed Connor.

"Kyra, please gather able-bodied men and women to deliver food to the East apartments. New Eden shall remain in lockdown until further notice."

Fillion pretended to busy himself with taking note of activities around the

Hall as Kyra continued to stare at him, unsettled. He didn't need her approval right now, or ever. He needed her compliance for the benefit of her community. If appearing submissive is what it took, then fine. Actually, it was the least he could do. New Eden needed to take back power, too.

"And what shall I tell each home, when they ask about the source of our suffering?"

"We shall courier news when we have definitive information," Connor replied, kindly.

Kyra shifted on her feet and coolly eyed Fillion once more. "Shall the Son of Eden extend apologies for so selfishly dishonoring all of New Eden?"

"Kyra—"

"It's all right," Fillion said to Connor. "I'm on your side, My Lady," he answered Kyra. "Valid question." The use of an honorary title warmed her neck and face. Or maybe it was because he was looking at her now. "My honor price," Fillion continued, "is my life."

He knelt on one knee and bowed his head. The Great Hall hushed, noticing his gesture, until Fillion swore the stones echoed his galloping heartbeat. Apologies weren't his forte. But he remembered three years ago when another had humbled herself in her time of trauma, simply to build trust. Even though her apology was authentic, he now understood the layers of compassion and empathy behind the gift she had laid at his feet. Not once had Willow twisted her apology into a manipulated excuse to defend and justify her behavior, or her needs.

Love has little to do with romance and everything to do with honor.

"I owe all of New Eden a life debt." Lifting his head to meet Kyra's eyes, he whispered hoarsely, "Please forgive me?"

Her shoulders relaxed and she blinked back shyness, then offered Fillion a curt, but reluctant, nod. Turning back to Connor, she said, "As you request, My Lord," and lowered into another shallow curtsy before trotting off toward the kitchens.

As Fillion rose to his feet, Connor brushed at another tear. "Any other requests, Your Majesty?"

"No. But I'm appointing you as temporary Regent. I'm going to investigate for leads and start legal action. But I'll remain here, by the stage."

"What has Hanley done?"

Fillion drew in a shaky breath. "I think inoculated second and third gens are in a state of cybernetic stasis. The injected nanotech is mimicking animal hibernation."

"Stasis…" Connor repeated under his breath.

"No torpor chambers means less fuel is needed." He rubbed his fingers together. "Mars transports can be filled with other colony needs instead. A lot, since equipment and supplies are lighter than torpor chambers too."

"Has NASA confirmed this practice, yet?"

"Only with coolant machines and animals." Fillion considered the bodies on the floor. "But to confirm my suspicions, record signs of cooling body temps and slowing heart rates when you check their vitals."

The corded muscles in Connor's jaw, neck, and arms tensed. "Shall we close their eyes as well?"

"Yeah, but make sure villagers understand it's *only* to protect their eyes. No symbolism in it. If eyes won't remain closed, they can dampen spare clothing or linen scraps to drape over the eyes. Keep nose and mouth exposed."

Connor placed his large hand on Fillion's shoulder and squeezed. The calm that Fillion was fighting to maintain began to unravel. "Years ago, I made careless comments of how you were just like your father."

"Forget it." Fillion sloped his head until hair fell over part of his face. "We can hug it out later."

A sad smile tugged the corners of Connor's mouth. "You are one of the most honorable men I have ever known, Fillion Nichols. Your great-grandfather would be proud of the man who stands before me now." He squeezed Fillion's shoulder one last time and then angled away to relay care instructions to the gathering villagers.

Aware of eyes watching his every move, expressions fearful or angry, Fillion kept his head down and moved back to the stage. His vision blurred with Connor's words and his throat tightened.

Focus.

Willow's chest rose and fell in a metered rhythm, a small comfort. Gathering his quickly deteriorating concentration, he ran his fingers down the length of her arm until his hand curled around hers. Beside her, Leaf's complexion grew waxen in the candlelight. The Son of Earth appeared so peaceful. In fact, Fillion tried to remember a time when Leaf had ever looked as serene or as young. Leaf wasn't that much older than himself, but the Son of Earth always seemed decades ahead of everyone else. The perpetual worry lines around his friend's eyes had smoothed. His mouth had relaxed and parted, as if staring at the ceiling in soft awe. Similar to Willow, Leaf's chest moved at a steady, predictable rate.

Tapping his Cranium, Fillion counted Leaf's breaths within a fifteen-second period and made a note. Then he did the same for Willow. He'd check again in twenty minutes to see if their breathing or pulse had changed and continue to log the vitals. The lab was probably already noting this data, but Fillion wasn't sure yet if Hanley had blocked access or wiped contents—something Fillion would do if roles were reversed.

Fillion's brows pushed together as he nibbled the inside of his cheek. He reached out his free hand and, with two fingers, attempted to close Leaf's eyes. A tightened breath whooshed from Fillion's lungs when his friend's lids remained shut. The action felt so final, so wrong. A shudder brushed along Fillion's skin, leaving goosebumps behind. "I'm sorry I failed to protect your family, brother. I'll make this right. Promise."

Could he close Willow's eyes? Bile burned his throat as he drank in her simple beauty and wild strength. Candlelight-gilded strands rippled down her arms and over the stage floor, decorated with small, corded braids. The edges of her laced-up bodice frayed above her breasts. Dirt stains, new and old, darkened the hem of her skirt. A smattering of faint, tiny freckles sprinkled over her nose; they would be unnoticeable if her skin wasn't so pale. Fillion peered at their entangled fingers and bit back the stinging tears.

He had never truly known the pit of fury and fear until now. Pockets of terror and rage had held his life captive since birth. But this? Peering at Willow, her brother, and the other fallen—imagining babies and toddlers crying over unresponsive parents in the apartments—pulverized his mind and heart to dust. There, in the writhing shadows and cold, obsidian walls, a new man was being made from these winnowed ashes. The war beat drummed louder in his pulse, an Aries rhythm both calm and feral. Clarity struck with each beat, each blow as he knelt before the woman who claimed his death, his life, and everything in-between.

"Maiden," Fillion whispered against Willow's cheek. "I'm counting down the seconds until you wake and fight with me." He kissed her cheek and then gently lowered her eyelids. "But I need to slay this dragon on my own before I'm worthy to battle your wits again. You keep winning," he ended, threading a smile into his voice to hide the tears. "Your name, Willow Oak Watson, is carved into the boughs of my heart." With his fingers entwined with hers, he lifted her hand and placed it on her chest, over her heart, and tucked the linden leaf charm into her fingers before slipping his away and standing.

Tiny amber lights glinted off a nearby latticed window. Fillion studied how the sinuous flames flexed and straightened in response to invisible air currents—the elements of wind. He narrowed his eyes. New Eden was a giant Faraday cage. Wi-Fi signals could *only* be broadcast from within. What would happen if he cut the signal and disabled the Techsmith Guild's production server? Would it harm the residents under digital torpor? Without knowing the programmed fail-safe, he wouldn't flip the server's kill switch.

Wind Element.

Where was Skylar?

Since Ascension, Skylar had sent videos to Fillion regularly. Had his cousin recorded the riots? Hanley? Just saying that bastard's name in his mind target-locked Fillion's vision onto the body of Skylar Kane on the opposite side of the stage. A muscle pulsed in Fillion's jaw as he marched over and stared down at the man who looked just like his dad, but a couple years younger. Red flashed in Fillion's vision and his fists curled at this sides.

Breathe. He needed to breathe.

His gut didn't care if the body before him wasn't Hanley. The reaction was visceral, perhaps even primal. Hands shaking, muscles taught, he reached out two fingers and closed Skylar's hazel eyes. Fillion sucked in a sharp, angry breath and exhaled on a choked sob. He could do this. He could face Hanley and win. The game wasn't over yet. To prove that he was in control, Fillion tapped on his Cranium and began recording Skylar's vitals. When done, he removed the Cranium from Skylar's ear, put it on his own, and then sat on the edge of the stage beside his cousin's body. Everything he would do to investigate and to take legal action, he would do in front of Hanley's image.

Biometric security features prevented Fillion from powering on Skylar's Cranium. But that was an easy hack. Grabbing Skylar's hand, he positioned his cousin's finger onto the device's bio-sensor and waited for the green light.

A user screen popped up, prompting a password. Fillion switched back to his own screen and launched a tool to link devices and inject data programmed to crack Cranium security features. Within minutes he was in and began roaming around files and content, pulling up the most recent data.

Message logs uploaded first. He read through each one and then closed out Skylar's message center. Tapping the air, Fillion opened up media files next, and his heart jumped. There, at the top, was a video of the Great Hall's warmly lit, smoke-filled room. Silhouetted bodies walked and crouched in the background, a scene eerily similar to the one before him. "Shit," Fillion breathed. The video was still recording and had been for *hours*.

Pressing "stop record," he dragged his finger along the recording's time bar until Hanley's face blurred by. Was this a trap? A honeypot to eat up Fillion's time? These past few weeks Fillion had discovered how most games moves were just that—a distraction. Not wasted moves, per se. They all had a singular point and wove into the unfolding plot seamlessly, which is why the leads were always so believable.

Something was definitely off. He just couldn't buy that Hanley would have allowed anyone to record the town meeting in New Eden without consent forms and other legal docs. Especially since a legal nuclear holocaust would ensue over the deaths of minors. History had already proved that reality during The Watson Trials. No, the *kisama* had jamming tools he used for this exact reason. But this was the second time a video slipped by Hanley's control-freak nature, the first being the handover speech.

Fillion hesitated. Did he spend time watching Hanley's town meeting and the resulting riots? Or did he contact Michael and Mack and check in with the lab to report the bio-cyber attack in New Eden? Whatever happened earlier didn't change anything. Yet, nothing Hanley planned was surface level. He played multiple plot points at once.

"A Gamemaster ponders the hidden," he mumbled to himself, deep in thought.

Whatever was in the video, Hanley wanted Fillion to know. He couldn't reason any other plot device, not fully and logically at least. Before self-doubt could creep in, Fillion hit play.

The slithering voice of his tormentor filled Fillion's head. Air hissed between Fillion's clenched teeth as he attempted, in vain, to regulate his fight-or-flight responses. War. He wanted war. And he wouldn't stop until this dragon was slain into an orange uniform, once and for all.

The Hall filled with angry, grief-stricken faces. Hanley stood before them on the stage and offered shallow, mis-directed apologies and charming lies for bitter truth. Leaf stood beside him, appearing pale and stricken. Purple shadows lined his friend's eyes while his lips, though pressed into a thin line, trembled. Then it happened. The riot. Fillion had heard the stories, but holy fuck. This wasn't the pacifist New Eden he recognized. The contorted faces and violence, especially against women and in front of children, was as unnatural as it was shocking. It was if collective grief had manifested into a blood-thirsty beast that then demanded equal sacrifices.

Wait.

Were the attacks that literal?

The part of his brain trained to spot patterns lit up. He turned down the volume to focus only on movement and counted. Four NASA reps and six scientists. Ten Outsiders for ten villagers. Fillion's eyes widened. Son of a bitch. Had Hanley programmed villagers to attack specific individuals? To ensure the riots happened?

"For every action, there's an equal and opposite reaction," Fillion said, thinking aloud. Newton's Third Law of Motion dictated much of nature's symmetry within a closed loop system. "Sick bastard."

Rewinding the video, he decided to backtrack to when Leaf spun toward Hanley and yelled. Willow's face flashed onto the screen. This wasn't far enough back, but he lifted his finger anyway and the video played just as she slapped Hanley across the face. Fillion's jaw dropped and, if sorrow didn't cling to every air particle right now, he would've burst into laughter. Instead, he played back the slap over and over. God, he loved her. She was so freaking cute when mad. But mad as hell? Hot.

The slap cracked in Fillion's head once again. He allowed a small smirk before rewinding the video until Leaf's body language changed from offense to defense.

"You have a choice," Hanley said to Leaf. *"Just like your parents gifted you a new life, a different life, you can do the same for your children and their children."*

"If I do not make this choice? What shall become of my children's generation?"

Hanley leaned close and quietly shared, *"Earth is already overpopulated, with virtually no jobs. Government contracts end with project shutdown. N.E.T. doesn't have other means of cash flow now that Fillion broke contract with the Hirabayashi family."*

"You would sacrifice an entire people?"

Fillion paused the video to collect himself. *This* was Hanley's plan for project shutdown? How the hell would their companies pay out all the lawsuits from project failure? From murdering hundreds of people? Joel's money was to secure New Eden Space Ventures. And Della . . . oh god. Her death. She was worth astronomical amounts of money. Hanley planned for this possibility. Of course, he had. Her death also meant Hanley would receive legal ownership of the T.R.U.S.T. Theory as her beneficiary, granting him one-hundred percent control over the second and third gens.

Haziness crept into his head. The same digital fog that arrived right before his mind glitched. "No." The word formed bright on his tongue and cut through the building kernel panic. His cybernetic system would obey him. A scowl formed between his brows. With concentration renewed, he hit play once more.

"In order to live, something must die," Hanley replied melodiously. *"Your generation is an integral part of a closed loop system. My solution, the one I'm offering you, involves*

resurrection and rebirth."

"*How is that even possible?*"

"*Mars.*" Hanley waited a beat, then continued. "*An entire biodome city on Mars needs citizens. I have the means to transport every resident of New Eden to a new home free of Outsider interference. Just think of it, Leaf. You would have complete control to rule in peace.*"

Leaf scrubbed at face. "*What of Fillion? What role does he play in this future scenario?*"

"*That is* his *choice.*"

Fillion stopped the video.

For a few seconds, he felt absolutely nothing. No external stimulation. No emotions. His body registered zero pain. His mind, however, looped on hyper drive. Images and snapshots of information and conversations strobed by—a fireworks-like explosion of endless details—before interlocking to build a single picture. Reality had never seemed clearer or as bright. Then he was moving, away from the stage, past discarded bodies, past first-gen villagers, and out of the Great Hall. Connor called after him from the lantern-lit path. Fillion lifted a hand to signal for Connor to back off.

Moves and countermoves.

To create a reality all my own.

Adrenaline surged. Muscles quaked as rage seeped from the marrow of his bones and hit his bloodstream.

The Rows were dark. Soft, ambient light from the biodome panes illuminated lighter-colored plants. Fillion didn't care if he trampled the garden. He wanted to kick up the living soil and set the dead free. Would they hear his call to action? Would the elements of their perished lives wake the sleeping? Before the living joined them in death?

Before an entire generation was wiped from this Earth?

Once inside the heart of the Ceremonial Garden, he screamed.

The war cry discharged from every cell in his body. Dragging in a deep, ragged breath, he screamed again. His throat burned; his stomach heaved. Another roar shook his body, the blistering sound raw and bleeding. He continued to scream, even when his voice grew hoarse and he began throwing up. Flames of pain engulfed his lungs and shot down his legs. But his soul wasn't done. Another dirge released from his gut, raspy and weak. Followed by another.

Only when he believed the deceased accepted his living death did he tap his Cranium, scroll through the contacts, and hit "video call." Let the dead hear. Let the life that sustained New Eden witness Hanley's message and Fillion's *choice.* Nothing was wasted in a closed loop cycle. And Fillion would be damned if innocence was tossed aside like common trash.

"Ashes to ashes. Dust to dust," he whispered to the wind, to the earth, to the fires in the distance, and to the water flowing through the gardens.

The line opened up.

"I warned you that your promises to New Eden were pointless."

To some people I'll always be the bad guy.

— Mike Mitnick, hacker, 2010 *

Reality is that which, when you stop believing in it, doesn't go away.

— Philip K. Dick, science fiction writer, 1978 *

Chapter Thirty-Four

ashing in prematurely, don't you think?" Fillion rasped, his voice shot. "Mom isn't dead twenty-four hours and already you're readying her product to ship off-planet like the capitalist pig you are. Gross. By the way, she hasn't been pronounced legally dead yet. Therefore, you're not technically her beneficiary of the T.R.U.S.T. Theory. The second gen are property of the lab until then, not *you.*"

A disappointed smile curled Hanley's mouth. "I wanted to share my empire with you."

"You wanted to use me to build your empire into something greater."

"I've given you *everything,* including your beloved New Eden, and still you think I'm the bad guy."

Fillion grimaced in angry disgust. "Spare me your narcissistic delusions."

"What of yours?"

"Did you love *her?* Or only what she could give you?"

"This isn't about Della."

"Like hell it isn't!" Fillion shouted hoarsely. "I look like her. My voice sounds like hers when I talk. I even have her emotional intelligence. Used to think my genius status was yours, but now I see reality. All of it."

Hanley rolled his eyes and fell back against his chair. "You sound *pathetic,* to quote you."

"Why her?" Fillion choked out, ignoring the barb. "Why so obsessed with Della? That . . . that you'd conspire to kill her brother, her lover, and all her friends? That you'd reduce her worth to sexual objectification instead of being valued for the mind you exploited?"

"Are you still seeing things? Hallucinated recently?" Hanley asked, leaning forward. "You realize how crazy you sound, right?"

"I'm not crazy!" Fillion screamed.

Hanley laughed, as if Fillion were a toddler having an adorable tantrum.

"I'm. Not. Crazy." Fillion thought of his visceral reaction when seeing Skylar's body earlier, and his lips trembled. "You wanted to share your empire with *her.* You gave *her* everything, even *her* beloved New Eden. And when that didn't work, you used *her* son as a form of punishment for mourning the loss of the son she had wanted and lost with Joel. And the sick thing?" Fillion spat. "The really sick part is that *you're* the one experiencing psychosis. You treat me like I'm Della, as if you actually believe I am. Hell, maybe you do. Even right now. Who do you see?"

Hanley's eyes winced.

You're an entirely different character, son.

"Answer me!" Fillion screamed when Hanley didn't reply. Silence ticked by. "That's why Willow could never be mine," he whispered, "because Joel could never be *hers.*" He sucked in a sharp breath to damn up his flooding grief. "Akiko is like you. A self-absorbed, power-hungry, bloodsucking leech. This whole thing is in your head." Fillion slashed at an angry tear with a trembling finger. "You tried to make me think it was all in mine. Convinced others I was crazy. So, let me ask you: Are you still seeing things? Hallucinated recently?"

Hanley clapped as a slow grin stretched across his face. "Well done." He cocked his head to the side, a predatory movement. "Is that what you want me to say?"

"Narcissists are incapable of remorse."

"Psychoanalyzing me doesn't change the second gen's future or my decision."

Fillion grit his teeth. "This conversation is about *my needs*, not yours. And I *need* to tell you that this game is over only when *I* say so."

"Is that all, Gamemaster?" Hanley lifted a bored expression and sighed.

"No." Fillion wiped at another tear. "*My* choice of what happens to the second gen for project shutdown is none of your damn business. I owe you nothing, except for one thing. My thanks."

Hanley now laughed, full and loud. "You're a predictable algorithm, son."

Fear prickled the hairs on the back of Fillion's neck. No. He wouldn't let Hanley get inside of his head. Straightening his shoulders, Fillion said, "You said one day I'd thank you. So here goes . . . *thank you* for preparing me for what's necessary to take you down."

His dad grinned. But, like usual, the smile never reached his eyes. "Your sarcasm gets you nowhere. Neither will doxxing me."

"The walls are listening," Fillion tossed out. "They have ears."

"I know it was you."

"Present your evidence in court." Fillion's smile dripped with arrogance.

Hanley shook his head and then sipped on a glass of wine. "Stock has dived. The experiment is over, unless the second gen goes to Mars." Hints of fury touched each word. But, on the surface, he maintained charisma. "We'll never financially recover from your scheme. Already investors are circling New Eden Enterprises for takeover. Think, Fillion. Drop all the poor-me drama and think like a goddamn businessman. If you want to save Leaf, Laurel . . . *Oaklee* . . . you'll do the right thing."

Fillion lost it. "I wouldn't need to save them if *you* hadn't placed them in a state of stasis!" Drawing in a deep breath, he released it slowly. "When's the ship date?"

"Whenever you sign off on release. Papers are with your lawyer."

"They're human beings, not consumer products."

"Then they'll be dead human beings and *that* will be on your hands, not mine."

As he gaped at his dad, Fillion's heart ached. "You . . . you'll kill them all. In cold blood. Literally." Bile churned in his gut and coated this throat. "Are the second gen even real to you? Or just figments of your imagination?"

"You've decided I'm the bad guy, so what's the point in answering? Think, Fillion. Use the brilliant mind *Della* gave you."

A sharp pain stabbed at his heart. "What life will resurrect from their actual deaths?"

"Not one you or I'll know, or any other person connected to N.E.T." Hanley sipped his wine again. "Either sign off on release or game over."

Dammit. He hated it when Hanley spoke as if the voice of reason. And Hanley knew it, patiently waiting for Fillion to admit defeat. God, that calm, cool psychopathic patience was infuriating. The man rarely raised his voice or physically lashed out in violence. He was glib yet charming, even while discussing the deaths of hundreds of people. Babies. Children. Men and women who were the same age as Fillion and Lynden. As if it were all so simple and logical.

Wait. Was Hanley mimicking Fillion's thought process? To gain trust? Had he been doing it all along and this is why people thought Fillion was "just like his dad"? Fillion wasn't charming, in public or private. He was a cynical, arrogant, grumpy ass who verbalized in sarcasms and who preferred solitude over crowds.

The war drum beat louder in Fillion's chest. Defeat wasn't an option. He wouldn't be absorbed by Hanley's impression management. Nor could Mars or death be the only two logical options. Fillion choked on another forming sob. Even after knowing how his dad suffered from toxic levels of narcissistic psychosis and antisocial traits, Fillion still fell for Hanley's manipulations.

He opened his mouth to reply and then stopped. Anything he shared would be twisted into something else. No, he wouldn't be emotionally baited to disclose his *choice* for Hanley to use against him, now or later.

"Are you done?" Hanley asked casually, slowly raising his eyes to meet Fillion's. Copper mesh walls glinted behind his head as he crossed a leg over his knee and leaned to the side of his chair. "We have court tomorrow, and I have your mom's funeral to prepare."

Time seemed to still in this moment. As Fillion looked at Hanley—truly looked at the man beneath the glamour—his heart began to ache for entirely different reasons. Norah's deathbed words to Fillion whispered fresh in his mind.

There is a difference between being able to love and believing your love is valuable, worth giving away.

Thoughts moved into focus and then faded into his mind's black hole as new considerations vied for attention. But one thought blared with clarity: Emotional mimicry wasn't the same as recognizing another's humanity. The kind of recognition that connected existences like communication devices. A fingerprint always remained. This is what Norah had been trying to tell him when he confessed that he didn't know how to love.

But he did, and always had.

Love wasn't a position to be earned or a boss who was entitled to their demands. Rather, love rebuilt the destroyed pieces of humanity in people when another demonstrated their own. This wasn't a conditional truth, either, based on what one deserved or gave away. Fillion couldn't regulate Hanley's cognitive dissonance for him. Or society's. But by ignoring the humanity in Hanley, he ignored his own. And Fillion respected himself too much now to let that pass without care.

"He has convinced you that the true battle is for your mind and re-directs your energy to defend your coherency and intelligence," Willow's voice called out from his memories. *"But it is your heart he wishes to own, for you were made to love and to love passionately."*

Willow's voice faded and Leaf's emerged . . . *"When she bestowed upon you her heart, I hated you. That was the only time I have ever felt contempt toward another. You toyed with her affection while she grieved and, still, she chose to lay down her reputation to honor you. I tried to speak reason to her, but she would not listen. Rather, she defended your right to feel loved and to know you were important."*

"This has been enlightening," Hanley murmured dryly, shifting in his chair again. "Make the right decision, Fillion. See you tomorrow in court."

"I love you, Dad."

Hazel eyes snapped to his and widened and then narrowed in confusion. Tears rolled down Fillion's face. He allowed Hanley to discern the unconditional truth a few seconds longer, and then he ended the call.

Millions of emotions detonated inside of Fillion all at once. Shattered, he fell to his knees and touched his forehead to the living soil. Pain slashed, stabbed, and exploded like shrapnel. He sank his fingers into the tilth and clawed. Violent spasms shook his frame as he silently sobbed. His mind glitched in and out of focus. His lungs gasped for air. And then a haunting, keening sound pushed through his convulsing grief and the building pressure released.

They were going to die. Leaf, Laurel, Willow. He didn't know a heart was capable of feeling such intense pain and could still beat. A severing, that's what it felt like. Layers of himself skinned and peeled back. A rip. A tear. The kind of pain that made him emotionally beg to die with them. Did he just let them all go peacefully while in a state of stasis? Possibly die during transport to Mars? Or did he bio-hack and live with the knowledge that he's the one who possibly pulled the fail-safe trigger?

A hand touched his back. His muscles flinched then relaxed as the hand moved in soothing circles. "Hey," Lynden's voice said near his ear. She leaned her head onto his, her hand still moving round and round.

"Lyn—"

"I heard everything. Starting with your screams."

Fillion straightened and wiped his face, feeling dirt smear over his cheek. "What? How?"

"Secret unicorn powers, Einstein."

Ignoring her sarcasm, he looked at his screen and stilled. When had he pushed the external volume button? Switching to Skylar's screen, he held his breath. Confusion muddied his head again. He had also pushed record? Fillion tapped "stop record" and then studied his hands. All he remembered was the puzzle clicking into place right before launching into berserker mode. He lifted his gaze to his sister's and released his tightened breath.

"I . . . I have to bio-hack."

"OK."

"What if . . . if I kill them? If I kill her?" He wheezed out the words. Talking was painful. Everything was painful. His sister remained quiet. "They're dead no matter what I do." Another sob wracked his body and Lyn pulled him into her arms. Her hand resumed tracing circles on his back while he wept.

"Fillion," his sister began when he eventually quieted. "What if Hanley isn't Mom's beneficiary?"

A chill wended its way down his spine. He pulled away enough to see her face. "You think she committed suicide?"

Lynden's eyes darted to the side. "I think she wasn't stupid."

"She knew she was going to die," he whispered.

Lynden simply nodded, staring at the black ring she twisted on her thumb. The ring he had gifted her several years ago. His brows knit together as his ash-fall of thoughts settled. His sister was here. In the Ceremonial Gardens. The hell? Fillion scrutinized every detail on her face—at least, the details he could make out in the limited light—hunting, searching, scanning for any tell that she was a digital rendition, or a hallucination, not real.

"You have that look." Lyn groaned. "The calculating one."

"New Eden is in lockdown. Only Mack has access." At his words, she flipped her hair with an eye roll and then arched an eyebrow. Fillion created distance between them. "How did you get into the biodome?"

"Ticketing," Mack said from the shadows as he moved into their circle.

"Shit!" Fillion's heart leaped to his throat as he gaped at his friend. "Your ninja skills cost me another life, mate."

Was his friend real?

"She went all alpha on the guard and shoved him to the wall," Mack continued. "While making out, Rainbow placed his hand on the bio-sensor, using her other hand to—"

Fillion cut him off. "I get it."

"Then she kneed him in the man bits and ran through the door."

"Again. Secret unicorn powers," Lyn drolled. "Don't listen to Mack. He's just jealous."

Turning to Lynden, Fillion blurted, "You ticketed your way into New Eden?!"

"Hire better guards," she snapped back, sticking out her tongue. "Body hack security breach."

"Whoa." Mack's eyes widened after sitting next to Fillion. "Uh, you look like your face is melting off."

Yeah, his friend was real. Fillion released another tight breath.

"I'm still hotter than you. Sexy *henshin* never lies."

Mack's lips twitched. "Clean up, smart-ass. The community has faced enough scary things today, *desu*."

Fillion touched around his eyes then looked at his fingers. Black. Shit. He was still wearing makeup from visiting the computer underground. He had professed his love to Willow while wearing makeup. Charged into the Great Hall, Willow limp in arms, while looking like a hell-bent demon. All his piercings were still in place, too. No wonder people in the Great Hall had watched him with spooked, fearful expressions. Mortified, he tipped his head back, closed his eyes, and moaned. "I'm such a freak."

"A smexy freak." Mack bit his tongue and waggled his eyebrows. His friend licked the hem of shirt and reached the corner out to Fillion's face and cooed, "Come to Mack the Mother Hen."

Fillion ducked, laughing, while swatting Mack's hand out of the way. His friend was such an ass and he laughed again. But the wrongness of laughing right now slapped his conscience back to reality, and his smile dimmed to a thin line as the pain returned.

He stared at his hands again. What in the hell was he going to do? God, he needed a cigarette. Think. He shook his head and hissed a few choice words. There really was only one answer. He may kill the second gen trying, but it was the only solution with a reasonable margin for reversing stasis. He locked eyes with his friend and held his gaze. Mack's face remained as bored and aloof as usual, but the concern darkening his eyes gave him away. It would be like his friend to break the tension so Fillion could re-focus. A slight smile softened Fillion's lips. Mack smiled back.

"Fillion," Lyn quietly spoke. "What you said to Dad? That was hella weird."

Dread pooled in his stomach once more. And embarrassment. "He's … he's…"

"Sick."

"Yeah."

"He just wanted Mom's love?"

Fillion swallowed. "And ours."

"Demented."

"He gave us what he always wanted"—Fillion said, gesturing to New Eden—"but is incapable of psychologically understanding himself."

"That makes no sense."

"Love." Fillion scooped a handful of living soil and watched the particles slip between his fingers. "Family. Community." He lifted a sad smile. "Our legacy."

Tears brightened Lyn's eyes as she absorbed his words. "That's beautiful."

"So, what's the plan, boss?" Mack asked, stretching out his legs and leaning back on his elbows. "You disappeared, and then everything went to hell."

"Thinking," Fillion murmured, running a hand through his hair. "Give me a sec."

"The lab's server is locked out," Mack said after a few nanoseconds. "Michael lit fires under the security team's ass. Amanda has a team on it too. But what's happened in New Eden? Did you say *stasis*?"

Turning off his and Skylar's Craniums, Fillion drew in a deep breath and then purged all the details he knew. "I need to wake them up without triggering the fail-safe."

"That bastard," Mack breathed. "You think the fail-safe is death?"

"Yeah. I think Hanley tested the fail-safe in New Eden earlier today and wanted to see with his own eyes if it worked." He considered Lynden a moment. Hesitated. Then asked, "Is Coal down?"

"No. He's helping Amanda."

The immediate relief was tangible. Fighting back more tears, he said, "Right before Willow fell my vision digitized. Only lasted a blink."

"The inner sanctum software is working," Mack said more to himself. "Man-in-the-Middle too. Good to know."

"The riots…" Fillion's voice was scratchy and cracking. "I think targeted villagers were programmed to attack specific reps from NASA and the lab to test future control or influence or something. Maybe for the military."

"Cybernetic zombies." Mack's brows hung low over his eyes. "That's some sick shit."

"Call Lewis Psychiatric Hospital and check on Andra," Fillion directed at Mack. To Lynden: "Contact Coal and tell him to find the MELISSA Project test subjects and move them into the hacker circle to be watched. State of stasis or awake. I don't care. Have Coal fill Amanda in on all the details, including how there's a possibility that test subjects could be mind-controlled. The awake ones need inner sanctum stat before they go into shutdown for stasis." He stood up and brushed the soil from his pants. "I'll be in the Great Hall."

"Wait," Lynden shot out. "You're leaving us here?"

"First-gen villagers are inside the Great Hall looking over the fallen. I don't want them to overhear these details." He pulled Lynden into a tight hug and whispered, "Thanks, Sis. You're my everything. Couldn't do this without you." Lynden's breath hitched. Fillion couldn't look at his sister or he'd start sobbing again. Instead, he stepped away and locked eyes with Mack and held this gaze for a few seconds. No words needed to be spoken. His friend knew.

It was a ten-minute walk from The Rows back to the Great Hall. Not nearly enough time to regroup his thoughts and crystallize a game plan. Every black, ticking second mattered. From behind, he could hear Lyn and Mack's voices as they made calls as directed. Amber lights twinkled and glowed around the Great Hall up ahead. The earlier gusts had calmed to a breeze which continued to skip across the landscape. Nature breathed easy. But Fillion? He was gasping for air, his chest wheezing as panic tried to crush his heart.

At the pump well, he stripped from the waist up and ducked his head beneath the small stream. The cold water startled his skin into a shiver while the breeze clawed icicles across his back. The shock forced air back into his lungs. One arm pumped while his other scrubbed at his face and hair. A part of him wanted to scrub until he bled. He still wouldn't be clean enough. By morning, hundreds of people may have died at his hands. And if he couldn't reverse stasis, they might die during reanimation Mars-side, if not during transport. Hell, they could still die during reanimation here.

He cupped a mouthful of water, drank, and then straightened, lifting his face to the fractured sky. Droplets dribbled down his face, neck, and chest until he shook his head of excess water. Air continued to burn his throat and lungs. He needed to focus on breathing—something—to calm the grief and fear twisting his insides.

Inhale.

Exhale.

He could do this. His mind was trained by the leading experts in the world. Everything could be cracked, even quantum computers. It wasn't a question of "if" but of "how."

Teeth chattering in the cold, Fillion turned his visual *kei* button-up shirt inside out to dry his face and upper body and then re-dressed. The now-dampened shirt clung to his back and upper arms, but he didn't care. The heat in the Great Hall would dry his clothing and, more importantly, bring feeling back to his body. Ugh. He was mentally rambling. Sighing, he quickly pocketed most of his facial piercings, save the small hoop in his nose and the pin in his eyebrow. Then, while combing trembling fingers through his washed hair, he began the final leg of his death march.

"This whole thing is in your head."

His steps faltered.

"Psychoanalyzing me doesn't change the second gen's future or my decision."

Was Hanley saying this to Fillion or Della?

The conversation continued to play back in fragments. He analyzed each word separately, then in pairs, whole sentences, followed by their conversation in its entirety, mentally mapping patterns and layered clues. He took even, clipped steps, but his surroundings faded into his swirling mind. He didn't even register the drastic change in temperature.

"What happened?" Connor asked when Fillion strode past him in the Great Hall. The older man studied Fillion's wet hair and freshly washed face.

Fillion rasped, "Hanley," and then continued toward the stage. Connor matched his strides. "I'm planning to bio-hack the second gen."

"Your voice." Connor stepped into his path and leaned close. "Are you well?"

"I . . . I, uh, Mack and Lynden will join us." Fillion didn't want to re-hash his mental breakdown in The Rows or his conversation with Hanley. Most of all, Fillion couldn't bear to share with Connor that he was going to lose his children and grandchildren, one way or another. He just wanted to focus on the hack. And breathing. "I'm setting up for a collaborative bio-hack," he redirected. "Could last all night. Not sure."

Connor pointed to a man nearby and gestured him over. "Fetch a meal for the Son of Eden."

"I can't eat—"

"Go quickly, sir," Connor insisted, ignoring Fillion. "His Majesty needs nourishment. Bring two pitchers of wine and three tumblers as well."

"Yes, My Lord," the man said and left for the kitchens.

Connor dug into the pouch hanging from his belt and then extended his hand. Fillion's blood nearly quivered at the sight. "You shall need these, yes?"

"I could kiss you." Fillion took the joints with shaking fingers, like the junkie he was. Just placing one between his lips was enough to calm an annoying sliver of anxiety. Connor lifted a candle from a nearby window and held it out. Fillion dragged long and slow, closing his eyes. Oregano and sage rolled across his tongue. So what? God, this never got old. Exhaling, he opened his eyes and leveled his gaze onto Connor, even though guilt demanded he look away. "Seriously. Kiss you. Your feet. Your ass. Name it."

"As tempting as that is, I shall pass. This time." Connor's smile was rascally yet fatherly, and Fillion soaked it up. A second later the warmth disappeared and fear returned. "Alder, the twins, Laurel, and Ember shall be relocated here and placed beside Leaf and Oaklee. I do not wish to leave any Legacy heirs or descendants of Joel out of sight."

"Smart."

Fillion opened his mouth to say more when a ping echoed in his head. The caller ID announced Coal. At least the man hadn't exploded and wound up shot. Another pinch of relief trickled through him. He accepted the call without vid feed. "Hey."

"I found Pinkie."

Fillion's pulse kicked up. "Where is she?"

A jumbled scratching sound fuzzed in his head and Fillion winced. Puffing on his joint, he waited, exhaling on a cough when Pinkie spoke.

"Ready to talk?" she asked.

"Not in person. I don't trust you. But we can chat over Coal's line."

She laughed and he narrowed his eyes. The laugh wasn't low and seductive as usual. It almost sounded . . . normal. And nervous. Clear. Had Amanda cut the strings and uploaded inner sanctum? She wasn't an idiot. Probably required that Pinkie disconnect all ties to Hanley before allowing her to step into the hacker's den.

"You won't see me anymore after this."

"After what, *Rebecca*?"

"Yes, my real name is Rebecca Nakamura. I'm thirty-seven years old. Born in Japan and moved to the States at age five. My parents died when I was fifteen, and foster care had no room for me. I've been a whoring underground rat ever since."

Fillion swore his heart stopped. "Why are you sharing this with me?

Pinkie laughed again. This time dark and hollow. "He promised me eternal youth, fame, all the money I wanted, and immortality. He made me think I was special. My sacrifice would change the world. All I had to do was give up my identity. He used my body for his business and personal pleasure." The last word ended on breathy hitch and Fillion felt the bile rise again. "I thought this was my *ticket* out of the underground."

"I'm—"

"Don't apologize!" she snapped. "Just don't."

He remained quiet.

"The nerve damage is reaching fatal levels. Drugs don't stop the pain anymore."

He closed his eyes, grieved. "What can I do for you?"

Pinkie's voice was faint. "Forgive me?"

Now his heart really did stop beating. "Were you under compulsion or did you do the things you did to me and my sister by choice?"

"Does it matter?"

"Yes."

"Both." Pinkie remained silent for two, long beats, then said, "He set it up. But tell Rainbow she was the only true friend I've ever had. Happy times."

Fillion's eyes flashed open and widened. "Rebecca, go to the safe house. Don't do anything stupid."

"Too late."

"I forgive you—" The line ended.

"Shit!" Fillion hissed between clenched teeth. He grabbed his hair and cinched his eyes closed to fight back against the wave of heartache and dizziness. After a few measured breaths, he called Coal back, but got no answer. He tried again. Then Amanda. Same result. "Dammit. Oh god…"

The wheezing returned to his lungs. He gasped for air. Fingers shaking, joint in his mouth, he opened up his contacts. It was after seven o'clock here, which made it noon the next day in Japan.

"Fillion." Akiko's voice purred in his head, delighted. "I knew you would come begging."

"Are you in Japan?"

"Breathless? Scream yourself hoarse while bedding—"

"Answer. Me." Fillion puffed on his joint and grit his teeth.

"Yes, of course." A thread of temper colored her reply.

Curious eyes watched him from all over the Great Hall. "*Hanley kara hana-rete inasai. Abunai tokoro ni irunda yo.*"

"Your father is not dangerous." Akiko laughed as if he were absurd. "He is a great visionary."

Fillion groaned, then continued in Japanese: "He used HiraMed Technology to put the second generation into a state of stasis. He might frame your family if anything bad happens."

"I did not realize you cared. Bored with your lab rat so soon?"

"I'm an asshole," Fillion practically growled. "But I'm not cold and heart-less."

"I warned that you would pay HiraMed one way or another. Your precious lab is in debt to my father's company. He is willing to forgive a portion of the debt as a wedding gift."

He swallowed. "Please tell me you're not involved in this shitstorm."

Akiko laughed again. "I always get what I want, and I had wanted *you*."

"Disgusting."

"Perhaps I would still want you if you had not pressed charges against me and made me into a worldwide fool."

Fillion's lips curled. "You threatened my sister and New Eden. What in the hell did you expect me to do? Write sonnets of endless gratitude for your media scandal pushback?"

"You were always weak and childish." Akiko sighed, bored. "I prefer a man who knows he is a king among men. A man who is visionary. Now that Della is out of the way—"

"What?! Akiko, he just wants your money!" he seethed.

"Yes," she cooed. "And I want his power."

Fillion gagged. He couldn't speak and ended the call, stumbling to the edge of the stage before bending over and dry heaving. Footsteps raced over. A crowd pressed in. An arm wrapped around his waist and held him up. Light and shadowed faces blurred and spun in nauseating motions. Sweat beaded on his forehead. He couldn't breathe. His stomach spasmed and dry heaved again. Air. He needed air. Voices slurred in his ears. Shouts echoed off the stones. An inferno crackled and burned hot in his chest.

The world glitched and digitized, his body convulsing, his eyes rolling to the back of his head. And, for the first time since age twelve, Willow didn't appear and beg to be saved as he PTSD system-crashed.

More likely, though, astronauts and space colonists will learn a few tricks from dehydrated snails, which survive for a year or more ingesting nothing; giant pandas subsisting on low-calorie bamboo; leeches that survive a liquid nitrogen bath; children who have been sub-merged in frozen ponds yet can still be resuscitated; or skiers buried in an avalanche and brought back to life ever so slowly, reborn from a super-cooled, dreamless state.

Scientists call this phenomenon "torpor-induced hibernation." Once considered outlandish, torpor induction—the old term was "suspended animation"—is under serious study for long-duration spaceflight.

— *Air & Space* magazine, 2017 *

Chapter Thirty-Five

Cold hands cupped his jaw and lifted his head.

"Look at me," a voice soothed and commanded simultaneously. A thumb caressed his cheek. "Come on. Look at me, mate. That's it. Gaze into my dreamy blue eyes. Make your heart flutter for new reasons." Mack peered over Fillion's shoulder and barked, "Give us space. Back up." Then his focus rested on someone behind Fillion. "Not you. Keep holding him up."

"Akiko…"

Mack's face darkened. "Come on, mate. You need to sit."

His friend took Fillion's hand in his and led him toward a shadowed corner beside the stage. Connor kept his arm around Fillion's waist for support. Lynden brought over a chair and knelt next to Fillion after he crumpled in the wooden seat.

"I can't—"

"You're hyperventilating," Mack said. "Fight the emotional overload. Leaf needs you." Fillion felt pressure on his back and he gave in until his head hung between his knees. "That's it. Deep breath. You got this. Not going to leave you."

From the corner of his eye, Fillion could see Mack light up a cigarette. Connor spoke but his friend cut him off. Mack grabbed his hand again and put the cigarette in his fingers. "Get a nicotine hit. Just a few puffs before Farm Boy's beefcake daddy puts it out." He didn't argue. The effect was immediate. Ironically, he started to breathe easier. Much too soon, Mack took the cigarette away but replaced one vice for another. "Bottoms up, mate." Fillion tipped the wooden tumbler back. Wine coated his throat and soured in his stomach. He almost retched. Almost. Instead, he handed the empty cup back to Mack who filled it up again. "Last cup for a while. Make it count." When empty, Mack put the herbal joint back in Fillion's fingers, re-lit. "Better?"

"Yeah," Fillion whispered. "No."

"I know," Mack whispered back, holding his hand again. "I know."

Fillion nodded his head and dragged on the joint, looking anywhere but at his friend, sister, or Connor. "I didn't protect the Watsons. I . . . I didn't cut strings before . . . God, I sat up in a tree and made out with Willow."

"No one could've predicted this."

Fillion's bloodshot eyes flashed to Mack's. "Don't blow sunshine up my ass. I can't stomach any more lies."

"Christ, you're allowed happiness, Fillion," his friend shot back equally as pissed. "This is what's going to happen. Your skinny ass is going to eat this yummy medieval hippie food before you pass out. I don't give a shit if you don't want to. Got that? I'm going to access the Techsmith Guild server and get a feel for what we're up against. And you"—his friend said, pushing a finger into his shoulder—"you're going to use that fancy MIT education to decrypt patterns. Do the math. Figure out the equations. Compare findings to the underground's analytics of your, Coal's, and Andra's cybernetic systems. Propose theories of how we can wake the cursed with your brain's True Love's Kiss." Mack lifted his eyebrows in question. "*Desu?*"

"You're pathetic," Fillion mumbled with a faint side-smile. "It's sexy."

"Whatever arouses the hell of you." Mack grabbed Fillion's face and kissed his cheek in a loud, comical smack, then hit him by the back of his head playfully. "Now turn me on, lover." His friend snatched the ordered food from the hands of a gaping village man and shoved the trencher plate onto Fillion's lap, then stuffed a pinch of greens into his mouth and chewed slowly in a look of ecstasy. "Hot damn. That's good." He winked at Fillion, then stood and faced Connor. "Try not to faint at our badassary, Beefcake Daddy."

"Oh. My. God," Lynden whispered in horror. "You didn't."

Connor sputtered and covered his mouth to hide his rumbling humor from the villagers. Especially when Lynden shot Connor a warning glare for encouraging Mack. The giant of a man had to walk away, his large shoulders shaking. Pleased, Mack tugged on a strand of Lyn's hair while on his way to the nearest wall, where he began setting up shop.

Leave it to his friend to make people laugh in the face of death. The light to Fillion's dark, and apparently Connor's too.

"Eat or he'll come back," Lyn mock-whispered.

Fillion forced himself to eat a bite of food. The vegetables moved around in his mouth, tasteless. The grains, too. When he was done, Lyn took his plate and handed him a clay goblet filled with cold water. His stomach rolled and he closed his eyes until the nausea passed.

"I *can* do this," he mumbled to himself. "Not 'if' but 'how.'" Lynden peered up at him from the floor, eyes red with unshed tears. "Hey," he said to her. "Sit with me?"

"I am."

"No, over there, by Skylar."

"Creepy, but sure."

On shaking legs, Fillion stood and walked over to the opposite wall and eased up on the stage beside Skylar. Rain was now laid out next to the Son of Wind, her eyes closed. "Do me a favor?" he asked Lyn. "Can you record pulse and intake breaths for fifteen seconds for each person on the stage?"

She scrunched up her nose while considering the bodies. "They're all alive?"

The muscles in his gut seized with her question. "Alive."

"OK."

When she moved away, he tapped on his and Skylar's Craniums. While loading up various software and the underground's collaborative hack group chat channel, he re-watched Hanley and Leaf's interactions during the riot, forcing himself to focus only on the words and body language. The riots distracted Fillion though. In his file folder, he touched a transcription tool and slid it over from his screen onto Skylar's. The software uploaded on Skylar's Cranium in a matter of seconds. Fillion selected the portion of video he wanted transcribed and hit "start." Transcription would take time, so he minimized that tool's screen and moved back over to his own.

Villagers watched him, many casting glares and scowls his way. Hanley had blamed the Son of Eden for all their hardships, a believable claim. Fillion had ended his betrothal to two women, one from this world and one from his. For safety reasons, the community had a zero-tolerance policy when it came to matters of the heart. But he couldn't be upset by their reactions. New Eden was groomed to behave this way, and they didn't have the full story.

Didn't matter now. He'd only be remembered for what happened this night—as the hero who saved their children, or the monster who ushered in their deaths. He was the Son of Eden, the man of bedtime stories. The one who would save them from the evils of the Outside world. Fillion wanted to laugh. The mentally twisted layers in just that single statement further soured his already sickened gut.

Time would tell if Hanley's prophecy rang true.

Information streamed upward on his screen. He tried to steady his wheezing breaths. In the group chat, he found the link to his, Coal's, and Andra's cybernetic analytics. The study was still live, but there was enough content already to dissect.

"Hey Mack," Fillion called out. His friend came trotting over. "I need to run my own diff report. Coal's cybernetics to another's in New Eden."

"Sure thing."

"Extract data from Skylar's system and two random villagers in the Hall. Send mirror files to the hacking circle and me."

"Why Skylar's?"

Fillion briefly met his friend's eyes. "He was part of the first rollout in New Eden and the Guild captain. I want to see how the code has changed."

"This," Mack drawled in a low, sultry voice, "turns me on. Keep it up."

Climbing up onto the stage, Mack knelt next to Skylar and began hacking into the Son of Wind's control center.

Fillion continued to busy himself with reading code. The underground had software to extract code differences. But Fillion wanted to read each line personally and catalog anomalies from one prototype generation to another and then compare his findings to the underground's. His fingers shook, but he managed to highlight key segments to paste into a notepad for later review.

Lynden returned and curled up behind him, resting her head onto his shoulder and wrapping her arms around his waist. He leaned back against her and she snuggled in closer. They remained this way for twenty-minute periods when she left only to check and record vitals again. She'd return and he'd melt into the comfort she quietly provided him, both ignoring the spiteful looks thrown their way by first-gen villagers coming and going in the building.

A message popped up on his screen.

<u>Mack</u>: Lab servers unlocked. Amanda's team.

Fillion clicked over to the group chat and watched disclosures and notes load.

<u>FNichols</u>: Damage report?

<u>Mack</u>: Still assessing. Calling Michael. Stand by.

Two hours had passed since they began hacking and he had finally made it to the new cybernetic samples Mack had provided him. The transcription completed minutes ago, too. Maybe he should stretch and take a smoke break. Fingers trembling, he pulled a joint from his pocket and approached the nearest candle, lighting up. Lyn stood and stretched as well, pausing before Willow. He pretended to stare at the floor but, from his peripheral, he could see Lyn studying the Daughter of Earth for several long seconds before moving on toward Mack.

He had refused to peer Willow's way since his conversation with Hanley out in The Rows. But, now, he found himself unable to look away. Invisible threads tugged him forward until he stood before her. The flickering candlelight did little to mask the torpor's affects. Her skin was even paler, if that were possible. The soft, flushed lips his own had worshiped hours earlier had also drained of color. A bluish color now tinged the tips of her fingers from slower circulation. And, still, he had never stood before anyone so beautiful in all his life.

"Your Majesty," a voice said from behind. Fillion peered over his shoulder before turning to face Gareth. "All of the unresponsive parents and their children are under supervision. Kyra trailed behind us with meals and is still delivering food."

Fillion released a relieved breath. "How many non-vaccinated children?"

"We counted thirty-four children, all babes under age one."

Exhaling smoke away from Gareth, he asked, "Do they need special care? Wet nurses? Goat milk? Mashed food?"

"Aye," Gareth quickly responded. "All is cared for, Your Majesty."

"Thanks, Gareth." Fillion placed a hand on his shoulder. "Let me know if any needs do arise."

"Your Majesty," the man said, dipping his head.

Fillion watched him leave to report to Connor as a group of villagers arrived carrying more people under stasis. Ember's familiar strawberry-blonde hair glinted in the candlelight. Connor approached and scooped his daughter's limp body into his arms and held her close to his chest, weeping. The gesture was intimate and many, including Fillion, turned away to allow the former Fire Element a moment of privacy.

> **<u>Mack</u>**: Content deleted. Ordered data recovery. 2 hackers
> on it.

> **<u>FNichols</u>**: Thanks.

The crowd followed Connor in a slow march toward the stage. Gently, Ember was laid out beside Leaf, with Alder placed between them. A woman directed the man who held Laurel to place her between Willow and Leaf. Lynden approached with the chair Fillion once occupied for a woman who held the bundled and sleeping Fia and Terra. The woman glared at Lynden, but his sister smiled kindly in reply, and Fillion's heart squeezed.

He'd never really recognized the depth of Lyn's courage until this moment. Or her compassion, even though she had dedicated her life to helping the lowest members of society be reborn. It was easy to overlook with her typically emotionless, timid state.

"New Eden does not desire your help," the woman spat at Lynden. "Our community has suffered enough scandal and grief because of your family!"

Connor placed a hand on the woman's forearm. "She is Coal's wife, *my daughter*, and you shall address her as 'My Lady.' Nor is she responsible for anything that has transpired in New Eden at any point in time."

The blood drained from Lynden's face before she warmed with Connor's defense and words. A look the woman mirrored. His sister's shoulders lifted as her head dropped. She swiveled on her heel and started to walk away when Connor grabbed her hand.

"Come here, daughter," Connor said. Lynden stared up at him like a frightened animal, her eyes spooked, her body rigid. "Lynden Hansen, I shall never hurt you," he quietly comforted. "Nor shall I allow others to harm you. I am proud you are my family."

"My Lady," the woman began softly. "My sincerest apologies for my unkind words. Thank you for fetching a chair for me and your assistance during our time of need."

"No prob," Lyn whispered in reply. She retracted her hand from Connor's and crossed her arms across her chest, staring up at the ceiling and blinking back tears, before walking away toward Mack and slumping next to him against the far wall. His friend, eyes locked on his screen, pulled Lynden close and she pressed her face into his neck.

Fillion glanced at the Watsons one last time and then trudged across the Hall, dragging on his joint. The stone scraped against his back as he slid down the wall beside Mack and turned his screens back on. The stage area was too crowded right now. And he wanted to give the woman space to care for the twins.

"Where you at?" Mack asked.

"No-leads land." The transcript loaded on Skylar's screen. "You?"

"Been busy working with Amanda and Michael."

"Thanks, mate."

Mack grunted. "What set you off earlier?"

"Pinkie," Fillion started and stopped. "Spoke to her and . . . and she sounded suicidal."

Lynden popped off Mack's shoulder, her mouth slack.

"Said something about nerve damage being at fatal levels and too much pain."

"She's transhuman?" Lynden asked. "Like them?"

Fillion puffed on his joint and shared a brief history of the MELISSA Project with Lyn while loading Skylar's cybernetic files.

"Then I called Akiko," he continued, "worried that her family might be framed if the HiraMed tech fails." Waves of disgust sloshed his insides and curdled his next words. "She celebrated Mom's death. Confessed an arrangement with Hanley to pay off debts the lab owes HiraMed."

Mack grimaced. "Ew. Didn't need that imagery."

"Arrangement, as in *marriage*?" His sister made gagging sounds when Fillion slowly nodded. "She'd be our stepmom. Oh hell no."

"*Evil* stepmom," Mack corrected. "Hanley is still living in a disgusting, psychotic fairytale."

A spark hit Fillion's brain with Mack's comment. But before he could comment, a woman barged into the Great Hall screaming. A child shook violently in her arms.

"My son!" she shrieked. "Help my son!"

Fillion dropped his joint and jumped to his feet. Vertigo hit him while running with screens up. The world tilted and spun for a moment. He stopped long enough to turn off his and Skylar's Craniums. The wheezing returned. He started gasping for air. But he mustered enough strength to rip a piece of his shirt off, rolled it up, and placed it in the boy's mouth while holding the ends tight. The small body stopped convulsing.

"Daniel?" she sobbed through rising hysteria, shaking her now stilled son. "Daniel!"

He looked at the boy's face and fresh pain tore through Fillion. Blood dripped from the child's eyes and ears. He removed the cloth from the boy's mouth and gaped at the bloodstains. Screams rippled across the Hall.

A fallen body on the floor near the mother and child released a choking sound before convulsing, similar to how the boy had died.

"Hold the victim's head!" Fillion pointed at a nearby man. "Take your belt off and put in his mouth!" Villagers leaped into action.

"He is dead," the mother sobbed. "My son is dead!"

A young woman beside the convulsing man started seizing next.

Mack's eyes grew large. "Oh shit."

"Get the boy and these two out of this room!" Fillion hoarsely shouted. "NOW!"

Connor's pulse visibly thundered in his neck. "Where should we take them?"

"The Rows. Quick! Every second matters!"

Connor lifted the convulsing woman in his arms and sprinted toward the exit. The mother continued to scream in hysteria, holding her dead son to her heart. Mack grabbed her by the shoulders and gently pushed her toward the exit. Lynden intercepted and took over. "Stay!" she commanded Mack. The mother fought and screamed, but Lynden eventually got her out of the building with the help of another woman. Two men carried the convulsing young man, accompanied by various family members, and ran out of the Great Hall.

Mack appeared on the verge of vomiting.

"The fuck?!" Fillion gasped for air. "He set up a triggered virus!"

"Signal range?"

"Hopefully just close proximity."

Mack closed his eyes and swallowed. "Damn. Quick thinking. I thought stasis was failing."

"What set the virus off?" Fillion blinked sweat out of his eyes. "Did the underground nick the fail-safe?"

"On it." Mack marched across the room, tapping his Cranium as he went. "Amanda," he heard Mack say, before his friend's voice tapered off while walking away. An eerie silence settled on the Hall.

Slowly, facing the living, the war drum in Fillion's chest beat anew. He couldn't hide his emotion, never seeing anyone, let alone a child, die so violently. Innocent lives were always victims in wars and had been since the dawn of mankind. But Fillion didn't care. Nothing was as cowardly or as evil as assaulting the lives incapable of fighting back—and all to establish the illusion of dominance.

"Our children..." a woman said and stopped, unable to finish.

A man stepped forward, jaw clenched. "Why?" One word, but a thousand questions and accusations.

"People aren't seen as real anymore in the Outside world," Fillion wheezed through tight, shallow breaths. "We're characters on the Net. Or corporate products."

"Our children are not products!"

"I agree." Sweat dripped in his eyes again. "Neither are you. But that's not how the Outside world operates. Everything is exploitable for profit, even me. The world sits on the Net and argues justice, declaring sinners and saints, but does nothing of value. *Nothing.* Justice is just another product to market for fake

Internet points and intellectualism while *real* people suffer."

Horror and tears lined the faces of the community as they listened.

"You want an honor price. But honor doesn't exist out there anymore," he spat, pointing to a window. "We traded it in a long time ago for instant gratification. People deny their own humanity because it demands personal sacrifice. Easier to treat life like a game and others as fictional characters."

Fillion pressed a hand to his chest, over his broken heart tattoo. "I . . . I won't stop fighting until your children are free. I don't care what the law says. The only person who owns your body is *you*." Dizziness swam circles in his head as he fought for breath. "But, right now, I need to focus on waking the second and third gens. So nobody leave the Great Hall without permission. We can't have mass panic and risk infecting others. Understand?"

He estimated around forty heads nodded or dipped in answer.

"You," Fillion continued, pointing at the man who had given up his belt. "What's your name, sir?"

"Peter, Your Majesty."

"Peter," Fillion rasped, "assign three different first-response teams to jump into action if other bodies go viral. And set up rotating guards inside and outside the Great Hall doors to prevent infected bodies from entering."

The man bowed and turned to his community.

Black shaded Fillion's glitching vision. He needed to sit before he passed out. Stomach rolling, he dragged his feet across the cobblestones.

Back next to Mack, Fillion listened as his friend conferenced with Amanda and her team. With a single tap, the transcript on Skylar's screen reappeared. The words blurred and warbled. Fillion squeezed his eyes shut and focused on breathing. The edges of his mind deadened. He wasn't sure how much longer he would last under the pressure. Seeing that innocent boy die so violently carved deep, gaping gashes into Fillion's resolve. His bleeding heart was now gushing.

A sob caught in his knotted throat. Fillion curled his knees up to his wheezing chest and dropped his head. His fingers gripped his hair and he pulled. Images of that boy played on repeat in his mind.

"Twist of Fate," he whispered to the dark. The spark that had flinted in his memories earlier now crackled for attention. Timothy had declared how Fillion was naive when Fillion had asked if the Techsmith Guild's server would reveal Hanley's plan to keep the business in the family. All this time, he had thought that Timothy's message was directed at Fillion. But what if it was a clue about Hanley, the second gen, and the MELISSA Project? And why did everything have to be so damn cryptic? He knew why, but it pissed him off.

Either Hanley was truly losing his grip on reality or something else was going on. Maybe the triggered virus was unrelated to Hanley's ultimatum and two dragons were now in play. Or always had been. Both circling and fighting over the same treasure to hoard. If Hanley wanted Fillion to know about a viral ticking time bomb, he would have stressed that point in their conversation. Instead, the man had thrown out casually for Fillion to make the right decision and that he would see Fillion the next day in court.

He grasped at that final thought and held onto it. The transcript wavered in front of his vision. He read through it once. Then again.

"How have the residents actually suffered by my experiment? Think, Leaf. You have heard the stories of Fillion's world. Seen the images. I gave the second and third gens life." Hanley's words floated around in the stratosphere of Fillion's mind. Later in the conversation, Hanley repeated the same sentiments. *"When have I personally harmed you or the residents? Others have, but not me. This colony is a lifelong investment of mine."*

Gross. The lies reeked, but Hanley coated his words with honey. So much so, Leaf almost swallowed them whole.

"It wasn't the underground." Mack leaned his head on the stone wall and stared at the ceiling. "They haven't touched the Techsmith Guild server."

"The lab is in debt to HiraMed," Fillion said, trance-like. "Why didn't I see these financials pre-Ascension?"

Mack held his Cranium straight and angled his head to peer at Fillion. "Maybe the lab isn't in debt, but Hanley?"

"Why would Akiko say, 'the lab' then?"

"Ms. Bat-Shit-Crazy is a first-class idiot."

"Won't argue that." Fillion re-read Hanley's words again. "So, you're suggesting that Hanley personally purchased HiraMed tech and contracted his supply to the lab?"

"Smart biz move." Mack took his Cranium off and twisted to fully face Fillion. "That's what I'd do. Get a medical supply wholesaler license and set up a sole proprietorship. Make investments to deploy in multiple companies while cutting out the corporate middleman. Maximizes profits."

"Probably how he operated in the underground without slime trails leading back to New Eden Enterprises."

"Right."

Made sense. Sole proprietorships didn't count in global economy laws. Hanley could own as many small businesses as he wanted.

Fillion raked trembling fingers through his hair, exhaling loud and slow, ending in a coughing fit. The swirling smoke in the Great Hall morphed into ocean currents. He was sinking, fighting for air. Bubbles left his mouth and obscured his view. But he knew his mom's corpse was floating before him. "No," he choked out. He was in control of his cybernetics and he'd fight his PTSD too. Deadened gray eyes stared directly into his and blinked. "No," he said again, more forcefully.

He couldn't save her or make right all the wrongs.

Focus.

The Great Hall pulled into view. A shudder caressed his spine.

He did it. He fought his coping mechanism's disassociation and won.

In the lingering mental haze, he could see Mack pull out his pack of cigarettes and lighter and toss them into the space between their bodies. Fillion considered the cigarettes and then looked at his friend, eyebrow arched.

"Suck hard," Mack said, biting down on his tongue piercing. "Beefcake Daddy might return at any moment."

With automatic movements, Fillion lit up and dragged, eyes closed. Once again, he started to breathe easier. God, he was so weird. A cold object touched his cheek and he jumped, swearing as his eyes flashed open. Mack's lips twitched, holding a clay cup filled with wine. How the hell could his friend joke right now? And he knew what Mack would say: It was fun to see potential energy become kinetic. Fine. Give the people what they want. Fillion flipped him off and then snatched the chalice from his friend's grip, downing the contents in a couple gulps before handing back the empty vessel.

Mack rolled to his side, lifted his utilikilt, and then scratched his bare ass. Like usual, his friend redirected Fillion's intense energy so he could refocus instead of overthinking himself into a grave. To play back, Fillion leaned close and kissed Mack on the cheek, surprising his friend, and then seductively whispered, "You have the ugliest ass."

"Rawr."

"Stop tempting me and get back to work."

"Your Dictator Mode is so arousing."

Fillion bit his bottom lip flirtatiously. "Everything about me is arousing."

"You're back," Mack whispered, his voice cracking. He touched his forehead to Fillion's. "Stay with me, OK? We'll get through this."

"To win."

"To destroy."

"Cut every string and walk—" Fillion's eyes widened and he leaned back. *"Narcissists are incapable of remorse."*

"Psychoanalyzing me doesn't change the second gen's future or my decision."

"They're human beings, not *consumer products."*

"Then they'll be dead human beings and that *will be on your hands, not mine."*

Ignoring Mack's inquisitive stare, Fillion switched over from Skylar's screen to his own. The mirror files for two random villagers loaded with a quick tap. Deflecting was Hanley's mode of operation. His narcissistic personality disorder fed his sense of reality with delusions of grandeur until he only saw people as reflections of himself. If the second gen died, Fillion would be tried for neglect and manslaughter. Just like Hanley had been during The Watson Trials.

"When have I personally harmed you or the residents? Others have, but not me. This colony is a lifelong investment of mine."

Dissecting subtext, Fillion could see how blame was being shifted to HiraMed. In Hanley's unrepentant mind, it was the technology, created by another, who had harmed the colony. Not him. God doesn't *personally* harm his creation. *He allows* trials and tribulations to test his subject's faith. A psychopath's explanation to victim-blame and control the masses through fear-driven devotion. But it was the narcissistic side of Hanley that Fillion feared had rigged the cybernetics.

"What're you looking for?" Mack leaned in and studied Fillion's screen.

"Dead Man's Switch."

Mack's breath caught. "You think—"

"Yeah."

"Wouldn't that mean Hanley ... died?"

"Or hacked to simulate death to the programmed code. Maybe to punish him for outstanding debts, or other reasons. Who in the hell knows?"

His friend nodded. "The triggered virus."

Fillion puffed on his cigarette and blew the smoke away from Mack's face. "Hanley never shares the spotlight, and HiraMed is positioning for corporate takeover."

"New message from Amanda." Mack sat back and tapped his screen. "Some of the deleted data has been recovered."

"Another goddamn honeypot."

"True."

"We need the data, though." Fillion groaned. "Tell Amanda to focus on re-establishing connection to the second gen. I want the lab to have access to vitals in real-time again."

Mack hesitated a beat. "They'd have to hack into Techsmith Guild server to do that."

"Shit." Fillion used the hem of his shirt to wipe the clammy sweat from his forehead. "I need to disarm the fail-safe first." He swore again. And again. The cigarette dangled from his lips as Fillion pressed his palms into his eyes. "If I trigger the fail-safe, they die. If Hanley's cybernetics include a Dead Man's Switch and he's hacked, they die—"

A scream cut him off. His gaze whipped across the Hall as a small group of people rushed to a convulsing body. Peter and two other men grabbed spasming arms and legs and ran toward the exit. A woman who guarded the entrance from inside yanked on the metal rings until lantern-lit night spilled into the hall, and then quickly slammed the doors shut after the group's exit.

Silence fell on the Hall again, save for the crackle of wood burning in the hearth. A collective breath was held. All eyes stared at the bodies on the floor, on the stage—waiting. Several seconds passed and nothing. And then shouts sounded from outside, followed by sharp commands. The quiet returned. Fillion released his breath. Whoever was guarding the door outside had prevented signal infiltration.

"I'm going to have nightmares for the rest of my life," Mack whispered. "This is so fucked up."

Fillion didn't respond. He couldn't. His gaze snapped onto his screen. Fury hissed from his pores. Strings of code filled his screen. In the upper right corner was a smaller, minimized notepad screen with his earlier observations. Simple function changes and updated medical coding were the only differences between Andra's and Coal's codes. But his own? Fillion's cybernetic system was riddled with traps. Any attempts to alter his code resulted in physical pain followed by vomiting, as if he were poisoned. No Dead Man's Switch in his personal code, though. So far, the two random villager samples resembled Coal's code exactly. Skylar's wasn't much different either. Just a few upgrades and new medical coding from the Son of Wind to the Son of Fire and villagers.

He bit the inside of his cheek until he could taste blood. Rivers of information rushed through his mind's eye. A new approach was needed. The obvious resulted in zero leads or fatal command codes. What was hidden?

Lynden returned and cozied up next to Fillion, watching him. Tears stained her cheeks. He wanted to ask her what had happened in The Rows, but he needed to remain focused.

The cigarette continued to dangle from his lips as his fingers manipulated information on multiple screens. Numbers, letters, and characters streamed upward. His eyes, burning from strain, searched for patterns. Reading programmer comments. He halted his scrolling. Was he seeing things?

Fillion highlighted a large segment from Skylar's cybernetics and pasted it into a fresh screen. Sections of unique, uncommented code had snagged his pattern-seeking gaze. A large section not recorded in the underground's diff reports or his own. Had it been hidden in an encrypted file until triggered?

He separated out each method to reverse engineer its functionality. The blood froze in his veins. Lynden lifted her head off his shoulder and leaned in closer, tilting her head. This once-encrypted section of code invoked a race condition while creating memory leaks in the hibernation program embedded in the nanotech—a virus transmitted wirelessly through short-range signals, like Fillion had theorized. One that, if triggered, resulted in brain hemorrhaging. He searched for the object method name, hoping for more clues. He clenched his teeth when he found it.

```
Initialize.InOrderToLiveSomethingMustDie();
```

A quick search, using the object method name, pulled up the same code in the two random villagers. But not his, Coal's, or Andra's. Probably not in Jeff's either, or any other MELISSA test subject's cybernetics who were born outside of New Eden. Or perhaps those whose strings were cut and now had inner sanctum software. The latter made the most sense, given the samples.

"Found the Dead Man's Switch," Fillion said to Mack. "Pull up a notepad screen."

Mack scooted closer until their screens touched, and then Fillion dragged the highlighted section over to Mack's notepad.

"Whoa." Mack's eyes moved back and forth as he read. "Complex."

"Ideas? We can't augment code on a live system."

"I've been thinking."

"Oh god," Lynden blurted. "I know that look, Mackenzie."

"Whatever, *kusogaki*," Mack deadpanned. "I'm smart and stuff."

Fillion rubbed his cigarette butt into the stones. "What about a counter-virus?"

"Well damn." Mack sighed heavily. "Steal my thunder." Then he winked. "Our hearts are linked. We are one now, never-really-happened-husband."

Lynden groaned while standing up. "I'm getting us more wine."

"We could write augmented bio-code," Mack continued. "To inject a counter-virus into nanobots from the lab and re-inoculate a sample of second and third gens. The sleeping will wake up in waves as the virus spreads."

"To destroy the fail-safe and Dead Man's Switch?"

"And destroy hibernation controls. For good."

The first touches of hope brightened Fillion's pulse. "But death makes way for the resurrection of new life." He locked eyes with Mack. "The object method name for *our* virus."

"You know, there's no guarantee they'll survive reanimation."

"I know." Fillion blinked back the flood of resurfacing emotions. "Hanley's too patient and meticulous. I don't think he'd ship defective product off-planet. Failure equals scandal. And HiraMed's corporate survivability hinges on superior technology."

"Unless he's become desperate for cash flow. The benefits might outweigh the risks."

"What would you do?"

A grim smile flitted across Mack's lips. "Locate and send me the Techsmith Guild's server fail-safe code."

"Will do." Fillion rose to his feet and embraced his friend before Mack left for the lab.

As the doors slammed shut, Fillion brought up a message screen.

FNichols: Mack is on his way back to lab. Needs sublingual vaccine printer. He'll explain everything. Give him whatever he wants. I approve.

Michael: Yes, Mr. Nichols. How are the residents?

FNichols: Traumatized. At least five more known deaths. Maybe more.

Michael: Oh my god!

FNichols: A solution is coming. /comm

The next few hours stretched on in agony. Three more slumbering people in the Great Hall suffered brain hemorrhages. First-response teams jumped into action and dashed the convulsing bodies out of the building to prevent wireless infection. The past forty minutes or so had been quiet though. He still wasn't sure of how many second gens from other parts of the village had suffered. The virus was unpredictable, programmed to hit living targets in a randomized time sequence. But all inoculated second and third gens were triggered. It was just a matter of time.

God, he couldn't think anymore. Reality was quickly becoming soupy. A hammer pounded in his brain. Grief spasmed in his neck and shoulder muscles. And knives shot from his eyes with the simple act of staring, at anything. He probably looked cracked out.

What time was it now?

A yawn teared up Fillion's vision, but he glimpsed the time on his Cranium—a little after two o'clock in the morning. Thankfully he had found the fail-safe code before he started going into shutdown mode. And helped co-write and encrypt augmented code with Mack via the underground's group chat. Community members now rotated watch shifts. A rest station was set up by the hearth and around twenty villagers stretched across the floor to catch pockets of sleep. He should, too. Nothing else for him to do but wait for Mack to return.

How the hell would he face Hanley? White-hot rage erupted and flashed to every point in his body. His muscles ached to fight, to demand reparations. They would face each other in court the next day. Fillion planned on pressing charges against both Hanley and HiraMed after protection orders were awarded. And they would be. There'd be no contest with the supporting evidence he had against the minority owner.

Fillion closed out screens, leaving notifications on, and shut his eyes. Lynden had curled up on the floor next to him thirty minutes ago, using his thigh as a pillow while she slept. He tracked a villager who walked by the stage to check on the Watsons, Skylar, and Rain. No, he needed to look away before another angle or problem demanded attention. His mind fogged with fatigue, but his heart refused to let go of awareness. Visions of Willow both comforted and tormented his mind as he slipped in and out of sleep. Finally giving in, his conscious state ran to her, and he finally faded from reality.

"Fillion," her lilting voice softly spoke. "Fillion, my love."

His eyes fluttered open and an image of golden hair and green eyes blurred into focus. Auric light haloed around her head and wreathed her body and linen dress in a soft, ethereal glow. Health had returned to her lips and warmed her pale skin in rosy hues.

Pain exploded in his chest at her angelic sight and he hiccupped back a sob. "I'm so sorry," he choked out in a hoarse whisper. "I couldn't save you."

She cradled his cheek. "I slumber no longer. How have you failed, My King?"

"I never believed in angels." He leaned into her touch and squeezed his eyes shut as tears slipped through. "When I die, we'll have our *forevers* together. Please don't forget me."

"When you die?"

"God, my heart aches. I . . . I can't breathe," he sputtered through more tears, opening his eyes to soak in her presence before she left him for whatever afterlife existed in the beyond. Even in death, she was so unbelievably beautiful. He reached out and wrapped a strand of her hair around his finger. "Forgive me?"

"Fillion Nichols," she huffed. "You are speaking utter nonsense. I am not dead."

His mind skidded to a complete stop.

"You're real?"

"Yes." She smiled. "You see me truly."

The Great Hall shot into sudden focus. Just behind Willow, by the edge of the stage, Mack pretended innocence and batted his eyes. Lynden no longer rested on Fillion's thigh but assisted villagers in the main Hall area. People spoke in hushed, excited tones. On the stage, Leaf, Laurel, and Ember still appeared under the effects of torpor. Alder, however, rested in his grandfather's arms, nibbling on a cookie. Fillion's gaze slid back to Willow's and he tensed as a tsunami of emotions surfaced.

"You're alive," he whispered. Unwinding gold strands from his finger, he touched her face and neck, before pulling her into his arms. "You're alive," he whispered into her hair.

"Your friend awoke me first," she whispered back.

"How did he know you wouldn't die?"

She softly kissed his lips. "He tested it on villagers in the apartments before treating those of us in the Great Hall. I awoke nearly two hours ago."

"Two hours ago?!" Fillion lifted an accusatory eyebrow at Mack who winked in return. A quick tap on his Cranium confirmed the time: a little after six o'clock. He'd been asleep for four hours?!

Willow blushed and dipped her head toward her shoulder. "I was rather disoriented when I awoke. The process took time, I was told. They moved me to the hearth to regain warmth and had me eat a small meal before I could rouse you."

He peered at the stage again. "Your brother?"

"He shall awake soon." Willow gnawed on her bottom lip, her neck and face warming even more. "The villagers were reluctant to wake you, as you have court this day. Mack shared that I should be gentle when I finally approached you, as you might cry and desire to publicly cuddle afterward."

Fillion laughed. That freaking bastard. Unable to resist, he pulled Willow onto his lap. "Pretty much," he said, and he kissed her—soundly—tangling his fingers into her hair. He didn't care about propriety or prudish onlookers. Over her shoulder, he flipped off his friend. He could hear Mack laugh before walking away.

Bittersweet emotions surged through Fillion as he savored the feel of Willow's lips on his. While most families would celebrate reunions this day, there were others who would experience the tearing severance he had tasted earlier. A pain so real, so all-consuming, he was unsure how anyone recovered from such grief to live on. And, yet, people somehow clawed their way out of the grave and back to a form of normalcy.

Fillion found the linden leaf charm dangling around Willow's neck and caressed the cool, metal surface. Her fingers entwined with his, trapping the symbol of love and truth between them.

"To be continued," Fillion spoke into their kiss. "I should help Mack and check in with Michael."

"When we find a pocket of solitude, you may drink your fill."

Oh god. How in the hell would he concentrate on anything now? Guilt began creeping in, but he remembered Mack's words: He deserved happiness.

Playing along, he breathlessly whispered, "Destroy me."

The hand on his chest balled his shirt into her fist.

"I'll beg on hands and knees if I have to."

The night sky exploded in his veins when her lips met his in answer. He wanted to lose himself to her touch, to fall endlessly in a bottomless sky. And Willow knew it as she pulled away. A mischievous glint flashed in her eyes while coming to a stand.

"Well, do you plan to laze about all morning?" she asked, hands on hips, eyebrows raised.

"You could've woken me up sooner."

Her mouth fell open. "I was under supervision."

"People can supervise you now?" He rose to his feet and dusted off his pants. "Good to know."

She lifted her chin a notch. "Others in this room. Not you."

"Ouch." He placed a hand to his heart. "This isn't what I meant when I asked you to destroy me."

Willow blushed but continued to boldly meet his gaze. "Pity."

He laughed. God, she was such a brat. "Come on, let's find Mack."

Hand in hand, they joined the crowd of villagers who held vigil while the living dead reanimated back into the folds of their waiting community.

A body of a woman, believed to be in her late teens or early twenties, was discovered curled up in a ditch on Mercer Island early Wednesday, and authorities are closing in on the nearby residence of businessman Hanley Nichols.

Skin genetically identified as belonging to Nichols, CEO and president of New Eden Enterprises, was found under the deceased's fingernails, according to a source with close access to the investigation.

FBI agents and a SWAT team have been spotted near the Nichols residence by an Associated Press drone. Neighbors reached by vid feed confirm the presence of heavily armored vehicles and describe officers surrounding the palatial residence.

The cause of the woman's death awaits an autopsy, but Seattle Police initially reported that they believed it to be a possible drug overdose. Authorities earlier Tuesday also said they also hope the medical examiner will be able to determine the woman's identity.

This is the first time in two decades that a body was discovered without bio-stat registration or DNA birth records.

— Associated Press, "Breaking News: Dead Body Linked to Hanley Nichols," April 16, 2058

Chapter Thirty-Six

El Centro, California

Wednesday, April 17, 2058

Fillion shifted in his chair and checked his Cranium again. Court proceedings should have begun twenty minutes ago, and Hanley had yet to arrive. He looked over his shoulder at Mack who shrugged. Weird. It wasn't like Hanley to be late, for anything. He didn't need gimmicks like this to command attention. And, after last night, Fillion had zero patience for anything. He wanted war, and he wanted it now.

Every single second and third gen under digital torpor had reanimated by the time he, Mack, and Lynden left N.E.T. for Imperial County Superior Court in El Centro. Guards had crowded N.E.T.'s large wrought iron gates as Fillion's driver slowly crawled through the protesters. People had thrown rocks at his car, pounded on the tinted windows, and screamed hateful slurs. Lyn cowered and tried to make herself as small as possible. But Fillion glared at the idiots. He wasn't afraid to make eye contact with them.

Tomorrow afternoon, he planned a marketing stint in front of the protesters to partially reveal Hanley's unlawful activity. Fillion wanted to publicly announce charges with promises of how he would fight to change the human property status of New Eden Township. Hopefully Leaf would be recovered enough for a public appearance. His presence would help cement Fillion's declarations and gain sympathizers. Maybe this was the angle Fillion needed to engineer results. The Green Morons would probably claim the social justice victory, but whatever. They had presumed Fillion's guilt long before without presenting actual facts.

After court adjourned today, he had originally planned to depart for Ireland. But now, he'd go once the cremation ceremonies were over. New Eden still teetered in a precarious position. Before leaving the States, he wanted to ensure the community understood—without question—that he would not abandon them in their time of need. Rebuilding trust was going to take time, he knew, but it would take longer if he didn't show good faith while the trauma was still fresh.

A strange shift in the atmosphere cut through Fillion's mental rants. Goosebumps prickled across his arms and torso. The media murmured in the gallery. Normally he'd ignore them, but the tone bleeding through the hurried whispers felt off. The courthouse blocked Internet access to everyone save government employees, journalists, and lawyers. Had they found his mom's body? Is that what held up Hanley?

"I'll be right back," Fillion said to his lawyer. He didn't wait for the man to reply and pushed out of his chair. Eyes tracked his movements as he strode over to John Abrams.

John was turned away from Fillion and didn't notice his approach. The man spoke into his Cranium. "When?" John asked quietly. The man shielded his eyes as he furiously scratched across his notepad. "No signs of forced entry? . . . Oh, wow. OK . . . Yeah, got it . . . New Eden Biospherics & Research wants a chance to examine the body too."

Dread pooled in Fillion's stomach. Body? And why was John speaking on behalf of Fillion and his legal team?

"I can't comment on that," John continued. "Yes, I'll inform Mr. Nichols." John looked over his shoulder and saw Fillion. His face fell. "OK. Thanks." He tapped the air and then drew in a large breath.

"What's going on?" Fillion asked.

"That was the FBI." John glanced around, fear darkening his eyes. "Get your lawyer. We need to talk privately." John stood and looked to the bailiff. "Permission to approach the bench?"

Fillion found his lawyer's eyes and waved him over, then Mack and Lynden.

John returned, sweat beading on his forehead. "They're preparing a mediation chamber for us. Let's go."

An officer led them out of the courtroom and down a short hallway. A million possibilities barreled through Fillion's mind. Had the underground uncovered evidence that led to Hanley's arrest? Or were hacktivist activities leaked so that Fillion now faced arrest? Who was "the body"? It didn't make sense that the lab would perform an autopsy on his mom, unless she had contained top-secret HiraMed tech as well.

Once inside the room, the officer left them alone, shutting the door behind him. Nobody moved. Not even when John slumped into a chair.

"You'll want to sit for this," he said, a slight shake to his voice.

Fillion swallowed and then eased into a chair across from their family friend. A man who had been like an uncle to Fillion and Lynden while growing up. Pain hammered in Fillion's head and competed with the pulse pounding in his ears. Muscles in his neck and shoulders continued to spasm.

"Is Hanley in Seattle?" Fillion asked, unable to take the tension a moment longer. John blinked back an unreadable emotion. "I spoke to him last night and noticed the copper walls from the hidden Faraday cage in his office. Did the FBI delay his flight?"

"You spoke to him last night?" John asked, eyes wide.

"Yeah. Do you know what happened in New Eden?"

"The riots?"

"After the riots," Fillion said, narrowing his eyes.

John shook his head. "I only know about the riots." He faced Colin Carlsen, Fillion's lawyer. "Do you know?"

"Yes," Colin replied simply.

"We'll circle back to this," Fillion said, biting back his building anger. "First, let's discuss your conversation with the FBI just now."

John drew in another long, shuddering breath, first looking at him, then Lynden, then back to him. "Hanley is confirmed dead."

"What?!" Mack blurted. "Holy shit…"

Lynden's jaw slackened. The fatigue coloring her eyes darkened as blood rushed from her head.

"Did you say *dead*?" Fillion asked, hearing the word but not comprehending it. Hanley was invincible. Untouchable. How could he be dead? Was he on the run after being doxxed and murdering people? The man had enough money to pay off the FBI and stage a crime against himself. Hell, he was already using a false name through witness protection. "How? . . . How did he die?"

"His throat was slit by a broken wine bottle in his Faraday cage room." John doodled on his notepad and cleared his voice. "A woman in her late teens or early twenties with pink hair was found in a ditch two blocks from your family home. Overdosed on meth. Skin under her fingernails and bodily fluid samples were identified as belonging to Hanley."

"Oh god," Fillion whispered, momentarily closing his eyes. Pinkie turned a whoring call into an assassination mission. While Hanley's wife rotted at the bottom of the ocean, and after he had watched children brutally die during Spring Harvest activities, he hired out for sex. Sickness knotted Fillion's gut while a bizarre sensation moved through him, as if he were floating in zero gravity. "The Dead Man's Switch," he said to Mack barely above a whisper.

"Yeah."

John continued, his voice shakier. "The police can't positively identify the female. No bio-stats or registered DNA birth records. Nothing." He locked eyes with Fillion. "She's—"

"Property of the lab," Fillion interjected. "MELISSA Project. Rebecca Nakamura. I've read her files."

"Yes," John sighed, as if relieved. "The Seattle Police can't know this."

"I don't want her identity released to the public." Fillion raked trembling fingers through his hair. "Or her underground handle."

"Dad is dead," Lynden whispered like she hadn't heard a word, not even about Pinkie. Maybe she hadn't.

Tears slipped down her cheeks as she stared at her hands. Fillion bit the inside of his cheek, thinking of what to say. What could he say? Every detail slithered and writhed with shame and disgust. Maybe just a simple confirmation would do, despite his own denial. And, strangely, she showed more emotion about Hanley's death than their mom's. Weird. He was about to open his mouth when his sister lifted her head and smiled.

"We're free."

Was that the strange floating sensation he was feeling? He'd never known freedom or a life without Hanley manipulating everything. It was as if Fillion had been pushing against prison walls for years, and his muscles now moved around weightless. At the same time, he couldn't reconcile John's information. Fillion had witnessed far too much death in the past twenty-four hours. Trauma was numbing his emotions, his thoughts, and his body dragged on autopilot.

Hanley was *dead?*

"Did the FBI send you images?" Fillion asked John.

John blanched. "Yes. They're gruesome."

"I want to see them—"

"Fillion, trust me. You don't."

"I *need* to know this isn't a trick." Fillion clenched his jaw as his hands curled into fists. "He's fucked with my mind for so long, I don't know what to believe anymore."

The older man gestured for Fillion to peer at his privacy screen. Mack followed and leaned over John's other shoulder. Hanley's naked body slumped in his favorite chair inside the Faraday cage room. Dried, dark blood crusted down his neck, over his chest, and pooled between his legs. His face was blue and bloated, eyes bulged. Fillion wanted to vomit and pressed fingers to his mouth. Mack started gagging and walked away to lean against the opposite wall.

It was real.

Hanley was dead.

Overwhelmed, Fillion trudged back to his seat and slowly sat, staring straight ahead, unable to focus. A spot on the table gained his attention and he studied the dark stain. Nausea swirled and bubbled, and it took all his energy to not bend over and retch.

"The FBI wants to talk with you once you leave the courthouse," John said to Fillion. The room remained silent. They all stared at the table for several long, strained seconds. "I'm sorry."

"Don't be," Fillion quietly answered.

"No..." John cleared his throat again and his eyes watered. "I'm sorry for all the pain Hanley caused you and Lyn. I couldn't stop him. But I did what I could to minimize his efforts."

Colin leaned forward. "You're admitting complicity."

"Hanley hasn't been charged with anything," John rebutted.

"Yet." Colin added.

"If he is, my hands are clean. I only work within the law."

"My client still hasn't located partnership paperwork between New Eden Biospherics & Research and New Eden Space Ventures."

"It doesn't exist," John said, flicking a glance to Fillion before returning focus back onto the lawyer. "Two days ago, I confronted Hanley when I discovered he still held onto the document that he had publicly announced was signed. All he needed was a signature from either Leaf Watson or Fillion Nichols for the partnership to be legal and binding."

Fillion swore under his breath. "He tried to gain Leaf's signature yesterday."

"Mr. Watson didn't sign?" John asked.

"No, he didn't. I have a video of their conversation, too."

John's forehead wrinkled. "Hanley allowed a video?"

"Yeah. I also have video footage of the handover speech. And my conversation with him last night."

"That's not like him," John said, the corners of his mouth dipping in a frown.

"Nothing is by accident," Fillion threw back. "And now we have solid incriminating evidence against him and HiraMed." He explained what transpired in New Eden last night, and John's skin turned a pasty shade of green. "I will prosecute every single person involved in the twenty-eight deaths that occurred yesterday. And I won't stop until those bastards spend a lifetime behind bars."

"Twenty-eight?" John said under his breath in horror. He studied his lap, his jaw working back and forth. "I had no idea."

"You knew about the MELISSA Project," Fillion derided.

"Consenting adults. Common in science." John doodled on his notepad again. Meaningless geometric shapes and patterns. Probably how the man organized his internal thoughts, Fillion realized. "Not the same thing as testing on minors without full parental consent."

"Even if property of the lab?"

John didn't answer. Instead, he aligned his pen with a faint line on his legal pad and leaned back in his chair. "I'm Hanley's executor on his will. Did you know that you're listed as the legacy beneficiary for New Eden Enterprises and affiliates?"

Mack leaned forward. "Including New Eden Space Ventures?"

"Yes."

Fillion shoved away from the table and paced the other end of the room. Happiness blended with fury over this news. More legal hell and public image rebuilding but, also, more control over project shutdown.

"Colin," he began, "I want you to work with John to decipher if my legal options for New Eden Township have changed. As the new majority stock owner of N.E.E., find out what constitutes conflict of interest." He locked eyes with John. "I planned to press charges against Hanley this afternoon. Can't prosecute the dead. But I will go after conspirators and accomplices. And I plan to file with the U.S. Supreme Court to change human property status for all non-first gens as well as refile New Eden's experiment status to asylum."

"I understand." John reached over the table and offered Colin his hand, who shook it. "It will be nice to work with you for a change."

"Agreed," Colin answered.

"Another thing," John directed at Fillion. "Della's lawyer will be contacting both you and Lynden."

A pang stabbed Fillion's chest at the mention of his mom's name.

"It appears she made you her beneficiary for the T.R.U.S.T. Theory patent and copyright over a week ago." Fillion peered at Lynden, who refused to meet his eyes. Did she know? Had their mom shared this with her? John picked up his pen, then set it back down, shifting in his seat. "Hanley had believed that he was the beneficiary. We found out yesterday."

"Before or after the first round of deaths in New Eden?"

"Before."

"Son of bitch," Fillion muttered. "He wanted to sabotage me," he said to Mack. "Traumatizing Leaf to sign the partnership and secure the deal before I could intervene."

His friend nodded slowly. "Hanley never shares the spotlight. Create new order from chaos."

"She knew," Fillion whispered to himself. "Goddammit, she knew Hanley wanted her out of the picture. In court, Hanley would win every case I brought against him if he were owner of the T.R.U.S.T. Theory, and he needed an alliance with HiraMed to pay off debts." Pissed, Fillion faced John. "Did they find her body?"

"No, not yet." John's eyebrows pushed together as his mouth dipped in another frown. "If they don't find a body by week's end they'll pronounce her officially dead."

"I plan to travel to Ireland after the cremation ceremonies in New Eden. First, I'll . . . I'll make arrangements for Hanley's body." Thick silence blanketed the room again at the reminder. The muscles in Fillion's legs grew weak and his chest tightened to wheezes, like last night. He crumpled into a nearby chair and lowered his head until his forehead touched the cool surface of the meeting table. "Oh my god," he choked out as his body shuddered with fresh grief as reality caught up to him.

Twenty-eight dead in New Eden.

Innumerable legal hells to battle.

One twisted parent to bury.

One parent's body absent, just like always.

He was an orphan. No more family existed on his mom's or dad's side. He and Lynden were the last of their line. And both of his parents had died violently within a twenty-four period. So much death in one day. This realization slammed into every angry, disgusted thought he possessed for Hanley, and even his mom.

Lynden pushed her chair over to his and wrapped her arms around his shoulders. God, he didn't think he had any more tears to shed. But the pain in his chest liquefied until the acute stress and ash-coated grief ran down his cheeks and salted his sister's shoulder.

The past could never be changed. What was done was final. For years, he'd wanted to lock Hanley up and see the man lose everything he'd swindled others to gain. But death? No. He never wished death on his dad or mom. Or on anyone but himself. And for what? All those dark emotions, all the coffined pain was the product of a goddamn illusion.

No longer would he have to look over his shoulder. Chains fell off his mind and his heart stepped into the sunlight. His body floated up into the endless blue until he touched every star of possibility.

Free the people, slave owners!

Reality was his to spin and weave, to clothe the future of his choosing.

"I'll let the bailiff know that we're done," Colin quietly said before excusing himself from the room.

Fillion studied the door as it closed. "You should know that Jeff is among the twenty-eight dead."

John's head fell and his eyes reddened.

After a few seconds, Fillion asked him, "Can you provide legal representation to the community as needed?"

John simply nodded then released a long breath, wiping away his own tears.

A few hours later, Fillion left Mack and Lynden at the lab and practically sleepwalked to the Watson apartment. He had to see Leaf and share the news. HiraMed was still in play, but the virus he and Mack created disabled stasis capabilities and disarmed the fail-safe and Dead Man's Switch. The inoculated residents would need inner sanctum though. A task he would employ the underground to handle once Techsmith Guild server data was fully recovered. Fillion still didn't trust all the scientists at the lab. It wouldn't be surprising if HiraMed planted one of their own at N.E.T.

He knocked on Leaf's door and waited. The biodome remained eerily quiet, as before. Fillion glanced over his shoulder and watched the trees dance in the breeze. Leaves fluttered, a violent movement. Yet they remained attached to the tender stem that in turn anchored their life to the tree. Fillion could relate. He was hanging onto his existence with every fragile thread of strength he could find.

The door slowly creaked open. He swung his attention forward and first watched as the wrought iron tree move away from him, then watched as Willow studied his disheveled state on her doorstep.

"Fillion," she said, a slight smile on her lips. The emotion slipped from her face, however, when he grimaced against his own.

He couldn't speak. All the words he planned to share vanished. Instead, he wrapped his arms around her and buried his face into her neck as grief and exhaustion took over. Again, he didn't know he was capable of more tears. God, it was pissing him off. Still, he cried until his body swayed and verged on crashing.

Gently, Willow coaxed him inside and shut the door. Her hand in his, she led him through the living room, down the hallway, and into her bedroom, then created distance. The door remained open, but he wanted it closed. He wanted to hold her and kiss her and find comfort in her touch. But he also wanted to shut down and defrag.

"You need rest," she said into her shoulder. "Please use my chamber, and I shall ensure you are left alone, even if you sleep through morning time."

"Where's Leaf?"

"Evening meal."

Fillion looked out her window and noted the shadows. "What would your brother think?"

"It matters not to me what he thinks concerning my life with yours." She drew closer, raised herself on tip-toes, and softly kissed his lips.

Fillion swallowed and turned away. "Hanley is dead."

She gasped. "How?"

"Murdered." He couldn't share details with her right now. The images were still far too raw in his mind and the information far too delicate for hers. "I need to let Leaf know."

"Are we safe?"

"Yes," he whispered. "We're safe."

Willow cupped his face. "Then rest, My King. You appear ill." When he nodded she wove her fingers with his once more and pulled him toward her bed. "Please, care for yourself, Fillion."

"Willow," he began and stopped, blinking back shyness. "I know I hurt your image. We can't marry in my world, but . . . but we can handfast in yours."

"I care not for the opinions of others," she said. "My reputation is mine alone, and I have already forgiven you."

He sucked in a breath to hold back more forming emotions. "I love this about you. But I want a future together, one that won't cause either of us more pain."

"Perhaps it is wishful thinking, but I had hoped your world offered an alternative to marriage." She looked him boldly in the eyes. "Since men and women do not tread on ceremony and do what they wish without apology. For I am not an object to receive or be given away."

"How about a compromise?" Fillion offered a bashful smile. "I never wanted to get married either. It's demeaning to 'husband' another. Disgusting. Be my life partner instead. My equal."

"Yes!" Willow threw her arms around his neck. "Thank you."

"You haven't heard the compromise yet," Fillion whispered into her hair.

She leaned back. "Handfasting?"

"OK, never mind," he quietly laughed. "But yeah. Handfasting. For Leaf's sake, if nothing else."

"As long as we are pronounced as partners in life and love, I shall consent."

Fillion kissed her softly, overcome. "I love you, Willow Oak Watson."

Willow grinned and gracefully stepped out of his embrace. "Now, you should rest." Her hand slipped from his while she backed away—her eyes communicating promises to his—until she said, "I love you, Fillion Nichols," and shut the door.

For once he fell into a bed without dreading the future. Hardships stacked the days ahead. But he was *free*. Fillion swept the chains away from his mind. Warmth touched his heart as redemption lit his battle-weary body. The feelings were foreign, but he enjoyed the rush of old, unwelcomed shadows being driven away. He turned on his side and faced the wall. Lavender seeped from the pillow and blankets, and he breathed deeply before falling asleep, with a smile on his lips.

This is a story of people who made a world in their image and of how it came apart. …

In the end, the environmental visionaries came up hard against an eccentric businessman whose funds may have seemed inexhaustible but whose patience was not. …

It started as a shared fantasy in an avant-garde theater troupe of environmental zealots and trust-fund hippies on a Santa Fe ranch in the early 1970s.

— Los Angeles Times, April 24, 1994 *

Chapter Thirty-Seven

New Eden Township, Salton Sea, California

Thursday, April 17, 2058

Leaf popped open a black umbrella from the safety of the main biodome's shadow. He traveled alone to the Outside world this day. The community prepared for a mass cremation ceremony and busied with gathering juniper branches, firewood, and preparing the gardens and ceremonial cloths for the bodies. Fourteen would become elements upon the morrow and fourteen more the day after.

The biodome mechanics were not equipped for so many deaths in a single day. But the Nobles, with the help of Michael, settled on a plan and the community approved. Travel bans were thankfully lifted the prior afternoon, allowing lab employees and villagers to cross between worlds as before. Scientists, led by Michael, arrived late morning and hand-tested New Eden's atmosphere to double-check the calibrations for the anticipated carbon emissions increase. Bio-rains were scheduled to cleanse the air during the night hours this week as well.

There was simply too much to do. But, first, he needed to focus on facing the media, protesters, and delivering his practiced speech.

Six guards were positioned a stone's throw from The Door, dressed in flexible yet form-fitting black material. Shiny dark shields covered their elbows, shoulders, chests, and knees. Gloved hands held weapons that fired machine-killing signals. Spooked, Leaf held his breath when he glimpsed his distorted reflection in their full-face helmets. Strangely, Leaf could handle holographic technology, for it was not real. But the guards? They were real, for all their unnatural appearance.

Upon noting his arrival, Fillion pushed off the paned wall and motioned for the guards to form a circle as they marched toward the protesters.

"Are the requested media channels here?" Fillion asked Michael when the scientist squeezed through the guard's formation.

"Yes, Mr. Nichols. All is ready."

"And you?" Fillion asked Leaf.

Leaf dipped his head. "I desire to disrupt the game further."

Michael sculpted the air with his finger. Satisfied with whatever was on his screen, he poked the air, touched his Cranium, and then matched Leaf's and Fillion's strides.

Early this morn, the Son of Eden rose from Willow's bedchamber and departed for the lab shortly thereafter. Leaf wanted to chastise his sister for offering an unmarried man her room without first consulting Leaf's permission. But, at this point, he knew the conversation would be useless. She and Fillion operated under different social rules than the rest of New Eden. And, if he were honest, he was happy his sister had insisted that Fillion rest after all he had endured. Willow had much to teach him about empathy and self-worth. Where Leaf often concerned himself with upholding rightful appearances, Willow allowed compassion to direct her choices, even at the cost of her good name.

Leaf adjusted the umbrella overhead and squinted his eyes at the bright, azure skies. Billowy clouds crowded pockets of the blue expanse and slowly floated past. Despite the partial cover, heat rolled off his skin and wavered upward from the parched soil . His heart, however, sank beneath the hard, desolate earth.

He had agonized over how to face the families who had lost children when his own family had remained whole. Yet he had. After Fillion left, Leaf and Ember had made rounds to each home in bereavement. The only hope he had to offer was that Hanley had perished the same night—that their colony was now safe. A cheap extension of sympathy. And, yet, the information brought a modicum of comfort. Their delighted, vindicated anger added to the heaviness Leaf carried.

"Justice is a word," he said to himself, "subject to the law."

He understood the wronged families. It was not losing a child alone, but losing a child to Hanley's delusions and greed. Still, Leaf could not condone celebrating a man's murder, even if the deceased had murdered others in his lifetime. At what point was justice served by murder being morally acceptable? These were thoughts he had never considered until now—not even with the news of Timothy's death—and he found his heart and mind struggled with how to appropriately respond.

Fillion lit a joint and exhaled smoke away from Leaf. The Son of Eden appeared lost to his own weighty contemplations. They had barely spoken a few personal words between them, only discussing business this morn before Fillion left to see his friend and sister off. Heaviness settled on Fillion's movements, even lifting his hand to his mouth seemed to take great effort. When he did speak, the words were softer than usual and tinged in a dark, rumbling anger.

"Changing your mind?" Fillion asked when catching Leaf's stare.

"No, not at all."

"Did you have a chance to read the speech Kerry sent Ember?"

"Yes, actually." Leaf drew in a deep breath. "I practiced after mid-day meal. I am impressed by her team's ability to capture my sentiments."

"Any changes?"

Leaf studied Fillion's shaking hands as he lifted the joint to his mouth once more. He knew Fillion despised dealing with the media and standing before the common judges of the world. "Perhaps one detail," Leaf eventually answered.

Dressed in black from head to toe, and with smoke circling his head, Fillion moved as though a shadow. Gray eyes flitted from object to object, before his anguished gaze rested on his boots as he abruptly halted. "Leaf," he choked out, lifting his head. "I'm sorry I failed you."

"The guilt is not yours to carry," Leaf offered with a sad smile. "You are not responsible for the actions of others."

"I . . . I knew an attack was imminent. For most of the day my mind was glitching. Della's plane crash provided the perfect distraction for . . . for—shit." Fillion cut himself off and puffed on his joint while staring up at the sky. "My intention was to warn you right away. But I sat up in a tree with Willow instead."

"Did you know what would happen?"

Fillion shook his head. "No clue. But I should have protected your family's cybernetic system. I didn't even secure Willow when I had the chance. And I was hyper-paranoid that afternoon because I hadn't given inner sanctum to the second gen yet, let alone your family. There just wasn't time the day I found out the truth. You were in the middle of the New Life Ceremony, and we had to hide Coal, and the police were trying to force their way into New Eden. Plus, Mack and I didn't have all the details yet. My cybernetics were different than Andra's, and hers was different than Coal's. Based on that, we figured it would be a person-by-person process. I guess . . . I guess I thought we'd have more time. Hell, I've only been owner for three weeks. Still…"

"You are *still* not to blame," Leaf insisted, placing a hand on Fillion's arm.

"I know it's not my fault. But I could have done *something*. So many people died…" Fillion allowed the words to trail off as he puffed on his joint to hide his thundering emotions. "Hanley feels nothing now. But me? You? All the families who lost their children? I'm so pissed. I can't tell him off. I can't fight Hanley to release my anger. The bastard gets eternal peace after all he's done and I get . . . I get to feel like I'm six feet underground, clawing at my coffin, while making right all the wrongs in front of the whole damn world."

A guard turned his head and considered Fillion a moment before resuming his post. But Fillion ignored him as well as the way Michael stared at the biodome panes, unblinking. Did the scientist feel guilt for his part in assisting Hanley? Did the man know what would happen? Though Leaf did not believe Michael would approve of violence against another, especially children, he also knew the Outside world did not measure human value the same as New Eden.

"You saved my generation from the evils of the Outside world, Son of Eden," Leaf quietly said. "You are our hero and our King."

Fillion threw his joint on the reddish dirt, gritting his teeth, and ground out the embers with his boot. "That's the thing," he snapped. "You've been programmed to accept my heroics even though you feel the violation of every crime that makes that statement true. Just think about those words, Leaf. Consider what is hidden."

When Leaf failed to reply, Fillion continued. "Heroes only exist because villains do. It's demented." He turned away toward the guards. "Let's go."

They resumed their march to the gates. A hot wind breezed past, and Leaf shuddered despite the heat. Perhaps they had not fully battled their way through hell yet.

Fillion's words tumbled around in Leaf's untilled mind. Since stasis, his mental clarity felt more wild than structured. Seeds of thoughts would begin to germinate then shrink beneath weeds of doubt and confusion. He had no recollection of his time in stasis. One moment he was directing dissenters in cleanup duties and, the next, he was waking, cold and disoriented, to a gathering of tears, both happy and sorrowful. The scientists reassured all that full cognitive functions would return. But Leaf understood the unverified promises for what they were.

"Hope," he said aloud. Brows deeply furrowed, Fillion slid him a sideways glance. "We need heroes for they restore faith in humanity. Deeds defend a man's honor, as Willow would say. A hero provides a selfless act of hope."

Fillion blinked several times, not breaking stride. "The very breath of life."

"Yes, indeed."

"It's still demented."

"Perhaps," Leaf replied. "But heroes allow people to heal, and that is what New Eden needs. The world may judge you as the son of a killer, but you are our Son of Eden, a son of life and prosperity. A son of hope."

Fillion stopped and locked eyes with Leaf. "I don't deserve this honor."

"Is anyone truly deserving of any honor?"

"Look, I get my self-worth. But it's ridiculous to praise a man for doing what any other person in that room would have done given the same set of skills. It was a group effort. It still is"

"Allow New Eden this hope, Fillion." Leaf lowered his voice. "And I forgive you, if that is what you need in order to feel released from guilt." Fillion sucked in a quiet breath. "Even so," Leaf continued, "no person can predict the future, not even the most heroic or intelligent among us. And you were doing something. But you can only do so much with what you are given."

"Fine. Be logical." Fillion's mouth hinted at a smile. "I rescind my unspoken offer to participate in my black parade."

"We are poor excuses for men, Skylar and I have decided. Political sons until the end." Leaf tipped a corner of his mouth up. "You are welcome to join our pity party instead."

Night faded into day as his friend released an earnest laugh. Even Michael smiled. The transformation was immediate and gratitude rushed through Leaf. It seemed such a small thing to grant this man a piece of happiness and, yet, his large response to acceptance always humbled Leaf.

"Deal," Fillion said, holding out his hand. "I hate parades anyway. Too many people."

Leaf gripped him by the forearm and leaned in close. "It is an *honor* to serve beside you, Son of Eden. Now, let us remind the world of our true worth." Fillion swallowed and dipped his head, before pivoting on his heel. But Leaf held fast and pulled him back, leaning in closer. "And I have decided that you and Willow shall handfast on Beltane."

A dark eyebrow arched. "How patriarchal of you."

"Yes." Leaf peered down his nose at Fillion with a playfully smug grin. "I have also decided that the world shall witness your union."

"Says the man who married in secret," Fillion threw out. "Nice knowing you, mate. Willow is going to destroy you."

"She has already agreed."

Incredulity twisted Fillion's blanching face. "You're shitting me," he whispered under his breath.

"Perhaps if the great Fillion Nichols considers a woman from New Eden his equal, so will the world."

"You came up with that all by yourself?"

Leaf's smile grew. "I might have had persuasion from a woman who is my equal."

"Look at you." Fillion smirked in appreciation then bit his bottom lip. "You're such a progressive bad boy, Leaf Watson."

"Unless you strongly object, I shall mention your union during my speech." He pushed Fillion forward. "And save your flirtations for Willow."

"My seductions don't make her blush as much you." Fillion winked at him and then continued walking.

A couple of guards stifled laughs, and Leaf ducked his head to hide his smile. Though his heart grieved and battled guilt, he was also experiencing joy. 'Twas the strangest paradox. But he had risen from the dead, as had his family and many others in New Eden. A resurrection into a new future, one of their making. Grief and gratitude, sorrow and celebration—he welcomed all the conflicting emotions. And he knew Fillion did as well. Despite the dark, rumbling anger, there was a scintillating light behind the sorrow in that man's eyes.

The protesters roared when their small group emerged from behind the biodomes. The angry mob spewed slurs and hateful words. Some even threw rocks—until they saw him. In the confusion, the crowd lowered signs and quieted to whispers. People murmured and pointed as Leaf approached where they had camped for several weeks now. Media were positioned within the gates, per Fillion's instructions. Also per his instructions, they waited to ask questions until after the announcements.

Fillion's publicist squeezed through the journalists and trotted over. "Mr. Nichols, here's your wireless mic." She clipped the tiny device to his collar then addressed Leaf. "And yours." Leaf blinked back shyness when she slipped fingers beneath his tunic's collar to attach the strange piece of technology, one no bigger than a bumblebee. "There. Say your names so we can test the volume." They both complied and journalists offered thumbs up. "You're all set."

"Thanks, Kerry," Fillion said.

Over her shoulder, she said, "Anytime, Mr. Nichols," then blended back into the media crowd.

"Monster!" a protester screamed, cutting the silence.

Another quickly followed. "Son of a killer!"

Fillion's head snapped up and he leveled a fiery gaze at the crowd.

"Anything else before we begin?" He blinked long and slow. "I'll wait." Heads turned left and right to see if another would speak out. "No?" When no one responded, he gave the media a faint nod and launched into his prepared speech.

"Free the people, slave owners," Fillion said. "Humanity is not an experiment." He took a step closer toward the gate, back straight, held head high, his voice even. "I agree, and I have been working since day one on the job to help New Eden Township. I don't say this to defend myself against your accusations, but because I don't represent *your* voice. I represent *his*." Fillion turned to Leaf and bowed, then faced the cameras once more. "It's hubris to declare what's best for another without consulting them first. Though we at New Eden Biospherics & Research appreciate all the sentiments in defense of Leaf Watson's colony, there are more constructive ways you can help. Mr. Watson, please share how the world can join me in supporting you and your community."

"Thank you," Leaf said, bowing in return to Fillion. He cleared his throat, his heart thumping against his ribs. "My mother and father believed in a world built upon the cornerstones of love and community. A world where every action had purpose and meaning, and each individual was treated as though their life mattered, even in death. I imagine it must be difficult to fathom how anyone would wish to remain enclosed as a tight-knit community when you are used to wide-open spaces and easy connection to anyone in the world. However, my generation views New Eden as a beautiful gift, and we are happy. Though this life was chosen for us, not a single resident of New Eden Township wishes to leave and rejoin Earth's modern society. I would ask that you respect our choice and not judge our lifestyle, though we live far differently than you. We are neighbors and share this beautiful world together."

Leaf bowed to the cameras and to the protesters. When he rose, he intentionally met as many curious eyes as possible while continuing. "Human property laws declare my generation and the one after me as less than human. But as you can see," he said gesturing to himself, "that is simply not so. Our clothing may differ, and perhaps our manner of speech, but I am made of flesh and blood, born of a man and a woman, same as you. Even Fillion Nichols views those in my community as his equals and always has. In fact, it is with great honor and pride that I invite the world on May the first to witness a partnership union between Fillion Nichols and my sister, Her Highness Willow Oak Watson."

Gasps and murmurs circulated almost immediately. Fillion shifted on his feet and lifted his shoulders a notch. A muscle pulsed along his jaw, but he remained steady.

"Your laws declare marriage between human property and those born free as illegal," Leaf said, allowing a thread of anger to color his tone. "Your laws also declare that my worth is only in providing evidence so that science and corporations may profit. I am a product of a theory, not a fellow human. This is where you can assist my community. Treat others different than you with human dignity. Continue to support our efforts in challenging inhumane laws, forcing research labs and corporations to treat their volunteers with the same respect and freedoms as you receive. Thank you." Leaf stepped back and nodded for Fillion to resume.

The Son of Eden's brows pushed together, his lips forming a thin line. "This morning I opened investigations with the FBI to uncover all inhumane practices at New Eden Enterprises and its affiliates. I will press charges against those who willingly conspired with Hanley Nichols against the residents of New Eden Township."

Shock rippled through the protesters and journalists. Mouths hung open and eyes rounded. Hushed exclamations swelled until whispers grew to chatter. Fillion carried on over the noise, nonplussed.

"I have also pressed charges against HiraMed Technology for knowingly selling a fatally harmful product to New Eden Biospherics & Research, which Hanley Nichols had used on the second and third generations with full knowledge of the fail-safe defect."

Outrage rose from the protesters at what Fillion insinuated. Were the people truly that invested in lives of New Eden? Or were they placating with an emotionally expected response over such news to maintain political ground? Leaf squinted his eyes as his mind absorbed body language and tone to better understand. When people quieted several heartbeats later, Fillion began again.

"The law firm of Colin Carlsen and Morgan Bishop have also filed, at my request, with the Supreme Court of the United States, to not only change human property laws but also to reassign the status of New Eden Township from an experiment to an asylum. This would grant New Eden Township full freedoms and would allow the colony to negotiate rent conditions as a commune located on the properties of New Eden Biospherics & Research."

He paused long enough to draw in a trembling breath and then said, "Thank you for supporting Mr. Watson and his community. I'll take a few questions now."

"Mr. Nichols," a holographic journalist shouted, "are you able to share any details of your father's murder?"

"Next," Fillion said, his gaze sweeping over the media. "You."

"Have people died in New Eden from HiraMed Technology?"

Fillion sighed and pointed at another journalist.

"Do you believe Dr. Della Jayne Nichols' death was an accident?"

Anger clenched Fillion's jaw, though he tried to posture with as much class as possible. "How about you," he said with a slight head nod.

"How are you able to marry Ms. Watson if the law prohibits unions with human property?"

"We're not filing for a marriage license and will be considered single according to tax codes. My residence is also not the same as hers. Next."

"Sources say that Coal Hansen is still wanted for using a fake ID and committing perjury. Are you in contact with Mr. Hansen?"

"No. And update your information. Akiko Hirabayashi fell for an April Fool's joke. Mr. Hansen's falsified ID and illegal marriage license were set up by hacktivists to bring awareness to inhumane laws." He lifted an eyebrow. "Any other questions?"

"Why is he still in hiding then?"

Fillion leveled a bored look at the journalist. "I can't answer for him absolutely but, my guess, based on the same information accessible to you, is that he's waiting for all the false charges to be dropped. Due process is a time vortex. Next."

"Did you end your engagement with Ms. Hirabayashi over suspicions of defective HiraMed product?"

"I refuse to align myself with someone who promotes inequality agendas."

The media and Fillion continued in a similar manner for another ten minutes. Unable to hide his annoyance, Fillion announced that he was no longer taking questions and removed his mic. Leaf removed his as well and placed the tiny technology into Kerry's waiting hands. Then, Fillion twisted away from the crowd and marched back toward the biodomes, his guards circling around them once more.

The protesters cheered as they walked away.

"Green Morons," Fillion muttered, rolling his eyes. "And, just like that, they worship me again." He shot a glance Leaf's way. "The world feels sorry for me right now. Easy hit."

"I am ever astonished by your world's disrespect of privacy, especially over sensitive topics."

Fillion grunted an ill-humored laugh. "You have no idea." They remained silent, lost to their heavy thoughts, until the The Door's etched metal glinted into view. Leaf closed the umbrella and placed it inside the holder. "See you tomorrow morning," Fillion said, barely above a whisper.

Their gazes touched briefly before Fillion, standing rigid, resumed his inspection of the parched ground, brows pushed together. Dark hair hid part of his face, but Leaf could see him gnaw the inside of his bottom lip. While Leaf had two funeral services to attend this week, Fillion had four and no community or family to attend him in the Outside world besides Mack and Lynden.

The word "family" pushed a new thought to the front of Leaf's mind. In two weeks, this man would become his brother beyond their own sworn oaths. Pride swelled in Leaf's chest, and he pulled Fillion into an embrace and held him tight. The Son of Eden stiffened at first, then he wrapped his arms around Leaf and released a shuddered breath.

"Until the morning," Leaf replied.

The sun dipped below the dome horizon line when Leaf stepped into the Great Hall. Chairs and benches scraped across stone as villagers stood upon his entrance. Then, to Leaf's surprise, the community lowered to one knee, even the Nobles at the head table. Moved by their gesture of gratitude, Leaf placed a hand upon his heart and bowed deeply in return.

They would mourn this week. But a new life awaited them in the days and years ahead. Slowly people rose and resumed quiet conversations, but hope fairly shimmered over each individual in the warm candlelight. Leaf breathed deeply the atmosphere of his community, and then made way to the head table to sit with his family.

Sorrow prepares you for joy. It violently sweeps everything out of your house, so that new joy can find space to enter. It shakes the yellow leaves from the bough of your heart, so that fresh, green leaves can grow in their place. It pulls up the rotten roots, so that new roots hidden beneath have room to grow. Whatever sorrow shakes from your heart, far better things will take their place.

— Rumi, 13th century A.D. *

Chapter Thirty-Eight

Dublin, Ireland

Saturday, April 27, 2058

Dust motes glinted as they passed through the dusky shafts of light that sliced through the shop's dank shadows. Lathes, various saws, and other equipment took up most of the room. Unfinished pieces of furniture piled in a corner heap, blanketed in sawdust. An end table. Chairs. Picture frames. A buffet. Water dripped from the ceiling and pooled beside the scraps. Several pieces had already swelled and rotted from the moisture.

Fillion placed his bottle of whiskey on a shelf then picked up a table leg and wiped off the cobwebs and grimy layers of dust. Sorrow touched his smile as his fingers trailed along the sanded wood grain. The very same hands that had tousled Fillion's hair, thumped his back, and pulled him into an embrace had also shaped this tree remnant into a work of art. Besides Lyn, Corlan Jayne was the only relative who had touched Fillion with genuine affection. And who spoke to him as if he mattered. Reverently, Fillion placed the odd end piece back onto the discard pile.

The warmth of the sun streaming through the skylight' touched Fillion's face and he closed his eyes. For a nanosecond, he pretended that it was his great-grandpa who embraced him. And, just like that, he was a little boy all over again. Sitting in the corner and listening to the old man sing as he worked, waiting for him to say "Fillion, my boy" followed by a lesson. Watching him toast the setting sun with a shot of whiskey after closing shop, saw-dust in his hair and wood stain on his fingertips.

Fillion opened his eyes and grit his teeth against the ache in his chest. The toe of his boot pushed rotten pilings aside. Dirty concrete floor lay beneath the disgusting layers of filth. Still, he searched deeper for his roots. For any sign that he inherited more than dysfunction and pain. But he already knew the answer, and it stirred up a strange mix of emotions.

He was free.

Somewhere in the shadows of his mind, he heard Leaf's deep voice: "Feelings are real. They often become one's reality. But they are not always based on truth."

Fillion whispered back, "What's the truth?"

The truth was embedded deep in his legacy: Love. Family. Community.

It was a truth he had come very close to missing. He was from a world that sought to transcend such mortal confines, and through artificial means at that. By contrast, New Eden cherished every nuance of life and honored death—and taught him how to live.

His generation had forgotten how to live. They died every day only to rise each morning and die again. The world was dying. So what was living? What new beginnings were nourished by this suffering?

His brows furrowed as he considered the discarded table leg again. The carved scrap of wood was once a living, growing thing. In order for the table to live inside someone's home, an entire ecosystem was sacrificed. If the community had moved to New Eden Mars-side, would societies of Earth feel a ripple of resurrection in the community's slow decay?

Hell no. Not even the slightest ripple.

Mars didn't deserve the people of New Eden. Earth did. His generation desperately needed reconnection to their humanity, to awaken to the physics that tied each human being to this orbiting rock in space—and to each other.

He wasn't a character on the Net.

And the villagers weren't characters at N.E.T.

Life wasn't a simulation. Humans weren't machines.

They were real.

Bleeding hearts and haunted souls, all of them.

"Fillion, my boy…" his great-grandpa's rolling Irish brogue caressed his mind. "Toast the setting sun and thank her for the day she gave us. Embrace the night with confidence of a day well earned."

Fillion reached for the bottle of whiskey he'd placed on the shelf. Unscrewing the cap, he tipped back the bottle and enjoyed a long swig. "To the sun," he said, finishing his great-grandfather's toast. "To the moon and to the stars. To the love of family and friends, near and far. Thank you for this day. Rise again tomorrow and the day after that. I'll be ready—"

"Fillion?" His sister slinked inside the shop. Sawdust blew across the floor from the change in air pressure. The rusted metal hinges creaked as she shut the door behind her. "Who are you talking to?"

"Myself," he said, holding back a chuckle.

"Weird."

"And cathartic."

Lynden arched an eyebrow. "OK. Sure." She wrinkled her nose as she took in the mold and rotting wood, arching her eyebrow higher when noticing his smile. "*This* makes you happy?"

"Yeah. It does."

"Sometimes I swear I don't know you."

Fillion's smile grew. "I've been thinking about Coal's words."

"Whoa. Hold up." Lynden flipped her hair and scrutinized Fillion's face, dubious. "*Coal's* words?"

"He mentioned about how Earth needs a reboot." Fillion enjoyed another swig of whiskey. "I'm going to make that happen."

"How?"

"Secret unicorn powers," he answered with a wink.

"Cool. I'm in." Lynden rolled her eyes. "Your happiness is stressing me out."

Fillion sighed dramatically. "I swear, I can't win with you."

"Aww, poor Fillion," his sister cooed before sticking out her tongue. "Hard to be a poor loser."

"Whatever, Rainbow." He raked fingers through his hair, annoyed when dust poofed into the air. "Ready?"

"Yeah. The guards secured the grounds for us."

"Let's go." He followed Lyn out, soaking up the sight of his legacy before closing the door. Both of them lifted hoods and lowered their heads to blend in with traffic.

A few minutes later they entered the church's grounds. Fillion announced on various media circuits that his mom's funeral would be held tomorrow. He even wrote an obituary announcing the date as April 28th. Later he'd apologize for the typo. But, today, he'd pay his respects with just his sister. The world wasn't invited to his family's suffering. They could climax at some other person's grief or scandal instead.

An empty coffin waited for him and Lyn at their family plot. At first, he balked over the waste of burying nothing. Now he was grateful for some semblance of closure.

Just over a week earlier, Hanley's body was incinerated to ash in a funeral home. No ceremony for him. No burial. Not that anyone would attend except those who showed for business or political reasons and, even then, only to appear sympathetic and woo the new business owner. Instead, Fillion requested a small urn with his dad's ashes, separate from the large urn. The vessel fit inside his pocket. At some point, he'd visit The Rows while the community slept and privately remember his dad.

New Eden may not want the elements of the man responsible for their pain in their garden. But he was also the man who gave them their world. For this, Fillion wanted his dad's elements to commune with the community. To honor the life who desperately wanted what he gave but couldn't understand.

Manicured grass softened Fillion's heavy footsteps. Up ahead, a curtained shelter sat over his mom's plot. *Gardai* drones hovered nearby or hid in the church's shadows. People passed by on the sidewalk but didn't pay them much attention. The ruse had worked.

Lyn slipped her hand into his as he parted the black curtain and entered. A solid oak coffin rested on a makeshift table. The twisting branches and grooved trunk of a linden tree carved a haunting design over the lid. When he made the request, he didn't realize how mystical the imagery would be. The otherworldliness settled in his bones and the hair rose on his arms and neck. They were burying a ghost.

His sister took in the coffin with large eyes and quick breaths. Giving death a ceremony was new to her, he realized. While he experienced anxiety as well, memories from his time in New Eden were forged into his soul. He understood what his sister didn't understand now but would in the years to come—he hoped. She didn't attend the Ceremonies of Death in New Eden. The idea was too traumatizing for her. He remembered feeling the same three years ago. But now? He embraced the beauty in watching a life being reborn into elements, allowing new life to flourish and continue.

Fillion slipped his hand into his pocket and caressed the ceramic urn. Since his dad's cremation, he carried Hanley's ashes with him wherever he went. It was creepy weird, but it allowed him an opportunity for his heart to grieve while his mind processed the millions of unanswerable questions he had, and probably always would have. He was the son of a killer. But the sins of the father no longer owned him or his future. People could say whatever they wanted about him. Fillion knew the truth.

His love was valuable, worth giving away.

He was a son of Eden, a man who would revolutionize the world and bring life back to the deserts of his generation's existence.

Reaching out his other hand, he brushed his fingers along the coffin's cold surface.

"A part of me feels like she's still alive," Fillion said to the eerie silence. As usual, Lynden didn't comment. He found his sister's bottled up responses strange. "How about you?"

"Yeah." She flicked her lip ring in and out of her mouth. "I like to think of her somewhere safe. Maybe starting a new life of her own."

Fillion thought of her answer for a few nanoseconds. "Is she?"

Lynden finally met his eyes. "I didn't think to bring flowers or anything. What the hell are we supposed to do?"

"I thought you could sing a song over her grave."

His sister's eyes bulged. "What?!"

Fillion laughed. "I don't know. Whatever the hell we want. It's not like she's here. We don't have to entertain her or anything."

"Cemeteries give me the creeps."

"I like them." Fillion lifted his shoulder slightly.

"You would like them," Lynden murmured, taking his outstretched hand.

"Good memories are buried here, too. Let's find them."

They left their mom's empty coffin and wandered the cemetery. When they found their great-grandpa's tombstone, they sat on his grave and exchanged stories. It was one of the best afternoons Fillion would remember. Hearing his sister's laugh, feeling her head rest on his shoulder, and holding her hand as they tried to outdo each other's ridiculous childhood memories in Ireland, made the muscles around his mouth shake from smiling so much.

Fate really did have a twisted sense of humor, he decided. Here, in a place of sorrow, joy had found him. Maybe now he could finally start to heal.

We have been rambling all this night,
And almost all this day,
And now returned back again,
We have brought you a branch of May.

— from "The Mayer's Carol," a medieval Maypole dance song

The minute I heard my first love story
I started looking for you, not knowing
how blind that was.

Lovers don't finally meet somewhere.
They're in each other all along.

— Rumi, 13th century A.D. *

Chapter Thirty-Nine

New Eden Township, Salton Sea, California

Wednesday, May 1, 2058

Willow's eyes fluttered opened to darkness. A voice had called her from pleasant dreams, whispering her name. Confused, she remained still and allowed her eyes to adjust to the shadows while her thumping heart attempted to steady. Mayhap she had only been dreaming.

A warm hand softly shook her shoulder. "Oaklee, time to rise."

Her skin jumped and she clutched her blankets. "Dear Lord, Ember!" Deflating back into her pillow, she released a relieved breath. "Is something amiss?"

"No, quite the opposite."

"What is the present hour?"

"Come," Ember said, kneeling beside her bed. "The women are waiting."

"The women?" Willow leaned up on her elbow and yawned. "The matriarchs should not arrive until after sunrise."

Though Willow could not see her sister, she knew Ember smiled.

"Do *the women* wish for me to sport ghastly shadows under my eyes this day?" Willow said. "Seems rather cruel."

Ember softly laughed. "We must be on our way."

"I shall blame you if I am listless come evening meal."

"Oh, I doubt you shall feel listless. He is a handsome man."

"Ember Lenore Watson, hush!" Willow tried to sound scandalized, but Ember knew better and soon they smothered giggles. Just the mere thought of Fillion dusted Willow's pulse in moonlight. Stretching, she rose from her cot weak-kneed, thankful the night hid her blush.

A few heartbeats later, they departed the apartment and tip-toed down the stairs. Willow shivered in the early morning chill, wearing only her slippers, nightgown, and a wool cloak. Terra, her eldest niece, protested the cold air as well. Ember adjusted the bundled twins that were secured in a wrap across her chest. The babies settled with her movements and Ember closed her cloak over their sleeping forms to seal in the warmth.

"Do you plan to tell me the nature of this adventure?" Willow asked.

Ember slid her a glance. "You shall see soon enough."

"I am not fond of secrets."

"Yes." Ember's voice held another smile. "Makes this all the more fun."

Silhouetted branches stretched overhead as they walked the trail along the apartments. The breeze hummed a merry tune, as if the wind, too, knew of this great secret. Mossy grass padded their footfalls. Only the leaves joined the breeze in making music this morn, the first of May.

In the distance, lanterns dotted the stone bridge and crowded around the linden tree. Reflected candlelight flickered across the North Pond's shores and Willow's breath caught. "Beautiful," she whispered.

Women rose from the grass and ferns beneath the linden tree at her and Ember's approach. Above the gathering, Beltane ribbons and unlit lanterns dangled from branches. The ends of several long ribbons held tiny bouquets of wildflowers, twigs laden with hawthorn blossoms, or ferns. A bower altar of flowering hawthorn branches arched before the trunk, also festooned in Beltane ribbons. 'Twas one of the most magical sights Willow had ever beheld, and far more decorative than other Beltane unions of her recollection. Was this for the world who would witness her handfasting vows this day with Fillion?

A ceremonial Beltane sash crisscrossed over the trunk's entire length, tied off into a bow mid-way up. After mid-day meal, the tails of the bow would bind her and Fillion's hands together. Even from the bridge, Willow could make out the embroidered Celtic knots threaded over the sash in various shades of green, framed in by stitched linden leaves and buttery yellow linden blossoms, completed by dark red lines that ran down the ribbon's edges. Red and white, the colors of Beltane, while gold and green represented New Eden Township.

"Welcome, Daughter of Earth," a matriarch greeted from the gathering. "Our Beltane bride and May Queen."

The women curtsied as she stepped off of the cobblestone bridge and onto the grass. She was the May Queen this year? Warmth spread to each limb as she thought of the significance. In New Eden, a bride was a symbol of Life as if Spring herself. But the May Queen was the goddess of Spring, *the* flower bride, the queen of the faeries. She represented wild, unfettered strength and perseverance, and the resilience of Earth as she healed after Winter's cold darkness.

Willow's gaze skipped over the smiling faces. Surely they had made a mistake, for her independence and temerity were deemed unladylike. May Queens past were genteel and possessed unparalleled moral character to inspire fellow young women of marriageable age. Though Willow now handfasted with the very man who had jilted her, she still remained the only woman in New Eden to have lost a betrothal—hardly a symbol of propriety.

On the edge of the gathering, a tall figure in a blue-hooded coat hugged her arms over her chest and stared at Willow wide-eyed.

"Lynden?" Willow asked, taking another step forward.

"Hey." Fillion's sister appeared as uncomfortable as Willow felt. Perhaps they could cling to each other in this strange pre-dawn ceremony of sorts. "Ember invited me."

"I am thankful you are here," Willow said. "Though, I know not why we gather before sunrise."

Ember placed a hand on Willow's forearm and guided her back into the circle. "Are we all present?" she asked the group.

"Yes, Your Highness," a matriarch answered Ember, placing a crown of flowers and ferns upon Willow's head. Taking her hands, the matriarch gifted Willow a small twig of flowering hawthorn. "For you, our Queen, a branch of May."

Willow dipped her head. "Thank you."

"Shall we begin 'Bringing in the May' now that our Queen is here?" Ember asked.

The women gently interlocked hands around the linden tree and hawthorn bower. Willow tucked the twig into her nightgown's laced bodice, then wove her fingers with Ember's and Lynden's. She shared an uncertain look with Fillion's sister and then returned attention back to the circle.

"Remember us poor Mayers all," a woman sang out in a lovely voice. Willow smiled and joined the women in singing the familiar May-Day carol as they stepped to the right.

...And thus we do begin
To lead our lives in righteousness,
Or else we die in sin.

We have been rambling all this night,
And almost all this day,
And now returned back again,
We have brought you a branch of May.

A branch of May we have brought you,
And at your door it stands;
It is but a sprout, but it's well budded out
By the work of our Lord's hands.

The beauteous melody wrapped around Willow in tender light despite the indigo darkness. Across the circle, Rain grinned at her and Willow could not help but return the happiness. The final refrain echoed softly in Willow's heart and she lifted her face and sang to the fractured sky.

The moon shines bright, and the stars give a light,
A little before it is day;
So God bless you all, both great and small,
And send you a joyful May!

Silence fell like dew drops upon their circle, each body awash in flickering lantern light. Tonight, after evening meal, the community would light a bonfire outside of the Great Hall and revel late and into the morning. While her family and friends drank and danced, she and Fillion would slip away. Beltane 'twas the only night a bride and groom could disappear without honeymoon blessings from the head of home, much to her relief. Mortification flamed her body at the very thought of Leaf joining her and Fillion's hands and kissing their foreheads before her chamber doorstep. How other maidens survived such indignity, she knew not.

Slowly, women turned to Willow and offered embraces, plucking flowers from their hair and placing them in her braid. All except Lynden, who continued to watch their ceremony with large, rounded eyes. She was tall for a woman, almost as tall as Fillion. Willow rose on tip-toes and tucked a wildflower into Lynden's ruffled red tresses.

"Merry May," Willow said to Lynden.

Lynden touched the flower in her hair. "Uh, same to you."

She took Lynden's hands. "We shall become family this day," she whispered. "I am honored to call you sister."

An uncertain smile pulled at the corners of Lynden's mouth as she stared at the ground. "Yeah," she whispered back. "Coal is sad to miss today."

"I sorely wish he were here," Willow whispered, pressing a hand to her mid-section. "I missed his union, and now he shall miss mine."

Grief and anger pooled in her stomach still. Her childhood friend would not need to hide all his days, she hoped. Fillion spoke of a future where her people were free. She would raise her sword and fight beside him until that fated day happened. Nor would she allow Hanley quarters to ruin this day from his grave, or any other day in New Eden.

"I am ever so glad you are here, My Lady." Rising on tip-toes once more, Willow kissed Lynden on the cheek. Then she lowered herself to the grass, as many others had done, inviting Lynden to join her. When all were seated, a matriarch began speaking once more.

"Willow Oak Watson, this day you shall *partner* your life with another. As fellow married women—well, all married women save one, but she is sworn to secrecy"—Rain ducked her head as women glanced her way—"we wish to endow timeless wisdom for a blissful Beltane union. As the eldest in attendance, I shall go first." The older woman adjusted her shawl, mischievous amusement curling her smile and twinkling in her dark eyes. "Always demand your own pleasures in the bedroom."

The women roared with laughter while a few feigned gasps, pretending to swoon. Willow clapped a hand over her mouth in horror, much to the wicked delight of the gathering. She could not look upon Ember or Lynden. But Rain? Her dear friend mirrored her own astonishment. Willow's head grew dizzy and she forced her lungs to draw in air. Women did not speak of such indelicate topics so boldly, or so she had always thought. Demand her own pleasures?

"Kiss him until he is breathless and then walk away," another offered.

"Better yet," a younger woman interjected, "join your friends so he cannot reciprocate until you are alone once more."

More humor colored the night.

"You suggest I manipulate him?" Willow asked, incredulous. "Play with his heart?"

"No, not manipulate," several women sang out in chorus.

"Just flirtations, Your Highness."

"A man's *heart* desires to give chase."

Peals of laughter and giggles followed the last piece of advice.

"You shall think only in love sonnets tomorrow morn," a younger woman said, "after he knows your heart in ways no other man has before."

The gathering murmured agreements then quieted, each lost to her own reverie. Moonlight touched Willow's pulse once more. Up in her tree, his kiss had awakened longings in her she had previously feared, though curious. But there was a melody to his affections and vulnerability despite his seductions. Willow lowered her lashes, afraid the others might read her scandalous thoughts as they flitted through her imagination.

"Let us now drink mead," a matriarch said, breaking the silence.

A goblet and berry tart were placed in Willow's hands. The honeyed wine coated her lips and she drank deeply. Spirited conversations sprang up almost immediately. Rain crossed the grass and sat before Willow, holding her goblet up. Per their tradition, Willow entwined her arm with Rain's, each drinking from her own vessel. They ended in giggles, especially when Rain fed Willow her tart as though feeding a babe. Unable to control her mirth, Willow covered her mouth while lifting her head to appear as regal as possible.

"Her Highness needs more mead," Rain called over her shoulder.

"Yes," Willow confessed. "Mead all day, otherwise I might faint at the hawthorn altar."

"Or fall over," Rain teased in reply. "Drunk on love. Oh, to kiss such a man on Beltane until the sun rose!"

"Rain Daniels!" Willow squealed. "Such things you say."

Lynden scrunched up her nose. "Yuck."

Willow and Rain laughed at Lynden's disgusted expression.

A village woman leaned over Rain's shoulder and poured mead into Willow's empty goblet. Rain raised her cup to the night. "To our May Queen!"

"To our May Queen!" the women cheered back.

As the sun tipped over the dome's horizon, the women led Willow in a procession back to her apartment. There, hot water and a copper basin awaited her, along with toiletries from the Herbalist and a selection of fruits and cheeses from Cook.

After prayers, the women undressed Willow and helped her bathe, followed by lathering her skin in lotions and oils. Lynden sat in a chair by the latticed window and ignored most of the commotion. Outside, little girls ran up to the window on occasion and tried to glimpse their Beltane bride and May Queen. When they pressed noses to the glass, Lynden leaned back and played with the silver linden leaf bracelet around her wrist.

Crowds were tiresome things, Willow thought, especially when one was the center of their attentions. Hiding a yawn, Willow desired nothing more than to curl up under her covers and slumber for a short spell. Hands continued to touch her, matrons fussed, and endless conversations and giggles filled her chamber. She would not know solitude until the moment before she left her apartment to meet Fillion by the North Cave.

A knock sounded. Laurel peeked her head inside Willow's chamber and took in the flurry of limbs and noise. Brows wrinkled, her amber gaze swept the room until she spotted Willow. "May I join your bridal party?" her little sister asked.

"Yes, darling," Willow answered. "I was about to send for you."

Laurel straightened her shoulders and lifted her chin to appear older and more mature than her twelve years, gliding across the room with practiced grace. Many women turned away to hide their knowing smiles from her sister, who seemed oblivious to it all. Rather, her eyes bespoke enchantment as she took in the ribbons and flowers and lotions.

"Your chamber smells heavenly," Laurel said on a sigh. She plucked a piece of cheese from a wooden trencher and popped it into her mouth. "Oh divine. I adore garlic and herb varieties."

"Shall you brush my hair?" Willow asked.

Laurel grinned and took the comb from Willow's hands. "The Great Hall is positively stunning. You shall swoon with appreciation."

"I am sure I shall."

"She shall notice nothing except for her groom's comely eyes and handsome smile," a woman teased.

Laurel released a loud quivering sigh, as though her heart fluttered violently, before draping herself across Willow's cot in a dramatic swoon. Women quietly laughed at her sister's romantic antics. "I fear I shall never breathe again," her little sister added in an overly dreamy voice. "To be a May Queen on the day one handfasts a dashing man."

"Laurel, darling," Willow drolled. "Continue to sigh so and you shall float away, never to tread upon earth again. Now, shall you brush my hair or shall I ask another?"

"Goodness," her sister playfully protested, rising from the cot and taking the comb from Willow's fingers. "Need you be so serious?"

"Someone must anchor your flights of fancy."

Laurel slid a disappointed look Rain's way. "I do believe my sister speaks truth how she possesses not a romantic bone in her body."

Her friend's smile was as indulgent as it was impish. "As I said before, she is a romantic beneath all the overtures."

Willow rolled her eyes and lifted her goblet. "I daresay I need more mead."

"Yes," Rain heartily agreed, pouring mead into Willow's cup. "Let us sweeten you up before you meet your groom."

The women erupted in laughter again.

"Where is your gown?" Laurel asked. To the room she said, "My *dear sister* would not allow me to see the gown she sewed every evening these weeks past, insisting her trousseau remain a surprise."

"Lynden?" Willow asked. Fillion's sister shrank back but met Willow's eyes with a level stare. "Would you do me the honor of revealing my gown? You are the only one present who has experience with such luxurious fabrics."

Titters and whispered chatter moved through the room at her words.

"Yeah, sure."

Lynden rose and walked to where Willow pointed. On her wall, the silk gown hung delicately on a peg, covered by a linen blanket and her nicer cloak. Carefully, Lynden removed the coverings until violet shades rippled in the mid-morning light. Gasps of delight echoed in her small room. Lynden removed the gown and placed her hands inside where the bodice would rest upon the edges of Willow's shoulders. Layers of silk swirled in the air and pooled onto the wooden floor.

"Now would be an appropriate moment to swoon, Laurel," Rain said among the excited exclamations.

Rimming the bodice's top and the skirt's hem, Willow had embroidered dark purple-blue wood violets as well as oak leaves in hues of gold and green over finely tatted lace. She repeated the same design on upper-arm and elbow cuffs, but stitched only oak leaves around the wrists. A silk tippet ribbon fell from the elbow cuff and reached mid-way down the gown's skirt, also covered in delicate tatted lace, violets, and oak leaves.

"Is this real China silk?" a young woman asked, touching her cheek in wonderment.

"Yes," Willow softly answered. "A gift from His Majesty, Fillion Nichols." She nibbled on her bottom lip as women continued to gush over the exotic Outsider item. Loosening a tight breath, she asked, "Do you think me pretentious for wearing this extravagance when clothing for many is thread-bare? I would not wish to cause offense."

A matriarch placed a hand on Willow's arm. "Daughter, you are allowed to enjoy highborn gifts from your groom without censure. Wear this dress to please him. In his world, it is customary for brides to wear silk. You are not only a union of hearts and souls, but also of worlds."

Willow nodded, feeling a blush rise over her face once more.

"Please save this dress for me, Oaklee," Laurel said, a wistful lilt to her voice. "I shall never tease your unromantic bones ever again!"

"Of course, Frog." Willow pulled her sister into an embrace, then gently placed her May crown upon Laurel's head. "Beautiful."

Hours later, shortly after mid-day meal, Willow stood alone in her chamber—finally. Henna now decorated her hands and feet and around her navel, the latter of which only brides received in a ceremony of nuptial blessing. Willow had silently begged for the floor of her chamber to open up and swallow her whole as the women incanted the ritual words of fertility. Her attendants had also curled her waist-length tresses, weaving portions into cords and braids with silk scraps Willow had saved. A bridal chaplet rested on her head as the finishing touch, made of fresh hawthorn blossoms, wildflowers, and golden willow oak leaves.

The sudden emptiness of her room increased the ache in her chest, one she hid from others. Their community had mourned enough and deserved a day of celebration and happiness.

In a secret pocket sewn into her gown, Willow clutched the prayer beads gifted by her father upon her fifteenth birthday. His deep voice rumbled in her mind, with familiar words of encouragement. "I have tried to be strong and resourceful, Father," she whispered to the shadows, closing her eyes. Peace trickled from the top of her head down to her toes. Fastened to curled strands and braids, her mother's carved bone dragon comb flew above the wreath of flowers upon her head. Willow could almost hear her carefree whimsical laugh, a laugh so similar to Laurel's. "Your faerie child is the queen of faeries this day, Mother." Her words ended in a choke. Willow blotted at forming tears with a handkerchief she had stowed in a separate pocket.

Movement redirected her attention and she drew in a ragged breath.

In her chamber door, stood Leaf. His eyes roamed over her gown and hair as his steady countenance gave way to emotion. Had he heard her whispers to the ghosts of their parents?

"You are most beautiful, Willow Oak."

"Thank you, Your Majesty," Willow lowered into a shallow curtsy. "I do not feel myself, if I am honest. I despair being trussed up and placed on display." She released a small laugh and touched her gown. "Though, I am quite fond of China silk and would relish many gowns made from this impractical fabric."

Leaf tried to smile, but it fell. "Mother and Father should see you this day."

"They do, I am quite certain of it."

He nodded, blinking back tears, and then held out his arm. "Is the May Queen ready to greet her community?"

"No. But lead the way."

Her hand rested upon his forearm as they traveled, in silence, down the hall and into the living room. Fingers of sunlight touched her spinning wheel. Carved oak leaves and acorns danced across the wood, and Willow smiled. Opening their front door, Leaf bowed. Sunlight brushed the chill from her skin and shimmered across her gown. She crossed the threshold of their family home and into Spring's warm embrace. Her legs shook and her pulse stirred into a gallop.

Cheers thundered from the biodome floor when she came into view at the top of the stairs, followed by gasps. She smiled to hide her distress and absently touched the silk. The only colors worn in New Eden were shades of white, brown, and black, natural tones from plant and animal fibers. Magic glimmered in the eyes of children and younger maidens gaped in awe as Willow descended the stairs as though a moving waterfall.

"Hail, Queen of May!" a woman called out.

"Hail, Queen of May!"

Susurrations of appreciation rippled through the crowd as she drifted past to the front of the procession. Willow placed a hand upon her heart at their sentiments and dipped her head in honor when she finally reached the head of the line. There, Brother Markus lifted a Celtic cross decorated in flowers, and they began marching toward the North Cave.

Children danced around Willow, throwing flower petals. A few dashed ahead to dot the grass in pinks, purples, and yellows. All along the apartments, Beltane ribbons fluttered from tree branches in the breeze.

The beauty overwhelmed Willow, and her entire being humbled at the community's display of affection. The merriment was infectious. New Eden celebrated their new life and the new life to come. Still, as she watched the children gambol about, throwing petals, and young maidens peer at her with romantic longings, Willow remembered those from their generation who should have shared this happy day with them as well. She touched the prayer beads in her pocket reverently and said each buried name in her mind.

A gentle breeze skipped by and she released her prayer beads, satisfied. But as one thought left, the wind carried to her another equally as profound.

The last time she had marched at the head of a procession was on Exchange Day when she had journeyed to the North Cave in a wedding dress to welcome a handsome stranger who would revolutionize New Eden Township. Now, she marched to the North Cave in a different wedding dress to welcome the same man who would exchange vows with her shortly thereafter.

Leaves and blades of grass quivered as the breeze whispered yet another wondrous memory.

At The Door that first time, she had parted with her golden tribute, an offering from a tree to comfort her tears. A wayfarer by nature, the leaf had accompanied its friend into the unknown. Willow smiled and touched her new companion, the silver pendant dangling from her neck. A different wayfaring leaf, also born of a maiden's tears. Strange how, when one story ended, another began.

A beginning, Willow hoped, that would be full of happy endings.

Around the bend, the North Pond glistened in the mid-day sun. Lanterns in the linden branches glowed in the shade and enchanted the tree and hawthorn bower. Cheers filled the glade and Willow peered toward the North Cave.

The breath in her lungs stilled.

Fillion stood beside Mack, shoulders elevated, his thumbs tucked into his pockets, tension knotting the muscles in his neck and jaw. Headiness swirled through her body as she drew nearer. A dark gray tunic trimmed in silver—the one he wore to the Ascension Celebration—clung to his toned frame and brightened his eyes. Those very otherworldly eyes that now held hers in veneration, his lips parted in appreciation. Midnight limned his slightly disheveled black strands in the filtered sunshine, which draped partially over one eye. He blinked slowly as if she were the light of day after a long dark night, and she smiled, bashful with the intensity of his silently communicated ardor.

Brother Markus halted a short distance from Fillion. Before the monk could make ridiculous statements of Fillion coming forward to receive his bride, Willow broke tradition and moved toward her groom instead. Leaf whispered her name in shock and the older man raised bushy white eyebrows at her boldness. Villagers murmured behind her as well. Did they now regret their decision to name her their May Queen?

The invisible thread connecting her to Fillion tugged hard, and she fairly floated to over him, desperate to breathe once more. He moved toward her as well until their hands wove together. Energy, fervent and heady, arced between them. And Willow's pulse feverishly throbbed with longing, love, giddiness, and myriad emotions she could not name, her thoughts lost entirely to him and him alone.

"To say you're beautiful is grossly inaccurate," Fillion whispered to her. "Words don't exist for how I feel this moment."

"I feel much the same, son of Della."

Fillion hoarsely whispered, "You honor me, daughter of Joel."

Swept away with sudden shyness, Willow dipped her gaze, furrowing her brows when discovering an unfamiliar tattoo. An elegantly detailed oak tree with Celtic knotted roots sprawled across Fillion's forearm. "Is this my tree?"

His shoulders rose a notch. "My sister surprised me with this tattoo a year ago. To remember you."

"Beautiful," she breathed.

Mack cut his friend a sly look and then leaned toward her. "If you change your mind about him, I'm available," he said, ending with a wink.

Willow bit back a smile. "You flatter me, sir."

"You're going to break my heart, aren't you?" Mack pressed a hand to his chest and whispered, "Be gentle."

Rather than reply right away, Willow deeply curtsied, her skirt rippling over the grass. "Thank you, for all you have done for Fillion and New Eden. You own my highest esteem and sisterly affections."

Mack grinned as she rose. "Do me a favor and never let Fillion win a fight. Drives him crazy, *desu*."

Fillion shot him a dark look. "Whose side are you on?"

"Told you weeks ago. Team Willow."

Mack wagged his eyebrows at Fillion who muttered words in Japanese. Seemingly pleased, his friend's grin widened.

"Shall we?" she said to Fillion, nodding her head toward the hawthorn altar. "My brother's impatient stare is burning holes into my back."

Fillion peered over her shoulder at her brother. "A parade? You shouldn't have."

"Well, I know how much you enjoy them so," Leaf quipped.

"Stop flirting with me, Leaf. People might get the wrong idea."

Mack sighed. "Jealousy activating." Then, as if bored, Fillion's waggish friend said, "No more stalling, *bishounen*. Let's do this thing before another Watson breaks my heart."

"Stop your jealous gritching. Pathetic." Fillion smirked at Mack. To Brother Markus, he said, "Go ahead."

Relieved to continue, the older monk lifted the flower-dressed cross and proceeded to march toward the stone bridge. Willow rested trembling fingers over Fillion's forearm, her shoulders straight, chin lifted. Skylar now walked to their side, recording the ceremony, much to her dismay. She agreed to Leaf's plan and desired to help Fillion win New Eden's freedom. Still, anxiety over so many watchful eyes bloomed bright in her mind and trickled to each limb. She knew Fillion felt much the same, using humor to diffuse his inner tension.

A few erratic heartbeats later, they stood beneath the hawthorn bower. Their family and close friends circled around the tree, except Skylar who stood in front of the altar, his Cranium now propped up on a strange three-legged contraption. The villagers crowded along the North Pond's shores and filled the glade.

Brother Markus reverently rested the cross against the trunk as people settled. He then lifted the ceremonial sash ribbons. "Daughter of Earth and Son of Eden," the monk began, "place your hands together."

Fillion covered both of her hands with his, as they had practiced briefly in her family apartment.

"Do you join together this day of your own free will?"

"Yes," they spoke in unison.

"Do you wish to voice any hesitations before your matri—er—*partnership* is sealed?"

Entirely reminiscent of the Dungeon Master, Fillion arched an eyebrow in blasé challenge, as if their handfasting bored him already though it had only just begun. She lifted her chin and narrowed her eyes to slits, her back straight. Pleased, he bit his bottom lip in a goading grin before mouthing the word, "brat." Laughter bubbled in her chest at his impertinence, but she could not allow him to have the last *silent* word. Narrowing her eyes farther, she mouthed the word, "knave," and then arched her brow to mock his.

Brother Markus looked between her and Fillion, forehead wrinkled and lips pursed. "Forgive me, but do you—"

"We hesitate no longer," Fillion deadpanned. "Carry on."

Humor sputtered from Willow's tight-lipped smile. Oh, how she loved this man's flippancy and wit.

"Let us begin, then," Brother Markus practically sighed in relief. "Blessed be this union with the gifts of the East." The monk draped one of the sashes over her and Fillion's joined hands. "Communication of the heart, mind, and body. Fresh beginnings with the rising of the Sun. The knowledge of the growth found in the sharing of silences."

Taking the other sash, he wrapped the ribbon under their hands. "Blessed be this union with the gifts of the South. Warmth of heart and home. The heat of heart's passion. The light created by both to illuminate the darkest of times."

Brother Markus looped the sashes together and pulled them into a loose knot. "Blessed be this union with the gifts of the West. The deep commitments of the lake. The swift excitement of the river. The refreshing cleansing of the rain. The all-encompassing passion of the sea."

The sash ends looped once more to form the final knot. "Blessed be this union with the gifts of the North. A firm foundation on which to build. Fertility of the fields to enrich your lives. A stable home to which you may always return."

The last line ended softly, and Brother Markus peered at Fillion with kindness. Quietly, just for their ears alone, the monk said, "May you find great peace in a stable home with Her Highness, Son of Eden."

Fillion swallowed and lowered his head. "Thanks," he whispered. Beneath dark strands, Fillion's gaze dropped to their knotted hands, his chest rising and falling in rhythm with hers. He desired family, she knew. To belong to a home where he was cherished and valued. The vulnerability and trust he community in that moment shattered any semblance of self-control she held. Tears gathered and fell, slipping down her cheeks and dripping onto their bound hands.

"I shall *never* tire of your love," she whispered to him.

His smile was shy and beautifully boyish as he met her eyes. "I'll *never* tire of loving you."

"I shall *forever* be your family."

"You'll *forever* be my haven."

Warmth deepened the wrinkles around the monk's eyes as he continued the handfasting rubric. "These are the hands that will love you and cherish you through the years for a lifetime of happiness.

"These are the hands that will countless times wipe the tears from your eyes—tears of sorrow and joy.

"These are the hands that will comfort you in illness, and hold you when fear or grief racks your mind.

"These are the hands that will hold you tight as you struggle through difficult times.

"These are the hands that will give you support and encourage you to chase your dreams."

The monk paused for breath. "We shall now exchange vows. Daughter of Earth, you shall go first."

For a moment, she could not find her voice nor remember the Outsider vows, plucked from ones Fillion had provided at her insistent instruction. New Eden's vows did not speak of equality or partnership, not like the relationship she and Fillion desired. The ones they settled on were written by a woman of Celtic descent. The knotted tie around their hands swept away the cobwebs rooting in her mind and she cleared her throat.

"You cannot possess me for I belong to myself," she began. "But while we both wish it, I give you that which is mine to give." The remembered words flowed from her soul to the tip of her tongue, and she smiled through her heart's tears. "You cannot command me, for I am a free person. But I shall serve you in those ways you require, and the honeycomb will taste sweeter coming from my hand."

Fillion repeated the same segment, eyes and lips flushed with emotion. His voice held the gentle loll of the wind, carrying her away to the moon and stars where her pulse danced. "I pledge to you," he continued on, "that yours will be the name I cry aloud in the night, and the eyes into which I smile in the morning. I pledge to you the first bite of my meat and the first drink from my cup."

She drew in a quivering breath, overcome as she echoed the new segment, adding, "I pledge to you my living and my dying, each equally in your care. I shall be a shield for your back and you for mine."

"I pledge to you my living and my dying," he quietly declared in return, "each equally in your care. I shall be a shield for your back and you for mine."

"I shall not slander you, nor you me," she proclaimed. "I shall honor you above all others, and when we quarrel we shall do so in private and tell no strangers our grievances."

Fillion paused half a heartbeat upon saying the word "quarrel" and she laughed at his devilish smile. "This is my handfasting vow to you," he finished. "This is the union of equals."

"This is my handfasting vow to you," she repeated in a thready whisper. "This is the union of equals."

For a blessed moment in time, she forgot about New Eden and court trials and the petty laws of men as she and Fillion stared at one another, enraptured.

"Now you are bound one to the other with a tie not easy to break," Brother Markus intoned, refocusing her attentions.

From a pouch on his belt, the older man retrieved ceremonial oil and poured a small pool into the palm of his hand. His bony finger drew a heart first onto Fillion's forehead and then onto hers, dribbling droplets of oil onto their hands. "May God be with you and bless you. May you see your children's children. May you be poor in misfortune and rich in blessings. May you know nothing but happiness from this day forward." With two fingers, the monk brushed the air in *signum crucis*. "*In nomine Patris, et Filii, et Spiritus Sancti*. Amen."

Willow released a laugh, unable to contain her joy.

"It is with great honor," Brother Markus announced, "that I pronounce you partners for life." To Fillion he said, "You may kiss your partner."

"May I?" Fillion asked her, leaning in close.

"You ask my permission to kiss me at the altar?" Willow asked, silently cursing the blush moving its way up her neck and face. "Is this customary in your world?"

"The old man doesn't decide how and when we kiss. Or any other goddamn person here."

"Oh." Willow blinked back the shock. "Yes, Son of Eden. You may kiss me, if you so desire."

"Desire," he whispered, his gaze slowly traveling to her lips, "is a weak word for what I feel."

A quivering rush of heat buckled her knees and inspired her breath to dance with his confession. He paused a heartbeat before her lips and celestial lights fell and twinkled in her pulse as she waited. Then his mouth brushed hers in gentle invitation. Honeyed wine had never tasted so divine as when coating his lips, she decided. And her heart burst into beams of moonlight as a heady emotion, an urge so utterly liquefying in its solidity, enthralled her senses. Much too soon, Fillion broke their kiss, his breath heavy on hers. She was not ready for him to move away, needing—*wanting*—more. A similar feeling softened his face as they studied each other's eyes.

"We have an audience," he whispered. "Until later, Maiden."

Cheers crashed through the melody dancing in her head and she swept a bashful glance over the friends and family circling around the linden tree. Their answering smiles and laughter deepened the flush warming her skin. Fillion ducked his head until black strands covered his face, though his smile remained unhidden—a smile that left her completely breathless.

Brother Markus tugged on the ceremonial sash ends to untie their knot. The sash fell away and Willow gingerly removed her hands, a bit faint. Any moment she feared her body might float into the heavenlies and never return. Grateful for a moment to gather her wits, she stepped back as Brother Markus retrieved a small knife from his pouch.

"You may carve your initials here," he said to Fillion, gesturing to the linden tree.

Sunlight glinted off the metal as Fillion inspected the carved pastoral scene etched into the bone handle. Falling to his knees gracefully, Fillion knelt before the linden tree, lifted the knife to the spot indicated, and paused. The community had reserved a space just below Joel and Della's initials. Fillion's eyes connected with Willow's in a bittersweet collision before he carved their initials into the trunk.

"As one story ends," Willow said to the wind, "so another begins."

"New Eden Township," Brother Markus shouted when Fillion rose and handed back the knife. "I present to you Fillion Malcolm Nichols and Willow Oak Watson, partners for life!"

Jubilant shouts and cries of celebration engulfed the glade. Coifs and ribbons streamed into the air. Fillion and Willow both grinned, receiving blessings and embraces from their close friends and family. Then, hand in hand, they took their first steps together as partners across the stone bridge and into the waiting crowd.

Showers of petal confetti rained down on her and Fillion and fluttered across the wild grass and ferns. Lifting her hand into the air, she caught a tattered blossom and considered the battered edges and spots of decay surrounded by shimmering life. "Delicate as hope and bruised with mourning," she murmured and then released Spring's delicate offer of renewal to the winds of change.

Under the old linden trees
Deep, fragrant dark spreading.
There were two of us
Yoshitsune and me
Silent
Silent
Silent

Linden blossoms
Quietly fell to the ground
And then, it was morning

— Ingrid, poet, 2012 *

I once had a thousand desires,
But in my one desire to know you
all else melted away.

— Rumi, 13th century *

Chapter Forty

Warbling amber light painted the meadow in hues of golden happiness. Willow sipped her mead and took in the swirling revelry from beside the crackling bonfire. The world tilted in pleasant dizziness and buzzed bright with each pocket of laughter offered to the night.

"Shall I have this dance?" Rain asked, bowing.

"Why yes," Willow replied equally as formal. "Sweep me off my feet."

Grabbing her hand, Rain tugged and mead sloshed from Willow's goblet. They squealed followed by bellows of laughter. Rain plucked the drink from Willow's hand and plopped it onto a nearby table. "We shall fetch you another after we dance! Now, come my May Queen."

The music held a natural pause and Willow used the opportunity to jump into the rollicking group of villagers, Rain beside her. The Celtic drum started up once more and they skipped to the beat through the grass and wildflowers. Merriment tipped her vision in swirls of fire and smoke. Light on her feet, she spun and clapped her hands along with the other dancers, falling onto Rain in laughter.

"Oh! Time to skip the other way!" Her friend sang out.

Willow straightened and clutched Rain's hands, dashing back toward the bonfire. Dark and light melded into blurry ribbons as she spun and clapped as before. Touching her head, Willow giggled and stumbled back a step.

"Spinning is dangerous sport, My Lady," Willow said. "The ground laughs and calls me closer."

"Come," Rain grabbed her hand once more and led her to a table laid out with spiced meats, sugared fruit, and various cheeses. "Nibble on this," her friend suggested, placing a Jack in the Green gingerbread biscuit into Willow's fingers.

"Handsome fellow," Willow said humorously. She picked off a raisin eye and popped the sweet, dried fruit into her mouth. "Shall I remove your green leaves next? I daresay I am ready to shed my own chaplet." She broke the head in half and sampled his parsley garland.

Across the bonfire from her, smoke hazed into the darkness beyond the halo of firelight. Fillion stood on the edge of the illuminated circle with Leaf, Mack, and Skylar, one foot in shadow and the other in light. He stared at the fractured sky while puffing on a joint, smiling at something Mack said, no doubt. That smile! The ground called to her once more as she melted into the moss and wildflowers. Fillion flicked the ashes and then looked her way in a single soft blink, holding her gaze. The invisible thread knitting her heart with his plucked with longing.

Ember sidled up beside her. "Go," the Daughter of Fire encouraged, peering into the darkness behind Willow. "He shall follow."

"Where shall I go?"

Her sister smiled in that knowing way of hers and Willow angled her head toward her shoulder. "You suggest I appear wanton before the community?"

"No one shall notice your departure." Ember gestured to the small groups engrossed in conversation and drink. "He is waiting for you to leave your friends."

Rain wove her fingers with Willow's and squeezed. "Shall I fetch you another goblet?"

She shook her head, not wishing to be any more addled than her current flush. Squeezing her friend's hand back, Willow smiled and then slipped into the shadows of the meadow, leaving her friends behind. Tingles warmed her back where she knew *he* watched until she faded into the shadows.

The night wove around her in threads of black and blue. Drum beats seduced her pulse and bewitched her steps as she swayed through flowers and grass toward a copse of trees near the South Cave. Unable to resist the beat, she twirled, giggling to herself. Mayhap she had indulged in too much mead.

The white bark of birch and cypress trees glowed in the reflective moonlight. Wrapping her arm around the thin trunk of a birch tree, she swung around to face the bonfire and her breath caught. Not too far in the distance, a shadow moved toward her, the orange glow of his joint dotting the smoke-smudged darkness.

"Hey," he said, leaning his hip on the birch tree beside her.

"Hay?" Willow sputtered through soft laughter. "Do you always great young women as though barn animals?"

He lifted the joint to his lips to hide his smile. "Says the young woman who called me a stunned goat."

She laughed and leaned her head on his chest. "You are a handsome goat, though."

"Mm..." Fillion murmured. "Are you saying I'm pretty, not smart?"

"You did confess that I make you stupid."

"True." He kissed her neck just below her earlobe and whispered, "Let's disappear."

"Where, my love?" A shiver of pleasure wended down her spine and settled in her core. "I shall follow you anywhere."

"I have a surprise for you in the rainforest."

Willow stepped back. "The rainforest? Why must all secrets happen in the rainforest?"

"Anywhere but the rainforest?" Fillion raised an eyebrow.

"The rainforest has snakes."

"You're afraid of snakes?"

"They are dreadful company." She shuddered.

A flirtatious smile flitted across his lips. "I didn't invite any snakes to our private party."

"Well, then, I suppose." She sauntered away from him and stopped. "The condensation shall ruin my dress."

"I guess you'll have to take it off." He winked as he passed by her, puffing on his joint again.

Willow's jaw slackened at his brazen suggestion. Amble through the jungle in only her shift? Memories of this morning around the linden tree floated back and she gnawed the inside of her lip. Since they were equals, it was only fair she demand her own pleasures in return. Warnings and lessons on propriety elevated her trepidations in behaving so. Still, she marched up to his side, head held high.

"'Twould be a shame for your tunic to ruin as well."

He spun on his heel, walking backwards, gray eyes fixed on her lips, and then he pulled the tunic over his head while somehow still holding onto his joint. Disheveled strands fell across his face in the fluid motion. He flashed his eyes at her, the challenge in his gaze as sensual as it was infuriating. "Any other requests?"

Her face flamed, not only with his question but with standing before a man half dressed. Silvered light softly touched his toned muscles and marks, and her eyes wandered over him unabashedly as yearnings quickly replaced manners. A slow grin appeared as he bit his bottom lip and winked. Then he swiveled on his heel to walk forward.

"Your move," he tossed over his shoulder.

Inked symbols cascaded down the length of his spine and she pressed a hand to her chest at the sight. His breeches were tight and hung low on his hips and she could not look away—nor did she wish to—though a lady should. Now she regretted turning away a goblet of mead. Dear Lord, he was beautiful for a man.

The South Cave soon swallowed their forms and Fillion felt for her hand. He flicked the end of his joint onto the path and ground it into the rocks without breaking stride. Fingers interlocked, they moved in silence toward the wooden door.

Besotted and weakened by his every touch, her breath came quick and her head swam in dizzy circles. More so when accepting the truth in his scandalous suggestion. She really should remove her silk gown before entering the rainforest. And, if she were to undress before a man, she would rather do so in the near-blackness of this cave.

Willow pulled her hand from his and slowed her steps. "I do not have attendants."

"I'll need to touch you."

"Yes," she whispered, turning her back to him. "You have my permission."

He gathered up her longs strands, pressing his mouth to the back of her exposed neck while lowering her hair over one shoulder. The Celtic drums reverberated off the stone walls of the cave in a seductive rhythm and danced in her pulse. Drowsy sensations intoxicated every nerve-ending igniting her body, especially when his fingers tugged and pulled on the laces of her dress. The silk slid down her arms and she covered her chest to catch the fabric.

Willow peered over her shoulder, though she could barely make out his form in the black. "Thank you," she said.

"No prob."

She appreciated his sensitivity this moment, not offering flirtations or witticisms. Slowly, she allowed the silk to fall to the cave floor and then she stepped out of the pooled gown. Cool air brushed along her skin and goosebumps prickled down her arms and torso. The simple shift she wore did little to warm what the thin fabric did cover. He said nothing as she folded the silk garment as small as possible and bundled the smooth fabric to her chest.

"I am ready," she said.

The large wooden door creaked open a breath later and sultry air chased away the chill. Birds and insects sang to the night in a raucous symphony. Fillion paused by the entry and she squinted her eyes to better see his silhouette. A small light flickered to life in his hands. Her breath hitched in delight at the personal mechanical torch. Outsider technology frightened her, mostly. But sometimes, such as now, personal devices of convenience sparked her wonder and curiosity. She tilted her head as he lit a lantern that he had stored by the biome door.

Golden light spilled over the bare skin of his chest, arms, and stomach. Her gaze roamed over his tattoos, captivated by each one. Feathers unfurled across his winged chest in intricate detail, singed and on fire as they collided with the tree ablaze on his upper arm. Stars began under his arm and traveled in a diagonal line down his side to his stomach, dipping below his hips. Bashful, she lifted her eyes to his face and almost forgot how to breathe as his gaze caressed her nearly undressed state as well.

Taking her fingers in his, he gently kissed the palm of her hand and then her wrist. "I have wine waiting for us," he said. "And chocolate truffles."

"Chocolate?" Her eyes grew wide.

His lips twitched. "Truffles."

"I have not had the pleasure of chocolate-covered truffles, though I have read of this fungal delicacy in books."

Fillion's smile grew. "No, not mushrooms. Even better. You'll see."

"Now that I know chocolate and wine are involved, I will surely follow you anywhere, even through the rainforest."

"Ouch." He placed a hand over his bleeding-heart tattoo. "Thanks."

"It would be immodest of me to confess *other* reasons, though I still have my reservations," she teased, surprised by her brazenness.

Fillion took a step closer. "Such as?"

"Not wishing to dirty my shift or stain my gown, naturally."

"Remove your shift and wrap it around your gown."

Her eyes widened and he laughed at the shock spreading across her face. But she could not allow him to win. "Be a gentleman and lend me your tunic instead." Fillion's humor faded into mock boredom as he handed over his discarded garment, which she quickly used to cover her gown. "Shall we?" She gestured to the path. "I am eager to sample chocolate truffles."

"Just the chocolate truffles?"

"Oh no, My King. You mentioned wine, did you not?"

Fillion playfully rolled his eyes at her wit and turned toward the path when boldness flamed through her veins. Willow tugged on his hand and pulled him back to her. Their bodies connected in the momentum and a delicious warmth spread to each of her limbs at the feel of his skin against hers.

"Fillion . . ." she whispered.

"Yes, Maiden?" he whispered back.

She placed a hand onto his bare chest and rose on tip-toes, capturing his lips with hers. Not expecting her assertiveness, he sucked in a ragged breath and then softly moaned into their kiss. A wild sensation rushed through her as though she were falling, weightless. His free arm wrapped around her waist and pulled her closer, his fingers clutching the folds of her shift. The falling sensation intensified, and she feared her legs would grow too weak to traverse the jungle if she did not stop.

Gently, she eased from his embrace and created distance, their eyes locked. She could not hide the tenderness in her gaze, nor the unadulterated *want*. The feeling was overwhelming and her chest heaved for breath as she drowned in one emotion after another. Fillion grinned at her unladylike forwardness, a look so utterly boyish it took all her self-control to tear her gaze from his and move toward the path.

They ambled through the jungle, fingers intertwined. Condensation dripped from leaves and gathered on her skin. Now damp, her shift clung to her body and she blushed, knowing the thinness revealed every dip and curve. Eventually the overgrown foliage cleared as the Dragon Bridge filled her vision. Mist shrouded the carved stones and shimmered in the soft moonlight. Her hand traced the curved arch of the dragon's spine and moss-covered scales. The waterfall roared before them in sheets of glistening silver and they paused their journey to appreciate the magic.

Fillion traced a single finger down her cheek with his free hand. Leaning down, he brushed a soft kiss across her lips. "Ready for the surprise?"

"In the hatch?"

"We're going to walk on water."

Willow leaned back. "You jest."

Fillion didn't answer her with words. His smile said it all. Tugging on her hand, he encouraged her forward to the banks of Step Stone Pond. Along the edge of the biodome wall, he unlaced his combat boots, pushed up his breeches, and then stepped onto the water. She covered her mouth, waiting for the splash, but it never came. His feet sank only a little as he took another large step. Then he held his hand out to her.

"Take your shoes off and hike up your skirt."

Willow followed his instructions and gripped his hand, grimacing against the unknown as she stepped where he indicated. Her foot touched stone and her gaze flew to his in wonderment. A laugh loosened from her chest as she practically skipped across the hidden stones with him. They ducked inside a larger-than-expected opening behind the crashing curtain of water and hopped onto the banks of a clandestine alcove.

Warbled light undulated across the stone walls, dressed in orchids of every color imaginable. Large pillows and thick blankets filled most of the available space, dotted by flower blossoms and petals. Two baskets occupied a corner, filled with fruits, nuts, cheese, and pastries. Beside the baskets rested several bottles of wine and two goblets. A blue instrument held her greatest attention, however, and she tip-toed over to the musical apparatus and inspected the wood and strings.

"Is this your gu-gui—"

"Guitar."

"You shall play for me?"

Fillion lifted his shoulder in a slight shrug. "If you want."

"This place is otherworldly." She sighed and turned in a slow circle and stopped when facing a door. "Where does this lead?"

"Into the technosphere. Here," he said holding out his hand. "Hand me your gown. I'll hang it up for you."

"Where?"

"On the door. I brought hangers for us. Ember packed a dress for you, too. In case you wanted to wear something different when we return tomorrow."

"You thought of all this?"

Fillion shrugged again. "I travel a lot. The flower petals weren't me, though. Mack is strangely romantic sometimes."

His friend was adorable, a trait she had never known in a grown man until now. Though she had never seen a man in a skirt, either. Everything about Mack challenged her society's ideas of men and women and she found the oddity refreshing. But it was Mack's playful banter and his unapologetic public affections for Fillion that won her heart.

Draping an arm across her chest, she gave Fillion her bundled gown. In many ways, Fillion carried similar feminine traits, though undeniably masculine. Perhaps the Outside world viewed gender much the same as other values: without ceremony or tradition. The very idea fascinated her as she watched

Fillion walk behind the pillows and blankets and proceed to hang her dress with care, hanging up his tunic as well. Then he poured two goblets of wine.

She accepted the cup, suddenly shy. "Thank you."

They sipped on the wine, both lost to their own thoughts. The thick jungle air seemed to thicken even more as the atmosphere charged with building energy.

Moonshine enchanted the waterfall in blues and silvers. Mist slithered across the pond in spectral ribbons. Water lapped onto the alcove's banks in a soothing lullaby compared to the roaring aria of the waterfall.

Here, she felt secluded, wholly transported away from the community. To be alone with a man—with *him*— without fear of public shame or discovery thrilled her sensibilities. And, she realized, as much as she had feared the idea of intimacy before, she was not afraid of him. And *that* changed everything.

Fillion's brows pushed together as he stared into his goblet. Clearing his throat, he asked, "So, the guitar?"

"Yes," she breathed, smiling. "I long to hear you play your beloved instrument."

He gulped down his wine and set down his goblet.

Beneath lowered lashes, Willow appreciated how muscle and sinew rippled across his back as he moved to fetch his instrument. The hard lines of a man's body intrigued her, only knowing the softness of a woman's. Looking away, she melted into the nest of blankets and fell back against a pillow, sipping her wine with a satisfied sigh.

This reprieve from normalcy felt gloriously indulgent. The alcove's magic washed over her in a warm embrace and she stretched out her legs and sank deeper into the pillows. Willow tipped up her goblet and drank heartily, removing her arm from across her chest to fall at her side.

Fillion settled beside her, situating a basket of treats, their opened bottle of wine, and his guitar. She refilled her goblet, curious as his head pressed to the body of the guitar and his fingers turned knobs. With a shy glance her way, he then began a haunting melody that echoed softly off the stones. His fingers flew across the lower strings of his instrument while different fingers slid in strange positions over the upper strings.

Sorrow and longing sang to the waters, the melancholy tune akin to falling bio-rain. Each note dripped from his fingers and splashed onto her soul. Closing her eyes, tears formed and slipped down her cheeks as a tragic tale of love and loss wove through the air. Just when she thought her heart could bear no more, he changed to a new song. And, oh, how the music danced within her blood and enthralled her mind. Entire worlds opened before her imagination. She could feel the rushing wind through a canopy of pine trees. She could glimpse snowfall on mountain tops. Her feet seemed to traverse cold cobblestone as she climbed a grand stairway in a castle tower that touched a pregnant sky.

He played song after song, each one equally as unique and haunting. His foot tapped to each beat and his body swayed back and forth, as if carried away by the very melodies his fingers plucked. Enraptured, she closed her eyes while toying with the linden leaf necklace dangling from her neck as a song transitioned from adoration to an emotionally charged silence. The air fairly vibrated with his energy. Her eyelids fluttered open and caught his gaze right when he began to sing.

Dear Lord in Heaven, his voice—it ached and smoldered.

At the sound, suns rose and set in her heart and ignited her body in glittering rivers of pleasure. Every part of her burned as his lyric's adulating heat kissed her pulse, only to blaze anew when he began strumming a fervent melody to accompany his song's poetry. The invisible thread connecting their hearts caught fire and she hummed a harmony. So lost was she to the passion his music stirred, she continued to sing her melody when his stopped.

Fillion lifted his fingers from the strings, beguiled. Her lilting voice was earthy and ethereal. Quietly, he set his guitar behind the pillows and knelt beside her while she continued to hum and sing unaware. Her lips flushed with wine. Thin fabric, transparent from the water vapor, clung to her breasts and draped over her body down to her ankles. God, she was unbelievably beautiful.

"I could listen to you sing all day," he said. Gently, he coaxed the wine from her fingers to set behind their pillows.

Willow's eyes flew open on a smile.

"And I you, My King." She repositioned to sit on her knees, like him. "Your music is magic to my soul."

"You're magic to my soul." Fillion wanted to cringe with his words. Seriously? His small-talk skills were forever the bane of his existence and his pulse groaned for him. Willow didn't seem bothered by his corny sentiments. He, however, was beginning to freak out. She had the power to break him this night. He knew the truth. He knew his value. But it was hard to shut off the voices in his head.

A pretty blush colored her cheeks as she whispered, "I long to know your love and give you mine." Her fingers trailed along his jaw, down the length of his neck, until her hand rested on the broken heart tattoo. His skin danced under her touch and his muscles tensed.

God, he couldn't breathe. He'd never "made love" before, whatever that actually meant. Didn't matter. Regardless, this was the point of no return in their relationship. She stared at him boldly, even though he knew she was just as nervous as him. But that was Willow—always brave, always strong, while he fought endless anxiety and self-doubt. He could tease, flirt, and kiss. Sex, however, was something else. Redemption would only come if he lost himself to her completely, he knew. To fall off the edge of reasoning. To learn what it meant to belong to someone he craved for all the right reasons.

Not sure of what to do, he opened his mouth to ask for consent—and froze. Looking away, bashful, she slid the straps of her shift down her arms until the thin garment fell to the ground. All words died off as his eyes roamed over the soft curves of her body, creamy white skin and shadows, long golden hair rippling to her waist, all made more alluring by the dim, silvered glow of the waterfall. And, he swore, his heart stopped beating. All vitals flat-lined. This very moment, he was certifiably dead.

"…Beautiful."

Willow ducked her head, shoulders raised, but said "kiss me," with a certainty that confirmed permission.

He drew in a breath. His heart rate sprang into a gallop. In a single touch, his lips rested on hers, and he drowned in sensations, intoxicated by the intimacy. Being on the edge of letting go had never felt so good. His fingers grazed her back, electricity sparking with each contact. Another breath, another heartbeat, and passion ignited into an explosion that set their bodies into motion. His mouth moved against hers, searching, wanting, and she replied, her kisses and touches drinking him in, matching his feverish longing.

Fillion lowered her to the blankets and pillows beneath him. Long, wavy tresses spilled over the small clusters of tiny white and pink blossoms. Their movements crushed several of the flowers and infused the air with their honeyed scent.

Reaching over their pillow, he grabbed a chocolate and placed the truffle against her mouth. She took a bite and moaned. He plopped the other half into his mouth, then sank into her kisses again.

"Chocolate and kisses," she said, breathless. "I am undone."

Her playful yet trusting intimacy held his mind captive while they ate more chocolate, sipped wine, and kissed as their foreplay transcended physical pleasures to something else entirely. It was if her soul touched his in a way only their hearts understood while his body discovered the rhythm of hers.

Slowly, erotically—unable to contain his building emotions—he traced his fingers over her breasts and down her stomach, confessing, "I want to worship every inch of you."

"In your worship, what shall you pray?" Willow whispered back between stirred breaths. "Make your confessions, and I shall grant you your heart's desire."

Damn. She wanted talk during sex? His aroused mind nearly fainted at her invitation to verbally play. Now *he* was undone. Tangling his fingers into her hair, he tilted her head back and kissed the exposed skin of her neck. "I pray," he began, brushing his lips beneath her earlobe, "that you would continue to show me what it means love and be loved."

"I shall love you until my last breath." She sighed deep and long. "And then, I shall love you for all eternity."

Tasting the skin of her neck once more, he traveled down and pressed a light kiss into her collarbone. "I pray," he whispered, "for your grace. I want to see myself the way you do."

"I am captivated with each perfection you possess," she murmured into his hair. "But I am in love with each and every one of your scars. Your soul, in all its complexities, is achingly beautiful to me."

Overcome, he stilled. She was in love with his scars? His imperfections? His impurities? Humbled, he met her eyes as acceptance flamed through him. Heat poured into his veins and set his heart on fire to a new rhythm—and he felt so alive, so in tune with her and life and everything around him.

"I pray," he whispered, his voice catching, "for your forgiveness. I'm . . . I'm going to make mistakes. Have made mistakes. God, I'm so scared I'll hurt you or ruin everything. Ruin us. You. I'm trying to learn, but I still don't know how to do this."

Willow caressed his face and brought his lips to hers. "There is nothing to forgive, My King," she whispered. "For we all make mistakes. I know your heart. Forgive yourself."

"How?"

Fingers moved up his torso until her hand caressed the bleeding organ inked into his skin. "Set me as a seal upon thine heart"—her hand moved to the willow oak tree tattooed into his forearm—"as a seal upon thine arm; for love is strong as death: jealousy is cruel as the grave"—her other hand slid up his arm to the symbol of New Eden Enterprises, and she traced the fire as it curled and licked up his arm—"the coals thereof are coals of fire, which hath a most vehement flame."

His breath caught then rushed from him. Willow's fingers left the flames on his arm and trailed over his bottom lip as she continued.

"Many waters cannot quench love, neither can floods drown it: if a man would give all the substance of his house for love, it would utterly be contemned."

He kissed the tips of her fingers, then the palm of her hand. "You honor me."

"'Tis the Holy Scriptures. They are pledges of love from a king to his bride, a powerful man of unspeakable riches and intelligence. He played the political games demanded of him by the world, but he gave his undying love to her."

Fillion locked eyes with Willow as the words played back in his mind. Somehow through the war of thoughts, he asked, "And the bride? How does she feel?"

Her mouth curved with a flirtatious smile. "Let him kiss me with the kisses of his mouth," she said, drawing him closer. "For thy love is better than wine."

An entire universe exploded into existence with her last words, searing and intense. Vulnerability faded into her nebula of rage, the one that had grieved over his brokenness and fought for him to know truth. And this . . . this passion. Holy shit. He thought pissing her off and kissing her anger was hot. He had played with fire then—a small, flickering flame. Now? He intimately knew the surface of the sun and burned, an unquantifiable damage that incinerated every desire to go back to the insecure man he was before.

A look of rapture softened her face as he explored her body. She gasped under his touch and he caught the sensual sounds in a provocative kiss. Willow clutched his hair as their kiss deepened into a hunger that could only be satiated by drawing closer. So, he pulled away. Wanting to tease her awakened senses. Smiling when her body arched for more of him. Quietly laughing when she threw a mock-glare his direction.

But he couldn't stay away for long.

Heady with longing, he dipped down for another kiss and she playfully turned her head away with a mischievous smile. He laughed again. She was such a brat. This was his game and he wouldn't let her win. His mouth fell onto her neck once more, moaning her name as her skin slid across his until nothing separated them. No *nevers*. Not different worlds. No inhumane laws.

Shit. She could win every time.

And, god, he couldn't get enough of her. His heart pounded her name with force, each beat hypnotizing. Pleasure throbbed and ebbed, whispered through ragged breaths and soft sounds, dancing from her body to his.

"I love you, Willow Oak," he said in between kisses. "God, I love you so much."

She whispered back, "You are my heart and soul, Fillion Nichols."

He smiled against her mouth and she smiled in reply. Then he rolled her on top of him, dying with want while her hair draped across his face. Delirious, his arms fell above his head as his eyelids slid shut, hazy with ecstasy. He was drunk on her. His head swirling, buzzing, consumed with how her breath pulsed across his skin. The way her body moved against his. The warmth of her kisses on his lips. Arrested, his broken heart colliding with hers again and again, he let go of all control, becoming whole, new—sanctified.

Love wasn't a fairytale or a painkiller that dulled with time. It was the most beautiful reality he had ever known.

New Eden Enterprises CEO and President Fillion Nichols celebrates a massive victory in court this morning. After three years of intense deliberations, the U.S. Supreme Court has ruled in favor of Nichols and overturned human property laws in a case that effects the majority of human experimentation cases across the nation. Those include Nichols' own New Eden Township, the famed Mars prototype commune, which is no longer under experimentations status. The residents, under the commune's leadership structure headed by Leaf Watson, are now free to explore asylum on the biodome's lab property.

Leaked sources confirm negotiations between Nichols and U.S. government agencies to create similar communities across the nation. After the human rights documentary, Eco-Crafting Eden II, *gained unprecedented Net ratings, economists believe the government will proceed with contracts to ease homeless burdens. These planned communities also would serve as Community Service Rehabilitation Programs for delinquent youths to work off their sentences and relieve overcrowding in the nation's correctional facilities.*

Sources close to Nichols say his goal is to rebuild purpose for his generation in an economy where automation and robots fill most of the jobs.

Also today, several individuals and corporations were indicted for conspiring with the late Hanley Nichols in negligence, fraud, and multiple counts of murder, notably Gen. Stephen Claussen, previously the director of Mars Operations at NASA who sold Stellar Dock Corp. to Hanley Nichols in spring 2058. HiraMed Technology also is under fire and involved in an international investigation, with an additional spotlight on tech heiress Akiko Hirabayashi who, after emerging evidence, is believed to be connected to Dr. Della Jayne Nichols' plane crash and disappearance.

— *Global Press*, "Nichols Claims Victory in Human Property Trials," July 11, 2061

Chapter Forty-One

New Eden Township, Salton Sea, California

Monday, July 11, 2061

Fillion pushed through the crowded vigil, dashed up the stairs to his second story apartment, and slammed open the door, out of breath. Villagers had clapped his back and congratulated him. But his mind couldn't process the external stimulation. Only Willow owned his thoughts. So much so, the town car had barely rolled to a stop inside the wrought iron gates before he jumped out and sprinted into New Eden Township, Mack close on his heels.

Candles flickered from wall sconces and cast the room in dancing shadows. His eyes didn't know where to settle in the room until Leaf, Coal, Lynden, and Laurel rose from their chairs.

"Finally," Coal muttered.

"Is she—"

A scream—more like a growl—echoed from his and Willow's bedroom.

Fillion's heart lodged in his throat then plummeted to his stomach. "Shit."

"She fares well," Leaf began, blinking nervously. "Perhaps worked up, but otherwise hale and hearty."

"Worked up?" Fillion asked, raising an eyebrow. "I flew here as soon as I received Lyn's message. Left in the middle of a press briefing."

Mack limped into the apartment and bent over his knees, panting. "Please . . . tell me . . . we arrived in . . . time."

"Where is that vexing man?!"

Willow's muffled shout soured the already nauseating pool of dread in

Fillion's gut.

"I love that woman," his friend murmured on a sigh, still short of breath. "Ms. Willow-o-the-wisp is a Scorpio, right?"

"Oh god." Blood drained from Fillion's head and the room tilted on its side. "How . . . how did this happen?" He didn't mean to speak his awkward rhetorical question aloud, realizing his mistake when Mack threw him a straight look.

"Well, *bishounen*, when a mommy and daddy love each very much—"

A loud thud interrupted Mack's speech. Laurel squeaked and jumped back. Something hard hit the wall in his room. Fillion lifted his shoulders, biting the inside of his cheek. Everyone in the room peered down the hallway then back to him.

Mack placed a hand on his shoulder. "Rest in peace, mate."

Fillion swallowed, unable to tear his gaze away from his bedroom door. Gradually, however, he met Leaf's eyes. "Is this normal?"

The Son of Earth shook his head, working hard to hold back an amused smile. Coal's sputtered laughter ruined the illusion of Leaf's control. Soon, both men shook with humor while Laurel gaped at them, horrified.

"Try to show some semblance of feeling, Your Majesty," Laurel snapped at her brother. Now fifteen, the newest Daughter of Earth glared at Leaf and then Coal. "This is our sister, after all. She suffers, and you laugh?"

This made Coal laugh even harder.

"They're laughing at Fillion," Lynden said to Laurel. "We'll let them." His sister stuck her tongue out at him. But he was panicking too much to give a damn. Or reply.

The bedroom door opened and Ember's voice softly called out, "Is he here?"

Leaf, Coal, and Mack all shouted, "Yes!" followed by stifled laughs.

"Send him back, please, before Her Highness decides to march out and demand an audience herself."

Fillion thought he was going to throw up. The whole idea of becoming a father was terrifying enough without watching Willow in delivery. What the hell was he thinking? He should have been sterilized years ago, like Mack.

He slammed the door on that thought.

It wasn't his child's fault Fillion didn't know what in the hell to do. Pregnancy was weird enough. Shit. Should he swear when thinking about his kid? Dammit. Maybe. No. Whatever. It's not like he was around that much to be a bad influence. These past few years were rough. He was so lonely while traveling for work—which was most of the time. Now he'd have Willow *and* their child to miss. There may be some reprieve, though, now that the human property law trial was done as of this morning. No more court for a while since guilty parties in a spin-off trial were just indicted this afternoon. The next court date wasn't for another couple of months. But today? He finally earned New Eden's freedom, and Willow wanted to destroy him.

"Shit."

He was mentally rambling.

And he needed to stop swearing before he entered his bedroom.

Wait. Fetuses began developing language skills in the womb. Fuck.

Focus.

But he couldn't. Positives and negatives warred inside his head. An innocent, codependent human being would be subjected to Fillion's nature and his nurture, not to mention his total lack of parenting skills. Too terrifying a thought. Better to rant about good things.

New Eden Township was free.

Free.

After years of deliberations and social campaigns, the U.S. Supreme Court ruled in Fillion's favor. His own child wouldn't be property of the lab. Neither was Fillion or any other resident. Robotics laws also no longer applied, based on their transhuman status. In fact, new laws were being written to protect their augmented existence and fully recognize their humanity.

Tears pricked the back of his eyes and the room dimmed around the edges. He shifted on his feet, bending his knees. Elation and terror combusted in his bloodstream and stole the air in his lungs.

"I think he's going to black out." Mack's voice was distant, like his friend spoke from a tunnel. Another muffled groan emerged from Fillion's bedroom. A chair was pushed up behind him and a voice encouraged him to sit. He stepped toward the hallway instead.

"I, uh . . ." Fillion took in a deep breath and released it slowly. "I'll be right back." Bile coated his throat and his head spun in orbit around the vacuum of space in his mind.

"He's going in," Mack's voice held a touch of awe despite the greenish shade to his skin. "Brave lad, going to the front lines."

Laurel sighed with annoyance and rolled her eyes.

Leaf and Coal both grinned.

But Lynden appeared as sick as he felt.

Willow groaned again and Fillion's steps faltered. From behind, he could hear Mack tell the room he was going to check on Andra and would return. Bastard. Running out on Fillion. Lynden quickly offered her company, but Coal asked her to stay with him. Seriously? Even his sister wanted to bail. God, Fillion needed a cigarette and a couple shots of whiskey. Then he rolled his eyes. Here he was being a self-absorbed coward while Willow writhed in pain on the other side of the wall.

At the door, Fillion held his breath and knocked before pushing in the iron ring. The lantern-lit room buzzed with activity. In the center, Willow sat on a wooden birthing stool and held a rope secured to the rafters of their ceiling. Sweat plastered strands of hair to her head as her teeth clenched in a grimace. Joannah dipped a rag into a bowl of water and dabbed Willow's flushed face and neck.

"You are doing well," Brianna encouraged. "Not long now."

Willow hissed through her teeth but stopped when noting him in the doorway, her eyes narrowing into furious slits. The women in the room spurred into action, grabbing any object nearby and moving them out of Willow's reach.

By his feet, remnants of the wall dusted the floor around a wooden tumbler she had hurled.

"Change your expression!" Willow gritted. "Stunned goats belong in the barns, not my birthing room."

Leaf and Coal snickered from the living room. Bastards. All of them. He'd flip them off if Laurel wasn't in the room. Gently, Fillion shut the door and faced Willow, trying hard to school his features and remain present.

She sneered his way once again. "Do not touch me."

"Noted."

The others in the room—Ember, Joannah, Timna, and Brianna—all busied with something and pretended he wasn't an awkward idiot pressed against his bedroom door.

Another contraction hit Willow and she yanked on the rope with shaking arms, leaning forward. A low growl shuddered from her body. The room blurred and Fillion gulped in a large breath.

"Come, Your Majesty," Brianna encouraged him. "You should sit before we have two patients in our care." She turned to Joannah. "Give His Majesty a mug of cider."

Fillion hesitated to move toward Willow, not wanting to piss her off even more. Timna, noting his uncertainty, sidled beside him and whispered, "Her neocortex has turned off, which happens to all women in labor. Over-stimulation is common in this state." He nodded, appreciating the explanation. Science he could process. Joannah placed a mug in his hands with a polite smile as the Naturopath continued. "Her limbic system has taken over, which controls basic functions and instincts. Side effects of this are intense focus and a driving need for space. The combination, however?"

"Makes her primal," Fillion answered. "Animal."

"Indeed." Timna smiled kindly. "Our Willow is already fierce without the hormones of birth influencing her tenacity."

"Thanks for the info," he said, taking a much-needed sip of cider.

"Fare better, Your Majesty?" she asked.

Surprisingly, he did. Refocusing his attention onto Willow, an understanding smile touched his lips. Ferocity glittered in her eyes as she challenged him from across the room, and he blinked at her slowly.

"May I sit by you?" he asked.

"This pain is—"

"My fault," he tossed out casually.

Fury flushed her already reddened skin. "You dare take credit for my pain?"

"Technically, I can take half of the credit."

All of Willow's attendants flashed warning looks his way.

"You arrogant, pigheaded arse!"

"Pretty much." He sipped the cider nonchalantly. But, really, he wanted to laugh at the shocked gasps at her language. "Now that we've established that I'm an asshole who causes you nothing but pain, can I sit by you?"

She bared her teeth at him. "So you may taunt me more with your insensitivities?"

Fillion wanted to snap back that it didn't matter what he said. He was already the bad guy. Instead, he remembered to focus on the positive.

"I want to share good news with you."

She tensed and growled through another contraction, her knuckles turning white as she gripped the rope and pulled. He'd seen a lot of medieval technology, but this one was the strangest. He thought women gave birth in beds, on their backs.

"Breathe through the pain," Brianna coached. "There you go. Think of holding your precious child. Work with your muscles to deliver your babe to you." Brianna shot him an irritated glare over her shoulder. "We need her to relax."

Fillion let out another slow breath. "Willow, I have news. I can share it from here or beside you. Your choice."

"There," she spat. "I do not wish to smell you."

"Smell me?" He looked to Timna for an explanation who nodded slightly with a crooked smile. Was this another primal instinct thing? Or something random in the delusions of pain? "Uh, OK. Sure. I'll stay back."

Fillion locked eyes with Willow and nearly stopped breathing. Again. God, she was beautiful. Her savagery was as otherworldly as it was humbling. For years, her warrior spirit had championed him. Now she fought for their family and he stared, moved by her strength and bravery.

"Our child," he began, choking back his emotion, "will be the first human born free in New Eden."

All the women turned slowly, eyes wide with growing smiles. Willow, however, began sobbing. The emotion that was knotted in Fillion's chest liquefied and his tears joined hers.

"We did it," he whispered hoarsely. "We won."

She started laughing and he softly smiled her way, overcome by the sound. He had cut all the strings and walked away. Well, all but one. Neither John or Colin had found a way to legally abdicate inheritance in the Legacy. But they had fourteen years to worry about this problem, when Alder Dylan Watson would take the throne as New Eden's King and Aether, six years before Fillion's own child would become majority owner of New Eden Biospherics & Research.

The smile slipped from Willow's face when another contraction hit. The joy, however, remained in her eyes.

"You are close," Brianna said. "Picture a beautiful, swaddled babe in your arms and push."

Joannah brought him a chair and gestured to the seat. "Many a man has fainted during delivery."

He nodded his thanks as he eased into the chair and placed the cider beneath the seat. Timna moved behind Willow, who now leaned against the Naturopath, eyes closed in concentration. Ember held her hand and spoke gentle words of encouragement.

"Exhale," Brianna instructed to Willow. "Now draw in a deep breath, hold it, and push."

They continued in this pattern for the next thirty minutes. Fillion remained quiet and tried to calm his thundering heart rate. The agony on Willow's face was killing him, especially because he knew his world could remove the pain. That wasn't New Eden's way, though.

"The head is crowning." Brianna smiled at Willow. "Just another push."

He'd taken a lot of science classes and seen a lot of things over the years. Nothing had prepared him for the actual violence of birth, or the amount of blood. "Holy shit," he whispered under his breath right before his stomach purged. He found an empty bowl and retched. The room began to spin, and he stumbled to his bed, sank onto the edge, and vomited again.

A baby's cry filled the room. Fillion grimaced with heartache, too afraid to look. Every fear battered his self-worth. Every memory of torment and pain. He did this. He helped create the life he could destroy. Voices shouted instructions to help Willow but Brianna's announcement rose above them all.

"You have a son."

Stunned, his gaze whipped toward Willow, and then Fillion saw him. His son. A sob exploded from Fillion's gut as his boy, his child, wailed and drew in his first breaths of life. Synapses pistoned at rapid fire as meaning and purpose expanded to include a definition of love that was incomprehensible to Fillion. It wasn't like how he felt for Willow, his sister, or Mack. The emotion ripped apart his life and fused back together a new man—a more complete man. A powerful bond had clicked into place. It was tangible, visceral. In these few nanoseconds, Fillion knew he'd live and die for his son. He'd fight for his every happiness and would be willing to destroy entire worlds just to protect him.

Small arms and legs pumped the air with each gust. Thick, dark hair covered his head and tiny red lips quivered as he cried out. Willow cradled the small body to her breast. Tears streamed as the most beautiful smile Fillion had ever seen lit her face.

"Welcome, Ashton Mackenzie Nichols. I love you," she said and laughed when their son released another angry cry. Lifting her eyes to Fillion's, she beckoned, "Come and meet your son, my love. He is a handsome lad."

Fillion didn't remember walking to Willow's side. He didn't even remember sitting down. Or that the cup of cider was once again in his hands. His eyes were riveted to the writhing bundle of anger in her arms. A laugh rumbled from him at the sound of his son's first rants—he was pissed. A boy after his own furious heart.

Willow met Fillion's eyes and they smiled at each other, both lost to their own storms of whirling emotions. "I love you, Fillion" she whispered, right before kissing him, her lips lingering softly on his.

"I love you," he replied, capturing her mouth back in a kiss he hoped conveyed the words he didn't know how to speak. God, this woman made him crazy. Everything was always so intense with her—their fights, their convictions, and their passion for each other. From the sound of their son's wails, Ash was no different.

"Your Highness," Joannah said, almost embarrassed. "My apologies. I do not wish to interrupt your celebration, but I need to help move you to your cot."

Their kiss ended in shy smiles, and Fillion leaned back and ducked his head until hair covered part of his face. He'd forgotten others were in the room. Brianna took Ash and swaddled him in blankets, singing to him the whole time. Still their son cried. Timna prepared the bed while Joannah and Ember assisted Willow in changing into a fresh nightgown.

"Your Majesty."

Fillion's head snapped up. Brianna offered him his bundled son and Fillion's stomach flipped. Hold him? Anxiety re-pumped through his veins along with a cocktail of other equally as potent emotions. His hands trembled, but he cradled his son close and fought for words. Anything. God, he was a mess.

"I don't know what to do," he whispered to no one.

Ash turned his face toward the thundering pulse in Fillion's chest and opened his eyes. The world dissolved that moment as their eyes connected. This was his flesh and blood. A new relative. His *son*. Hope and humility swelled in Fillion's chest as he touched Ash's tear-stained face in wonder. The sins of the father might fall on the son, but Fillion wasn't like Hanley. He wasn't like Della, either, even if his work life called him away from home more than he wanted. Ash released another angry cry and Fillion thought his heart would shatter into a billion pieces.

"Hey, Ash," he said to him. "Be as pissed off as you want. I won't judge you." His son's cries calmed at the sound of Fillion's voice and then Ash blinked, as if trying to focus on Fillion's face. So Fillion lowered his face closer to Ash's, his own vision blurring. "I love you." A tear slipped down Fillion's cheek. "I love you so much. Don't ever forget that, OK?"

The women helped Willow onto their bed. Brianna turned back toward him, but Fillion wasn't ready. He didn't want to let go of his son. Not yet. Not ever. Before Brianna arrived, he whispered once more to his Ash.

"I'm going to make mistakes. You deserve better than me. But I promise you this…" Fillion offered a shaky smile. "I will honor you every day of your life."

Fillion Nichols, CEO and president of the New Eden Enterprises empire, died in his sleep early Sunday at the age of 56. Biometric readouts show cardiac arrest, common in others who received HiraMed technology from 2054-2058. But sources close to the family say he died of a broken heart after losing his partner of 35 years, Willow Oak Watson, to an incurable type of brain cancer just nine days prior, another flaw from the same generation of HiraMed bio-cybernetic technology.

Memorials are springing up all over the world in honor of the man who revolutionized the Anime Generation's response to unemployment and hunger crises. Heir to the famous Mars-prototype biodome city, New Eden Township, Nichols expanded the model to every continent of Earth. At least a thousand planned communities now house transient populations, including incarcerated youths as well as Mars-bound civilians and government employees who use the facilities as training grounds.

Nichols is survived by his children, Ashton Mackenzie Nichols, Ronan Dylan Nichols, Autumn Laurel Saulness and Corlan Sage Nichols; his grandchildren, Corlan, Drew, Meadow, Kai, Ivy, Forrest, Cadence, Geneva, Olivia, Andrin, Talon and Aiden; his sister, Lynden Hansen, his brother-in-law, Coal Hansen, and his sisters-in-law, Ember Watson and Laurel Daniels; his nieces and nephews, Alder, Terra, Fia, Solstice, Flint, River, and Reed; and his lifelong friend and business partner, Mackenzie Patton Campbell Ferguson III.

Ceremonies of Death will begin at 10 a.m. Monday and continue throughout the week. The ceremonies are closed to the public but will be broadcast live on the Eco-Crafting Eden II site.

— *World News Today*, "Fillion Nichols Dies In His Sleep," September 27, 2093

Love is
The funeral pyre
Where I have laid my living body.

All the false notions of myself
That once caused fear, pain,

Have turned to ash
As I neared God.

What has risen
From the tangled web of thought and sinew

Now shines with jubilation
Through the eyes of angels

And screams from the guts of
Infinite existence
Itself.

Love is the funeral pyre
Where the heart must lay
Its body.

— Hafiz, *The Gift*, 14th Century *

Epilogue

New Eden Township, Salton Sea, California

Monday, September 28, 2093

Ashton Mackenzie Nichols dipped a rag into a bowl of vinegar and squeezed. Droplets plunked into the wooden bowl and echoed in the sorrow-filled silence. On a litter stretched across a table, surrounded by tallow candles, lay his father's lifeless body. Lips, tinged blue, rested in a stiffened hint of a smile. Had his Mother risen from the grave and called him to her?

"Synchronicity. Quantum entanglement," Ash said, remembering Father's tale of his and Mother's love story. From the dark corners of Ash's mind, his father's soft voice continued. *"What happens to one happens to the other. Even death."*

All his life, Ash believed this science-inspired poetry to be nothing more than romantic embellishments. Quantum physics belonged to theory and engineering, not relationships. Yet the complexities of life often felt more like the pages of fiction than real; and love, like a fairytale.

Happily ever after was subjective, Ash concluded. For what was happy for one could bring sorrow for another. Only two days prior, his father's own grief had still haunted these walls. How the stench of death infuriated Ash. He didn't know a heart could hurt so much. His muscles ached from battling each intense emotion until his eyes burned from endless tears and sleepless nights.

In one week, he had lost both of his parents to fatal flaws in biotech no longer in circulation. New Eden Enterprises was his family's life and had become his parents' death. And god, the twisting pain in his chest nearly brought him to his knees.

Jaw clenched, Ash dragged the rag reverently across the tattooed broken heart and angel wings inked onto his father's chest. As a child, he remembered touching the feathers in wonder, thinking his father could truly fly. He was the Son of Eden, after all. A man of magic. It wasn't until he was older that he understood what was meant by "flying out in the morning." A small smile tempted the corners of Ash's mouth with the memory, but it failed to fully form. Now his father really did fly with angel wings, and Ash cursed as fresh pain stabbed anew.

How was he to do this? How was he to move on in life without his father's passion inspiring his own? Run New Eden Biospherics & Research without his guidance and insight? Ash loved him deeply and had from his earliest memories. They shared a bond he foolishly believed was unbreakable. Others had lost their parents, but not him. Never him. Their family was untouchable, or so he thought.

The cycle of life was no respecter of persons, however. Life, death, and rebirth was the heartbeat song of New Eden and her sister communes. The earthly melody flowed in his veins as he now honored a man in death who had honored him in life.

Drawing in an angry breath, Ash brushed the rag over the flames on his father's upper arm. Vinegar dribbled down the pomegranate's trunk and pooled onto the litter. Shoulders shaking, he brought the rag over the other arm and caressed the willow oak tree tattoo, then paused.

His younger brother, Ronan, reminded him most of Mother, aside from his blond hair and green eyes. He was carefree yet fierce, and connected to nature in philosophical ways that Ash, Autumn, and Sage didn't understand. It was as if every blade of grass, each leaf, and every tuft of moss spoke personally to Ronan. Perhaps they did. Autumn often teased him for being so melodramatic, but Ash had always thought Ronan was otherworldly.

Sage, on the other hand, was highly cerebral and preferred the company of technology over nature. His features, much like Ash's, were reminiscent of Father, with silver-gray eyes and dark hair that reflected mahogany in the sun. Classic Jayne traits, they were told. Uncle Mack spent most of his time training Sage when their father wasn't available. His youngest brother's humor always flirted at the edge of propriety in New Eden as a result. Though the matriarchs loved him. Sage could do no wrong, even as a grown man.

Full of smiles and daggers, Autumn most embodied their parent's wit and tenacity. Her hair shone like rays of sunshine, and her eyes glinted steel. His sister had the uncanny ability to make you laugh one moment and then slice you into quarters the next. Her mastery of language was legendary in their home. Father often hesitated before sparring words with Autumn, for several times he was tricked into ridiculous promises or dares. But with Mother? Autumn knew she was outmatched, in both tongue and spirit. Rather, she studied Mother and practiced her education on her hapless brothers. Ash loved her for it.

Candles flickered with his movements, and Ash's mind blinked back in-to focus.

With a grunt, he rolled his father onto his side, then ran the freshly dipped rag along his father's back. A tattoo in Japanese characters was inked down his father's spine. On his shoulder blades were Ash's and his sibling's names and dates of birth. Ash touched the rag to his own name and grit back a forming sob. Fury rushed through him at the injustice of this situation. Unable to hold back, he rolled his father gently once more onto his back and then Ash screamed, throwing the rag across the room as the grief burning in his chest found its voice.

"Why did you leave me, Father?" he sobbed. Grabbing his father's stiffened, blue-tipped fingers, Ash asked in hoarse whisper, "How am I to do this without you?"

For twelve years, Ash had worked alongside Fillion Nichols as a majority owner within the New Eden Enterprises empire. But, for thirty-two years, he had watched this remarkable man heal from years of emotional abuse while rebuilding what progressive society had left behind, giving hope and purpose to millions. Ash relished the fingerprints of his father's legacy in both worlds. And, despite his present pain, he knew it was that very legacy that would carry him forward in the days and years to come. They were terribly difficult shoes to fill, but he was willing. And, if he were considered half the man his father was, he would consider it a life well spent.

"Spin the tales," he said to himself. "Weave the stories together. Create a reality all my own."

A Gamemaster didn't focus on the obvious; they pondered the hidden. His father had woven plot layers so intricate and complex, it would take a lifetime for Ash to uncover each one. But the invisible threads linking their lives tugged and pulled. He felt their invitation to explore every glittering facet of love, each cut and angle of family, and the binding tapestry of community.

Loosening a tight breath, he released his father's fingers and trudged over to retrieve the rag from the floor. A whirlwind of emotions spun violently in his heart. But Ash forced his fractured mind to focus on the duty and honor in carrying forth his father's legacy while he spun and wove his own for his children and his children's children.

Two hours later, Ash stood on the edge of The Rows beside his siblings as pallbearers lowered their father's corpse onto a funeral pyre before all of New Eden Township.

A rare storm moved through the desert. Wind battered the biodome panes and raindrops fell and marched across the reflective glass. From their view, it appeared as though a wave washed over the Township. Water ran down the curved structure. Warbled light moved over the meadow and gar-dens in an eerie dance. Muffled thunder rolled and shook the biodome, fol-lowed by an intense flash of light.

Villagers murmured and stared at the fractured sky. Ash, however, hardly noticed the weather, too consumed by his own raging storm. Ronan, ever perceptive, took his hand and squeezed while they waited for the Ceremony to begin. They didn't have to wait long.

Brother Aaron's robes flapped in the bio-breeze as he moved before the funeral pyre and lifted the Holy Scriptures in opening prayer. "Thank you,

Heavenly Father, for gifting us with Fillion Malcolm Nichols, an extraordinary and honorable man. His life will forever bless our souls, and his memory will re-main alive through the love and good deeds we now extend to one another. It is with a heavy but thankful heart that we commit his spirit unto you." Opening his eyes, the monk brushed the sign of the cross into the air as the community chanted, "Amen," then he gestured for Ash to approach.

A tiny drone followed him to the funeral pyre. The Ceremonies of Death were being recorded live for the world to witness. Another gentle bio-breeze swept by and feathered his father's dark hair. Blinking back heavy emotion, Ash placed a hand on his father's chest one last time. This was it, the last time he would see his father's form whole. The shape of his face, the graceful height of his body, and that barely-there smile would soon belong only to memory.

Per tradition, Ash slipped his hand into his father's pocket and laughed through the forming tears as he pulled out a pack of cigarettes. Villagers and visiting scientists laughed with Ash. He knew who placed them there, finding Uncle Mack's eyes. The older man winked at him, but the grief etched onto his face brought fresh tears to Ash's eyes.

Collecting himself, he slipped a hand into the other pocket and sucked in a ragged breath. The tears he tried to hold back fell as he revealed his mother's carved bone dragon comb and her silver linden leaf necklace. Muffled cries circulated from the crowd. He rubbed his thumb over the silver linden leaf wistfully. His parents had a strange romance. They fought while they flirted and flirted while they fought. Often, while growing up, he thought his father was crazy for eliciting his mother's ire intentionally. But it was their language. Their affection.

God, would denial always be this difficult?

Ash couldn't look at his siblings or at his wife and sons. If he did, he would collapse on top of his father's corpse, begging and screaming for him to return to the living. Instead, he pocketed the items and stepped away as the matriarchs came forth with ceremonial funeral cloths and began wrapping the body. Little by little, his father disappeared until only his white-draped outline remained. Once complete, the residents formed lines on either side of the funeral pyre and bowed while placing juniper branches over the shrouded body.

Far too quickly, honors ended and Ash stared at the mound of branches and piles of wood. He couldn't do this. He couldn't light his father's body on fire and watch him burn. The haunting memories of his mother's service last week still lingered vividly in his grief-stricken mind.

And, yet, he must.

Flint Hansen, the Fire Element and his cousin, handed Ash a lit torch, tears streaking down his cheeks as he did so. The hurricane ripping inside of Ash gained speed and the world spun in nauseating circles. Above, rain crashed against the geometric glass. Below, wind rustled the grass by his feet. The muscles in his legs shook as he marched north and lit the torch representing the Earth Element. Turning on his heel, he forced his feet east and lit the torch for the Wind Element, then south for the Fire Element and, finally, west for the Water Element. Similar to the office of Aether, his father represented all Noble families and houses.

The torch weighed heavy in his trembling hand as he faced the funeral pyre once more. Biting back a sob, Ash raised his arm and dropped the torch onto the pyre. He stumbled back when a wall of heat curled in a furious roar of smoke and fire. Flames quickly licked the sky and crackled in the wind.

Fresh sorrow convulsed through Ash as he forced himself to watch. His knees buckled and he collapsed until kneeling before his father's burning corpse. That same moment, a breeze skipped through the meadow and billowed the smoke into a black cloud. Through the haze, his gaze landed on a leaf as it twirled and tumbled in the air above the flames.

His breath caught. He wasn't sure why, but he felt as though his mother and father were reaching out to him while nature extended a beautiful gift of thanks for receiving his parents as the cycle of life demanded. Ash squinted his eyes, reached out, and caught the leaf when it flew his way. The ragged edges and veins of life fascinated him and called up memories.

"As one story ends, so another begins," his mother often said. Her words trembled into textured shape in his mind as understanding dawned bright in his heart.

Ashton Mackenzie Nichols tore his gaze from the leaf and the funeral pyre and peered at his sons along the circle, his chest swelling with love. One day, they would prepare the soil for his life's elements. But, until then, they were an integral part of the story Ash spun and wove for his life's happy future.

The leaf fluttered in his fingertips and he smiled through the tears rolling down his cheeks. The song of New Eden Township pulsed from his heart to each limb.

"Ashes to ashes, dust to dust," he whispered, and then he released the leaf to the winds of change to complete the ephemeral journey it began.

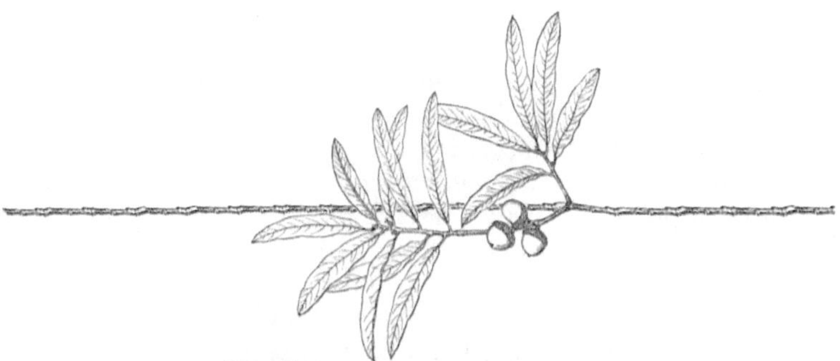

Appendices

1. Author Notes

2. Hacker Terminology

3. Anime and Japanese Terminology

4. Additional Definitions

5. Translations

6. The Elements of YOUR Life: Blog Fun with Readers

7. Selected Bibliography

Read THE CODE at
www.jesikahsundin.com

PLEASE LEAVE A 1-2 SENTENCE REVIEW
on Amazon to help others find my series. Reviews
increase an author's and a book's searchability.

THANK YOU!

AUTHOR NOTES

Whew. I'll be honest, guys. I didn't think this book was going to make it. The last half of 2017 and first few months of 2018 proved to be significantly difficult thanks to several incidents, including a concussion that plagued me for months. Writing with brain damage is like running a race through a park in a dense fog and tripping over everything. You make progress s-l-o-w-l-y.

But, if I'm really, really honest? I was afraid to finish. Terrified of letting down readers, many of whom have followed and supported me since LEGACY was published in January 2014. Terrified of what my life would look like without Fillion, Willow, and the gang filling my page each day. I've dedicated six years of my life to The Biodome Chronicles. And what an amazing ride. When I finished writing the epilogue, I ugly-cried for hours, complete with dying donkey sounds. It was epic, haha! The few days that followed, I looked like a twitchy, puffy-eyed zombie. I had to laugh, though. Here I was grieving about finishing a book that's all about grieving. Oh irony, how I adore you . . .

Speaking of irony, it was Willow's words that pulled me out of my funk: "As one story ends, so another begins." I have many more stories to pen. Seriously, folks . . . my weird brain is exploding with a galaxy of story ideas. My poor writing partner, Melissa. She hears my imagination's rants and rambles so often, patiently sipping her 15th cup of coffee as I word-vomit all over her. And, yeah, the MELISSA Project and even Mel, the underground's PM, was me poking at my bestie of twenty-five years. Because I can. She's now immortalized in strange ways that are nothing like her at all. And, that folks, is what it's like living with me, lol.

Melissa: Per tradition, here are five happies for you: 1) melodramatic music moments; 2) faerie cordial; 3) writerly womance getaways; 4) surviving a 300-foot climb up a cliff with no safeties as the tide rushes in #badass; 5) loving you. *There is no sidekick'n. We are equal partners in badassary and goofyism #SugarPacket*

Readers: THANK YOU for all the laughs, loves, and shenanigans over the years. I cherish every moment and look forward to a bazillion more. You make all the blood, tears, and sweat worth it. Smooch!!

Dad: I've wanted to tell you for six years now that I planned on dedicating this book to you. Keeping this detail to myself was killing me! But I couldn't think of a more perfect story to dedicate to you. Thanks for the legacy of love, family, and community you gave Adriel (ahem, *Nicki*) and me. Our late-night talks about Bigfoot, aliens, science, and our fantastical religious, historical, and philosophical convos are the absolute best. Love you!

I have several friends who have made GAMEMASTER possible, from giving advice, beta reading, brainstorming, encouraging me when my inner-tortured artist would emerge, supporting me during my concussion, and who continually share my books with the world: Melissa Patton (*says like Coal* Naturally), Tracy Campbell, Jennifer Newsom, Katie Kent, Selah Tay-Song, Rob Slater, Raven Oak, Elise Kreinbring, Jessica Jett, Hannah Miller,

Tyffany Hackett, Becky Moynihan, Andra Perju, Artis Fricbergs, Jennifer Ross, Barbara Simonds, Erik Saulness, Sarah Saulness, and many more friends and family who were not directly involved but still impacted my life and this book in meaningful ways. *bows to you*

Amalia Chitulescu: This cover, oh my goodness! Hearts are shooting out of my eyes *le sigh* I am honored to have your artistic magic clothe one of my novels once more. THANK YOU for always caring about my world, characters, and ensuring the cover is perfect. <3

Emily Newman: I am forever thankful to you for translating segments of Fillion and Mack's dialogue into Japanese. *Doumo arigatou gozaimasu.*

Jennifer Cook and Marjolaine Gagnon: My heartfelt gratitude for your assistance in transforming a few fun pieces of Leaf, Willow, and Coal's dialogue into French. *Merci beaucoup.*

Sunil Patel: Thanks for breathing life into my characters with your "sexy British Barry White voice." The audiobooks are amaaaazing!

Andra Perju: Not only do you make an awesome institutionalized transhuman from the MELISSA Project, you are also an incredibly talented digital artist! Thank you for this beautiful, fantastic map of New Eden Township. Hugz and Kissez!

Lori Collins of LoriofPandora Studios: That print of Fillion and Willow!! And the Eco-Crafting gaming cards!! Wow. Just wow. Endless gratitude to you for bringing the gaming elements of my series into reality and the romance of Team Willion, too <3

Nali of A Court of Candles: I loooooove the custom-made Biodome Chronicles candles. Oh. My. Gawd they smell divine. Thank you so much!!

Leah McNatt of Uppercase Bookshop (Snohomish), Emily Newman of Main Street Books (Monroe), Aly Tornblad of University Book Store (Mill Creek), Kristina Twiss and Adam from Barnes & Noble (Bellevue): Thank you, thank you, THANK YOU for your endless support of my series. I am continually humbled by your desire to introduce your readers to my characters and worlds.

Myles Sundin: Your name is written on the boughs of my heart. Thank you for supporting my dream these past six years. I love you.

To my children, Myles, Colin, and Violette: Spin the tales. Weave them together. Create a reality all your own. And never forget your legacy of love, family, and community.

Although I draw on the expertise of others in various subjects to build the near-future world of Seattle and the quasi-historical world of New Eden Township, all errors are entirely mine. In the famous words of Nennius, a ninth-century Celtic monk, "I have made a heap of all that I could find."

Owari …
(The End)

HACKER TERMINOLOGY

HACKER – A hacker is an individual who breaches security in a computer system or computer network to capitalize on exposed weaknesses, for beneficial or nefarious reasons. Sometimes the term is applied to an individual with expert knowledge of computers and computer networks. A subculture now exists for hackers, formed by a real and recognized community known as the computer underground. This subculture of tech-savvy individuals has also developed a unique language and slang terms defined and collected in The Hacker's Dictionary (originally known as the Jargon File), which is searchable online.

A Lefty's Catcher Mitt – Net jargon for something people think exists, but doesn't. The term came from the anime show *Laughing Man* ("Ghost in the Shell"), where a character owns a left-handed mitt inscribed with a quote by Holden Caulfield, title character in the novel *The Catcher in the Rye* by J.D. Salinger

Bagbiter – a person who always causes problems, is a whiner, and is never satisfied. Comes from the hacker term for a piece of equipment, hardware, or software that fails

Black Hat – someone who maliciously hacks into secure systems to corrupt or gain unauthorized information. The hacker subculture often refers to this person as a "cracker" rather than a "hacker"
F
Bletcherous (bletch) – disgusting, makes you want to vomit, usually in reference to an object, and rarely regarding people

Defragment (defrag) – an action to reduce the fragmentation of a software file by concatenating parts stored in separate locations on a disk

Faraday Cage – a grounded metal screen (usually copper) that surrounds a piece of equipment to exclude electrostatic and electromagnetic influences

Fatal Exception Error – an error that closes down and aborts a program, returning the user to the operating system

Frobnicate – to manipulate or adjust, to tweak for the fun of it, goofing off

Gabriel / "Pull a Gabriel" – [for Dick Gabriel, SAIL volleyball fanatic] An unnecessary (in the opinion of the opponent) stalling tactic, e.g., tying one's shoelaces or hair repeatedly, asking the time, etc. Also used to refer to the perpetrator of such tactics. Also, "pulling a Gabriel", "Gabriel mode"

Glitch – a sudden interruption in electric service, sanity, or program function, sometimes recoverable

Gritching (gritch) – to complain; a blend of "gripe" and "bitch"

Gubbish – nonsense; a blend of "garbage" and "rubbish"

Hack-back – Loosely defined, "hacking back" involves turning the tables on a cyberhacking assailant: thwarting or stopping the crime, or perhaps even trying to steal back what was taken

Kernel Panic – an action taken by an operating system when detecting an internal fatal error from which it cannot safely recover; also known as "the blue screen of death"

Loser – an unexpectedly bad situation, program, programmer, or person

Mumblage – The topic of one's mumbling, often used as a replacement for obscenities, "full of mumblage"

Parse – Slang for to understand or comprehend

Uncanny Valley – The hypothesis in the field of aesthetics which states that some humans feel revulsion or disturbance when robotics or 3D animation look and move almost, but not exactly, like natural beings

White Hat – someone who hacks into secure systems and instead of corrupting or taking unauthorized information, exposes the weaknesses to the system's owners so they can strengthen the breach before it can be taken advantage of by others (including **Black Hats**)

ANIME and JAPANESE TERMINOLOGY

ANIME / MANGA – Anime is a distinctly Japanese style of animation, while manga is the term for comic books that feature anime-stylized characters. Anime differs from American cartoons in that it is more often created for teens and adults with a range of topics that typically explore serious themes. It has been criticized by parents in the United States for discussing such taboo topics as teen suicide, violence, social rebellion, spiritual ideas, and sex. However, anime and manga include many genres, including romance, comedy, horror, and action, and feature several series for children, Pokémon being the most notable and successful in the U.S. Many video games, for general or mature audiences, feature anime-style characters and themes. In Japan, and even in the U.S., anime fans have formed a subculture with punk undertones emulating goth, emo, or cyberpunk movements.

Bishounen (bishonen, bish, bishie, bishy) – literally, "pretty boy" in Japanese, a term used to describe a young man—including those in anime, manga, and video games—who is notably beautiful and attractive

Bakayarō – dumbass, idiot, fool

Chikara – strength, power

Desu – Japanese for "it is," often said at the end of sentences to seem cute or unwitting

Dokyun – a derogatory internet slang term that spread from Japan's 2ch.net, which mostly means dumbass or idiot

Henshin – "to change or transform the body"; in anime and manga, this is usually when a character transforms into a superhero

Hikikomori – someone who purposely stays in their house all day long, isolating themselves from society, and who usually spends all their time on the Internet, playing video games, or watching anime

Jitsu – martial arts term for "technique" or "art"

Josei – woman

Kawaii – cute, Japanese culture reference.

Kiai – a Japanese term used in martial arts for the short yell or shout uttered when performing an attacking move

Kisama – No direct translation, but a good English equivalent might be "motherfucker." It is an extremely hostile and rude address, mostly toward males, that begets the air of "hate" or "detest" to whom it's directed. Historically, it was what a samurai called their enemy

Kono Yaro – translates to "that bastard"

Kotatsu – a low, wooden table frame covered by a futon, or heavy blanket, upon which a table top sits. Underneath is a heat source, often built into the table itself

Kureejii – translates to "crazy," as in a person

Kusogaki – little shit, shitty brat, damn child

Origami – The art of paper folding

Otaku – in Japan, originally a very negative term to describe a recluse who has no life, usually because their world revolves around fictional characters, such as in anime and manga; in America, the word has been applied by anime fans as a positive term for fanboy/girl

Nakoudo – translates to "matchmaker" or "go-between" and is the person who contracts a marriage between the man and woman who hope to marry

Nettomo – slang term for a friend made on the Internet

Nosebleed – used by fans about someone whom they think is hot or exciting; when an anime or manga character has become sexually excited, it is portrayed with a sudden nosebleed

Sakura – translates to "cherry blossom"

Samurai – a member of a powerful military caste in feudal Japan, especially a member of the class of military retainers of the daimyos

Sekushī – sexy

Senpai – someone who is of a higher social standing. "Notice me senpai" is usually a junior hoping he/she would get the attention of the senpai.

Tesaki – translates to "fingers," but is slang for "minion"

Yaoi – "boys love" manga and anime typically aimed at a female audience

Yuinou / Yuinou no gi – translates to "betrothal presents" and is the ceremony where the groom and bride to-be swear their engagement publicly, followed by an exchange of gifts between the two households

ADDITIONAL DEFINITIONS

Cob – a type of structural mud made from clay, sand, water, and straw that is applied wet between stones or in clumps to form walls. Cob homes, shops, and barns became the preferred building type during the Middle Ages, especially in the British Isles. The mud structures reached the height of popularity with Tudor-style architecture made famous for its external geometric timber designs, stone or brick accents, oriel window boxes, and lead multi-lit latticed windows. This is the most commonly featured style of building in fantasy storybook villages.

Cyberpunk – a literary and visual media genre that takes place in a future or near-future Earth and is most notably known for the film noir detective-like qualities of the story, high technology (computers, hackers, robotics, artificial intelligence), and a degraded society. The world or place setting is typically regulated and influenced by large corporations and wealthy elite rather than traditional governmental bodies. The protagonist is usually a rogue/misfit, a loner in society with a dark past. The cyberpunk genre is prominently featured in anime and manga in Japan.

Dungeon Master (DM) – individual in charge of organizing and planning the details and challenges of a given adventure in the table-top role-playing game "Dungeons & Dragons." He or she also is a participant in the game, but their key role is to make all the rules and control the story, telling the player characters what they hear and what they see. The only part a DM does not control are the decisions/actions of the player characters.

Emo / Emocore – an alternative rock subculture influenced by the punk music scene that emerged in the 1980s, featuring lyrics about self rather than traditional punk themes of society. The Emo scene exploded in the 1990s with the indie rock grunge scene and popularity of pop punk, and was later brought back to mainstream teen culture in the early 2000s through the Internet social media site MySpace. Individuals belonging to this subculture have a unique and notable fashion, the modern looks and trends believed to have been influenced by the anime and manga subculture. The Emo's (sometimes called Scene Kids or Ravers) are described as being "emotive" in nature, giving rise to the idea that the boys possess more feminine traits and qualities than their non-emo counterparts.

Gamemaster (GM) – an individual who officiates and referees multi-player role-playing games (table-top or live action), sometimes with other Gamemasters. They arbitrate and moderate the rules, settle disputes, create and define the game world/environment, blend and weave player character stories together, and oversee the non-player character roles and influence in the story. The Gamemaster's specific job and function is unique to each game.

Live Action Role-Playing (LARP) – a style of game that transcends traditional table-top or video game role-playing into live action where people physically become a character and act out their role in a defined fantasy setting. A LARP must contain three consistent ideas in order to be considered true live action role-playing (expanded in more depth by larping.org): collaborative (a mutual operation where everyone understands they are a character and must work together toward a common goal); pretending (a necessary element for each LARP, such as the game world/space, weapons and characterization, to name a few); and rules (agreed upon by the community of gamers and refereed by Gamemasters but usually sustained by an honor system among players).

Mundane – an object or person that does not belong to the fictional game or setting, such as a cellphone in a medieval community, or the President of the United States in ancient China. In the LARP and role-playing subculture, mundane also refers to one's "real" life versus his or her character life/world.

Visual Kei ("visual music" or "visual system") – an alternative rock music movement in Japan that features band members who typically try to emulate a unified androgynous appearance. They embody unique makeup, hair styles, and clothing that is punk in nature with mainstream success and influenced by Western concepts such as glam rock, goth, and cyberpunk. Some argue that Visual Kei is no longer about a music genre but about a subculture of individuals who reflect this fashion style and trend.

TRANSLATIONS

Chapter 2

She kissed Corona on the cheek and said, "I shall see you at mid-day meal, *soeur de mon coeur.*"
Translation: *Sister of my heart.*

"I am beyond grieved and know not what to say," Leaf whispered. He considered his brother-in-law a heartbeat, then asked, "*Vous avez trouvé le bonheur à l'extérieur?*"
Translation: *In the Outside, you have found happiness?*

"I am a product of myself, Your Majesty. No man can steal my life, although they might try," Coal answered in English. He then peered Lynden's direction surreptitiously and added, "*Malgré les circonstances, j'ai la chance de connaître le bonheur.*"
Translation: *I am fortunate to know happiness, despite my circumstances.*

Chapter 3

He tried to restrain a smile as he intensified his gaze, knowing it was comical at best. "How about now, *mon joli petit dragon?*"
Translation: *My lovely little dragon*

Chapter 4

"*Tabako wa iya na kuse desu yo. Kekkongo toriaezu yameta hou ga ii deshou. Watashi ni haji wo kakasemasu.*"
Translation: *Smoking is a disgusting habit. After we are married first of all you should quit It embarrasses me.*

"*Kiiteimasu ka?*" A dainty hand, clad in rings and white-painted nails, brushed the petal off his pants in a single sweep.
Translation: *Did you hear me?*

"*Are wa Fillion deshou?*" a teenage girl asked her friend.
"*Hontou da!*"
Translation: *Is that Fillion? / It's him!*

Chapter 8

Fillion swung her direction with lightning speed. "*Ore ga shitteiru ichiban kouketsu na hito da yo. Kare ya New Eden no juumin o hiningen no you ni atsukatte ikemasen. Wakatta?*"
Translation: *He is the most honorable man I have ever known and you will not dehumanize him or any others in New Eden. Am I clear?.*
Chapter 9

Narrowing his eyes at her, Leaf said, "*S'il te plait, prend sur toi et montre un peu de modestie. Dévisager quelqu'un n'est pas distingué ni apprécié par notre invité.*"
Translation: *Gawking is not ladylike nor does our guest appreciates such gestures.*

She scoffed and pushed him toward his bedchamber. "*Tu seras père encore aujourd'hui et ce petit enfant aura la chance d'avoir ton amour pour la vie.*"
Translation: *You shall become a father again today. This wee babe is fortunate to have a lifetime of your love.*

Leaf's eyes filled with tears and he lowered his head. "*Et ce qui appartient à sa mère.*"
Translation: *And her mother's.*

Chapter 11

His friend shot him a dark expression. "*Ittai doushitattenda yo?*"
"*Kanojo o touzake te iru. Kibou o sute tame.*"
Mack stared at his friend, long and hard. "No shit."
"*Hanley o shinjirarenai. Jibun jishin mo.*"
"*Shoujiki ni iu hou ga ii deshou. Otona dakara daijoubu.*"
Fillion shook his head as he dismissed his friend and turned to leave.
Translation: *What the hell is wrong with you? / Pushing her away. Ending any kind of hope. / I can't trust Hanley. Or myself. / Be honest with her instead She's a grown up, she'll be fine.*

Chapter 15

"*Mon coeur,*" she whispered followed by a gentle shush.
Translation: *My heart*

Chapter 23

"I am deeply honored." She lowered into a curtsy, a hand draped across her heart. *"Merci beaucoup, mon cher frère et soeur"*
Translation: *Thank you, my dear brother and sister.*

Chapter 32

Shyly, he placed the gift in her hand, saying, *"Korekara zutto, ore no jinsei wa anata no mono desu. Zutto eien ni sasagemasu."*
Translation: *I now see that you have always owned my life and always will. I give it to you.*

Chapter 34

Curious eyes watched him from all over the Great Hall. *"Hanley kara hanarete inasai. Abunai tokoro ni irunda yo."*
Translation: *Stay away from Hanley right now. He's in a dangerous place.*

SELECTED BIBLIOGRAPHY

Chapter 1

Bikel, Theodore. *Theo: An Autobiography.* Madison, Wisconsin: The University of Wisconsin Press, 2002.

Bradford, John. "Torpor Inducing Transfer Habitat for Human Stasis to Mars." NASA.gov. July 19, 2013. https://www.nasa.gov/content/torpor-inducing-transfer-habitat-for-human-stasis-to-mars

Chapter 2

Abbey, Edward. *A Voice Crying in the Wilderness.* New York: RosettaBooks, 2015. Electronic version.

Chapter 3

Hurley, Dan. "Trait vs. Fate." *Discover,* May 2013.

Javelosa, June. "Memories Can Be Inherited, and Scientists May Have Just Figured out How." Futurism.com. April 13, 2016. https://futurism.com/memories-can-inherited-scientists-may-just-figured/

Chapter 4

Smith, Richard Gordon. "The Holy Cherry Tree of Musubi-no-Kami Temple," in *Ancient Tales and Folk-lore of Japan.* London: A & C Black, 1908.

Chapter 5

Shakespeare, William. *A Midsummer Night's Dream.* "No Fear Shakespeare," SparkNotes.com. Accessed April 2018. http://nfs.sparknotes.com/msnd/page_10.html

Sharma, Sheena. "Uncomfortably Numb: Why I'd Rather Feel Pain, Than Feel Nothing At All." *Elite Daily.* July 20, 2015. https://www.elitedaily.com/dating/rather-feel-pain-than-nothing/111577

Chapter 6

Curtis, Adam. "How the 'ecosystem' myth has been used for sinister means." *The Observer.* May 28, 2011. https://www.theguardian.com/environment/2011/may/29/adam-curtis-ecosystems-tansley-smut

Chapter 7

Curtis.

Chapter 8

Martine, Christy Ann. "Transformation." http://www.christyannmartine.com. 2017.

Chapter 10

Carroll, Lewis. *Alice's Adventures in Wonderland*. Boston: Lee and Shepard, 1869.

Chapter 11

Bedier, J. *The Romance of Tristan and Iseult*. Translated by H. Belloc. Portland, Maine: Thomas B. Mosher, 1904.

Paz, Octavio. "A tree within." Translated by Eliot Weinberger. In *Twentieth-Century Latin American Poetry: A Bilingual Anthology*. Edited by Stephen Tapscott. Austin, Texas: University of Texas Press, 1996.

Chapter 12

Gaskin, Ina May. *Spiritual Midwifery*. Summertown, Tenn.: Book Publishing Company, 2002.

Joseph, Eve. *In the Slender Margin: The Intimate Strangeness of Death and Dying*. New York: Arcade Publishing, 2016.

Chapter 13

Erickson, Jim. "Biospherians return to world." *The Arizona Daily Star*. September 27, 1993.

Chapter 16

Martine, Christy Ann. "Metamorphosis." http://www.christyannmartine.com. 2017.

Chapter 17

Mitnick, Mike. "They call me a criminal." *The Guardian*. February 22, 2000. https://www.theguardian.com/technology/2000/feb/22/hacking.security

Chapter 20

Metz, Cade. "Elon Musk Isn't The Only One Trying to Computerize Your Brain." Wired.com. March 31, 2017. https://www.wired.com/2017/03/elon-musks-neural-lace-really-look-like/

Chapter 21

Conrad, Andrew. Presentation at WSJD Live conference, Laguna Beach, Calif., October 28, 2014. Posted November 16, 2014. https://www.wsj.com/video/google-andrew-conrad-speaks-at-wsjd-live/09A6323E-5802-4360-ADDB-7FD8AC04C5BD.html

Chapter 22

Paz, Octavio. "Coda" from "Letter of testimony." In *A Tree Within*. Translated by Eliot Weinberger. New York: New Directions Books, 1988.

Chapter 23

Gandhi, Mahatma. Quoted in *Wisdom of Gandhi*. Compiled by Prashant Gupta. New Delhi: Ocean Books, 2009.

Rumi, Jalal al-Din. Quoted in *The Sufi Path of Love: The Spiritual Teaching of Rumi*. By William C. Chittick. Albany, N.Y.: State University of New York Press, 1983.

Chapter 25

Gibson, William. *Zero History*. New York: G. P. Putnam's Sons, 2010.

Westworld. "Contrapasso." Season 1, Episode 5. Directed by Johnny Campbell. Teleplay by Lisa Joy. Story by Dominic Mitchell and Lisa Joy. HBO, October 30, 2016.

Chapter 27

Rumi, Jalal al-Din. "Every Tree." In *The Glance: Sons of Soul-Meeting*. Translated by Coleman Barks. New York: Viking/Arkana, 1999.

Chapter 28

More, Thomas. *Utopia*. London: Cassell and Company, 1909.

Chapter 29

Cymreas, Winter. "Tree Lore: Willow." The Order of Bards, Ovates & Druids. Accessed April 2018. https://www.druidry.org/library/trees/tree-lore-willow

Chapter 31

Mitnick, Mike. Interview by Dean Takahashi. *VentureBeat*. October 21, 2011. https://venturebeat.com/2011/10/21/interview-with-the-former-worlds-most-wanted-hacker-kevin-mitnick/view-all/

Chapter 32

Shakespeare, William. *Romeo and Juliet*. "No Fear Shakespeare," SparkNotes.com. Accessed April 2018. http://nfs.sparknotes.com/romeojuliet/page_80.html

Chapter 33

Jung, C.G. *Aion: Researches into the Phenomenology of the Self*. Translated by R.F.C. Hull. Vol. 9 (Part II) of *C.G. Jung: The Collected Works*. Edited by Herbert Read, Michael Fordham, and Gerhard Adler. London: Routledge, 1991.

Chapter 34

Dick, Philip K. *I Hope I Shall Arrive Soon*. Edited by Mark Hurst and Paul Williams. New York: Doubleday, 1985.

Mills, Elinor. "For Kevin Mitnick, staying legal is job No. 1." *CNET*. August 5, 2010. https://www.cnet.com/news/for-kevin-mitnick-staying-legal-is-job-no-1/

Chapter 35

Emmett, Arielle. "Sleeping Their Way to Mars." *Air & Space/Smithsonian*. April 2017. https://www.airspacemag.com/space/hibernation-for-space-voyages-180962394/

Chapter 37

Hotz, Robert Lee and Adam S. Bauman. "Biosphere 2: Trouble in Paradise." *Los Angeles Times*. April 24, 1994. http://articles.latimes.com/1994-04-24/news/mn-49890_1_biosphere-project

Chapter 38

Rumi, Jalal al-Din. Quoted in *Sacred Wounds: A Path to Healing from Spiritual Trauma*. By Teresa B. Pasquale. St. Louis, Mo.: Chalice Press, 2015.

Chapter 39

"The Mayer's Song." From *The Every-Day Book*. Compiled by William Hone. London: A. Applegath, 1825.

Rumi, Jalal al-Din. "The minute I heard my first love story…" *In Rumi: The Book of Love: Poems of Ecstasy and Longing*. Translated by Coleman Barks. New York: HarperSanFrancisco, 2003.

Llywelyn, Morgan. Handfasting vows. In *Finn Mac Cool*. New York: Tor, 2010.

Chapter 40

Ingrid. "Yoshitsune." *Hello Poetry*. December 2012. https://hellopoetry.com/poem/269770/yoshitsune/

Rumi, Jalal al-Din. "All My Youth Returns." In *Rumi: In the Arms of the Beloved*. Translated by Jonathan Star. New York: Jeremy P. Tarcher/Penguin, 1997.

Song of Solomon 1:2, 8:6-7. King James Version.

Epilogue

Hafiz, Shams-ud-din Muhammad. "Love is the Funeral Pyre." In *The Gift: Poems by Hafiz, the Great Sufi Master*. Translated by Daniel Ladinsky. New York: Penguin Compass, 1999.

Jesikah Sundin is multi-award winning Ecopunk SciFi and Forest Fantasy writer mom of three nerdlets and devoted wife to a gamer geek. In addition to her family, she shares her home in Monroe, Washington with a red-footed tortoise and a collection of seatbelt purses. She is addicted to coffee, laughing, Doc Martens shoes… Oh, and the forest is her happy place.

Discover the worlds and characters
of *The Biodome Chronicles* at:

www.jesikahsundin.com